FOXMASK

Juliet Marillier

TOR
fantasy

A TOM DOHERTY ASSOCIATES BOOK
NEW YORK

FOXMASK

Copyright © 2003 by Juliet Marillier
First published in 2003 by Pan Macmillan Australia Pty Limited

Edited by Claire Eddy

Maps by Bronya Marillier

A Tor Book
Published by Tom Doherty Associates, LLC
175 Fifth Avenue
New York, NY 10010

www.tor.com

Tor® is a registered trademark of Tom Doherty Associates, LLC.

ISBN 0-765-34591-9
EAN 978-0-765-34591-2

First hardcover edition: August 2004
First trade paperback edition: April 2005
First mass market edition: November 2005

Printed in the United States of America

0 9 8 7 6 5 4 3 2 1

Also by Juliet Marillier

THE SEVENWATERS TRILOGY
Daughter of the Forest
Son of the Shadows
Child of the Prophecy

Wolfskin

For Godric

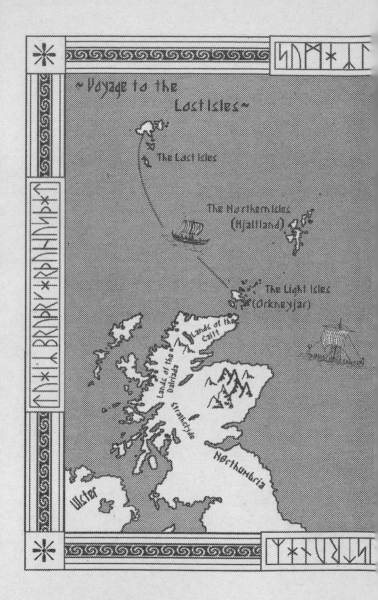

~Voyage to the
Last Isles~

The Last Isles

The Northern Isles
(Hjaltland)

The Light Isles
(Orkneyjar)

Lands of the Caitt

Lands of the
Dalriada

Strathclyde

Northumbria

Ulster

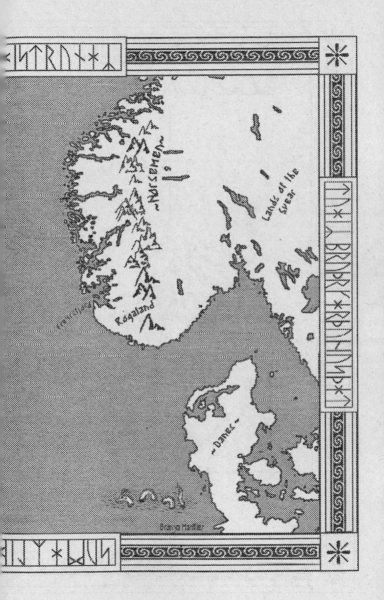

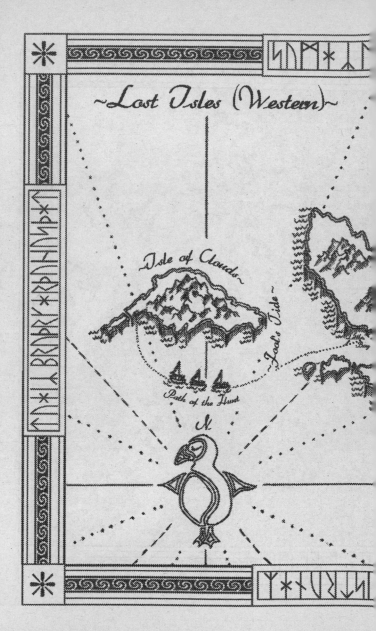

~Lost Isles (Western)~

~Isle of Clouds~

~Seal's Tide~

Path of the Hunt

~Isle of Streams~

To Outer Isles ?

~Isle of Storms~

Brightwater

Blood Bay

To Isle of Shadows
and Isle of Dreams

Bronya Maxillier

ONE

*. . . if anyone can understand, it will be you; I have always
respected your intellect. I had so much to offer here. I could
have achieved great things, and in time all would have
thanked me for it. Yes, even the Wolfskin. That he has been the
one to wrench the possibility from my grasp is bitter indeed . . .*

EXCERPT FROM LETTER

The day Thorvald's mother gave him the letter, everything
changed. Creidhe was weaving, hands busy on the loom,
shuttle flying, a fine web of blue and crimson unfolding before her in perfect pattern, testimony to the skills Aunt Margaret had taught her. So industrious was she, and so quiet,
that it seemed she had been forgotten. The bestowal of such
a perilous gift as that letter was surely best suited to a moment of complete privacy. Aunt Margaret spoke to her son
quietly, in the long room before the hearth. Creidhe could
see them through the doorway from the weaving chamber.
They did not argue. Voices were seldom raised in this most
orderly of households. But Creidhe heard the front door
slam open, and she saw Thorvald go down the three steps in
a single stride, then vanish across the yard and out over the
spring fields as if hunted by demons. She saw the blood-
less, driven look on his face. And although she did not
know it at the time, that was the moment Thorvald's life,
and her own, took a twist and a turn and set off on an entirely different path.

Creidhe knew Thorvald better than anyone. They had been
childhood playmates, and they were fast friends. Thorvald
had few friends; the fingers of one hand would be more than
enough to count them. There were perhaps only two to whom
he ever spoke freely, and whom he allowed close: herself,

and Sam, the fisherman on whose boat Thorvald sometimes helped. As for Creidhe, she understood Thorvald well: his black moods, his lengthy silences, his sudden, brilliant schemes and his rare times of openness. She loved him, for all his faults. In her mind there was no doubt that one day they would marry. He wasn't a real cousin, just as Margaret wasn't a real aunt. The tie was one of old friendship, not kinship. If Thorvald hadn't seen yet that he and Creidhe were destined to be together forever, he'd realize some time. It was just a matter of waiting.

The shuttle slowed to a stop. Creidhe stood gazing out the doorway across a landscape dotted with sheep, new lambs at foot. From Aunt Margaret's house you could see all the way to the western ocean, where stark cliffs marked the margin of land and sea. Far off now, there was the small, dark figure of Thorvald, running, running away. Creidhe had seen a terrible change in his eyes.

"Finished?"

Creidhe jumped. Margaret had come up beside her without a sound.

"N-no, but maybe I should go home. Father's due back from Sandy Island, and I should be helping—" Creidhe fell silent. Aunt Margaret had tears in her eyes. Such a phenomenon was astounding. Her aunt was a model of propriety and restraint. She never lost control.

This household, run by Margaret's long-time retainer, Ash, but ordered by Margaret herself, operated to a strict routine, with little allowance for errors. This approach was reflected in Margaret's own appearance. She was a handsome woman of around six-and-thirty, her hair a rich auburn, plaited neatly and pinned up under a snowy lace cap. Her linen gown was ironed into immaculate pleats, her woolen overdress fastened with twin brooches of patterned silver polished to a moon-bright shine. She bore the accouterments of a good housewife: knife, scissors and keys hanging from a chain. Margaret was capable. Some found her intimidating. She had never remarried after her husband died in the very first year of Norse settlement here in the Light Isles, before Thorvald was born. Creidhe did not find her aunt frightening; there was a bond between them. Creidhe might not be skilled in the arts of a priestess, as her sister Eanna was. She might not be beautiful in the style of the island girls, slender, dark and graceful. But she had other abilities. Young as she was, Creidhe had the best hands for midwifery in Hrossey, and had advanced quickly from assisting the island expert to taking a full share of responsibility. The women valued Creidhe's deft touch and cool head; these made her youth irrelevant. The same clever hands gave her a talent for spinning, weaving and embroidery. Margaret valued that talent, and over the years she had taken pleasure in fostering this buxom, fair-haired niece's skills.

If Thorvald never comes round to marrying me, Creidhe told herself sourly, *some other man surely will, just so he can say his wife's the best weaver in Hrossey.*

It wasn't as if nobody was interested. Creidhe was never short of partners for dancing. Sam had made her a whalebone comb with sea creatures carved on it. Egil had composed a poem for her and recited it, blushing. Brude had kissed her behind the cowshed when nobody was looking. The problem was, she didn't want sweet-natured Sam or scholarly Egil or handsome Brude with his merry blue eyes. She only wanted Thorvald. Thorvald had eyes dark as night and smooth auburn hair like his mother's. Creidhe loved his cleverness, his wit, the way he could always surprise her. She loved his moments of kindness, rare as they were. She wished, sometimes, that he were a little less aloof; she'd heard other girls call him arrogant, and she didn't like that. He did keep himself to himself; she was lucky to be one of those he considered a friend. Creidhe sighed. Thorvald was taking a long time to realize she could be more than just a friend to him. At sixteen she was a woman, and ready to be married; more than ready, she thought sometimes. If Thorvald didn't wake up to himself soon, her father would start suggesting likely husbands for her, and what could she say then? As her mother's daughter, she must wed and bear children. It could not be long before Eyvind began to apply subtle pressure.

"Creidhe?"

"Oh! Sorry." She'd been daydreaming again. "Are you all right, Aunt Margaret?"

"Well enough." The words belied the red eyes, the tight mouth. "Go on then, if Nessa's expecting you home. This can wait for tomorrow. The design's coming out well, Creidhe. You're quite an artist."

Creidhe blushed. "Thank you, Aunt." She paused. "Aunt Margaret—"

Margaret raised a hand. It was a gesture that said plainly, no questions. Whatever it was that had sent Thorvald out of the house like a man pursued by dark dreams, it was not going to be shared just yet.

"Creidhe," said Margaret as her niece hovered in the doorway, small bundle of belongings in hand, "don't go after Thorvald. Not today. Believe me, he's best left alone awhile."

"But—"

"If he wants to tell you, he'll tell you in his own time. Now off home with you. Your father's been away a long while. I expect he'd enjoy some of his daughter's fine cooking, perhaps your roasted mutton and garlic, or the baked cod with leek sauce. Off with you now."

The tone was light, kept carefully so, Creidhe thought. It was her aunt's eyes that gave her away. Thorvald's had held the same shadow.

Sometimes Creidhe did as she was told, and sometimes she didn't. Thorvald was sitting on the ground, his back to a low stone dike overlooking the western sea. He had his head in his hands, his face concealed. His sleek red hair had escaped its neat ribbon, and the wind whipped the strands like dark fire in the air around his head. He was very still. Behind him in the walled field, sheep bleated and lambs answered. Above in the sky, birds fluted songs of spring. Creidhe climbed over the wall and sat down by his side, saying not a word. She had become quite good at this kind of thing.

"Go away, Creidhe!" Thorvald growled after a while. He did not open his eyes.

There was a little boat out in the swell, coming in from

fishing. The wind was picking up; the scrap of sail carried the vessel forward on a fast, rocking course southward, perhaps to Hafnarvagr, or some point closer. Creidhe raised a hand in greeting, but they did not see her.

"I mean it, Creidhe," snapped Thorvald. "Go home. Go back to your embroidery."

She took a deep breath and let it out, counting up to ten. It was useful to have wise women in the family; one might not learn the mysteries, for those were secret, but one did at least pick up techniques for staying calm.

"What is it?" she asked him quietly. "What did she give you?"

"I don't want to talk about it. Not to you, not to anyone."

"All right," Creidhe said after a moment. "I understand. When you do want to, I'll be here to listen."

Thorvald balled his hands into tight fists. His eyes were open now, staring out to the west. It seemed to Creidhe that what he saw were not cliffs, gulls, clouds, a wind-stirred ocean, but something quite different and much farther away.

Time passed. Father would be home soon; the remark about roast mutton had been true. Such simple pleasures had the power to bring a smile to Eyvind's lips and a light to his eyes that warmed his whole family. It was not so much the good food that did it, as his daughter's thoughtfulness and skill. Creidhe rose to her feet, picking up her bundle.

"Creidhe?"

It was a dark whisper. She stood frozen in place a moment, then sat down again without a sound.

"A letter," Thorvald said. "From my father. She kept it all these years. She never even told me."

Creidhe was at odds to understand the bitterness in his tone. His father had died before he was born, and that was indeed sad, though surely sadder for Margaret than for this son who had never known the father he had lost. From what folk said, Margaret's husband Ulf had been a fine, noble chieftain who had led the first Norse expedition here to the Light Isles. He was a father to be proud of. A letter was good, wasn't it? It seemed not inappropriate that Margaret had saved it until her son was a man.

"From Ulf?" Creidhe asked gently. "I suppose that is distressing; it reminds you of what you might have had. It is a sorrow he was not here to watch you grow up."

"I didn't say it was from my mother's husband, the worthy Ulf Gunnarsson." Thorvald's voice was sharp-edged. "I said it was from my father. The man she tells me was my real father, that is. Here, if you're so interested. Why not find out all about it, since it seems half the island knows already?"

He drew the little roll of parchment from the breast of his tunic and thrust it into her hand. Creidhe was mute. What could he mean? She untied the cord that bound the letter and uncurled it to reveal row on row of neat, black script. It was old, the edges worn, the characters smudged here and there as if by drops of water. There was a pale line all across the outside where the cord had fastened it, as if the small scroll had lain long untouched.

"You know I can't read, Thorvald. What is all this about?"

"I'll tell you what it's all about. It means I'm nobody. Worse than nobody, I'm the son of some evil madman, a crazed killer. Forget Ulf; forget a conception in the respectability of marriage, and the sad demise of my father before I saw the light of day. Ulf was not my father. She kept that from me all these years. And they knew: your father, Nessa, Grim, everyone who came here in those first days. Even that stick of a serving man, Ash, knew the truth and kept quiet about it. A conspiracy of silence." His voice was shaking; he stared fixedly at the ground by his feet. "How could my own mother be so cruel?"

Creidhe was lost for words. She wanted to put an arm around him for comfort, as she would do if this were one of her sisters. But she did not; Thorvald would shake her off the instant she touched him. This news was indeed terrible, if true. What if such a thing had happened to her? Her own father was the center of her world, the warmth at the core of the family. Indeed, sometimes it seemed Eyvind was father to the whole community, guardian and loving protector to them all. To hear your father was not your father would be like the snatching away of everything safe. It would be like sundering the heart from the body. There seemed no way to comfort him.

"You're very quiet," Thorvald said suddenly, turning his head to glare at her. "No ready words of advice? No quick solutions to my problems?" His eyes narrowed; his mouth went tight. "But perhaps you knew this already. Perhaps I am indeed the last to be told the truth about my own heritage. Did you know, Creidhe?" His tone was savage; Creidhe shrank back before it.

"Of course not! How could you think—?"

Thorvald's shoulders sagged. His anger was turned inward again. "That's just it. I don't know what to think anymore."

"Who—who was he?" Creidhe ventured. "Was this letter written to you? Where is he?"

"Ask your father. He knows the answers."

"But—"

"Ask Eyvind. He was the one who exiled my father from this shore, so that he never knew he had a son. The letter was to my mother. It says nothing of me. It attempts to explain to her why her lover killed her husband. It tries to justify his murder of his own brother. You see the delightful heritage my lady mother has chosen to make me aware of now I'm deemed to have reached years of maturity?" Thorvald picked up a stone and hurled it out beyond the cliff edge. A cloud of gulls rose, screaming protest. His face was sheet-white, the eyes dark hollows.

"What was his name?" Creidhe asked, playing for time as her mind searched frantically for the right thing to say. In such a situation, there probably was no right thing.

"Somerled." He threw another stone.

"Why don't they speak of such a man? They must all have known him."

"Why don't you ask them, if you're so interested?"

She breathed slowly. "Thorvald?"

"What?"

"Aunt Margaret was wise not to tell you this before. You're grown up now. Couldn't you see this, not as a reversal but a challenge?"

His brows rose in scorn. "What can you mean, Creidhe?"

"You could find out about Somerled. As you said, there

must be plenty of people in the islands who knew him back then. Maybe he wasn't as bad as you think. Everyone's got some good in them."

"And what comes after that?" Thorvald snapped. "I jump in a boat and go off looking for him, I suppose?"

The words hung between them as the silence stretched out, giving them a weight Thorvald had not intended. Blue eyes met black; there was recognition in both that this crazy idea was, in a way, entirely logical.

Thorvald rolled the letter up and knotted the cord around it. He put it away and leaned back against the wall, arms hugging his knees, eyes firmly closed. She waited again. At length, not opening his eyes, he said, "I know you're trying to help, Creidhe. But I really do want to be by myself." There was a pause. "Please," he added.

It was not possible to bestow a gesture of affection, a quick hug, a hand-clasp, although Creidhe longed to touch him. "Farewell, Thorvald," she said, and made her way home under darkening skies.

She couldn't ask them straightaway. This was not a topic that could be broached amidst the general joy and chaos of her father's return, with dogs and children jumping about making noise, with Nessa failing to hold back her tears, and Eyvind himself doing his best to hug everyone at once while burdened with axe, sword and large pack of belongings. He was not a man who asked others to fetch and carry for him, not even now he bore such authority in the islands. When he had married Nessa, he had allied himself to the last royal princess of the Folk. This had conferred a status above that of ordinary men, and Eyvind had built on it by dedicating himself to the establishment of a lasting peace between the two races that had once been bitter enemies— the Norse invaders and the Folk who had inhabited the islands since ancient times. It was due more to Eyvind than anyone that the two now lived so amicably side by side, and indeed together. It was almost possible to forget that it had all begun in blood and terror. As for Nessa herself, she had never lost the respect due to her as both priestess and leader of her tribe, a rallying point in times of terrible trial. Now Eanna was priestess, Nessa no longer enacted the mysteries nor withdrew to the places of ritual. She had her husband, her four healthy daughters, her household and her community, and played a part in councils and negotiations, as befitted her special status. For all that, there was a sorrow in it. Eanna had been the first child for Eyvind and Nessa. The next had been a son, and the sea had taken Kinart before he'd seen five years in the world. After him there were only girls: Creidhe herself, then Brona and Ingigerd. That was not as it should have been; not as the ancestors foretold it.

Despite their near-royal status in the islands, Creidhe's family dwelt in a compound that was more farm than palace, a sprawling set of low stone buildings surrounded by walled infields, somewhat east of the tidal island known as the Whaleback. The Whaleback had once been the center of power in the Light Isles. Nessa had lived there; her uncle had been a great king. When the Norsemen first sailed out of the east, Margaret and Nessa and Eyvind had been not much older than Creidhe was now. That voyage of discovery across the sea from Rogaland to the sheltered waterways of the Light Isles had begun as a search for a life of peace and prosperity. It had turned, in the space of one bloody year, into a bitter, destructive conflict that had come to an end only after most of Nessa's folk had been cruelly slain. It was Eyvind and Nessa, Norse warrior and priestess of the Folk, who had won that peace: the two of them side by side.

What different lives they had had, Creidhe thought, watching her mother and father as they stole a quiet moment together. Nessa brushed Eyvind's cheek with her fingers; he touched his lips to her hair. The way they looked at each other brought tears to Creidhe's eyes. Their youth had been full of adventure: journeys, battles, struggle and achievement. Looking at them now, she could hardly imagine that. One did not see one's own parents as heroes, even if that was exactly what they were. One simply saw them as always there, an essential part of one's existence. Where would one be without that?

She had to ask them. But not yet. Supper first. There were men and women who lived in the household: housecarls, Eyvind called them, in the manner of his homeland. These were capable folk who seemed almost part of the family. The women had become used to Creidhe taking charge in the kitchen, especially when she wished to prepare a special meal for her father. Today someone had been fishing, and there was fresh cod; Creidhe sent Brona out to the garden for leeks, and fetched garlic and onions herself. Small Ingigerd was soon persuaded that cutting vegetables and stirring sauces and grinding herbs would be tremendous fun, and it was possible for Nessa and Eyvind to retreat to the inner room for some time alone. Creidhe told her sisters a story as she prepared the fish. It was a tale about the Hidden Tribe, those tricky spirit folk who were seen from time to time in ancient, underground places, and she made sure it was long and exciting, and allowed the children to interrupt with questions as often as they liked. It grew dark. The folk of the household gathered around the table for supper. Creidhe's efforts were rewarded by Eyvind's smile and Nessa's quiet words of approval. Brona ate every scrap and carried her platter to the wash trough without being asked. Ingigerd was falling asleep even as she finished her meal.

Respecting the family's need for privacy with Eyvind so newly returned, the men and women of the household did not linger after supper, but retired early to their sleeping quarters. It was night outside, and a sudden chill crept into the longhouse, though its walls of stone and earth were thick and sturdy. Eyvind put more turf on the hearth and they moved in closer. One on either side of the flickering oil lamp, Creidhe and Brona worked on their embroidery. Brona was making laborious progress with a row of small red flowers across an apron hem. Creidhe's project was more complex and more personal. She called it the Journey, and worked on a small section at a time, keeping the rest folded out of sight.

It was quiet now. Ingigerd drowsed on Eyvind's knee, held safe by the arm he curled around her. It was a shame, Creidhe thought, that the whole family could not be here to-

gether. That would happen increasingly rarely now that
Eanna had completed her training as a priestess of the mysteries and retired from ordinary life to dwell in the hills
alone. She must ask them tonight. This could not wait.
Eyvind carried Ingigerd to her bed and tucked the covers
over her. Brona pricked her finger and yelped; she sewed
doggedly on for a while, then sighed, yawned, and packed
her work away.

"Goodnight, Brona," Creidhe said a little pointedly. "I'll
help you with that in the morning if you like."

Brona flashed a grin and turned to hug first Father, then
Mother. She bent to light her little oil lamp with a taper
from the fire, then disappeared along to the sleeping chamber she and Creidhe shared.

"More ale?" Nessa queried. "What about you, Creidhe?
Don't strain your eyes with that fine work, daughter. You
look tired out."

"Come, sit by me," said Eyvind. "I've missed my lovely
girl. Tell me what you've been doing while I was gone. I expect Aunt Margaret's been working you hard."

Creidhe sat; she took the cup of ale her mother offered.
Her father put his arm around her shoulders, warm and safe.
If the topic were to be raised, there could be no better time
for it.

"Father, Mother, I want to ask you something."

They waited.

"It's about Thorvald."

Silence again, though there seemed a change in the quality of it, almost as if they had expected this.

"Today—today he was very upset. It was because—because Aunt Margaret told him about his father. His real father."

She felt the sudden tension in Eyvind's arm, and heard
Nessa's indrawn breath.

"I tried to help him. I tried to listen, but he was too angry.
He said—Aunt Margaret told him his real father was a mur-
derer. That's what he said. That he killed his own brother,
Aunt Margaret's husband. And he said—" She faltered.

"What, Creidhe?" Eyvind's tone was calm enough.

"That you sent Thorvald's father away," she whispered. "Banished him from the islands, so that he never knew he had a son."

"I see."

"Father, why is it none of you told us that story? Is it true? And wasn't it cruel of Aunt Margaret not to tell Thorvald until now? He's so angry and bitter. I've never seen him like this. There was nothing I could do to help."

A look was exchanged between her parents, a complicated look. Eyvind took his arm away from Creidhe's shoulders and clasped her hand instead.

"Did you talk to Margaret about this, Creidhe?"

"No. She told me to wait until Thorvald was ready to tell me. But . . ."

"But you couldn't wait." Nessa's tone was dry, but not unkind. "Creidhe, this is Margaret's story, and Margaret's secret. It was her choice to wait and tell Thorvald when she judged he was ready. Those were terrible times. To dwell on what had happened was to set a barrier between your father's people and mine that would keep us at enmity all our lives, and would be passed on to our children and our children's children. There had been enough hatred and cruelty. We made the decision, in those early days, to put it behind us. We didn't forget; one carries such memories in one's mind forever. But we chose to move on, all of us. I suppose now it will be discussed more widely. Thorvald is sure to talk to his friends, you included."

"Eanna knows what happened, Creidhe," Eyvind said quietly. "One cannot follow the calling of priestess without the knowledge of history. She has kept it to herself, as we promised Margaret. That was for Thorvald's sake."

Creidhe said nothing. It hurt, sometimes, to be nobody special, even though she had no great ambitions for herself. It hurt even more that her parents hadn't trusted her to keep a secret.

"I had an interesting talk with a man called Gartnait at the Thing on Sandy Island," Eyvind remarked, apparently changing the subject completely. "A chieftain from the

Northern Isles, a fine-looking young fellow of around two-and-twenty, very well-mannered and courteous. He asked me about you, Creidhe. It seems talk of you has spread quite far."

"Talk? What talk?"

Eyvind smiled. "Nothing bad, or I'd not have spoken so fair of the fellow. You were described as a model of young womanhood, highly skilled in all the domestic arts, and far from ugly into the bargain."

"Eyvind!" Nessa frowned at him.

"His exact words were a good deal more complimentary than that. In fact, your virtues were enumerated at quite some length, but I won't repeat them for fear of giving you a swollen head, daughter. It was clear the young man's interest had been sparked by what he'd heard of you. He's looking for a wife."

"Oh."

"You'd have liked him, Creidhe," her father said. "He was an honest, open sort of man, with a ready smile. And handsome—did I say that? You will need to start thinking of this some time soon. You know how important this is, not just for yourself but for all of us. For the islands."

"This is not the first such inquiry your father has had," Nessa put in.

Creidhe stared at her mother, sudden hope making her heart race. Had Thorvald said something at last?

"Creidhe," Eyvind said quietly, "we wondered how you would feel about going away for a while, perhaps with your Aunt Margaret to chaperone you. A stay in the Northern Isles would do you good, expose you to a wider circle, allow you to mix and give you some respite from your domestic duties here. You work yourself very hard, my dear. A visit over the summer would be easy to arrange. We have friends there. I'm not pushing an alliance with this Gartnait; you'd meet many folk. It would enable you to be seen, and put you in a position to get to know both him and others. You could make your own judgments then."

"You know the importance of a good choice," Nessa said.

"If we do not nurture the blood line, the identity of the Folk is quite lost. It is your children, as well as Brona's and Ingigerd's, who will carry forward the royal line."

Creidhe did know; one did not grow up in such a family without an understanding of the royal descent, and the significance of marriages. Nessa had been the only surviving kin of the great Engus, last king of the Folk in the Light Isles. She was his sister's child, and as the royal succession came through the female line, it was vital for her daughters to marry men with impeccable credentials, since their sons would have a claim to kingship. As Nessa herself had no surviving sons, this was doubly important. It still mattered, even though the islands were governed by council now and no longer chose kings.

"You must wed wisely," Nessa added.

There was a silence.

"I thought we were going to talk about Thorvald?" Creidhe blurted out suddenly, finding herself on the verge of tears for no good reason.

"We are talking about Thorvald, Creidhe," said her father gently.

She felt herself grow cold; a weight lodged in her heart. There seemed to be nothing to say.

"You asked for the story," said Nessa. "We'll tell it, but I suggest you take Margaret's good advice and keep it to yourself. This is Thorvald's dilemma and hers. They are best left to deal with it in their own way. Thorvald's father was a man called Somerled; he was indeed Ulf's brother, and came here to the islands in that first expedition, the same that brought Eyvind to this shore."

"Ulf wanted peace." Eyvind took up the tale. "He made a treaty with King Engus, Nessa's uncle. All seemed well. But Ulf died. He was murdered under very odd circumstances. My people blamed the islanders, and war broke out. There was—there was great ill-doing. Many died."

Nessa glanced at him, a little frown on her brow. In the soft lamplight, with her pale skin and wide, gray eyes, she looked very young, not at all like a mother of four daughters. She reached out and took her husband's hand. "My own people were all but wiped out," she said gravely. "My uncle died, my cousin, everyone close to me save Eyvind and Rona." Nessa paused. The loss of her old mentor, the wise woman who had taught both Nessa and her daughter Eanna the mysteries of the ancestors, was still fresh, for Rona had lived long, passing peacefully with the coming of last spring. "It grew clear to me and to your father that Somerled, who had become leader after Ulf's death, was responsible for the wave of fear and hatred that had gripped the islands. Your father was very brave. He confronted Somerled at risk of his own life and proved him guilty of his brother's murder."

Eyvind smiled faintly, though his blue eyes were troubled. "As I recall it, it was your mother's courage that tipped the balance. Without her, all would have been lost."

"I don't understand," Creidhe said, struggling to make sense of this. "Where does Aunt Margaret fit in?"

"Despite what he did," Eyvind said, "Somerled was not a wholly evil man. At least, I did not believe it of him, and nor did Margaret. We saw some hope for redemption in him, a spark of kindness, of goodness that might become more, given the right nurturing. There was a time when Margaret was very lonely. Ulf, fine man though he was, was always busy with his own projects, and I think she suffered for that. Somerled admired her greatly. Subtlety and cleverness had great appeal for him. In Margaret he saw something he found only rarely: an equal. But in the end theirs was not a happy alliance. She could not tolerate what he did in his quest for power."

"But she bore his child. And yet you exiled him." It seemed very cruel, even if the man had been a murderer. It seemed not at all the kind of penalty loving, generous Eyvind would impose.

"I was faced with a choice. Under the law he himself had instituted, I could have sentenced him to death. That was what Somerled wanted. He had always been fiercely ambitious. For a season he had been king here. Now he was defeated; even those who had supported his actions were deserting him. He had nobody left. He begged me to kill him. The sentence I decreed was a measure of the fact that I still had faith in him, even after the terrible havoc he had wrought. It gave him another chance to change his path: to learn to walk straight. I thought I was being merciful. To Somerled, the punishment I imposed seemed cruel beyond belief."

"He left this shore without knowing Margaret carried his child," Nessa said. "Rona knew. I guessed. But Margaret did not tell him, nor did she speak of it to me until Somerled was gone. That would have made no difference to Eyvind's decision. Somerled was not fit to remain in the islands. He treated my people with contempt. Many thought Eyvind's decree too merciful; they feared Somerled's return. He was a man who could wield great power. He influenced people through fear, and fear is a potent weapon. But Eyvind made him promise never to come back. He made him promise to do his best to change. Whether Somerled kept to that, I suppose we'll never know."

"Why would he promise such a thing?"

"Because of this," Eyvind said, rolling back his left sleeve to show the long scar that ran up his inner forearm. Creidhe had always thought this a legacy of the life her father had once led as a Wolfskin warrior; his body bore its share of the marks of combat. "Somerled and I were blood brothers, sworn to lifelong loyalty. He challenged me with that bond at the end, and at the end I held him to it. Then I sent him westward across the ocean. Perhaps it was, after all, a sentence of death. In all these years, we've never had any word of him."

Creidhe was speechless. This was like something from an old saga, the kind full of gods and monsters. It was surely not real life.

"It's true, Creidhe," her mother said. "Those were terrible times. Eyvind and I were lucky; our love for each other made us strong. The ancestors warned us all along that our path would be hard, yet they told us we were doing right. Some very old powers stepped in to aid us in the end, but it was human courage that won the day. You must not think harshly of your Aunt Margaret, although she lay with a man who was not her husband. She's a strong woman, and proud. Her life has been lonely because of the error she made then. She has never forgiven herself for it."

"She has Thorvald."

"Yes. And she loves her son, even though he is a daily reminder of the sorrows of the past. I imagine she will speak of this to him, and explain it as best she can. I hope he will listen, and not judge her too severely."

"He spoke little of her," Creidhe said slowly, "except to call her cruel for holding back the truth for so long."

"Would Thorvald have dealt with it better last year, or the year before?" asked Eyvind mildly. "He's still a boy, for all his eighteen years. He'll come to terms with it in time. The lad still has some growing up to do." His expression was thoughtful.

"Father?" There was a question Creidhe knew she must ask, although she did not want to hear the answer.

"Yes, daughter?"

"I would not like to think folk would judge Thorvald on the strength of what his father did. It seems—unfair—that people might think him—unsuitable—because his father performed an ill deed all those years ago. It seems to me— I think a person of good judgment should disregard that, and assess Thorvald on his own merits." This was very hard to say. "That is what I plan to do. He's still the same person he was yesterday." Tears were close; she blinked them back. "I hope you will remember that, when you speak of sending me away to the Northern Isles."

"Oh, Creidhe," Nessa said with a sigh. "We wouldn't be sending you away; don't think of it like that. It's an opportunity. Your circle is so narrow here in Hrossey."

"Father?"

"Daughter, I am taken aback that you would think me capable of such prejudice. You should know I always judge a man on his own merits, not on his lineage or the deeds of his kinfolk. Thorvald is not Somerled; he is his own self, and far more Margaret's son than anyone else's. I do not weigh him with the burden of the past on his shoulders."

"And yet you want me to go to the Northern Isles and make friends with some chieftain I've never met?"

He smiled. "And yet I want you to go, although I'll miss that roast mutton terribly."

"I have to think about it," Creidhe said, swallowing hard. It was as good as an edict, what they had said and what they had so carefully not said. *We do not think Thorvald a suitable husband for you.* She almost wished they were not so sweet and tactful, the two of them, so she could scream and yell and stamp her foot at them. Inside her head was a jumble of feelings clamoring to be released, and there was no way to let them go. Creidhe rolled up her embroidery and rose to her feet.

"Goodnight, Father. Sweet dreams, Mother."

"Creidhe—" Nessa began. But Creidhe had turned her back, heading for bed. It was only when she had snuffed out the lamp and wriggled under the covers next to the sleeping Brona that she let her tears fall. It wasn't fair. None of it was fair. The ancestors played tricks sometimes, and turned things all awry. If she'd been at all interested in Gartnait from the Northern Isles, this would have been simple, since the fellow seemed to view her as a catalog of feminine virtues without so much as meeting her once in the flesh. Gartnait was probably exactly as her father had said, a fine specimen of young manhood and utterly suitable to father a future king. Why did she have to love the one man in the world who hardly seemed to see her on some days, and on others treated her as if she were no different from a boy? It just wasn't fair.

"Creidhe?" Brona's voice was muffled by layers of blankets. "What's the matter?"

"Nothing," sniffed Creidhe, moving closer to the warmth of her sister's body. It might be spring, but the air was bitterly cold, and even in this well-made house, little drafts stirred in corners. "Nothing. Go back to sleep."

It was like a curse, a darkness that would hang over him for the rest of his life, shadowing every step he took. It was one thing to have a heroic dead father whom one had never met, a man who was remembered, still, as leader of the first bold voyage from Norway to the Light Isles. It was quite another to discover your father was a crazed murderer, a tyrant who had unleashed a tide of blood and terror on the islands. Thorvald did not want to acknowledge, even to himself, what that seemed to mean. Striding along the track toward Stensakir with a violent wind whipping his hair out behind him and tugging at his cloak with insistent, cold fingers, he shrank from the terrible truth that had hit him like a hammer blow after the first numbing shock of his mother's news. But he could not shut it out. *This made sense of everything.* His legacy was not Ulf's but Somerled's, not light but darkness, not order and sanity but discord and chaos. This was the missing piece of a puzzle. It told him why he had always felt outside the world of other people, why he could not smile and clasp hands readily, why he turned on those who tried to befriend him, despite himself. It gave the reason why, some days, he felt as if he carried his own gray cloud of misery with him, which nobody else could see. No wonder he'd never fitted in. No wonder he'd never felt a part of things. No wonder he had so few true friends.

Thorvald shivered. As his father's son, by rights he did not deserve friends, most certainly not loyal ones like Creidhe, who could always be relied upon to listen and wait by him even when his dark mood made him snap and snarl like a feral cur. Creidhe would be better off staying right away from him. Who knew when this bad blood would surface? It was not safe for any man to befriend him, nor any woman, least of all a guileless girl like Creidhe with her cozy domestic pursuits. She was a child, and knew nothing of the world. She was innocent of such destructive forces as those he bore hidden inside him. From now on nobody would be safe. Unless . . . unless, against all evidence, what they told of Somerled was somehow wrong. If the tale had been twisted and changed, as is the pattern of stories over so many years, if that were so then maybe there was a glimmer of hope. If his mother said Somerled had killed Ulf, that fact must stand. But perhaps there was a reason for it, a justification. Why had Somerled acted as he did? And what had become of the man? He'd been cast out to sea from the west coast, near the Whaleback. Trackless ocean was all that lay before him then, until he reached the rim of the world. What a punishment that was, a penalty grand and terrible enough to belong to an ancient saga, like a burden imposed by a vengeful god or thwarted monarch. That it was Eyvind who had determined it was unbelievable. Creidhe's father was widely respected in the islands, not just as husband of a royal princess of the Folk, but also as a mainstay of the group of landholders who assembled twice yearly at the Thing to maintain order and administer justice. Eyvind was known as scrupulously honest and absolutely fair, a model of strength and honor. But he was most certainly not a man of devious imagination or cunning irony. To devise such a method of exile seemed to Thorvald quite out of character. Maybe there were parts of the story Margaret hadn't told him.

Asking Eyvind was just not possible. Pride forbade it. He couldn't talk to his mother. The thought of what she had done disgusted him. If she had such a model husband as Ulf, why lie with some misfit wretch of a brother-killer? And how could she not tell her own son, all these years? It was this that hurt Thorvald most. Up till now, when he was angry or upset, he had relied on Margaret's grave advice, her calm words to soothe him. When he could see his mother was lonely or out of sorts he had done his best to divert her with a game or a walk or a tale of what he'd been doing. It had been thus ever since he could remember: mostly just the two of them, unless you counted Ash hovering silently somewhere in the background. Why his mother kept Ash, Thorvald couldn't comprehend. It was quite clear to him the fellow wanted a bit more than the relationship of trusted servant to mistress of the household, and that Margaret was not in the least interested. A man who would hang around like a stray dog for years and years, waiting for table scraps that never came his way, seemed to Thorvald a lost cause. But silent, poker-faced Ash stayed while other servants came and went. All the same, they were a small family of two, Thorvald and Margaret, neither much given to open displays of affection, yet trusting and depending on each other. Until now. That closeness was destroyed forever now. She might as well have thrust a blade through his heart, Thorvald thought, kicking savagely at a stone that lay on the track in his way. She might as well have cast him out like his father, away from the paths of right-thinking men and women, so he could be conveniently forgotten. How could he ever forgive her for this?

It was late afternoon when he came down the hill past the small settlement at Stensakir, where smoke from cottage fires was whipped sideways by the wind, and the heather thatch shivered, straining at its bindings. Thorvald could see the *Sea Dove* making a steady course back to shore, the red-striped sail taut before the gale. His timing was perfect. He must talk to Sam; must tell him as much as he needed to know. He'd have preferred to keep his news to himself, but this was necessary. Thorvald needed a boat. Sam had one. He just hoped Sam would be able to keep his mouth shut.

It would be a while before his friend reached the jetty, doubtless with a good catch from the treacherous waters between this northeastern shore of Hrossey and the rising ground of Hrolfsey, which the old folk called Queen's Isle. It was most certainly not the safest place to fish, but Sam was an expert sailor and an astute judge of currents and tides. He had prospered and built his own cottage in Stensakir; he talked of marrying and starting a family. Thorvald thought that ridiculous, and had told his friend so. Being an equable sort of fellow, Sam had only smiled.

Not only was this waterway a perilous fishing ground, it also housed the strangest of dwelling places. On the level ground of Holy Island, situated halfway between the larger isles, lived a community of Christian hermits. The brothers had traveled across the ocean from a land far to the southwest, in tiny, frail shells of boats. This small isle with its weight of lore had been their chosen home. Folk had shunned the place for generations; it was known to be a dwelling place of the Seal Tribe, a dangerous people at home both in water and on land, the women of unearthly beauty, the men so fearsome they could scare a person to death with a single glance of their dark green eyes. Shielded by the courage of their faith—or by blind ignorance, depending on how you looked at it—the brothers had settled on Holy Island nonetheless, and now lived in a well-ordered though simple fashion, running a few sheep, a goat or two, some chickens. As far as anyone knew, the Seal Tribe had never bothered them, though it was said that the sea folk were immensely patient and had long memories. Say someone offended them, or received a favor. Generations might pass and all seem forgotten, and then suddenly there they'd be, demanding vengeance or asking for payment. Because of that, there were very few visitors to Holy Island, and those who made the trip always carried a piece of iron with them for protection. If you forgot this essential item, there was no saying you'd ever get home safely. Sam was one of the few who put in regularly to the brothers' small jetty, with a message or a gift of bread or fresh fish. Sam was a big fellow and not easily frightened.

Thorvald waited on the shore, watching as the *Sea Dove* bobbed closer. This was a superior kind of craft, a vessel such as a young fisherman like Sam might dream of all his life and never hope to own. Sam had built her for a man called Olaf Egilsson, who had wealth enough to buy in the fine oak from Rogaland. The *Sea Dove* was perfect in every detail, from her eye-sweet lines to the sturdy strength of her keel. The lower strakes were of oak, the sheer strake of lighter pine. She was a haaf-boat, an ocean-going craft, though small. The two pairs of oars she carried were seldom employed, for she went far better under sail, with one man stationed near the stern to handle the steering oar, which was mounted on the starboard side, the other adjusting the trim as required. Sometimes they rowed in and out from the jetty; that was all. Sam had made the sail himself, not trusting any other man in Hrossey with such a critical piece of craftsmanship. On the day she was finished, Olaf Egilsson had taken sick with an ague, and within seven nights he was dead, but not before he told every one of his kin that nobody was getting their hands on his boat but the man who had made her with such love. If he were to die, the *Sea Dove* must be Sam's, for only Sam would use her as she deserved.

The haaf-boat was as well maintained as any vessel in the islands; her master had a reputation for thoroughness, for all he was barely twenty years of age. The boards that formed the small decks fore and aft had been replaced last autumn when squalls drove a handy supply of pine trunks up on the beach at Skaill. The mast could be lowered to rest on a low, crutch-like frame, though Sam never undertook this maneuver at sea; the mast remained in place save when the *Sea Dove* was hauled up for work in winter. Every year Sam's pride and joy was recaulked, her hull scraped clean, her thwarts rubbed down with coarse sand then oiled against the saltwater. In the right conditions the boat could be handled comfortably by two, at least in the coastal waters around Hrossey, which were not without their challenges. All in all, Thorvald thought the *Sea Dove* seemed up to a longer voyage. He hoped very much that his friend would agree.

Sam had a passenger today. The gray-haired priest stepped out neatly onto the jetty while Sam and the deckhand tied up the boat and began to unload their catch in a seamless sequence of well-practiced moves. Of all the brothers, it was Tadhg who was best known in the islands, for it was his practice to travel widely, telling his tales of the Christian faith. Tadhg was an old friend of both Eyvind and Nessa. A long time ago he had known Nessa's uncle, the last great king of the Light Isles. His appearance now was remarkably convenient; Thorvald must make the most of the opportunity it offered.

"Go on up to the house, Thorvald!" Sam yelled as he hefted a crate of fish onto his shoulder. "Take Brother Tadhg with you, and stir up the fire for me. I'll be done here soon."

Thorvald made his way up to the settlement and let himself into Sam's neat cottage, main room open and light with a shuttered window to the east so you could read the moods

of the sea, back room housing sleeping platforms and a separate small hearth, and a snug little shelter beyond for stores
of various kinds. Today there appeared to be a broody hen
in there, grumbling to herself in a cozy basket of straw.
Brother Tadhg came in behind Thorvald, the skirts of his
brown robe blown crazily about him by the fierce wind. He
shut the door with some difficulty. Thorvald raked out the
embers of the fire, fetched turf, set a kettle to heat. Because
there was limited time, he decided to dispense with the
niceties.

"I want to ask you something."

"Go ahead," said Tadhg, seating himself by the fledgling
fire and reaching down to warm his hands.

"I found out about Somerled. That he was my father. My
mother told me. You must have known him back then. I
want you to tell me what sort of man he was. I want to find
out why he killed his brother. And . . ."

"And what, Thorvald?" The brother did not sound at all
perturbed by this volley of difficult questions.

The fire was starting to pick up now. Thorvald put on
more turf. "And I want you to tell me where you think he
would have gone, when Eyvind set him adrift. On Holy Island you've got men who sailed here from far away, men
who must know the pattern of the currents out there in the
western ocean, and where the islands and skerries lie. Tell
me what you think. Could he have survived?"

Tadhg did not reply immediately. It looked as if he were rehearsing the words in his head, choosing each one with care.

"Tell me!" Thorvald demanded. "Don't bother to couch it
in comforting terms. If you think he would have died, just
say so. If you think he was evil and depraved, tell me
straight out. My mother held back the truth for eighteen
years. I've no patience for falsehoods nor for polite half-
truths. Whatever you have to say, it can be no worse than
finding out I've lived a lie my whole life."

"You're a young man, Thorvald," Tadhg observed, regarding him gravely. "You have many years ahead of you. It
is those years that matter, not the ones that are past. What

your father was, and where he went, makes no real difference. It's your own life you are living, not Somerled's."

"Spare me your philosophy!" Thorvald snapped. "Give me facts. Why did my father kill Ulf? Is it true that he single-handedly wiped out most of the islanders before Eyvind stopped him?"

"You wish me to answer before your friend arrives home? These are big questions, Thorvald."

"Please." It took some effort to get this word out; still, he saw understanding in the priest's gray eyes, and heard compassion in his voice. It was expedient to take a deep breath and attempt calm if he were to have a chance of getting the answers he needed.

"Only Somerled could tell you why he killed his brother," Tadhg said. "There seemed obvious reasons: the lust for power, jealousy, frustration that there was no real role for him here. His feelings for your mother, perhaps. There were older reasons, which he brought with him from Rogaland, matters of the distant past. You'd need to ask Eyvind about those."

"Eyvind? Why?"

"The two of them were close friends: blood brothers. It was in a sense of responsibility for Somerled's ill deeds that Eyvind banished him. He could have killed him. Instead he chose a way that gave his friend a second chance. It was a wise and generous decision."

"A second chance! A chance to sail over the edge of the world and perish."

"That is one possibility," agreed Tadhg evenly.

"You think there are others? Tell me!"

"I will, Thorvald. One answer at a time. Somerled brought a weight of trouble with him when he came here with his brother's expedition. Ulf was a friend of mine; we spoke much during his all too brief season as chieftain here. For all Somerled was his own brother, Ulf feared him greatly. It was not on his invitation that Somerled came here, but at the behest of the Jarl back home. Ulf was under pressure to agree, since the Jarl had financed his venture.

The result was catastrophic. Somerled did terrible things as leader here. He was a clever man, subtle, ingenious. He was also completely ruthless. It seemed to me he had no awareness at all of the suffering of others; it was as if some essential part of a man's understanding were closed to him, and always had been. It is troubling to consider that, had it not been for Eyvind's intervention, and Nessa's, he would have remained king here, and none of the island folk would have survived. Your father believed the Norse people to be superior in every way, and far better fitted to rule. He saw no place here for folk he believed to be primitive, weak and ineffectual. He'd have wiped them out entirely. Somerled never understood them; he never understood the islands. He'd have killed Nessa; she was too influential to be left alive. Eyvind, too. At one point both the Wolfskin and myself were imprisoned and on the verge of execution. Somerled did not take kindly to hearing the truth if it happened not to suit his own purposes."

There seemed to be nothing for Thorvald to say. He had asked for answers, after all. Too bad if it hurt to hear them, when he had believed nothing could hurt much after what his mother had told him.

"King," he said finally, his tone hollow.

"Indeed. That was his lifelong ambition, so Eyvind told me. For a short while, he achieved it. The cost was high."

Thorvald felt a bitter laugh escaping from his throat. "Hah! Just think, if he'd stayed on here, I might have been king after him. King Thorvald. Very amusing, that. And Eanna would never have been born, nor Creidhe, nor the others. Thank the gods he was sent away. As ruler here I probably would have turned out just like him."

"We must concern ourselves with the path that was taken, not the one abandoned," Tadhg said, using an iron hook to lift the kettle's lid and see if the water was boiling. "You want to know where he might have gone. Why?"

This one must be answered carefully. "He was my father. It is of some interest to me whether he lived or died."

"I can speak of possibilities, Thorvald. But nobody can say what happened. Your mother told you, I imagine, that there has been no news of Somerled since that day, no sign at all that he ever reached safe shore. All I can give you is surmise."

"That'll do," Thorvald said, trying not to sound too interested. It was important that nobody got any hint of what he intended to do.

"Very well. Under conditions such as were apparent that day, my guess is that the boat might have traveled somewhat north of due west. Perhaps sharply north. We have no proof that there's land of any significance to the west, but there are some very strange tales. I heard that a fellow came in to the Northern Isles some time back, in a state of shock so severe it was almost as if he had lost his wits entirely. He was one of our own kind and had sailed the same path as I did, but was blown off course by contrary winds and failed to touch shore in the Light Isles. His words were a stream of nonsense, but he seemed to be telling of a sojourn of two or three seasons on another group of islands further to the northwest. They'd be several days' sailing from here at least, and maybe considerably more, since we've heard so few reports of such a place. One or two other accounts do seem to confirm their existence. That would be the last land to the west, a marginal place. It would be easy to miss it. Should your father's craft have drifted somewhat northward, it is possible he may have reached that shore."

Thorvald's heart was thumping. "Why was the man in such a state of mind?" he asked eagerly. "Was he deranged by the journey itself, or something more?"

Tadhg frowned. "My account is third-hand, of course. The fellow was terrified out of his wits; they could get little sense from him. He was frightened of staying by the seashore, as if he expected an enemy to come from the water. He spoke of stealing children, and of some kind of singing. It was quite odd. Very probably his long voyage and the isolation had caused these waking nightmares. It's not the easiest experience. A man's faith can be sorely tested."

"Yes, well, that's why you do it, isn't it?"

Tadhg smiled. "Indeed. And I will be honest with you, I

have often wondered whether such a voyage would change Somerled for the better, as Eyvind hoped it would."

"Perhaps he was unable to change," Thorvald said. He could hear the crunch of Sam's boots on the path outside. "Maybe he was so evil that he could never redeem himself."

"Ah," Tadhg observed, "while we cannot say what did happen to your father, I can tell you one of God's most profound truths, and you would be wise to ponder it, Thorvald. No man is quite beyond salvation. God's grace is in all of us. If nurtured well, that little flame may grow into a radiant goodness. We are all his creatures; we are part of him. To change, all we need do is learn to love him. Even Somerled could do that. You must believe it possible that he did so, in his own way."

The arrival of Sam with a string of pale-bellied fish dangling from one hand and his bundle of gear grasped in the other put an end to that conversation. Cups were filled with ale, a meal was cooked, and easy talk flowed: of the weather, of the arrival of new lambs on the brothers' small farm, of a forthcoming wedding and the death of an old man down at Hafnarvagr. That was where Tadhg was heading: quite a way. Sam offered him a bed for the night, but the priest refused. He'd a lift arranged with a local farmer; indeed, he'd best be heading over there now, before it got too dark. They'd sleep at the fellow's house and take the cart on in the morning with a load of vegetables and some chickens for the market. Tadhg wiped his plate clean with a scrap of bread, then rose to depart.

"Remember what I told you, Thorvald," he said mildly. "Take time to consider. On reflection, a monster can become no more than a fleeting shadow, an unassailable mountain a gentle rise. You are young; you rush to seek answers, heedless of the cost. If you allow time, you may find that all you need to do is wait."

Thorvald let him finish. There was no point in arguing. The truth was simple. He bore his father's legacy, and it marked him as surely as Eyvind's courage and goodness had marked his small son Kinart. If that child had not been snatched by the sea, he'd doubtless have grown up into the sort of leader folk followed to the ends of the earth. Tadhg had missed the point. To know himself, to look into his own spirit, Thorvald must find out what kind of man his father truly was. And there was only one way that could be done. It was perilous. His mother wouldn't like it. Sam would take a lot of convincing. Nonetheless, he must attempt it, or forever live with the knowledge that he had not faced up to the truth. If his father still lived, he would find him. It was a quest: grand, challenging, heroic. Do this, and his life might come to mean something after all.

Sam was not easily surprised. He listened calmly to the story: Margaret, Somerled, Ulf, battles and blood, murder and exile. From time to time he sipped his ale and nodded. Once or twice he frowned. One of the reasons Sam had remained a friend for so long was his talent for calm. He was almost as good a listener as Creidhe, and a lot less inclined to make helpful suggestions when they weren't wanted. When Thorvald came to the end of the tale, Sam did not comment at once. He poked the fire, topped up his friend's ale and let a cat in the back door, all in complete silence.

"You want to borrow the *Sea Dove*," he stated eventually, his blue eyes thoughtful.

"Not exactly," replied Thorvald, a wave of relief sweeping through him that Sam had understood this part of it without needing to be told. "I'm not enough of a sailor to take her there myself. You'd have to come with me. I could pay you, if that would help."

Sam's brows lifted a little. He took a mouthful of ale. "How long do you plan being away? From full moon to full moon, or maybe a season? Perhaps more if the wind carries you astray? There's a lot of fish to be caught in such a time, enough to pay for a fellow's wedding and furnish his cottage nice and snug: best woolens, fine linens, a piece of seasoned wood for a cradle. Enough to cover his hand's wages. What if the boat's damaged? That's my livelihood down there, Thorvald. She may be a sturdy craft, but she's not made for that kind of ocean voyaging."

The words were less than encouraging. On the other hand, there was a certain note in Sam's voice, and a certain glint in his eye, that showed his interest had been sparked.

"It needn't be long." Thorvald leaned forward, elbows on knees, keen to press what little advantage he had. "Brother Tadhg didn't seem to think it was very far. We could be there and back again almost before anyone knows it. We could tell them—"

Sam raised a hand, cutting off the flow of words. "Not so fast. What about when we get there, *if* we get there? You planning to pop in, announce that you're this fellow's son, then sail right home again? What if you can't find him? What if you do and he wants you to stay? Where does that leave me?"

The smile that curved Thorvald's lips felt like a mockery. "I can assure you that won't happen. I'm not expecting to be greeted with open arms, even supposing we do find what we're looking for. I've no intention at all of staying there. All I want is the answer to a question."

"And what question's that?" Sam asked, stroking the cat, which had curled itself on his lap in a ball of gray-striped contentment, purring like a simmering kettle. But Thorvald did not reply, and the silence lengthened between them.

'I'll think about it," Sam said eventually. "But I'll be straight with you, Thorvald. I can't see much in it for me, beyond helping an old friend."

"One last adventure before you settle down?" Thorvald suggested. "One last foray as a single man? You worry me with your talk of cradles. I did say I'd pay."

Sam nodded slowly. "If I agreed, it'd be as a favor to a friend. I'd expect that to be returned some time."

"Of course. I'll do whatever you want," Thorvald offered eagerly. The fact was, such a favor would be easily repaid, since Sam never asked more of him than a day's help on the boat or a hand with laying thatch. His friend was easily pleased.

"Mmm," Sam said with a funny look in his eyes. "I'll hold you to that, Thorvald. Give me a day or two to think about this. One thing, though. In open water you'll need a crew of four, at least. We'd have to get another couple of fellows in on it. And they'd certainly want to be paid."

"No." Thorvald had wondered when Sam would get to this; he had known there needed to be a good answer to it, but the look on his friend's face told him none of those he had thought up was going to be sufficient. "I can't have anyone else. Asking you to come along is one thing, getting other men to do it is another thing altogether. As soon as we started asking about, the whole island would know. This is secret, Sam. It has to be just you and me. You've told me often enough how well the *Sea Dove* goes under sail. And it's not very far. We could do it easily. Don't you go out every day with just your deckhand to help you?"

"You're crazy," Sam said flatly. "I wouldn't so much as consider it, not without one more man at least. You seem pretty confident about how far it is. I thought we didn't know that for sure."

"Brother Tadhg said a few days' sail. Folk would hardly get the chance to miss us." A lie, that, almost certainly. "Come on, Sam. This is a once in a lifetime opportunity: a true adventure."

"An adventure isn't worth having if you never get back to tell the tale," Sam observed flatly. There was a brief silence.

"So you won't even consider it?" Thorvald asked, watching his friend closely. "Not as a test of your boat, or of yourself? Not at any price?"

Sam's mouth stretched in a faint grin. "At any price? You're not as rich as that, Thorvald, however good a farm your mother runs. Now tell me, did you mean what you said about returning the favor? Say I do it, and then what I ask you isn't to your liking? Will you stay true to what you promised?"

Thorvald's heart leaped; evidently there was still hope. "Of course," he said with complete confidence. He could not think of a thing Sam could ask for that he would not be prepared to deliver. "I gave you my word, didn't I? I know how much you'll be risking, Sam. If you do this, I'll be in your debt forever."

"If I do it, I'll be as mad as you are," Sam muttered. "Well, I'll give it some thought and let you know. Maybe we could pick up a crew in the Northern Isles, fellows that don't know you, if that's what matters. There'd be a lot to organize."

"It must be kept secret," Thorvald put in quickly. "I'd be stopped if they knew—my mother, Eyvind, any of them. You mustn't tell Creidhe."

"You're a grown man," Sam observed, rising to his feet. The cat, dislodged, fell bonelessly to the floor and strolled away unperturbed.

"All the same. They'd think this foolish, dangerous. They chose not to speak of my father all those years; they made a decision to forget him. It's hardly likely they'll want him brought to life now, when he's so conveniently faded into the mists of memory."

"Still," said Sam, "your mother did tell you."

Thorvald shivered. "So she did," he agreed. "More fool her."

"A bit hard on her, aren't you?"

Thorvald did not reply, but later, while Sam slept as tranquilly as a babe, he lay awake pondering this, wondering if he had been entirely fair to Margaret. There was no doubt in his mind that she should have told him the truth earlier, not saved it for now, then expected him to absorb, understand and forgive as if this were a small, everyday matter. On the other hand, she'd been young back in those days, younger than he was now. And perhaps Somerled had not been what people said. Perhaps there'd been reasons for what he did, reasons nobody else understood. Maybe he'd been like Thorvald, an outsider, a man with few friends, a person too clever for his own good.

Thorvald lay staring up at the roof thatch, listening to the purring of the cat as it kneaded the blankets behind Sam's knees. The fisherman sighed, turning over. Thorvald considered the implications of his plan. There was no doubt he would hurt people he cared about, his mother and Creidhe especially. It was a long voyage, almost certainly longer

than he had given Sam to believe, and there were no guar-
antees of safe landfall. Somerled might not be there; might
not ever have been there. He might have perished long
since, somewhere out at sea alone in his little boat. When
she learned what he had done, Margaret would be horrified.
Creidhe would be hurt that he had not confided in her; she
was accustomed to sharing his inmost fears, his frustra-
tions, his schemes and plans. This he could not tell her. He
must hope she would forgive when he returned. If he returned. One thing was certain. This was a journey he was
bound to undertake: bound by his blood.

TWO

Three tides on western shores
Whale harvest, blood tide
Night of voices, death tide
Isle of Clouds, fool's tide

MONK'S MARGIN NOTE

Creidhe's weaving was almost finished, a soft blanket of
finest wool, vivid red on deepest blue. The decorative
borders with their pattern of foxes, owls and little trees had
already been done on the strip-loom; Creidhe would sew
the pieces together to produce a seamless effect. Margaret
asked her what project she would start on next, but Creidhe
could not answer. For some reason there didn't seem to be a
next, not right now. Perhaps she would go to the Northern
Isles as her parents wanted, she told her aunt. It might not
be a good time to embark on a new piece of work. And
there was always the Journey, that very private embroidery
which seemed to grow and grow and never quite be finished
to her satisfaction.

"Don't worry about Thorvald," Aunt Margaret told her

bluntly one afternoon when the two of them were beginning to fasten off the warp threads, working side by side as late afternoon sun slanted in through the open doorway, touching the colored wool to fiery brightness. "He'll come home when he's ready. He told you what this is about, I suppose."

"Some of it," Creidhe said awkwardly. It was difficult to approach such a subject, even though Aunt Margaret was a trusted friend. This was not just about secrets, it concerned murder and betrayal, and it was beyond imagining that neat, self-sufficient Margaret, a woman who displayed none of the signs of a passionate nature, had ever been embroiled in such high drama. "I know he's unhappy," Creidhe went on. "I'd like to help him, but . . ."

"A man can't be helped if he doesn't want it," Margaret said. "You'd be best to leave him alone, Creidhe. Thorvald has to work this out for himself. Your father's right, a trip away would be good for you."

Creidhe said nothing. Margaret might think Thorvald was off brooding somewhere and would come home when he'd forgiven her. Creidhe knew better. Thorvald was away visiting Sam again. Sometimes it seemed to Creidhe that Thorvald thought she was stupid, just as he thought the pastimes she loved so much—weaving, sewing, cooking—were women's pursuits requiring little in the way of cleverness. She knew she was not stupid. She could tell Thorvald was planning an expedition. He was going to find his father, and Sam would be traveling with him; it took two men to sail the *Sea Dove*. If Margaret had not worked that out, she knew her son less well than she imagined.

This was going to be a challenge. It might be quite a long way, and Creidhe had never enjoyed the motion of a boat, not even the small faering they used to take out when they were children. But one thing was certain. For all his eighteen years, Thorvald was not very grown up at all, and had no idea how to look after himself. And whatever anyone might say about him, he was deserving of her help, of her love. People looked at Thorvald and saw only the bad side, the gloomy moods, the sudden anger, the silences. Creidhe knew him better. He had been her friend as long as she could remember. He had been there the day Kinart died, a terrible, long-ago day when her parents were too shattered by shock and grief to take heed of their little daughter. Creidhe had stood quietly in the shadows, watching as the cold, pale form of her brother was laid out on the table to be washed and dried, and prayed over and cried over. Margaret had come, and Thorvald with her, himself still a small child. It was Thorvald who had settled by Creidhe's side, wiped away her tears, warmed her hands in his. It was he who had kept away the terror of the unknown that day when her whole world went awry.

And later there were many more times, times when she had been sad or upset and he had heard her catalog of woes in accepting silence, and told her it would be all right. Times when he had got her out of trouble. She could remember a trip out on the lake in a forbidden boat, a capsize, and an embarrassing rescue. If not for Thorvald that day, she might herself have drowned. If not for his help, she'd most certainly have had to go home in wet clothes and confess her stupidity to her parents.

Then there was the reading and writing, something Creidhe had always found immensely difficult. She'd struggled with Margaret's lessons, for her attention kept straying to the things she'd rather be doing: baking, embroidery or just being out of doors in the fresh air. Thorvald had helped her then, adding his own unofficial tuition to Margaret's formal sessions. He'd sit with Creidhe down by the western dike and watch gravely as she made the letters in the earth with a pointed stick. He never got cross when he was teaching her. It was her own fault that she hadn't been able to learn.

There was no doubt in Creidhe's mind that that patient teacher, that kindly child represented the real Thorvald, the essence of the man he would become. Other folk might see him as arrogant, unfeeling, even cruel. There was no doubt he could be all of these. His true face, Creidhe thought, he showed only to those he trusted, and there were precious few of them.

All the same, right now he was still unpredictable and

moody, and still prone to sudden, illogical decisions. He must not undertake such a grand adventure without her by his side.

Once she had decided this, there were plans to be made. There was no way Thorvald and Sam would agree to take her with them, so she'd have to stow away. That meant finding out when they were leaving and getting to Stensakir the night before. How long would they be gone? Which way were they going? And how could she do it without worrying Eyvind and Nessa half to death?

The very thought of it made her belly churn with unease. There was such danger in it, peril and uncertainty. Thorvald must have asked around, of course, though she knew he had not spoken to Eyvind. He must have found out the likeliest route, the probable landfall for Somerled's lonely voyage. Surely Sam, the most practical man in Hrossey, would not have agreed to take him if there had not been suitable safeguards. All the same, there were questions hanging over the very idea. What had it come from, after all, but a chance remark of her own about finding out the truth? Perhaps their destination was far away. Perhaps they would be gone a long time, a whole cycle of the moon or even two. Her mother would be anxious, her father shocked. Eyvind would be furious with Thorvald, even though her presence on the boat would be all her own doing. He might even take it into his head to come after them, though there was no other vessel in the Light Isles that could match Sam's for speed and maneuverability. Her father could hardly commandeer a longship. And what about Margaret? Who would help her with the weaving? Who would comfort her when she discovered her son had abandoned home and hearth in a wild search for a father he had never known? All the same, Creidhe knew that she must go. It was a knowledge that owed little to logic, but was nonetheless deep and strong, a conviction that beat in the heart and flowed in the blood. She must be there. Without her, Thorvald could not do this. Without her, this quest would fail.

She was careful to follow her usual routine, making herself useful at home, walking or riding down to Aunt Margaret's most days. Her parents talked about her trip to the Northern Isles again and she pretended to be thinking about it. It was not a good feeling to deceive them. The household was built on trust and truth; she longed to seek their wise advice but could not, knowing they would never agree to let her go on such a voyage.

Her sister Brona was the only one who sensed there was something wrong, and it was Brona who helped Creidhe find a way. A wedding was to be held near Stensakir: Grim's eldest daughter Sigrid was marrying a farmer from West Island, and the whole family was invited. The day before they were to head eastward for the festivities, a messenger came with news that the chieftains of the Caitt had sent a delegation to Hafnarvagr, wanting to speak with Eyvind about some kind of arrangement to protect the straits between the Light Isles and their own northern coastline. The traffic of Norse and Danish vessels in those parts had picked up considerably, and one could never be sure whether an attacker might decide to help himself to a cargo of livestock or fine timber, furs or thralls. It was necessary for Eyvind to travel south immediately, and Nessa, who was looking tired and pale these days, made a sudden decision to stay at home with Ingigerd rather than go to the wedding without her husband.

Nessa did not want to disappoint her daughters. Creidhe and Brona could still go, she decreed, as long as they traveled there and back with the three men Eyvind had chosen to accompany and guard them, and stayed with Grim and his wife Eira until the celebrations were over. Margaret was not going, and nor was Thorvald.

At around the same time, Creidhe had an amazing piece of luck. One of Eyvind's housecarls, a girl called Solveig, was walking out with the fellow who worked on the *Sea Dove* as deckhand. When Solveig happened to mention that Sam was giving her sweetheart an unexpected holiday soon after the coming wedding, it all fell into place. There could be only one reason, Creidhe thought, for a decision that would cost Sam dearly in lost fish. The *Sea Dove* must be almost ready to leave. And she herself would be close to Stensakir at just the right time: perfect. It almost seemed meant to be.

The hurt she was about to inflict on her family weighed heavily on Creidhe, but her mind was made up. The two girls packed their bags: a good gown each for the wedding, Creidhe's prized string of amber beads, Brona's favorite yellow ribbon, two pairs of fine stockings of white wool. Gifts for the happy couple had already been stowed away. There was a box carved with images of whales and seals in pale soapstone, holding a good weight of silver pieces, and a woolen wall-hanging of Creidhe's own making which showed a magical tree whose limbs held fruit and foliage of many shapes and hues, apple, pear and berry all springing from the same branch. Creidhe was glad the blue and red blanket had not been given away as yet. She was pleased her handiwork was so prized, but it was always sad to see it go, for there was a part of herself in every piece she crafted. Thorvald would think that silly; it was the sort of thing she could not tell him. Her mind wandered ahead to the time when the two of them would be man and wife. Perhaps the blue and red blanket might cover the bed they would share. She imagined waking as the dawn light streamed in across the rich colors of the wool; she felt the warmth of Thorvald's body against hers, the strength of his arm around her . . .

"Creidhe?"

She started; Brona must have said something, and she hadn't even heard her.

"Why are you packing that?" Brona asked, staring at the rolled-up linen of the Journey, which Creidhe was tucking into the outer pocket of her bag. "We'll only be there a few days, and there'll be feasting and dancing every night. You won't get any time for sewing. I'm not taking mine."

"It can't hurt," Creidhe said, glad her sister had not noticed some of the other items she had packed: a sharp knife, a length of strong cord, a bar of soap, a roll of soft cloths in case she had her monthly bleeding before they sailed back home, a pair of shears, a piece of flint, bone needles, colored wool, herbs to counter seasickness. At the bottom of the bag was an old shirt and trousers of Thorvald's, removed surreptitiously from one of Aunt Margaret's storage chests, and a warm felt hat with ear flaps. Thorvald's clothes did not fit her very well; her figure was not of the kind one could call boyish. Still, she suspected this would be a voyage ill-suited to her fine linen gowns and soft woolen tunics. It would be wet and cold until they got there, wherever *there* was. She must be practical.

"Creidhe?" queried Brona, staring as her sister fastened the strap around her bundle of belongings.

"What?"

"That's a big bag."

"So's yours."

"Not as big as yours."

"What is this, a competition?"

Brona frowned. She was a slight, wide-eyed girl with soft brown hair like Nessa's, and a sweet look about her that did not quite conceal her sharp mind. "Creidhe, you wouldn't be planning something, would you? You've been acting very strangely this last little while."

"Planning? What could I possibly be planning?" Creidhe raised her brows in what she hoped was an expression of innocent surprise.

Brona put her hands on her hips. "Planning to run off with Sam, that's what," she snapped. "You'd better not be doing that, because if you marry Sam I'll never speak to you again, not even when I'm a wrinkled old crone with no teeth."

"There wouldn't be much point in speaking to me if you had no teeth," Creidhe retorted as relief swept through her, closely followed by the spark of a very useful idea. Brona had come alarmingly near to the truth, and yet had missed it entirely. "I wouldn't be able to understand a word. Mind you, I'd probably be deaf as a post myself by then."

"Well?" glowered Brona. "Are you?"

"Of course not!" Creidhe said, seeing that her sister was almost in tears, and marveling that she had not noticed how much of a woman Brona had become, so wrapped up had she been in her own concerns. "Sam's not exactly the running away kind, Brona. If he wanted something, he'd just ask for it."

"So has he?"

"Has he what?"

"Asked. Asked you to marry him. Asked Father for your hand. I know he made you a comb. I've seen him looking at you."

"No, Brona," Creidhe said, sitting down on the bed and putting an arm around her sister's slender shoulders. "Sam hasn't asked, and I don't expect him to." This was not the time to tell Brona that it was possible their father might consider kindly, hard-working Sam no more suitable as a prospective son-in-law than he did Thorvald. "But I do have a secret; you've guessed that right."

"What?" Brona's attention was instantly seized by this; the calculating look on her face showed she was sifting the possibilities, all of which probably had a young man in them. Brona had always been fond of tales of romance.

"I'll tell you when we get to Grim and Eira's. But only if you swear to keep it secret."

"Why should I swear?"

"I'll tell you that when we get there too." Told just enough and no more, Creidhe thought, her sister might prove immensely useful both to cover for her own departure and to soften the bad news for Eyvind and Nessa. Judging by the look in Brona's eyes whenever the name Sam was mentioned, it wouldn't be very hard to dream up a return favor. "Now let's take these bags out to the horses and say our goodbyes. I hope it's not going to rain. Make sure you put your winter boots on."

Eyvind had already left, riding away to Hafnarvagr at dawn with a group of his most trusted men. They would collect Ash on the way. Margaret's taciturn steward was a man valued for his ability to ease the awkwardness of negotiations on tricky subjects by summarizing, clarifying and suggesting useful compromises. Eyvind had once remarked that Ash had acquired this useful skill by living in the same household as Thorvald and Margaret, neither of whom was known for a pliant disposition. If Ash could survive that, the fearsome chieftains of the Caitt should present him with little difficulty.

Nessa bade her daughters farewell with a grave kiss on either cheek. She spoke quietly, first to Brona, then to Creidhe while Brona was hugging her small sister one last time.

"Be safe, daughter," Nessa said softly, her gray eyes gazing with alarming clarity into Creidhe's own. "This is a branching of the path for you. I've seen it. There will be a choice of ways, and some of them trouble me."

"You looked in the fire for me?" Creidhe whispered. Her mother had once been a powerful priestess. She'd given that up to wed Eyvind, but the skills she had learned were deep and enduring. She had helped to train Eanna in the arts, and Creidhe knew her mother still used them herself when the need arose. The images in flame, the voices in earth, the song of wind and waves each told a little of the ancestors' wisdom and the paths ahead. "What have you seen?"

"A journey. A finding and losing. Death. Love. Hurt. I cannot tell if this is a tale encompassed in a single waxing and waning of the moon, or over a far longer span. There's a strangeness and terror in it that makes me want to keep you here at home, safe where you belong. But I can't. The ancestors don't lie to us."

Creidhe shivered. Her mother's eyes were shadowed now. "Have you told Father about this? About what you saw?"

"No," Nessa said.

"I'll stay home if you want." Creidhe's words tumbled out in a rush. "You don't look well. I did wonder—"

Nessa smiled, and the sudden chill was gone as quickly as it had come. "I'm fine, daughter, and I'll do well enough here with Ingigerd to keep me company until you girls come home. Enjoy yourselves; it will do you good to have some dancing and fun. Perhaps, for you, the path branches only as far as the Northern Isles and a certain fine young man. What happens will be your own choice. Now go on, the men are waiting. Is this your bundle? What have you got in here, a loom and a sack of wool?"

Then small Ingigerd began to cry, and Nessa gathered her up with soothing words, and all at once it was time to go. Creidhe looked back over her shoulder as her mother's slender figure grew smaller and smaller, standing in the doorway with Ingigerd in her arms and a brave smile on her face not quite concealing the unease in her eyes. A shiver ran through Creidhe. How long would it be before she saw them again? And what, oh what would her mother say when she learned Creidhe had sailed away in a little boat toward the edge of the world?

In the end it was almost too easy. The first night of the wedding celebrations, Sam came up from the settlement in his best tunic with the red embroidery and joined in the dancing. It was quite a party; Grim's wife Eira had not stinted on the ale, and Grim himself had slaughtered a couple of pigs to complement the usual spread of fish and baked goods. A woman called Zaira, who was famous for her cakes, had made a splendid confection with bere flour and honey, and nuts and spices brought over on a knarr from Norway. The goods had their origin in markets far east, places so far away they were like something in a dream. Zaira herself had come from just such a distant land. She was a fine dancer and, as her husband Thord was away at the same council as Eyvind, she partnered one man after another with her dark hair flying and her red lips smiling. She was a little flirtatious, Creidhe judged, but there was no harm in it. Scarred, gap-toothed Thord, a man built like a monolith, had kept this lively woman's heart since he'd been awarded her as some sort of prize, long ago in another land. Pairings did not follow any strict pattern of culture or kinship in the Light Isles. Look at the bride herself: her father had once been a Wolfskin warrior, and her mother, much younger, bore island blood at its purest. Look at Eyvind and Nessa. Creidhe herself was part of two races. A suitor who could show he was strong and good, and able to provide for a family, might gain approval regardless of his origins. It was a little different for Creidhe and her sisters. If one's sons were to be some kind of kings, one could not wed just any man, though it might seem to some people that Nessa herself had done just that. Eyvind was a Norseman, and had once been a warrior servant of Thor. His people had been the enemy, the invaders who had brought devastation to the islands before valor and magic had put an end to that brutal season of conflict. But Eyvind had been as carefully chosen as any princeling or Jarl. Both Nessa and her old teacher, Rona, had subjected him to trials of their own, trials in which he had proved his mettle not just as warrior but as stalwart protector, strong in courage and goodness, wise and loving. If ever a man were fit to be a father of kings, it was he.

Creidhe sighed. Today she had extracted Brona's promise of silence, and in return made a promise of her own. Yes, she had told her sister, if Sam asked you-know-what, Creidhe would say no. In addition, she'd do everything she could to ensure Sam turned his attentions to Brona herself, who was nearly fifteen after all, and would be quite ready for marriage in a year or two. Everyone knew Sam wanted to settle down as soon as he was satisfied the house was cozy enough; he was saving his profits and making it all perfect for just that purpose. Seeing the look on Brona's face, Creidhe knew her sister's determination. It was going to be Brona lying under those fine woolen blankets, cooking a hearty meal for her man's return and providing a bouncing baby boy for the new cradle, and not any other girl on the islands.

So Creidhe promised, and did not say perhaps a fisherman was not the right father for a king, however pleasant a fellow he might happen to be. And in return Brona gave her word to keep quiet for a certain length of time, long enough so it would be too late for someone to take a boat and set off in pursuit with any likelihood of finding the *Sea Dove* in open water. After that, Brona would tell Nessa and Eyvind what Creidhe had instructed her to tell, a task that would demand no little courage. Creidhe knew the bargain was unfair. Though Brona wouldn't believe it, she'd never wanted

Sam for herself. She liked him, everyone did, but Creidhe could never put another man before Thorvald. It was as simple as that. A pity Sam himself didn't see it the same way; he was coming across the room toward her with a purposeful tread now, and there was a certain look in his steady blue eyes that worried her. Brona was down the other end with a group of girls. Brona was watching.

"Will you dance, Creidhe?" Sam asked politely, sketching a little bow that, from another man, would have looked ridiculous. Sam had a natural dignity and could get away with it. Creidhe took his hand and they moved into the circle. Brona was frowning. This was not part of any bargain.

The music struck up again, and the circle began to move this way and that, hands clasped, feet light or not-so-light in the steps of a chain dance. There was a lot of noise, folk chattering, whistles and drum in lively discourse, boots stamping on the earthen floor.

"You're looking well, Creidhe," Sam yelled above the general din.

"You, too," Creidhe shouted back. "I didn't think you'd be here."

"I like a good party." Sam grinned as the circle broke into couples and began a weaving in-and-out motion.

"A late night," Creidhe observed, "if you have to take the boat out at dawn, or before."

"Ah, well," said Sam, whirling her around in a circle rather faster than the other men were doing with their partners, "I might take a day off, work on the cottage."

Creidhe nodded. She needed to ask just the right questions, not to sound too inquisitive. "Will you be coming again tomorrow night? Grim says there will be games; I don't know what kind."

Sam drew her adroitly back into the circle. Now Brona was on his other side, partnered by young Hakon, Grim's son. Sam winked, and a delicate blush rose to Brona's cheeks. Sam turned back to Creidhe.

"Games, is it? Well, I suppose I'll miss those. Going on a bit of a trip; I may be away a few days, perhaps longer. Up north. No late night for me tomorrow; heading off at sunup next day."

"Oh?" Creidhe said lightly, though her heart was thudding with excitement; it had been easy, after all—he'd come right out with the information she needed. Only another day to wait, and then she would creep out while the games were on, and . . .

The pattern of the dance changed again, and she found herself with a tongue-tied farmhand while, behind her, Sam danced with Brona. A glance over her shoulder showed her the two of them were not talking at all; indeed, her normally voluble sister appeared quite lost for words, though Brona cut a graceful figure as she moved to the music, her large gray eyes fixed on her partner's with a sweetly solemn expression. Brona's pale complexion was still touched with pink in the cheeks. At least Sam was looking at her. It was a start. The unfortunate part of it was that Brona did not quite comprehend Sam's role in the expedition to come; how could Creidhe tell her that she was, indeed, running off with the object of her sister's affections, though not at all in the way Brona would have understood it? There would be some explaining to do when she got back.

Well, fate had delivered exactly what she wanted. Games tended to be noisy, and accompanied by a generous flow of ale. Nobody would notice her slipping away. She must trust Brona to hold her tongue until long after it was discovered she was missing. Brona knew she would be with Thorvald and why, and the general sort of direction they were going in. As long as Eyvind did not leap into a boat and head straight after them—always possible—then the voyage would unfold as it must. So she just had to creep out of Grim's house, find the *Sea Dove,* get on board and hide, put up with a certain amount of discomfort until the right time came, and then . . . She would deal with that part of it when it happened, Creidhe told herself. She must put her fears to the back of her mind; that the weather would be bad, that the boat would sink, that they would sail on and on and never find their destination. She must set aside the guilt; she could not afford to picture her father furious, her mother frantic, Margaret grieving, Brona in trouble because of her. If she thought about these things, she might be tempted to change her mind. And that inner voice, the powerful, deep voice that was both part of her and at the same time outside her, was making it very clear that she must go on with this. She had made the decision. Thorvald needed her, and she would be there for him, as so often in the past her friend had been for her. She would be strong. As for the aftermath, she would deal with that when it came.

Frightening, it was, he had to admit it, frightening and exhilarating, as the *Sea Dove* fought a precarious way north-westward, now sliding down to the dark trough of a wave, as if she would carry them relentlessly on into the very depths of this watery kingdom; now riding high, steeply rising over the peak of a monstrous surge that surely, surely she could not breast, surely they'd be smashed in splinters. Sam barked out terse instructions and Thorvald, tight-jawed in a strange blend of excitement and terror, obeyed them as best he could, fighting to keep the quivering boat on some sort of stable course, and realizing it had not been very wise to talk Sam out of taking a third man with them from Stensakir. The plan had been to sail as far as the Northern Isles and pick up a crewman or two who didn't know either of them. That way they'd have sufficient numbers for the difficult bit. The trouble was, things were already more difficult than anything Thorvald had experienced. The sky was wild with shredded clouds; the sea was a fractious monster with a mind and a will there was no gainsaying. If it wanted to gobble them up, men, craft, provisions, it would do so as casually as a dog snatches a morsel dropped from the table.

In truth, Thorvald loved it. The gale whipped all confusion from his mind; the ache in his back, the blisters on his palms, the constant struggle to keep firm footing emptied him of all but the will to stay alive just a little longer and not lose Sam's fine boat for him. He was on a mission. It was good; today he was a man.

Their course was somewhat farther westward than Thorvald had expected. Once out of the sheltered waters of the Light Isles they'd made good speed, for the wind had been favorable for a straight course to their destination. After a quick debate with himself, Sam had made the decision: they would head northwest, abandoning the plan to go by the Northern Isles and pick up one or two extra men, since that would add at least two days to the trip either way. Things were going well; they were managing. And the sooner they got there, Sam said, the sooner they'd be home again. He didn't want his deckhand defecting in the absence of paid work; it would take him too long to train another. When they found these islands, Thorvald could talk to his mysterious father, Sam would do a spot of fishing, and then they'd come home. From half moon to full should see the trip accomplished and the two of them back where they should be.

So it was straight out into open sea, with no more than guesswork to guide them. Sam did not use sunstones, since the *Sea Dove* fished solely in the coastal waters of the Light Isles, where cliff, dune and skerry were the only markers a man needed. But he watched the light and the clouds, and eyed the birds passing overhead on their wind-harried journeys, and as dusk fell Thorvald could see him squinting upward, working out what the patterns of sun and moon could tell him. It had grown calmer; for a while, Thorvald had wondered if they would both have to stay awake all night, clinging to line or thwart or steering oar as the sea clutched and released, heaved and subsided. But the gods had had enough of playing for now, and the *Sea Dove* settled, creaking, to a gently swaying movement. They lashed the steering oar in place and dragged a sea-anchor, heavy rope with a conical bag attached, to slow their progress. It might be possible for each to snatch a little sleep, while the other kept watch for reefs and skerries, whales and sundry creatures of the deep. Who knew what lurked in these untraveled waters? Somewhere to the west, perhaps not far at all, was the very rim of the world; a man might be swept over before he knew it, and find himself falling away into the true unknown. Perhaps, after all, they would not sleep.

"Food," grunted Sam, kneeling to retrieve a skin water-bottle and an oiled bag of provisions from the box where he'd stowed them. He was used to long days on the water; he and his hand were often out from before dawn until nearly sunset, and Sam was a big man with a big appetite. Salted mutton, flat bread baked hard, an egg or two boiled in the shell—his hens were laying again—under the circumstances, it was a feast. Sam leaned across to pass the water to Thorvald, and froze suddenly as if turned to stone.

"What?" Thorvald queried, somewhat alarmed. "What is it?"

"Shh," hissed Sam, now staring intently at the pine decking between his feet. "Listen."

At first Thorvald could hear nothing beyond the constant creak of the boat's timbers and the wash of the sea. But wait; perhaps there was something else, a sound like a faint moan or a sigh, and a sort of scrabbling noise, very small, down there under the boards.

"Rats?" Thorvald suggested, brows raised.

Sam, it appeared, had something other than vermin in mind. His broad, amiable features had turned pale, and now he was levering up the boards that lay loosely over the boat's ribs to allow for easy adjustment of cargo or ballast. One short plank, two, three, and Thorvald, taken aback by the speed and intensity of his friend's reaction, moved forward to peer down into the shadowy hull of the *Sea Dove*, near the bow. There was a smell; someone had been sick. And a sound, not the animal scrabbling now but a voice, a girl's voice, shaky and weak. "Sam?"

Without a word, the two men clambered down into the open hold between the fore and aft decks, where their load of provisions was stored; they scrambled over the cross-beams, moving sacks and bundles until they had made a narrow way through under the foredeck. Creidhe was crouched on the ballast stones behind the fish crates, in a hiding place that seemed scarcely big enough for a mouse. They hauled her out, Sam with a modicum of gentleness, Thorvald with hands that shook with fury.

"What in the name of all the gods are you doing here?"

he demanded. "How did you get on board? Odin's bones, what will your father say?"

"Not now," Sam said. "She needs water, and we'd better light the lantern; it'll be dark soon. There's a flint down yonder in the small bag, and a bundle of dry tinder. Take care. A fire's just what we don't need." His tone was level, held carefully so, Thorvald thought, not to further distress the filthy, cheese-pale, sniveling Creidhe. Distress, huh! He could scarcely believe she had done something so stupid. Why, by all the gods, why? It defied all common sense. She had put his whole venture at risk, as if she truly wanted him to fail. And what about her own safety? This was no place for a girl. What if she got hurt? What if she got sick? Creidhe was supposed to be his friend. Friends didn't do things like this.

His hands were still shaking as he made fire and lit the small enclosed oil lamp that had been stored just so, like all the rest of Sam's gear. Now Sam was talking softly to Creidhe, getting her to drink water, wiping her face, making her stretch her cramped limbs. There were tears in her eyes, Thorvald could see the glint of them in the lamplight. Odin save him, what reason could a girl have for dreaming up such a foolish trick? Especially a girl like Creidhe, with her fondness for trivial pastimes such as fine embroidery and fancy cooking. How could Sam be so placid about it? He should have come alone, thought Thorvald savagely. You couldn't trust anyone, not even the people you thought understood you.

Creidhe was calmer now, sipping water from the bottle, responding to Sam's patience, stretching her arms and legs with a groan and sucking in lungfuls of fresh air. Gods, she looked terrible, her tunic all stained with vomit, her hair in a tangle and her face ghost-white in the lantern light. Her eyes had great shadowed circles around them.

"What—" Thorvald began, but Sam silenced him with a gesture.

"Food first, questions after," the fisherman said, rummaging in the bag. "I should think they can hear my belly growling all the way back in Stensakir. Drink it slowly, Creidhe, just a bit at a time. You'd better try a mouthful of this bread too. Emptied your stomach pretty well from the looks of it. Come on, just a nibble or two. Feeling any better?"

Creidhe gave a weak nod; she held the bread in her hand but seemed unable to do more than sit shivering, clutching the water bottle and sniffing from time to time. In silence Sam cut bread, sliced meat, shelled eggs, handed Thorvald a portion of each. Hungry as he was, Thorvald found it hard to eat. Finally he could hold back no longer.

"Tell us, Creidhe. Give us your explanation. Don't you understand how dangerous this is? Don't you realize where we're going?" He could hear the harshness in his own voice, though he was trying to keep it calm. Sam was looking at him with an expression that could not be described as friendly. "What reason could you possibly have for doing something like this? It'll only make everything more difficult."

"You're going to need me," Creidhe said, squaring her shoulders and lifting her chin in a way that was all too familiar. "I know it. You'll need me before the end." Her voice belied her attempt at confidence; it was very small, and wobbled.

At that moment Thorvald knew that what had gripped him in the instant he heard and recognized her voice, down under the decking, was less fury and frustration than fear: fear for her, and for what it might cost her to be his friend. It was bad enough to have coerced Sam into coming, into risking himself and his fine boat. But to have Creidhe in peril, Creidhe whose world was all handicrafts and family and blithe sunny days, that was truly terrifying. It was as if his father's hand, the hand that had turned all in the Light Isles to darkness in one terrible season, had somehow crept out to touch his son's voyage; to turn it, too, to shadow. For a little, Thorvald could think of nothing to say.

There was still no moon; the small lantern that Thorvald had hung carefully in the bow cast a circle of pale light just sufficient to show how tiny they were, men, woman, frail vessel, in the immensity of dark ocean that surrounded them.

"Not used to this," observed Sam. "Keeping her out on open sea at night, I mean. No sign of land, any direction, doesn't feel right. Doesn't feel comfortable."

"Yes, well, I don't suppose it was comfort you expected when you agreed to come," Thorvald snapped, unable to contain the conflict of feelings that was building inside him. "It's a trip of high risks, a voyage into the unknown, not a—not some sort of family outing up the coast on a fine morning."

Sam did not respond to this. Indeed, it had not really been meant for him. Taking his time, he finished his meal, wiped his hands on his tunic, tidied away the loaf, the knife, the oiled wrappings. He moved across to adjust the lantern, and gazed into the sky a while. The stars were almost imperceptible; even so early in the spring, the nights were washed with the pale afterglow of the sun. Eventually Sam turned back to the others.

"Well," he said quietly, "no two ways about it, is there? Sunup, we put about and head straight back home."

"No!"

It was as if one voice had spoken; Thorvald and Creidhe had rapped out the response in perfect, vehement unison.

Sam blinked. "One good reason why not," he said, regarding his companions mildly. "One each."

There was an extended pause while Thorvald, scowling, folded his arms and stared out across the heaving ocean, and Creidhe looked down at the water bottle as if it were an object of intense fascination.

"Well?" queried Sam. "There aren't any, are there?"

"Ah," said Thorvald, "that's just where you're wrong. I can see you're concerned about Creidhe's state of health, not to mention her safety. I have to say, bearing in mind how long we've been traveling and the force of that gale we encountered earlier, that I'd guess we're a deal closer to our destination than we are to the Light Isles. Isn't our first priority getting Creidhe to the nearest place of refuge?"

Sam did not comment. "Creidhe?" he asked.

"She has no good reason," Thorvald said, before she could answer. "She shouldn't be here. It's as simple as that."

Creidhe cleared her throat. "I imagine you made him a promise," she told Sam. "A good man keeps his promises." She did not look at Thorvald.

"I did," said Sam, frowning. "Trouble is, your father'll kill us if we don't get you back safe. He'll probably kill us even if we do. I really can't understand why you've done this, Creidhe."

Her voice was firmer now. "I know you're looking for Somerled. I know you're heading for wherever he might have gone. I knew you wouldn't let me come with you. But I needed to come. It's not something I can explain very easily. It's more of a feeling, a deep-down feeling. I know I have to be here."

"I can't imagine why." Thorvald's tone was blunt. "You can't sail, you can't fight, you can't help us in any way whatever. All you've done is put yourself in danger and upset your family."

"Isn't that what you've done?" asked Creidhe quietly.

There was another silence, during which Sam unrolled two blankets, put one around Creidhe's shoulders and settled himself among the fish crates.

"All right," he said. "My boat, my choice. Only thing is, it's the wind makes the choice for us at times like this. I'm going to sleep for a bit; the two of you can practice tearing each other to shreds all night if you want, as long as you keep your eyes open. Wake me when you want a rest, Thorvald. I'll make a decision at first light."

Thorvald was to remember that night, later, as a strange lull in the storm of his journey. He recalled his confusion, the guilt and anger and fear warring within him. He remembered how serene Creidhe had seemed with the lamplight playing on her wan features; how, despite the need to creep to the side of the boat every so often and retch helplessly into the swell, she still regarded him with a calm gravity that annoyed him more than anything, since it told him she was far his superior in self-control. As for conversation, there was little of it. He did not trust himself to speak; she appeared to think further explanations unnecessary.

For a while she slept, cheek pillowed on an arm, fair hair

fanned out like strands of pale silk, and he watched her, wondering how he could possibly manage to keep her safe and still achieve his quest. His quest: it remained foremost in his mind, though another man might have turned for home without hesitation. Perhaps that was his father's legacy, condemning him always to put his own interests first. Sam's reaction to the crisis had been swift and kind. Thorvald was painfully aware that his own response had been somewhat lacking in compassion. Sam now slept the sleep of a man whose conscience was free from burdens, while Thorvald sat alone with the night and the ocean, pondering the way fate seemed determined to turn his steps astray and make him a misfit. Fate, he thought grimly, never passed up a chance to remind him he was his father's son. Creidhe shivered, sighing in her sleep. It occurred to Thorvald that there had been a certain bravery in what she had done, wrong-headed though it was. There weren't many girls he knew who could have stayed silent under the deck like that through such a rough passage, nor planned well enough to be there in the first place. None, in fact. If they'd *had* to have a girl with them, Creidhe would have been the only possible choice. Absently he tucked the blanket over her and resumed his solitary watch. He prayed for an easterly wind.

There was, indeed, no decision made but that of the gods themselves. In the darkness before dawn the gentle rocking of the *Sea Dove* became a harsher movement, the sea-anchor near useless against the insistent pull of the current. The wind came up, whipping a fine spray into every corner of the boat, drenching their clothes, their blankets, their stores. The *Sea Dove's* timbers groaned and creaked; her sheets whined in protest. Sam gave directions, Thorvald obeyed them. Creidhe crouched down, doing her best to keep out of the way. They made a choice—speed over safety—for if Tadhg's directions were right, this wind would bear them straight to their destination. They hoisted the sail. The gale drove them westward, or perhaps north of westward; the lowering clouds made it too dark to tell. Sam held the steering oar in a death grip, and the others clung like barnacles to whatever they could find.

The expanse of sailcloth above them bellied out to within a hairsbreadth of tearing asunder; the mast bowed, its strength tested almost to the limit. It came to Thorvald that they had no control at all of the vessel's course; the wind would bear them where it fancied. The best they could hope for was to turn the *Sea Dove* into the monstrous waves and keep her afloat until the storm abated. What chance had they of finding a small group of isles, about which they knew nothing save that they were somewhere northwest of the Light Isles? Beyond those islands, which might themselves be no more than a crazed man's fevered imaginings, all knew there was nothing but empty water. It was as well the wind sought to snatch the very breath from their mouths, for what was in their minds was better not put into words. Best think only of the task in hand, staying on the boat, gathering themselves for the next impossible surge of water, and the next, and the one after, being ready for the sheeting, freezing rain when it came, somehow forcing the hands to fasten and unfasten the lines, shifting position to balance the *Sea Dove* and in between, praying with clenched teeth and narrowed eyes, straining to see some change in the elements, some small hint of mercy.

The boat on which Somerled had made this journey was a tiny curragh like the ones Tadhg and his brothers sometimes rowed across to the mainland. Beside the *Sea Dove*, such a vessel would be like a duckling to an albatross. The imagination could scarcely encompass how it would be to travel thus. A terrible truth crept into Thorvald's mind. *Somerled could not have survived.* Following that thought, another, starker still: *We're going to die, all three of us.* Oh, for a faith like that of Brother Tadhg, simple and sure, the unshakeable belief in your god's eternal mercy. Had not the brothers, too, come this way, guarded by the hand of that selfsame god? Somerled had had no such faith; how could an evil man expect the favor of any deity? If Somerled had completed this journey, it was something else that had given him the will to do it. Hatred? Pride? Ambition? Yet he had never returned; never come home to confront the friend who had sent him into this nightmare.

Sam was maintaining his vise-like grip on the steering

oar, the muscles of his arms bulging with effort. His face
was white in the faint predawn light. He was shouting
something, but Thorvald could not hear the words in the
howl of the wind. Creidhe's hair streamed in the gale like a
flag of gold; she clung, tight-knuckled, to a rib. *The sail,*
Sam seemed to be telling him. *Lower the sail.* For the mast
was flexing dangerously, the pressure too great, and they
must give up any effort to control their path lest they lose
their rigging entirely and render the boat unable to make a
course for land even in calmer weather. Thorvald lurched
forward, his sodden boots like lead weights, his fingers
numb with cold as he fought to unfasten one rope, then another from the iron hooks that held them. The *Sea Dove*
shuddered; a mountain of dark water arose before them.

"Hold on!" someone screamed, and an instant later the
wave crashed over them. Thorvald's nose and mouth, his
eyes and ears were full of water; the sea lifted him in a
fierce, chill embrace and he felt pain scythe through his
arms as he strained to keep his grip on the rope, clutching as
a terrified child clutches its mother in the face of the fearful
unknown. Long moments passed; he held his breath until
his chest was fit to burst, until the agony could surely be
borne no longer, until he knew he was as close to death as
he had ever been, and then with a sound like the groan of a
wounded animal the *Sea Dove* righted herself again, and
there was blessed air to breathe, and as the light of a new
day crept cautiously into the stormy sky Thorvald dared
open his eyes once more.

The mast was snapped to a splintery stump, the sail gone.
Creidhe lay sprawled on the deck, gasping and choking, a tangle of rope across her bedraggled form. Between the falling
timber and the rush of the water, it was a miracle she had survived. Sam. Where was Sam? The boat rocked violently, her
erratic course no more than the ocean's whim; the steering
oar swung uncontrolled. Thorvald's heart went cold. *Not this,*
he prayed, though he had never set much store in gods. *This is
not right, maybe I wanted a challenge, but not this, please . . .*

"Sam!" Creidhe shrieked, leaping to her feet and lurching
across the hold toward the stern. The *Sea Dove* pitched;

Creidhe fell to her knees and scrambled up again, clambering to the aft deck. Now she was crouching down; the steering oar jerked and shuddered, swinging free not far from her
head. "Don't just stand there!" she yelled over her shoulder.
"He's out cold, and bleeding! Don't you know how to sail
this thing?"

Goaded out of his shock, Thorvald now saw Sam's bulky
form slumped on the deck, looking more dead than alive. The
bright stream of blood moving down cheek and neck, soak-
ing shirt and tunic, made a note of vibrant color in a dawn
storm-dark, ocean-green, shadow-gray. Thorvald edged aft
and seized the steering oar, knowing his puny efforts to maintain control were useless against the malign force of the elements, but understanding the need to try. A fight to the
death, this was, man against nature; he must hang on and
hope some higher power, if there were such a thing, would
eventually grow tired of toying with them. He'd sought
a challenge and he'd got one: the hardest game he'd ever
played.

Creidhe was tearing something up, she was wrapping a
bandage around Sam's head and pressing on the wound
with her hand. Her mouth was set very tight; the rays of
dawn light creeping between the heavy clouds showed her
even paler than before, as if she, too, would lapse into unconsciousness any moment. Now she was trying to move
Sam away, just enough to give Thorvald room to maneuver
in his desperate efforts to keep the *Sea Dove* under some
kind of control, though indeed, without the use of oars or
sail, the best he could hope to do was keep her from being
swamped. Creidhe subsided onto the decking with Sam's
head in her lap; he was too heavy for her to shift, and now
she held one hand over his crudely bandaged injury and
hooked her other arm around the nearest timber as the sky
rumbled above them and the water surged and retreated,
rose and fell, determined to dislodge them. A stain of blood
already marked the linen—Creidhe's shift?—that circled
Sam's head. Creidhe looked up at Thorvald where he
strained against the shuddering pull of the steering oar.

Strands of wet hair were plastered across her face, and her eyes were full of shadows.

"Sorry," she said. Whether it was for the plight they were in, or simply for being in the way, there was no telling.

"Me too," said Thorvald.

The *Sea Dove* fled through another lowering day, another chill night in which Sam lay groaning under the two blankets. Thorvald and Creidhe stared into the darkness, numb with exhaustion but still doggedly maintaining their watch, one over the injured man, the other on the water, the stars, the movement of the battered craft. They did not talk much. Creidhe wiped Sam's brow, fed him sips of water, helped him roll from one side to the other. He seemed to be improving just a little. Thorvald did his best to keep some control over their course, though it seemed to him the boat was not responding as it should. He thought the steering oar was damaged, but he did not mention this to Creidhe.

They sighted no land on the second day after losing the mast. The wind died down, the seas became calmer, and the chill crept deep into their bones. They covered Sam with all the warm clothing they could find, for in his weakened state it was important that he not surrender to the cold and give up altogether. The fisherman was sleeping a lot, but when he woke he was talking sense now, and trying to make helpful suggestions, which was a good sign. The next night, Thorvald heard Creidhe muttering from time to time, and wondered if she was losing her mind; that would surely be the last straw. But after a while it came to him that she was praying, or something very like it, though she spoke in the old tongue of the islands and he was not fluent in that language. He remembered that Creidhe's sister was a priestess; that her mother, too, was skilled in the ancient ways of their faith, which had to do with earth and ocean, the ancestral lore of standing stones, the paths of moon and sun. Creidhe chanted with her eyes closed. There was no telling whom she addressed, nor what she asked them.

If it made her feel a little better, Thorvald thought grimly as the sky paled toward another dawn, fine. As for himself, it was becoming rapidly apparent to him that he could not hold on much longer. The ache in his arms was intolerable, his palms were raw with blisters and, worst of all, his head was throbbing with a fierce, insistent pain that came close to blinding him. This happened from time to time at home, and he knew the only cure was to lie down in darkness and wait for it to pass. The sun was coming up; its pale light transformed the headache into a vise closing on his temples. It made his gorge rise and spots dance before his eyes.

"Thorvald?" Creidhe's voice pierced his skull. "Thorvald!"

He closed his eyes; *Just hold on,* he told himself, *just hold on, just keep going . . .*

"Thorvald!" Creidhe's voice was so loud, his head was fit to split asunder with the pain of it. "Land!" she yelled. "I see land!"

His eyes snapped open. Creidhe was half standing beside him on the aft deck, cautious still, and gesturing, pointing to the north, where—yes, it was true—islands rose in the distance, islands of daunting steepness, grouped close like a ring of fortress towers set in defiance of this inhospitable sea. Something welled in his heart, something kindled in his spirit: an improbable hope.

"Wha—?" Sam was trying to get up; he fought to his knees, his hands grasping a line for purchase.

"Land," Creidhe told him reassuringly. "Islands. Not far off at all. There'll be shelter, food, help." She turned back to Thorvald. "You can get us there, can't you?" she asked.

Bitter laughter rose to his lips; he suppressed it. An easterly wind, no mast, no sail, a steering oar that was only half working, and himself fit for nothing with his screaming headache and worn-out arms? Get them there? Those mist-shrouded isles were no more a reality for them than some fabled land of story, which retreated even as a mariner approached its shore. The silence drew out.

"I know we can't sail," Creidhe said in a small voice. "But I did think maybe we could row." There was another pause. "We could try, anyway."

Sam was struggling up again, a hand to his head. "Oars,"

he mumbled, gesturing to the forward racks where they were stowed. "Come on . . ."

Thorvald looked at Creidhe, and she gazed solemnly back. There was no way she could handle an oar; in these conditions he wasn't sure he could himself. And who would steer?

"Here." Sam had lurched across the open hold, unsteady on his feet but with a seaman's instinctive sense of balance. He lifted one long oar from the rack by the forward deck and set it in place. On this craft two men must stand side by side to row. Sam's massive arms gripped the pine shaft at chest height. He jerked his head toward the other oar, and rolled his eyes in Thorvald's direction. "Steady does it. Creidhe . . . steering oar. Wind's easing up. Got . . . chance. Damned if I lose . . . *Sea Dove* . . ."

It was a source of amazement to Thorvald later that he managed to go on. Friends, he thought, were both curse and blessing. Perhaps all that had spurred him was the desire to seem no weaker than wounded Sam or exhausted Creidhe, each of whom set to with gritted teeth and eyes ablaze with new hope. He rowed, and Sam rowed, and Creidhe wrestled with the steering oar, her eyes narrowed as she sought to keep their course in line with the distant points of land. The wind died down; the sun glanced between scudding clouds. Birds circled the boat and flew off again with derisive cries. Nobody asked if they were getting any closer. The grip of damaged hands, the pull of aching arms were all that existed, those and the steady movement of the sun across the sky. After a very long time there were skerries to be seen eastward and westward, and a few seals hauled up on them. After a longer time an island loomed close, and for a while they pulled hard toward it, but there was a persistent current tugging them offshore. In a moment of grinding despair, they stilled the oars and stood in silence, watching the green-clad slopes recede to impossibility. There were tears in Creidhe's eyes. She blinked them back, speaking very firmly.

"Drink some water, rest a moment, then we'll go on.

We're a little west of that main group now, but there seems to be another to the north of us. We'll aim for that. It's not far at all. You're doing very well."

Sam looked at Thorvald, and Thorvald looked at Sam. Through the sheen of sweat, the pain of bone-weariness, each managed to stretch cracked lips in a feeble grin.

"Stop laughing at me," commanded Creidhe. "Now come on, put your backs into it. Trust me, I know what I'm doing." If there was a slight tremor under the commendable briskness of her tone, both men chose to ignore it.

They passed to the west of other isles, bigger ones, smaller ones, farther off a tiny one with monstrous cliffs all around, rising to a desolate plateau where, improbably, sheep could be seen grazing. They struggled against the current; the thing had a mind of its own. At times the surface of the ocean showed a strange margin, farther off silver-green, closer at hand the natural darkness of deep water. It was westward across that divide that the current sought to draw them, and it took all their flagging strength to resist its will. Perhaps they had moved somewhat closer to that northern isle; they were too tired to tell. Thorvald thought there were cottages, but he could not be sure. It seemed unlikely folk would choose to settle in so stark a spot, where there was hardly a level scrap of land to be found, and the waves pounded the rocky shore as if to split the very stones asunder. Who would be stupid enough to put out to sea here? he thought sourly as he pulled and pulled, and the *Sea Dove* plowed her sluggish way through the choppy waters. Who would come here at all save an exile or a fool?

In the end there was a bay, and a small beach, and a current that carried them forward. At last they began to believe that they would not die after all, not today. It was not Creidhe's fault that the *Sea Dove* scraped her hull on rocks coming in and began instantly to list alarmingly. The waters were turbid and the undersea reefs invisible. Nonetheless, Thorvald scowled at her as he hauled on his oar. Creidhe appeared to be working hard to keep tears from falling. As for Sam, when he heard the unmistakable, sickening crunch of the boat's timbers cracking on the reef, he flinched as if he himself had received a mortal wound. He put his back into rowing, snarling at Thorvald to pull harder, for if they could beach the *Sea Dove* before she sank, he had at least some chance of patching her up. The landscape was bleak; these islands seemed no richer in trees than the Light Isles, and a great deal less hospitable. No doubt, as at home, logs washed in from time to time, a gift from the sea more precious than any fine-wrought gold or silver. They had nothing to bargain with save the *Sea Dove* herself. Still, they were alive, and now, by dint of a last desperate effort with the oars, they felt the boat's hull slide onto sand, and Sam, less than his usual buoyant self, clambered over the side to secure ropes to two massive boulders perhaps set there for just such a purpose. There was no jetty, but other craft were beached farther away, small, ungainly vessels that seemed ill suited to these capricious waters. Beyond the sheltered bay rose forbidding, rock-layered hills. There was nobody about. Further back, tucked into a fold of the land, there seemed to be buildings of some kind; smoke drifted above their turf roofs.

It was, in fact, beyond their energy to go there, to seek help. Sam inspected the damage to his beloved boat, his livelihood and treasure; he shook his bandaged head, but it was clear he was working out how soon he might fix the great rent in her hull, replace the mast and be on his way again. The jagged rocks had pierced both garboard and second strakes near the stem; where might one find oak in these tree-poor isles? He ran his hand over the planks, muttering to himself.

Creidhe could scarcely walk. The instant she set foot on land, her knees buckled, and she stumbled through the shallow water to collapse, white-faced, onto the fine shingle of the beach. Thorvald felt little better himself. His arms and shoulders throbbed as if branded; as for his hands, he would not look at those, for fear the sight would sicken him. He knew they were raw and bleeding; he had seen Sam's. One must hope the people here were friendly, and had healers. He sprawled on the shore beside Creidhe, his eyes closed.

"Are you all right, Thorvald?" Despite all, her small voice was desperately polite.

"Mmm," he grunted. "You?"

"It's my fault," she whispered. "Now the *Sea Dove*'s smashed and we can't go home."

"Nobody's fault but the sea's," Sam said calmly, coming up beside them. "I can mend it, given time and the right bit of wood. Means we'll be here longer, though. Need to look for shelter. And I could handle a roasted mutton shank or two, I can tell you. Looks like some kind of settlement up yonder, though the folk don't seem in a hurry to come out and welcome us. Shall we try?"

Thorvald sat up abruptly. "Just one thing," he said.

The others looked at him.

"You know why I'm here, to find him, to find Somerled. I have to believe he could have reached this place, otherwise it's all been for nothing. I know it's a slender chance, but it's not impossible. Maybe he's right there, in one of those cottages, maybe not. I want you to keep quiet about that. It's my search and mine alone, and I've my own way of going about it. Do you understand?"

"What do you mean?" Creidhe asked, putting her head in her hands as if she were simply too tired to think. "Not tell him you're his son?"

"Exactly. And not tell anyone the real reason I've come here. If Somerled is on these islands, I want to observe him, to weigh him up before I tell him the truth. I can't do that if someone blurts out who I am and what I'm looking for the moment we clap eyes on the locals."

"Probably not even the right islands . . ." Creidhe murmured.

"Never mind that," Thorvald snapped. This was taking too long, and his head was throbbing. "This could be the place. How likely is it there are two such groups of isles in these parts? Now, do the two of you understand me or not?"

"I understand all right. You expect us to lie for you," said Sam flatly. His face was ghastly pale under the stained bandage, and his eyes bore a disapproving look.

"You don't have to lie. Just don't mention Somerled. That should be easy enough even for you, Creidhe." Thorvald saw her flinch, and instantly regretted this barb. But why were they taking so long to comprehend what was blindingly obvious? The gods protect him from friends.

"Listen, Thorvald," Sam said wearily, "I've got a sore head and a broken boat, and Creidhe's close to fainting from exhaustion. We're in the middle of nowhere, and neither of us cares right now about your little games. Just tell us what our story is, so these folk won't think we're crazy, then let's try to find some help."

Sam was slurring his words. Thorvald realized he had entirely forgotten his friend's injury. "Went out fishing, got blown off course, dumped the catch when it started to stink," he said succinctly. "Now we ask for shelter while we repair the boat. Easy."

"And Creidhe? Why is she here?"

"Your sister? Your wife?"

Sam's features tightened a little. "You're very ready with your answers, Thorvald. I won't mention Somerled, if that's the way you want it, but there's no need for more lies. Now come on, the two of you. I'm soaked through, my head's killing me, and my belly's complaining again. Let's find out what kind of folk choose to settle at the end of the world."

"Brona!" The name rang through the lamplit chambers of the longhouse like a battle cry, as the door slammed shut behind Eyvind. An instant later, Ingigerd began to whimper, roused abruptly from her sleep. It was the first time she had ever heard her father's voice raised in anger.

"You got the message then." Nessa was seated by the fire, hands relaxed in her lap, gray eyes wide as she regarded the big, furious form of her husband, axe on his back, sword by his side, wolfskin cloak long and shaggy across his massive shoulders. His face was a picture of distress. "Don't be angry with Brona. She's shed enough tears over this already And she was just keeping a promise. You've taught them to keep their promises." At that moment Brona herself appeared in the hallway, carrying her weeping small sister. She gave them a look; her eyes were swollen, her expression quite wretched.

"It's all right, daughter." Nessa's tone was calm. "Take Ingigerd back to bed now, tell her a story. Your father will talk to you in the morning." She turned back to Eyvind. "Come, sit down, and I'll pour you a cup of ale. You've journeyed fast, dear one; this has driven you hard. Come now. Sit down a while. Perhaps things are not as bad as they seem."

"How can that be? Our daughter, our good, dutiful girl, running off with a couple of irresponsible young men, out on a coastal fishing boat into waters unknown? What can Creidhe have been thinking of?" He paced restlessly as he divested himself of cloak and weaponry. "This is quite unlike her, quite out of character. I blame Thorvald. The boy's unpredictable and unreliable. We should have sent her away."

"Sit down, Eyvind." Nessa used the tone her husband could not refuse. He sat; she placed a cupful of ale in his hand and reached to tuck a stray curl back behind his ear. "Now listen to me."

"I should not stay here—I should go north, find a boat, head off after them. They can't have got far—"

"Eyvind. Listen to me."

He was silent.

"It's possible this was meant to be. I saw something of it in the fire; I could not avoid the vision the ancestors granted me. There is a strange pathway ahead for our daughter, dear one. Strange and perilous."

"You saw this? Saw it and did not tell me?"

"I could not tell you. You know how these portents are; they can be imprecise, misleading. I saw Creidhe on a long and arduous journey, and I saw signs and symbols—a little, ragged child; a creature like a fox . . . no, I will not tell all."

"There's worse than this?"

Nessa saw the look in Eyvind's eyes and took his hand

in hers. "Worse, and better," she said. "Our daughter will have a wondrous tale to tell, if she comes through this. You ask why she would do such a thing, why she would run away. Creidhe has not run away. She seeks only to aid her friend. She will sacrifice much for Thorvald. You know she loves him."

Eyvind frowned ferociously. Such a look had often turned his enemies' bowels to water. Nessa waited, expression tranquil.

"I thought we agreed Thorvald was the last man we wanted for her," her husband said. "The boy is clever, I acknowledge that, but the legacy he carries is a dark one, and he has few of the qualities I would seek in a husband for my girls. The lad is selfish and volatile, and quite lacking in kindness. How can you say—?"

Nessa smiled. "Thorvald will need her help before this journey is done. You should pray for the two of them, and for Sam. They will suffer and become wiser, all three, before this is over."

Eyvind shifted restlessly. He had not touched the ale. "I must go after them. Those waters are wild and unfamiliar; even Sam would be hard put to find the place they seek, that's supposing it's more than a madman's vision. No father worth his salt just lets his daughter go on such a foolhardy quest. I must try to find her—"

"No, Eyvind." Nessa put a hand up to his face, laying it softly against his cheek, and looked him straight in the eye. "You will not go. You cannot. I'm going to need you here."

He blinked in confusion. Nessa was wise and resourceful; she ordered the household effortlessly and played a confident part in the councils and dealings of the islands, as befitted her royal status. "But—" he began.

"Eyvi, dear one, I have some news for you. I have waited to tell you until I was quite sure." Her voice had become suddenly quiet, hesitant. Her fingers stroked his temple; he took her hand and pressed it to his lips. She saw the alarm in his eyes, and spoke quickly. "I'm going to have another child. It surprised me; I thought there would be no more chances. I think, if I can carry it safely, this one will be a boy. I hope . . . I hope so much . . ." Her lip trembled; the tears that began to roll down her pale cheeks were mirrored by those in her husband's eyes. He gathered her close, stroking the long, soft fall of her hair.

"Oh, Nessa," he whispered. "Oh, my dove. Of course I will stay, of course, but—"

"Creidhe will get through this," Nessa said shakily. "Our daughter is strong and capable; this may seem a foolish escapade to you, but she would not have gone without sound reasons. Brona said her sister hated the need to lie to us. Brona is very sorry, Eyvi. Don't be too harsh on her. They are good girls, the two of them."

"A son," Eyvind murmured. "I did not believe we would be so blessed, after the sea took our little one from us. But . . . will this be safe for you? You must rest, perhaps you should be in bed now—"

"Hush," Nessa told him, smiling even as she wept. The loss of Kinart had cut him deeply; he would bear that wound within him forever. His small son had been the light of his life for four summers, until the morning the Seal Tribe had snatched him away. She had always thought that was a kind of payment, a reckoning those strange sea dwellers exacted in return for the aid they had once given her. If it were so, the price had indeed been high. "I may be a little past the best age for this, but I am well and healthy, and I know how to prepare for it. Creidhe has good hands for midwifery; she'll help me when the time comes. Don't look so anxious, dear one. Be glad of this wonderful gift."

"I am glad. Glad but concerned, for you, for him," he laid a gentle hand on her stomach, which was barely rounded with the new life she bore, "terribly worried for Creidhe, despite your reassurances. And there's the treaty; I don't trust this princeling of the Caitt people, and nor does Ash. We'll be much occupied."

"So you see, you could not sail off into the west on a foolish quest of your own," Nessa told him. "Trust your daughter. She will surprise you."

"That she's done already," he said grimly. "Tell me, when will this child be born? How soon?"

"In autumn, by my reckoning. Perhaps two cycles of the moon before the time of the women's ceremony. Creidhe will be home long before then, and your worries set at rest. Now drink that ale, husband, and then go and bid your daughters goodnight. Tell Brona you've forgiven her. We must not let the moon rise on our anger."

Later, as Nessa slept in his arms, Eyvind stared out through the narrow window into the pale silver sky of the spring night. He thought of his bright-haired girl, out there somewhere on the wild sea, or washed up on some strange shore, with only her courage and common sense to aid her. By all the gods, a lovely young woman of sixteen set suddenly amidst whatever wild and desperate men might make their home in those distant islands—the very idea appalled him. Nessa could not see how dangerous it would be; Nessa did not think the way a man thought. A cold shiver went down his spine. Somerled. Somerled might be there. If the man had survived that perilous journey, who knew what he might have become through the long years of exile? Perhaps he would have changed, as Eyvind had charged him to, and grown to be wise, good, a man of peace. Or perhaps he would merely have built on the qualities that had won him kingship here in the Light Isles: ruthless ambition and a complete disregard for the welfare of others. Somerled had no respect for women; he believed a man should take what he wanted. He had much cause for bitterness against Eyvind and Eyvind's kin. It must be hoped, then, that they did not find the isles; that Thorvald never located his father. And yet, they must find them. There was nothing else out there but a slow death on empty seas. Gods protect Creidhe, and gods protect this little son now growing inside Nessa's belly. Let Creidhe be home in time to deliver the child safely, for if she were not, he did not know what he would do. There were no other hands he trusted so well to undertake this task. Let them not lose another child; he could not well survive that. Not a day went by without images of Kinart in his mind, not a night without dreams: his son learning to walk, sturdy legs moving in confident, uneven gait, fair hair sticking up in an unruly halo, infant features wreathed in a huge, triumphant grin. Kinart riding before him, a proud, small warrior sitting very upright in his father's arms as the old horse ambled across the gentle pasturelands. Kinart sleeping on Nessa's lap, worn out by a long day out of doors, and the firelight gentle on the two of them, his dear ones. Kinart lying on the shore, limp and white, and a terrible howl of anguish that must have come from his own lips, though he had felt his heart stilled by terror. There had been losses before, but none like this. *I will give anything,* he vowed silently, scarcely knowing to what god he spoke, only that this was a plea from the very depths of his being, *anything you want, if you let this one live.*

THREE

Brightwater bell tolls
Which does it mark
the birth of a child
the sighting of whales
or the coming of strangers?

MONK'S MARGIN NOTE

There was a bell ringing somewhere, its note dull and regular. There were men coming down from the settlement. Creidhe could hear their voices. She could tell from Thorvald's face that he had one of his headaches; nothing else could give him that sickly pallor, that grim tightness of jaw. Beyond that, everything was starting to blur. She was managing to walk, her feet seemed to keep going, but her legs were half numb and she couldn't stop shivering. In the teeth of death, cold and hunger had been forgotten for a while. Now she knew a chill like winter's harshest frost, deep in the marrow; her clothing was soaked through, and although she walked on solid ground, her head reeled and her belly churned with nausea. Sam was grasping her by the arm, helping her to keep going, and Thorvald, face white as chalk, was walking forward with commendable steadiness as the reception party of three men came down the path toward them.

"Good day to you." Thorvald's voice was firm; evidently his teeth were not chattering uncontrollably as hers seemed to insist on doing. "I hope you can help us. As you see, we are cast ashore here and our boat is damaged. We seek food, water, shelter. Can you help?"

The three men had halted in a line across the path. They took no notice of Thorvald; each of them had his eyes fixed intently on Creidhe. They said nothing. Through the haze of dizziness, Creidhe observed that they wore thick clothing of dark-dyed wool and boots of sheepskin. There was a certain hardness of countenance common to the three of them, two young, one older, perhaps their leader. There was no telling what race they were, nor what tongue might be spoken here. The oldest man had gray hair and was clean-shaven; the others were fair and bearded. How they stared; did she really present such a spectacle, disheveled and sick as she was? One might expect such folk to be surprised at the unexpected arrival: shocked, even. But this silent scrutiny went beyond that; she felt she was being examined, somehow measured, and she did not like it. One man had front teeth missing, and one a torn ear. Each man bore scars on his right cheek: neatly incised parallel lines, four or five of them. No aftermath of combat, these, but ritual markings. Two carried spears; all three wore knives. If Thorvald and Sam had brought weapons, they were still on the boat.

"I hope you can help us," Thorvald said again, more slowly. He spread out his hands, palms open. "We mean you no harm. There are just the three of us, my friend here," nodding at Sam, "and—the girl. As you see, she is sick and cold, and my friend has an injury to his head. Can you offer a night's shelter?"

Now the eyes of the three men turned to take in tall, blond Sam, who stood stolid under their searching gaze, and then moved back to the shivering Creidhe who leaned on his arm. She felt the force of that stare through all her misery, felt it like a blade scraping away her surface to lay bare what was within. They could hardly have been impressed; she was aware of how bedraggled she must appear. Their eyes traveled over her once more, assessing, calculating; it seemed to her they made some decision with not a word spoken. The silence became uncomfortable. Sam shuffled his feet.

"They can't understand you," he hissed to Thorvald. "Use signs. Sleep, eat, you know. Keep it simple."

"My name is Einar." It seemed that, after all, they did understand; the older man spoke now in a barely accented form of the Norse tongue. His eyes were deep-set, their expression guarded. "The woman," he went on, gazing at Thorvald. "Your wife? Your sister?"

Thorvald blinked; perhaps the answer to this had been ready, but it evaded him now.

"Our friend and kinswoman," Sam put in. "Under our protection. We want to mend the boat and sail back home. That's all. Got blown off course, heavy storm to the southeast."

"You have wood for this mending?" one of the younger men asked bluntly.

"Perhaps you didn't understand," Thorvald said. "The young lady needs rest and dry clothes—"

It was at that moment Creidhe felt the world spinning before her eyes, and for a while darkness overtook her. She awoke to find herself naked under woolen blankets, which was somewhat alarming, though it was blissful beyond description to be dry and warm. She lay still, aware of the aches and pains in her hands, her arms, her back; the stint at the *Sea Dove*'s steering oar had punished her body sorely. By all the ancestors, if she hurt this much, how must the others be feeling after rowing all that way? Creidhe rolled

over cautiously, opening her eyes. She was lying on a rough
pallet; whatever filled the mattress, it did not make the soft-
est of beds. Above her were the low roof supports of a cottage or hut, poles of driftwood holding up a latticework of
withies overlaid by turf. The place was dark. She turned her
head. This was a small sleeping chamber; there were several bed spaces crudely marked off by slabs of stone, but
the only occupant other than herself was an old woman sitting on a high stool by the cloth-hung doorway, plying
distaff and spindle by the light of a simple seal-oil lamp, no
more than a shallow bowl with a floating wick. The lamp's
glow accentuated the crone's deep wrinkles, her gnarled
hands steady at their work, her dark hooded eyes. Creidhe
cleared her throat.

"Excuse me—where are my clothes?"

The woman turned toward her; her hands did not halt the
movement of the spindle, the twist of the wool. Her expression was blank, uncomprehending.

"Clothes," Creidhe repeated, sitting up carefully with the
blankets clutched across her chest. "Tunic, trousers, shoes?
My things?" She tried to illustrate what she meant with one
hand, while gripping the blankets with the other.

The spindle twirled slowly down. The old woman jerked
her head toward the foot of the bed, then looked away.

"Oh," said Creidhe, somewhat disconcerted. There was a
little heap of clothing there, certainly, but it was not her
own, neither the old ones of Thorvald's she'd been wearing
nor the others she had carried in her bag. Indeed, her bag
was nowhere to be seen; as far as she knew, it was still
tucked into a dark corner under the decking of the *Sea
Dove*. A shiver ran through her. "I need my bag! Where are
my things?"

There was no reaction at all. Very well, she'd have to
scramble into these garments, whatever they were, and go out
there in search of her belongings. There was no way she'd let
these dour individuals get their hands on the Journey.

Abandoning the attempt at modesty, Creidhe got up and
dressed herself, aware of the biting cold raising goosepim-

ples on her exposed flesh, and conscious of the old woman's sunken eyes scrutinizing every move. You'd think they'd never seen a girl before, the way they looked at her. Well, it was a different land; one must allow for different customs, different manners. There was a shift here, and a gown of coarse gray cloth, not elegant but warm at least, and a thick woolen shawl. The sheepskin boots were too big, but they would have to serve for now.

"Comb?" she inquired without much confidence, running her hands over the damp, salty tangle of her hair. The ribbon that had held the single, thick braid in place was gone in the storm; only a thorough washing with soap, followed by lengthy, painful combing could restore her hair to its usual well-kept state. One might as well go about with a haystack on one's head. "Wash? Soap?"

The old woman grunted disapprovingly and jerked her head again. This was becoming irritating. There was a length of gray cloth on the bed, finer and softer than the gown's fabric. At Creidhe's blank look, the crone ceased her spinning and gestured, making it clear what was intended. *Take, wrap, cover your hair.* She was frowning; it was not possible to tell why.

"Comb?" Creidhe mimicked the action, doing her best to look polite and friendly. "Please?"

The old woman glared. She spat out a single incomprehensible word with such intensity that Creidhe flinched. Very well; she had a comb in her bag, if indeed her bag had not been washed into the sea in those last days of storm. She hoped very much that it had not, for to lose the Journey would be a cruel thing indeed.

"I'm going out," Creidhe said as calmly as she could. "I need my bag, and I want to see my friends. Thank you for—" She could not decide how to finish this. For guarding me? She stepped over to the doorway, but the woman was there before her, alarmingly quick for one so old, her arms stretched out to bar the way.

"I want to go out." Creidhe's heart was pounding. "My friends, I need to speak to them."

The crone shook her head, making the same gesture as

before: *Wrap your hair.* Of course, thought Creidhe, she could simply push her way past, but something in the dark, beady eyes made it clear that would not be a wise move. She had not forgotten those men with their assessing gaze and their spears. Creidhe retreated to the pallet, took the cloth, wrapped it around her head loosely. Was it really only days since she had worn her best blue linen with the border of silver braid, and danced at a wedding with silk ribbons in her hair?

"May I go now?" she asked quietly, doing her best to look demure and contrite, though a slow anger was building in her.

The crone did not reply, but gripped Creidhe's arms, turning her around. The old hands, hard as tree roots, shoved her hair up under the scarf, every bright thread out of sight, and fastened it in place with alarming bone pins drawn from the depths of a pocket. In the front, the scarf was tugged down, and stray wisps of hair pushed back under it. Creidhe stood silent, a flush of indignation rising to her cheeks. The words were on her lips, *Do you know whose daughter I am?* but this was a far island, a wild place of the utmost margins. Here they had never heard of the brave and noble warrior Eyvind who had made peace in the Light Isles, nor the wise and lovely Nessa who had sustained the hopes and identity of her people through the darkest time. To these folk, Creidhe and her companions were just travelers washed up in the wrong place: a nuisance. She must be grateful for what help was offered them. She was warm and dry, and had slept a little. And now the ancient one stepped aside from the doorway and let her out.

Creidhe crossed a small yard where scrawny chickens were foraging in the mud and, following the sound of voices, entered a larger hut. Men were gathered around a central hearth. Thorvald and Sam were eating. At least, Sam had a mutton bone in his hand, and his mouth full; there was a platter on the bench by Thorvald, but Creidhe saw from the way he looked, pallid, distant, that he still fought the crippling headache, and would be unable to contemplate food. She had learned to read him very well over the years since childhood. By now he would be near blinded by the pain but doing his best not to show any weakness in front of the small group of island men who had gathered to share this evening meal and take a look at the strangers suddenly arrived in their midst. And there was another thing; she'd thought of it when those three met them on the pathway from the shore. From now on, Thorvald would not be able to look at a man of middle years without thinking, *Are you my father? Are you Somerled?* By all the ancestors, this would be a tortured journey indeed if he insisted on their silence and maintained his own until he was quite sure. But that was Thorvald's way; he had never sought the straight and easy path.

On the crude hearth burned a small fire fueled by animal dung. Creidhe walked across to stand by it, deciding she would not be intimidated by the wild look of the folk gathered here, nor the fact that there was not a single woman among them. Perhaps this was merely a gathering place for fishermen; their real settlements were probably farther away, in more hospitable parts of the islands, hidden valleys, rolling grasslands like those of the Light Isles. She shivered, remembering the sheer cliffs, the pounding waves, the high, steep peaks they had seen from the *Sea Dove*. These men's closed faces, their guarded eyes, told of a life of struggle, an existence carved out in the face of the elements. All of a sudden, home seemed a very long way away. Maybe she was just a little frightened. This would not do at all; she was here to help Thorvald, not hold him back.

"Good evening." She made her tone courteous and confident as she spread out her hands to warm them at the fire. "Thank you for providing us with shelter."

There was a silence, as if she had said something either quite astonishing or entirely inappropriate. Then one man turned to Thorvald and muttered something about food and drink.

"You want something to eat, Creidhe?" Thorvald asked in the constrained voice the headache imposed on him.

Creidhe stared at the man who had spoken. "Thank you," she said. "A small amount only. I've been ill." Indeed, she felt the weakness in her legs, the dizziness in her head now.

"Here," said Sam, moving along the bench to make room for her. "Sit down, you look washed out." He glanced at the scarf wrapped around her head, but made no comment.

"Thank you." She sat; the young man on the other side edged away like a nervous animal, and the one standing behind moved too, as if she would pass some malady on to them. Perhaps she smelled bad; lacking water for washing, there wasn't much to be done about that. Every man in the chamber was watching her; that strange expression was on all their faces, as if the smallest move she made were of intense interest to them. The older man, Einar, had ladled some meat from a stew pot into a bowl; he did not pass it to Creidhe, but gave it to Thorvald with a roll of the eyes in her direction.

"Here," Thorvald said, putting it in her hands. His eyes defied her to mention the headache. She held her tongue. The stew was gray and beaded with fat, and there was nothing by way of a spoon, not even a hunk of bread to scoop with. Still they watched her.

"Better eat up," Sam advised. "They say we're moving on in the morning. Got to visit some chief; find out where we can get wood for the *Sea Dove*. These fellows are just passing through on their way to a place called Council Fjord. Lucky we came in when there were folk around. Here."

He rummaged in a pocket and brought out a little spoon carved from whalebone; he had ever been a resourceful fellow. Creidhe ate in silence, feeling the pressure of so many eyes on her. There seemed no reason for such discourtesy.

"Tell me," Thorvald said after a while, "how many folk live on these isles, and where? You speak as we do; we must share ancestors. How long have you dwelt here, and where did your people come from?"

Einar was sitting opposite Thorvald, using a finger to scour the last of the meat juices from his platter. "You have many questions," he observed, frowning.

"I don't wish to offend," Thorvald said carefully. "If I have kinfolk on these isles I'd welcome the opportunity to greet them, that's all. I'm sure my friends here feel the same. Have any of you come from the place called Orkney-jar, also known as the Light Isles? Are there men here from Norway? From Ulster?"

"None of our business, of course," muttered Sam, tearing the last shreds of meat from his bone. "But interesting. Good meal, this; best I've had in days. How's the fishing in these waters? Tricky tides, I'll bet. What do you take mostly? Cod? Redfish?"

Several men began to speak at once; this topic, apparently, was both safe and interesting. In no time at all, Sam was the center of a lively conversation that included much waving of hands, though there were no smiles; there was a universal grimness about these men. Creidhe applied herself to her meal. The standard of the cooking fell far short of her own, but she could hardly afford to be fussy. She just hoped she would keep it down.

"Thorvald," she hissed under the talk of boats and nets and winds. "You look terrible. Tell them you need to lie down."

"I'm fine." He was seated near her, leaning back against the wall with eyes closed. His face was the color of goat's cheese.

"Then I'll tell them. You're being stupid."

"I'm fine, Creidhe. Eat your supper."

The meat was rich and greasy; perhaps the sheep here carried an extra layer of fat to help them cope with the cold, which even now penetrated this small chamber with probing fingers. Warm gown, woolen shawl, headscarf and sheepskin boots could not alleviate Creidhe's shivering. She was thirsty, terribly thirsty. There was a jug on that far table, perhaps water, but in the din of voices nobody was going to hear a polite request for a drink. She started to get up, to fetch it for herself, but there was a lad in front of her now, the one who had moved away before, and he was extending his hand shyly, offering a cup. His hand was shaking so much the water slopped over the side; what was it about her that caused such strange reactions?

"Thank you," Creidhe said, smiling at him and taking

the cup. The youth ducked his head, a fleeting grin flashing across his features, and scuttled back to a corner. If the others could ask questions, Creidhe decided, then so could she.

"Where are the women of your community?" She addressed this to Einar, who had not joined in the talk of fishing, but had kept his attention on Thorvald and herself, almost as if fearing they might run away, though there was indeed nowhere to run to. "Do they not come to supper with you in the evenings?"

Einar's hard eyes looked into hers. He shook his head, then turned back to Thorvald.

"Tomorrow," he said curtly. "Tomorrow we walk to Brightwater. The Ruler will meet us there. It's for him to answer your questions, not I."

"The Ruler?" Creidhe asked. "What ruler?"

Even to that, she did not receive a direct answer; the fellow still addressed himself doggedly to Thorvald, as if she were invisible.

"The Ruler of the Isles," he said gravely. "Leader of the Long Knife people. All strangers must be seen by him; he will decide your fate."

It was a measure of the grip the headache had on him that Thorvald gave no visible reaction to this. It was Sam who sat forward, frowning, talk of nets and tides abruptly abandoned.

"Fate? What do you mean by that? All we want's a couple of pieces of wood and a roof over our heads while we do the fixing. We'll pay for it, as I told you; by work, it'd have to be. Whatever you need doing, we'll give you a hand. Nobody's talking about fate here."

"That is a strange name, the Long Knife people," observed Creidhe. Her shivering didn't seem to be stopping, and it was not entirely due to the cold. "Who are they?" An instant later the answer came to her, for there had been a certain pride in the way the odd name was spoken, and there were the weapons they wore in their belts, every one of them, for all this seemed no more than a fishermen's out-

post. With their dour expressions and scarred skin, these islanders were entirely suited to such a title.

"This ruler," Sam put in. "Got a name, has he?"

Einar spat neatly on the earthen floor; he had been picking the remnants of mutton flesh from his teeth with a splinter of bone. "Ask your questions tomorrow. Early start; you
can sleep alongside us. Steep climb; can the girl do it?"

It was becoming impossible to disregard the fellow's
rudeness. "If you are referring to me," Creidhe told him in
icy tones, rising to her feet, "I have ears and a tongue of my
own and am well able to use both. I'm quite capable of
walking wherever Thorvald and Sam go, and have every intention of doing so. Now, my kinsman here has a bad
headache and needs to lie down. And we want to go back
down to the boat, to fetch our things—"

"No!" Einar said sharply. "Not safe for you—" He
sprang to his feet and took a step toward her. He may not
have intended to lay hands on her, but she shrank back, and
at the same instant Sam interposed his large form between
them. Thorvald had opened his eyes, but seemed too dazed
by pain to realize what was happening.

"Now, then," Sam said levelly, "no need for that. Different lands, different ways, I know. But we don't take kindly
to men who threaten womenfolk, back in the Light Isles.
You'll keep your hands off Creidhe if you know what's
good for you. Descended from royal blood, she is: a lady."

The islander's attention had been captured by the action,
if not the words. His eyes were on Sam's square jaw and
sturdy body, his well-muscled arms and look of determination under the strip of stained cloth that still bound his head
wound. "You a fighting man?" he queried.

Creidhe saw Sam open his mouth to answer, no, he was
just a fisherman and wanted no fight with anyone, but he did
not get the chance. Thorvald was on his feet, a hand against
the wall to steady him.

"Of course we are," he announced with a firmness quite
at odds with his alarming pallor. "Where we come from, no
lad reaches twelve years without a mastery of spear and

sword. An island people without the ability to defend itself can expect only annihilation."

"Good," said Einar after a considerable pause, during which several conflicting expressions passed over Sam's usually placid features. "That will please the Ruler."

The time seemed right to press what little advantage there was, though Thorvald's words had troubled Creidhe; to call them exaggeration was an understatement. She summoned up her courage. "I want my bag, the one I had in the boat. And we need a bed for Thorvald, he's ill. And a promise we'll be kept safe until we get to this—this—"

"Brightwater, wasn't it?" Thorvald supplied the name in a voice that was no more than a whisper. His earlier effort seemed to have drained his last strength.

"Sleep," the fellow said, pointing to the far end of the chamber where a doorway opened into a further space within the hut. Some of the men were already retiring there; their yawns suggested they'd had a long day. One was damping down the fire. The cold room grew even chillier. That old woman was back, standing by the outer doorway like some messenger of Bone Mother, with her sunken eyes and knotted fingers. "Sleep," said the man again, jerking his head toward the crone. "Safe here." It was a kind of answer, but not enough.

Creidhe clutched at Sam's arm. "Sam, ask him! I need my things." It sounded girlish and petulant, and she did not want to be a nuisance; her role was to help Thorvald, not hinder. It wasn't the comb that really mattered, the clean clothing, the useful bits and pieces. It was the Journey; she could not let these people set their hands on it.

"Don't fret, Creidhe," Sam said. "I've no intention of going to bed without checking on the *Sea Dove*. It's light enough, this time of year. I'll bring up what you need if I can find it."

True to his word, he was back not so much later, at the door of the little hut housing Creidhe and her grim guardian. Before Sam could so much as open his mouth, the old woman snatched the bag out of his hands and shooed him away.

By the flicker of the same tiny lamp that had lit the ancient one's steady spinning, Creidhe spread out her sodden clothing, her roll of wools and needles, her other small possessions to dry as best they could on the empty bed-shelves. The Journey seemed unscathed, and was perfectly dry. The other things were a mess, and so was her hair. Still, she must be glad her belongings had survived at all; if she had not jammed them tightly into her hiding place, they'd surely have been lost in the storm.

She struggled to draw the comb through her disheveled locks. It seemed to her that teasing out the implacable knots was a little like trying to get useful information from these odd, tight-lipped folk with their strange approach to conversation. She knew the old woman could understand her, just as the men had. Yet the crone only muttered and frowned, and Einar seemed to believe women quite lacking in the skill of comprehension. He had been quick enough to anger when she had challenged him. As for the others, their sidelong, nervous glances annoyed her almost as much as Einar's rudeness. She didn't like this. She didn't like it a bit, and when they got to see this Ruler of the Isles, probably another jumped-up fisherman, she would tell him so straight out, Thorvald or no Thorvald. Her father had taught her honesty was the best way; her mother honored courage and a forthright manner. How could she aid Thorvald's cause if she were alternately ogled and intimidated?

"Ouch!" Creidhe winced as the comb caught another tangle. The job was nearly done; in the morning she would wear the headscarf without argument, just to stop the wind putting all the knots back in. She yawned. What a godforsaken place this was. It was unthinkable that Thorvald's father would actually have chosen to stay here, if he could have sailed anywhere else at all. The people were as capricious and strange as the winds and tides, impossible to read. She hoped they would find Somerled soon, or at least learn what had become of him. There was nothing in the world would induce her to remain on these islands an instant longer than she must.

* * *

A steep climb: it was certainly that, in parts, and a long walk. Thorvald's head was clear this morning, and he thought he made a passable show of strength, forcing himself to match the brisk pace of their minders, although he could see how hard it was for Creidhe in those ill-fitting boots. To survive here, it seemed to Thorvald, one must earn these folks' respect quickly. They understood winds, tides and fish, and they understood strength: the only thing that had impressed them so far had been Sam's quick defense of Creidhe. Creidhe. By all the gods, Thorvald thought as he watched her dogged, white-faced struggle to keep up with the line of men climbing the precipitous, slippery track, what had possessed her to come here? Premonitions and vague feelings were no basis for such a journey. Surely she knew that; she had ever been a practical girl. Her presence here would be more hindrance than help; she was going to cause all manner of complications with these islanders, he could see it. Everything in their manner screamed their unease with her presence, and worse still, he could tell she was frightened, for all her show of confidence. He knew her well; he had seen the change in her eyes when the fellow, Einar, would have touched her. Wasn't this hard enough already, with the *Sea Dove* smashed and themselves under armed escort? How could he get on with what must be done here if he had constantly to be worrying about Creidhe?

They halted on a small patch of level ground near the top of a particularly steep section of track. On one side the slope fell away, on the other it rose sharply. Rangy island sheep grazed there, heedless of the long drop to the base, though they stayed downhill of their lambs. The men brought out water skins and passed them around; some squatted by the track, some sat on the rocks, easing their legs. In the distance, far ahead, a plume of smoke arose. Below them a broad, glinting lake spread, wide and peaceful, under the light sky, its margins rising steeply to grass-clad fells and bare, craggy peaks. They had climbed high enough to see far to the west, where a long, narrow bay seemed to cut between dark cliffs. At its mouth were more islands; a small, improbably steep one not far out, and another, more distant, which seemed to wear a shawl of cloud even on this clear spring day.

"Council Fjord," said Einar, pointing to the west.

"Your people have their main settlement there? A council house, where the Thing can be convened?" Thorvald queried. There were many islands—he had seen them from the *Sea Dove*—scattered to north and south, though that cloud-wreathed isle was the farthest point west, he judged. Fighting men. Did they face the threat of invaders here? Surely not; the place was too remote to attract such unwelcome attention. And it was as stark and bleak a realm as one could imagine; what could be here worth taking? Of course, the peril might come from within. Such a realm might harbor many small settlements, each with its own inhabitants and codes. But how could a serious dispute be sustained in this desperate terrain? There was scarcely a scrap of flat land to be seen. It was not fighting men they needed, but creatures of legend that could fly like eagles or swim like seals. "Your home?" he added.

"Long Knife people dwell here on Isle of Storms, on Isle of Streams and East Island," Einar said, sweeping a hand around. "A few further north. In the south, the others."

"Others?"

"A scourge; an accursed race." These words were spoken in a hushed undertone, as if even to name such a threat were perilous. "The Unspoken."

Thorvald felt the hairs on his neck prickle. "They are— not human?" Stupid question; it was the sort of thing a girl would ask, not a man who had boldly declared himself a warrior not so long ago.

"I will not talk of this here," Einar whispered. "Not safe. We are at war; there is no time for councils. Come on, we must go."

Thorvald shouldered his pack and moved on in Einar's wake. The track was steep here, rising to skirt the slope above the lake; some distance ahead, it dropped again toward what seemed to be a small settlement. Sam walked up near the front of the line. Thorvald observed his friend was carrying Creidhe's bag as well as his own, and managing to keep up a lively conversation as he strode on. Thorvald's own legs ached, and his back still felt the strain of that last, desperate effort on the oars. His hands hurt, too, though a fellow called Skolli had slathered them with some sort of evil-smelling grease last night, and it appeared to have helped a little. He fixed his mind ahead. Ruler of the Isles. The title seemed possible for a man who had once possessed a burning desire to be a king. He rehearsed what he might say, what questions he could ask. He considered what information he might offer. Not much: even his mother's name could give too much away. Perhaps he should play dumb, and hope Sam and Creidhe could hold their tongues when required. Perhaps he should let Somerled do the talking. If it was Somerled. Would he know? Was there something in the blood that called, this is my father, this is my son, some instant recognition that went beyond a voice, an appearance, matters of probability and logic? He shivered. Soon enough he might get his answer, and he might regret the wild impulse that had drawn him here. What if you sought out your father and found only a monster?

There was a sudden, sharp cry from one of the men behind and below him. The line came to an abrupt halt, strung out along the narrow pathway. Thorvald turned, and felt his heart leap to his throat. Creidhe had stepped off the track. She was standing on a tiny shelf that protruded from its outer edge, an uneven, slippery surface scarcely large enough for her two feet. She was gazing westward, seaward, her eyes fixed on that far-off, cloud-swathed island as if it had the power to draw her through the air toward it. The smallest move and she would plunge down the sheer hillside to be smashed on the protruding rocks, or swallowed by the lake waters far below. The man behind her was shouting in alarm; the one above her was running back. She reached out her arms, not for help but as if to fly, as if to embrace the very air separating her from the vision that held her, some wondrous thing nobody else could see. Thorvald knew she would fall the moment anyone touched her.

"No!" he called, his tone urgent but low, so as not to startle her. "No, not like that! Let me!" He began to edge down the track; the islanders pressed back to let him pass. His heart was hammering, his brow ran cold with sweat. He knew such trances, and the danger of breaking them abruptly. There were wise women in Creidhe's family, priestesses; one did not grow up as a neighbor of such folk without some understanding of the power of the seer and the havoc it could wreak. He made himself go carefully, suppressing the instinct to run. Behind him he could hear the sounds of Sam's descent—who else would be scrambling back down the path so fast, sending a shower of small stones over the edge?—though what Sam could do to help him he could not imagine.

"Stay back," he hissed over his shoulder. Now he was quite near Creidhe, moving slowly closer, making sure he did not let his shadow fall on her face, or frighten her with sudden movements, unexpected noises.

"Creidhe?" He kept his voice quiet, calm. "Creidhe? What do you see?"

Her face was turned away, eyes still rapt on that distant island. It seemed numinous, otherworldly, its slopes of gray-blue, dusky violet and moss-green rising gracefully from a wide expanse of mist-shrouded water. A shawl of white clung close about its upper reaches.

"What is it, Creidhe? What do you hear? Tell me. It's Thorvald. Tell me."

He sidled closer, easing his feet silently across the rock. It would be so easy to get this wrong, to lunge and grab, to miss by a hairsbreadth; he could see her falling, the wide, terrified eyes, the bright hair like a banner, the wind snatching away her last scream. "Creidhe?"

Behind him, Sam had slid to a halt and now stood motionless. The other men had fallen silent. Even the gulls that had followed their path, circling and calling, had stilled their cries; it was as if the whole island held its breath.

"Creidhe?" Thorvald took another step forward. Now he was close enough to touch her, but he would not touch, not yet. He could see her eyes, wide and strange; perhaps a man could glimpse her vision in them, if he looked deep enough. Her cheeks were flushed; the wind had teased out strands of her fair hair from the cloth that swathed her head and tossed them across her brow. There was a kind of radiance in her features that terrified Thorvald; it was as if she belonged in another realm entirely, one that he could never reach. He saw her draw a deep, shuddering breath, and then another, and he saw the change in her face, the doubt and confusion suddenly overtaking the vision as she returned to herself. She put her hands up to cover her eyes and began a stumbling step forward. He moved then, quicker than he had known he could, seizing her around the waist and hauling her back to safety. He could feel her trembling; she was crying now, shielding her face with both hands as if, while she could not see what was before her, she might still return to whatever strange realm had captured her. Thorvald gripped her tightly by the arms; might she not simply walk away from him and over the edge if he let her go? The islanders had moved in closer, before, behind, silent no longer. The buzz of talk seemed to have a note of approval in it. Thorvald could think of easier ways to earn their acceptance.

"Creidhe! Wake up! Come on now!" He gave her a little shake; their position was still precarious, and now that the worst danger was over, he found sudden anger had replaced his terror. He swallowed the next words that came for, after all, they still had to get down to the settlement.

"That's enough, Creidhe. Wipe your face and get going. You're slowing us down."

Shivering, she did as she was told, though a flood of tears was rolling down her cheeks. Thorvald could not tell if it was the vision, or the loss of it, that made her weep. Perhaps it was no more than artifice. Women did these things for their own reasons. "Come on," he said, pushing her ahead of him along the path.

"Here." Sam's voice sounded odd, gruff. "Take my hand.

It's not much farther. So they say anyway. Lovely island, that. Wouldn't mind going there myself, taking a look."

"Huh!" The exclamation came from a stocky, weathered-looking fellow with a bristling beard, who stood next to Sam. "Isle of Clouds? You won't be going that way in a hurry. Worst patch of water this side of the snow lands, between Council Fjord and that place. Fool's Tide, they call it. Lucky if you can get across once a year, at hunt time."

"Really?" asked Sam, making a steady way along the path with the two bags on his back, and one arm stretched out behind him to clasp Creidhe's hand and guide her. "So it's uninhabited? Looks a fair sort of place. But strange."

"It's strange all right. Home to freaks and sorcerers. They call that peak over there the Old Woman. Old Witch, more like. Nobody goes near the Isle of Clouds. It's forbidden even to the Unspoken. A death place; cursed."

"Except at hunt time," another man put in.

"That island gobbles up men," said the first. "Chews them up and spits out the pieces. Keep your woman's eyes off that place; it's evil. We don't sail out that way."

"Only at hunt time."

"I see," said Sam thoughtfully. "When is hunt time?"

But there was no answer. Einar had barked a stern command; his men fell silent, and they made their way slowly down the track till the slope flattened out at the lake's edge and a cluster of turf-roofed cottages came into view, squeezed together between a gushing stream and the rising, grass-clad hill. The western fjord with its view of the mysterious Isle of Clouds could not be seen from here. Creidhe walked now with her gaze on the path before her, following in Sam's steps. If she'd done that all the way, Thorvald thought grimly, she'd have saved them a lot of trouble. It was odd: she had never had visions before, not that he knew of. Indeed, it had always been Creidhe who was the practical, sensible one, busy with cooking or sewing while her older sister Eanna learned the ways of the spirit. Creidhe did not go into trances and step off cliff paths as if she expected to take wing. He must hope it would not happen again, or she would be even more of a liability than he had imagined. His heart was still thumping, even now; he must be less fit than he had thought. And they were almost there. He must collect his thoughts; he must be ready.

"Remember," he hissed to the others. "Remember what I said. Leave the talking to me."

They were on level ground now, and the path was wide enough for two to walk side by side. Sam was supporting Creidhe with his arm; both turned their heads back toward him. Thorvald saw, to his surprise, that big, burly Sam was pale as a ghost. Creidhe's face was marked with the tracks of tears; she seemed exhausted and sad. They looked at him, then turned away, walking on. There had been something like reproach in their eyes. What was wrong with them? He'd saved Creidhe, hadn't he?

They entered the settlement, if that was the right name for such a ramshackle collection of tiny dwellings and narrow, twisting paths. Someone was ringing a bell from higher up the hill: a welcome, perhaps, for rare travelers. Why was it, then, that it seemed to him like a warning tocsin? Thorvald gritted his teeth. This place was getting to him, and he must not allow that. He was leader of this expedition, and a leader must be strong. He squared his shoulders and held his head high, addressing the men who had brought them here. He made his voice firm and confident: not a plea, but a challenge.

"Take me to this Ruler of the Isles," he said. "I would speak with him."

It was not quite so easy, for it transpired one did not seek out this potentate but waited for him to arrive in his own time. In due course, their escort told them, they would be sent for. Meanwhile there would be a place to rest, and food. The girl would go elsewhere; it was not appropriate she be housed with them. Briefly, Sam and Thorvald protested. Creidhe was not well, she needed her friends close by, they were responsible for her safety. As for Creidhe herself, she was unusually silent, clutching her bag with both hands. Her eyes were oddly vague, as if the last shreds of her vision still lingered there. At length a couple of women appeared, and Thorvald, reassured by their practical, down-to-earth look, allowed them to lead Creidhe away to one of the little houses. It was one less thing to think about.

The two men were led to a building somewhat larger and better maintained than the others. They waited in a small anteroom. Islanders stood casually at either door, but whether to prevent others from entering or the new arrivals from departing, there was no telling. An attempt to engage these men in conversation proved fruitless. All Thorvald discovered was their names: the man with the bristling beard was Orm; the other, younger fellow, Svein. Food was brought: a blood sausage, rich and dark, and a dish of eggs. They ate gratefully. Water was provided; they'd have welcomed ale. Perhaps these folk were without the wherewithal for brewing, for it did not seem a promising terrain for crop yields. They waited longer, as the day wore on. There was plenty of time for thinking: too much time. In the end Sam stretched out on the floor, head pillowed on his bag, and fell asleep. He muttered from time to time, perhaps dreaming of storms. Thorvald knew his friend was anxious about the *Sea Dove*; it had been a wrench to leave her unguarded.

Dusk was falling when they were finally summoned. There had been good signs: water brought for washing, more dry clothes, a warm cloak apiece. All the same, Thorvald recalled the talk of fates being determined here. He must take control from the start; he must not forget that this was his own quest, to make of what he could. These islands were a proving ground. Here, he would find out who he was. Maybe his father was here, and maybe not. Perhaps Somerled was still the man he had been, ruthless, driven, cruel. Maybe he had changed. Could such a man change? Could he break free of that dark legacy and make himself anew? And if that were so, could not his son, too, strive to do well, to make his mark in the world, to find his true purpose and calling? Thorvald shivered. Possibly the truth he would discover might only confirm what he already suspected: that his father's blood was tainted, his spirit irretrievably steeped in evil. That this was the legacy he had passed down, an inescapable shadow, rendering Thorvald, too, incapable of fine deeds, of worthy thoughts. Still, at least he would know, one way or the other. He would know the truth.

"My greeting to you." The man who stood in the lamplit chamber, waiting for them, was not surrounded by courtiers or warriors, nor by fishermen or folk of his household. He had just one guard by him, a very large man with shoulders like a bull's and small, alert eyes. Thorvald and Sam walked the length of the room, two islanders behind them. Thorvald noted the low roof, the small hearth, the lack of wall hangings. If this were the Ruler's domain, it was a poor thing indeed beside the grand council chambers and assembly halls of the Light Isles. As for the man himself, he was formidable enough. He regarded them levelly as they approached, his dark eyes assessing, his mouth a thin line, giving nothing away. He was of middle height, not strongly built but wiry and lithe-looking. He was the right age, or could be: the hair dark as a crow's wing, with a thread or two of gray at the temples, the right cheek marked with the same parallel scarring they had seen on the other men, a five-line pattern drawn with neat precision. The robe he wore was not kingly, but of plain wool, its only trim a narrow, patterned border, lighter gray on darker. His hair was tied back with a strip of the same woven braid. The impression was austere. They halted a few paces away. The big guard shifted slightly, fingers moving on the haft of his axe.

"And ours to you," Thorvald said, matching the coolly courteous tone in which the fellow had addressed him. "You are the man they call Ruler of the Isles?"

"My lord," Orm spoke quickly, his tone apologetic, "these are the two travelers who landed at Blood Bay. The woman—"

"You can leave us now." The Ruler spoke without emphasis. A moment later the islanders were gone; obedience was evidently automatic and instant. The bodyguard made no move. "Please, be seated." The Ruler motioned to a stone bench, and sat down himself on the one opposite. "Your names?"

Sam opened his mouth, but Thorvald was quicker. "We

are from the islands to the southeast, which some call Orkneyjar, and some the Light Isles," he said, never taking his eyes off the Ruler's. "As we told those who brought us here, we were blown off course, and our boat is damaged. I am Thorvald; my friend here is Sam."

"Sam Olafsson of Stensakir. The boat's mine, and I'm keen to get her mended and sail for home. We were hoping—"

The Ruler lifted a hand; Sam fell silent. "And you?" the Ruler queried, his eyes intent on Thorvald. "His brother? That seems unlikely. His deckhand? I think not; your manner of speech suggests at least a rudimentary education. Your friend here gives his father's name with pride. Why do you not do the same?"

"From you," Thorvald replied, his heart racing, "we have heard neither name nor lineage. The title of Ruler was not given you in the cradle, I imagine." Sam jabbed him sharply in the ribs; he ignored it. "As for me, I am my own man and go my own way. I need no other identity." He wished it were true; life would be so much simpler.

"I am Asgrim," said the Ruler. "We are of all kinds here. We call our home the Lost Isles: a place of fugitives and outcasts, men who see the world beyond these shores through a veil of bitterness and mistrust. Not content with that, we war with one another."

Rapidly, Thorvald rethought what he had been about to say. "Asgrim," he mused. "A fine Norse name. Were your antecedents from that land? How long have folk dwelt in these parts? Where we come from, the existence of these isles is no more than the subject of conjecture: a thing of legend almost."

Asgrim steepled his fingers, his dark eyes intent on Thorvald's face. "Einar mentioned your fondness for questions," he said mildly. "I have some for you, and before you answer them, you'd do well to note who I am and what power I wield here. The Long Knife people obey me in all things. But for my guidance they would have perished long ago. This is an unforgiving land, and we are not its only dwellers. My people have much to contend with. They have

learned to play a single game only, one they must play for
survival: my game. While you remain here, you will do the
same. The weak or disobedient cannot survive in such a
place. Now answer me. Why have you come here? What do
you want?"

There was a brief pause. "Sam spoke the truth," Thorvald
said. "We're here quite by chance; there was a storm, and
our boat was carried to this shore despite our efforts to turn
her back eastward. As for what we want, we made that plain
yesterday: enough wood to mend the *Sea Dove* so we can
leave here."

"We understand wood's in short supply," Sam put in.
"That's no surprise, it's the same at home. We'll work at what-
ever you want doing until we earn the price of what we need.
I've got tools; I can do the fixing, it's just the materials—"

Asgrim raised a hand again, cutting Sam's words short.
"Yes, I heard the tale. Fishing, wasn't it? And I was told
enough to recognize that you, at least, are no more than you
seem. These folk know their own kind. But you," turning to
Thorvald, "you are another matter. Tell me, why would you
bring a woman on such an expedition? A woman of exceptional beauty, and very young at that? I can think of only
one reason, and it does not match what I read of you, nor of
your friend here. Is the girl indeed only with you to warm
your beds at night, each in turn?"

Sam flushed scarlet. "You insult her, and you offend me,
my lord, with such a suggestion. Creidhe's a good girl;
there's nothing of that sort going on, nothing at all, and I
hope you make your men aware of it, because if anyone
lays a finger on her—"

"Sam," Thorvald warned, and Sam's torrent of words
subsided to an angry muttering.

"I have heard no answers as yet," Asgrim observed
coolly. "The girl is this man's sweetheart, maybe, that a
simple question provokes such a flood of emotion. She is
comely, no doubt of it, shapely and fair. Such a woman cannot fail to draw the eye. Who is she?"

"A childhood friend, my lord." Thorvald found himself

somewhat taken aback at the repeated emphasis on Creidhe's looks. He had never thought of her in those terms. Exceptional beauty? Hardly. Creidhe was—well, she was just Creidhe. He decided truth was the best option here. "She is sixteen years old, of high birth, and not yet promised to any man. Untouched."

"And it'd better stay that way," growled Sam.

"But, my lord, to be quite honest with you," Thorvald went on, "the girl did not accompany us with our consent. Creidhe stowed away on our boat; by the time we found her, the storm was already bearing us far from our home shore. We had no choice but to bring her here with us. You know women; once they take an idea into their heads, there's no gainsaying them. Creidhe thought it would be an adventure, I suppose."

"Really?" Asgrim's dark brows rose in derision. "A fishing trip? The women of your island must indeed be short of diversions."

Thorvald managed a nonchalant shrug. "She's young," he said. "She hardly knows what she's doing sometimes." The sight of Creidhe on that little ledge, arms outstretched, eyes blind to the world, was imprinted starkly in his mind.

"So I've been told," Asgrim observed. "An incident on the way here, and the woman nearly lost. That was very careless. I questioned those who accompanied her; there has been appropriate punishment. Such visitors are rare on our shores and must be protected."

"Punishment?" Sam sounded quite taken aback. "It wasn't their fault. Creidhe did it herself. It was like something took hold of her, something none of us could see."

"Indeed. It does seem to me the young woman is more than a little capricious: wayward, one might say. She presents a danger to herself, or to others."

"Oh no!" Sam said anxiously. "Creidhe's a good girl, a reliable girl. Great little spinner and weaver, wonderful cook, the sort any man'd want for his wife." He caught Thorvald's penetrating look and blushed violently. "It's this place," he added with a note of apology. "Getting to her, you know, the strangeness and all. I mean, how does a peaceful cove earn the name Blood Bay?"

"A simple matter of whales," Asgrim said mildly. "In past times, the men of that settlement prided themselves on the size of catch they could herd into the shore with their curraghs: the sand has run red in many a season. These days we are occupied with other pursuits; there has been no whale harvest for over five years. As for Creidhe, we must ensure she is kept safe. She's a creature of rare loveliness and, if you speak truth, remarkable skills as well. A prize indeed. Fortunately this settlement is well protected, and there are women here, company for your little friend when you move on."

There was a brief silence.

"Move on," Thorvald said eventually. "Move where?"

Asgrim stretched, arms linked behind his head. "You know," he said expansively, "I don't think you've answered a single one of my questions. Fortunately, the young lady was a great deal more communicative. Shall we continue this in the morning, when you've had some time to think? It grows late, and you've had a long day. Let it not be said that the Ruler of the Isles has forgotten what it means to be a good host."

He gave a single sharp clap of the hands, and there was the sound of men approaching, vessels clinking, and a smell of roast meat.

"Just a moment," Thorvald said as a chill of misgiving went down his spine. "You've spoken to Creidhe already? Why didn't you tell us that? What kind of game are you playing here?" Odin's bones, perhaps Asgrim knew the truth about this quest already; Creidhe might have told him everything. But no, Creidhe would be true to her word. If there was one thing you could say about her, it was that she was completely trustworthy. She'd have kept quiet, true to her promise.

"What, still more questions?" The Ruler gave a thin-lipped smile. "It's quite a simple game, Thorvald. Not beyond you, I'm sure. Information is exchanged, question for question, answer for answer. Don't they do that where you come from? The other part is easier still. You want something, and I can give it to you. But you must earn it. As this is my domain, you will earn it on my terms. I'm told you have some skill in the arts of warfare. We can use that; indeed, it's precisely what we need. But you will find the kind of battle we wage here strange and frustrating, for all is at the mercy of wind and tide, and the uncanny powers of our enemies lie beyond the reach of spear and knife. We have the smallest margin of time to act; that requires the planning to be meticulous."

There were islanders coming in now, bringing jugs, cups and platters of mutton and boiled fish.

"Tell us," said Thorvald urgently, "tell us more. Who are these enemies, and where do they live? Why do you war with them? What is the nature of their attacks?"

"Perhaps," observed Asgrim, "you will learn patience during your stay with us, Thorvald. I hope you do. This constant questioning could soon grow wearying. Come, have a bite to eat, a little to drink, and let us speak no more of this until morning."

"Still," Thorvald was taken aback to hear Sam speak up, for their host's tone had grown dauntingly chilly, "I'd feel better if I knew Creidhe was well. I take it the women won't come here for their supper; that doesn't seem to be your way. But, you understand, she's a girl, and we're responsible."

Asgrim had walked over to the stone table where the dishes were set; he was using a small, sharp knife to slice off strips of meat and lay them neatly on a platter to the side. Most of the men who had walked with them from the bay were in the hall now. Suppertime it might be, but there was no sense of conviviality; all were silent and grim-faced. Thorvald could not see the man who had walked in front of Creidhe that morning, nor the one who had followed her.

"Rest assured, lad," Asgrim addressed Sam with a quirk of the lip that might have been a smile, "there can be no safer place for your friend in these isles but here at Brightwater. Don't distress yourself. She has a warm hearth, good

food and female companionship in abundance. I imagine
it's a great deal more comfortable than your boat. Trust me.
The girl's a treasure, and I know how to look after precious
things. Now eat, drink; we've work ahead of us, and you
need your strength."

Much later, as the two of them settled in the narrow
chamber they had been allotted for sleeping, Sam hissed to
Thorvald, "Did you hear what he said? Arts of war? Why
did you tell them that anyway, about every lad in the Light
Isles being a fighter before he's twelve years old? You know
what'll happen now. We'll end up in their front line, and be
stone dead before it's summer."

"Shh," whispered Thorvald. "Keep your voice down,
there's men sleeping on the other side of that partition, and
I'll bet he's ordered them to report every single thing they
hear. Maybe I did exaggerate just a bit."

"A bit? I may be handy with my fists when pushed, but
I'd be precious little use with a sword in my hands. Arts of
war? Only art I know's throwing out a net and hauling it in
again."

"It's all right, Sam. I know what I'm doing."

There was a pause.

"Could've fooled me," Sam muttered.

Thorvald made no response.

"You think it's him?" Sam asked.

"I don't know." That was a lie, of course; he was almost
sure, as sure as one could be after so short a time. Not that
the man resembled himself in any way that was obvious,
save perhaps the eyes. It was more a feeling, not the calling
of the blood he had imagined, but a recognition at once
more alarming and more heady. This man had hidden
depths; he harbored secrets, plots and plans. Thorvald
would uncover them; he would find out what lay behind that
mask of austerity and control. Asgrim intrigued him. The
whole place intrigued him: an island of sorcerers and
freaks, a war waged against an enemy with powers beyond
the merely physical, a hunt that must be carried out at precisely the right time—there was indeed a quest for him

here, a challenge far beyond what he had envisaged. And he would do it; he could show this fellow Asgrim, who might or might not be his father, what stuff he was made of. They would achieve victory together perhaps: like and like.

"It's an opportunity," he said softly, not sure if Sam was still awake. "A chance to find out what kind of man this is. Maybe he's my father, maybe not. Maybe I'll tell him and maybe I won't. We've got to earn our wood anyway. Going farther afield is good. I can talk to people, find out who came to these parts back then. Anyway, it sounds as if they really need us, half-baked warriors or not. It sounds as if we can help them. It's a strange place, an interesting place. I want to find out more." He rolled over, knowing sleep would be a long time coming.

"Thorvald?" came Sam's whisper in the darkness.

"What?"

"What if the two of us get killed and Creidhe's left here on her own?"

"Trust me," said Thorvald. "It'll be fine. Now go to sleep; you heard what the man said—we're going to need our strength."

The light was fading. Margaret sat before the loom, shuttle idle in her hands, the fine-woven strands in their subtle shades of gray and dun blurring before her weary eyes. It was too late for work; she should give up the pretense and go to bed. Yet she sat on, staring blindly at the woolen web and picturing another, a bold swathe of blue and red, and her niece's small, deft hands moving like graceful birds across its flawless surface. Why couldn't she weep, as a normal woman would? Why did it all just build up and build up inside her, when already her heart bore a lifetime of burdens? By all the gods, it was a long punishment she had been set for her one error. On days like today, it seemed to her a doom that was forever.

"Come, you must eat a little. Leave that for now."

Ash's voice was quiet and even, as always. She did not turn her head, but knew just how he stood in the doorway behind her, knew every crease and line of his grave features, the concern in his eyes, the plain, serviceable clothes he wore, garb that reflected his role as something between guard and companion, household steward and familiar friend. Over the years she had watched as his hair turned from russet brown to gray. It was no life for a man, a half life at best.

"Come now," he said again, gently insistent. "You can't see in this light; you'll strain your eyes."

She got up reluctantly, turned to face him knowing he would read the pallor of her cheeks, the unshed tears.

"He will come back, you know," Ash said. "Sons have a habit of sailing away; they learn about the world, and about themselves into the bargain. Thorvald loves you. He will remember that in time."

Margaret shivered, walking past him into the long room. Bread and ale were set on the table, with a round of sheep's cheese and a platter of little onions. Ash was so good to her; she did not deserve such kindness. "He hates me," she said flatly. "He told me so. I looked into my son's eyes as he said those words, and I saw Somerled staring back at me. I can't escape what I did; it is a curse that lies not just over me but over Thorvald as well."

"Come, sit down," Ash said. "This bread is good, let me cut you a piece." His hands were long-fingered and capable, wielding the knife, slicing cheese, setting a platter before her.

"I can't eat," Margaret said, feeling the churning tension in her stomach. Since Thorvald had gone away, a cloud of uncertainty had shadowed her thoughts by day and haunted her dreams at night; there was no escaping it. "It's my fault this has happened, Ash. If I had chosen to tell him earlier, when he was little, he might have come to terms with it. Then he would not have done this." She put her head in her hands, hating her own frailty.

"You are concerned for him; I, too," Ash said. "But Thorvald is no weakling. You have taught him to be resourceful, to accept challenges."

She managed a wan smile. "And, thanks to you, my son

is able with sword and bow, though he was ever less than gracious to you for the years of tutelage you gave him."

"Thorvald resents my presence here," Ash remarked calmly, taking a mouthful of bread and cheese. "I have long known that. He does not understand how it is with you and me. He wishes to be the center and sole focus of your world; he is unaware that he is indeed precisely that."

Margaret sipped her ale; why was it everything tasted like ashes? It was as if a pall had descended since the day she told Thorvald the truth. She had not known then what she would bring down on herself, on her old friends, on everyone. On that day she had brought Somerled back to life.

"It seems different here without Creidhe's visits," Ash observed quietly, crumbling his bread with his fingers.

Suddenly Margaret was unable to stop a tear from spilling down her cheek. She wiped it away with furious fingers; even here, even with nobody but Ash to see her, she would not be weak. She must not be weak. Her strength was all she had left.

"You miss her," he said, eyes intent on her face. "You miss her most of all: your bright light, your almost-daughter."

"You've been here too long, Ash," Margaret said bitterly. "Sometimes I think you know me better than I know myself."

He said nothing. Now neither of them was pretending to eat, and the silence drew out.

"You should leave," Margaret said eventually. "You know that. There is nothing for you here, no life, no future. You should move away, get yourself a farm, take a young wife, have a family of your own. You are not yet so old that you cannot find that kind of contentment."

Ash smiled; there was such sadness in it, such resignation that guilt and sorrow settled on Margaret once more like a heavy cloak.

"You know I will not," he said simply. "You know how it is with me. Besides, why should I heed your good advice if you yourself will not? We spoke of Creidhe, who is like a daughter to you. All the same, she is not yours, although you love her. Why do you not move on, make a new life free from the shackles of the past? It was a long time ago. And you are still young enough to bear another child, if you choose: your own daughter."

She laughed, a harsh, bitter sound quickly suppressed. "Bring another child into the world to share the curse I carry with me? I think not."

He regarded her gravely. "What will it take," he asked her, "to lift this burden from your shoulders? A lifetime of loneliness? When is it enough?"

"I don't know," she whispered, wrapping her arms around herself. "I fear to see my son grow into his father. That I fear above anything. I fear for Creidhe now; she has been drawn into something that can swallow and destroy her. Her love for Thorvald lays her open to great harm. If only she had not gone with him—"

"A traveler needs a light to show him the way," Ash said, wrapping the bread in its cloth and covering the cheese. "While she is with him, our home hearth is a little darker. Perhaps she has a part to play. You look weary; you should rest."

"I have dreams. I am not overeager for sleep when such shadows attend it."

"Margaret?"

She looked at him, seeing the steadfast goodness in the gray eyes, noting new lines on his weathered features, knowing what he was about to say.

"Each of us sleeps in a cold bed." Ash's voice was very soft. "There is no need to be alone with your dreams."

She shook her head helplessly. "I can't. You know that. I have nothing for you; nothing to give. I cannot shake off the darkness of the past; Somerled would always lie between us."

"All the same," Ash said, rising to his feet, "I will be close by, should you need me. You know that."

"You are too good, Ash. I am not worth such care."

He said nothing. There was a code between them, a pattern of restraint that did not allow the touching of lips to palm, a kiss to the cheek, nor even the clasping of hands in the manner of serving man and lady of the house. She got up: another day over, another night to be endured. Where were they, her son with his intense, pale face and his driven eyes; her dear Creidhe of the golden hair and clever hands? Had the ocean even now devoured them, or did they stand on some far shore, confronting the pitiless gaze of the man she had once believed she loved? Gods treat them kindly; gods be more merciful than they had been to her, trapped as she was in a web of her own making.

"Good night, Ash," said Margaret.

FOUR

They call us; it is time.
Have they learned nothing?
Not holy cross nor cold iron can prevail against these
shadows.
God grant me the gift of detachment.

MONK'S MARGIN NOTE

She managed to pretend. She didn't cry; she didn't beg them to stay, or at least not to leave her behind in the settlement with these strangers who, despite their efforts to make her welcome, continued to behave very oddly indeed. There were men standing guard all around Brightwater, and nobody would say why. There was a war; that was as much as she could get out of the women. Those men who did not guard the settlement had to go away. It was terrible to have to smile and clasp hands with Sam and Thorvald as they stood there with packs on their backs and staves in their hands, clad in thick outdoor gear that spoke of a long journey to come. It hurt to pretend she didn't mind, to hold her tongue when everything in her was screaming, *Take me with you, oh please!*

There was a moment when Sam asked her gently if she was sure she'd be all right, and she came close to telling them how uneasy she was and pleading with them not to go. But she smiled again and said everything was fine. She knew they had to work for the wood they needed. The Ruler had explained to her that in a place like this there were always huts and boats that needed repair after storms, tracks to be strengthened, stock to be tended. Asgrim had seemed a courteous man, both authoritative and kindly. He had asked after her health and assured her she would be safe at Brightwater. It had been hard not to scrutinize him too closely, seeking signs of likeness to Thorvald. She had tried not to stare. As for conclusions, she had reached none. This might be Somerled and it might not. All in all, it seemed unlikely such a pleasant sort of man would have a catalog of evil deeds in his past. Since they were going away, it would be up to Thorvald now to find out one way or the other.

She managed her farewells and watched the long line of men snake its way up the track to the west, watched the bright auburn of Thorvald's hair, a solitary note of color against the green-gray of the hillside, moving farther and farther away until he rounded a corner and was lost from view. There had been a light of challenge in his eyes; that was good. The bitterness of those last days in Hrossey was gone from his face and he was looking ahead. Surely it would not take them long to do their work and come back with the wood. To speak of her worries would only have delayed them, and she was here to help, not hinder. Besides, her concerns were probably baseless, just homesickness and the aftermath of what had happened that first morning on the cliff path. Often she tried to recapture the dream, closing her eyes, willing it back, but it was fading now to no more than a lovely half-memory. It had been like a voice, like singing, but only in her head; wordless, magical music that tugged at her, calling, crying, *Here, I'm here!* Sometimes she thought it had been more like hands reaching toward her, hands stretching out in love, or friendship, or need. *Come,* the hands were saying. Yet, as well, the hands were clasping that mist-shrouded island closely, surrounding it with a barrier of protection. She would have gone if she could, winging her way there on invisible pinions, bridging the gap with only a dream to hold her.

She had not spoken of what she felt, not even to Thorvald. She doubted she would have shared something so strange and powerful even with her own mother, her own sister. Now Thorvald and Sam were gone, and so was Asgrim the Ruler along with most of the men. The small force armed with throwing spears could be seen patrolling the pathways of Brightwater by day and standing guard at night, but all remained quiet.

Creidhe applied herself to embroidery. There was no exploring; the women had made that clear. A walk down to the lake was allowed, and up as far as the corner overlooking the walled vegetable patch, but no farther; she had tried one day and had found herself escorted back by two of those fellows with the spears. It was for her own safety, the women said. None of them went wandering.

The vision that haunted her, coming with clarity only in her dreams, found its place in the Journey. At first the women had been curious, crowding around to see. It was clear no seamstress here had the gift for such fine and detailed work. Creidhe was obliged to show them a little, unrolling the fabric a hand's breadth to reveal the vibrant colors and meticulous detail, a pattern not at all in the mode of traditional craft with its mirror images, its formal motifs and regular borders, but an organic, evolving, everchanging flow. They exclaimed, amazed, impressed, perhaps a little fearful: it was like nothing they had ever seen. One admired the tiny trees, one the creatures hiding in the foliage, one the figure of what seemed a girl flying, and the moon within her grasp. One reached to touch; Creidhe rolled her work up again, leaving only the empty part exposed. The dream, the vision, crept onto the cloth in wools of violet and dusk blue, soft green, moss and lichen shades,

the gray of rocks under a wash of tide, the subtle hue of a
seal's pelt. The Journey moved on; it was as well she had
packed her bag with ample supplies of needles and wool,
for many days passed and she had need of occupation.

One could not sit at such demanding work all day. Early
on, she had seen the others spinning and offered to help; this
seemed to surprise them, but when it became evident she
was more than capable at it, they found her a distaff and
spindle and let her ply them in the communal work hut of a
morning. She offered to cook; indeed, she ached to take
charge in the kitchen and produce something more palatable
than the endless diet of boiled fish and overcooked mutton.
But Gudrun, in whose house Creidhe was staying, made it
quite plain her guest should not dream of exerting herself in
such a way. Creidhe must rest, eat well and recover from her
illness. Protests that she was fine now fell on deaf ears.
Creidhe grew restless. At home her days were filled with activity; she was always busy. The idleness made her uneasy,
and she took to walking the allowable section of track four
times over every morning, thinking miserably of her daily
trips to Aunt Margaret's and back, and how much she
missed them. Poor Aunt Margaret; she would be so worried
about Thorvald. As for Creidhe's own family, she shuddered
to imagine their distress, made worse by every one of these
endless days that prolonged her absence. For the weather
had turned foul, with sheeting rain and dense, lowering
mists, and nobody seemed to be expecting the men back.
Sometimes the women talked of this in undertones, nervously. Creidhe questioned them, but they were good at answers that told her nothing. She spun and sewed and waited.

There weren't many children in the settlement. A couple
of boys seemed to go to and fro a lot, bringing fish and eggs,
and there was a lass of twelve or so with a terrible squint and
a furtive, sidling manner, but not a babe or infant to be seen.
Creidhe missed her small sister Ingigerd, and she missed
Brona with her quick wit and ready smile. She could imagine how Brona would be feeling, knowing Sam had made
this journey with Creidhe and waiting out day after day of no
news.

One of the women was heavy with child; when her time came, and it could be no more than two full moons away, that would at least swell the numbers a little. Creidhe remarked on the matter to Gudrun and, as usual, got a response that told her nothing. She commented on it to the others and received blank stares. It was a challenge even to make conversation about the weather here, let alone broach more serious topics. She told the pregnant woman, Jofrid, of her own experience in midwifery, and offered her services should they be needed. Truth to tell, she hoped fervently that before this babe was ready to make its way into the world she would be heading for home again; who would have thought another voyage on the *Sea Dove* could seem so attractive? Jofrid nodded nervously as Creidhe told her of the twins she had delivered back in Hrossey, the breech births safely accomplished, the many straightforward cases, as Jofrid's own would likely be, for she seemed young and sturdy, if disproportionately afraid.

"Is this your first child?" Creidhe asked her, certain the answer would be yes; it did take them like this sometimes, especially if their mothers were not at hand to reassure them. Jofrid shook her head, eyes down. Creidhe looked at Gudrun; there had been no children at Jofrid's skirts as they sat with their spinning, no babe on her back as she walked from hut to cottage.

"Her third." Gudrun spoke matter-of-factly, her hands busy winding wool into a ball. "Lost two. If she holds on till summer she may keep this one."

"Oh," said Creidhe. "Oh, I'm sorry. As I said, I have delivered many babes; I can help—"

"We can always use another pair of hands, if it comes to it," Gudrun said. She was one of those women whose age seems indeterminate; the hatchet features, thin, scraped-back hair and shrewd eyes were matched by a certain terseness of manner. "Of course, you may well be gone by then. Perhaps there'll be no need for a hunt this season. We must pray Jofrid doesn't come early to her time."

Perhaps she was missing something, Creidhe thought. She

framed her words carefully. "Tell me about the hunt. The men spoke of it too. What do they hunt? Are there deer or foxes here? Wolves?" She had never seen any of these creatures, but knew them from her father's tales. Long ago in Norway, Eyvind had been unequaled as a hunter. "Or is it a whale hunt you're talking about? I've heard that was common here, before the war."

"You'll find out if you stay here long enough," Gudrun said. "We've lost husbands and brothers, sons and fathers to it over the years. Of course, this year may be different."

"Why would it be different?" A sudden misgiving came over Creidhe as to the nature of the task Thorvald and Sam had been called to assist with.

"Let me plait your hair for you, Creidhe." A woman named Helga, one of the friendlier of this dour bunch, came forward with a comb in one hand and a length of twine in the other. "Turn around for me—that's it."

With that the answers dried up. Nobody would speak further of the hunt, or of the absence of children, and Creidhe sat there thinking very hard as Helga combed out her hair and braided it up again. Creidhe's long, fair locks were the object of much admiration among the women: not one of them had hair of such a hue or of such a glossy shine and thick abundance. Somber and silent as they were most of the time, they still delighted in combing and dressing it, almost as if she were some kind of toy they had previously been forbidden. She noticed, too, the offers to lend a favorite shawl, a best skirt, to provide her with what passed for delicacies here: fresh eel meat, wind-dried lamb. It was almost like being fattened up for market; not a comfortable feeling. She would have traded any of these things gladly for some honest talk. How she missed Thorvald and Sam. Boys might be somewhat blind at times, and lacking in subtlety, but at least you could get straight answers out of them. With any luck they would be back soon, for the moon had waxed and waned since they had marched away, and surely in that time they must have earned the price of a few lengths of driftwood.

The days passed. A pattern had established itself; she'd be up at dawn to walk the track through the settlement, with a pause at the westernmost point to scan the way up the steep hillside in case she might catch a glimpse of Thorvald and Sam coming back. After the walk she returned to Gudrun's to be plied with breakfast, and then she joined the others for spinning. All spent the mornings working at such crafts, save for the few women who took small boats out on the lake for fish every day; odd, this, but with all the men away or on guard duty, essential. Creidhe was not invited on these expeditions. Later in the day, when the women went back to their cottages to prepare food or tend to animals, Creidhe would take out the Journey and let her mind float free as her fingers took up the complex tale, the intricate puzzle of images. At dusk Gudrun prepared another meal, watching her guest as every mouthful went from platter to lips, almost as if Creidhe were a sick child whom she feared to lose. It was hard to summon much enthusiasm for the food; the island cheese was of poor quality, lacking in flavor and unreliable in texture, and sometimes Creidhe felt she might kill for a loaf of fresh-baked bread. Grain was scarce here, such goods a feast-day luxury. After supper there was little to do but retire to a fitful sleep. They did not allow her to feed the stock or tend the straggling, untidy garden. They stopped her from cleaning fish, from scouring dishes, lest she spoil her hands.

With so little to fill her day, Creidhe determined to undertake one more task at least, and that was to supervise the last stages of Jofrid's pregnancy and make quite sure this babe was delivered safe and well. She rehearsed in her mind the possible complications. A breech presentation: tricky but manageable, she'd look out for the signs and turn the babe in the womb before it settled in place. Twins: she did not think Jofrid bore more than a single babe but, just in case, she must make sure the other women knew how to help. Other complications that might occur: she practiced dealing with each in her mind. She would cope. Meanwhile she bullied Jofrid into drinking milk, eating fish and resting with

her feet up in the afternoons, for all the woman's protests
that she had animals to feed. The others could do that for
her, Creidhe told Jofrid firmly, at least from now until the
child was safely delivered and taking the breast. Jofrid
stared at her, face wan, saying nothing; sometimes Creidhe
wondered if she was a little simple.

Gudrun, as the senior woman of the settlement, organized others to tend to Jofrid's cow and calves and keep her
hut tidy. All the same, Creidhe felt the weight of their stares,
as if her efforts to help were in some way bizarre, inappropriate and doomed to failure. She squared her shoulders and
got on with it. One had to do *something*.

It was late in the spring. Back home, lambing would be
over and the days long and light. Here, it might almost have
been winter still, for one never knew what the morning
might bring: rain, sleet, storm, lowering cloud and eldritch
mist were all common, yet from time to time the sun
showed its face, as if to remind them of the season, and on
the precipitous slopes above Brightwater ewes called to
their wayward lambs. If there were indeed wolves or some
other fierce creatures to hunt, it seemed they did not frequent these parts, for the sheep went their own way by day,
untended by boys or dogs. The girl with the squint had
geese and chickens to look after; the two lads disappeared
each morning, returning before dusk with a haul of shellfish
or eels or eggs of varying hues and sizes. They, it seemed,
were allowed to wander where Creidhe was not. The rules
were hard to understand. There was an expectation, still,
that Creidhe would wear her headscarf out of doors, covering every strand of bright hair, yet the other women seemed
subject to no such edict. She asked, and got no answers except that it was a rule and must be obeyed. In fact, the scarf
was useful. In this place, one never knew when the heavens
might open and rain pour down by the bucketful.

On such a morning of late spring storm, Jofrid's pains
began. It was early for her, dangerously early. They called
Creidhe, not, she thought, from any confidence in her ability as a midwife, but because Jofrid had asked for her. The

pregnant woman lay now on a pallet in Gudrun's cottage, her eyes wide with fear, her brow pallid and dewed with sweat. Creidhe examined her, muttering reassuring words. The birthing was not yet advanced; surely the pain should not be troubling Jofrid so much? Briskly Creidhe bid her get up and walk around between the pangs; not only would it speed the process, it would take her mind off her belly for a little. Gudrun, more dour-faced than usual, if that were possible, set a kettle to boil and rummaged in a chest for cloths. Helga came in bearing a jug of milk and a round of coarse bread to be shared after the hard work ahead of them. Helga's face was almost as anxious as Jofrid's own. As she walked the expectant mother up and down the chamber, Creidhe looked across and saw men in the doorway, dressed warmly for travel, and beyond them, rain teeming down.

Gudrun went over to them and an urgent conversation took place in undertones.

At one point Gudrun looked back at Creidhe and asked, "How long?"

"She's barely started. The child will not be born before dusk." Of course, an infant could always take you by surprise, but Jofrid's pains did not seem strong. It was far more of a concern that the child was coming now, at least a moon-cycle before its proper time. It would likely be small and weak. Creidhe hoped Jofrid could shake off her unreasonable panic in order to deliver it safely, and that her milk would be copious. This child must survive; Creidhe had promised herself Jofrid would not lose yet another infant while she had the power to do something about it.

"Keep walking," she urged as Jofrid paused, panting, after the mildest of spasms. "It will go more easily for you if you move about in this early stage, I promise you . . ."

In the entry, Gudrun still held conference with the men, their hushed voices now raised slightly. *You must fetch him . . . track . . . impassable . . . not until tomorrow . . . what about her?*

Then Gudrun said, "Without Asgrim here, this child is doomed."

It did not make a lot of sense. The men left, the door was closed against the weather. They walked up and down, up and down.

"Why do you send for Asgrim?" Creidhe ventured. "Is he the baby's father?" These women spoke little of personal matters; they were as tight-closed as limpets. She had learned that Helga's man was called Skolli, and that he was a smith. She had discovered that Gudrun was a widow with grown sons. But Jofrid had never mentioned a husband; if she had one, he was certainly not at Brightwater. If the Ruler were indeed the husband of this frightened young woman, and the father of her lost babes, it seemed to Creidhe that tilted the balance still further against his being Somerled. Asgrim had seemed far too civil to be a murderer. A wife and child would render him too ordinary.

"It is not his child," Gudrun said, putting an abrupt end to Creidhe's speculations. "And he can't be here in time. The child wasn't due until summer. He would have been back by then; he could have done what has to be done. They'll go, but they can't fetch him here before morning. The infant's doomed. It can't survive."

Creidhe was seized by sudden anger. "Don't say that!" she snapped. "How can you utter such nonsense? I told you, I've delivered many infants, and I see no reason why this one should not do well, even if it is before its time. We must help Jofrid, not upset her. A man can make no difference, surely."

"The child's cursed." Helga spoke from her place by the table, where she was folding cloths in readiness. Her tone was resigned.

"How, cursed? Have you no priests here, no wise women who can cast a circle and speak words of ward?" Creidhe had seen no sign of either during her stay in Brightwater. It had surprised her, but was one of many things she had decided not to ask about, since these folk were ever less than ready with their answers.

"This is beyond any priest," Gudrun muttered, but a note of uncertainty had crept into her voice.

"My mother is a wise woman, my sister too. The simplest

of rituals can help at such times," Creidhe said. "I have no power to summon the spirits myself, but surely there are some here who—?"

"Not in the village," Helga said, glancing to left and right as if afraid there were listeners in the shadows. "Besides, Asgrim doesn't like them to come here. He doesn't trust them."

"Doesn't trust whom?" Was there no end to the complications here? Why couldn't they see none of this was doing Jofrid any good? She was moaning now, her face milk-pale, and Creidhe was forced to let her lie down once more, a limp, pathetic figure on the hard pallet, the swelling made by the unborn child round and tight as a ripe fruit.

"Hermits. Christians. They'd come, if we sent up the hill for them. Streams are in spate; not the easiest of walks. The boys could go. But the Ruler would be angry. He says they do more harm than good. Meddlers."

"The Ruler is not here," Creidhe said firmly. "If Christian prayers will help, then let us summon those who can offer them. How far away are these hermits?"

Gudrun stared at her a moment, nonplussed, then forced the door open against the harsh wind and whistled shrilly, fingers in mouth. Not long after, the two boys came. They got their instructions, and a sack each to keep off the worst of the rain. It was coming down so hard now the day seemed like dusk, and the pathway outside Gudrun's cottage was a gurgling, muddy stream. The door was fastened again. The women waited.

After a morning of hard work and little progress, Jofrid slept. It was a long time since the lads had set out into the storm. The women ate some of the bread, hard and musty-tasting but welcome nonetheless, and a watery fish soup Helga had prepared. Even Gudrun, whose iron features never showed much emotion, looked drained and tired; she sat with her soup bowl in her hands, staring into the hearth where dried cow dung made a sputtering, flaring fire lacking in real warmth. Seal-oil lamps were set on stone shelves around the room, casting gentle light over the form of

Jofrid, now mercifully peaceful in her slumber. Creidhe
willed her not to wake awhile yet; for all Creidhe's calm encouragement, Jofrid had endured the morning in a state of
what seemed utter terror.

They had told Creidhe a midwife was coming, named
Frida, but her arrival had provided no reassurance. Indeed,
it was more the opposite, for the old woman who had arrived at midmorning, swathed in shawls, was none other
than the grim ancient who had guarded Creidhe that first
night at the unpleasantly named Blood Bay. She'd lifted her
brows in apparent disdain at the way Creidhe had arranged
things, and would have assumed complete control at once
but for the way Jofrid had clung to Creidhe's hand, her eyes
so wide with fear the whites showed all around.

Now that Jofrid was sleeping, Frida had relaxed a little.
She sat by the table, dipping sippets of bread into the soup
and sucking them through her gapped and blackened teeth.
Her hands were filthy, the nails encrusted with grime.
Creidhe drank her own soup and listened to the small
crackle and spit of the fire and the relentless drumming of
rain outside. After a while, she thought she could discern
another sound, a distant, howling cry, as of someone
trapped in a deep place with no escape. It set a chill on her
heart; she thought instantly of Thorvald. She forced her
breathing to slow. It must be the wind, what else? This was
indeed a day of winter in spring, and with luck both Thorvald and Sam were snug and secure indoors somewhere, in
whatever corner of the islands Asgrim had led them to. Perhaps the hermits would not come after all. The gale tore at
the cottage, rattling the shutters. A man would be a fool to
walk out on such a day; he'd be blown off those cliff paths
like a leaf whipped away by an autumn breeze.

"Only a madman or a Christian would go abroad in such
a storm," Gudrun observed dryly, rising to her feet with
some reluctance.

"Or one of *them*," Helga added in a whisper.

"Hush!" Frida hissed. "Don't say it; don't tempt fate."

"She's awake." Creidhe had been watching the pallet; she

saw Jofrid's eyes open, at first tranquil with the recollection of good dreams, then on an instant alert, the face blanching to sickly pallor, the terror returned stark and real in her eyes. Jofrid opened her mouth and wailed, a heavy, harsh sound from the depths of the belly, a noise of utter despair that made the blood turn cold. Grasping Jofrid's hand once more, easing the pillow, it came to Creidhe suddenly that, lost infants or no, Jofrid would give anything not to be having this one; that it was the prospect of a birth of any kind that horrified her. Creidhe dismissed the thought quickly; surely it could not be so. Didn't every woman want children? She had often imagined what it would be like when she herself bore a son for Thorvald, a little red-headed babe as like his father as two peas in a pod. She knew she would not shiver and whimper as Jofrid did but would handle the process as efficiently as she did everything, with minimal bother to anyone, though it would be good to have Nessa there; a girl needs her mother at such times. She had pictured Thorvald with the infant in his arms, a smile of pride replacing the dark, furious look that so often shadowed his features. Creidhe frowned. It was much harder to capture those images now. If Thorvald was not ready to marry her when at last they got safely home, was it possible he might never be ready?

By evening, the storm had darkened the sky so heavily that the setting of the sun behind the clouds made little difference, merely layering shadow on shadow. Creidhe had heard it again through the afternoon, that distant, eerie wailing that set the teeth on edge, and she knew the others had, too, though they did not speak of it. She noticed what they did; the first time, Helga built up the fire and checked all the lamps, while Gudrun busied herself with Jofrid, talking loudly and constantly until the howling ceased. When it was over, Gudrun opened the door and called, and men came, some of those who were standing guard in the settlement. Creidhe heard Gudrun's orders with dismay: keep watch all around the house, storm or no storm, until it was over. On no account were they to leave their posts, no matter what they heard, no matter what they saw.

The second time, Gudrun went to the windows and put iron bars up across the inside of the shutters, where slots were made in the stone to take them. Frida sat by the fire, watching, silent. Indeed, Frida had scarcely stirred from there; Creidhe suspected the midwife would leave all the work to her, then claim the credit for a safe delivery. No matter. The child must live, Jofrid as well; nothing else was of importance. The third time the strange sound came it was louder, closer.

"What is it?" Creidhe's heart was racing; no wind sounded like that, as if there were hungry voices in it. "What is that crying?"

But they would not answer her. Gudrun looked at Helga, and they both looked at Frida, and all three made a sign together, tips of the fingers against the brow, two-handed, then a crossing of the arms over the breast, a charm of ward, Creidhe judged, though it was unfamiliar to her.

"They're coming," Gudrun said.

A moment later there was a sharp rapping on the door. Jofrid gave a strangled scream, while Creidhe herself could not suppress a gasp of fright. They sat frozen. The knocking came again.

"We come in God's name!" a man's voice called above the storm. "Let us in, if you will!"

Gudrun moved to open the door, while Helga hastened to screen Jofrid's pallet from sight. Creidhe rose to her feet as three men came in. One was very young, no more than a youth, his brown hair not yet shaven. The second man wore the tonsure Creidhe had seen on Brother Tadhg and his companions back home; the front of the head bald as a babe's, the hair at the back trimmed short and neat. This man had ugly, pleasant features and a soft voice with a burr of accent in it; he was, Creidhe guessed, of the same origins as Tadhg himself, and had doubtless made his own perilous sea journey from his home shore of Ulster. The third man stayed by the doorway, a hood covering his head. His cape dripped onto the earthen floor.

"I did not expect a call," the second man said, untying his own drenched cloak and passing it into Helga's willing hands. "Not on such a wild day. God scourges us hard at such times; he reminds us of our weakness, of how small we are before the force of his creation. I hear an infant is expected."

Helga had taken the younger fellow's cape now, and hung the two garments by the fire; rivulets of water trickled from the heavy woolen cloth. The cloaks were much patched; it was just so with Tadhg and his brethren, who lived in utmost frugality. Creidhe felt the unease that had gripped her beginning to abate; perhaps, at last, here was someone she might trust. At home in Hrossey it was unheard of for men to be present at a childbed, but she was learning every day that this place had its own rules.

"Jofrid's child is coming before its time," Gudrun said tightly. "You've heard the wind, how it torments us. We thought maybe a prayer or two." Her tone was diffident now. "It can't hurt."

"Asgrim's back at the encampment, then." The hermit's voice was calm; he showed no sign of offense at Gudrun's curt manner. "I don't imagine you would have sought our help if he had been here."

"Asgrim's about his own business," Gudrun said, hanging the iron kettle over the fire. "Too far to get here in such weather. The girl said to ask you. No real harm in it."

"But no good either, you think?" The hermit had come forward now, but not too close; the small screen concealed Jofrid only partially. "There is great power in prayer, Gudrun. Our Lord watches over all his creatures; we need only turn to him. A message that has fallen on deaf ears, unfortunately, in Asgrim's case. I am glad you summoned us." He turned his gaze on Creidhe, who stood by the screen. "I am Brother Breccan," he said. "With me I bring Brother Colm here," he nodded toward the youth, "and Brother Niall. I do not know your name, though we've heard tell of your arrival and that of your companions. A long voyage."

"My name is Creidhe, daughter of Nessa." She answered him almost without thinking, for she was becoming increasingly aware of the silent scrutiny of the hooded figure who still stood quietly by the outer door. She could not see any-

thing of his face, and yet she knew all his attention was
fixed on her and her alone. It felt most uncomfortable. "I'm
glad you have come," she managed. "In my home we have a
community of holy brothers much like yourselves. Our people hold them in great respect. I hope you can help here."
She would have liked to explain, *Jofrid is frightened, they
keep speaking of curses and doom and we really should just
be getting on with things,* but one could not speak thus before Gudrun and the others. Brother Breccan had an honest
face; his crooked, bulbous nose and ruddy complexion did
not disguise the goodwill in his eyes.

"I, too," he said mildly.

"The girl says she's a midwife." Frida's tone suggested
profound distrust.

"I can deliver the babe safely," Creidhe said steadily. By
all the ancestors, why didn't that other fellow come into the
room properly and stop staring at her? These islands
seemed a breeding ground for strangeness. "We were hoping you could offer up a prayer or two, something to banish
the ill they all fear. I don't know what it is, but Jofrid needs
to concentrate on what she's doing, and if you could—"

Brother Breccan smiled again. "You arc of our own
faith?" he asked her. The young one, Brother Colm, had sat
down at the table, eyes carefully averted from the screen
and pallet, and was wrapping his chilled hands around the
steaming cup of fish soup Helga had given him. The other
had not moved.

Creidhe shook her head. "My mother is—was—a priestess of the Folk, my sister too," she said. "We are of an older
faith. But we respect yours. The brothers have done nothing
but good in the Light Isles. Please help us."

"What occurs is God's will; we will ask for his mercy."
Was it her imagination or was the tone of this equable, smiling priest shadowed with the same color of inevitable doom
that had hung over Gudrun's words, and Helga's, and
Frida's? Creidhe shivered, and at that moment the man by
the door slipped back his hood and took a step forward.

"Well, well, Gudrun," he remarked softly, "you do get
some interesting items washed up on your doorstep. I never

heard the women of the Folk had such heads of hair; aren't they supposed to be little, dark people?" He doffed his cape in a fluid movement and dropped it on a bench, heedless of Helga's scurrying move to take it for him.

Creidhe stared. The fellow's manner could not have been more different from Breccan's; his words seemed some sort of challenge. She had forgotten about Somerled. Now, as she looked into a pair of fine, dark eyes of penetrating intensity, Thorvald's quest sprang back into her mind, and she felt a pang of misgiving. Had she said what she should not have? But no, it was safe after all. The man who walked across the lamplit room to seat himself by Colm at the table was too old by far. At the back of his tonsured head, Brother Niall's hair was purest white. His brows were of the same snowy hue, incongruous over those black, piercing eyes. The face was fine-boned, thin, and relatively unlined. She had noted the same phenomenon at home; whether it was the simple life they led, toiling in their fields, subsisting on a fish or two, a crust of hard bread, sleeping on ungiving stone, each moment of the day a prayer of joy for their god's blessings, or whether it was simply the openness of their hearts and minds, the brothers of Holy Island all possessed a serene, untroubled youthfulness in their features, as if their years hung more lightly on them because of their goodness. All three of these men had the same look; it seemed to Creidhe they brought a light to this place that had been sorely lacking.

"My father came from the snow lands," she offered, since some kind of reply seemed necessary. "A warrior of considerable note. I think you'd better get on with it."

For Jofrid had gripped her hand suddenly with fingers cold and iron-strong, and had uttered a gasping, grunting sound that Creidhe recognized instantly. Soon Jofrid would need to push. There wasn't much time left.

This might be the grandest cottage in the settlement, but it allowed little privacy, screen or no screen. She could see how pale young Colm was, as if he would rather be anywhere but here.

"Do it quickly," she urged the men as Jofrid howled in pain, her grip like a vise. After that she was so busy she registered only vaguely that Brother Breccan was walking the edges of the room, uttering prayers in a tongue she recognized as Latin but understood none of. Colm, eyes stolidly directed downward, went after the Ulsterman with a little flask of water, from time to time sprinkling a few drops onto the floor, the hearthstone, the table, the door that shivered in the gale as if it would burst from its frame and come crashing down at any moment. Breccan's voice was steady, clear, infinitely reassuring. The third man, Brother Niall, stood in the shadows by the wall. Glancing over, Creidhe caught the gleam of metal by his side, within the folds of his well-worn brown robe: a knife? Since when did a Christian hermit go armed? As if aware of her scrutiny, the white-haired man turned his head a little; he looked at her and a small, droll smile curved his lips. The flash of silver was gone, his hands folded peacefully together. And yet she had not grown up in a Wolfskin's household for nothing. She recognized his pose, outwardly tranquil but aware in every sinew, in every corner of his body. Ready to move in an instant: ready for trouble. Brother Niall, she sensed, had not always been a man of God.

Against the howl of the wind and Jofrid's straining groans, the flow of quiet prayer continued. Gudrun's hatchet face looked drained and weary, Helga's softer features flushed and anxious. Frida sat like an ancient, disapproving statue, and that man, Brother Niall, maintained a silent, watchful presence in the shadows. Jofrid was exhausted, her eyes glazed to an unseeing stare, and it seemed futile to bully her, but Creidhe battled on. The child must be born, or both mother and infant would surely die. *Try a little harder . . . push . . . keep on pushing . . .* Was it Creidhe's imagination, or were the woman's efforts growing weaker? Creidhe prayed it were not so; Jofrid must retain enough vigor to expel the child. She had heard of cases where the mother lost her will, and the child must be cut from her body; she knew she could not attempt such a feat.

Even if the most skilled of surgeons attended such a childbed, it was unheard of that the woman could survive. The child, sometimes. Usually both expired in a pool of blood.

"Now," Creidhe said, "next time, one really good push, and hold it as long as you can. I thought I could see his head a moment ago. Sit her up," she commanded Gudrun. "You," nodding at the glum-faced Frida, "help support her back. Helga, fetch a clean cloth; take the babe when it comes, and make sure it's breathing. Now . . ."

Then Jofrid screamed, and pushed, and briefly they all worked together, and the child's tiny head appeared, crowned with sticky, dark hair, the little face blue-white. Creidhe's heart lurched.

"Stop pushing!" she snapped.

"Cord's around its neck," Frida observed flatly, peering close, touching a grimy finger to the small, closed features. "Wee bairn's stone dead."

In the background the steady flow of words went on, a plea for mercy, a deathbed lament, who could tell?

"Don't say that! Don't touch him!" Creidhe felt her face flush, the tears welling in her eyes, and she felt the surge of utter rage. "Helga, make sure she doesn't push, it's vital. Jofrid, this might hurt a bit. Keep as still as you can. You've been very brave; just hold on a little longer."

It must be done very quickly, before the next spasm seized Jofrid's belly and sent the infant's body violently forth, strangling him with the very cord that had nourished him, robbing him of life in the moment of birth. A pox on Frida. The infant was not dead; Creidhe would not allow it.

She sent up a silent prayer to whatever spirits might be prepared to aid her. Her hands steady, she placed one palm beneath the tiny skull for support, feeling the fragility, the tenuous mortality, and slipped her hand within the folds of Jofrid's body, searching for the cord, easing a finger beneath. Jofrid screamed, a shrill, animal noise of pain and fright.

"Don't push," Helga said, her voice shaking. "Breathe slowly, Jofrid. You mustn't push."

Quick now, one finger, two between cord and small neck,

holding firm against the slippery coating of mucus and blood, ah, she had it now; and as Jofrid gasped and Helga soothed her with trembling voice, Creidhe slipped the cord over the child's head and freed him.

"Aaagh!" Jofrid expelled the air in her lungs in a shuddering rush, and with one last, groaning effort, the child was born. He lay, limp and blue, in Creidhe's hands.

"I told you," Frida said.

"Stop it!" This time, astonishingly, it was Gudrun who spoke. "Hush your voice!"

They stood for a long moment, looking down on the newborn: a boy, small, perfect, utterly still.

"Where—?" Jofrid whispered. "Give—?"

Creidhe's cheeks were wet. She could not speak. This was no good; there was work yet to be done.

"Give him to me," Helga said. She took the child; he hung from her hands, limp and unresponsive as a fish on the chopping block. Helga opened his mouth and stuck in her finger, clearing away the debris of birth.

"Pointless," Frida muttered, but nobody was listening: all eyes were on the infant. Even the wind had stilled beyond the cottage walls.

Helga took hold of the tiny ankles and swung the boy upside down. The young man, Colm, sucked in his breath. This practice was common enough, to clear the lungs and start things right; but what youth of sixteen was ever witness to such women's business? Again Helga swung the infant, and a third time; there was no sign of life.

"Cursed," Frida mumbled, and at that moment the small mouth stretched to reveal gums already turning from deathly blue to violet to pink, and a mewling cry cut across the lamplit chamber, a gasping, hiccupping proclamation of presence. Jofrid burst into noisy tears.

"Good," Creidhe said, sniffing. "Wrap him warmly, he's very small. You did well, all of you."

Sheer relief blotted out other things for a while. She supervised the delivery of the afterbirth, the washing, the changing of linen. She kept an eye on the child, now snuggled close to his mother and mumbling weakly against the breast; he would feed well in time, he was a little fighter. She made Jofrid drink some warm milk. She wondered, through a miasma of weariness, why Jofrid had not stopped crying; why Gudrun could not summon so much as a small attempt at a smile; why Helga, now busy cutting bread and cheese and pouring watery ale, still glanced nervously at door and windows every time a gust shook them. The wind was rising again. But it was all right now. Whether it was Breccan's prayers, or Creidhe's own skills, or the fact that, in the end, they had all worked together, the child was safely born and the threat was over.

She became aware that she was too tired to go on, and, since all was tidied to her satisfaction, she sat down at the table, food and drink in front of her. The others stood or sat around the room. Why were they so quiet? On the pallet Jofrid still sobbed softly, the tiny child held close against her. Gudrun sat by her side, stone-faced. On the other side Frida made a pair. With such grim guardians, Creidhe thought wryly, perhaps any woman would be reduced to tears. Helga was cutting the last of the bread. The knife shook in her hand. Breccan and the boy seemed calm; they were eating with enthusiasm. Creidhe suspected these plainest of viands were a feast for them. The other one, Brother Niall, had partaken of neither food nor drink. He had hardly moved from his place in the shadows this whole time.

Creidhe was too tired to eat. Indeed, she could not help folding her arms on the table and laying her head down on them, just for a moment . . . She would get up soon and let Helga rest. . . .

It was quick: oh, so quick. A sudden shift in the wind, a sudden change in its voice; above its howling, the shouting of men outside, not words of bold challenge but cries of fear. The lamps flickered and went out, every one, plunging the room into darkness save for the small, struggling glow of the fire. Cold terror clutched at Creidhe's heart, and she half rose to her feet, not knowing what this was, what she could do, but seeing in the strange, half-lit eyes of the others not shock, not fear, but a terrible fatalism: an acceptance of the dark inevitable.

"What is it?" she whispered, but nobody answered. Brother Breccan was praying again, voice less steady than before, and, breathlessly, young Colm joined in, the two speaking the words together, not Latin this time but an older tongue, *Kyrie eleison, Christe eleison . . .*

The voices came. They were here, inside this hut, though door and shutters had held fast against the fierce onslaught of the wind. Such forces find their own way; they require no admittance. It was a cry, a song, an awesome, terrible music that played inside the head, ringing its harsh tunes on the very bones of the skull, vibrating in the ears, wresting sound from nose and mouth, pulsing in the very breath, wrenching its wild anthem from every corner of the listener's body, as if it would suck out the life force to feed it. It thrummed in the blood, it throbbed in the veins, it raced in the heart. Creidhe squeezed her eyes shut, though there was indeed nothing to be seen. She put her hands over her ears, but the song was still there, ripping at her spirit, shredding her will, seeking to steal away her very identity. She took a shuddering breath, held it a moment, let it out. One could not be the child of such parents as hers without learning courage. *Kyrie eleison . . . Christe eleison . . .*

"Begone!" Creidhe stood, hands still clutched over her ears, eyes open now on the darkness as her breath faltered, then steadied again. "By all the ancestors, by all that is good, begone from this place!" To expect obedience to such a command was foolish; she was no wise woman. Still, one owed it to one's upbringing, to the love and wisdom of one's mother and father, at least to try.

The terrible sound ebbed and flowed, as if a malevolent force circled the darkened chamber. Creidhe thought there was a kind of laughter in it, a bitter, sorry laughter, and a lament of utter desolation, and a taunting, mocking cry, all at the same time. Around the room it traveled, once, twice, three times, and in a last, eldritch scream of shattering intensity, it seemed to whirl into the fire, up through the smoke hole and away. The fire sputtered and died, the darkness was complete.

For long moments nobody spoke. Even Jofrid was silent

now. Then there was movement, and a little flicker: someone putting a taper to the smoldering embers that lay beneath the ashes. A lamp was lit. The light touched Brother Niall's white hair as he walked about the chamber, bringing fire to each small bowl of seal oil. His features were impassive.

Creidhe was cold. She was colder than she'd ever been, even crouched wet and wretched under the *Sea Dove*'s decking after an endless day of voyaging. They were looking at Jofrid, all of them. Jofrid was not crying anymore. She sat on the bed, her face an ashen mask, her eyes empty. The babe lay on her lap, still warmly snuggled in his fine wool blanket. Nobody said anything.

They were the longest five steps Creidhe had ever walked: across to Jofrid's bed. She made herself look down. The boy lay still, small mouth no longer eager for milk; vague, infant eyes no longer searching to discern light and shadow; tiny, flower-like hands motionless now, paler than the linen on which they lay open. She did not need to check further to know that he was dead.

After that, all was confusion for a while. Creidhe did not weep. Indeed, she could not tell if what she felt was grief or fury or merely a cold recognition of failure. Her whole day's work, her whole night's effort had been futile from the start. There was hurt, most certainly. Whatever fell power had wrought this, why had it let her save the boy first, why grant her that small triumph only to snatch it away? No wonder Jofrid had not wanted the child born. They had merely waited, then taken him.

She sat, head in hands, and let the others do what must be done. Jofrid was conveyed to her own cottage, Helga by her side. Frida disappeared. Men came in, spoke with Gudrun and left, taking the hermits with them: even priests had to sleep. Creidhe was aware of Gudrun moving about, stacking platters, removing the straw that had been laid about the pallet, taking things away. It was late; she should retire to bed, or it would be morning. She did not seem to be able to move. Gudrun had gone through to the northern end of the cottage, where her best stock was lodged for the winter; a sound of lowing, a clanking of buckets suggested she might be there a while. Creidhe felt the weight of weariness, the longing for home settle on her. By all the gods, how had she managed to get everything so wrong? She had been so sure she could help them. There was evil sorcery here, horrors beyond her worst nightmares. *Come back,* something cried within her, a voice she could not silence, though it shamed her. *Oh, please come back soon. I want to go home.*

"It is difficult."

Creidhe started; she had believed herself alone, but it seemed Brother Niall had not left with the others. He stood now, grave in expression, facing her across the table.

"You weep; or would do, if you had the strength left. It is not so much the death of this child that grieves you, as your own failure to prevent it. That can be the hardest lesson in the world, to stand back and let the inevitable play itself out. To watch while others bungle the task you know you can do for them, and do perfectly. It is a lesson long in the learning. For some, it seems impossible not to act, not to strive. One sees what is right, what must be; how can one not attempt to make it so? And yet, in such a case as this, the action only makes things worse. A conundrum."

Creidhe felt anger awaken once more. "I suppose you're going to tell me it's the will of God that child died and I should just accept it?" she challenged, and saw the corner of his mouth twitch, as if he found her amusing. "How dare you? What god could will it that Jofrid should lose all three of her children? What god decides a little boy's life should be snatched away almost before he has the chance to draw breath? Why would I be allowed to save him, and then—" Her words trailed away.

"As I said"—there was no judgment in Niall's voice—"it is your own pride that is damaged most here; you thought you could be a hero, could do what all these folk knew was impossible, and you failed. Now you really are crying. I suspect they tried to warn you, and you wouldn't listen."

The tears came more quickly now; she rummaged for a handkerchief, sniffing. "They never told me; not what would happen. What was that, anyway? That wind, those voices?" Beneath her distress Creidhe felt a surge of gratitude; harsh he might be, but at least he was talking to her and making sense.

"Their enemy has been sorely wounded and strikes back in the only way he knows," Niall said, seating himself opposite her and folding his hands together on the stone table. "Asgrim's folk have never understood what it means to live here, an old place, a wild place. One does not disturb such a realm and walk away unscathed. On the surface the Unspoken seem much as we are; ordinary men and women. They speak our language; outwardly, they resemble us. But they are not the same. The first of our own race to journey here found an older people already in the islands, a people steeped in magic and possessed of powers beyond those known to our kind. The Unspoken come from a union of these two races. Unchecked, they are dangerous indeed. We do not know how they achieve this, the singing of charms so terrible they snatch the very breath from the body. We have not discovered how this uncanny music can reach us here on the Isle of Storms when the singers dwell across the water in the south, setting foot on our shore but rarely. All I know is that this is magic gone awry, a great power misused for lack of proper controls, for want of suitable guidance. The Unspoken have not always warred with Asgrim's tribe. The Long Knife people made an error, and now they pay for it with the lives of their newborn."

"An error?" Creidhe was both repelled and fascinated. The hermit's voice had remained measured and calm; he seemed unaffected by the strange visitation and might just as well have been discussing the weather.

"Indeed. By a quirk of fate, something was stolen: an item of great value to the Unspoken. Until it is returned or replaced, these voices will be heard at each childbed, and the Long Knife people will be bound to the hunt. In the first they lose their future; each time the second runs its course, their tenuous grip on these islands loosens, for the hunt greatly depletes their numbers. A misguided people; their Ruler serves them poorly."

Creidhe struggled to comprehend, her head dizzy from

lack of sleep. "An item of great value? What sort of item? Treasure? Weaponry? A talisman of some sort?"

Niall gave his thin-lipped smile. "The last is closest to the truth. The Unspoken lost the very core of their faith: their lodestone, their key to wisdom. They lost what can keep their wild powers in check. It was Asgrim's kin took it from them and placed it beyond anyone's reach, though not with Asgrim's blessing. Now his folk are bound to this, until they find a solution."

"Why didn't they tell me? Why wouldn't they explain anything?"

Niall's eyes narrowed. "I've a theory on that; it's something I must discuss with you, but not here where others might hear us." The sounds of Gudrun tending to her stock could still be heard. "A knowledge of the true situation, I suspect, would not have changed your actions in the slightest. Am I right?"

Creidhe felt her cheeks flush. "You think me a fool," she said, chastened.

"Foolish in your courage, perhaps."

"You mentioned a solution. The Ruler spoke of war. That worries me. My friends have gone away with him. They are not warriors; one is a fisherman, the other a—a scholar, I suppose you'd call him. What war? Do Asgrim's people fight against these Unspoken, the ones who can wield such terrible magic? What chance have ordinary men against such evil charms?" The thought of Thorvald in battle was bad enough; Thorvald at the mercy of some kind of demon was unthinkable.

"Evil? It's all relative." Niall gave a little frown. "Asgrim should open his mind to the possibilities, expand his view a little. He spends a great deal of time sharpening his men's skills for the hunt. He makes no effort to investigate alternatives, to find another way."

"The hunt: they speak of it often, yet they tell nothing. What is it they hunt?"

He widened his coal-dark eyes at her, raising his brows. "Asgrim's folk hunt what was lost and cannot be found, yet must be, if they are to survive. They seek that which the Unspoken desire yet cannot reach, since the island is forbidden to them. Their—what was the word you used? Their talisman."

"Oh." She tried to imagine what this might be: a stone, a jewel, a sacred bone in the shape of an animal. "So, it is more of a—a treasure hunt, than the tracking and killing of animals? I thought—"

He smiled; it was an expression quite without mirth. "Both," he said. "Two in one."

There was a rustling, the creak of the half-door from the back of the cottage. Gudrun was returning.

"I really should be going," Brother Niall said, rising easily to his feet. He had shown no signs of weariness. "There's no point in flagellating yourself. One cannot stop the inevitable. These folk have brought it on themselves."

Creidhe was shocked. "That is a strange view for a Christian priest," she could not help saying to him.

"You think?" He was putting on his long cloak; it had not dried much and hung about him heavy and dark. "Creidhe?" His voice dropped suddenly to a whisper. "We must speak privately in the morning. It may not be safe for you here. You should consider—" He broke off; Gudrun was back, yawning widely as she moved to damp down the fire. "I'll bid you goodnight, then," the hermit said smoothly, making for the door. "I might look in tomorrow early, before we set out for home. These are sorry times, Gudrun." And with that, he was gone.

Dark thoughts kept Creidhe wide-eyed and wakeful until the first traces of dawn were creeping into Gudrun's cottage, and then, abruptly, exhaustion won the battle and she slept. She had intended to be up early, walking the length of the settlement according to her usual pattern. She had hoped to catch the hermit alone, out of doors; his words of warning had worried her. Besides, it was sheer relief to be able to conduct a conversation that made sense, even if Brother Niall's comments sometimes cut a little close to the bone. As it was, a web of troubled dreams held her fast until much later, when she was aroused by the sound of angry

voices. She rose quickly, donned her overdress, slipped on
her shoes and tidied her hair as best she could in the darkened sleeping quarters. She was alone there: Gudrun's
voice was one of those she could hear from the outer chamber. Creidhe made to walk out, then froze where she stood,
hearing what they were saying.

"I should have banished you from the isles long since!"
This voice was sternly authoritative: Asgrim was back, too
late for the child, but returned nonetheless and, from the
sound of it, furiously angry. "You're a pack of ignorant
fools. What did you hope to achieve here? I made it clear
Brightwater is forbidden to you, yet you walk straight in
here regardless, spouting your foolish doctrines of tolerance
and forbearance. What good could that possibly be to
Jofrid, or to any of us? Has a single one of the Long Knife
people turned to your holy cross in all the years you've
clung on here like an irksome parasite? Last night's episode
merely serves as another illustration of what we've all long
known: your prayers are entirely powerless. Our enemy still
harries us, and another child succumbs even as you mouth
your meaningless litanies. As for you, you should have
known better. There are rules, and rules are to be obeyed
unless we are to sink into total lawlessness. It's for your
own protection."

"The girl persuaded us." Creidhe barely recognized Gudrun's voice, it was so subdued. The woman sounded almost frightened.

"The girl?" Asgrim's tone was scathing. "How could she
influence such a choice? Her part in this is already mapped.
You know what is right; you know the way this unfolds."

"Since we knew you could not take action in time," Gudrun said, "there seemed no harm in a prayer or two, for
Jofrid's sake."

"Rules, Gudrun," Asgrim chided. "None of us can afford
to weaken on this."

"It won't happen again," said Gudrun.

There was a polite cough. "To the matter in hand." This
voice was calm and measured: Brother Niall's. A wave of
relief flooded through Creidhe, and she stepped out from

the sleeping quarters. They were standing, the three of them, Asgrim still in heavy outdoor cloak and muddy boots, with a knife at his belt, Gudrun by the fire, the hermit caped and tranquil near the door, ready for travel. There was no sign of Brother Breccan or the youth, Colm. Surely the Ruler had not come here alone. He must have brought a few men with him. Perhaps . . .

"Thorvald and Sam," she burst out, "are they here? Have they come back?" Home; she could go home, and the nightmare would be over. Brother Niall was regarding her somewhat quizzically; she realized she had forgotten her manners.

"I'm sorry." Creidhe addressed the hermit. "I overslept. Are you leaving now?"

"Ah," said Asgrim before Niall could reply. "Creidhe. I'm told you did your best to help in the sad events of last night. We're indebted to you. I'm afraid I've come alone, but for Skapti, my guard. Your young men are much occupied. Brother Niall was just going. Then, I think some breakfast would do us good."

Gudrun turned her back and began purposefully clanking pots and pans.

"Don't let us keep you, *Brother*." There was ice in Asgrim's voice.

"Ah." Niall's tone was an echo of the other's. "We have a little unfinished business; I don't recall your responding to my suggestion, save by losing your temper. I find silent meditation an excellent aid to self-control. You should try it some ti—"

"Enough!" Asgrim thundered. Platters rattled on the table. "Leave now! Your suggestion does not deserve an answer, it is patently ridiculous. A young unwed girl, alone up on that hilltop in a household of men? Sheer lunacy!"

"We are sworn to celibacy, every one of us," Niall said mildly. "Creidhe's safety would be assured in the hermitage, far more so than it can be here. What about last night? Such visitations do not cross our own threshold. You should at least give your young guest the choice." He was looking straight at Creidhe, trying to convey some message with those cryptic, dark eyes.

"Oh," she said, taken aback. "Oh—could I go there?" This was a reprieve from imprisonment: no more strange silences, no more eerie manifestations, no more glum Gudrun and grim Frida. Best of all, there would be folk she could talk to, honest, good men in the mold of the brothers of Holy Island. "I don't mean to sound ungrateful," she said to Asgrim, "but I would like that. Just until Thorvald and Sam come back. I will go, I think; thank you so much." She gave the hermit a smile; he inclined his head courteously.

There was a quality in the ensuing silence that made her very uncomfortable indeed. Gudrun had ceased pretending to cook and now stood very still; Asgrim was drawing a deep breath.

"That's settled then," said Brother Niall calmly. "I'll wait while you pack a bag. We live frugally, but you'll be warm and well fed. As you say, it's just until your friends return. This is much more suitable." He set a hand to the door.

"I don't think so." Asgrim was not shouting now: he held his voice very soft. "Creidhe," he said, turning toward her and taking her hands in his, "would you not wish to be here in the settlement when your friends arrive? It can be only a day or two until their return. Why not stay with us a little longer? I'm sure Jofrid would like that; I'm told she has taken a fancy to you, and of course she will be in need of comfort after her sad loss." He sighed. "Another fine boy; another future snatched away. Jofrid weeps without cease. Creidhe, I know you will not want to miss your friends' homecoming. They'll have so much to tell you." He glanced at Gudrun.

"Asgrim's right," Gudrun said. "Besides, you've helped us beyond what anyone would have expected; what happened wasn't your fault. You did your best. Let us repay that if we can. Stay a while longer; won't your menfolk be expecting to find you here?"

Creidhe had never heard her make such an extended speech before. "Oh," she said. She thought of Thorvald's long journey back to Brightwater; she imagined his smile when he saw her again, safe and well. That, surely, was worth a day or two of waiting. And yet Brother Niall had said it wasn't safe here; what about those voices that brought death on the very heels of life? What if they came again? He had not had the chance to tell her what he meant. "I don't know. Will Thorvald and Sam really be here so soon?" It felt as if she'd been waiting forever.

"Undoubtedly, my dear," Asgrim said, smiling. "I have this very night come from the encampment where they're staying. They speak of you often, and with affection. I'll take pleasure in relating their exploits over a little breakfast, if Gudrun hasn't forgotten how to cook, that is."

"Creidhe should come with me," Niall said firmly. "I am certain that is the best course. It isn't so very far, after all; I'm sure we—"

"Enough." This time the Ruler's voice had an edge as sharp as a blade. "Let the girl wait for her sweetheart; she's been patient enough, don't you think? Besides, there'll be plenty of time after they return for her to come up and visit your establishment if she chooses. The young men can accompany her: nothing improper in that. What do you say, Creidhe?"

"Please stay, Creidhe," Gudrun said. "Jofrid needs you." This was so unexpected, Creidhe could hardly summon a reply.

"I think you've outstayed your welcome, Brother Niall," said Asgrim, and at that moment the door opened to reveal a very large man clad in garments of leather and armed with a thrusting-spear. "Good-bye, Brother Niall," the Ruler added.

"I'm sorry." Creidhe found her voice. "I would have liked to come; I would have liked to talk to you and the others. But I must be here when Thorvald and Sam get back; that's what they'll be expecting."

Brother Niall nodded. He seemed quite unperturbed by the fierce-looking giant at his back and the grim glare of the Ruler. "Remember," he told Creidhe quietly, "we're there if you need us. Our door is always open. Just take the track up the eastern side of the valley and you'll find us. Good day to you, Gudrun." The white-haired man turned and went out; the big guard stepped back to let him by. Beyond him, Creidhe glimpsed Brother Breccan and young Colm waiting on the path. The rain had abated to a fine drizzle. She turned back to the Ruler.

"Tell me," she said eagerly. "Tell me about Thorvald and Sam."

On the Isle of Clouds, the rain came in a cool, refreshing whisper, blanketing the slopes, silvering the grasses and setting small birds chattering. Keeper stood on the eastern hillside with Small One at his heels, looking across to the Isle of Storms. His eyes were keen: small boats hugged the far shore, driven hard before the gale as they made their way in from fishing. Smoke came sideways from the shelter at Council Fjord. Gulls screamed above Dragon Isle, competing for the best spots. Here on the island, the birds had no need to war thus. Here, they understood him, and he them. They gave him what was necessary to keep Small One alive: a few eggs, carefully chosen; their own bodies, taken gently, with love. There was a way to do the killing, a right way, with soft, strong hands and words of respect for the sacrifice made. Men were different. They came in anger, came where they did not belong. When he killed a man, he saw no reason for mercy.

Later, Small One stirred in his sleep, whimpering. Keeper did not sleep. He sat by the remnants of the cooking fire, still glowing red in its stone-lined pit, and listened to the voices. There was a storm over Council Fjord, but his ears were a hunter's, finely tuned. This song carried far and deep, threading through the turmoil of gale and deluge. He laid his hand over Small One's ear where it showed above the threadbare blanket. His other hand went to his own neck, touching the ornament he wore, a narrow circle of plaited hair, once brightest gold, now soiled and faded to no color, but strong: the strongest part of him. *Sula*. Her name was a talisman to keep them safe. The voices keened on the wind, ebbed and flowed with the waves, sobbed their bereavement deep inside him. He would not heed them. *Sula, I keep my promise still. I am true.*

The music rose to a screaming, a frenzied wailing that tore at his heart. Small One cried out in his dreams, and Keeper lay down by him, curving his body to accommodate his, stretching an arm across in protection. He waited. At length the voices faded and were gone, their harvest complete until the next time, and the next. How many seasons, how many children for the Long Knife people? He would not think of that. What had befallen Asgrim's folk was their own doing; their own folly had made it so.

Small One moaned again, shifting in the darkness.

"I'm here," Keeper whispered. "Sleep. You are safe. I will always be here."

FIVE

With whom shall a man keep faith?
A silent god, an absent brother?
Into the void the heart cries, enough.
                    MONK'S MARGIN NOTE

They were camped at the head of the long western fjord, at a place where there had once been a settlement with turf-roofed huts and a substantial hall suited to councils and gatherings. Though it was not so far from Brightwater, it might have been another land, so different was the pattern here. Many men were staying in the encampment and sleeping communally in the hall. Their days were employed in what appeared to be preparations for war. There was a rule nobody broke: no leaving without Asgrim's consent. As it was, nobody ever asked to go anywhere. There was an unvoiced understanding that trips out of camp happened only when the Ruler had business to be done. Generally, two or three men stood guard on the single track eastward, just to be sure. Thorvald came to understand that, from early spring to midsummer at least, these islanders had no contact at all with their wives and children, their old folk, their home communities. This was necessary because of the hunt.

The days were spent in refurbishing boats, fashioning weapons, preparing the accoutrements of combat. They were all kept busy, though Thorvald watched the pattern of it with a critical eye, seeing much room for improvement. He kept quiet, for now. As for the Ruler, he stalked about the encampment inspecting the men's work, always shadowed by one or other of his big bodyguards. Thorvald almost never heard Asgrim praise his warriors' efforts. His criticisms, on the other hand, were sharp and wounding. The Ruler seemed on edge, as if waiting for something. He kept himself to himself, sleeping apart in a hut reserved for the purpose, taking his meals for the most part in silence. He would appear in the evenings to give brisk orders for the next day's work. The pair of formidable warriors who served as his personal guards were an additional spur to obedience.

Asgrim's rule was absolute, and he did not hesitate to enforce it by physical means when necessary. Once, a fellow was caught helping himself from the ale keg. Thorvald did not witness the punishment, but whatever it was, the culprit was unable to stand straight for three days afterward. The two men deemed responsible for Creidhe's near fall from the cliff path had never reappeared. When Thorvald asked after them, Orm muttered something about the mouth of the lake and a certain precipice, and then retreated into tight-lipped silence.

Asgrim or no Asgrim, they needed materials to patch up the *Sea Dove*. It seemed appropriate, therefore, simply to do as they were bidden. As soon as he made his background known, Sam was put to work mending the small boats drawn up on the tidal flats below the shelter. There was a reasonable supply of wood: lengths of pine and ash, other bits and pieces, some already shaped, some just as the tide had delivered them. Sam found friends of a sort and set to his tasks willingly, observing to Thorvald that it shouldn't be long at all before they were headed for home with the *Sea Dove* as good as new. The mast was going to be a challenge, but he'd spotted a piece he could work with; he'd made a mark on it, just to be sure. Once these poor excuses for boats were watertight, he'd ask politely for what he was owed, and that would be that.

It was not so simple for Thorvald. Back home in Hrossey he had moved in his mother's circle and that of Eyvind and Nessa, the group that maintained the order and culture of the Light Isles. He was used to the open discussion of strategy, the planning of endeavors in trade or alliance, the airing of matters of justice and law. Debate excited him; ideas intrigued him. Here, there was no possibility of that. These islanders were no more than simple farmers and fishermen; they never questioned the Ruler's judgment and apparently never sought to know more than the little he chose to tell them.

It was evident that part of the rule Asgrim imposed on them related to the keeping of secrets. Sam appeared to be chattering away all day, and his fellow workers answering readily enough, yet at suppertime Sam had nothing to tell but tales of wind, tide and improbably large codfish. For Thorvald, making conversation with these men was like blundering through a maze full of blind corners and dead ends. He needed to know what this was all about. He wanted to know. As the son of this man who called himself Ruler, there could be a place for him here, a place and a purpose, if he did things right. It was clear to him the way they were going about their work was less than efficient, and he had ideas on how they could fix that. But these people were universally dour, sad and silent, and he could not work out how to break through the barrier they set around themselves.

Many days passed and still Thorvald had gleaned little information as to the nature of the hunt they spoke of. He had worked alongside the men on the preparation of

weapons and had moved through the steps of battle, watching how they went about it, storing away what he learned.
He wanted to talk to Asgrim. It seemed ever more probable
that this tight-lipped autocrat was Somerled; his ruthless authority and caustic tongue underlined it. In his mind, Thorvald placed the man in the tale Margaret had told him, a
story of cruel conquest and coldblooded fratricide, and
found Asgrim fitted there too well. And there was the manner, guarded, evasive, cryptic. In that, and in the watchful,
dark eyes, Thorvald saw, uncomfortably, a reflection of
himself.

He planned to ask Asgrim a few penetrating questions,
without quite stating the truth of his mission here. He would
make sure he obtained answers that proved it one way or the
other. If Somerled had become Ruler of the Isles, he had
done better for himself than anyone would have expected.
He had forged a life; he had made himself once more a
leader of men. On the other hand, the flaws in Asgrim's
leadership became clearer to Thorvald every day. He itched
to step in, to start making changes. All he needed was an explanation. If the Ruler would just tell him exactly what this
hunt entailed, he was sure he could offer many helpful suggestions, starting with something that would wake these
would-be warriors out of a state of mind that seemed to accept defeat before battle was ever joined. But Asgrim chose
to make himself unavailable. He had shown no inclination,
after that first meeting, to engage either Thorvald or Sam in
conversation, and Thorvald began to believe they would
simply earn their wood and go back to Blood Bay with no
more said. His frustration grew. He needed to learn whether
Asgrim was worthy to be told the truth. After a while, he
began to suspect that perhaps Asgrim knew it already and
had chosen not to recognize it publicly. The Ruler was definitely avoiding him.

Meanwhile there was work to be done, and at a certain
point Thorvald found he simply could not let them continue
to do it so badly. If Ash had taught him anything it was to
make best use of what you had, whether it be raw materials

or talent and enterprise. Besides, their attitude was irritating him. Why bother fighting at all if you didn't believe you could win?

They were finishing off a batch of spears. The shafts had been hewn with axe, adze and knife from the limbs of a great, dead ash, a treasure of immense worth cast up in spring storm and weathered until another spring. The spear-heads were of iron. The upper reaches of this island held bog ore, and on the hillside above this sheltered cove a small forge worked night and day. Its glowing fire, fueled by dung and peat, was the beating heart of this settlement of men.

These were throwing spears, the points long and slender, some leaf-shaped, some triangular and barbed. They were cruder than the ones Eyvind's men used back in Hrossey, the quality of the metal inferior, the shape without refinement; still, they were capable of damage, if used skilfully. Thorvald was shaping the end of a shaft, where the spearhead would be pinned in place. Today they had made ten or more, and arrows as well. His adze moved carefully, smoothing the wood.

"I've noticed," he observed casually, "we're concentrating on these, and the arrows. Yet you have a big supply set by already. Lose a lot, do you?"

The man next to him gave a grunt of assent. Others nodded, their hands never pausing in the steady work.

"Of course," Thorvald went on, "you know about loosening the pin?"

They looked at him without comment, hard faces expressionless.

"No? It's pretty simple, just a way of making sure your enemy can't throw too many of these back at you if you miss. Keep the pin in place to hold the head on the shaft like this, see, until you're ready to throw, but leave it loose enough to be easily knocked out. Then, just before you throw, remove the pin."

"Spear without a head never killed a man," observed bristle-bearded Orm, looking at Thorvald blankly. "Unless you got him in the eye, maybe."

"Watch this," Thorvald said. The finished spears were propped against a low stone wall; he chose one he had put together himself, one with a good weight to it. There was a target set up for testing the weapons' balance before they were deemed complete: a man of straw, with an outer skin of coarse sacking. Someone had used colored clay to draw on rough features, staring dark eyes and a grinning mouth.

Thorvald took the pin from the spear, making sure they could all see what he was doing. He lifted his arm, balancing the weapon, took aim, and threw. There was a whistling sound, and a thud.

"Told you," said Orm glumly. "Falls off."

But others were running to the straw man, pointing and exclaiming.

"See! Straight into the target, and then shaft and point come apart."

"Like magic," said Ranulf, with an edge in his voice. "Uncanny."

"All the same," Wieland spoke up, coming closer and thrusting his finger into the hole the weapon had made in the straw man's chest, where the heart would have been, "he's not likely to return too many of these, not if he needs to find the heads and put them back together before he can throw." He looked at Thorvald, eyes narrowed. "How does it work? How does it hold together?"

Thorvald managed a smile. "Not by witchery, I can assure you. It's all in the movement forward. While the spear travels quickly, its very force holds the head in place. It is only when the weapon finds its mark that the two separate. After the battle, it is possible to retrieve the parts and make these spears anew. It's simple enough, but it will slow your enemy in the initial phase of the attack and give you an advantage." They gazed at him silently; he thought he detected a slight change in their eyes. "Want to try it?" he asked.

From then on they started putting the pins in differently, so they were easier to remove. At Thorvald's suggestion, Ranulf and Svein fetched the stocks from storage and spent some time modifying those as well. Buoyed by his small success, Thorvald went on doggedly with his questions.

"What weapons does the enemy have? We seem a bit short on swords, knives, even thrusting-spears. This stuff's all very well for the first stage, but what about after you move in?"

Silence again, not unfriendly exactly, simply blank. Einar, who had first greeted them at Blood Bay, was the oldest of the men and the most ready to contribute more than a grunt or a sigh. He looked at Thorvald, eyes narrowed, jaw set tight, then turned his attention back to the bowstring he was testing. Not to answer seemed a kind of defense, a protective wall they had learned to build around themselves. They were not stupid: Thorvald had seen how quickly they could learn, once their interest was sparked. Wieland, in particular, a youngish man with close-cropped hair and sad eyes, seemed ready to embrace new ideas. This was more like a deeply formed resistance, as if somewhere within them lay a belief that their lot could not alter, no matter how hard they tried. That infuriated Thorvald: it was pointless, time-wasting, and he determined to change it even if it took him all summer. He would work on the men first, and then concern himself with their leader. These fellows needed help; for now, his own quest must take second place. Besides, what better way to show his father his own mettle, his own qualities, than by throwing himself into this endeavor? If it was his father.

"Do these enemies have axes? Swords?" he asked them. "Or is it some impregnable fortress we're supposed to be attacking?"

A long pause. Perhaps, thought Thorvald, he had got it wrong, and the islanders were just very slow thinkers. "It would help," he added, summoning his last shreds of patience, "if I knew what we were up against."

Orm cleared his throat. "Ask the Ruler," he mumbled. "Best if he explains it to you."

"The Ruler isn't talking to me these days," Thorvald said. "Why can't you tell me?"

They glanced at one another, their eyes furtive, fearful.

"Spears of living bone," someone whispered.

"Poison darts," hissed someone else.

"Stones," muttered another, and several nodded assent. "Big rocks, hurtling through the air; took a man's head off, last summer."

"Wind, waves, tides," said Orm. "The enemy's got what we haven't got: sorcery. But we shouldn't be telling you. Ask Asgrim. He knows. The Ruler knows what to do."

"Anyhow, what do you mean?" someone challenged, voice rising in distrust. "*It would help,* you said? Help who? Help what?"

Thorvald found himself suddenly without an answer, for he could not say what was in his head: *If I knew the truth about this situation, I could help you to win your war.* And after that, another thought, though where it had come from, he did not know. *I could lead you.*

"Never mind," he said casually. "It's none of my business, of course. I'm only passing through, after all." The pretense of nonchalance didn't seem to be working: now the lot of them were staring suspiciously. "Let me show you a way you can fit more arrows into these quivers. Did you say poison darts? Ever thought of trying a bit of the same yourselves?"

He knew, of course, that Asgrim was watching him. Asgrim watched everyone. That was not unreasonable, for Thorvald in his turn watched this grim chieftain. He learned the Ruler's daily habits, his disciplines, his ways of making sure the men remained a little wary, a little frightened, so they did not think to question his orders. He noted the differences between the one group, more ready with talk and smiles, set to work exclusively on the boats at the far end of the bay, and the others, Einar and his fellows, united in their reticence and that set, grim expression. Thorvald wondered if they could see only death in their future: he had gleaned enough information to know that many were lost each time they confronted this strange enemy. Between keeping an eye on the Ruler and trying to get it across to these men that nothing was going to change unless they grappled with a few new ideas, his days were pretty full. As time passed he found his mind dwelling less on Somerled and on questions of character, his own, his father's, and more on practicalities such as ensuring the men knew basic techniques for stemming the flow of blood or refletching an arrow. Oddly, he seemed to be enjoying himself.

It had been almost two turnings of the moon since they came there. Thorvald knew all the men's names now, and he had learned a little about the individuals to whom the names belonged, but not much. It was as if they found the exchange of words somehow pointless. He had not been able to lighten the look of despondency all of them seemed to wear, as if their efforts were doomed to inevitable failure. To change that look became something of a quest for him, for he did not like to see men sunk in despair thus, especially when a great part of the cause seemed to be no more than poor leadership.

He worked on them one at a time. Wieland might have seemed the obvious one to target, for this young man watched with attention when Thorvald was explaining something new, and could occasionally be seen showing the others different ways to bind on an arrowhead or to balance a shield. But Wieland was a reserved man. His habit was to watch and not to speak. So it was to Skolli the smith that Thorvald went first, knowing that, even in times of despair, a craftsman has his pride. He stood in the doorway of the little forge, watching with folded arms as the smith hammered a lump of rough iron into the leaf shape of a spearhead. Skolli used the tongs to lift the darkening metal and plunged it into a barrel of water. Steam arose.

"You worked here all your life?" Thorvald asked casually.

Skolli gave a grunt, turning the iron in the water. "Council Fjord, Blood Bay, outer isles."

"How did you learn the trade?"

"My father." The spearhead came out of the barrel and was laid back on the anvil and inspected closely. "He came

from over the sea. Always complaining. Said the iron in this
place was poor quality, second-rate stuff. I see it's true.
Your own weapons are fine. Superior. Give me a bit of that
to work with and I'll turn out something a man can be
proud of."

Thorvald was encouraged by the smith's readiness to
talk. "Of course," he said, offhand, "if these islands had a
trading arrangement, say with my home islands or with
those that lie to the north of them, you could have as much
top quality iron as you wanted. Has the Ruler investigated
that?"

"Huh," Skolli grunted, laying the finished piece to one
side and stooping to wipe his brow with a grimy rag. Sweat
was pouring off him. "Trade? Who's got time to think of
that, with the hunt hanging over us? A man doesn't think of
trade when he's struggling for survival. Not that a few decent weapons wouldn't help; you've got that much right."

"So, no chance of improving on the materials," Thorvald
said, seating himself on the bench by the door. The heat
from the fire was intense; he eased the cloak off his shoulders. "But how about the design? I don't know much, but I
did work with men who had been in a Jarl's personal guard,
and I have a few ideas . . . Of course, you'd need to tell me
if they weren't practical. I think, with this iron and your
skills, we could produce a different kind of spearhead, one
more suited to this terrain . . ." He picked up a charred twig
and began to draw on the bench, ready for Skolli's scorn, or
his silence. "Two kinds, maybe, one with a flange around
here, and the other very long and narrow, easy to thrust,
easy to withdraw. Longer, lighter shafts for these ones, so
the fellows can carry them readily across country. What do
you think?"

"Interesting." Skolli took the twig from Thorvald's hand,
rubbed out the diagram and started again. The look in his
eye surprised and heartened Thorvald; this had indeed
sparked his attention. "I could angle the flanges down and
leave a ridge along the center, that would give it a bit more
weight for throwing," the smith went on. "That one would
have the removable pin, the other would be fixed in place,

for hand-to-hand combat—not that we see much of that on the island."

There was a pause as Skolli mused over his drawing.

"The island?" Thorvald queried.

"The Isle of Clouds," said Skolli absently. "That's where it is. The hunt. Here, I think I've got it. What do you think of that?"

"Excellent," Thorvald told him. "When can you make a trial batch?"

"Tomorrow. I'd want to work on this design a bit first, make sure it's just right. You get the fellows busy on the shafts—Hjort's your best man for shaping the wood, and that young fisherman, Knut, isn't bad either. And work out how to test them. Set something up so the difference is plain; new version, old version. It can be hard to convince the fellows to change their ways."

"What about Asgrim? Can he be persuaded to change his ways?"

"Don't know," mumbled Skolli, who was drawing again. "Nobody ever dared to try."

The new designs were good. Tested on the run, and against stationary targets, and by men of different heights and builds, they proved superior in every way, and once Einar had given them the nod of approval it did not take so long for the others to agree, and to slap Skolli on the back and congratulate him for his work. Skolli told them that although the making was his, the idea was Thorvald's. At the time, nobody commented. But Thorvald detected a subtle change from that point on. They were reluctant to let him take the lead in the rehearsal of actual maneuvers; indeed, they seemed to do very little battlefield training. But they began to listen seriously to his advice on weaponry and on tactics, and occasionally one of the more confident men, Einar or Orm, would offer an opinion or acknowledge the sense in Thorvald's suggestions.

He began to glean information. On his own, Einar was prepared to speak more openly of what was to come; and one morning on the tidal flats below the shelter, Thorvald found the older man walking by the water, his boots setting their prints beside the delicate markings of gull and tern, and he asked him direct.

"Skolli tells me the hunt will take place on the Isle of Clouds." From here, the shape of the western isle could be clearly seen out beyond the mouth of the fjord, its cloud-shawled slopes dark and mysterious across the silvery expanse of water. "I can see the difficulty you face in leading the men; they seem defeated, and they don't train as warriors should who are heading into such a challenge. Asgrim doesn't make it easy for you."

Einar glanced at him, frowning. "You should be careful what you say, Thorvald. There's no special treatment for incomers here. The Ruler doesn't care for talk of that kind."

Thorvald spoke calmly. "I mean no criticism of the Ruler, nor of you. I see both of you trying to do what must be done under considerable difficulty. I don't want to be forward, but I do believe I could contribute something, if you'd let me."

Einar said nothing. He lifted his brows in question, expression wary.

"Would you allow me to take the men through some exercises in battle-craft? Perhaps discuss with you and Orm some ideas for organizing their working day better, so all of them are fully tested in both body and mind? I think, if we could do that, if we could occupy them better so they didn't have time to let their fears overwhelm them, perhaps we could change the way they think about this—this hunt."

"Oh yes?"

"Yes. I believe it, Einar. But I can't do it without more information. I need you to tell me about the hunt, or battle, or whatever it is. Who is the enemy, what weapons does he have, what advantages? Tell me about the terrain and the difficulties you've encountered there. Tell me how soon we have to be ready. Tell me why the men are so despondent, so terrified they can't work properly. Tell me that, and I will help you change things."

Thorvald waited somewhat nervously. This had been quite a risk. Of all those here, Einar was the one who

seemed to have the men's trust. He was the closest thing
they had to a true leader. Asgrim could not be counted. He
made his own rules and took no heed of others' opinions.
As Ruler he was ineffectual, insulated from his men's concerns by his own arrogance and by the two hulking guards
who shadowed him, their very presence striking fear into
all. A chieftain could not lead properly if his men did not
know him. He could not lead well if his men were scared of
him. Perhaps that was what had gone wrong for Somerled
before, in the Light Isles. Thorvald's stomach twisted into a
knot. He could help his father win this war, he was sure of
it. But perhaps his father was beyond helping, beyond
reaching. Perhaps Asgrim did not want a son.

"Difficult," Einar said in an undertone. "Asgrim prefers
us not to talk about it. Certainly not to incomers. You'd
need his approval to do what you say. Can't act without
him, not unless you fancy a beating from Hogni or Skapti,
or both."

"Well, no." Thorvald thought of the two bodyguards with
their menacing eyes and their thick, muscular necks. "But I
can't let things go on like this either. It's not right."

"Why would you care?" Einar asked blankly.

"Because . . ." Momentarily Thorvald was at a loss. "Because they're good men, all of them, and I don't like to see
good men give up. That's all the answer I have for you."

"Mmm," Einar said, looking at Thorvald with a somewhat different expression on his weary features. "I suspect
you don't know what you're taking on, but I salute your
courage. And some help certainly wouldn't go amiss. Still,
there's a right way and a wrong way to go about these
things. I won't go against the Ruler's commands. I haven't
survived five trips to the Isle of Clouds by being stupid."
His hand moved to touch the parallel scars on his cheek.
Thorvald had learned already that these were a badge of
honor, one new line earned each time a man got through the
hunt and returned to tell the tale. Five was the highest number borne, sign of a veteran warrior. "A couple of things you
need to know," Einar went on. "It's not so much about win-

ning a battle as staying alive while we find what we're looking for."

Thorvald's heart quickened: real information at last,
something he could use. "And what is that?" he asked.

"A child," Einar said with some reluctance. "A prisoner."

"One of your own? Kept captive by the tribe that lives
there?"

"The fact is," Einar said, "it's less a tribe of warriors than
a force of nature, an enemy that uses sorcery and tricks to
fend us off. There's only a certain amount spears and arrows can achieve, when all the enemy needs to do is open
his mouth and the men's bowels turn to water."

"What do you mean?" This was strange indeed. A child!
What child could possibly merit the loss of so many lives,
the expenditure of so much effort? There was a tale here,
and he must have it.

"Said more than I should already," Einar muttered. "If
you want the story about the hunt, you must get it from Asgrim. After that, come and talk to me again."

Thorvald was silent. Half of the story was almost worse
than nothing. He had hoped for better than this.

"And," Einar went on, turning back toward the shelter,
"I'll have a word with some of the others, Orm in particular. We know you've got new ideas. We know you want to
help. But the fellows might take a bit of persuading. You'll
understand that when Asgrim tells you about what we're
facing here. If we look as if we've given up before the battle begins, there's a good reason for it. You'd be taking on
quite a job."

"Not I, we," Thorvald corrected him. "*We'll* be taking on
quite a job. A challenge."

"We'll see," said Einar.

There had been scant opportunity to talk to Sam. The fisherman worked a long day, either on shore refurbishing the
beached vessels or out in the fjord gleaning the men's supper from an ocean full of tricks and surprises. At night they

all slept in the one long building, on the raised earthen platforms to either side. Conversation was never private there, and always interrupted with plaintive calls to shut up, couldn't they, and let a fellow get some sleep.

Sam caught Thorvald late one afternoon, when the weapon makers were packing up and the fishermen bearing the day's catch back to the shelter. Rain was starting to fall in heavy, spattering droplets; in these isles, one could have all four seasons in a single day. Sam bore a damp-looking sack on his shoulder; he stood by the pathway in the dark sand, his guileless blue eyes shadowed with anxiety. He was looking thinner; older, somehow.

"Good catch?" Thorvald asked.

Sam regarded him in silence.

"Don't tell me you've developed it too," exclaimed Thorvald in mock alarm. "The inability to speak, I mean. It's driving me crazy. But then, your lot do talk, don't they? I've seen them."

"Thorvald." Sam put the sack down. He sounded alarmingly serious.

"What? What's bothering you?"

"You shouldn't need to ask that," Sam said.

"Well, come on then. What is it?"

Sam sighed. "Can't you count? Haven't you noticed the season passing? Don't you know how long we've been here?"

Thorvald stared at him. What was this all about? "I told you this would take time," he said carefully. Sam's placid features looked almost angry; for him, this was most unusual. "I have to assess the situation, work out what the man's up to. It's not so easy to talk to him—"

"Have you forgotten about Creidhe? She's all by herself, and nobody will tell me when we're going back there. What if she comes to some harm? I mean, we just went and left her—"

Thorvald could not stop his brows from rising in disbelief, though he was doing his best to be understanding. "Is that what this is? Creidhe will be fine, Sam. She did say she didn't mind us going, don't you remember? Creidhe's a strong girl. Besides, what's to harm her back in that village? She's got all the things she likes—women's company, domestic comforts, time to weave and sew and potter about the house. I expect by now she's organized the whole community to her own design. She'll scarcely have noticed we're gone. Don't bother yourself about Creidhe."

"I do bother myself," Sam said doggedly, "and so would you if you could think beyond your own little world for a moment or two."

Thorvald did not reply. His friend had never spoken thus to him before.

"If that sounds bad, I'm sorry for it, but it's the truth," Sam went on, his cheeks flushing red. "There's something going on here that I don't like, and I don't want to be part of it. Mending a boat or two is all very well, helping these fellows haul in their catch and so on, but they're scared, scared out of their wits, and if you think Creidhe's safe from harm, making herself at home among these folk and forgetting all about her family and friends, you're just plain stupid. Some of the stories I've heard here would curdle your guts." His tone fell to a whisper as men passed close by, on their way to ale and supper. "That fellow, Asgrim, he's up to no good. I know he might be your father, and you might not like me to say this, but I have to. He's got them eating out of his hand, but it's not like the way folk are with Eyvind at home: not from respect. These men are frightened of the Ruler, and no wonder."

Thorvald found his voice. "What do you mean, stories?" Maybe Sam knew more of this odd tale about a captive child and sorcerous powers. "What have they been saying?"

"They want to go home, like us. But they can't. They've got wives in the settlements but they don't see them. Only in winter. He won't let them go."

"It's a war," Thorvald said, frowning. "Men don't take little trips home in a war."

"That's another thing. There's some kind of battle coming up, some kind of test. Nobody says, *when we win,* or even *if we win*. It's more, *If I die, tell Helga there's a bit of silver hidden under the hearthstone,* or, *If I die, you can have my second best net.* It doesn't sound good. These fellows are no more warriors than I am, Thorvald. I didn't come here to fight."

"We are improving," Thorvald offered. "The group I work with has made big advances, both in skills and the standard of weapons. You may not need to be a warrior, Sam. Perhaps none of your fishermen need be a part of it."

"Heard what happens when a fellow tries to leave?" Sam asked heavily.

Thorvald waited.

"Asgrim makes all the rules here. A game, isn't that what he said before? Some game. You know what happened to those two that were walking over to the settlement next to Creidhe? A quick death and a quicker consignment to the sea, that was the price for their mistake in nearly letting her fall. It wasn't even their fault. Of course, if Asgrim decides you're too useful to get rid of, there's a beating instead, bad enough to stop you disobeying again, not bad enough to cripple you, since cripples can't fight. The two big fellows, Skapti and Hogni, do the dirty work for him. I don't want Creidhe staying on these islands, Thorvald. I think we should go home."

"Of course," Thorvald said after a moment. "But there's the question of the *Sea Dove.*"

"Surely we've earned the price of a bit of wood by now," Sam said. "We need to ask for it at least."

"So ask."

"Me?"

"Why not?"

"You ask. This is your trip, not mine. Ask for wood, ask if he's your father, ask why he takes a whip to fellows who just want a peaceful life with their nets and their family. You brought me and Creidhe into this; now it's for you to get us out." Sam's voice cracked; he sounded quite unlike himself.

"I have a suggestion," Thorvald said. "What if you go back with your wood, see if all's well with Creidhe, and get started on the repairs? I'll come later, after—"

"After the battle? You *want* to be in it?"

"We've worked hard; these men have learned a lot. They can win, with what I've started, with what I can still do between now and midsummer. From what I've heard, it sounds as if all they have to do is retrieve one prisoner from over there. That can't be so impossible."

Sam shouldered the bag of fish and turned up the path toward the shelter. "Enjoying yourself, aren't you?" he asked over his shoulder. "Can't drag yourself away, not even with Creidhe's life at risk. If you're looking for proof of whose son you are, maybe you've found it."

"Oh come on, Sam," Thorvald protested. His friend's odd behavior was making him increasingly uneasy. "Creidhe's life at risk? Hardly. If you weren't sweet on her yourself, such a notion would never have occurred to you."

"Just ask him," Sam growled. "Ask him tonight."

There was a simple pattern to that last part of the day, between dusk and bedtime. The season had indeed advanced and the working day was long. Sleep came quickly on the heels of supper. A sunken hearth ran down the center of the big hut, with a rudimentary opening above that dispelled some but not all of the smoke. A couple of lamps would be lit, and the men would gather around the fire where one or two cooked the day's catch, generally in the form of a kind of fish stew containing a generous share of small, sharp bones. There might be a shred or two of vegetables in it, onion mostly, if someone had brought across a supply from one of the settlements. A pair of skinny lads ran between with messages sometimes. Thus one fellow learned of his mother's death from a spring chill, and another that his cow had produced twin calves, one male, one female. Neither man asked for leave to return home. There was no leaving: not until the hunt was over.

While supper cooked, there was some talk. Mostly it was the fishermen who exchanged comments, always concerning the day's work, the catch, the weather, perhaps a joke relating to an obscure point of net-mending. Thorvald had noticed Sam's popularity among this group, and he had observed, as well, that Sam was always very careful, giving nothing away, asking no probing questions. It came to him that perhaps he had underestimated his friend.

The weapon makers spoke little. Already weary by the time they made their way up to the shelter, they sat hunched and silent, and when supper was ready, ate with no apparent enjoyment. To work, to feed, to sleep seemed no more than necessary steps in an existence set out for them in unchanging, joyless inevitability. Night after night Thorvald had sat among them and wondered if, given sufficient time, he, too, would become like this: no better than a beast yoked to a heavy load, obedient to the whip and the master's call. He shuddered. Not true; already he was making them change. He was showing them new tricks, new ways. He would awaken a spark of something in their dull eyes no matter what it took; he would make his mark before he left here.

Asgrim's habit was to come down from his hut just in time to eat. There were no formal tables here, no benches, just the long earthen platforms that served as bed, seat and storage for a complement of close to thirty men. The only one to dwell outside this dark, smoky hall was the Ruler himself. Then there were his two personal guards, Hogni and Skapti, biggest and most silent of all. Broad-shouldered, stone-faced, they were brothers, and took it in turns to spend the night on duty outside the Ruler's hut.

Many times Thorvald had thought to seat himself close to Asgrim and engage him in conversation as casually as possible, to glean what clues he could as to the strange patterns of life and conflict in these islands. There were so many questions to be answered: what was the nature of this enemy, exactly? What numbers did they have? Did they truly use sorcery to aid their assaults, or was that account merely a product of superstitious fear? Why were Asgrim's forces gathered here in a single place, sitting targets should the Unspoken move on them from the sea, as was said to be their habit? And why weren't the men supposed to talk about it?

All he needed to do was be there at the right time and ask.

But somehow, wherever he placed himself, Asgrim was always on the other side, or farther down the hall, and seated between taller, bigger men so that Thorvald could not attract his attention. And with so many men gathered in so small a space, and sleep the foremost thought in all their minds, it never seemed possible to squeeze past the others and seek out the Ruler; indeed, there was something about the thick, smoky, defeated feeling of those silent suppers that quashed the urge for independent inquiry almost before one felt it.

Thus Thorvald had let time pass: too much time. He did not think he had wasted it entirely. Over his bowls of tasteless stew he had done a great deal of observation. He knew now which men had Asgrim's favor: Orm, Skolli and Einar. He knew which ones the Ruler watched with a little frown on his brow: Svein, Wieland and, rather oddly, Sam, who as far as Thorvald could see had not set a foot wrong since they got here. The man who had been beaten for stealing no longer attracted Asgrim's attention; one lesson seemed to be enough.

Tonight there was no choice. A pox on Sam and his silly anxieties. If Thorvald didn't broach the question, his friend would probably do it for him, and get them both sent straight back before Thorvald could finish what he was doing; before he found out what he wanted to know. Tonight, then, he must confront Asgrim and hope he had the skill to make the man answer him.

He waited. They sat; they cooked and ate the meal; they unrolled bedding, took off boots, settled in huddled heaps on the earthen shelves. One or two went outside to relieve themselves, and Thorvald slipped out behind them. Asgrim was on his way up to his solitary hut, the looming forms of Hogni and Skapti on either side. It was raining; in the west, lightning speared the dark sky, and after it there was a fierce, low rumbling like the angry voices of earth giants: *Who dares disturb our slumber?*

"I want to talk to you," Thorvald said crisply, stepping out of the darkness into Asgrim's path. An instant later

Hogni had him in a hold that did something exceedingly uncomfortable to his neck, while Skapti, breathing heavily, waved the point of a thrusting spear a handsbreadth before his eyes.

"Ah, yes," Asgrim observed easily, coming to a halt. The rain had increased to a steady, drenching downpour. "Thorvald. You've been quite a busy fellow."

Hogni moved one hand slightly: pain lanced through Thorvald's neck and into his head, the kind of pain that suggests unconsciousness is not far off.

"You kill men for daring to speak to you?" he gasped, trying to recall if Ash had ever taught him how to get out of such a grip. "No wonder your army is so small." The spear point was so close to his face, he could see every pockmark in the iron, every drop of rain running across the dark metal. He would not close his eyes.

"Should I retain you, do you think?" Asgrim's tone was light. The spear point trembled.

"Depends on what you want," Thorvald wheezed. Ah, he remembered now: the bluff, then the knee, that was the trick. "To win your war, or merely to keep things the way they suit you." His whole body went suddenly limp; for an instant, no more, surprise unclenched Hogni's hands, and in that moment Thorvald rolled, striking his captor hard in the back of the knee with a well-placed kick. Hogni howled; Skapti thrust wildly with the spear.

"Not quite quick enough," Thorvald said breathlessly from where he now stood on the path behind the Ruler. "You'd want to counter that with a low, sweeping blow and follow up with your boot. If you like, I'll show you tomorrow."

There was a roar from the two guards as they closed in from either side, teeth clenched, features contorted in identical grimaces of furious frustration.

"That will be all, men," Asgrim said calmly. "No likelihood of disturbance in such weather; this rain seems fit to drown us all. Go to your beds, now."

"But—" Skapti began, his eyes flicking toward Thorvald and back again.

Asgrim looked at him.

"Yes, my lord," Skapti muttered. Hogni was flexing his fingers in a manner that suggested he had unfinished business with Thorvald, and it didn't include lessons in hand-to-hand combat. The two bodyguards turned without another word and were gone into the night.

"Well," Asgrim said coolly, "I don't imagine your plan was to stand here in the rain all night. Follow me."

Inside, the Ruler's hut was comfortable without ostentation; the practical, solitary quarters of a seasoned war leader. It housed a stone table, two small benches, a sleeping platform where bedding was neatly rolled. There was a hearth with the remnants of a fire. Asgrim stirred the embers, set on dried cow dung, lit oil lamps with a taper. The light revealed further details: it seemed the Ruler was a man of learning, for there was a roll or two of parchment laid away in a niche beside knife, sword and bow. Asgrim fetched ale in a stoppered flask and poured it into a pair of crude clay cups.

"Sit down, Thorvald. Get your breath back."

Thorvald sat. Now that he had his chance, he wasn't sure where to begin. Get this wrong and he'd be thrown out with not a single question answered. Asgrim's face was shuttered, his eyes unreadable. Still, he had asked Thorvald in.

"A long time ago," Thorvald said, "you explained a process to me. Question for question, answer for answer. I have many questions, and little information to give that can be of any interest to you."

Asgrim gave a murmur that might have been agreement. He seated himself opposite Thorvald, a cup between his hands.

"How do we play this game?" Thorvald asked. "Perhaps you should begin, since we're on your territory. What do you wish to know of me?"

Asgrim's thin lips twisted in a smile. "I see you have learned something after all. Well done. Why are you here, and what do you seek?" The question was rapped out, sudden as a blade in the dark.

Thorvald's heart thumped, then quieted in obedience to his will. "I believed I might have kinfolk here. I was told of a man who sailed to isles such as these, a Christian monk who spent many seasons away, and returned crazed by what he had experienced. I determined to voyage here and learn what it was that could confound even a man of faith. I hoped at the same time to discover whether my kin had indeed traveled this way, and what had become of them."

"Your companions?"

"As I said, one came because the boat is his and I needed him to sail it. The other accompanied us uninvited."

"So you told me."

"It's the truth. I have no reason to lie to you. Indeed, I'm here tonight because Sam wants to leave. He wants his length of wood so he can go back and start mending the *Sea Dove.*"

Asgrim nodded slowly. "And you?"

"That's three questions."

"Answer, and you shall have three of your own."

"It's a long-winded way of exchanging information on the eve of a battle. No wonder—" Thorvald fell silent at the look in the Ruler's dark eyes. This was a man who dispensed life and death as easily as he poured ale. "Very well," Thorvald said. "I would prefer to stay on a while. I've been trying to work with the men, to improve the weapons and the way they use them. There's a lot more I want to do here. I think I can help you. But not without better information. The men don't talk much."

"The men obey. An army must obey."

"How long have you been fighting this war? How many battles have you actually won?" Thorvald forgot to be cautious. "These men are worn down, defeated before they even begin. They can see only failure. You can't get the better of your enemy like that—"

Asgrim raised his hand again. "Are these your questions?" he asked smoothly.

To his annoyance, Thorvald felt a flush rising to his cheeks. He took a mouthful of the ale: it was of considerably better quality than the watery brew served down in the shelter. "I'm sorry," he said. "I would be grateful if you would explain to me the nature of this enemy you call the Unspoken: his numbers, his location, his manner of attack. I cannot help you effectively unless I know that. Sometimes I hear of a battle and sometimes a hunt; how are the two connected? Who is the child we seek? I understand we have to travel out to the Isle of Clouds. Why is it we are so ill-prepared for close combat? These men don't practice with sword or thrusting spear unless I make them. They seem to think it's pointless."

"*We* are so ill-prepared?"

Thorvald looked down at his hands, "I don't like to see such potential wasted. There's strength here, and talent, if we could just get past their attitude. I think I could do that, given the chance. Given the information."

"Hmm," said Asgrim, sipping his ale. "And you could be a spy, though generally spies don't march straight into the enemy's headquarters demanding full details of his plans. Thorvald, perhaps you've forgotten what you told me when you first arrived here. Fishing, a storm, a profound desire to mend the boat and head for home at the earliest opportunity, wasn't that it?"

"This is another question," Thorvald said. "You owe me some answers first, I think." He felt a trickle of cold sweat on his neck: here in this isolated hut, it was all too easy to believe the tales of sudden, final punishment. It was all too simple to look at the pale, impassive features, the shrewd, dark eyes, and see his own reflection. *Why don't we work together, like and like? Father and son?*

"There's a small difficulty, as I see it," Asgrim said, rising to fetch one of the rolled sheets of parchment from the recess in the stone wall. "Sam wishes to return home, you want to stay. We don't know the girl's mind; possibly she is happy to wait for you, possibly not. This could be awkward to reconcile."

"Sam doesn't care for fighting. He could go back to Blood Bay now if you'd instruct the fellows on guard to let him pass. He could visit Creidhe on the way, fix his beloved boat. Then, when I'm finished here . . ." Thorvald's words faltered to a stop as the Ruler unrolled the parchment on the table, setting small stones on the corners to hold it flat. Asgrim moved one of the soapstone lamps to rest beside the drawing that flowed, meticulous in its neatness and complexity, across the coarse, cream-brown surface of the parchment.

It was a map fashioned by a master, a map that showed the islands in every detail, curves and fissures of coastline, lakes, streams and sea currents, hills and dales and tiny isolated settlements. Here and there words were written, words Thorvald could read: Isle of Storms, Isle of Streams, Dragon Isle. Troll's Arch, at the mouth of Council Fjord. Witch's Finger. Out to the west, all on its own, lay the Isle of Clouds. In the south were islands with no names, realms marked only by a subtle shading of the pen, as if these territories lay beyond some barrier that could not be shown by image or text. They were the lands of the Unspoken. The small, neat script held Thorvald fast; he stared at the page, unable to speak. He knew this writing: he had seen it before.

"Some of your answers lie here," Asgrim was saying calmly.

"This is a fine piece of work," Thorvald croaked. He cleared his throat. Now was not the time, he must get a grip on himself. "I congratulate you."

Asgrim did not reply. His hand moved to hover above the shadowed isles of the south. "Such a chart cannot show all," the Ruler said eventually. "It cannot show the years of failure, the deaths, the bitterness. Our enemy has a power we cannot match; my men know that, they have seen it. Their despair is not surprising. Each of us has his own losses: father, brother, comrade. I, too." He bowed his head.

"I'm sorry," Thorvald said, still struggling to control his voice, now that he had seen the proof, now that he knew. "You have lost family?" Somerled could have married again, probably had done just that; a decree of exile was not necessarily one of total isolation. Strange, though: this possibility had never occurred to him. He might have a step-mother here and a whole tribe of half-siblings. He had imagined Somerled alone.

"A daughter," Asgrim said quietly, his fingers still trailing gently over the map, across the Isle of Storms to the empty realms of the north. "A girl every bit as lovely as that young friend of yours, with the same bright hair and innocent smile. Taken, despoiled, slaughtered. A boy, also. He was no more than a fool. His blundering efforts to put the world to rights set a dark curse on our future. He'd never have come to anything; he was too much his mother's son. You?"

The question came so abruptly after this flat statement of loss and bitterness that Thorvald hardly understood what was meant by it.

"You have family?" Asgrim asked, gazing at him across the table. Between them, the map lay in all its complexity and wonder, the last piece of a puzzle to which its maker still did not understand the solution.

"Yes," said Thorvald, heart hammering. "But I will not speak of them until you answer my questions. The rules of your game are to be obeyed, are they not?" The moment he mentioned Margaret, the truth would be known, and everything would change. Now that he had come so close, he felt curiously reluctant to take the next step. As a stranger, it would be up to him to prove his worth entirely on his own merits. Far better, he thought, to take up the challenge, to make this rabble of dispirited islanders into a real fighting force with heart and discipline, far better to win the battle and then, only then, to make the truth known. *I have achieved this, and I am your son. I will not disappoint you as the other did.*

"As you know," Asgrim said, "this is a realm of secrets, of strange past, difficult present, unknowable future. We are reluctant to share our story; it pains us to tell it. I have watched you, waiting until it might be appropriate to reveal this tale to you, for if, as you say, you wish to take a role in aiding our endeavor, there are certain matters you must be aware of."

"And what have you concluded?" Thorvald managed to make his question nonchalant, as if he cared little whether he heard the tale or not. In truth, he could hardly wait. As-grim was going to tell him the truth at last. His father trusted him.

The Ruler gave his thin-lipped smile. "I've concluded that you may indeed be useful to me. I had thought your talk of expertise in arms merely a young man's bragging, a wild exaggeration designed to impress. Your actions, however, and your evident commitment to improving the men's ef-forts, seem to prove me wrong. If your will to help me is genuine, then I believe we can work together. If that is to occur, you must first know the truth."

Thorvald waited.

"Understand," Asgrim went on, "that it has not always been thus in these islands, the Long Knife people against the Unspoken, the battles, the hunt, the murder of children—"

"Wait a bit," Thorvald interrupted. "I know the purpose of the hunt is to retrieve a child, but nobody said anything about murder."

"It is all part of the tale; another thread in the long pattern of suffering. When our kind first settled in the Lost Isles, it was not thus. We came to the islands as exile, as outcast, as farmer and fisherman and hermit, all of us fleeing some-thing, all of us searching for something. Bonds of a kind were forged; one cannot survive long in such a realm with-out them. We made our settlements and built our boats. We ran our stock on the hills, we scraped a living, we bred our sons and daughters. In those southern isles, the Isle of Shadows, the Isle of Dreams, the others dwelt, those who were here before us. We saw them little."

"There's been talk of sorcery, of magic," Thorvald said diffidently. "I was given the impression that this tribe you call the Unspoken are not entirely human."

Asgrim's finger moved again on the map, coming to rest on the small, isolated shape of the Isle of Clouds. "We have long winters here," he said, "summers of mist and storm. It's a climate that breeds superstitious fears. I keep the men occupied as well as I can, but their imaginations tend to get the better of them. The Unspoken come from the same stock as we do. They speak our tongue. But they are not as

we are. It's thought there was an older race here, a race possessed of unnatural power and unusual savagery. They in-
terbred and in time became one people: a people like none
you have ever encountered, Thorvald. They are a scourge, a
curse."

There was a brief silence while Thorvald decided which
question to ask first. "There was some suggestion," he ventured, "that this tribe prevails by the use of hexes and spell-
craft. How can we counter that? I believe it is those charms
the men fear, not the prospect of an honest battle."

Asgrim gave a crooked smile. "This is a real enemy and
a real threat. My daughter died; I lost my only son. I have
known the pain of this conflict, as they all have. The ancestors of the Unspoken dwelt in these islands long before our
kind sought refuge here. The lineage of these folk has given
them faculties we do not possess, an ability to tap into a
strength that emanates from the land itself. Those skills
they employ to their advantage, with devastating effect."

"Winds, tides, weather," mused Thorvald.

"Exactly. Call it magic if you will; my men think of it as
just that. It is beyond us to counter it, Thorvald. Each con-
frontation reduces my numbers further; and there are the
children. That was the final blow. It is no wonder you see
despair in these men's eyes. The Unspoken rob us of our
very future."

Asgrim sat down once more, hands clenched before him.
At last Thorvald could see some spark of feeling in the
coal-dark eyes.

"Tell me the story," he said, taking up the flask unbidden
and pouring more ale for the two of them. Outside the stone
hut, the wind was rising; the rain beat down like a many-
toothed flail.

"It is a sorry tale, Thorvald, a tale that has turned us old
before our time. Once, we lived peaceably enough. They
left us alone; we did not venture across the water to the
places where we knew they dwelt. There were chance en-
counters from time to time, a sudden squall driving a boat
to shore where it did not belong, a request for a sheep or
two in years of bad harvest. There was tolerance between

us, but no formal bond of friendship or alliance. There was a council of sorts, held once a year at midsummer on their Isle of Shadows. They are a people of many secrets; their ritual observances are governed by complex networks of laws. They would let no more than three of our people attend the gatherings: the Ruler and two of his chosen men. In my early days as chieftain here, I attended several such councils; Einar, too, has witnessed them. We discovered something of their ways." Asgrim's voice dropped suddenly to a whisper. "It was thus we learned of Foxmask."

"Foxmask?" This grew stranger and stranger.

"Their priest or holy man. A visionary, a teller of ancient wisdom. At the time when I became Ruler, Foxmask was old. Old, blind and crippled. He did not venture forth, but they held him in utmost awe and reverence, as if he were a creature unearthly in his power, part elder, part feral thing, able to pass to them the wisdom of standing stone and deep well, wild beast and eternal stars. Foxmask was the center of their existence, the cornerstone of their belief. Foxmask kept them safe; he told them how to live their lives, how to survive. You understand, this crippled priest, this old blind man was but one in a long line of such seers. Foxmask is not a single individual, but a title; a position, one might say."

"Such as Ruler."

Asgrim nodded. "Indeed, though not a leader such as we appoint from among the Long Knife people. Foxmask does not bring his folk forth to war. He sings his wisdom: they listen, and follow the path he decrees."

"It sounds harmless enough," Thorvald observed, thinking that, indeed, it sounded not so very different from the ways of Nessa's people, another ancient race of island dwellers. Such folk cling to the lore of earth and sky, ocean and fire. Privately, he thought them doomed to be overrun some day by people more flexible in their ways, more amenable to change. This was not a sentiment he would express before his mother. He would not speak of it to Eyvind, who, Norseman though he was, was fiercely committed to the preservation of his wife's ancestral culture. He had never aired his views to Creidhe, a child of two races.

"Harmless it was," Asgrim said, "until Foxmask died. That was some time ago. I was a young man then, my son and daughter mere children. It is the custom of the Unspoken, after such a death, to select another to take the seer's place. That they do with some ceremony. But this time there was no suitable candidate. There is a circumstance of birth by which Foxmask is chosen; a test follows to determine his aptitude. If no member of the tribe fits this mold, the Unspoken are without ancestral wisdom, without the guidance they need to lead their lives, to survive in this harsh realm. There was no visionary among their own, not this time; and so they sought elsewhere."

"I see," Thorvald said softly, never taking his eyes from Asgrim's hard features, his tight mouth. "A child? This is what you spoke of, the stealing of children?"

Asgrim shook his head. "We did not know why they had begun to attack, to sink our fishing boats, to raid our coastal dwellings, to howl their songs in the night and fill our heads with evil dreams. We called for a council; I sailed to the shore of the Isle of Shadows, with two others, and entreated the Unspoken to sit down with us and explain themselves, to try for an agreement. They drove us off with hurled stones and arrows of bone, with witching music that set our minds full of foul visions. After that we prepared ourselves for war. We countered their raids as best we could; I taught my own folk what I knew of battle-craft, and we tried to protect our fields, our stock, our boats. We lost many good men. The pity was, I did not understand what they wanted until they took her." The Ruler's control was slipping now; his voice shook, and lines of pain bracketed the severe mouth.

"Your daughter?" Thorvald ventured.

Asgrim nodded. "My only daughter. Not as seer: Foxmask must be of their own people. They stole my girl away by night. We could not fetch her back: wind and tide defeated us time after time. They used her, Thorvald. Waited only until she had her first bleeding, then passed her from man to man, so that the child she bore would be the son of each of them, the true offspring of the tribe. That is the hideous practice they follow. Sula bore a son for them, and died of it. Little matter to the Unspoken. They had their seer: Foxmask was reborn."

Thorvald cleared his throat. He had come here in search of answers; this was almost more answer than he was ready to hear. No wonder the Ruler seemed a little odd at times. This was a weight of grief and guilt to rival the burden Somerled had borne with him from the Light Isles.

"I'm sorry," he said, knowing any words he might summon would be inadequate. "You pursue this war now for the sake of vengeance? To make them pay for your daughter's suffering?"

Asgrim gave the bleakest of smiles. "No, Thorvald. I've no wish for more men to die simply so I can be at some peace with my conscience. My daughter is gone; no amount of blood-letting can bring her back. If it were up to me, I would seek to negotiate, to make terms for truce. Indeed, I have already attempted that and will do so again. It is not I who desires to continue this conflict, but the others: the tribe of the Unspoken."

"But why? They have what they wanted, their seer—"

"Not any longer. For a little, there was peace of a kind, a peace that simmered with unease. Then, suddenly, Foxmask was gone. Stolen. The seer was removed to a place where only the boldest or most foolish could seek him. He was encircled by a barrier of protection only the cleverest and most devious could penetrate. It is so to this day. The Unspoken cannot fetch him back: the place where he is kept is forbidden to them. To set foot there is to transgress their oldest law. Foxmask himself lies above and beyond law; he may set his foot where he chooses. They say he still lives, somewhere on that western isle, and since their attacks on us are based on that belief, we must honor it, though his survival would be something of a miracle. The island is perilous, surrounded by the most treacherous of waters, studded with tricks and traps, a place we dare visit but once a summer when a particular conjunction of wind, tide and time occurs. And yet we must attempt it. Until we fetch him

back, the Unspoken punish us by stealing our hope: by robbing us of our newborn."

"What? But that's outrageous! How can you stand for
that? Surely your warriors can prevent it, it would be
easy—"

"This is a matter that goes beyond the merely physical,"
Asgrim said levelly. "It cannot be halted by sword or
spear. A curse has fallen upon the Long Knife people.
There is no longer a need for the Unspoken to set foot on
our land, or to raise a hand against us. The voices come,
howling in the night. In the five years since Foxmask was
taken, not one of our infants has lived to see a second sunrise. Unless we return the seer to his true home, our folk
are doomed."

Thorvald could think of nothing to say. He had hoped to
hear of weapons tonight, of campaigns, of strategy and advantage. To that kind of conversation he could have con-
tributed much. This, this seemed like something from an
ancient tale, part truth, part bizarre imagining. And yet it
was conveyed as baldly as if Asgrim had been presenting
him with tomorrow's plan for combat training. "Who took
the seer away?" he asked. "And who guards him now?"

"Who took him? A meddling fool who should have
known better. That was a dark day. We had believed the
time of death and suffering over at last. That it was one of
our own who betrayed us cut very hard. Because of him,
Sula's sacrifice was in vain. To the Unspoken this punishment is appropriate, I suppose—their child is taken, so they
will rob us of ours, each and every infant, until we find Foxmask and return him to his true home. Without their seer the
Unspoken are a dangerous force indeed. Without his control, their wild music wreaks such havoc as could drive us
all mad. They cannot govern themselves, it seems, unless
this living heart beats again to the pattern of their ancient
lore, safe in the midst of their strange circle. I have witnessed this myself, in my futile efforts to treat for peace.
There is one elder of the Unspoken who, in the past, was his
people's voice at the council, and spoke wisely, wild man

though he is. Given the right conditions, covert meetings can be arranged between this elder and myself; there are rules to be followed, and it's somewhat risky. I've been there once or twice with Skapti. Through this man I was informed of Sula's fate, of the stealing away of Foxmask, of the curse they had laid on us until the child was returned. The end is very close for us if we cannot achieve that soon. This is the purpose of our preparations, Thorvald: to travel to the Isle of Clouds, to do battle, to rescue this visionary and take him back where he belongs."

"Forgive me," Thorvald said, wondering if he had missed something, "is there yet another tribe on this Isle of Clouds whom you must fight to reach the seer? Isn't this Foxmask still quite young? Wouldn't it be easy to go and get him, tricky currents notwithstanding?" Already, he could see himself sailing there, accomplishing the task with ease, returning triumphant to set all to rights. Sam would help him; Sam liked children.

"Easy? No, Thorvald, it is far from easy. For five summers my men have pursued the hunt, on those few days each year when conditions make it possible. Our losses have been severe. The one we seek is guarded by an elemental force of great strength. You would not call such a task easy if you knew the Isle of Clouds."

"Asgrim," Thorvald asked with some hesitation, for there were further secrets here, old hurts that ran very close to the bone, "who was it that stole Foxmask away? And why?"

At that moment the howl of the wind and the drumming of the rain were joined by a rapping at the door and the sound of a loud, hoarse voice: Skapti's, or maybe Hogni's. "My lord! A messenger, my lord!"

After that, things moved very quickly. Two rain-soaked men were admitted and conversed briefly, breathlessly and inaudibly with the Ruler as their clothing dripped onto the floor around them. Skapti stood by the half-open door, glaring at Thorvald. All that could be heard of the message was a woman's name, Jofrid, and something about being early. Whatever the meaning of the messengers' words, it brought a look to Asgrim's face that Thorvald found disquieting: the furious glare of a man thwarted in some long-held plan. An instant later the Ruler could be seen to draw a deep breath and force his expression to calm. He was rapping out orders even as he reached for his cloak, his heavy boots, his sword and spear.

"Skapti!"

It seemed the guard was to accompany Asgrim wherever he was going on this night of screaming wind and drenching rain. The Ruler was heading out the door before he remembered Thorvald. He turned.

"I'm called away, as you see. I'm sure I need not tell you that what we discussed isn't for open airing. The men know of it, but we don't speak of it; such talk only unsettles them. Now, Thorvald. Somewhat to my surprise, the men do appear to be responding to your efforts at training them. That can only be to our advantage in the hunt. I want you to continue, though in my absence it's Einar who's in charge. If you can work with him, so much the better. As for Sam, see if you can persuade him to stay on a bit. He's a big, strong fellow. I'm sure you understand how useful that might be. Give him my guarantee he'll get home safely when all this is over." With that, Asgrim vanished into the night, shadowed by the looming form of his bodyguard. The messengers looked at one another, pallid and wheezing. Both seemed fit to drop with exhaustion right where they stood.

"Come on," Thorvald said to the two men, moving to snuff the lamps and damp down the small fire. He was tempted to stay in the hut to investigate what further secrets Asgrim's private quarters might reveal. On the other hand, Hogni was around somewhere, and Thorvald could still feel the imprint of large fingers on his neck. "You need a bite to eat and a warm place to sleep. Follow me." It did not feel at all odd to be assuming a kind of responsibility. Indeed, it seemed to Thorvald entirely appropriate.

There was no need to talk to Sam, for the very next day Sam came back early from the boats with his arms around the shoulders of two other fellows and his right foot swollen up so badly they had to cut his boot off. An anchor had fallen, or been dropped: a nasty accident. Sam was considered to have been extremely lucky. There were no broken bones as far as anyone could tell, but the injury was painful and he could put no weight on the foot. Orm applied the pungent green salve that seemed to be a universal remedy; Hjort wrapped a length of cloth around the injured extremity. Sam took his misfortune with a good will, as he did most things. It did not need to be spelled out that there would be no walking back to Brightwater, let alone Blood Bay, for quite some time. It was almost as if the fates were conspiring to keep them at the encampment; the timing of the accident made Thorvald uneasy, but he said nothing of that to Sam. In his turn, Sam did not ask Thorvald about the night before, and Thorvald welcomed his restraint. He was far too busy for explanations.

With Asgrim away and Skapti with him, a brief opportunity presented itself. Hogni remained in camp, and Hogni's attitude to Thorvald could not be described as cordial. Hogni's role was critical, and time was short.

There were three ways of tackling this. One, Thorvald could wait for Hogni to challenge his authority, fight as well as he was able, and hope to salvage some kind of reputation from it. If he survived. Two, he could ignore the look in Hogni's small, angry eyes, and offer to share a few of the tricks he'd learned from Ash, with him as well as the rest of them. That might perhaps win the bodyguard over. There was another choice, and that was the one Thorvald took: the first step in a strategy that, if he played it right, would carry him all the way to the Isle of Clouds.

They had a good stock of the new thrusting spears now. The first type was based on a model Thorvald had seen Eyvind using, the blade an elegant leaf shape with a ridge down the center and what might be called wings at the base. This could be inserted effectively and withdrawn with relative ease. The second was narrower, a long triangle with a very precise tip. Thorvald had explained the particular advantage this offered at close quarters when one's opponent was wearing protective clothing, such as a mail shirt. This had drawn blank looks. Or a leather jerkin, Thorvald had added, like the garments Hogni and Skapti possessed. He demonstrated how the spear point could be inserted neatly into a vulnerable spot, its small head being designed for that purpose. Of course, a man needed to develop some skill in its use. He would show them.

A day or two after Asgrim's departure, Thorvald made a request of Hogni. Before he did so, he made sure everyone was within earshot. The men needed practice at hand-to-hand combat, he said, to sharpen them up for what lay ahead and to test the weapons properly. You couldn't expect your enemy to stand still like a straw man. Everyone knew Hogni and Skapti were the best among them at close fighting. Hadn't Thorvald witnessed it himself, not so long ago? Indeed—he rubbed his neck ruefully—he'd taken away more than one little reminder. The men laughed. So, he told them, from now on they should have a few bouts every day, in pairs, and watch one another and learn. Since Hogni was a talented fellow, he should be first to demonstrate what he knew.

Hogni grunted and spat on the ground. There was no telling if this signified agreement or derision.

"Thing is," Wieland said diffidently, "there's not much of it. Hand to hand, I mean. Even on the island. Not much close work. We never get the chance."

"Not that we wouldn't welcome it, if it came to that," Orm put in, scratching his chin. "But . . ."

"Mostly arrows," Knut said. "Took out six men last time. Then there's the spears, and those other things . . ."

"This time," Thorvald made his tone confident, strong, the voice of a leader, "we'll have better spears and better arrows. And we'll know how to use them. This time we'll attack with our wits as well as our weapons. We'll take the battle right up to the enemy. This time we'll be ready."

"So who's going to fight Hogni, then?" One of the fishermen spoke up. There was a general muttering, a little laughter, a nudge here, a gesture there. At least this had their interest. "And when are we starting?"

Hogni rose to his feet. He was a head taller than anyone else, and built like a plow ox. "Why not now?" he inquired, looking straight at Thorvald.

"Why not indeed?" Thorvald gazed back steadily. "And since I was silly enough to come up with the idea, I suppose the first challenger has to be me. I just hope you don't kill me. Skolli's got a new batch of spearheads cooling up in the smithy, and I'd like to be here tomorrow to see if they're any good. Well, now." He summoned a nonchalant grin, though his heart was racing; Ash's tuition may have been thorough, but there were limits to what one might achieve against an opponent of such daunting size. "Shall we start?"

It was not necessary to win, only to survive. That was just as well. His escape the other night had owed as much to lucky timing as anything, and Thorvald was uncomfortably aware of it. He was no more than average as a fighter; he had got by so far on his ability to learn quickly and his talent for observation.

It was clear from the way Hogni flexed his arms and bent his knees in preparation that this giant had no intention of letting him off lightly. The men formed a circle around the two combatants. Thorvald caught a glimpse of Sam at the rear, propped on another fellow's shoulder and pale as goat's milk. Orm was taking wagers; men jostled to get a better view. If he were to die today of a cracked skull or a snapped neck, Thorvald thought as he eyed the bodyguard's massive arms, his formidable shoulders and little, vindictive eyes, at least he would have achieved one of his goals. This had woken them up; it had kindled a spark within them. That was exactly what he needed. He could use this, if he came out of it in one piece.

It was important, he told himself as Hogni moved in, dodging low then levering up with a punishing shoulder, it was important to keep it going long enough to show a modicum of strength and skill; to provide excellent entertainment, so the men were both diverted and heartened. It would be good, he mused as Hogni threw him painfully down on knee and elbow, jarring every bone in him, it would be good to appear to be winning at some point, just to maintain a little credibility. He rolled, twisted, came up on his feet and managed a kick or two; Hogni grunted in surprise, perhaps pain, and took a step back. The main thing, Thorvald told himself as his opponent locked his hands together and prepared for a crippling, hammer-like blow to Thorvald's neck and shoulder, the main thing, apart from not dying, of course, was that Hogni must win. The way this was going, that part of it wouldn't be a problem.

He parried the blow with his left arm; it was a bone-breaker, and he reeled away, fighting to keep a steady footing. Hogni roared and charged at him with head lowered, a battering ram of sheer muscle. The crowd howled with excitement.

Thorvald jumped. The maneuver was not in Ash's repertory: it came in a flash, the only possible option. He sprawled awkwardly on Hogni's back, his legs around the bigger man's neck, his face level with the fellow's buttocks and staring into the tightly packed group of onlookers. Hogni straightened, hands fastening like clamps around Thorvald's crossed ankles. Thorvald squeezed his thighs together and prayed. He was hanging now, his head against Hogni's odiferous trousers, his arms flailing for purchase. He could hear Hogni wheezing, gasping, struggling for air as his assailant's legs pressed ever tighter against his neck.

The noise from the crowd was deafening. Some of them had started a rhythmic chant, *Hog-ni, Hog-ni,* but others shouted encouragement, "That's the way, youngster!" and helpful suggestions, "Sink your teeth in, lad!"

Hogni shook him, setting his teeth rattling. Hogni turned, spinning him, hazing his head with dizziness. *Hold on, hold on . . .* Hogni's grip was weakening, Thorvald could feel the fingers starting to loosen, he could hear the whistle of Hogni's agonized attempts to draw breath. The big man would be red in the face by now, close to passing out. Hogni staggered; the ground lurched below Thorvald's head.

Now was the time. Thorvald slackened the death grip his legs had on Hogni's neck, grabbing his opponent's belt to keep himself from falling. A moment, that was all that was needed: the bodyguard might be brutish in appearance, but he was a skilled fighter. Hogni sucked in a single, shuddering breath and whirled in place again, then with a deft twist of the arms, a stylish flick of the huge hands, he plucked the smaller man from his back and launched him through the air to land, with a painful thud, flat on his back in the very center of the circle.

"Ouch," said Thorvald after a moment. "I think you may have broken something."

A chorus of cheers erupted, and a renewal of the war cry: *Hog-ni, Hog-ni.* Many hands dragged Thorvald to his feet, dusted him off, ruffled his hair and slapped his shoulders. Men like a good loser.

Straightening up, Thorvald found himself looking directly into the eyes of the warrior who had, inarguably, been the outright victor in this contest. Hogni's face was an alarming shade of crimson; sweat streamed down his broad brow. He was beaming.

"Not a bad trick, that," he observed, putting out a large hand. "Not bad at all for a runt of an incomer. Couldn't hold it, though, could you?"

Thorvald shook the hand; even after that bout, Hogni's grip was crushingly strong. "Ah, well," he said, grinning back, "there'll be other chances. I don't suppose you'd teach me that lock you used on me the other night, would you?"

As the sun slipped down toward the margin of sky and sea, Keeper sharpened his spears: heart of ancient tree, laid at his feet by ocean's giving hands; splinter of bone, carven from a great, dead giant of the deep, taken with a prayer. Some were iron-tipped, wrenched from the bodies of those who would sully his shore and steal the precious thing he guarded. Small One feared the smell of iron; while Keeper scraped away, smoothing the metal, the other watched from between the stones, a pair of bright eyes in the shadows.

"It is not the spear that kills," Keeper said. "Man's hands kill, holding the spear. Only tools, these."

Small One made no answer; his was a different kind of wisdom. Over the years, Keeper had learned to touch the edge of it, no more than that. He understood, at best, the mystery of Small One's gift, and the peril it carried with it.

The spears were propped in a line against the moss-cloaked rock wall; the setting sun touched them with a blood-red gleam. He had prepared them lovingly, to make of each death an act of cleansing, a sacrament, a cry of truth. Thus had he sworn, long ago, and he would keep faith until the day he died.

In the shadows, Small One shivered.

"Come," Keeper said. "Fire; food." He held out a hand, encouraging, and after a little, the other crept forth and came to wait by the fire pit, still trembling in sudden bursts, as if shaken by some unseen force. Keeper stirred the embers, remade the fire; the fish he had caught at first light lay ready, weed-wrapped, beside the flat cooking stones.

As dusk fell, the flames set a warmth on Small One's anxious features, and the shivering ceased. Under his breath, Small One began to hum, and the fire burned deep ocean green, and summer sky blue, and dark as the flank of an ancient whale. The stones grew hot. When they were ready, Keeper set the fish to cook on top, covered with ash and earth. The hum grew slowly to a song. The sky dimmed, and against the gray of the spring night faint stars appeared, distant, solitary, sweet as the notes Small One threw up to them, call and echo, question and dazzling, perfect answer.

SIX

Three eggs today: a bountiful harvest.
After breakfast, this slow calligraphy.
Memory stirs, cruel as a knife.

MONK'S MARGIN NOTE

Some days, the Journey flowed under her fingers, so that it seemed to make itself. If she squeezed her eyes almost shut, she could see its figures moving, changing, living a life of their own within the confines of its narrow borders, its dyed-wool landscape, and yet possessing a freedom beyond that offered to folk who walked their way on solid earth and breathed plain air. Some days, she was too dispirited to attempt so much as the threading of a single bone needle, the fashioning of a solitary stitch.

They hadn't come. Asgrim had promised, and they hadn't come. Creidhe knew she was behaving like a child thwarted of some long-anticipated treat, but she could not shrug off the gloom that had settled over her, nor the anger that went with it. Asgrim had been kind to her, taking time from his busy day to sit down and tell her everything Thorvald had been doing: rebuilding walls knocked down by winter storm, helping ferry much-needed supplies to isolated communities, digging drains. That had made her smile; Thorvald possessed a certain sense of his own importance and was not known to be especially forthcoming where he felt himself overqualified for a task. Such hard and basic work would be good for him.

Their piece of wood was already more than earned, Asgrim had assured her, and the young men simply helping with some final duties before returning to collect her and tend to the *Sea Dove*. They had made themselves well liked with their easy manner and general willingness. Both had mentioned her often, with evident concern and obvious affection. Asgrim had undertaken to let them know she was quite well and perfectly safe. A pity she had had to witness what she did with Jofrid; it was a difficulty caused by the other tribe, a scourge and a sadness, but not something visitors need concern themselves with. The Long Knife people were used to it. Some day they would find a solution. She must forget that, put it behind her. It could be no more than two days, at most three, before Thorvald and Sam returned, Asgrim had said. Creidhe would be doing him a personal favor if she would keep Jofrid company for that small time, and perhaps stay on while her young friends were mending their boat. Gudrun would like that, too, and the other women. They had become fond of her.

So she had waited, two days, three, walking to the western end of the settlement each morning, eyes scouring the hillside in vain for signs of life beyond straggle-coated sheep and scrawny goats. Asgrim departed, on his way back to wherever they were; his bodyguard, a very large man, padded silently at his side. This fellow had looked Creidhe up and down thoroughly and expertly with his small eyes, as if she were a prize heifer or likely breeding sow, until Gudrun scolded him out of her cottage. Now he was gone, and the Ruler with him, and it was not two days or three, but seven, nine, fifteen, another full turning of the moon, and Thorvald still did not come back. Sitting in the workroom, plying distaff and spindle as Jofrid combed the fleece in preparation, Creidhe was forced to recognize what it was she felt. Thorvald had not met up to her expectations. He had been unkind to her, and to Sam. They were both used to that; it happened often, and could be excused because Thorvald did not understand how it made them feel. He had left her behind. She could forgive that as well; Sam had known how ill at ease she was, his concern could be seen in his eyes, but Thorvald had believed her blithe assurances that she didn't mind a bit. This time, however, Thorvald's selfishness could not be explained away. She had tried to do just that; indeed, she realized how many times she had made excuses for him, had justified what he did, simply so she could go on believing him perfect. The days passed and Thorvald stayed away. Yet he was free to return: Asgrim had told her so. That could only mean one thing. Thorvald didn't care a bit how she felt. Indeed, he probably hadn't given her a single thought since he walked away that morning with his staff in his hand and his eyes fixed on his personal quest. Not only did he disregard Creidhe herself, but her whole family, and Sam's livelihood, and everyone who waited, back in Hrossey, to know if the three of them lived or died. What about Margaret? Had he spared any thought for her, for the pain and guilt she might be feeling, knowing that it was her action that had sparked this journey? Creidhe was forced to reassess Thorvald, and the result left her somewhat dissatisfied, not just with the object of her affections, but with herself as well.

"You look angry," Jofrid said softly, easing the oily tangle of uncarded wool through the wide comb.

Creidhe set the spindle turning, drew the twist of fiber between her fingers. The good thing about spinning was that, once you had the knack of it, you didn't need to think; your hands simply went ahead and did the work.

"Not angry, just a bit sad. I want to go home. I don't understand why Thorvald and Sam aren't here."

A flicker of expression crossed Jofrid's pale features, and died. Jofrid had barely begun to talk, so long after that terrible night of loss. Her voice was an apologetic whisper, her whole demeanor one of exhausted defeat. She clung to Creidhe's side like a wan shadow. It had become habit for the two of them to work together in the mornings; for Creidhe to sit in Jofrid's cottage and sew in the afternoons, while Jofrid tended to her stock, or sometimes just sat in silence, watching. Returning to Gudrun's for supper and sleep had become a relief. Big, dour Gudrun had mellowed somewhat; there was a reluctant kindness in her terse comments, her attempts at special cookery.

"I'm sorry," Creidhe went on, talking more to herself than Jofrid. "It seems selfish to fuss about such things, I know. I didn't expect to be away so long, that's all. I miss my family." She could see them as if they were right there before her: Eyvind striding up and down, wracked with worry and guilt, though her plight was none of his doing; he would believe he had somehow failed in his fatherly duties to let such a disaster occur. Nessa quiet with Ingigerd in her arms, holding her concern inside as always, looking for signs in fire and water, seeking her inner wisdom for answers. Brona, trying to do all her own tasks as well as Creidhe's, and biting her nails to the quick over Sam. Aunt Margaret, Creidhe's second mother, standing stern and silent on the steps of her house, gazing out to the west. Ash would be in the background somewhere, maintaining a faithful watch over her. "I miss them terribly."

Jofrid bowed her head, apparently intent on her task. She laid a handful of carded wool in the basket at Creidhe's elbow; between the two of them they had prepared enough twist this morning to make a good start on a blanket or a warm tunic for one of the men.

"Jofrid?"

There was no reply; Creidhe had not expected one.

"Have you a husband? Is he away with Asgrim's men?" Creidhe had not tried this direct question before; now seemed as good a time as any.

A nod. Jofrid's hands stilled, the soft, teased-out wool like thistledown between them.

"What's his name?"

"Wieland," Jofrid whispered, making a little sigh of the name, a small sadness.

"Is he a fisherman?"

"Not anymore," Jofrid said. "He is a warrior now." A moment later, a single tear rolled down her cheek. "He—" Her voice cracked; more tears fell, and she put her hands up over her face.

"Oh—I'm sorry, I didn't—" Creidhe began, but as soon as it had started, the moment was over. Jofrid scrubbed a hand across her cheeks, took up the comb again and retreated back into silence.

After that, Creidhe swallowed her frustration a while and went on waiting as late spring turned to early summer and the lambs on the hillside grew sturdier. There was no news at all from Thorvald and Sam. As for Brother Niall and his fellows, she had seen no more of them; she supposed Asgrim had forbidden them access to the settlement at Brightwater. She thought, herself, that the women would have welcomed such voices of calm and common sense among them. Maybe Breccan's prayers had been powerless to hold off those voices of death, but they could at least provide solace. When it came to such times of loss and grief, Creidhe thought it mattered little which gods one believed in, which faith one adhered to. Anything was good, as long as it helped.

As time passed, it seemed to Creidhe that the women were growing accustomed to her presence, almost as if she were one of them, and because of that she began to hear things that were not intended for her ears, scraps of conversation that worried her. At first she dismissed them. She was lonely, upset, disappointed with Thorvald. She was overreacting. All the same, being her father's daughter, Creidhe had learned how to listen, and the more she listened, the more a sense of dread, of dark secrets and dangerous shadows, began to creep over her.

Gudrun, clanking pots on the fire, talking to Helga as Creidhe was changing her shoes in the inner room: *good little thing . . . seems a shame really . . .* and Helga's response, a sudden hissing, *Shh . . .*

Frida, invited to share their meal on another evening, silently chewing the overboiled mutton and watching Creidhe with her beady, inimical eyes. Ale poured later; a joke shared with Gudrun, something about the size of men's noses, that had them all laughing, all but Frida whose shriveled lips never so much as attempted a smile. Then later, words overheard as Frida donned her shawl and Gudrun opened the door for her: *careful . . . too friendly . . . just makes it harder . . .*

Helga, in the workroom one sunny morning, and Creidhe offering her help with weaving. There was a much more efficient way to beat the weft threads up, a particular grip on the whalebone weaving-sword, a flick of the wrists that was easy to master, once someone showed you. Creidhe demonstrated: the threads aligned themselves, perfectly even and regular. She watched as Helga did it, once to try, twice to be sure; she congratulated her on her quickness to learn.

Helga beamed. "Oh, thank you. You're such a clever girl, Creidhe, and so kind, it seems a pity—" She blushed crimson and turned away.

"What seems a pity?" Creidhe asked quietly. All of a sudden, the room had gone very still.

"That you won't be staying," put in Gudrun from where she sat on her stool, spinning. "That you'll be off as soon as your young men get back."

It was a logical answer. But Creidhe knew it was not the one Helga had come close to blurting out. There was something afoot, something they were not saying, and it had to do with her. She wished Asgrim would come back so she could ask him straight out.

Then, at a time when the air was growing appreciably warmer at last, with a hint of real summer in it, they presented her with a gift. It was a gown of finest wool, not made on these islands, she suspected, but borne to this shore from far away and set aside for some special purpose. These women had neither the ability nor the tools for such delicate work. It was palest cream in color, with a narrow green border to neckline and hemline, embroidered with little flowers and birds: both skill and love had gone into its making. The sleeves were narrow, the skirt fell in graceful folds from a wide girdle. There were green ribbons for the hair, to set off the trim. It was a lovely thing, and entirely inappropriate as a gift.

"I can't take this," Creidhe said flatly. "It's like a—a wedding dress. You must save it for one of your own, your daughters . . ." She faltered. This settlement had few daughters; the pair of lads, the awkward, squinting girl made up its full complement of children. "You must not waste such a precious garment on me," she went on, "though I thank you for your generosity—"

"Take it," said Gudrun, sounding almost angry. "Try it on. You'll look bonny in it, with your yellow hair and all."

"When your young man comes back," put in Helga, "wouldn't he like to see you in such a gown?"

"Go on, lass," said Gudrun.

Creidhe was pushed and prodded through into the sleeping quarters, and found it impossible to refuse their polite, insistent requests to undress and put the gown on. The fit was not bad, the bodice a little tight, the waist a little loose, but comfortable enough. Now that she was doing as they wished, the others had retreated; Jofrid remained, combing Creidhe's hair, tying in the ribbons, stroking the folds of the skirt so they fell more cleanly from the girdle. It was a

strange fashion, showing somewhat more of the figure than
was considered respectable at home. Even for dancing,
Creidhe and Brona always wore gown and overdress, properly pinned, or the straight skirt and long tunic that were
the traditional garb of their mother's people. This was
more like a nightrobe, low-necked, clinging at breasts and
hips, a garment she had absolutely no intention of wearing
in front of Thorvald and Sam, though it would have been
interesting to see their faces. She stared at herself in the
dull bronze of Gudrun's mirror; her face gazed back, dimly
candlelit, shadowy, worried eyes in a pale oval. Her hair
was a haze of gold, falling across her shoulders and down
her back unbound. Jofrid stood behind her like an anxious
wraith.

"Creidhe."

Jofrid's whisper was so soft, Creidhe thought at first
she'd imagined it: tiny and intense, a breath of danger.

"What?" she whispered back.

"You must go away. In the morning. Go."

"What?" Shock made her voice louder.

"Shh!" Jofrid hissed. "Not safe. You must not stay here."

Creidhe's heart was thumping. She opened her mouth to
ask, what is not safe, where must I go, but the moment was
past. Jofrid, hearing the others coming, had lapsed back
into silence; she moved the comb steadily through
Creidhe's long hair, smoothing the shining strands, her eyes
once more blank of expression. It was as if nothing at all
had happened.

Creidhe allowed herself to be admired, petted, fussed
over. She submitted to the twining of more ribbons in the
hair, the small adjustments to the dress, the presentation of
a pair of soft slippers deemed more appropriate than her
workaday shoes. It became apparent that refusal of the
gown would not be allowed; reluctantly, she accepted it,
knowing that she could never wear such a garment, save
perhaps in the privacy of her own bedchamber, to laugh
about with Brona. In this outpost, among these grim folk,
to dress in such extravagant clothing was to single oneself
out as different, special, and she could see no reason at all

for that. When every detail was to their liking, the women stood about and admired her, with little comments about how kind she had been, how helpful, how clever, and how pleased they were to be able to thank her thus. Jofrid wasn't saying anything now; she stared at the ground or into the corner, as if she were pretending to be somewhere else. But after it was over, and Creidhe was permitted to remove her finery and fold it away neatly, Jofrid looked at her from the doorway, and in Jofrid's shadowed eyes the message was once more stark and plain: *Go! Go now, or it will be too late.*

Creidhe passed a sleepless night, trying to set her mind in order while her heart drummed in panic and her body ran with cold sweat. In the pre-dawn she rose in silence. Across the small chamber, Gudrun still snored under her coverlet; the ale had flowed generously last night, and with luck the woman would sleep later than usual. Creidhe packed her bag. There was not time to find everything, but she stuffed in what she could: her knife, her sewing things, a shawl, the comb Sam had made for her, and into the pocket on the outside, the closely furled roll of the Journey. Then, sheepskin boots in one hand, bag on her shoulder, she tiptoed out to the main room of the cottage, where the fire lay in cold ashes and the merest sliver of gray light could be seen through the chinks and cracks around the door. This was all in the timing, and the ability to keep quiet. For all she was a girl, and not destined for life as hunter or warrior, Creidhe had learned a thing or two growing up in her father's household. For such a big man, Eyvind had an uncanny knack of moving swift as a shadow, silent as a hawk, when there was the need for it. Creidhe had learned, as well, how to watch and listen, how best to seize an advantage. She slipped the bolts on Gudrun's front door, opened and closed it without a sound, set rocks in place to stop it from swinging and banging. Hood up over her hair, she stood by the wall, every sense alert for danger. The place was quiet; no dog stirred, no bird sang yet in salute to the rising sun, though it was light, the traces of first day a sensation of pallor somewhere beyond the blanket of damp that clung low around the houses. If there were men set to guard the settlement today, they were nowhere to be seen. At such a time, on such a morning, it was probable they sat by a fire somewhere, warming their hands and sharing a flask of ale and a mutton chop or two. One could only hope.

The first part was easy, mist or no mist. She had passed this way daily in rain or shine since her first arrival in Brightwater. Soft-footed as a ghost, Creidhe slipped past cottage and outhouse, pigpen and fowl run, up to the place where a stile in the stone dike marked the end of her permitted territory, the border of forbidden land. She glanced behind her. Down the track, shreds of mist cloaked Gudrun's dwelling, the communal craft hut, the cottages of Jofrid and Helga. Creidhe hitched up her skirts and clambered over the wall by the straggling vegetable patch. A bird sang suddenly, high above, in confident recognition of morning. Creidhe drew a deep breath, feeling the moisture in the chill air, sensing something odd in her heart, fear maybe, mingled with an awareness of freedom that went far beyond the fact of leaving the small settlement, silent women and half-spoken secrets. She could not capture it yet, not quite: it beat within her, strong but elusive, beautiful and dangerous. Beyond a doubt, this feeling was akin to the vision that had seized her that morning on the cliff path, something wondrous, powerful and ineffably sad. What it was, she did not know; she knew only a profound gratitude that it still lived, somewhere inside her. Shifting her bag higher on her back, Creidhe set her steps forward and began to stride up the valley, away from Brightwater. In time the morning mist lifted, and the squint-eyed girl drove her geese out to forage. By then there was nothing to be seen on the hillside beyond the settlement but the pale, slow forms of grazing sheep.

"She's not here." Brother Niall spoke calmly, lying with a practiced ease that sat at odds with tonsure and habit. "Not a sign of her, and Colm's been outside all morning digging the vegetable patch. He'd have seen Creidhe if she passed by. I did tell the boys when they came up looking. Now you've climbed all this way for nothing."

The two lads had appeared at the hermitage around midday, breathing hard, and had been sent on their way again with a brief answer and a drink of water. Now Gudrun herself had made her way along the valley and up the hill, redfaced, sweating, with a note of real fear in her voice.

"Where else would she go?" she panted. "She must have come this way."

Brother Niall spread his hands in a gesture indicating helpless perplexity. Funny, that, thought Creidhe as she stood very still, watching through the crack in the inner door of this small, neat dwelling. She'd never known a man who seemed less helpless, except her father.

"I can't imagine," said Brother Niall. "I do understand your concern. One's mind tends to play tricks at such a time. Let us hope Creidhe has merely gone wandering along the lake shore, or into the fields to pick flowers. Girls will do these things. Of course, she may have attempted the path back to Blood Bay. And we all know the danger for a girl of walking alone by the sea. I'm afraid it may already be too late. Asgrim's not going to be happy."

Gudrun wrung her hands. Creidhe had never seen her like this, not even on the night of the voices. The large, capable woman seemed at her wits' end.

"You're very welcome to join us at prayer," put in Brother Breccan from the far end of the chamber where he stood at a table that held scrolls of parchment, soapstone pots of ink, quills in a jar. "God may have answers for you. A little quiet reflection can provide great comfort to the troubled spirit."

By all the ancestors, he was as bad as Niall: bare-faced dissemblers, the two of them. Creidhe watched in silence as Gudrun scowled at the hermits and peered into the corners of the hut as if to seek proof that they were tricking her.

"As you see," offered Brother Niall in mild, kindly tones, "there are just the two of us here, and Colm out in the fields somewhere. If you like I'll call him in so you can ask him yourself. Unless you wish to inspect the sleeping quarters of a household of three men, all of them sworn to celibacy in God's service?" He lifted his brows. *Don't say yes,* Creidhe willed Gudrun. If the woman took one step through this inner door, Creidhe would be in plain view. This white-haired hermit certainly seemed to enjoy taking risks.

Gudrun growled a response in which Creidhe could discern the name Asgrim, then turned on her heel and headed off down the hillside. It was a long walk back to Brightwater, and by no means an easy one. They waited in silence. After a carefully judged interval Brother Breccan moved to close the front door, a massive, heavy thing that had perhaps once been part of an ocean-going vessel, for it was studded with rivets in unlikely places.

"Oh dear," observed Brother Niall as Creidhe came forth from her hiding place and resumed her seat by the table. He fetched a jug from the stone shelves at the far end of the room, filled a cup, set it before her. "Trouble does seem to follow you, doesn't it?"

"I'm sorry," she said. She had explained herself already, the reasons for her sudden, unannounced arrival, the way her disquiet in the settlement had grown to a real fear. Remembering Brother Niall's veiled warnings and his offers of help, she had hoped they might take her in. Here, surely she would be safe. Folk did not harm men of faith, nor those whom they sheltered. The brothers had received her calmly, heard what she had to say, fed her vegetable broth and warm flat bread. While she was eating—the hard walk had brought back the appetite that had deserted her in recent times—Breccan had made a few adjustments to the sleeping arrangements in the cottage. Colm would share the outhouse with the cow and calf, he'd announced blithely; it was the warmest place anyway, and a good lesson in humility besides. He and Niall would spread their blankets here in the outer chamber, leaving the sleeping quarters to their guest. Creidhe had begun a protest, but after the walk she'd been weary enough to drop, though it was not yet midday, and she had fallen asleep on one of the hard shelf-beds the instant she lay down. She'd been not long awake when Gudrun had come rapping at the door. Now Gudrun was gone, but others might come; and she realized, sitting here beside these quiet men, with the late afternoon sun streaming in warm and golden between open shutters, that on no account was she going to return to Brightwater, not for Gudrun, not for Asgrim, not for anyone.

"Don't be sorry," Breccan said. "Our home is open to you; you are safe here."

Niall made no comment.

"It's only until the others get back," Creidhe put in quickly. "Not long; Asgrim said—" She fell silent.

"Asgrim said two days, I seem to remember." Niall's tone was thoughtful. "That was some time ago. I'm afraid, my dear, that the Ruler may have plans for your friends, plans that will keep them by his side until midsummer at least."

Creidhe was horrified. "What plans? He said they'd already earned what they need. He said they were coming back."

"Yes," agreed Niall. "The Ruler says many things, and every one of them with a purpose."

"A pox on him!" Creidhe rose to her feet, fists clenched. "I'll just walk on over there and find them, that's what I'll do. I'm sick of these rules: cover your hair, stay in the settlement, don't ask awkward questions. Thorvald and Sam should come back; folk need us at home."

"Did you ask anyone why?" Niall's voice was soft. "Why cover your hair? Why not walk about freely?"

Creidhe gave him a cross glance. "Of course I asked. But nobody would tell me anything. I suppose it's to do with the—the spirits, the voices, whatever it is the other tribe sends that does such evil work. I'm not afraid of them." Now she was the one who was lying; she was deeply afraid, but for the moment her anger was stronger. "I'm going to go and find Thorvald and Sam, and nobody's going to stop me."

"Mmm." Niall regarded her levelly, his dark eyes assessing. "Not today, though. You wouldn't get there before dark, and if you want to avoid Brightwater, you need to take the steep track. That can be treacherous, even when your shoes fit properly." He glanced at Brother Breccan, and Breccan moved to busy himself over at the hearth. "I can provide answers to some of your questions, Creidhe. Guesswork, maybe, but informed by my years of living on the islands, close to both Asgrim's tribe and the other. I think, really, it would be wise to learn what you can, before——"

Creidhe grimaced. "Before I go rushing off trying to change the world?" She sat down, folding her hands on the table before her. Its stone surface was scrubbed shining clean; the pens and inks, the sheets of parchment lay in orderly fashion at its far end, ready for a scholar's touch. "You're right, of course; I'm behaving like Thorvald, dashing into the fray without studying the lay of the land." That was exactly what Thorvald had done, she thought, when he had followed Asgrim away from Brightwater. Though he had said nothing to her, he had already decided the Ruler was his father; she had seen it in his eyes. Perhaps he was right. By now he would know one way or the other. There was a simple means of ruling people out, one that required no questions at all. "My father would be ashamed of me," she added.

"Would he? Well, then, let us do this as he would wish it done, calmly and carefully. Myself, I have learned the great value of foreknowledge; one cannot defeat an enemy one does not understand. Unfortunately, Asgrim has never grasped that. So the situation grows ever more tenuous for the Long Knife people, season by season. These folk deserve better."

Breccan had taken a bucket and gone out, closing the door firmly behind him. Of the boy, Colm, there had been no sign save a head ducked in the window earlier, and a bit of bread and cheese passed out with a few explanatory words. Breccan had gone to warn him, perhaps, in case anyone else came searching.

"We have a few days at least," Niall said, perhaps seeing something of her anxiety in her face. "He will know where you are; he and I have a long history. He will anticipate my keeping you here, out of his way; he won't rush back. Asgrim's busy. He's getting his forces ready for the hunt. At this precise moment, I'm informed he's preparing to sail your boat around from Blood Bay to his encampment for a bit of refurbishment. I would suspect he has a particular job in mind for this vessel. Asgrim has plenty to occupy him for now. Nonetheless, we must be ready for him. That means, I'm afraid, that you are still within prison walls of a kind. You'll have to stay indoors until we decide what to do."

"Oh." Perhaps, after all, she had made a terrible mistake. Perhaps they were not Christian monks in the mold of peace-loving Brother Tadhg at all. This one still wore a dagger; she had seen his hand move to its hilt when Gudrun hammered on the door. She had seen him adjust his robe later, to conceal the bright metal.

"Not good, I know. You are an active girl, I suspect. You made the walk here in remarkably good time."

"At home I'm used to walking to my Aunt Margaret's house every day so we can work together. Sometimes I ride; it's a fair way. I hate being cooped up." She flushed. "I'm sorry, that sounds terribly ungrateful. Please, do tell me what you can about all this. I'm so worried about Thorvald, he gets caught up in an idea sometimes and forgets everything else. He can't really look after himself very well. And Sam's just a fisherman, and expects everyone else to be as honest as he is. That's why—"

Niall gave a half-smile. "That's why you came with them?"

"Well, yes. I suppose it sounds rather silly, but it seemed to me they needed someone—" She faltered again.

"Someone who could see the situation from outside and come up with answers? Not this time, I fear. The three of you have walked into a web that is dark, complex and very old, a struggle that has come close to annihilating all who live here, both Long Knife people and Unspoken. And, sad to say, because of what you are, it will be no simple matter to extricate you."

"What we are?" Creidhe echoed, not understanding.

Niall reached across and took a strand of her hair between his fingers, twisting the bright gold gently. "Not the others, just you. They bade you cover your hair with good reason. Asgrim's daughter had such a head of hair, fair and shining as ripe wheat. Asgrim's daughter was stolen for her golden hair, stolen and borne away by the tribesmen of the Unspoken. She was used by each of them in turn, over the nights from one full moon to the next. Thus does the tribe make a child, a very special child, whose conception and birth are integral to their lore. They call this one Foxmask, a powerful visionary, their priest and wise man. Such a child can be born only of a maiden who is sun and moon in one being: hair like rays of morning light, skin white as moonbeams on snow."

Creidhe stared at him aghast. "His daughter? How terrible! What happened to her?" But she seemed to know the answer already; it was in the gravity of his austere features, the careful neutrality of the eyes.

"She died; she was a young thing, perhaps thirteen when they took her. Younger than you, Creidhe. The Unspoken had been without a seer for some years, since the old one died. They were in turmoil; they require this kind of guidance to maintain their order, their whole pattern of being. Without it, they are like a sharp axe in the hands of a crazy man, striking at random, as ready to destroy a friend as an enemy. You've heard their wild music; you've seen what damage it can inflict. They did not use their powers thus when Foxmask dwelt among them. The girl served her purpose: her death would have meant little. She was merely a vessel for them."

Beneath her outrage, Creidhe was thinking hard. "Golden hair, all right, I suppose I have to cover up because they might see me, because I might be at risk of—abduction." She shivered, recoiling from the image of it: that little girl all alone among those monsters, her whole world destroyed. Herself, perhaps taken and used the same way . . . It was disgusting, impossible. Such things just didn't happen. "Why only me?" she challenged, hearing the shrill note of fear in her own voice. "Why don't all the women have to

cover up? And how do you know all this anyway? I thought
the three of you were banned from the settlement."

"As to that," Niall said, "we are unwelcome in Asgrim's
domain, that much is true. But I've been here many years,
Creidhe, since well before these troubles began. There was
a time in these isles when men plied their trades without
fear; when folk traveled freely from settlement to settlement and spoke openly of their business. In those days,
Long Knife people and Unspoken met yearly for a council.
Hard to believe now, but true. Latterly, the information has
come through Asgrim himself, for only he can speak with
the enemy now, and that with some difficulty, I gather. My
young messengers, bringers of fish and news, keep me up to
date, and they don't tell tales at the other end. You ask, *Why
only me?* Fair-haired women are rare in these isles. In all
the time I have been here, Sula and yourself have been the
only two young girls with such a head of hair. Your mother,
I expect, had her origins in some land far to the east: Norway, perhaps."

Creidhe managed a smile. "My mother is one of the old
race in the Light Isles: a dark-haired woman, and slightly
built. You know that already. It is my father who has the
butter-yellow locks and the eyes like pieces of sky."

He did not reply. There was a quill in the jar by his side,
and he took it out and rolled it between his fingers absently.

"You are a scribe? A draftsman?" Creidhe asked, trying
to fix her mind on something normal, to reassure herself
this was not some living nightmare. She had wondered at
the tools of scholarship set out here; they seemed incongruous in the brutal, ungiving landscape of these far isles.

For a moment she thought he was not going to answer.
Then he put the pen down and said, "All three of us practice
this craft, in one way or another. It passes the time. You
read?"

"Oh no. I would like to, of course; Thorvald can read, his
mother taught him, and I wanted to learn, but I don't seem
to have the knack for it. Aunt Margaret said it didn't matter,
that I put my talent into the other things I do. But it would

be very fine to be able to make my name; to cipher, and to scribe."

"Other things? What are these other things Aunt Margaret values, Creidhe?"

She was blushing again: stupid. "Girls' pursuits. Spinning, weaving, embroidery. Cooking and midwifery. Looking after children, and teaching them. Thorvald thinks those things aren't important, but they are. They have to be. They are the heart of a community, they hold it all together . . ." She was babbling; what interest could he possibly have in this?

"You have some handiwork with you?"

"Yes. But I don't show it. Not usually."

His smile was guarded; something had set a constraint between them. "Nor I mine, Creidhe. We are both slow to trust, and rightly so. Perhaps, when we know each other better, we may work side by side. Now it grows late and I think the others are returning; perhaps there will be eggs."

"Oh—but you didn't finish! What about Asgrim, and the boys—why is he keeping them there, and how—?"

The door rattled and opened, admitting Breccan and Colm. The latter shot a glance at Creidhe, then retreated to the fireside, milk pail in one hand and egg basket in the other. Creidhe supposed he was still young enough to find the presence of a woman at close quarters disturbing; the others, by dint of age or discipline, seemed to have no trouble with it. The cowshed would probably be a blessing for Colm, judging by the way he was looking at her under his lashes like a bashful suitor.

"As I said," Niall folded his arms casually, "we do have a few days, and with the restriction on outdoor activities, plenty of time to talk. And you need more food and more sleep. Let us come at this slowly. There is layer upon layer here, and not all are so easily unfolded. Ah, four eggs today. The hens must have seen you coming."

"I'm going back," declared Sam, testing his weight on the heavily bandaged ankle and wincing in pain. The injury was taking a long time to heal; maybe something was broken after all. "I'm going if I have to crawl there. This is just ridiculous. I want my boat, I want to see Creidhe, and I want to get home. Since the Ruler's not here, I needn't ask permission, need I? Or is it you I'm supposed to ask, since you seem to have set yourself up as leader in his absence?" He glowered at Thorvald and hobbled another step along the shore. The two of them were alone; on the higher ground by the shelter, the men were engaged in mock battle under Hogni's supervision. Thorvald had moved them on from one-to-one bouts, and now they rehearsed the possible flows of a real skirmish, eight men attacking, eight defending, the rest observing. By midsummer they would be ready; he would make sure of it.

"Leader?" Thorvald lifted his brows. "Hardly, I'm what they call an incomer, after all. I merely share what little knowledge I have. You've seen what they're like, Sam. They'd have been sitting targets in this battle. The least I can do is give them a bit of help."

"Mmm. You lap it up, though, don't you? Being treated like you're someone special, the hero that'll see them through and solve all their problems? I don't know about you, Thorvald, I really don't."

"Anyway," Thorvald said, finding himself more than a little rattled, though Sam's comments were nonsense, of course, "you know you can't walk more than six or seven steps on that foot without falling in a heap. You know you'd never make it over to Blood Bay, especially not with a load of wood on your back. I presume that was the plan, since there's a certain question of boat-mending to be addressed. You know I can't go back yet. These men depend on me. Without my help they stand to be beaten yet again: beaten, maimed, killed and sent back into despair until this enemy wipes out every last one of them. You expect me to let that happen when I can do something to prevent it? Try to look past your own concerns, Sam. This is far bigger than you and me and the *Sea Dove*." It was so big, in fact, that it had begun to consume his thoughts, night and day. In the Light Isles, the closest he had come to influencing men, to making decisions of any importance, was in joining the debate when invited to councils with his mother. His contributions, while always received with respect, had been at best peripheral. It had never been possible to believe himself essential to any discussion, to any endeavor. He had never been part of a venture in which life and death hung in the balance; he had never had men depending on him. This was vital. He could almost believe he had been sent to do this.

Sam set his jaw obstinately. He had given up the attempt to walk and stood leaning on the length of driftwood he used for support. "What about Creidhe?" he challenged. "Forgotten her, have you, in your quest to impress this father of yours?"

Sudden anger seized Thorvald. He lifted his hand as if to deliver a blow, and lowered it at the look in Sam's eyes. "Hold your tongue!" he snapped. Then he made himself draw a deep breath. A leader does not lose control so easily, and he was a leader here, for all his denials. In that, Sam had been quite correct. The men turned to Thorvald increasingly for guidance and encouragement, and he saw a flowering in them, both of skills and of hope. "Creidhe came here by her own choice," he said, forcing his voice calm. "You know that. There is no reason why she should not wait for us a little longer. Provided we sail before the autumn storms, we can reach home safely. A passage across to the Northern Isles, I think, then a cautious trip down to Hrossey. There'll be plenty of time." Creidhe could wait. His mother could wait. This was a quest, a challenge bold and real.

"You'll do what you want, of course," Sam muttered. "Don't you always? But you won't make me do it, not this time. I have a bad feeling, and it's got to do with Asgrim, and this whole hunt business, and Creidhe as well. Soon as this leg's fit for it, I'm off back over there, and if you're not ready by the time the *Sea Dove* is, we're going home without you."

Thorvald smiled thinly. "That'll be cozy, just the two of you." It hurt somewhat that Sam did not support him, that

Sam could not comprehend the magnitude of what he was doing here, the huge significance of it. Win this summer's battle, retrieve Foxmask at last, and he would deliver the long-sought peace and freedom that Asgrim craved for his tribe. Surely no boat, no girl was more important than that?

"Blind, are you?" growled Sam, turning away. Thorvald had no idea what he meant, and no inclination to ask. The injury, the forced inaction, had turned Sam rather odd; his sunny, equable disposition had been replaced by ill temper and restless brooding. Well, that was Sam's problem, not his. Asgrim would be back again soon, his latest trip merely to check outposts and call in a few more men to swell the number Thorvald was training at the camp. He must ensure that when the Ruler returned, they had something to show him.

As their trust in Thorvald had grown, the men had begun to talk more openly, and he had learned enough about the nature of the coming battle, and the terrain on which it must be fought, to narrow his strategies to those appropriate to such challenging conditions. What was the size of the enemy forces? Big: they came from everywhere, appearing and vanishing at will. Last summer they had accounted for many of Asgrim's men before the broken remnant of the islanders' army had raced the Fool's Tide back to Council Fjord. So, this tribe had numbers, and they were well armed, resourceful and clever. They had the advantage of knowing the territory. The timing of the hunt? Two days if they were lucky; the boats would stand off the Isle of Clouds overnight, for the ground was treacherous even in full light, and there were presences. Not a man among them wanted his foot on that shore in darkness. Two days, and then home again, whatever the result; fail to cross over while the strange midsummer calm lulled the roiling currents of the Fool's Tide, and the sea would have them if the enemy did not. The terrain? A beast of a place, full of sudden, sheer drops, holes, cracks and caves. Not much cover, and the enemy knew every bit of it like the back of his hand. There were birds everywhere, the ground in some areas slick with their droppings, the air full of their screams and pecking beaks. They'd have young to protect; it was an additional hazard. Anything else he should know? Well, there was the mist, the drenching rain, the chill; there were the hands under the water, and the voices . . .

It was a kind of warfare in which organized formations, the wedge, the swine's head, were entirely inappropriate. He could have made use of Wolfskins. Fear of the enemy seemed a primary barrier to success here, and a small force of elite professionals would have served him well, not least those fanatical followers of Thor with their total disregard for self-preservation. It was interesting, Thorvald mused, to recall that Creidhe's father had once been such a fighter; indeed, although Eyvind was now more arbiter and family man than soldier, folk throughout the Light Isles still referred to him as "The Wolfskin," as if there had only ever been one. Well, there were no such warriors here; even the best of Asgrim's men still viewed the coming conflict either with trepidation or with a certain blank-eyed acceptance. Thorvald was working hard to change that. He had made it his task to get to know each man better, and to give each man a sense of purpose. It was starting to work. Einar had become a friend, and Skolli an ally. Wieland was more ready to share his own ideas than before, though he was still unnaturally somber.

Skapti had been a challenge. It had been necessary to set up a situation in which the second of the big guards, whom the men feared still more than his brother, Hogni, could be commended for his expertise, his own particular skills, and convinced that he was vital to the endeavor. Hogni himself had been helpful. Skapti, he told Thorvald quietly, had a deft touch for knife-throwing. There wasn't much call for such a skill here; brute force and minimal scruples were what Asgrim wanted from his guards. But Skapti was an artist with the knives.

Thorvald gave the men an afternoon off work and had them set up a competition, in which games of various kinds featured: wrestling, running, jumping and climbing, a race to haul up boats, escaping from bonds, and to crown the contest, the hurling of knives into a target. This was a wooden door on which was sketched the outline of a man, with his heart done in red clay. There were five points for the head, ten for the heart and one for a hit anywhere else on the body. With each round, Thorvald moved the target farther back.

In the final turn, only four throwers managed to hit the wooden man at all, two in the leg and one in the arm. Skapti's huge hands wielded his knives with delicate precision. He landed his missiles in a neat triangle, each of them piercing the small red heart. Thorvald congratulated him warmly and offered him a drink, and then another. By the end of the evening, he had persuaded the big warrior that the hunt's success would depend on Skapti's ability to teach the men all the tricks he knew, not just knives, but every kind of fighting in his considerable repertoire. If both Hogni and Skapti worked with him, Thorvald said, they'd have a first-rate band of warriors by midsummer.

Some of the men had glanced at Thorvald sideways; Skapti's history had little in it to commend him as a teacher, and they were thinking, no doubt, of the beatings that might ensue if they did not come up to standard. Thorvald ignored the looks.

"We need you, Skapti," he'd said at the end, with simple truth, for without this most formidable of warriors as an ally, the men must continue to work under the shadow of Asgrim's harsh authority. "Will you help us? Will you be part of this?"

Skapti, curiously hesitant, had spoken with unusual restraint. "You sure?" he queried, small eyes intent on Thorvald's. "Sure it's me you want and not some other fellow?"

"I am sure, Skapti. I trust you. Indeed, I don't think I can manage without you. What do you say?"

Skapti's ferocious grin, his crushing hand clasping Thorvald's, had been all the reply necessary. And Thorvald's confidence in him appeared well founded, for now. Both Hogni and Skapti delighted in their new roles as tutors in warcraft. All Thorvald needed was time. He just hoped there would be enough time.

Skapti and Hogni carried out their duties with little need for words. They knew their trade; had it not been so, Thorvald would not have trusted this to them. They had the men's respect already for their size and strength, a respect that would always be touched with fear, for these two had long been the instruments of Asgrim's rough justice, and there was no forgetting that.

Asgrim had a habit of staying a while, barking a sharp order or two, stalking about the encampment watching the men's endeavors and making them fumble with nervousness, then heading off again for two days, three, sometimes longer. He always took Skapti or Hogni with him, sometimes both. Of recent times, Hogni and Skapti had drawn straws to determine who would stay and who would go, and it was the loser who walked away at Asgrim's side, though they did not tell the Ruler so. Thorvald had put Hogni in charge of the daily mock-battle sessions, while Skapti had been given responsibility for ensuring each man, fishermen included, came up to a certain basic level of skill in both armed and unarmed combat. There were rewards for improvement: a better knife, a warmer blanket, the privilege of leading the after-supper singing, if singing it could be called. Thorvald had dredged from his memory a store of old sagas of heroic warriors and seductive women, fierce hill-trolls and menacing ice-giants, and passed them on as best he could. He encouraged the composing of more, and a certain element of competition arose, with Orm being the champion so far.

The Ruler's absences became more frequent, and lasted longer. It was whispered that he was trying to arrange a truce with the Unspoken. When in camp, he observed in silence, eyes narrowed, lips tight. He made no attempt to curb Thorvald's endeavors, nor did he praise them. At one point he suggested that Thorvald might as well make use of his hut while he was away; no need to waste a good bed. That seemed in itself indicative of a certain recognition. But

Thorvald said he would prefer to sleep alongside the men, and he meant it.

Even the fishermen were actively involved now. Today they were using the newly made shields to fend off the blows of the opposing team, trying to advance by sheer, stubborn persistence beyond a certain line marked out by a pair of iron posts driven into the hard earth. The defending team had thrusting spears. There were no practice weapons: those were a luxury this army could not afford, being poor in both wood and iron. Watching the press of bodies, hearing the shouting and the thud of spear point on shield, Thorvald only hoped Hogni would stop them before they really injured each other. Each man must play his part in the hunt: a couple would guard the boats when they got there, and the rest move out across the Isle of Clouds. Using every farmer, every fisherman, he could muster a fighting force of twenty-seven men. He'd send Hogni and Skapti in with a group each, and Einar would lead the rest, with Orm or Wieland by his side. Each of them had shown certain qualities suggestive of leadership. If they kept their nerve, the chances of overrunning the enemy were better than good. Finding Foxmask and taking him alive would be his own task.

Sam was squatting down on the rocks now, big and awkward, and fiddling with the cloth that bound his damaged foot.

"What are you doing?" asked Thorvald. "Don't take it off. You're supposed to keep the salve on and keep it covered—"

"I've had enough of it," Sam said heavily, unrolling the stained length of bandage. "I've had enough of the whole thing. Let's try a dunking in plain seawater and some fresh air. Never did me any harm before." He sat on a flat rock and lowered the swollen, reddened foot into a small pool that lay like a round basin there, reflecting today's sunny sky. They had had few days of real summer; one would not be drawn to these isles by their climate, though the fishing was unsurpassed. "I'm doing things for myself from now on," Sam said. "If that fellow Asgrim gives me orders I don't like, I'll tell him no. Ruler he may be, but he's no chieftain of mine. I want out, Thorvald."

"Yes, you've made that extremely clear." Thorvald's voice was tight. "Sam?"

"What?"

"You should do as you're asked. You should be part of this. We need every able-bodied man."

"Able-bodied?" Sam queried, studying his foot which lay among the clinging shellfish and fronds of fine-leafed weed like a bloated sea creature.

"That will mend before midsummer. Don't desert me, Sam, I need you. Think how it will look to the others if you walk off. And don't defy Asgrim. That really wouldn't be sensible at all."

"That a threat, is it?"

"You can take it however you like. Folk don't disobey him and get away with it, that's all. You know that, you told me yourself."

"I know he's cruel," Sam said. "The man's got no heart."

"That's not fair. These are extreme circumstances, and he acts as he thinks he must to maintain discipline among his men. These fellows are not warriors. There's something about the enemy that scares them witless. Asgrim believes his strict approach is holding them together, I think. He doesn't realize the key to a good performance is respect and trust, combined with solid preparation."

"Performance." Sam spoke flatly. "Like a horse or a hunting dog, you mean? You may have your own methods, Thorvald, but it's Asgrim who's in charge here. If a man doesn't perform, the Ruler simply gets rid of him. If you still want evidence that he's your father, that might just be it. Didn't Somerled kill his brother in cold blood and run roughshod over anyone else that got in his way? Seems like he hasn't improved much since then." He paused. "I should be sorry I said that, but I'm not. I know you think he could be your father, but there's something not right about him, Thorvald. I don't trust him."

"You're wrong. Stay here and help me and I'll prove it. Asgrim's been struggling under impossible odds. Imagine how it must feel to lose your one battle, year after year; to see more and more of your men cut down for no gain at all.

Imagine an enemy who kills your children on the day they take their first breath. He's doing his best, but it's desperate, and desperate men get cruel sometimes. He probably thinks it's the only way."

"Then why's he letting you do his work for him?" Sam asked bluntly. "Seems to me he's just making use of you."

Thorvald did not reply. There was one obvious answer to this, but he would not say it.

"Proud to be his son, are you?" Sam's eyes were bleak in his honest face.

"If he is my father," Thorvald said in a whisper, "it seems to me I must be the best son I can to him. That's all. Will you stand by me?"

Sam opened his mouth to speak, and closed it again. One of the men had shouted something, and now the combatants had laid down shield and spear and were running to the shore, pointing out to sea. Sam stood up carefully, using Thorvald's shoulder for balance as he gazed across the water. A boat was coming in, rowed by two men standing, a boat of greater size than any of those assembled here on the tidal flat. She was listing heavily, her course somewhat erratic. The rowers were Egil and Helgi, who had gone with the Ruler on his last trip away. Holding the steering oar was Asgrim himself. The rowers hauled, muscles bulging with effort, and the *Sea Dove* crunched over shells and small rocks to beach herself at a drunken angle on the dark sand. Where the hole had been in her side there now sprouted a hodgepodge of planking and patching, crudely pinned and nailed together, as if a finely wrought sword had been mended with a lump of scrap iron, or a delicate embroidery with hanks of uncombed wool. Sam stared in horror.

First over the side and up the shore toward them was Asgrim.

"Thorvald, Sam. She's still watertight, as you can see. How are the men progressing?"

"To schedule," Thorvald said absently. His eyes were on his friend. Sam had taken one faltering step forward, and another. The expression on his face was comical in its stunned disbelief.

"Who mangled my boat?" he breathed. "What sort of repair do you call that? Odin's bones, a child in swaddling could do a better job. Where did you fellows learn your boat-building skills, from a cook or a shepherd?" He stumbled down to stand by the *Sea Dove,* one large hand reaching to stroke the undamaged timber, to touch with disgust the ragged line where the ugly overlay began.

"Temporary, of course," Asgrim said smoothly. He was watching Sam closely, Thorvald noticed, perhaps waiting for some particular response. "We do need her here; she's capable of carrying more men than any of the others, and her sturdier construction will give her an added advantage in the strong currents off the Isle of Clouds."

"Nobody's sailing her anywhere with that lump of ordure on her hull," Sam said baldly. "She's not going out on the ocean until I have that off her and a decent repair done. And nobody touches her without my say-so. That goes for all of you." He glared defiantly, turning his head to take in not only Asgrim and Thorvald, but the semicircle of others, warriors, fishermen, guards, who had gathered on the shore to watch the *Sea Dove* come in.

"Fine boat," grunted one of the fishermen. "Never seen a better."

"I hope you heard me," said Sam, blue eyes turned straight on Asgrim's.

"Indeed." The Ruler appeared quite unperturbed. "Certainly you must do this your own way and choose your own helpers, remembering, of course, that all men must continue to complete their daily quota of combat and weapons training. I'm sure Thorvald will see that's not neglected. My apologies for the repair. Foremost in my mind was the need to get her fixed—you did speak of it rather often—and your own inability to make your way back over to the place where she was beached. So, an emergency solution, I'm afraid. And there's still the mast to replace; we do have a length of spruce for that, not perfect, but serviceable. It's a big job, Sam, and you don't have a lot of time. Sure you can do it?"

The expression in Sam's eyes was answer enough. "I'll get started now," he said. "Who's got my bag of tools? Knut? Get down here, and step lively."

"Thorvald?" Einar spoke with some diffidence as the two of them stood next morning watching the men at target practice. Farther along the beach, the *Sea Dove* was swarming with Sam's chosen helpers; already, most of the patchy repair job had been undone.

"Yes?"

"Need to tell you something in confidence. Hope you won't take it amiss."

Thorvald turned to look at the older man. Einar's expression was unusually grim, even for a man who seldom smiled. "Of course not," he said calmly, even as unease clutched at him. "What is it?"

"You'd want to be careful," said Einar, lowering his voice to a whisper. "Very careful. He asked me to keep an eye on you, make sure you weren't overstepping the mark."

"What do you mean?" Thorvald felt suddenly cold. Hadn't Asgrim trusted him? Hadn't the Ruler more or less asked him to take charge?

"Can't say much more. The problem is, you're useful to him, very useful, and if you can win this for him, he's not going to stand in your way, not till it's over. But he sees how the fellows look up to you, and he doesn't like it. He's weighing you up: advantage or threat, help or, in the long run, hindrance. I've seen that look in his eyes before, Thorvald. He's not a man to get on the wrong side of."

"Why are you telling me this?" Thorvald hissed. He was torn between anger and hurt. "Doesn't that put you in danger too?"

"Why do you think, you fool?" Einar responded, laying a hand on the younger man's shoulder. "Just be careful, that's all I'm saying." His tone changed abruptly. "That's the round finished, and every man with at least one shot in the mark. They're getting better."

"Yes," Thorvald said, recognizing in that moment that whatever else had possessed his thoughts, his father, his identity, his own future, nothing was more important than the flowering of these men's skills and courage, the reawakening of their hope. "And will get better still before the end. Come, let's tell them so."

Creidhe felt uncomfortable if her hands were idle for long. After a good night's sleep, she sat at the table, bag by her side, the Journey on her knee. The fabric was unrolled just far enough to show where she had last formed stitches some time ago at Jofrid's house. She threaded a fine needle with moss-green wool—she had cluttered the hearth of Aunt Margaret's workroom with dyes and mordants before she was satisfied with this color—and began to sew. This part of the pattern was gentler, a lull in the swift flow of the Journey. What she made signified trust and openness. There had been precious little of either in recent times. She stitched a hill, and a small building with a cross on top. The next part was still in her mind: clasped hands; a dagger, veiled; an egg, its shape simple and perfect.

On the other side of the table sat Brother Niall, watching her in silence. The others had gone outside; after their morning prayers there was work to be done tending to stock and walled gardens, for they must support themselves in everything, Breccan had told her over supper. They even had their own small boat, which had brought himself and Colm to this shore from their native land, praise God, and was now kept safe in a place not far from Blood Bay. If Colm had not decided to take the cloth, Breccan smiled, he could certainly have earned his living netting cod.

After a while, Niall unrolled one of the pieces of parchment and set small white stones on its corners. He fetched water in a little jug, scraped powder into an ink pot, poured, mixed, waited. He took up a quill and began to write. Glancing up, Creidhe saw the words flowing across the parchment, neat and regular, cryptic and lovely as the tracks of otter, hare, gull or swallow. At the top of the page there was a bigger letter, with patterns set around it in colors as deep, as subtle as those she made for the fashioning of her own work. There were leaves, spirals, twisting snakes and small, strange-eyed creatures with wings and scales. The quill moved on; today Niall was merely adding text in perfect rows. And yet, within this order she could see disorder: around the neat framework, signs of escape. She turned her attention to her own work. Her hands moved industriously, making a flower, a cloud, a little sheep. For a while they sat in silence, each intent on the task.

"I've noticed," Niall's voice broke the stillness, "the small irregularity in your work—deliberate, I suspect— where there's a gap in the border pattern, a pathway out, one might say, amidst the trail of vines there. That interests me."

Her first reaction was to roll the fabric quickly over, to cover what she had made; it was secret, not to be shared, most certainly not to be discussed. But then, had she not put into today's labor what she felt most strongly in this small house of men: trust? She unfolded her work again, touching the part he had mentioned with her finger.

"You have good eyesight," she said.

"For an old man? Yes, I still seem to manage. Will you explain the pattern to me? A thing of wonder, it seems to be. Some might even call it a talisman of power. Not your Thorvald, evidently. His eyes are less acute, for all his youth."

"I will tell you what this means, this gap in the border, if you will tell me what those little writings are, the ones that flow into the margins of your manuscript. It looks as if the letters are trying to get out."

The quill stopped moving. Niall smiled; Creidhe caught her breath, for his expression was a wondrous blend of sadness, regret, acceptance, touched with a slightly guilty look, like that of a boy caught out in a small misdemeanor.

"Oh, Creidhe," he said quietly. "Your eyesight surpasses mine, I think; it goes straight to the heart of things. Very well, I will tell if you will. Ladies first."

"All right." She laid the Journey on the table, unrolled just a little, so he could see the parts she had made today, and the last time she had worked on it. The images from before were dark and strange; her fear and disquiet showed in the shadows, the half-glimpsed clutching hands, the faces that both smiled in welcome and screamed in furious repudiation. She did not show him the place where she had made the Isle of Clouds.

"It is difficult to explain," she said. "Because of what this is, the power it holds within it, there's a need for a safeguard. I make a new part every day if I can. I call it the Journey. There is so much in these stitches, these images, far more than wool and linen, that it is necessary to provide a—an escape route. If I did not do so, the love, the hate, the fear and joy would simply build and build, until it could not be held in so small an object. It would become too dangerous, too powerful. So I make this little path, here in the border: a way out. It is not regular; it must not be a pattern, or it risks becoming lost in the whole. This is the way with everything we make. Each blanket, each hanging, each garment possesses such an irregularity. It is a form of protection for those who use these items later. Even Aunt Margaret does it now, though this is a tradition of my mother's people, not of hers."

"You respect this aunt greatly, I can see. She is your father's sister?"

It seemed to Creidhe there was a studied casualness about this question; she began to feel an odd sensation in her spine, a kind of tingling anticipation. "Oh, no," she told him. "Aunt Margaret is not my blood kin; she is an old friend of my parents, that is all. I think of her as both aunt and friend; she has no daughters of her own, only Thorvald, and she has been very kind to me, and taught me all she knows of spinning and weaving. She enjoys my company, I think; her life would be rather lonely without our times together."

"Your young friend Thorvald—he is her son?"

Creidhe nodded. "The only one, yes. Aunt Margaret's husband was killed. She never married again, though she had plenty of offers. Will you answer my question now?"

"Oh, yes. What was the question again?"

She looked at him, surprised, and he gazed back, eyes

bright with some emotion she could not interpret. Creidhe shivered; this felt like the brink of a precipice, like a moment of discovery. It came to her that perhaps she had got things entirely wrong. "Tell me what these are, these places where the writing flows into the margins of your work."

"Ah, yes," Niall said softly, rolling up the sleeves of his coarse robe so that the fabric would not smudge the wet ink, and reaching to touch one such irregularity near the top of the page. The manuscript was a work of wondrous artistry, a creation to rival the Journey itself, and surely made with equal fire and equal love. "In a way, the answer is the same as yours. Our rule is strict here: kind, but strict. My own rule is more rigorous still, imposed in accordance with a vow, as indeed is the discipline we all follow, but somewhat harsher and more particular in my case." His gaze had left the parchment now and was fixed on the middle distance, as if he saw something far away, or long ago. The dark intensity of those eyes conjured an image of Thorvald on the clifftop, hair wild in the wind, his father's letter in his hand and bitter words on his lips. "For some men, and some women, I imagine," Niall went on, "the most difficult constraint can be not to act when one sees how one could have some influence in the world; not to solve puzzles when the intellect cries out to stretch itself thus; to ignore solutions when they appear right before one's eyes. But some men should not act; some men, it seems, can wreak only destruction, whether that is their intention or not. These small verses you see, crawling off the page like creatures escaping the confines of a cage, are the ramblings of one who chafes at such self-imposed fetters, that is all. The words are safe enough, I believe; indeed, if they take the place of actions, they perform much the same function as your hidden escape hatches, allowing what is perilous to dissipate before any real harm is done. There is some cost to me, and to you, as makers of these maps of the soul, but that is a price we pay willingly; not to fashion such things is to wither and die. I'm rambling, Creidhe. Does that answer the question?"

She nodded, unable to speak. It seemed to her a number of questions had been answered, and the knowledge was, for the moment, overwhelming. "I don't know what to say to you." It was a lame enough response to what had been, in its essence, a revelation of his inmost self.

"There is no need to speak further of these matters," Niall said quietly, rolling his sleeves back down to the wrists and reaching for his pen. "We understand one another, I think. I regret very much that I did not meet your friends before Asgrim took them away. Very much."

They worked on in silence a while, and if a confusion of thoughts and feelings caused both quill and needle to move less than freely, neither the white-haired hermit nor the young woman put this into words. It was Creidhe, eventually, who broke the silence.

"There are some things we do need to discuss. You left your explanations half finished yesterday. Asgrim, and the threat from the other tribe—I don't entirely understand that, and I need to, if it places me in danger. And the boys— I need to know what it is he plans for them."

"Yes, Creidhe, we must indeed come to grips with this, for increasingly I fear for your safety here. I think in a day or so we may need to move you elsewhere, before Asgrim decides you have enjoyed our hospitality for too long. I have earned his deep distrust over the years; I am one of the few who is prepared to challenge his authority here; though, being the mild-mannered cleric that I am, I do so only with words, never deeds." He gave a crooked smile. "We shall call Breccan back shortly, and the two of us will set it all out for you; then we'll decide what to do. But not just yet. I have a small favor to ask you." A touch of diffidence had crept into his voice.

"What favor?" asked Creidhe.

Niall hesitated. "I don't wish to speak of the past," he said. "Will you respect that?"

"Of course." Thorvald would most certainly want to speak of the past. But Thorvald was not here, and she herself had no business prying into this man's secrets. Besides, she had made Thorvald a promise, and the more Niall told her, the harder it was going to be to keep it. "If that's what you want."

"On the other hand," he said, "I would very much like to hear a little of your life at home: your family, your friends, the world you inhabit when not sailing the seas in search of adventure. I hope you will indulge an old man's foolishness."

"An old man?" She raised her brows at him.

"It was what you thought, wasn't it?"

"You do have white hair. One assumes—"

"I was a young man when I began my journey here. By the time I set foot on this shore my hair was of the hue you see now. If that makes me old, then I am old. Will you—?"

"It might be rather boring for you. A lot of my life is spent in front of a loom, or surrounded by cooking pots."

"All the same."

She set her tale out carefully, painting a picture for him: of the times of peace in the Light Isles, the breeding and rearing of fine stock, the nurturing of good crops, the governing of a society that had grown from two races—the ancient one of the Folk, her mother's people, whose kings had ruled there for generation on generation; and the Norse newcomers, her father's race, who now dwelt in the isles alongside the others, and indeed outnumbered them. She spoke of the existence of several faiths: Christian hermits such as himself dwelt in the Light Isles cheek by jowl with the priestesses of the ancient way—her own sister was one such wise woman—and the adherents to the gods of the snow lands, Odin, Thor, Freyr. She told of her father, how he led the people in the ways of peace and justice; of her mother, whose wisdom and insight had mended many a quarrel between the disparate folk of the islands over the years. Because Niall did not interrupt, did not cut her short, she went on to speak of her sisters, and the one small brother who had died before he reached his fifth birthday. She spoke of Margaret, and of Thorvald, close in age to her own elder sister, Eanna, the one who was a priestess. After a while she saw that he had stopped pretending to write and sat with chin in hand and eyes distant, simply listening.

"I am bound by a promise, you understand," she said, near the end. "Thorvald was eighteen last autumn. Then, in spring, his mother gave him a certain piece of information. It was this that sparked his journey here. I cannot say if he will find what he seeks. It is a matter of great importance to him; a search for identity, one might say."

"Mmm," said Brother Niall. "Difficult, and not just for the young man himself. You are a loyal friend, Creidhe; your father's daughter, no doubt of it." His voice was so quiet she could hardly hear it, even in the silence of the cottage. "One might carry such a search to its logical conclusion and find oneself bitterly disappointed with the result. He'd better have stayed home and got on with his life, I think."

"Like you," Creidhe said carefully, "Thorvald is a man who finds it hard not to act. That's why I need to know what he's doing now, away with Asgrim. I have a terrible feeling he's getting himself into some sort of trouble."

"Let us call Brother Breccan," Niall said, rising to his feet, "and think of a plan of action. I'm afraid trusting our future to God's mercy will be inadequate in this particular case."

"Just one thing before you call him." Creidhe hesitated. This must be said; she must hope he would not be offended. "Don't you believe a man can change? You said something about—about wreaking destruction, as if that were the only path possible. Aren't you a Christian? Brother Tadhg tells us the Christian God loves even sinners; that a man need only turn to him and he can start his life anew. If he has done ill, God forgives it and lets him try again. If you believe that, how can you speak thus of a man locked into evil-doing?"

"Ah. You speak from your own experience; you have grown up among the brave and virtuous, and it has clouded your judgment somewhat, I think. I am as much of a Christian as Breccan has been able to make of me since he came to this shore. His intentions are good." His tone was bleak as frost, his eyes without expression. "Can a man change?

One could spend a lifetime debating that point and never come to a conclusion. Shall I call the others?"

Thus it was that Creidhe learned the full and twisted story: how, after the girl, Sula, had produced the child they needed, the Unspoken had lost him before his second summer in their midst. He'd been stolen, taken away by Asgrim's own son, Sula's brother, not back to the settlements of the Long Knife people but over the water to the Isle of Clouds, where he had been kept in hiding ever since, for five long years. That isle was forbidden to the tribe of the Unspoken: their lore decreed that it was death to approach the place. Being a holy man, Foxmask himself was apparently exempt from this rule. For the rest, perhaps it was death anyway, lore or no lore. The sea currents between the island and the shore by Council Fjord were feared by every fisherman of the Long Knife people and shunned in any season, save for a brief time around midsummer, when a strange hush would descend on the churning ocean and one might cross over and return in safety between one day's sunrise and the next day's dusk. Even so, they did this only because they must. The Unspoken had set a curse on the Long Knife people when Foxmask was stolen. Until he was recovered from his captors and returned to his own tribe, no Long Knife infant would live to see the sun rise twice. The voices came and sang them into darkness.

So, the hunt: every summer they embarked on it, year after year, and every summer the bleeding survivors limped back with the broken bodies of the fallen—those they had managed to recover. Asgrim had led them into this death trap five times now; this summer would be the sixth. In all those years, not one infant born to the Long Knife people had survived. Nobody was quite sure what tribe it was that dwelt on the Isle of Clouds, only that they were fierce as wild beasts, numerous, and skilled in magic. The Long Knife people were not even sure that Foxmask himself still lived, but it was evident that the Unspoken believed it to be so and would continue to punish them until the seer was found.

"I see," said Creidhe. As Niall and Breccan told the story, she had been cooking; now she took the flatcakes from the iron pan suspended over the fire and set them on a platter. Colm was here too; his eyes lit up at the sight of the crisp, golden dough, the savory smell of herbs and sizzling butter. It was, in fact, merely a concoction of eggs and flour and a bit of this and that. The trick was all in the beating. "Do you think Asgrim has persuaded Thorvald and Sam to help him in this endeavor? To be a part of it? I cannot think Sam would do so willingly."

"But Thorvald might?" queried Brother Niall, cutting his flatcake and regarding it with appreciation. "Yes, Creidhe, this seems the likeliest explanation for their extended absence. A trade, perhaps—they assist in preparations for the hunt and they earn what they need to repair the boat. I did hear Asgrim had come over to move the boat to Council Fjord. That gave me pause for thought."

Creidhe felt her heart thumping. "They should not fight—I mean, Sam knows nothing at all of warcraft, and Thorvald—"

"Strangely, it's not that I'm concerned about," Niall said. "Mmm, you certainly do know how to cook. No, I fear that the prompt whisking away of these two young men, followed by their lengthy absence, is no more than a strategy to remove them from you, Creidhe. You are in danger. If Asgrim can finish this struggle without the loss of any more lives, he will do so. After five years his men grow dispirited. It cannot be long before they start to question his authority openly, to challenge his role as chieftain. The women too; this conflict not only robs them of their infants, it slaughters their men and leaves them with the entire burden of maintaining stock, fields, the very structure of community here. There are only boys to do the fishing once Asgrim gathers his force together, and few enough of those. The women themselves spend weary days out on the lake now, with scant harvest to be taken. It is a heavy load for the Long Knife people. Asgrim cannot afford another hunt."

Creidhe waited.

"It seems to us," Breccan spoke in his soft brogue, "that with you here among us, Asgrim has the means to make a bargain with the Unspoken. His men have shown quite clearly the impossibility of retrieving Foxmask from this island fortress. What can this summer bring but another expedition doomed to defeat? So, he seizes the chance to offer an alternative. He calls a meeting with the Unspoken, something we know is still possible for him, though they will no longer attend council nor speak to others of the Long Knife. He meets with their elders and presents them with the chance to breed another seer, a new Foxmask. In return, there will be no more deaths, no more voices in the night. To buy this peace, he offers them another fair-haired girl: yourself."

There was silence. Creidhe could feel the rapid beating of her heart, the chill crawling across her flesh. If she had not fled the settlement, perhaps even now she might be suffering the same fate as Asgrim's daughter.

"But wait," she said, frowning. "It was his own daughter they stole before, stole and treated so cruelly. Surely no father would seek to have that happen to another girl, surely he would recoil from such an idea, even though I am a stranger. He was kind to me."

"Perhaps," said Niall. "But I believe this is just what Asgrim plans. He would have acted before the birth of Jofrid's son, if he could, and so prevented yet another loss. The early arrival of the child made that impossible; as I said, in this time of conflict the Unspoken will deal only with the Ruler himself, and I imagine it takes time to arrange such a parley. So that infant was lost, but he can save his men and allow the womenfolk of his tribe the chance to bear children without fear once more. He must offer his adversary this prize before hunt time. We don't have long."

"I can't believe he would do it," Creidhe breathed. "After he lost his own daughter. How could he?"

"You judge him by the measure of men you have known, Creidhe: your father, perhaps. I have reason to doubt Asgrim. There was a certain—irregularity—at the time of his daughter's abduction, which did nothing to improve my opinion of the man. As Ruler here, he is clinging to the power he has, but his fingers are slipping. In such desperate times, men's boundaries change."

"Niall's right, Creidhe," said Breccan. "If not for Asgrim's persuasion, I imagine your friends would have come back for you long ago. He's keeping them out of the way until he can make this—arrangement. We don't have much time. Tomorrow, or the day after, we must move you to a place of protection."

"Where?" she asked blankly, a picture of stark, precipitous hillsides, tall cliffs and pounding seas in her mind. "And what about Thorvald and Sam? How will they find me?"

"I could take a message," put in the young man, Colm, cheeks turning pink with shyness. "I could go in and offer to say prayers; with luck, there'd be time to slip in a word or two before they kicked me out. I'd need to go when the Ruler was away. Those two lads can tell me when it's safe. I know them."

Breccan smiled. "Good. Do it carefully. We must ensure Creidhe has time to reach her destination before we draw Asgrim's attention. He went to Blood Bay, didn't he, to fetch the boat around to his encampment?"

"So I'm informed," Niall said. "And may well have left again by now. Possibly with a small side trip on the way." He turned to Creidhe. "The bay where your ship was beached is conveniently located for the crossing to the Isle of Shadows, where the elders of the Unspoken dwell. If I were the Ruler, I would not pass up this opportunity to sound them out, possibly even to finalize an agreement. I think we must expect a visit fairly soon."

"Where can I go?"

"To our brothers in the north, initially. Oh, yes"—he had seen her look of surprise—"we are not alone here. This place attracts those who seek God in solitude and hardship. We have two brethren on the far side of this island, with a boat, and there's another hermitage on the Isle of Streams. Best that you go there until we can get word to your friends.

I'm sorry, Creidhe. This is frightening, I expect, but I will not insult you by offering less than the truth."

Creidhe shivered. "I'd be lying if I said it doesn't scare me. I just wish there was some other solution, one that didn't involve death or suffering. If my father were in Asgrim's position, I know he would arrange a council, get all parties together, talk openly about the situation and try to agree on a course of action that suited everyone. He wouldn't do things secretly, all by himself."

"Asgrim has not been acting alone," Niall said grimly. "It is apparent the women of the settlement must have known what was intended for you."

"Yes." Creidhe's voice was sober, remembering the special meals, the combing of the hair, the green-trimmed gown. "And one of them warned me. One was brave enough to do that, even though she had just lost her child. There are good people here. Why doesn't Asgrim seek some other way?"

"He believes, perhaps, that there is no other way. Do not forget, his adversary deals in curses and spells, voices that bring death, and armies of superhuman strength. I have long considered whether another solution could be reached. I am inclined to believe a substitute might well be acceptable to the Unspoken; it would be a matter of presenting it in a way they understood, that is all. Persuading them to a slightly broader interpretation of their own lore."

"It is a barbaric faith," said Breccan. "Their ears are closed to God's word, and so to his infinite mercy. I would give much to be able to reach them, but they will have none of us. Asgrim's tribe is little better: he fears God's truth."

"Mmm." Niall's response could have meant anything. "You should go in the morning, I think, Colm. Make sure you're there and away before Asgrim sails the boat into Council Fjord. Be unobtrusive; don't upset anyone. I don't suppose your young men are of the Christian faith, are they?" he asked Creidhe, brows raised.

"Well, no. Sam adheres to Thor, a good god for fishermen. Thorvald doesn't think much of religion. He says that if a man cannot depend on himself, he is not much of a man."

Niall's mouth quirked at the corner. "Indeed. Ah, well, Colm must do the best he can. A word or two is all we need: a warning, specific enough to let them know the urgency, but not too detailed. We don't want anyone challenging Asgrim to a fight."

"And Creidhe must be gone soon after. We must wait long enough to be sure she won't be likely to run into Asgrim or his men, but we need her away from here before he comes looking. The best time would be at first light, the day after tomorrow. Colm will be back by then and we'll know if he has been able to speak to the young men." Breccan frowned. "One of us must travel with Creidhe, the other remain here to answer questions." He exchanged a complicated look with Niall. "If he's going to come in person, you are the one best able to deal with it."

"You mean I tell lies with impunity, risking God's disapproval, every day of my life? Yes, I understand. In addition, you are less advanced in years. I suspect I might have difficulty matching our young friend's pace across country, judging by her impressive speed up this hill. Very well, that's the way we'll do it. Now let us turn our attention to the remains of this extremely fine breakfast. What a pity we can't keep you, Creidhe. I'd love to see what you'd do with a catch of fresh mackerel."

The plan had seemed, if not foolproof, at least reasonably likely to succeed. The man who went by a name he had borrowed from a tale heard in childhood waited in the hermitage alone, waited for the arrival of the Ruler, angry, imperious, demanding the return of his prize bargaining piece. Colm had left one day, Creidhe the next, walking on up the valley at first light with Breccan by her side. Breccan would not carry a weapon, only his stout staff of ash wood. They had vanished across the hills like shadows, the girl's yellow hair closely hooded, and her bag on her back: the strange web she made traveled with her everywhere. Colm had not come home. Niall milked the cow, fed the chickens, cast an inexpert eye over the vegetable patch and returned indoors. Writing appeared to be impossible; his mind was elsewhere. The sun passed overhead and began to descend into the west, and there was still no sign of the boy. He was almost a day late. Niall collected the eggs, mucked out the byre, forking the soiled straw onto the garden. Colm was proud of his leeks and onions; one should not neglect them. The cold glow of the long summer twilight spread across the sky. Niall lit a solitary-lamp, more for reassurance than from necessity. All was quiet. The last plaintive cries of birds sounded through the air, and beneath them roared the old, deep song of the sea. He waited, alone in the night.

At first light he made a decision and, staff in hand, set out to the southwest on the high path toward Council Fjord. Before the sun had climbed two fingers' breadth into a clear sky, he stumbled over Colm, face down among stones, young hands open and helpless on the pebbly scree of the hillside. A single blow had felled him; there wasn't much blood. Niall turned him over and closed the sightless eyes. He tried to do what was appropriate, kneeling, hands together, whispering a prayer: *Pater noster . . .* but the words deserted him. Breccan was the one this lad needed to speed him to whatever reward awaited him, not some ill-fated pretender who could not set his hand to anything without turning it all to ashes. The boy was tall, heavy. Niall could not get him up onto his shoulders. He settled Colm as best he could, hands gentle on breast, wooden cross between them, rocks wedged by his side so he would not tumble down the sheer slope. When Breccan returned, they would come back with a board and carry the lad home.

More waiting. Long; too long. He sat into another night, listening to the silence. The house was cold. He did not light the fire. One lamp burned; Breccan would need that to find his way across the hillside, when he came. If he came. It occurred to Niall that, if the truth of his heart had matched the exterior he showed the world, he could have prayed and taken some good of it. The gods, however, were not on his side and never had been. That was no more than just: he had long dismissed their efficacy. Tonight he desired faith, but desire in itself is not enough.

Time passed. At some point in the night he heard foot-steps outside, and was instantly by the door, knife in hand.

"Niall?" said a voice that was barely recognizable, and when Niall pulled the door open, Breccan staggered in to collapse on the earthen floor, wheezing and shaking. Niall lit lamps, made a fire, fetched blankets. He waited; the other could not yet form rational speech. When the words came they were accompanied by tears, and the russet-haired Ulsterman made no attempt to brush them away. "Set upon . . . going over the pass . . . the Unspoken . . . too late to help . . ."

"It's all right," Niall said. His own voice sounded distant and small, as if it came from some other place. "It's all right; you must drink—here—and warm yourself. Let me see if you are injured."

Breccan had an angry lump on his head, and one wrist was badly twisted. Niall fetched salves, bandages, bound the arm, swabbed the head wound, got his friend, at last, to bed.

"Colm?" whispered Breccan as his lids closed over eyes full of shadows.

"Not home yet," Niall said quietly. "Now sleep. We'll talk in the morning."

He smothered the lamps then and stood in the darkness, listening to the beat of his own heart, pounding relentlessly on and on, strong and insistent. One would think it would have given up by now: what was the point? If one were doomed to fail, to turn gold to dross and squander what was most precious, why go on at all? And yet, for some reason, he had done so before and did so still. Perhaps he had been waiting all this time, all these long years, to learn what it was he must do. It whispered in his mind somewhere, a terrible thing, an extreme thing, one that froze the blood even of a man who believed his life to be entirely without value. He would not allow it to take shape yet, not while Breccan lay wounded and the boy out on the hill unburied. Still, the half-formed thought edged at his mind. Sooner or later he would have a choice to make.

SEVEN

Who would awaken the past?
It shines like a sunrise
And cuts like a fine blade.

MONK'S MARGIN NOTE

The moment their hands seized her, Creidhe's mind was filled with a single thought: she would survive, no matter what. They came out of the mist in total silence, long-armed, pale-faced, dark-hooded, their eyes bright and wild, their mouths set with grim purpose. Breccan began to lift his staff; then, with a grunt of surprise, he toppled to the ground as his assailant tapped him on the skull with a short, stout club. Creidhe's heart was pounding; she could feel cold sweat breaking out all over her body, she could smell her own fear. Their hands, gripping her arms from behind, were cold as ice and iron-strong. Her instinct was to fight, and for a few desperate moments she did, wrenching away from their grasp, stamping and kicking, using her nails to scratch and rip. Soon enough she noticed, through a haze of mind-numbing fear, that they simply loosed their hold, avoided her blows, then apprehended her again. There were many of them, tall, silent and strong. One thing became starkly clear: to try to escape this way was completely pointless. Breccan had been laid out senseless, and her efforts to resist might simply precipitate the same treatment for herself. Then she'd have no hope of getting away. A second insight was more worrying. It was evident they were at some pains to ensure she was not hurt, not marked. They held her carefully and moved with caution, so she could in no way bruise or damage herself in her frantic struggles.

They were shepherding her off the track now, still without a word spoken. Breccan they left where he had fallen.

Two walked by her on either side, thin fingers encircling her arms. Others went before and behind. No weapons had been drawn save the club that had felled her companion. She hoped he was not badly hurt. At least he would be able to take word back, when he came to.

The pace was brisk, and after they had gone a certain way the direction veered westward, apparently back toward Council Fjord. They followed the course of a fast stream that hurtled along between rocks. Here and there the ground was boggy, saturated; they made sure she did not slip and fall, though her boots were coated with dark mud. Creidhe ventured a glance to left and right; she did not like the look in her captors' eyes. It was clear enough who they were and what they wanted. Their faces, their eyes, their strange garb fashioned of ragtag skins told her they were not of the Long Knife people, but those others Niall had spoken of. And she knew what it meant, this careful handling, this avoidance of damage to their newly acquired prisoner. She must be delivered to the tribe unmarked: a perfect trophy. Stumbling over jagged rocks, sliding across pebbly scree, Creidhe weighed it in her mind. A girl who was sun and moon in one form sounded very poetic, but what it actually led to was less than dreamlike. What had been done to that girl, Sula, was crude and hideous. Perhaps they had believed it justified in order to allow each man of the tribe fatherhood over the child she was to bear for them. That did not lessen its brutality. Now it was Creidhe's turn; it would be her fate to provide their new seer, Foxmask remade. She saw it in the way these men were looking at her, for all the cautious touch of their hands. Their strange eyes mingled superstitious awe and avid lust. Creidhe shuddered. This simply wasn't going to happen. She wouldn't allow it to happen.

She used a trick her mother had taught her, breathing to a pattern, slowing her heartbeat, summoning strength of purpose and clarity of mind. She considered the situation as she marched on, with her grim captors maintaining their relentless, silent progress all around her. There was no point in screaming. Who would help her? They were all in this together, Long Knife people and Unspoken. She must make her way out of the trap alone and unaided.

It was a long walk, on top of the distance she had already traveled with Breccan from the hillside hermitage above Brightwater. Creidhe tried to keep track of where they were, knowing such knowledge would be vital if she managed to escape, but the thick mist clung close in the air, blotting out all useful landmarks, and she had to resort to guesswork. She judged they had crossed a high pass and come back down toward the shore of the western fjord, if shore it could be called: steep cliffs fringed the narrow waterway for most of its length. Today the mist veiled that lovely isle to the west, the mystical, cloud-swathed realm that still called to her in her dreams. She could catch a glimpse of other, closer islands: a narrow, improbably steep one, and by it a squat, sturdy arch. Now they were coming down to a place across the fjord from those small isles, a place where there was a narrow strip of flat land by the water and a couple of crude cottages on the hillside above it. The small dwellings looked bleak, deserted. Her captors had begun to whisper among themselves; she could not make out the meaning. There was only one word she caught clearly, and that word was Asgrim. That did not surprise her. She had seen already that among the tall, disheveled figures of the Unspoken walked one who was not of their kind, one who was familiar to her from a morning at Brightwater, when the Ruler had come back in a hurry and Jofrid's small son had been laid in the cold ground. This hulking warrior was none other than Asgrim's personal bodyguard, and his presence here among the enemies of the Long Knife told her Niall's suspicions had been well founded. She wasn't being abducted. She was being traded: peace for Asgrim's tribe had been bought, and the price was her own future.

Unfortunately for the Ruler, Creidhe thought grimly, she had no intention of letting herself be anyone's captive for longer than was strictly necessary. She'd better come up with a plan soon, for she could see now that on the narrow strip of ground below them, perhaps the only landing place in all this sheltered waterway, lay a long, low boat of tarred skins over a wattle framework. Beside it more men of the Unspoken waited. Each was tall, lean and ghostly pale of visage. Each stood utterly still. It was a stillness that spoke of ancient things, of an identity that was part of the very bone of these stark islands, enduring and deep-rooted. A dark power seemed to emanate from them. They bore weapons: spears of bone, bows and quivers, short clubs. There was nothing made of iron. Their garb was of crudely cured skins over coarse wool, with here or there a tattered cloak, a strand of shells around the neck, a small bone threaded on a cord. The tight discipline of their mouths stood at odds with the hunger in their eyes, shadowed, feral eyes that returned, over and over, to Creidhe's own figure, well covered though it was by gown and cloak, boots and scarf. The wind had teased a lock of her hair from under its neat wrapping and it drifted, golden and fine, across her face. It was this, above all, that drew their gaze, and Creidhe saw in their mask-like faces that disturbing blend of awed veneration and open desire. For a moment, terror and revulsion came close to overwhelming her. She must disregard that; she must not let fear paralyze her. Only weak people did that, and she was strong.

A plan, that was what she needed. Nothing immediate presented itself. The boat was being readied to depart under oars, with seven men to accompany her—six to row and one to guard her, she supposed. Brother Niall had spoken of the Isle of Shadows, to the south. On the shore, the big bodyguard stood still, watching. His face might have been carved from a lump of stone, so little did it reveal as the wild men bundled her into the boat and settled her in the stern with one fellow seated beside her.

The options darted through Creidhe's mind, to be discarded each in its turn. Try to run for it: she wouldn't even get off the boat before they stopped her. Scream for help: a wasted effort, she knew that already. Probably every single one of the Long Knife people knew what was happening to her and welcomed it. Gudrun had known, and Helga, for all their smiles and their little gifts. She made an exception for

Jofrid, a woman of surprising courage. That big guard had known even when he ran his eyes over her, back at the settlement. Niall and Colm were far away, beyond reach, and Breccan lay injured up in the mist somewhere. As for Thorvald and Sam, they seemed almost like ghosts from another life, so long it was since she had seen them. All the same, the moment seemed to call for some expression of what she felt.

"Shame on you!" Creidhe yelled at the bodyguard. "You're nothing but Asgrim's puppet, and Asgrim is not fit to hold the title of Ruler! How can you do this to me? I only came here by chance!"

The big warrior strode toward the boat. For a brief, heart-stopping moment she thought he was coming to help her, to make them let her go. Then he and several others set their hands to the prow, pushing with all their strength. The low craft ground over the shingle and out into the water. The men of the Unspoken clambered in over the sides and took up their oars. They turned the vessel expertly and began to row steadily out into deeper water.

One of her father's early lessons had been in keeping calm in difficult situations. Creidhe sat quietly awhile, listing in her mind what advantages she had. She was not tied up. They were not holding her, not anymore: now that they had her safely in the boat, they probably thought any restraints unnecessary. After all, apart from her initial struggle and brief outburst, she had appeared compliant. She had her bag on her back, and in her bag were some useful items, only getting to them unobserved was not possible. Unfortunately there were seven of the Unspoken and there was only one of her, and now they were well off shore, and the small craft was bouncing and bucking in a distressingly familiar way, putting Creidhe sharply in mind of her arrival in these lonely isles.

The mist was dissipating now, and as she looked westward, she saw it in the moment the veil parted, rising like a distant, lovely vision: the Isle of Clouds, still wearing its shawl of clinging damp, still somehow calling, crying out to her, *Here! Here!*

And that, of course, was the answer. That was the one

place where they could not follow, the one realm they could not enter to fetch her back. There she would be safe from Long Knife people and Unspoken alike. In order to make a southerly course to their home islands, these boatmen must first row out of the fjord, close to those two small isles, the tall, jagged one and the squat archway. They must skirt the edges of the Fool's Tide.

Very well; she would forget, for now, what she'd heard about the body of water separating that western island from the Isle of Storms; she would forget that no fisherman who valued his life went out that way, winter or summer. She would not dwell on the probability that the water would be freezing cold, save to ensure that her plan kept her in it for as short a time as possible. She would not think of sharks or sea serpents, nor of currents that might drag one down to the depths or sweep one away beyond the intended destination and over the rim of the world.

She watched the sea. Gudrun's brother had been drowned in the Fool's Tide, just one of many men of the islands lost to its fickle currents, its capricious gusts of wind and sudden, sucking whirlpools. She watched the rowers, observing how they struggled to maintain a straight course. Even here, on the far rim of the sea path between the fjord and the Isle of Clouds, the current still drew them hard to the west, as if the Fool's Tide were demanding a tribute, warning them that they were close enough for a toll to be exacted. She blessed the childhood summers in the Light Isles, when she had played in the lake waters with Eanna and Thorvald and learned to swim. Never mind that the lake waters had been warm and sheltered. She could do this. She had no choice.

Behind them, the landing place had shrunk to a smudge at the foot of the steep, rock-layered cliffs. The small figure of Asgrim's guard could be discerned on the shore, gazing after them. The boat was level with the tall, narrow islet; the crew were attempting to change their course, skirting the western margin of that island and making for the south. Out of the corner of her eye, Creidhe watched the movement of the oars. She sensed the pull of the current, recognizing the

same tug, the same insistence she had felt as Thorvald and
Sam had labored to bring the *Sea Dove* safely to shore
against impossible odds. Had she been a wise woman
steeped in ancient lore, as her sister was, she could have
sought help from the powers beneath the surface, the Seal
Tribe perhaps, for no doubt even here they had their
dwelling places under the waves, and might come to the call
of a priestess in time of direst need. Lacking those special
skills, Creidhe made use of what she had. She judged her
moment finely, waiting until the swell picked up and the
men of the Unspoken were fighting hard against that
strange current. One of them spoke harshly, snapping an order, and for just a moment the fellow who sat beside her was
distracted. Creidhe stood up; the light-fashioned boat
rocked violently. The men shouted; her guard sprang to his
feet, grabbing for her arm as the vessel tilted in the swell.
He was too late. Snatching a breath, Creidhe jumped.

The sea's touch was like a hard clamp around the chest,
squeezing out the air; it was only after she struggled to the
surface, gasping for breath, that she realized how cold it
was. Already the current had carried her some distance
away; now the tribesmen of the Unspoken were ignoring
the danger and turning the boat to row hard after her. The
vessel drew closer; Creidhe sucked in another desperate
breath and dived, trusting the ocean to hide her, to carry her
beyond her pursuers' reach. By all the powers, this was a
chill beyond any she had known before; no wonder so many
had been lost in these waters. She held her breath as long as
she could. Her skirts were dragging her down; she fought to
shed the sheepskin boots. Her bag, not to be discarded, was
like a leaden weight on her back. Again she sought the surface, coughing, choking, her hair plastered over her face.
The boat was close by, and they gazed this way, that way,
oars held poised, eyes ferocious: such a loss would be bitter
indeed for the Unspoken, and more bitter still for Asgrim's
people. Her strength was already flagging; she could not
keep this up for long. The current that carried her westward
was pulling pursuit after her; that was not the way she had

intended it to be. They still hadn't seen her, though they were very close now, the blade of that first oar almost within reach of her hands . . .

The water swirled, a gust of wind shivered the surface. Creidhe reached up and, grasping the oar shaft, tugged with all her might. Taken by surprise, the oarsman let go, and the length of pine tumbled into the sea. There was a shout, followed by a general movement to the side of the craft, which listed perilously. Clutching the oar, Creidhe gritted her teeth and gave herself up to the current, and the Fool's Tide bore her away. Looking back, she watched what unfolded through scarce-believing eyes, for it had the quality of some ancient tale of nightmare deeds and monstrous consequences. A wave arose: not a big wave at all, quite a moderate swell of water, but moving as if guided by an inexorable will. The sky darkened; the wind began to howl. The water lifted the boat, slowly turned it and tipped it gently over, and the tribesmen of the Unspoken were cast out into the ocean. Creidhe did not see what happened to them after that. Maybe they drowned; certainly, they disappeared from view almost instantly. Maybe they swam toward the shore, but if they did, there was no sign of them. All she knew for a time was the thudding of her heart, the rasp of her breathing, the weight of her clothing pulling her down, the fierce pain in arms and hands as she clutched at the oar, desperate for its aid to keep her afloat long enough. The water pulled strongly now, its westward current moving her in a kind of helpless dance; here a circle widdershins, here a circle sunwise, here an arc, a loop, a spiral, as the shadowy form of the Isle of Clouds drew gradually nearer, and her body grew colder and colder, and her mind clouded and wavered, refusing to obey her will. She chanted to herself, over and over, a charm of survival: *I won't die, I won't die.*

As the numb feeling spread through her arms and crept up her legs, so that she could not kick anymore, she recalled what Nessa had said after Kinart died. Creidhe had been very small herself, not quite four years old, but she remembered. Kinart had drowned: a simple matter of wandering off and not being found until it was too late. It was an accident, folk said. But Nessa was sure the Seal Tribe took her little son as the price for a favor they had once done her. If that were true, Creidhe wondered what it was she was paying for now. Her own foolishness, perhaps, in thinking her presence on this cursed voyage could have been of any assistance to Thorvald at all. Thorvald . . . she would never see him again, nor her parents, nor her sisters . . . she would never go home . . . by all the ancestors, she was cold . . . maybe it would be easier simply to let go, for this was really starting to hurt quite a lot, and nobody knew where she was, and all she wanted to do was sleep . . . easy really . . . just let go . . .

Something loomed up beside her. Her heart contracted; she was suddenly, sharply awake, anticipating any moment the rending bite of some voracious sea creature. But no: what lay in the water by her was a familiar construction of wattles and hide, floating upside down, buoyed by trapped air and festooned with a network of tangled cords. The boat floated alone; no men, dead or alive, clung to its hull or lay twined in its ropes. None could be seen in any direction on this wide sea. Now the shore she had left seemed more distant than the graceful, cloud-capped shape of the isle to which she journeyed.

I won't die. I refuse to die. Clambering up seemed beyond her. All the same, she must try, for escaping the chill clutch of the water was surely her best chance of survival. Climb up, cling on with the aid of those shreds of rope, and she had at least some chance. One hand . . . two . . . one foot . . . by all the powers, her body would feel the aftermath of this if she came through it alive . . . now pull . . . it was too hard, she would never be able to haul her own weight up . . . draw breath, once, twice . . . now, a gentle wave, coming from behind her, lifting her in its kind embrace, and a last, wrenching effort . . . grasp, twist, quick now, arms and legs through the ropes, heart thundering, quick, grip on while you can . . . and then the sheer weight of complete exhaustion . . . the wondrous, solid bulk of the boat's hull beneath her . . . the lulling rock of the swell . . . the bone-deep cold . . . the darkness . . .

* * *

Something had changed since Asgrim's return. Thorvald sensed it, though he could not quite put his finger on what it was. The Ruler seemed edgy, distracted; he strode about the encampment, up to the forge, along to the boats, but it seemed to Thorvald that most of the time Asgrim was not really seeing what was before him. There was a brooding look in those dark eyes, a frown on the pale brow that suggested the Ruler's mind was much taken up with other matters, secret matters. Skapti had not returned with him this time, and when Hogni asked where his fellow guard had gone, Asgrim snapped that Skapti was off on personal business and would return all in good time. That momentary loss of control, so unusual in this man, interested Thorvald. It seemed to him Asgrim was waiting for something. There had been talk of negotiations. Had Skapti been dispatched to the realms of the Unspoken to treat for peace? Most unlikely: the Ruler had said the enemy spoke only to himself. Besides, such dealings would require subtlety, cunning and cleverness. The bodyguard possessed all three qualities in the arena of combat, but he was no diplomat.

In Skapti's absence, Einar took his place as personal guard, since Hogni could hardly be on duty day and night. Now Hogni, too, began to wear a frown; he missed his brother, and it showed, for all his pains to conceal such weakness. The men began to whisper, and the talk was of some kind of agreement, a treaty; maybe they would not have to fight, but could go home at last. Asgrim was saying nothing. He paced and scowled and, quite clearly, waited.

Thorvald found himself growing irritated. While Sam had been working frantically to undo the botched repair on the *Sea Dove* and restore her to something like her old condition, he himself had been putting in long days on Asgrim's behalf. Einar's warning had done nothing to change his approach: a leader was useless if he did not earn his men's respect. If there was a personal risk involved, so be it. When he was not ordering the rehearsal of battle, coaching, encouraging, sometimes bullying to get the results he wanted, he was talking to the men: finding out as much as he could about the Isle of Clouds and the campaigns they had undertaken there, working out how they might achieve decisive victory where before there had been only numbing defeat. When the long day was over and the last lamp quenched, and the ill-assorted group of men snored in the half-light of the pale summer night, Thorvald lay wakeful, his head full of plans, schemes, strategies. There was much to lose here; if they failed in yet another hunt, he doubted these men would have the heart to try again. That meant this must be perfect to the last meticulous detail. Once they reached the Isle of Clouds, he must be prepared for anything.

And he would be. They would be. It was unfortunate that Asgrim seemed incapable of showing a genuine appreciation of their efforts; he remained grimly detached. As chieftain here, Thorvald thought, it was time the Ruler demonstrated some real leadership. If Margaret's account was accurate, Somerled had been misguided and cruel, but he had been a real leader. He had achieved things. Asgrim's lack of support dampened the men's enthusiasm and sapped their confidence. It came to Thorvald that, very soon, he must confront the Ruler openly; must ask him the question straight out. Surely, as a son, he could count on his father's full support in this endeavor. Perhaps all Thorvald needed to do was tell him the truth.

They made a map with wet sand, Orm and Skolli describing the contours of the island, its narrow coves, its one towering crag, its cliffs and outlying skerries, while Thorvald constructed it with careful fingers. Wieland prepared the mixture so it would hold its shape without crumbling. Knut, biting his lip in concentration, added detail in the form of small stones, twigs and greenery as instructed. Others stood around them in a circle, scratching heads or chins. Many were perplexed by what seemed a childish game, but as the Isle of Clouds took shape, complete with its caves, its rocky outcrops, its places of concealment and its places of danger, they began to nod and make suggestions: wasn't there a spot near the cliff there where a waterfall came down, and a hollow close by where two men could crouch under cover? The holm at the western end should be bigger, the channel splitting it from the main island narrower. There were rock stacks here and here, where gannets roosted. Yes, that was it. Odin's bones, the construction was a marvel: all it lacked was the breath of life to make it perfect.

"Now show me," Thorvald said, when all was fashioned to his satisfaction. "Where is the settlement of this nameless tribe that dwells on the Isle of Clouds? It's clear that we have only one possible landing place, and that severely limits our initial options. Einar tells me they sometimes attack as soon as you set foot on shore. But not always; some years, they've waited until you progressed to a point well inland. Where, exactly?"

"Don't know about a settlement," said Orm, squatting to peer more closely at the sculpted sand. "We never found one, nor much sign of habitation beyond the traps they set for us. You'd think it would be here." He motioned toward the westward end of the island, between the landing place and the sharply rising ground a short way inland. This was the only place where there seemed to be sufficient level ground for dwellings to be built, though they would have little shelter from the fierce lashing of westerly gales. "Where else, unless they dwell in the sea? There's not a hut, nor a hovel, nor any boats to be seen in those parts. Tumbledown ruin or two, that's all."

"What about these caves?" Thorvald queried. "They must live somewhere. Other concealed places on the island? Don't they have a child there? They must make fires. Have you seen any signs of smoke?"

Einar shook his head. "Only the mists they conjure up, to lead a fellow off his path and over the cliffs."

"I see," said Thorvald after a moment. "Then which direction do they come from when they attack? Maybe that is a clue. We must get this into our heads in a new way this summer; we need to reach a better understanding of the enemy before we go in. I intend to minimize casualties. We're going to win, and we're going to do it with as few losses as possible. Now let's run through the pattern of last year's hunt again. Orm?"

"It was bloody slaughter," Orm grunted, his eyes fixed on the shape they had made, elegant, ephemeral.

Thorvald waited, but nobody seemed to have anything to add. He drew a deep breath and let it out again. "Step by step, that's what I need," he told them calmly. "I know it was bad. I know it was frightening, and that many of your comrades were killed. That's why we need to fix in our minds just how it unfolded, so that we can avoid making the same errors next time." He looked up, alerted by some change in the quality of their silence. A circle of faces gazed down at him where he knelt by the sand map on the level ground above the shore: Orm's, grim with the memory of loss; Knut's, younger, lips curved in a tentative smile, for he had enjoyed his task as helper here; Wieland's, scarred, sad, resigned; many men, all of them watching him, all of them seeking something, a solution, a way out. He could give them that, if only he could make them understand.

"There may not be a next time." The Ruler had come up quietly; now he stood in the circle, shadowed by the larger form of Hogni behind him. Hogni craned to see what Thorvald had made; Asgrim's glance flicked over it dismissively.

Thorvald rose to his feet. Sudden anger possessed him, and he struggled to appear calm. "Yes, I heard talk of a treaty. That surprised me. Had I suffered such reversals, such losses over the years, my mind would be set on vengeance, not truce. There is a chance to defeat this enemy once and for all, to show him you are warriors of skill and courage. A red-blooded man does not shrink from such an opportunity, but strides forward to meet it."

"It seems to me," mused Asgrim, his dark eyes now fixed on Thorvald, his expression impossible to read, "that there may be a little self-interest here. You've done a good job, nobody's questioning that. All the same, one struggles to understand why. It's a lot for an incomer to take on himself."

Thorvald felt a flush rising to his cheeks, for all his efforts to contain his anger. Words spilled from his mouth before he could stop them. "What did you expect? That this *incomer* would stand by and see your men blundering their way toward yet another bloody defeat? That I would amuse myself tinkering with ill-fashioned spears and poorly strung bows, knowing all the while that the whole venture was headed for certain disaster? If that was what you thought, I can't imagine why you brought us here. You should simply have given us our piece of wood and waved us good-bye." His foot moved, trampling the little isle of sand into an amorphous heap; a general sigh went around the circle.

"You didn't need to wreck it," Knut said, outraged. "After all that work."

"Indeed." Thorvald heard the chill in his own voice. He could not remember being so angry for a long time, not since the day Margaret gave him the letter and changed his world. "The work has been for a purpose, and the purpose is victory and self-respect. After that comes the peace these men crave. Is it so hard for you to comprehend that a man may wish to put his talents to such a use, to lead others toward that goal?"

There was a frosty silence. After a little, the men started to edge away down to the shore or up to the sleeping quarters, with not a word said. Thorvald's heart was beating like a drum; he was caught between fury and fear. The Ruler's face was pale, his jaw tight. Probably nobody had ever spoken to him thus before. Thorvald held himself still, keeping his eyes on Asgrim's, waiting for a stinging volley of retaliatory words.

"You will never do that again." The Ruler's voice was deathly quiet. "If you feel you must express doubts as to the quality of my leadership, you'll do it in private. I will listen, as long as your arguments are based on fact and not ill-considered outpourings of emotion. You know less of the mastery of men than you think, if you imagine such an exchange will not damage your reputation among them. They know me. They trust me. I am one of them. You are young, untested, untried. You've kept them occupied during a difficult time, and that has been useful to me. But you have not fought alongside them, you have not suffered and wept with them, laid brother, father, comrade in cold earth beside theirs. You have not endured the wrath of the Unspoken. You have not seen the light go out in a child's eyes on the very day he first draws breath. How can you know what they want? You cannot even begin to understand how it is for them."

Thorvald felt as if Asgrim had struck him in the face. Hogni stood at a little distance, shifting his weight uneasily from one foot to the other. Farther away, the men's voices could now be heard as they went into the shelter.

"You're wrong," Thorvald said. He was unable to keep his voice from shaking. "It is at just such an extreme that good strategy and sound technique come into play. At such a time, when men risk becoming swamped in a tide of emotions, an incomer is exactly what you need. I stand outside this; I see it with clear eyes and can devise the necessary solutions. Give up and make a truce, and your men may survive a little longer, until the next time these other tribes decide to turn on you. Mount a solid attack, planned with precision and executed with discipline, and they can win back both peace and their belief in themselves. You would lead a stronger people forward on these isles of yours if you could do that. I believe I can make that possible for you." More words trembled on his lips, *Don't you know I am your son? Don't you see how we can change the future, make it good at last?* He bit them back.

"You speak with some passion," said Asgrim, "for all your talk of standing outside. I fail to comprehend your reasons for this dedication to a stranger's cause. You've worked very hard this past season; I've observed that. Your friend too"—he glanced along the shore to the place where Sam still labored on the *Sea Dove's* hull—"but his passion I do understand; the boat is his livelihood. You are more of an enigma. It seems that no sooner do you set foot on this shore than you are striving to control our endeavor, to prove you know better than we do how we should live our lives.

Did they cast you out of the Light Isles for meddling?" The Ruler's dark brows arched in query.

Thorvald flushed again. "Since we are on that tack, I have a question for you. Are you not, also, an incomer? Is not each of you a refugee from some other place, come to this shore to forget? The Lost Isles: a realm where a man can put his past life behind him, his errors, his misdeeds, the crimes he committed, the good deeds he never managed to do, all of that conveniently set aside now he lives where his past cannot pursue him. Surely only the youngest among you were born and bred in these islands. The tongue you speak is our own; your manner of life does not suggest to me an exile of many generations. It seems to me the Long Knife people are outsiders here just as I am. I'm only trying to help you. How dare you judge me?" He found he was shivering. The conversation was slipping from his grasp, something he had been at pains to prevent.

"I don't judge you, Thorvald," the Ruler said quietly. "I merely seek to discover whether, in my plans for the future, you represent an opportunity or a threat. Your manner, your words make it plain you see yourself as a leader. The Long Knife people have only one leader."

"I am no threat to you," Thorvald replied, wondering even as he spoke if this were the truth. "I have not acted thus from any desire to harm your cause or undermine your authority. Perhaps my motives are hard to understand. At home I was—I had—I felt I was outside affairs, in a way cut adrift. I—" Gods, he was sounding like a stammering, confused child. He forced his breathing to slow. "My father was lost to me; I never knew him. I have struggled to find a place for myself, a role and purpose. I traveled here at least partly in the hope of discovering both."

"Mmm," said Asgrim, frowning. "The question is, do you desire simply to step into another man's shoes? You know me a little by now, Thorvald. You know, surely, that such an ambition would set a very short term on your life."

"I've heard you can be ruthless, yes. I understand that, at least in part. A leader must act decisively in such a realm or quickly lose his authority."

The Ruler nodded. "Tell me," he said, "why here? Why not southward to Ulster, or back to the east? This is a dark corner of the world, Thorvald, dark and forbidding. It does not welcome strangers. Such a choice seems wayward: not the decision of a rational man."

Thorvald drew a deep breath. "I thought it possible a kinsman had made his way here long ago," he said. "I wished to discover if it was true. That was the sole reason for my choice. I have told you this already, I think. I suspect Creidhe may also have mentioned it to you."

Something flashed across the Ruler's face, a shadow, a swift change, and was gone as rigid control was imposed on his features once more.

"I had forgotten." Asgrim spoke lightly. "What kinsman was this? These isles are not well populated; nobody arrives without my knowledge. What manner of man?"

Thorvald swallowed. "He'd be of about the same years as yourself now, perhaps forty or somewhat less; a fit, able young man when he came here, and of Norse extraction."

"His appearance?"

Thorvald could not prevent his mouth from twisting in self-mockery. "Somewhat akin to my own, I imagine. I never met him. He traveled to this shore in the year before my birth."

Asgrim's eyes narrowed. "I see," he said slowly. "And could you put a name to this fellow?"

"A man can change his name." Thorvald could feel his heart thumping in a crazy dance, as if it sought to leap from his breast. "Probably did, I imagine, seeking this shore as so many others did, in order to forget."

"All the same."

"Somerled," Thorvald said. "His name was Somerled."

There was a lengthy silence. Hogni gave a little cough and shuffled his feet; from the shelter, now, came a smell of fish frying in oil, and a plume of smoke arose from the hole in the roof, to be quickly snatched away by the wind. The sky was glowing red, the sun sinking in the west beyond the dove-gray shadow that was the Isle of Clouds. Thorvald watched Asgrim's face. The man was a master of control;

for a considerable time he seemed to react not at all. When he did, it was with a fleeting, humorless smile that set a chill on Thorvald's heart.

"Really," Asgrim said. "Somerled. There is no man in these isles who answers to that name now. What was this Somerled to you, that you seek him so far from the safety of home, though he was gone before you ever clapped eyes on him?"

Thorvald turned away, unable to bear the malice that had awoken in Asgrim's dark eyes, the cruelty in the set of his thin lips. "It doesn't matter," he said, hardly recognizing his own voice, which seemed to come from somewhere far distant. "It's of little importance."

It was only after he had walked away, ten, twelve paces up toward the shelter and the false comfort of companions who probably thought even less of him than the Ruler seemed to, that Thorvald heard Asgrim's voice behind him, light, mocking.

"Your father?"

So this was what it came to. He had traveled this far, had given all he had in an attempt to achieve something worthwhile and lasting, to prove himself. He had found his father, and his father cared so little for the bond of kinship that he didn't even take the trouble to acknowledge it. Yet it was there, and Asgrim knew it: Thorvald had recognized that in the supercilious lift of the brows, the cruelly bantering tone of voice. This was Somerled all right. Somerled had found his own place in the Lost Isles, a place with no room at all for a son.

Thorvald sat alone on the rock shelves above the pebbly shore. Small waves washed in and out in the half-light, the sound they made a sighing, sorrowful, resigned. *We change, and are the same. This is as it was. This is as it is. This is as it will be.* He threw a pebble into the water, and another. The sky had darkened to the gray of sealskin, tinged with a faint glow that was both memory and anticipation of day. This was as dark as it seemed to get in summer here. He could hear the solitary calls of birds, somewhere up there winging from cliff to cliff, a mournful counterpoint to the whispering of the sea.

There was no more to say. There was no more to be done. If your own father did not want to recognize you, even when you had tried your best to please him, that said something pretty clear about your value in the world, didn't it? If he wasn't prepared to acknowledge you even though he himself was an exile, a man who understood, surely, how it felt to be cast aside as if you were rubbish, then what did that make you? Thorvald shivered. Why had he come here? Why had he trusted his instincts instead of thinking this through properly? He had been angry: angry with his mother for holding back the truth, for being less than the perfect creature he had believed her, for . . . he did not know what. Margaret was human, after all. She must have been barely seventeen when she lay with Somerled and made a son who would grow up as dark and twisted as his father. He had been furious with Eyvind, who had been his father's dearest friend and who had banished Somerled forever from the land where he had once been king. What man would take so drastic a course of action? The boat, they said, had been a frail curragh of wattles and skins, the provisions minimal. Such a repudiation had been heartless. It had been quite out of character for Creidhe's father, known as the most wise and just of men. He wished, now, he had talked to Eyvind. Most of all, Thorvald had been angry with himself, because the day Margaret told him the truth, he had recognized that he was his father's son. He bore within him Somerled's cruelty, his ambition, his single-mindedness. Somerled had become king because he was ruthless and driven. He was Ruler here for just the same reasons. His talk of sharing sorrow and regret with his men was sentimental rubbish, no more than a play for Thorvald's sympathy. Asgrim remained leader here not through any fellow feeling, but because of his iron fist and the way he fueled his people's fear of the Unspoken. Thorvald knew, to his shame, that he carried the same determination, the same grim sense of purpose within his own breast. He knew it made him snap and snarl at those who sought to curb him. He knew it made him blind, sometimes, to the needs of those around him. Creidhe had told him so, and Creidhe never lied. At the time he had pretended not to hear her. But he had heard, understood and accepted; accepted this dark energy inside him, which could work to achieve more wondrous goals than an ordinary man might dare to aspire to, and could work to send him spiraling downward into a deep pit of despair.

Gods, how he wanted Creidhe here now, sitting quietly beside him in that way she had, still and calm, just listening. He could say anything to Creidhe and know she would understand and forgive. She was the only one he could talk to when this black mood was on him; tell his true thoughts to anyone else and he would be judged as crazy. There were times when he would have believed that himself if Creidhe had not been there to comfort and reassure him. True, she was a little free with her advice at times, but nonetheless in some strange way she was essential to him. He realized he had missed her a long time, without recognizing what it was he lacked.

Well, if Asgrim got his truce, Thorvald thought savagely, hurling another stone into the sea, he would see Creidhe soon enough, for this would all be over, his work with the men completely wasted, the neatly made weapons set away in storage, the tribe of the Unspoken and their ghostly counterparts on the Isle of Clouds allowed their victory without even a token resistance. Orm, Wieland, Knut, the rest of them would think they were safe, would think this was an easy peace, until it all started again. And it would start again; such feuds did not die after so lame an ending. Something would reignite the burning anger, and these tribes would be at war once more, and the Long Knife people would be vanquished because he had not been allowed to lead them, because by then they would have forgotten what he had taught them. Pointless, useless, all of it. He tossed another stone. Futile and wasteful. A pox on Asgrim and his treaty. A curse on his cynical laughter. How dare he mock? Thorvald sat there a long time, his thoughts turning in a familiar pattern. One step forward, two steps back, that seemed to be the way of it for him. It was as if a shadow had been cast over his life before ever he left his mother's womb: a kind of curse, almost, that Somerled had bestowed on him as a reminder, for the rest of his days, that he was flawed, damaged, unable to set his hand to anything without all turning to ashes. He had allowed himself to forget that in the challenge of making this disparate rabble of islanders into a disciplined fighting force. He had believed in the task and, for a little, he had believed in himself. That just went to show how warped his own judgment was, for it had taken Asgrim—Somerled—only a moment to destroy his son's vision. How much of a man were you, when your own father dismissed you as a meddling incomer?

In his mind, somewhere, he could hear Creidhe's voice, quiet, careful, saying, *There are others who love you, Thorvald, others who believe in you. Your mother . . . Do not forget Margaret, and Ash, and your friends*. But he closed his thoughts to those half-remembered, half-imagined words, for tonight he was beyond such comfort. Creidhe was not here, nor Margaret, nor anyone but Sam who snored among the others in the shelter, worn out by an honest day's work on the boat. Thorvald was alone with the ocean and the night, alone in a place well suited to a man whose spirit seemed no more than a small echo of the desolate shores, the harsh, bare-topped hills, the monstrous cliffs and voracious surges of this most ungiving of realms. One could make an end of things, of course. On such an isle the means were readily at hand, the answer as easy as stepping off a cliff or entering the water at night when nobody else was at hand to cry, *No!* Thorvald pondered this, considering the methods, and which would be quickest and least untidy. Somerled could have killed himself, all those years ago. His voyage of exile had been desperate, a far greater challenge than that terrible journey on the *Sea Dove*. Sam's boat was big and sturdy and there had been three of them to handle her in the end. Somerled had been alone. He had not known

if there was any land at all to be found to the west of that
shore where his dearest friend had cast him adrift. Yet he
had not taken the easy choice of a sharp knife and a quick,
bloody trip to oblivion. Somerled had gone on; had gritted
his teeth and followed some inner voice to this wild place to
make his life anew. Why? To become Ruler of a sad collection of dispirited folk at the mercy of the Lost Isles' earlier
and more dangerous inhabitants? To father a daughter and a
son and then lose both in a futile struggle for survival?
There was no reward in that, no satisfaction at all. But he
had stayed here. He had chosen this, and chosen to survive.
And Thorvald knew that he, too, would choose life, for all
the dark thoughts that hedged him around. There was no
saying why; there was no sense to it. It was simply the
steady beating of the heart, the regular pulsing of the blood,
and at the point where outward breath pauses and becomes
inward, the decision each time, the knowing. *I will go on. It
is not yet my moment of darkness*. Even in this, it seemed he
was his father's son.

Dawn came eventually, and not long after it Sam, with a
frown on his usually placid brow.

"Been out all night, have you? Not the best start to the
working day."

Thorvald said nothing.

"Cold, too, summer or no summer. Here." Sam dropped a
blanket over his friend's shoulders. It would have seemed a
gesture of childish petulance to shrug it off; Thorvald gathered it around him, not trusting himself to speak, for all of a
sudden he seemed to have tears in his eyes: utterly foolish.

"Heard you and Asgrim had a little disagreement," Sam
said without any particular emphasis. "Did you tell him?"

Thorvald nodded. "More or less," he managed. "He
chose not to recognize it; I should have expected that, I
suppose."

There was a short silence.

"I'm sorry," Sam said quietly. "Sorry, but not surprised.

He's got his own little world out here, and no room for anything else in it."

They sat awhile as the sky lightened above them, and
one or two of the fellows passed by on the way to the
boats. It would be a good day for fishing: fine, mild, a day
on which the Lost Isles wore a face that belied their true
wildness.

"Thorvald?"

"Mmm?"

"The *Sea Dove*'s all but ready. The fellows have shaped
the mast better than I could have expected, and it turns out
there's a sail of sorts ready-made, from a boat they salvaged
a year or two since. I'm not overkeen to have her used in
Asgrim's crazy hunt; she's likely to end up on the bottom of
the sea, and us with her, if we sail her across this Fool's
Tide of theirs. And I'm not a fighting man, you know that. I
could have her ready to go, day after tomorrow. What I
think is, we should go back and pick up Creidhe from that
settlement, guards or no guards, and then sail away off
home. Weather seems set fair for a bit. Don't get me wrong.
I'm not pushing you. I know this is hard for you, and you've
got to make your own choices. Just quietly, there's one of
the fellows willing to come with me in your place, providing Asgrim doesn't get wind of it before we're safely away.
Still, if I were you I wouldn't be staying. There it is."

Thorvald did not answer for a while; to do so seemed to
be to put his own failure into words. Eventually he said,
"I'll give you an answer tonight. Will that do?"

"Of course," Sam said gravely. "Tell you what. Why
don't you work with me today, finishing off the *Sea Dove*?
You've a good eye for detail; I could use that. Knut's keen,
but he's better on the rough jobs. Give you some time to
think. I promise not to talk too much."

The simple kindness of this offer left Thorvald without
words for a reply.

"No privileges for friends, mind," Sam said with a grin.
"I plan to work you hard so we can get the job finished. Best
go up and have some breakfast, it'll be a long day."

* * *

Thorvald recognized later that Sam's suggestion had been not only kind but also remarkably wise. The hard physical labor stopped his mind from going around in circles; he was just too busy to think beyond the next rivet, the next plank, the brush and tar. No sooner had he finished one job than Sam gave him another, or sought his help with heavy lifting or his advice on whether the joint between the timbers was perfectly aligned and properly watertight. Knut worked in cheerful silence, content to do as he was told. It was with genuine surprise that Thorvald noticed, as he smoothed off the inner surface of the last of the replacement timbers, that the sun hung low over the Isle of Clouds once more, and that it would soon be too dark to continue. He realized in the same moment that, without being aware of any process taking place, he had made up his mind. He was going home.

Knut had run out of tasks and was heading back for supper. Sam was packing away his tools; being far from home had made him, if anything, still tidier and more methodical. Thorvald climbed down from the *Sea Dove* onto the coarse sand of the beach.

"Sam?"

"Uh-huh?"

"I wanted to tell you—" Thorvald broke off at the sound of angry voices from the encampment; there were running footsteps now and the flare of torches. He thought he could hear Skapti's rumbling tones, but the man who had shouted was Asgrim.

"What's going on there, I wonder?" muttered Sam.

"Better find out," said Thorvald. A strange sensation gripped him, a chilling premonition of change. "Come on."

They began to walk back.

"What was it you were going to tell me?" Sam asked.

"Never mind. It can wait." That sense touched him again, excitement, dread, anticipation. Perhaps this was not over yet. Perhaps the plans for a truce had fallen through; what else could make Asgrim lose his temper in front of all the men? *Give me this chance,* Thorvald found himself praying to whatever god might be prepared to listen. *Give it back; let me lead them. It is only right.*

When they reached the shelter the Ruler was nowhere to be seen. The men were very quiet. The usual routine of cooking, eating, preparing for rest was unfolding, but Hogni and Einar were absent, and did not appear as the fish stew was served and consumed. Thorvald asked Orm what had happened, but Orm, like the rest of them, knew little. Skapti had come in not long ago and given the Ruler some news, news that had evidently not pleased him at all. Skapti had been looking grim and tired, not himself. Asgrim had taken him up to his private quarters right away, and Einar and Hogni too. They were not to be disturbed. That was all anyone knew.

"You think this means no truce?" Thorvald ventured, keeping his voice down.

Several men turned to look at him: Orm, Wieland, Skolli. Where his own heart was filled with dawning hope, with purpose rekindled, their eyes held only a terrible, sorrowful resignation.

"What else would it be?" said Wieland flatly. "The Unspoken have rejected the offer; the hunt's on after all."

"You can't know that yet." Thorvald felt obliged to say this, though he was certain the other man was right. It would be hard work to persuade them that this was, in fact, good news.

"I suppose he'll tell us in the morning," grunted Orm. "And we'll go on, like always. I'm for bed. Put out that lantern, will you?"

Thorvald had been a long time without sleep. Tonight, however, it did not seem appropriate to give way to it. He sat on the earthen shelf by the others, a solitary seal-oil lamp that burned by the doorway the only light save the glowing embers of the cooking fire. He saw that Sam, too, was awake, lying blanket-swathed among the men, eyes fixed squarely on Thorvald himself. They did not speak. Perhaps each knew the other's thoughts. The *Sea Dove* was finished and ready to go; all hung in the balance.

The summons, when it came, was a subdued one. Hogni stood in the doorway, gave a little whistle, jerked his head.

Thorvald rose and went out, careful to avoid stepping on the close-packed ranks of slumbering men; he was aware that Sam had followed him, and waited for Hogni to send the fisherman back, but the bodyguard shepherded the two of them up the track in the moonlight and into Asgrim's hut. The Ruler stood there waiting, with Skapti and Einar by him. The lines bracketing Asgrim's mouth and furrowing his brow were starkly visible tonight; he looked old. Einar was withdrawn and pale, the big warrior Skapti nervous as a boy, restlessly moving his feet, clenching and unclenching his hands. Hogni had remained outside by the door.

"Thorvald, Sam." The Ruler regarded them levelly, his eyes giving nothing away; his voice, however, was less than steady. "You'd better sit down. Einar, give them some ale."

They sat; one did not disobey Asgrim. Thorvald was confused. He had expected to be called, if the truce were not to go ahead; he had hoped to be given instructions: *Get the men back into training, continue what you began, for I need you now.* But why had Sam, too, been summoned here? Why were they all behaving so strangely, as if this news was almost too hard to tell?

When they were seated on the bench with ale cups before them, Asgrim cleared his throat and spoke again.

"There's no good way to put this. I have some bad news for you. Shocking and distressing news. Skapti has borne it back from Brightwater." He fell silent, clasping his hands together in front of him; the other men were as still as stones. It was Sam who broke that dreadful hush, Sam's voice bursting out harsh and uncontrolled as Thorvald had never heard it before, a sound that clutched at the gut, though Thorvald did not know why.

"What?" Sam cried, springing to his feet. "Tell us now! What?"

"Hush, hush, please, sit down," Asgrim said, moving forward with hands outstretched to ease the distressed Sam back to the bench. Sam shook him off, raising a fist, and in a flash Einar was in front of the Ruler, a shield against attack. Sam's face flushed scarlet.

"Sit down, Sam," Thorvald muttered. "Do as he says. And let us hear this news, I beg you," he addressed Asgrim with exaggerated politeness. "If you think us unable to bear it, whatever it is, rest assured that postponing the moment of truth will do nothing to allay our misgivings."

"It's Creidhe, isn't it?" Sam blurted out. "Something's happened to Creidhe."

And as the silence descended once more, and Asgrim bowed his head to stare at his linked hands, Thorvald felt a terrible cold spreading through him, starting in the vicinity of the heart and seeping gradually outward.

"What?" he croaked. "What's happened?"

"Your little friend was taken." Asgrim's voice shook. "Taken by our enemies. And—"

There was no stopping Sam this time. He lunged forward, seizing the Ruler by the shoulders and shaking him hard. "What!" he roared. "You told us she would be safe! When was this? Why aren't you going after her? You know what they'll do to her—"

The words were stifled as Einar clapped a hand over Sam's mouth and, with Skapti's help, dragged him away from Asgrim.

"Hush, Sam." Something had gone wrong with Thorvald's voice; the most he could summon was a whisper. "We need to hear this. Let Asgrim finish." For this wasn't all. He could see that in his father's eyes.

"She wandered away from the settlement early one morning, while all were abed. The women said she had probably gone to visit the hermits, those crazy Christians who live up in the hills. Skapti was in the area and saw her taken. The Unspoken came from the sea; it was very quick. Their boat was in and out almost before you could blink."

Thorvald looked at Skapti, who still held Sam in an iron-hard grip, though Sam, in fact, had stopped struggling altogether. "What were you doing?" he heard himself say. "Why didn't you help her? She's only a girl." Curiously, he felt that perhaps it was to himself he was speaking.

Skapti's blunt features went red. He opened his mouth and closed it again.

"He did try, Thorvald," Asgrim said gently. "But he could not reach her in time. And then . . ." He paused.

"She drowned," Skapti said, releasing Sam suddenly so that the fisherman slumped back onto the bench beside his friend. "I saw it. They were well out, and she stood up, and the boat tipped over, right into the Fool's Tide. They were all swept away and drowned. I saw her go under. This is a cursed place. I wish I had never come here—"

"Yes, all right, Skapti," Asgrim said a little curtly, and the bodyguard fell silent, wiping his nose on his sleeve. "It's true, I'm afraid," the Ruler went on, seating himself opposite Thorvald. "It is dreadful tidings; I hardly know what to say to you. Such a sweet girl, and so beautiful. She had become well liked in the settlement. This is typical of our enemy, I'm afraid; I suffered a similar loss myself, and understand how you must feel."

"You?" snarled Sam. "How could you hope to understand, you selfish—"

"Sam." Thorvald laid an arm around his friend's shoulders, and Sam, with a strange, sobbing groan, put his head in his hands. Thorvald would have welcomed the chance to weep himself, or shout his grief and fury aloud. But this was a moment that called for something else and, digging deep within him, he found it. "I want to know exactly how this has been allowed to happen." His tone was chill, precise. "We were assured of Creidhe's safety. We were discouraged from returning to Brightwater to visit her. You say she wandered away. Creidhe is a grown woman and far from stupid. She doesn't wander."

"Perhaps not," Asgrim said quietly. "But her behavior is—was—unpredictable, you cannot deny that. Didn't she almost step off the cliff path on the way over from Blood Bay? Maybe she had another of her visions, one that led her into the hands of the Unspoken."

"What about these hermits?" Thorvald queried. "I've heard no talk of any Christians. I want a proper answer here; I sense we've been denied the full truth. If such a death occurred in my homeland there would be a thorough investigation and compensation to be made. I am extremely displeased." The words came out smoothly; a calm cold seemed to have descended on him, allowing him to continue this dark game, though within him a terrible, wild thing was building, like a trapped animal struggling for release. He must not allow it to break free. He must maintain control here.

"The hermits? No more than a nuisance, generally," Asgrim said. "They've been here a long time. There are more of them in other parts of the isles, mostly from Ulster. They seem content to keep themselves to themselves, except for one meddler who doesn't know when to hold his tongue. He has persuaded your little friend to stray, perhaps. I'll arrange for him to be questioned, if that is your wish."

Thorvald lifted his brows, compressed his lips. Beside him Sam now wept in open misery; Einar had come forward to crouch beside the fisherman. Thorvald's arm still lay across Sam's shoulders; the sobs seemed to go through his own body, jolting the heart, unmanning the will, but he kept his arm where it was. He could do this. He was a leader.

"I take it there is no chance," he said, "not even the smallest chance—?"

Asgrim shook his head. "In the Fool's Tide? None at all. I'm afraid she's gone, Thorvald. I'm sorry, so very sorry. What more can I say?"

This was getting harder; Thorvald forced his breathing to slow. He looked the Ruler directly in the eye, and Asgrim stared back at him unblinking.

"The repairs are finished on the boat," Thorvald said. "We've decided to go home. We must bear this news to Creidhe's family. The weather seems fine just now. We thought we'd leave the day after tomorrow."

"But—" Einar and Skapti both spoke at once, and both bit back their words.

"I see," said Asgrim. "And I understand why you would wish to do so, though I recall some words of yours, spoken not so very long ago. You said, *Had I suffered such losses, my mind would be set on vengeance, not truce.* Do you change your mind so quickly?"

Sam had fallen silent, though his shoulders still heaved. Einar fished in his pocket, drew out a square of cloth, crumpled and gray, and handed it to the fisherman. Thorvald did not speak.

"You realize, of course, that after such a terrible event, I can no longer think of a truce with this enemy," Asgrim said. "Who could consider peace with the Unspoken now? To snatch one of our girls in broad daylight, at a time when we had treated for peace and were merely awaiting their response—that was barbaric, outrageous. After this, it can only be war between us."

Another silence. Skapti sighed; Sam used the handkerchief to wipe his eyes and then, noisily, to blow his nose.

"I had hoped," Asgrim spread his hands in appeal, "to have you by my side in this venture, Thorvald, to lead my men. I had hoped Sam would lend us his fine boat, to spearhead our advance across those treacherous waters where Creidhe died so cruelly. His skills in seamanship, too—we have no such experts among our own men. You could aid us immensely, the two of you. It could make all the difference in the hunt. Still, I do understand if you wish to leave now. No attempt at revenge is going to bring Creidhe back, nor my Sula either. You must do as you think best."

Thorvald waited. He saw the signs of uncertainty begin to appear, a slight change in the Ruler's eyes, a shifting of the hands on the table before him. Asgrim knew he could not do this without Thorvald's help. It was a gift; it was the opportunity for which Thorvald had been longing, despite himself. To accept it was to accept the price it had cost.

"We'll stay." Sam's voice was muffled, but the words were clear enough. "We'll stay until the hunt's over. We'll wipe the scum off the Isle of Clouds, and then we'll go for the other ones. By Thor's hammer, if any of those animals that laid their hands on Creidhe survived this, they'll be lying in their own blood when I get the chance to come near them. You can count on us. Creidhe deserves no less."

After that there was nothing more to be said. Asgrim offered them sleeping space in his hut, and they declined.
Hogni and Einar shepherded Sam back to the shelter, one
on either side; there were no clenched fists or threatening
gestures now. Once there, others were woken and ale produced; it was apparent they intended to drink long into the
night and thus offer the fisherman a temporary oblivion.
Thorvald did not linger there. Getting away seemed to be
imperative right now, as far away from the others as he
could, but it was night, and the paths were dangerous above
the bay. All the same, he walked a fair distance by moonlight, until he found a small hollow below the clifftop where
he could look back down and see the lamplight from the
shelter, and the lesser light from the open doorway of Asgrim's hut, the looming form of Skapti standing outside, his
shadow lying huge and strange across the uneven ground.

Thorvald sat and gazed over the dark sea. What was inside him was growing stronger, fiercer, clamoring to be let
out; he forced control on it, for to be a true leader, one must
first learn to master oneself. A real man does not scream his
pain, does not rail at the stars, at the gods, at the evil of enemies or the frailty of friends. A real man is strong. Even
alone at night on a clifftop in darkness, he does not put his
heart on display. So he sat in silence, breathing as he had
seen Creidhe do when he had upset her and she was trying
hard not to cry: one, two, three in, one, two, three out. It
seemed to work for him, or almost work; he managed to
hold the sound in, to stifle what he knew would be an eldritch howling of grief, the cry of a wounded animal.
Strange, though: he did not seem to be able to stop the tears
that were running in a hot flood down his cheeks, tears
whose origin he could not understand, for surely within him
there was only emptiness.

Keeper had not expected a goddess to be washed up on his
island. He saw the boat coming, saw and distrusted his eyes,
keen as they were. From the watch point high on the hill, on

a good day, it was possible to make out quite small things: the little whales dancing in the swell, a flock of terns sweeping like a silver banner over the Troll's Arch, smoke from the cottages at Council Fjord. He watched awhile, seeing the flash of gold, the draping of pale cloth across the dark skin covering of the boat. He tried to make sense of it. Then, when it became apparent the Fool's Tide was delivering this gift to his own island, Keeper went out to take possession of it.

At first, Small One had bounded ahead, glad of an expedition, for they had been a long time still, simply watching. Tide and wind had told Keeper it was not yet hunt time, but those days were coming soon. Not the smallest sign must escape his observation, not the least clue, or he might not be ready for them. His spears waited, his missiles, his traps. But foremost among his weapons were his own ears and eyes, his fleetness of foot, and the island itself. They had spent many days watching, and Small One was growing restless.

So, he was first on the stones of the tiny inlet; first by the upturned boat with its cargo tangled limply in the ropes that twisted over the hull; first to stop short, then back away, staring. Keeper, too, was halted by something he could not name: a sense of turning, of changing, which was both wonder and dread. His fingers moved to touch the plaited circle around his neck, faded to the hue of dust; his eyes were on the limp figure that lay sprawled on the curragh. Her hair was darkened with water, tangled and wild; nonetheless, it lay across her face, her shoulders, down her back like a waterfall of sunlight. He swallowed. Sula was dead; she would never come back. He had seen her, little and gray-faced, like a shrunken mockery of his laughing, merry sister. This was someone else, someone who lay still and silent, pale hands twisted in the ropes, clothing sodden and dripping, and one narrow, white foot exposed below the hem of her woolen gown. She bore a small bag on her back; this, too, looked wet through. It was late in the day, the sun three fingers' breadth above the ocean. Could a goddess drown, or perish from cold? Keeper made himself move forward, past the spot where Small One stood trembling on the shore, right up to the dark form of the beached boat. He took his knife from his belt and began to cut, though he did it carefully: nothing could be wasted here, for they lived on what the sea gave them, and what the hunt left behind. He would use the ropes, the timbers, the tarred covering, everything.

At a certain point it became necessary to support the weight of that limp figure with his body, and Keeper realized she was a mortal woman. Not long after, the screening curtain of golden hair fell back from her face, and he discovered that she was wondrously fair, and still alive, but only just. He changed what he was doing then. Salvaging the boat could wait for morning; if the tide reclaimed it in the night, perhaps that was only as it should be. Of these unexpected gifts from the sea, it had become quite clear which was the most precious.

He called to Small One, "Quick! Blankets!" but Small One was being difficult, and had gone to ground among the rocks above the shore. That was not so surprising. When other folk came to their island it was always to hurt, to kill. They came with their iron-tipped spears, their forest of arrows and their angry eyes. Of course Small One was afraid. He could remember only the years of the hunt, nothing of the time before. He had been barely one year old when Keeper brought him here, his mother's golden hair no more than a faint warmth in his infant mind. In this world, strangers meant terror, blood and death. So he cowered in the shadows, watching, as Keeper took the woman in his arms and carried her up to their safe place.

It was necessary to be quick. She was moon-pale, her breathing slow and uneven. Keeper felt the chill touch of her skin, observed that she was not shivering: she was close to giving in, then, allowing her spirit to slip away. Still, she breathed. He called to Small One again, but there was no answer. The other would come when he was hungry; there was nobody else to provide for him. Keeper moved with the efficiency of a man who has lived long alone and is used to finding solutions. He raked the embers, made up the fire in the pit within their little shelter. He fetched the blankets; they only had a few, and these were very threadbare now, but there was a store of other things, trophies of the hunt: cloaks, tunics, a jacket of sheepskin. After he got her warm enough, after she woke, he would delve deeper into the items he had laid away. Somewhere among them were two gowns of Sula's; why he had brought them here he did not know, save that once he had discovered she was dead, it had not seemed right to leave the smallest memory of her among those who had stolen her childhood, her innocence and, eventually, her life. He had her little shoes as well. He would offer those: make a gift of them. But not yet. He'd have to take those wet things off the woman, wrap her in the blankets and let her lie by the fire a while.

He knew, once he had undressed her, that she would not be able to wear his sister's clothes. Sula had been frail, slight, scarcely more than a child. This girl was . . . she was . . . his hands shaking, he laid her on a cloak spread by the fire, covered her with two more and then the blankets. He reached to brush the strands of sun-gold hair back from her pale brow. This girl was, quite simply, the loveliest thing he had ever seen in his life, or might hope to see. He sat by her a little, watching her face, willing a touch of rose into her cheeks, a flutter of awareness to her long lashes. She was a miracle of sweet curves and elegant planes, of white and pink and gold; a graceful, tantalizing, terrifying creature whose presence by his fireside filled his heart with a tumult of feelings and his body with a confusing mixture of pleasure and pain. It occurred to him that perhaps he had been right the first time: maybe she really was a goddess. What human woman could wreak such instant havoc simply by lying there?

The fire was glowing warm now. He could tell Small One was back; the light the flames cast picked out the two bright points of his eyes between the rocks outside the hut. Small One was still frightened; he would not come back to himself until Keeper could convince him it was safe.

There were the wet clothes to deal with. He spread them out, a gown, an overtunic, a fine shift for underneath. All were ripped and damaged from the sea. He would find her something, make her something; he had become good at that, caring for Small One, who had come away with little. There was the bag she had worn on her shoulders, a precious thing to her, Keeper judged, or she would have shed it in the water. It was completely saturated.

Out of the corner of his eye, he saw Small One creep in, sidling to the far end of the fire pit. Keeper fetched the night's fish, ready in its wrapping of weed, and set it by the fire, knowing Small One would find reassurance in this familiar activity. He could not cook it yet, the flames were too high; but he must keep them thus to warm her, to bring her back. What he would do then, he could not imagine.

The bag: her things would be ruined. He unfastened the strap that held it and began to unpack the contents with careful fingers and lay them out to dry on a flat rock near the fire. Each seemed an object of wonder, secret and magical. A whalebone comb, carven with little sea creatures; there was still a thread of her bright hair in it. Shears made of iron, well sharpened, and a small, businesslike knife. He dried these thoroughly, knowing how quickly rust would dull and blunt them. Small One had moved closer and was watching intently; the iron made him flinch. Keeper, too, felt deep unease at the touch, the smell, but he had made himself grow used to handling this bane, since it was essential to their survival here. A length of strong cloth, which unfolded to show many small pockets holding bone needles, other delicate implements whose names he did not know, and skeins of colored wools, beautiful colors, the hues of his island: evening blue, night sky purple, sunrise gold, seal gray. The magic here was powerful indeed. He set them on the rock, arranged with care, light to dark, dawn to dusk to night. This little bag held a whole world: what was she?

There were other items here, useful ones: some clothing, a coiled rope, a flint, a jar firmly corked, which he did not open, a shallow vessel of soapstone and a length of wick.

There had been herbs, too, in an oiled bag, but the bag had split and they were ruined. Keeper sat a while, simply looking at what lay before him. For a goddess, she had a very practical turn of mind; he could hardly have packed better himself. She lacked only a fishhook, he thought.

Small One came closer, nudged at Keeper's arm. His nose was cold.

"You're hungry? I know, I will cook the fish soon. Soon. When she wakes—"

Small One nudged again, making a little sound. He touched his nose to the bag, sniffing. And now that Keeper looked, he could see there was another compartment to it, a pocket on the outside, itself firmly tied with a length of string. One could not have imagined a receptacle that seemed so small could encompass so much. They unfastened it together, and Keeper drew out the roll of fine linen that had been tucked securely inside. It was very strange; where all else was wet through, as was only natural after such a sea journey, this felt completely dry, pale and clean. He made a space on the rock and slowly unrolled it.

For a long time he only stared, entranced into a deep silence, his eyes moving slowly along the intricate pattern of tiny images and vivid colors, a whole world of mystery and wonder revealed in complex fashioning of fine wool. He could see it moving, evolving, as if the tale it told, the truths it held, were ever-shifting, even as the heart and spirit of man or woman grows and changes and strives toward what is new. He thought that he might sit there forever, as the sun rose and fell above him and the seasons painted new colors on sea and sky, and still never quite see all of it. Her own tale was here, and others, for there was a man at the start of it, a fine warrior with yellow hair like hers, and a mark on his arm. There was a woman, a priestess he thought, for creatures floated in the air around her, an owl, an otter, a dog, and at her feet was a little child, her own Small One. The goddess herself was in this pattern, flying in the sky, touching the moon, her golden hair streaming out behind her. A boat, in a storm; the goddess and her companions were in it . . . and there, the Isle of Clouds . . .

He became aware, at some point, that Small One had decided it was safe at last and had climbed onto his knee in order to see better. They studied the magical web together. After a while, Keeper began to tell Small One the tale, as he saw it. It was important to use language, to make sure Small One could understand it, even though, so far, he had not seemed to master speech himself. Keeper was young and strong, but he would not always be young. What would become of Small One then? So Keeper tried, as often as he could, to impart to the one he guarded whatever might be useful: to make fire, to find shelter, to speak and be understood. It was not easy. What Small One knew, he knew deep in the bone. What he could do, nobody had needed to teach him. The other things, the skills a man required in order to survive, had so far eluded his grasp.

"Here is her father," Keeper said in a whisper so as not to disturb his goddess, "see, a fine man with sun-colored hair, as she has. Here her mother, a wise woman; these creatures are her spirit friends, as the puffins and seals are ours. Here is her little brother—like you—but she had to leave him behind. See where she journeyed, far, far across the sea . . . much farther than we did . . . with two strong companions. One has hair as red as fire, the other is wheaten fair, perhaps her big brother. She came to the islands, but she was hurt, frightened . . . See here, the voices, the faces . . . they scared her, so she ran away . . ."

Small One had his thumb in his mouth; his eyes were intent on the picture, his body warm and relaxed against Keeper's. His fear was gone. He mumbled something, not words, just a sound meaning *More*.

"You must remember," Keeper said, "that there are many stories here, countless tales; each time a man looks into this web, he sees another, and another behind it. You could spend a lifetime looking, learning. I tell only one tonight. She climbed a long way, up the hill to a little house where there were friends." He knew the house, he had been there himself, long ago. Brother Niall he remembered, a white-haired man, and another, younger. They had been kind to him. His father had beaten him for going there. "Friends . . .

but . . ." The pattern ended there. The last thing he could see was a hand, reaching out into emptiness. "But in the end, they could not help her," Keeper said, and he looked up. The goddess still lay by the fire, the curves of her body not quite concealed by the warm covers he had heaped over her. The light from the glowing embers touched the golden sheen of her hair and the faint pink of her cheeks, and showed him a pair of eyes the blue of a summer sky, wide open and watching him.

EIGHT

Fair is the prattle of a child
Fair a woman's voice, singing
Fairer still, silence.

MONK'S MARGIN NOTE

When she came out of the fever at last, Creidhe wondered if she had imagined it: the young man, tall, lean, scarred, dangerous-looking, with tattered garments and a wildness about him that suggested something less, or more, than human; and the ragged child on his knee, half-asleep, sucking its thumb, held safe by this most improbable of keepers. She recalled the look in their eyes, dazzled, enchanted, caught in the vision, her vision; she could still hear the gentle flow of his voice, telling, extraordinarily, her own story. No one had ever seen the Journey fully unfolded, save herself; no one she knew could have related what it signified as this feral creature had with his soft words and graceful, gesturing hands. She remembered that, and the way he had started, falling abruptly silent, as he had realized she was awake. After that she recalled a few things, his kindness, her fear, not of him so much, for it was plain from the moment she heard his voice that he meant her no harm, but of the island and those others who dwelt there, the ones that held Foxmask captive and, every summer, gave fierce battle to Asgrim's troops. She had come here because she had sensed it was safe; unfortunately there was little logic to such a decision. The Unspoken could not follow her here; the same could not be said for others. She remembered her alarm at discovering she was naked under the blankets, and the way he had averted his gaze when he needed to come close, as if he knew just how she was feeling. He had fed her with baked fish, morsel by morsel as if she were a chick in the nest; he had held a cup in his long fingers, tilting it for her to drink. Above all, she had noticed that, as soon as the young man knew she was awake, the child had vanished. Simply, it was there, and then instantly not there. She concluded that this, at least, was no more than imagining.

Soon after that, lying by the fire in the tiny hut, watching through the open doorway as the summer half-dark washed across the sky, she felt fever grip her, seizing her as the sea had not, and she began to shiver and burn, and everything became a blur. That went on for quite some time, and she ceased to worry about such minor details as being thirsty or exposing her nakedness before strangers; these things were no longer of consequence. Her body ached and trembled, her head throbbed, she was running with sweat, she was freezing cold . . . she wanted to die, or if that was not possible, she wanted to go home, oh, so much . . .

The fever lasted several days, days in which the season continued to advance steadily toward midsummer. If there were other tasks her guardian was supposed to be doing, evidently he had set them aside for now. He sponged her brow, made her swallow water, changed the blankets that covered her, performed the most intimate requirements to keep her body clean. He kept the fire glowing warm; he cooked food that she could not swallow. In her rare moments of lucidity, it became increasingly plain to Creidhe that there was no child here; how could there be? Seeing that little figure on the young man's knee, she had thought of Foxmask, six years old and apparently captive somewhere on this island. But all she had seen through the mists of fever was a small, wild creature of some kind, perhaps a dog, although it was not so very hound-like, edging its way delicately up to the place where the young man baked supper in the hot coals, snatching a morsel or two, slinking off again into hiding. She thought little of that; the illness had stolen away her sense of what should be. If not for that, she would have felt alone, deserted and afraid. As it was, life existed only of the heat and the cold.

There was a night when her very bones seemed made of ice and her teeth chattered in a wild dance, and although the young man piled blankets and cloaks around her, still she shivered and trembled as the cold crept deep inside, long fingers probing, reaching to steal the small part of her that clung to life. She saw terror on his hard features that night. In the end he lay down beside her, wrapped his body around hers, arms and legs, held her close, heart to beating heart, and slowly the terrible cold went away and she drifted into a longed-for, dreamless sleep. When she awoke, soon after dawn, he had moved away, but behind the crook of her knees the little doglike creature lay curled asleep, a ball of disheveled gray fur, pointed muzzle tucked under folded tail. She knew that morning that the fever was gone and that she would get well again.

There hadn't been much talk. The young man's words had been restricted to, *Eat, Sleep now, Drink this*. Creidhe suspected she herself had babbled incessantly through the days and nights of her illness, of what she could not imagine: perhaps of home, or of her worry for Thorvald and Sam, who would not know where she had gone. Now that her head was clear, and the young man sat across the fire doing something to a knife and glancing at her with those odd, luminous eyes, eyes the color of the deepest parts of the sea, it was hard to think what to say to him. Indeed she was not even sure he would understand her. Sometimes he gave the impression of a creature poised for flight. And yet he had told the tale of the Journey: her tale. Perhaps that, too, had been merely some fevered hallucination.

In the end what she said was entirely practical. "I need

some clothes. I think I could get up now, try to look after myself. You must have other things to do."

He ducked his head in a sort of nod. "Skirt, tunic, small shoes," he said. "I have those; I will bring them. A gift."

"My own old things will do—" Creidhe began, then stopped herself, for it sounded churlish. When a man's eyes wore such an expression as this, without a trace of guile in it, one did not shun his kindness. "Thank you," she said. "I suppose mine were ruined. Anything you can manage will be fine." She watched him a little longer, the spare, lean planes of his face, a young face but wary and self-contained, the clever, dirt-ingrained hands, the odd eyes. "You saved my life," she added quietly. "I am grateful."

His long mouth softened a little, not quite a smile. "The sea carried you to my shore," he said. "I am Keeper; this task was given to me. You are safe here."

It was a little awkward sitting up; Creidhe held the blankets around herself, hoping he would do something about the clothes as soon as possible. It was one thing to know that he had touched her, washed her, cleaned her during the sickness; it was quite another to be exposed and vulnerable now that she was herself again. He had a store of his own old things, maybe. She tried to imagine herself clad as he was, in garments sewn over with feathers, but could not quite see it. It occurred to her that there were many questions to be asked, important questions, and that she had no idea at all where to start.

"Safe," she echoed. "But it's not safe here, is it? What about the hunt?"

His eyes met hers, level and steady over the low flames of the fire. "I am Keeper," he said again. "You will be protected. I swear this by stone and star, by wind and wing. They will not come near you."

His words, his tone sent a chill through her, like a memory of something dark and old. She did not doubt for a moment that this strange creature spoke the truth.

"Keeper?" she queried cautiously. "This is your name?"

He nodded gravely, then took up the knife again; he was

fashioning a binding around the handle, an elaborate woven pattern of cord.

"Have you another name?" she asked him. "The one your mother and father gave you?"

There was no response to this.

"My name is Creidhe," she offered. "I am from a far place, it's called the Light Isles. I came here because . . ." She was not quite sure how to finish this, not quite sure how much he would understand.

"You flee Asgrim?" There was an edge to his voice now, a danger in it; his care of her, Creidhe thought, had probably been far outside his usual pattern of living. There was the mark of a warrior about him, a kind of warrior who exists principally in tales and dreams. Perhaps she had indeed been drowned in the Fool's Tide, and all of this was some vision from the other side of shadow.

"You flee the Unspoken?" he added.

"Both," Creidhe said after a moment. "I was—traded. They were taking me away. That was when I tipped the boat over and escaped."

He waited a little before he spoke again; his hands were busy, weaving the cord over, under, looping here, twisting there. "You carried your web to my island," he said.

Creidhe nodded, feeling an odd constriction in her throat. "I don't show it to people," she told him. "Nobody's ever seen more than a small part of it before. It is—secret, private."

He said nothing; his hands continued their steady work, deft, fluid. Behind him in the corner she could see a small, dark shadow and two bright eyes.

"I think—I think maybe I was dreaming," Creidhe said. "I thought I heard you telling the story, my story. But how could you have known? How could you recognize my mother, my father?"

He looked up then and smiled, and it seemed to her a message came with that smile, something nascent, sweet, profoundly dangerous. "It is all there in the web," Keeper said. "I knew why you had come: to be safe."

Creidhe wished then for her mother, or for her sister, Eanna. Only a wise woman had the skills to understand this, and she herself was no more than an ordinary girl with a clever hand for needle and loom and a few strange ideas in her head. There was nothing she could say. The more questions she asked, the more there seemed to be waiting for answers.

"Clothes," Keeper said, rising to his feet and setting his handiwork aside. "Ready for you, Creidhe." His voice was hesitant, trying out her name; he glanced at her sideways, shyly, as if he were not quite sure whether he might address her thus.

"Thank you," she said, and managed a smile in return. It was not a very good one; she was still weak, her head felt strange, and she was acutely aware of her nakedness under the coarse blanket she held clutched around her body. All the same, her smile made him blush scarlet like a bashful boy. Muttering something she did not catch, he turned his back and strode out of the small hut.

She waited. Under the low stone shelf by the doorway something crouched, watching her. She sensed rather than saw it now, for as Keeper had left the hut, it had withdrawn deeper, farther in, fearful if the man was not present. Creidhe wondered what kind of creatures lived on the Isle of Clouds besides puffins, gannets, seals. She wondered how long it would be before the rest of the tribe showed itself, and what role Keeper played within their number. He seemed neither follower nor leader, but very much himself. Perhaps he stood entirely apart. She should ask him about the tribe again, and about the hunt. She should ask him about Foxmask. She did not want to ask. She did not want to contemplate the future, for it seemed to her that, between them, the Long Knife people and the Unspoken had cut her path to shreds before her feet. She had come to the Lost Isles to stand by Thorvald, her best friend, whom she loved. She had thought to support him in his quest and see him safe home again when it was done. Indeed, it was she who had found his answer for him, an answer she could not give him, for here she was, washed up on the farthest of shores alone, hunted by tribes on both sides of this long feud, cut off from her friends, helpless to aid them and, it appeared, quite unable to go back. In addition, she was weak as an infant; in Keeper's absence, she tried to rise to her feet and felt her legs collapse under her.

Yet there was a strange sense of calm over her, a certainty that she had done the right thing. As a little waft of breeze came in the door and whispered through the fire, it came to Creidhe that she was alive and safe and that, ridiculously, she was more content than she had been for a single moment since she left the shore of Hrossey. She imagined Nessa back home by the hearth, casting on a handful of dried weed and searching for answers in the flames. She saw Eanna in the lonely hillside dwelling of the wise women, standing before her own small fire with arms outstretched and eyes shut, the better to use the eye of the spirit. Could they see her, her mother, her sister? Perhaps if she concentrated very hard, if she fixed her mind fully on them, they might catch a little of her presence. Creidhe closed her eyes, rocking in place, humming under her breath. *Some things have no boundaries.*

When she came to herself once more, a little dazed, for it had been longer than she intended, she saw that Keeper had come and gone quite silently without her knowing it. He had left a pile of folded cloth for her, placed with care on the flat stones by the fire pit. That first evening he had unpacked her colors; she had seen how he set them out to dry in a sequence of light to dark, day to night. Her own order for them might have seemed random, blood-red nudging midnight, periwinkle blue edging up to sun yellow, yet within that apparent chaos she had her own pattern: she knew just which went where. Now, when she checked, she found the skeins of wool back in their holder, each in the precise spot where she was accustomed to storing it.

There was no sign of Keeper now. Even the little presence in the shadows was gone. She unfolded what he had left for her, expecting some kind of tunic and breeches, a cape of old skins, perhaps boots if she was lucky. The first touch told her she was wrong. For a moment, as her fingers encountered the soft woolen weave, a shiver passed through

her; it was not so long since the women of Brightwater had
made her a gift of a fine gown. A robe of sacrifice, that had
been. This was simpler, plainer, but, in its way, as beauti-
fully made. There were no feathers. A man's long shirt had
been cut shorter in the hem and sleeves, and neatly finished;
the fabric was old but still good, a faded blue, and the new
stitches were done in a darker shade, more akin to the hue
of sea under autumn cloud. The thread, she was certain,
came from her own supply; this color had been difficult to
achieve. The work was remarkably fine. There was a long
skirt, cunningly pieced together from several different garments, she thought, with a corded tie for the waist. Another
shirt had been altered to form an undergarment of sorts, a
sleeveless shift with borders in another thread. She had
named this color heart's-eye, after a flower that bloomed in
spring on the clifftops near her home in Hrossey. A deep,
bright hue it was, somewhere between red and purple, a
shade that shouted its gladness in the green and dun and
stone gray of the fields.

He might be back soon, and his strange small shadow after him. A little wobbly on her legs, Creidhe scrambled into
shift, skirt and overshirt. There was a belt, a wide strip of
wool in gray and blue, and she tied this around her waist. It
was odd: odd enough to set a shiver through her again.
When the women of Brightwater had made her put on the
green-embroidered gown, the one that marked her as a
valuable trade item, it had been loose here, tight there, as
one might expect with a garment made for another. These
things fit her perfectly. The sleeves came exactly to the
wrist, the skirt flowed neatly to the ankles, the belt tied perfectly with just enough left over for the fringed edging to
hang down a little below the knot. Creidhe's scalp prickled.
She tried to imagine Thorvald dealing with such a situation:
saw, immediately, her friend scowling with irritation and
throwing her the nearest garment he could find. *Here, put
this on,* he'd snap, then turn his back and get on with something more worthy of his time.

She ran her fingers over the neat, colored stitching at the

wrist of the shirt. Most young men she knew wouldn't even know how to thread a needle. Fishermen did, of course, but that was not the same. It was clear this had taken time and thought, care and imagination. She thought of those eyes: deepest green, mysterious, unfathomable; those hands, long-fingered, dexterous, dangerous . . . The Journey had yielded up secrets to him almost unasked. Why was Keeper here? It seemed to Creidhe that he was Other; that he stood outside what she knew of the Isle of Clouds—the fierce tribe, the hunt, Foxmask, the long, bitter dispute. Her mother had a gown, an old one, tucked away deep in a corner of a carven chest. It was a garment whose folds held all the hues of the sea, a shimmering swathe of dark enchantment and ancient power. It had only been worn once, on a night when Nessa worked deep magic to save her people and the man she loved. The gown had been a gift: a gift from the Seal Tribe. For their aid in a time of utmost need, Nessa had paid a terrible price.

Creidhe wrapped her arms around herself, moving to sit on the rocks by the fire pit. This soft covering of wool, these carefully prepared garments, lovely in their very plainness, these gifts were surely not perilous as Nessa's fine robe had been. These little stitches, made so delicately with threads from her own supply, seemed to offer protection rather than threat. Besides, to be quite practical about it, she had nothing else to wear, and it was a lot better than feathers.

She stirred the fire. The peaty fuel Keeper used burned with little smoke, keeping this small space dry and warm. She looked outside, venturing to circle the neat dwelling, trying to work out where exactly on the island it was. A narrow, barely perceptible track led down across glass-clad slopes toward the west. Eastward the land rose sharply to cloud-blanketed crags; a chill wind swept down from them, setting the grasses shivering. On the north side of the hut there was a sudden, alarming drop to the sea; many birds circled there. One would need to be careful not to wander at night. Like the Isle of Storms, this place offered scant shelter; it seemed at the mercy of storm and gale, and Creidhe could see nothing growing above knee height. For man and beast, rocky outcrops might allow cover, sudden gullies furnish hiding places. Standing by the doorway, Creidhe could see right down to the tiny cove where the boat had come in.

By all the ancestors, she hoped this muzzy head would clear soon, so she could start making herself useful. Keeper's seemed an existence both solitary and difficult. She had already taken up a great deal of his time, time that would have been better spent on—on fishing, or hunting, or whatever else he did. She picked up the blankets and folded them, tidied things as best she could. Even that small effort left her back aching, her legs weary. She could have begun to cook supper, but that was to disturb the pattern of things. Cooking was later; she had observed that despite her illness. Still, there was one task that was all her own: the Journey. Though her hands were shaky after the fever, the linen and wools called to her, eager for the new fashioning, the picking up of the strands. She rolled it out, rainbow colors on gray stone, a flashing brightness in the small space of the hut. She glanced from the complex interweaving of her pattern to the single, stark line of color that threaded its way around her new clothing, at neckline, at sleeve, at hem. She did not want to acknowledge the truth to herself, but there it was, plainly visible. Brother Niall had noticed the escape hatches in her work, the places that allowed the pain and joy of what she depicted to spill out and dissipate before their power built to a dangerous level. But here on the island, something else had happened. The Journey had broken its boundaries and was no longer contained. Now other hands were helping to move it forward.

Creidhe threaded a needle, selected soft gray, darkest green. She tried to show what she had seen, there in the corner: the same small creature that had slept on her pallet, and had fled the moment it knew she was awake. The little face was difficult. Sometimes it seemed one thing, sometimes another; now like a shaggy small hound, now more like some hunting animal, one of those from her father's tales, a weasel, a fox, a cat, for the muzzle was pointed, the ears large, the eyes quite feral. Yet at times it had a form not quite like any of these things, but nebulous, as if what it showed the world were only a hint or suggestion of what lay behind. When she was well enough to venture out farther, Creidhe thought, perhaps she would find whole flocks or tribes of such animals on the island. Maybe it was only her own weakness that made its shape so hard to distinguish. Keeper she could see clearly, but she would not put him in the Journey. To do so seemed in some way dangerous.

She plied her needle steadily, forgetting time and place as one does when deep in such work. What she made, in the end, was less depiction than suggestion, less image than idea: the eyes, the delicate muzzle, the shadows and timidity, the utter strangeness. She thought it conveyed, at least, the difficulty of actually seeing such a creature as it really was, with its concealment and its changing. When she had finished that part, she made the Isle of Clouds again, very small this time, encompassed in a pair of circling arms, hands curved inward to keep the precious burden safe. Outside that protective wall the storm raged, lightning-bright, blood-crimson; beyond the barrier, the Fool's Tide washed mercilessly over all those who dared approach. Within the cradling arms the island remained: apart, alone, inviolable.

He came back with fish, up from the western end of the island where great waves pounded the base of a bird-thronged holm. Beyond its cliffs and rock stacks there was empty ocean to the edge of the world. Creidhe was still sewing, bringing the creeping, twining border along to the place where she had made the wondrous, mysterious things. She made no attempt to fold her work over. It felt strange to leave it in view, as if she were letting Keeper look right inside her to a place nobody else had ever seen, not even Thorvald. Her mouth twitched in amusement. Keeper had certainly seen a great deal more of her outward self than Thorvald ever had; there really had been no choice in the matter. It was just as well he seemed to be painfully shy as well as dauntingly capable.

"Why do you smile?" He had gutted and scaled his

catch down by the shore; now he was cleaning it further, and spreading out pieces of seaweed to wrap it in, ready for the fire.

"Nothing, really." Not something she could tell him, certainly. "I was just thinking how strange it is to be here, the two of us alone. Last summer I was at home with my parents, my sisters, my friends. I could not have dreamed the ancestors would have led me here."

"Not two of us," he corrected her gravely. "Three."

"You mean the—?" Creidhe glanced across the fire; the doglike creature now sat by his master, eyes intent on the juicy, pale fish.

"My brother, yes."

Creidhe swallowed. Keeper was undeniably somewhat unusual, as one might expect of a man who chose to dwell in such a remote place. She had not, until now, considered that he might be somewhat lacking in his wits. "Your brother?" she choked.

"Not really my brother," he said, "but I think of him as that. We are kin."

Her mind did another twist, another loop, tried to put this into some acceptable shape. Was he a priestly man of sorts, and this his companion creature? She knew of that. Back home, the wise woman, Rona, who had been Nessa's teacher and then Eanna's, had possessed a strange affinity with dogs. Creidhe chose a safe question to ask. "Has he a name?"

"Small One."

She thought about this a little. "The same kind of name as Keeper," she commented.

Across the flames, he regarded her soberly. "Our chosen names," he agreed. "We have no need for those others give us. This is our island, our safe place."

She must tread delicately here. "I take some pride in my own name," she said, "and in my mother's and father's. Creidhe is the name they chose for me. I might also call myself Daughter of Nessa, and Daughter of Eyvind, and feel joy in that, knowing I bear their courage and goodness in me. That does not make me any less myself."

Keeper fell silent, his long fingers rolling the fish into a parcel, skewering it with what seemed to be sharpened bone.

"I'm sorry," she said, thinking perhaps she had upset him. "I don't want to pry. I am a little anxious, that's all. I don't really know who you are, or—or Small One, and I was told there is a very dangerous tribe on this island; the women at Brightwater said many men die each year, fighting here. I think it's possible that if Asgrim's warriors don't find Foxmask, they may find me. They had planned to offer me as some kind of substitute, so they didn't have to hunt this summer. I don't know if you are familiar with the story—?"

"I know the story." His tone was grave, calm. "It is true, many men die at hunt time. But you will be safe. I have promised."

"Yes, but—"

"I have promised. You should not be afraid."

"Yes, I know," she said after a moment. "And I don't doubt that you mean it. Still, I am—troubled. I came to these islands with two friends, two young men. Asgrim took them both away. The Ruler lied to me about several things. He may have been lying when he told me my friends were merely helping to repair storm damage in the settlements in return for the wood they needed to fix our boat. I'm afraid he may try to involve them in the hunt. And while I may be safe under your protection, Thorvald and Sam are not."

He was raking out the embers, putting the fish on the hot stones. "They are warriors, your companions?" he asked.

"No," Creidhe said. "That's just it. Sam's not a fighter at all, and Thorvald just plays with it really. It would be dangerous for them to get caught up in all this. But—Thorvald has a habit of doing this kind of thing, and it can be quite hard to make him see sense sometimes."

"If they cannot fight," Keeper said, "Asgrim will not bring them to the Isle of Clouds."

"I hope you're right." Creidhe shivered. She began to pack the Journey away, needles and threads in their pockets, the bright tapestry itself rolled up and stored in safety.

"If they come here," Keeper said, "they will die. And Asgrim's men will die. If not last summer, this summer. If not this summer, next."

Creidhe found this bald statement less than reassuring, but she made no comment.

"Tell me," Keeper sat back on his heels, regarding her, "why would you bring with you protectors who cannot fight for you? What purpose is there in choosing such companions?"

"Oh. Well, the thing is, I didn't exactly choose them. It was Thorvald's expedition, and Sam came because he owns the boat and knows how to sail it. I was not invited. I went with them because I thought they would make a mess of things without me. As you can see, I was quite wrong about that. I'm the one who has made a mess of it." She had tried to keep her tone light, joking; unfortunately, tears had appeared from nowhere as she spoke and were ruining the effect. She reached with angry fingers to scrub them away; she was supposed to be strong, capable. This just would not do.

Keeper had risen to his feet and slipped away without a word. By the fire pit, Small One sat gazing at her with his big, strange eyes.

"All right for you," she whispered fiercely. "Sit by the fire, sleep on the bed, meals provided, and then run off and hide when it all gets too hard." His ears twitched; he blinked at her. It was the first time he had not fled rather than be left alone with her. "Sorry," she said. "I don't mean it really. I'm worried, that's all." By the ancestors, this creature was truly odd; the more she looked at him, the harder it became to discern just what kind of animal he was. "What are you?" she whispered. "Tell me; show me." But Small One only looked at her, eyes glowing in the firelight.

Keeper was back, somber-faced. He had something in his hand.

"Small shoes," he said, coming to kneel by Creidhe and setting them on the ground. "Right for you, I think; you have little feet, little hands. Please wear them. A gift."

She saw the way his fingers moved on the soft leather of the boots, most certainly a girl's boots, for they were indeed small and delicately made, the seams neat and strong, the skin supple and well kept. His hands seemed reluctant to let these go; they were precious to him.

"Are you sure?"

"Please. A gift. Tomorrow, if you are well, I will take you, show you, so you can understand that you are safe here with us. For that, you will need shoes. Try them."

She slipped her feet in; the boots were a good fit, not as perfect as the other garments, for these had been made for a different girl, but certainly comfortable enough for walking. Creidhe began to think very hard indeed, to turn several possibilities over in her mind and reassemble them in an entirely different way.

"Thank you for the gift," she said, brushing Keeper's hand with her own. She regretted that instantly; he started like a frightened animal, and she felt her own heart do a strange kind of somersault. "These are lovely. I'll be proud to wear them. You are generous with your gifts; I have none in return."

He had moved to put the safe distance of the fire pit between them; he busied himself awhile with the fish, with laying on turf, with pouring water into a bowl for Small One. "You could . . ." he began, hesitant. "You could give . . . I should not ask . . ."

"You'd better go ahead," Creidhe said dryly, imagining just what a young man in his situation might expect of a girl who had no worldly goods with which to pay for her supper, and knowing that was the very last thing Keeper was likely to ask her for.

"The web," he said, "the story . . . He likes a story at bedtime. If we could look again . . ."

Once more his simplicity robbed her of words. She gazed at him across the fire, and he looked back at her, very solemn.

"It is too much to ask," he said. "This is a magical thing you make, and secret. But we have seen our island in this story. To look again would be . . ."

"After supper then," Creidhe said quietly. "A bedtime story is not such a bad idea." She looked down at the little boots, scarcely worn. A child's boots, almost; lucky she had such small feet.

"You are crying again," Keeper said in consternation. "Don't, please—"

"It's all right, it's nothing—" Creidhe tried to brush the sudden tears away, tried to halt their flow, but she could not; it was only now, seeing the shoes, so small, so lovingly preserved, that the reality of what had almost happened to her entered her heart in all its terror. "Oh gods, oh, I'm sorry—" She put her hands over her face.

She heard him come back around toward her, heard the rustle of the feathers on his garments, the soft touch of his feet on the earth. But it was Small One who reached her first, scrambling onto her lap, all hard little dog-paws and thrashing, hairy tail, and Small One's cold tongue she felt against her cheek, licking away the tears. Creidhe could not tell if she was laughing or crying, or both. Keeper sat down beside her, his thin features pale with concern, his deep eyes shadowed with anxiety. He lifted a long hand toward her face, but would not touch; his fingers hovered by her cheek, curving as if in echo of its shape. Creidhe's breath caught in her throat. The urge to put her own hand over his was strong; she had been a long time without gentleness. But she would not be so foolish. Without quite understanding why, she sensed she had the power to wreak havoc here, that this strong young man was a great deal more vulnerable than she was, even if it was she who was weeping now.

Small One helped by getting in the way; he had put his front paws on her shoulders and was washing her face thoroughly. The moment of danger was over.

"I'm all right," Creidhe said, rising to her feet and setting Small One down by her skirts. "I'm sorry; I'm not usually a crying sort of girl. It was the shoes. You've been so kind to me; I think that was what started it off."

"My fault?" Keeper had backed away a couple of steps: still too close for comfort. "I have upset you?"

"No, Keeper," she said, drawing a deep breath. "Your kindness reminded me of home. That's why I was upset."

"The priestess of the creatures? The man with a mark on his arm?"

"Yes. But they are far away, and I know I cannot reach them; there's no point in weeping over it. Perhaps we should rescue the fish; it must be suppertime."

"There is a man with a mark on his arm in these islands," Keeper said, watching her. "I knew him once, long ago."

"Yes. I know."

"You have met him?"

She nodded. "He is my friend's father. Thorvald's father. The scar revealed that: it is a mark of blood brotherhood. My own father bears its twin. After I saw it, I knew who Brother Niall was; the way he spoke made it still clearer, though he never put the truth into plain words. But Thorvald doesn't know, not yet. He went away with Asgrim. Everything went wrong. Our whole voyage, you understand, the whole venture was for that purpose, so that Thorvald could find his father. Thorvald wanted this kept secret. After what has happened, I see no more point in secrets."

"A kind man," Keeper said quietly. "A lonely man. His whole world will change when he knows he has a son." There was a terrible sorrow in his voice.

"Yes," she said. "There could be great hurt in it, and great joy, I think. But they need me, and I am not there to help them."

"No," said Keeper. "You are here. Is this why you weep, because the Fool's Tide brought you to my island, and took you from your friend?"

Creidhe looked at him; the ancestors only knew what he could read in her eyes. "No," she whispered, then cleared her throat. "Now," she added in a good attempt at a normal tone, "I think we should eat that fish before it's spoiled. I could cook tomorrow, if you like. They say I'm quite good at it, given the right ingredients."

* * *

Later, when the frugal meal was over and the three of them sat in the quiet of the summer half-night, Creidhe took out the Journey and spread it flat on the rocks by the fire. There was space, still, on the strip of linen for more work; the intricate pattern could grow and develop yet awhile. But the fabric would not roll on forever; the colored wools would come each to the end of its length, in time. There would be no such materials on the Isle of Clouds.

Creidhe looked across at Keeper, who sat on the ground by Small One, long legs crossed, his hands busy once more on the corded pattern of the knife hilt.

"It's ready," she said. "And he looks tired."

"You tell." Keeper's voice was low. "Please."

"Oh. But I'm not sure—"

"You tell as you wish. Many stories here."

"Yes, there are," Creidhe agreed, her fingers touching the small depiction of a man with a scarred arm, and thinking of another whose brand was twin to this. It had begun with those two, all of it: Eyvind and Somerled. When those small boys had taken a knife to their arms and made a vow of life-long loyalty, who would have thought it might at length have led here, to the islands at the end of the ocean, where Eyvind's daughter had drifted in the arms of the Fool's Tide, and Somerled's son still walked on into danger, blind to the truth she had discovered?

"Once upon a time," Creidhe said, "there was a boy called Eyvind, who had always wanted to be a warrior. Not any old warrior, you understand, but a very particular kind . . ."

Not all of what she told was in the Journey, at least, not precisely and exactly. On the other hand, all of its essence was there: the look in her father's eyes, the wolf pelt she had shown on his broad shoulders, the two hounds that stood by him like guardians. The scar. At a certain point, Small One came up to her, more cautious than he had been when she wept, and climbed onto her knee where he settled, apparently intent on the images of the Journey as Creidhe touched one small part or another, and told the tale behind it. Later, she was aware that Keeper had set aside his work and moved in silence to sit at her feet, knees drawn up, arms around them, like a child. He, too, watched the images on the cloth as if they were alive. He was very still, and very close; if she had reached out a hand she could have touched his hair, hair dark as a crow's wing, matted and wild. There was a feather in it, shining green-blue, and a strand of dried weed.

The tale was close to its end. "That was how Eyvind became the greatest Wolfskin that ever was," Creidhe said softly, "and learned that it was his destiny to be something quite different. In the Light Isles he learned that love, not war, is the heart and essence of a life well lived." She was getting a very strange feeling; while her eyes told her the small presence on her knee still had a pointed muzzle, and doglike ears, and a hairy gray coat, what she could feel there in her lap was the form, the shape, the weight of a child, leaning relaxed against her, its head touching her breast, its legs dangling across her thigh. Even so, on countless evenings by lamplight, had her own small sister Ingigerd snuggled against her, listening to tales of bravery and magic. Creidhe caught her breath in astonishment. Could she believe what her hands touched, what her senses told her? It was impossible; logic said so, and yet her heart recognized the truth of it, a truth that was deeper than human understanding.

"So," Keeper said, his voice oddly constrained, "the scar he bore was not merely a promise, but a mark of love."

Creidhe had closed her eyes; she moved a hand cautiously to touch the small person who sat on her knee. Her fingers moved over a child's delicate neck, a neat, round skull, a mat of tangled hair that had evidently seen a comb no more often than Keeper's. She stroked the disheveled locks as gently as she could; she had felt the shock run through this frail being when she moved.

"Yes," she said, "it was a mark of love, though neither knew it at the time. It bound them together always. It links them now, across the span of oceans, across the arch of years. The past follows us; we bear it in our bones, in our blood." The child sighed, turning its head into her breast;

she sensed it had put its thumb in its mouth and closed its eyes. One small hand had reached to grasp a fold of her shirt. Small One curled against her, drifting into sleep. Creidhe did not open her eyes. The wonder and terror of it gripped her: a sad, sad story, a terrible path for the two of them. "He must be six years old now," she said quietly, "or nearly that."

"One year, almost, when I took him." Keeper's voice was so soft now, she could barely hear him, for all he sat so close. "Five times we have endured the hunt."

Ingigerd was six. Ingigerd could hem a cloth and milk a goat and do up her own shoes. Ingigerd could run and swim and collect the eggs in a basket.

"He seems—very fragile, and easily frightened," Creidhe ventured.

Keeper was silent. Possibly her words had sounded like criticism.

"Why doesn't he show himself?" she asked. "Even now, I can't see him—" She opened her eyes, looking down. "Oh," she said, and heard the shaking of her own voice. Here on the Isle of Clouds, the impossible had indeed become reality.

"To be hunted is to be afraid." Keeper stood up, moved away.

"I-I'm sorry," Creidhe stammered, seeing the way his mouth had tightened. "I know I cannot even begin to understand how it is for you here, how difficult the life is, how hard it must be for you to keep him safe and well. It is a harsh place, and lonely. What about the other tribe? Do they help you?"

Keeper regarded her in silence. He stood in shadow, a tall, remote figure; long, pale face like a mask, with dark smudges for eyes. The feathers on his clothing stirred a little in the draft; all else about him was quite still. The child on her knee was asleep. His small form was clearly visible now, his limbs stick-thin, his face triangular and odd, but certainly human, his hair a miniature version of Keeper's wild locks. The clothing was the same, a motley construction of skins and feathers, though underneath, Creidhe could see the boy wore a garment of warm woolen stuff, tailored to his size as her own clothing was. His small shoes were fashioned from pieces of larger boots, sewn with strips of leather.

"He's a fine boy," she said, managing a smile. "A lovely boy. I know you have looked after him well. I understand why he is—not like other children. Your sister's son?"

Keeper nodded, frowning. "You say the past follows us, that we bear it with us. We are free of the past, Small One and I. We have our own names, our own place. Only one thing I carry forward: my promise to her, to keep him safe. The rest is set aside." His hand moved to touch what he wore around his neck: a circle of plaited hair, old, faded. "One task I was given; that is my life now."

Creidhe moved a hand to roll up the Journey; with the other she cradled the slight weight of the sleeping child. "I understand," she said, "why you would not wish to acknowledge that you are Asgrim's son."

"I am no man's son," said Keeper. "And my brother is no man's son." Something in his tone of voice was deeply chilling; Creidhe had not thought she could be afraid of him, but now she was not so sure. She wanted to ask, *What will happen when he grows up, what sort of future can there be for him here?* She was thinking again of Ingigerd, plump and healthy, bonny and clever, growing up amidst the lush pastures of the Light Isles, surrounded by love. Perhaps the only way to ask him was to put it in the Journey.

"This must be over some time," was what she said. "The fighting, the voices, the hunt. Then maybe he will not be so frightened."

"When all are dead, then it is over." Keeper had an odd way with words: not, Creidhe thought, the speech of a man whose native tongue is other, but more the manner of one who has not been used to speaking much at all. She wondered, again, about the tribe who dwelt on the Isle of Clouds.

"When *all* are dead?" she asked him, alarmed by the grim finality of his tone.

"Asgrim's men. When all are gone, there can be no more hunt. We are in peace then, Small One and I; then I make his life for him."

"Here, on the island?"

"There is nowhere else." He came to lift the sleeping child from her knee; she felt the inadvertent touch of his hands as if it were a lick of flame, and saw his face change at the same moment. Small One's presence, she thought, was in some ways a blessing.

"Will you show me tomorrow, as you said?" she asked. "The island, the other tribe, and what happens when hunt time comes?"

"If you are strong enough. I would not weary you."

"I'm used to walking," Creidhe said. "I'll be fine." She rose to her feet and a wave of giddiness swept over her. The fever, after all, was not so long past. "Fine . . ." she murmured as her knees buckled under her.

He was very quick. He laid the child down on the blankets, took two strides back, and caught her before she hit the ground. She felt herself picked up bodily and placed on the warmth of a folded woolen cloak. Her vision was behaving oddly; the walls of the hut seemed to be slowly moving above her, and the firelight's glow on the creviced surfaces of the massive cornerstones made patterns of light and dark, forms of men and beasts, an ancient dance from somewhere in their monolithic memory. Keeper's features were blurred; he leaned over her, and she thought she could see the ocean in the depths of his eyes.

"Sorry," she whispered. "Thought I was all right . . ."

"Shh." He settled himself beside her, cross-legged, and reached to put a blanket over her, up to the chin. "Tired. My fault. I asked too much."

"No," she said softly. "My fault. I did not see, at first, how much you love him. How much you loved her. Sula. These are her shoes, aren't they?"

"Yours now," said Keeper. "Tomorrow I walk with you, show you my place. Sleep now."

She waited for him to move away, to settle on the other side, across the fire, or down by the entry. But he stayed where he was, quiet beside her, sitting straight-backed in the half-dark. Creidhe closed her eyes. She was indeed weary, and yet sleep seemed far off, for her mind was full of questions, and her heart, for some reason, was thumping as if she had run a race. She tried to think of calm things: a gull gliding on currents of air, the tiny bright jewels of heart's-eye blooming in the fields at home, her mother's voice telling her all would be well . . . No, that would not do; there were tears in her eyes again, brimming over to roll down and lose themselves in the tangle of her hair. And now a hand reached to brush the tears away, so lightly she might have thought it was no more than a whisper of breeze, save that it was his hand, and she felt it in every corner of her body. She held her breath. His fingers moved to touch her hair, stroking it back from her brow, gentle, careful. Slow, sweet. She breathed again, and sighed, and, against the odds, was immediately claimed by sleep.

How are you supposed to feel when the prize you deserve falls into your lap, and you discover the cost of it is beyond what you are able to pay? How can you go on, knowing your opportunity to shine has been bought with your best friend's life? The day after Asgrim gave them the news of Creidhe's death, Thorvald went back to the Ruler and told him he was not prepared to lead the men, that it seemed to him there were others apter for that role; Einar, for instance, or Orm. He did not in fact believe this, but forced himself to say it, if only to deny that part of him that still cried out, *Yes! This is your time!* For it seemed to Thorvald that was a part of him which would better have been strangled at birth.

"After reflection," he said, keeping his gaze steady on Asgrim's impenetrable dark eyes, "I think it inappropriate that Sam and I should play any part in this. Creidhe would not have wished us to exact revenge at the cost of your men's lives, nor our own. Besides, it was not the tribe on the Isle of Clouds that killed her, but the Unspoken. Why should we do battle to retrieve their seer for them when they have acted with such savagery against us? It makes no sense. We will go home."

In the back of his mind, perhaps he expected Asgrim to put up some argument, to beg.

"Very well," the Ruler said. "If you're sure. I'm disappointed, I have to say. I thought better of you, Thorvald. Still, we have managed without you before, and will do again, I suppose. I fear the losses will be great. This news will dishearten the men. And you may have trouble persuading Sam."

"That's not your problem," said Thorvald. "Sam will come around. Not so long ago he couldn't wait to be off home."

That day he avoided the others as much as he could, speaking little, staying behind in order to go through his meager belongings in half-hearted preparation for departure. Hogni was hanging around, not working with the men, not on duty either, leaning morosely in a corner of the shelter, then sitting outside on the rocks with his arms around his knees, his big-jawed face like a sad dog's. Finally Thorvald felt compelled to go out and ask him what was wrong.

"Nothing," Hogni grunted, brows knitting in a scowl.

The bodyguard was a man of intimidating size and manner, but Thorvald saw the lost look in his small eyes. He sat down by Hogni's side. "All the same," he said, and waited.

Hogni's hands were restless, fingers drumming on knees, then twisting together. Thorvald watched the men down by the shore, practicing with knives; he felt curiously detached from it, now that he had decided not to go on after all. Nonetheless, he noticed how much Wieland's skills had developed; his throw was vastly improved and he was beginning to demonstrate real style. And Orm wasn't looking half bad, either. He'd just given Hjort quite a fright with the accuracy of his aim.

"M'brother," Hogni blurted out suddenly. "Skapti. He's gone all funny. Quiet. Not like himself. Something's eating him and he won't talk about it."

Thorvald had suspected something of the sort; it had been visible in Skapti's demeanor last night.

"Mmm," he said. "Awkward for you."

"Not right." Hogni scratched his boot sole on the earth, scattering small pebbles. "Something's not right. Never known him like this before. Almost never."

"Did you ask him straight out what the trouble was?"

"Tried to. Nothing, he said. It's bothering me, Thorvald. I don't like the look in his eye. Hunt coming up, all of us need to be our best. You'd agree with that."

A chill passed over Thorvald, like a breath of cold wind that trembled through the bones and was gone. Perhaps it was a premonition, but of what, he did not know. He drew a deep breath. This was not his place; these were not his men. He had been foolish to think he belonged here. The hunt was Asgrim's business.

"Thing is," said Hogni gruffly, "I thought Skapti might talk to you. He thinks a lot of you. Looks up to you. He might tell you what he won't tell me."

Thorvald opened his mouth to say no, there wouldn't be time, for he was going home tomorrow. He met the anxious, close-set eyes of the guard, saw the mournful expression on the big, bony face. Somehow the words just could not be spoken, for they seemed yet another betrayal.

"Skapti looks up to me?" he croaked. "I shouldn't think so. He could squash me with his little finger."

"Been good working with you. All of them agree. Not the jumped-up incomer we thought at first. Skapti too. Said you've got brains and guts. Will you talk to him?"

"I'll try." There was simply no way to refuse.

"Knew I could count on you," Hogni said, a grin stretching his mouth to reveal two rows of crooked, broken teeth. He had fought more than his share of battles.

Anything that was to be done must be done today: not only talking to Skapti, which Thorvald thought privately would not be much help at all, but also convincing Sam that they must follow the original plan and head for home while the weather was set fair. Sam could now be seen among the warriors, trying his hand with the spear. The fisherman's amiable features were set in a hard, fierce expression quite alien to him. His eyes were red and swollen. There would be a few sore heads today; they had drunk late into the night while Thorvald sat on the clifftop alone. In the morning

Einar had roused them at the usual time, no concessions,
and they'd been out working soon after without complaint.
These men were learning discipline. Some among them
were learning leadership. All the same, Thorvald reminded
himself, it was Asgrim who was their chieftain, not him.
Asgrim had said they could manage. Thorvald was dispen-
sable. He would go, then, and if he never did see the force
he had trained win its battle, so what? He had been foolish
to get involved, foolish to start caring so much, to think
there might be a place for him here. Stupid and arrogant.
The gods had demanded a terrible price for that arrogance,
a price he would spend the rest of his life paying for in guilt
and sorrow. He must return and tell Eyvind and Nessa their
daughter was lost because of him. He must tell Margaret
what his pride and ambition had wrought. No amount of
brains and guts was going to help with that.

Sam seemed to be making sure he was never alone today.
If he was not throwing knives with Orm, he was rehearsing
a cliff-scaling exercise with Wieland, injured foot or no.
Knut and several of the other fishermen were involved in
that as well; of the entire complement of men, the only ones
not engaged in some practice for the hunt were those who
had taken a boat out to catch something for the communal
supper. And Skapti. The Ruler had come down to watch,
shadowed by Hogni now; he stood close by the knife
throwers, expression grim, making a comment now and
then. The men seemed nervous in his presence and were doing less well than before. Thorvald itched to go down and
join them, to reassure and encourage them, but he did not. If
Hogni was on duty that meant Skapti was on his own somewhere. He set off to find him.

Instinct carried him to the selfsame clifftop where he had
kept vigil last night, alone with his grief. It wasn't hard to
spot Skapti, a veritable giant of a man. The guard stood perilously close to the edge, staring out to the west. Thorvald's
heart skipped a beat; a vision of Creidhe was before his
eyes, Creidhe with her gaze locked on the Isle of Clouds
and her feet slipping on the cliff path. He approached with
caution.

"Skapti," he said quietly, coming up to seat himself on the rocks not far from the warrior. "Sit down, man, you're scaring me. Come on, sit by me awhile."

Skapti growled something exceedingly coarse that equated to, *go away.* Thorvald stayed where he was, saying nothing.

"I mean it," Skapti snarled after a little. "I've got nothing to say to you. I'm sorry the girl died, and I'm not going to say any more about it. Now leave me alone. If I decide to take a quick jump into the waves down there, it's surely none of your concern." He took a step; his boot was overhanging the edge. Thorvald swallowed.

"It is, though," he said in a reasonable attempt at an everyday tone. "Haven't we been training the men for the hunt all season, you and me and Hogni? You're telling me you don't care if you live long enough to see that good work come to fruition? Come on, Skapti, I'm counting on you. Who else has a chance of taking in a raiding party unscathed? We need your team on one flank and Hogni's on the other. There's nobody else the men trust for the job. You can't just throw that away."

Skapti teetered on the cliff edge, putting out an arm for balance. His face went suddenly white. Several options flashed through Thorvald's mind, none of them promising. It had been all very well to grab Creidhe and drag her to safety. Creidhe was a girl and narrow-waisted. This giant would pull him over bodily, merely by leaning a little too far.

"Tell you what," Thorvald said. "I'll make a deal with you. Talk first, just a bit, then I'll go off and leave you. What you do after that's your own choice."

Skapti made an unintelligible sound.

"Thing is," said Thorvald in casual tones, "you'll have to sit down first. Watching you wobbling on the edge there is making me seasick. Come on, man, sit down here by me. That's it. That's the way." He heard his own breath expelled in a sigh as the warrior stepped away from the brink and moved to slump down on the rocks. Skapti, too, was breathing heavily, and his complexion had a greenish tinge.

"Bet Hogni sent you up," the bodyguard ventured, scowling.

"I did speak to him, yes, but it was my own idea to talk to you. The hunt's getting close; if you're angry, or sick, or not satisfied with something, I need to know about it, so I can help."

"Not what I heard."

"Oh?"

Skapti shook his head. "Asgrim says you're going home. Says you don't want to lead us anymore." He turned suddenly to fix his small eyes fiercely on Thorvald's. "Is it true?"

"How can I stay?" The words burst out angrily, against Thorvald's better judgment. "Creidhe's dead. She's dead because I was over here doing this and not looking out for her. I have to go home. I have to go back and tell her father. In its way, that will be worse than any battle. He's a formidable man. You'd admire him, I should think."

"Oh? What is he, a chieftain, some kind of king?"

"Not exactly. A leader of men, certainly. He was once a Wolfskin, back in Rogaland. That carries a certain reputation. I don't know if you—?" He broke off. It was clear Skapti knew exactly what a Wolfskin was, and found it more than impressive.

"That explains it." The big warrior nodded, eyes full of sorrow and something new, which Thorvald could not quite read. "A Wolfskin's daughter. No wonder."

"No wonder what?" asked Thorvald, ice trickling down his spine.

"Nothing," Skapti mumbled, looking at the ground.

"It's not nothing. You were there. Tell me!"

"Don't know if you'd want to hear, being a friend and all. It wasn't pleasant. Gave me bad dreams. Shook me all up."

Thorvald made himself breathe. "Tell me, Skapti," he said quietly.

"Well, you see, it wasn't exactly as Asgrim said. The way he told it, sounded as if the girl did something silly, standing up in the boat, causing a nasty accident, all hands lost and so on. But I could see. I could see what she did, and I wondered. Now I know. Wolfskin's daughter; all makes sense." Skapti shivered. "Just makes it worse. Makes it harder to go on."

"What?" Thorvald struggled for calm. "What did Creidhe do?"

"Deliberate. Not being stupid at all. Trying to escape. Stands up, dives in. Looks like she's gone under for good at first, then she bobs up a bit farther away. When they see her they row after, across the line, into the Fool's Tide. She did that on purpose. So they flail around with the oars, trying to reach her, trying to keep control. The girl grabs an oar and pulls, gives the fellow a good whack with it, he loses his balance and the boat goes over. Then they all disappear. Brave little thing. She gave it her best try. Fighting spirit. Good looker, too. Shapely." There were tears trickling down Skapti's cheeks; he made no attempt to conceal them. "Don't think I can go on, Thorvald. Don't think I can go on doing this."

"Doing what?" Gods, he would almost rather not have known this; it was so like Creidhe to keep on struggling, to keep on clinging to hope right to the very end. She would simply refuse to give up. He could see her in the water, fair skin turning slowly blue with cold, fingers cramping on an oar, whispering to herself, *I won't die, I won't,* as the waves rose greedily to drag her down, to snatch away her last breath.

"Everything," muttered Skapti, staring at his boots. "His business. Asgrim's business. What's the point? We carry out orders, we obey, we fight his battles and die in the hunt because we've got no choice. But where does it end, that's what I want to know? How long? How many times? Look at Wieland. His wife's lost three infants now, three springtimes the Unspoken have sung her babes away, and Asgrim won't even let him go home to comfort her. The hunt's too important." Skapti clenched his fists. "But how long? Five years, it's been, and more before that, when we were beating off their raids. And the other things . . . he thinks he can ask me to do anything he wants, anything at all. I've always obeyed. He's the Ruler. He knows best. But I don't think I can anymore. Think it might be better if I wasn't here. Then he couldn't make me do it." The big man was a picture of misery.

"This summer could be different," Thorvald said. "I've told you before. It's just a matter of changing the way you think about the hunt, and being properly prepared. When I first came here the men were all over the place, no discipline, no technique. I'm not a fighter by trade the way you are, but I've been well taught. I could see plenty of potential. I could see Asgrim wasn't making proper use of what he had. It happens when a leader starts to give up hope. Now look at them. They're strong, well trained and focused on the task. They work as a team. The weapons are better, the way they use them is better, their whole attitude is changed. This can be the hunt that's different, Skapti, I know it: the one they win."

Skapti mumbled something.

"What did you say?"

"Not without you," Skapti said.

Thorvald's heart clenched. "Asgrim can lead you—oh yes, I know what you said—but he can lead you to victory this time. The groundwork's been laid. Besides, he doesn't want me. Not really."

"Say he does do it," said Skapti, now looking straight into Thorvald's eyes; the warrior's own were reddened with tears. "Say he leads us in, and we get Foxmask out and return him. Say not all of us die in the attempt. That's good, anyone would agree. But what then? I'm sick of it, I'm sick of him and his rules, fed up with following orders I don't like, because I'm too scared to say no. And if I'm scared, how do you think the rest of them feel?"

Thorvald felt a chill again, a touch of something both heady and extremely dangerous. "I don't know why you're telling me this," he said. His voice had dropped to a whisper, though there was nobody around.

"Thing is," said Skapti, glancing nervously to right and to left, "we never had a leader like you before. Nobody ever stood up to him before. If you go off home, there's no chance of changing things after."

The words hung in the air between them, those that had been spoken and those that were too perilous to utter aloud. "Yes, well," Thorvald managed, "I—I don't think we should be discussing this. Not even up here. It's not that I don't want to stay. It's that I can't. It's my fault that Creidhe died. I'm going to bear the burden of that on my conscience forever. I need to face up to it and go home; recognize that I was never more here than a meddling incomer."

"Have more on your conscience if you leave," Skapti said. "That's my opinion."

The two of them walked back together in the end, Skapti drawn and silent, Thorvald working hard at keeping his mind fixed on one thing: he had made a decision, the only right decision, and he would stick to it. They could win their fight without him; he would make himself believe that. As for the tantalizing prospect Skapti had alluded to, of *afterward*, he must on no account allow himself to consider that. It was fraught with danger.

They'd been gone longer than he'd thought. Supper was cooking, the men sitting around the fire, looking as they used to in the first days after he came: weary and dispirited. They were probably worn out. It seemed to have been a busy day, though Thorvald had played no part in it. He'd missed his opportunity to catch Sam alone, and they were running out of time. The weather had a habit of turning bad here, and there often wasn't much warning. He'd have to try later tonight, call his friend outside on some pretext. They must go tomorrow; there was a limit to his own capacity to remain firm on this.

Asgrim had not come down yet. Hogni, too, was absent. Gods, they looked bad: Einar grim, Skolli glaring into his ale cup, Wieland pale and exhausted. As for Sam himself, the expression on his face could only be described as furious. Clearly, a day's rehearsal with the tools of combat had done nothing to damp down his rage. Of course, most of them had been up drinking late into the night, Thorvald reminded himself as he sat down by Skapti on the earthen shelf. Still, he felt distinctly uneasy. It was becoming ever plainer that the sorrow, the disapproval, the animosity were directed squarely at himself.

Little was said until the suppertime stew had been ladled from the great iron pot, the hard loaves split and shared. Thorvald found the food impossible to get down; his stomach was churning. Beside him Skapti ate stolidly. It was Einar, the senior among them, who broke the awkward silence.

"So, Thorvald. Asgrim tells us you're off home in the morning. Walking out on us."

"Not if I have anything to say about it," Sam snarled under his breath.

Thorvald said nothing; what was the point? They could not understand his reasons.

"We couldn't believe it," Wieland burst out, surprising Thorvald, for this was a reserved man, a man of very few words. "That you'd turn against us right at the end, abandon us just like that. Especially now. How could you?"

"I mean," Skolli put in, "we know about the girl, terrible thing, upset all of us, that did. But I'd have thought that would make you keener to go on. Makes you one of us, in a way."

"That's just it," Orm said. "Now you know how we feel. We've all lost someone: friend, brother, father. Infant in the cradle. Look at Wieland there, his last was taken only this spring, the child they say your girl helped to birth. Sounds like she did her best for us. Why can't you?"

"Thought better of you," growled Knut, the young fisherman. "Thought it was going to be different this time. Just goes to show, you can't trust an incomer." There was a general rumble of assent; its tone was ominous.

"Anyway," Sam said, "if I won't go, you can't go. Did you think of that?"

There was a brief silence.

"I suppose I need to explain," Thorvald said reluctantly. He had gone through this twice already; he felt a profound desire for it all to be over, and the *Sea Dove* on her way home, even though that voyage could only end in pain. "I don't expect you to understand. It's just—it's just—" He made himself stop and draw breath; they were angry, and there were a lot of them. This was not a moment to come out with some rambling, scattered statement about his own feelings. It was time to demonstrate some real leadership, if he were still capable of it. He rose to his feet, spread his hands. "You know," he said, "when I first came here I didn't know what to make of you. So much strength, so little application; so much potential, so little will to develop it; so much ability, so little cohesion. There were leaders among you, but they were too dispirited to lead. There were skilled fighters wasting their time on guard duty. There was intelligence, but you weren't using it. I saw an army without hope. Nonetheless, I saw an army."

The men were quite silent now.

"Well," said Thorvald, turning his head to meet each of them in the eye. "Look at you now. What a team! What a fighting troop! You've got cunning, cleverness and skill; you've got cooperation and discipline and the will to go on. You've got what gets a man up at dawn uncomplaining and out onto the practice field, even when his head aches fit to split asunder." There was a faint ripple of laughter. "You've got leaders like Einar here, and Skapti and Hogni, who'll drill you until you're half dead on your feet, and stand by you through thick and thin. You're not a dejected rabble anymore, you're a force to be reckoned with. You've got what you never had before: the will to win. I didn't give that to you, you did it yourselves, by hard work and determination."

There was a moment's pause, then an outbreak of applause and a muted cheer. Thorvald noticed Asgrim and Hogni standing in the doorway, watching. Then Einar spoke.

"Well said. It's true, we've a far better chance this hunt, and we know it. And it looks like we've no choice but to put it to the test, since there's no possibility of a truce now. But you underestimate yourself, Thorvald. There's only one thing different this year from last year and the one before;

that's you. Without you, we'd have been the same—what was it you said—?"

"Dejected rabble," put in Skolli.

"Exactly. You can't leave us now. You're the one who turned us around. You're the one with all the bright ideas—attack from three points at once, doctor the weapons, disable the traps. We can't do it without you."

"Told you," Skapti murmured at Thorvald's side.

"Stay till after the hunt," Einar urged. "Then we'll load up your boat for you, and the two of you can be off home if that's what you want."

"Or you can stay," Skapti said, eyes flicking nervously in the general direction of Asgrim.

"Or you can stay," agreed Einar gravely. "What do you say, man?"

There was a chorus of voices then, and many men pressing forward, each to make his own personal plea to Thorvald, all of them with that same look in their eyes, a look that made it starkly clear to him that what he had wrought here was far bigger than he had ever imagined. He had put hope in their hearts, had shown them a future without fear. Now he was taking it away again. He had not realized how closely he himself was bound up in their vision; had not dreamed of it until Skapti had uttered the fateful words, *If you go off home, there's no hope of changing things after.* These men saw a future in which Asgrim was no longer leader. It was a future in which his own part was critical. It came to him that Asgrim would be a complete fool to let him stay.

Thorvald raised a hand, and the hubbub quieted. "You forget, maybe," he said, "that a friend of mine was drowned here. I take the responsibility for that on my own shoulders. I should have protected her and I did not, for my mind was all on our own work here and I had forgotten her. It's my duty to take the news of her death home to her kin as soon as I can. That is the main reason why—"

"We understand your grief, Thorvald." Asgrim had stalked over to the top of the central hearth and now stood there wrapped in his dark cloak, his gaze sweeping them all. Total silence had fallen. "All of us have felt something of the same. In the Lost Isles, bereavement is our daily bread. But let us be practical. Your young friend is gone; we cannot bring her back. You've been away from home a long time, more than a season now. What difference can it make to Creidhe's family whether you bring them this sad news now or after midsummer? None, I think. Let me add my own voice to those of the men. You speak only truth, and you speak with a rousing voice, a young man's voice. We have sore need of true battle leaders here, those who can carry us forward with hope and purpose. Earlier, I accepted your decision to leave us, since I could hardly compel you to stay. But I regret that I did so. Can I not press you one last time to remain with us until after the hunt? We need you, Thorvald, you and Sam." The Ruler gave a cursory nod in Sam's direction. "Stay with us. Avenge your friend. Help us capture Foxmask. This, I believe, is the reason the gods sent you to the Lost Isles on the breath of the east wind. This, I am convinced, is your quest."

A cheer went up, louder this time. Someone put a cup in Thorvald's hand. He had the curious sense that he was no longer in control of his own life, that some malign force had taken over and was playing games calculated only to wound him, and to highlight his weaknesses. He wanted so badly to say yes, and he knew he must not.

"I don't—" he whispered.

Asgrim's dark gaze met his across the fire. "Please, son," said the Ruler. "Do this for me."

Thorvald felt his heart stop altogether and his breath cease. Despite himself, he gave a half-nod; it was enough. It was only after the men began to cheer again fit to lift the roof off the shelter, that the steady thud in his chest resumed, and he sucked in his breath and stared back at Asgrim, wondering if this was just another cruel trick. The Ruler smiled, the merest twist of the lips. He said something more, but Thorvald missed it, for he was enveloped in a huge bear-hug—Skapti—followed by several vigorous slaps on the shoulder and a number of friendly punches in the arm, as all came to offer their heartfelt thanks. Tight-lipped Wieland had tears in his eyes. Hogni was beaming. Einar wanted to sit down then and there and discuss a tactical plan he'd been working on. Orm wanted to drink with him. And Skolli, it seemed, had a gift: a gift that had waited for this moment.

"From all of us," the smith said gruffly. "Blade's my work, of course; saved a bit of good quality ore for it, better than the usual. Einar made the hilt; narwhal tusk, that is. Knut did the binding, being handy with knots. The fellows made the cord, polished it up, fashioned the sheath and all. Hope you like it. Kind of a thank you. You didn't have to help us. Would have given it, even if you'd left. Better like this, though. You can use it on the hunt. Should be good luck for you."

Odin's bones, now he had tears in his eyes. What was wrong with him? The knife was perfectly crafted; it sat in his hand as if it were an extension of his arm, finely balanced, elegant and plain. The hilt was warm, the yellow-white bone conforming cleanly to his palm. Even the sheath was a thing of beauty, the leather tooled in a pattern of vines and creatures. He had not known these men had such skills among them. Last spring, they could not have done this; a man worn down by loss, a man who believes himself a failure, has not the spirit to create lovely things. Was it true? Was it actually he who had changed them thus?

"Thank you," he said gruffly. "I'll bear it with pride; I'll lead you with still greater pride. You're fine fighters, and fine friends. Now, did someone say something about ale?"

After that he allowed himself to drink, which he had not done earlier, but he kept it in check, for a leader cannot afford to lose control. Once he saw Sam watching him with a funny expression on his face, but he decided to ignore it. Sam had wanted to stay, hadn't he? Well, it looked like they were staying, at least until midsummer. So Sam had got what he wanted; there was no reason for him to look so disapproving. As for the Ruler, Asgrim had called him son. Probably just another sort of game, that. It was one that two

could play. First he would lead the hunt and win back Foxmask. After that, Asgrim was going to find the rules had
changed.

On a western shore in Hrossey, soon after sunset, three
women stood quietly around a little fire. One was young,
slender, pale. Her expression was remote and grave; her
brown hair hung down her back in a severe plait. She wore
a skirt and long tunic of plain gray, and a little leather bag
around her neck. This was Eanna, priestess of the mysteries, sister of Creidhe. Her eyes were closed, her arms outstretched; the smoke arose before her, twisting in visions of
past, present and possible future.

Margaret and Nessa stood together, waiting. They had
sought answers; whether Eanna could give them remained
to be seen. The wise woman did not usually come down to
enact her rituals here; she dwelt alone in her sacred place,
and if folk wanted truth, they came to find her. But Nessa,
who was Eanna's mother, was now well advanced in her
pregnancy, and this child could not under any circumstances be put at risk. The piercing desire of Nessa and
Eyvind for a son was well known, although it was not
something they spoke of openly. And that was not all.
Nessa was the last princess of the Folk, the ancient race of
the Light Isles. Had the coming of the Norsemen not
changed the islands forever, the son of such a princess
would have been king here, for thus was the royal descent
of the Folk determined, through its female line. There
were no longer any kings in the Light Isles; nonetheless,
this child would be a potent symbol of survival for the old
race and the old faith. Nessa had given up riding; she
would not travel in a cart, either, and it was too far for her
to walk to Eanna's sanctuary. So the wise woman had
come down to the shore not far from the family's
dwelling, and had chanted her invocation as the sun set in
the western sea. They had chosen this spot for a reason.
Nessa believed the child would be at risk from the Seal
Tribe, the ocean-dwelling race that had snatched small Ki-

nart from her. She feared that above all as the infant grew apace within her and could be felt kicking vigorously against the confines of the womb. She was not sure the Seal Tribe had been adequately appeased by the taking of her only son, though when they had helped her, all those years ago, they had seemed to do so willingly, for love of the islands. She feared for the unborn babe, and she feared for Creidhe. On this occasion it had not seemed appropriate to seek out the ancestors herself; Nessa knew she lacked the detachment to see the vision and unravel its meaning calmly and coolly. Her daughter was the priestess now, and Eanna would bear this burden for her.

Margaret did not set much stock in gods, nor in ancestral spirits. On the rare occasions when she had requested their help, she had found the result less than useful. Besides, she thought grimly, watching as the wise woman raised her hands slowly toward the violet-gray sky, she suspected she would have made just as many errors in her life even if she had possessed faith, even if Freya or Thor or one of the others had decided to take a hand in her affairs. She seemed fated to get it all wrong. So most of the time she simply performed the tasks required to live a life: overseeing the fields, the barns and byres, the neat, orderly home, the vegetable patch; setting her skilful hands to spinning and weaving, embroidery and the fashioning of fine garments. Before, there had been Thorvald: both boon and bane, her only child, Somerled's child. Now he was gone, and she could not believe the emptiness he had left behind him, a gaping hole that spoke a truth she had long denied: she loved her son, no matter who his father was. He was hers, a good boy, a fine boy for all his flaws. She did miss Creidhe, her golden girl, her sunny apprentice; but it was Thorvald's loss that cut deepest. So she had come, not only to support her friend, but knowing that news of Creidhe was also news of Thorvald.

Out of sight, over a rise of ground, Ash and Eyvind were waiting to accompany them home. The wise woman's rituals were not for men, though long ago, so long it seemed another life now, Eyvind had come very close, when Nessa and the old priestess, Rona, had sheltered him. Ash had been looking tired this morning. Margaret suspected he had not been sleeping. Perhaps she kept him awake, the way she paced in the night, her memories tormenting her. There was a solution of sorts, a simple one; these last dark times, she had found herself drawn toward it with an urgency she had never experienced before, not even in the early days of her widowhood, when she was little more than a girl. One would think the urgings of the flesh, the hot cravings of the body, would wither and die, denied so long. She was six-and-thirty, surely too old for passion, surely past being comforted so easily, with gentle hands and the hard, fervent body of a man. Nonetheless, the longing was there, and she seemed to be getting worse at smothering it. Stupid woman, she was, foolish woman with a grown-up son and a household to run, and a body that wasn't admitting it was too late for everything to change. If she had not lain with Ash in all the eighteen years they had lived in the same house, why would she suddenly do so now? The answer came into her head instantly, quite uninvited. *Because, after eighteen years, he is still there, and he still loves you.*

Eanna was emerging from her trance, moving her arms, her hands in slow gestures to awaken the clay self, humming a scrap of melody under her breath. Nessa was sitting on the rocks now; she grew easily tired, for the babe was large and she had ever been slight and frail in build. Eanna's eyes snapped open: gray, wide, blind for a moment as she made the change from spirit-vision to ordinary sight. She blinked and bowed her head. Then, straight-backed, she sank to sit cross-legged by the small fire, and Margaret moved to pass her a cup of water. Nobody asked, *What did you see?* Answers to such questions come in their own time.

Eanna drank deeply, shuddered, and cleared her throat. It is no easy matter to return from a profound trance; it exhausts the body and numbs the will.

"This was confused," she told them eventually. "Many small images tumbled together. I could hazard a guess as to what was close this time, rather than yet to come: Creidhe with a little ragged child on her knee, and colors in front of her, beautiful colors, as if all the hues of the four seasons rippled and changed around her, passing by. A man at her feet. Not Thorvald, not Sam, but another, wild-looking, though he sat quiet. They were alone; sea, sky and magic separated them from the world of men." Eanna paused; she would not tell all, not even to her own mother. One must weigh the possible consequences of sharing such visions in their entirety. The seer bears a heavy burden.

"Was Creidhe well? Did she look happy?" Nessa asked shakily.

"Well enough. She looked tired, but not discontent. Thinner. The child was odd, a little birdlike creature."

Nessa nodded. "I, too, have seen that image."

Margaret did not speak; would not ask. She waited with her hands clenched together.

"I saw nothing of Sam," said Eanna. "Thorvald I saw, on a clifftop at night, weeping. And a white-haired man clad like a Christian priest. Darkness and light, a link of some kind . . . death and life in the balance. I saw men armed, and the spilling of blood."

"No sign, nothing to tell us when they will come home?" asked Nessa. "Not that I expect such neat answers; I have enacted this rite often enough myself to know its images are never easy to untangle."

"Folk singing at the birth of a babe," Eanna told them in a whisper. "Not a joyous sound, but one fit to wrench the heart, an unearthly lament. Creidhe's voice then, defiant, full of courage. And tears. That is all I can tell you. I felt Creidhe's presence strongly. I know she has had no training in a wise woman's arts, but it seemed to me she was trying to reach me, to tell me something. Perhaps that she loves us and holds us in her heart. Perhaps only that."

Nessa nodded soberly, rising to her feet. She gave a little bow of formal thanks; although this was her own daughter, the respect due to a wise woman must be demonstrated. "Thank you," she said. Nessa would not give in to tears. The news had been mixed; she would ponder it awhile and see what insights came to her.

"Thank you," said Margaret, thinking she had never seen her son weep, not even as a small child. It seemed to her such scant news merely made the heart ache more painfully; she would almost rather have none at all.

Eanna spent the night with her family. In the morning she returned to her own place, a tiny stone dwelling in the hills, set in a fold of the land where one wind-bent willow grew by an outcrop of stone that somewhat resembled a gnarled old woman. A streamlet trickled close by her door; her fireplace set among flat stones overlooked a green-robed valley and, farther down, a glinting, circular lake. Eanna made up her fire and sat awhile, quiet under the wide bowl of the summer sky. Her mother had laden her with provisions; fine bere bread, fresh vegetables, a round of sheep's cheese, a sack of beans. Eanna's little cat had been quite put out that she had spent a night away from home. Somewhat mollified by a sliver of cheese, he now sat on the rocks close by her like a smoky shadow, washing his face. Margaret had given the young priestess a warm cape of her own making, plain gray with a narrow border of blue, little dogs and flowers.

Eanna considered her vision. What she had told them was exactly what she had seen; one did not falsify the ancestors' wisdom. On the other hand, there were parts of it she had not told. Her mother's health must be safeguarded; Nessa must carry her child to term, and even then there were risks, for she was well past the best age for safe delivery. It would be important to have Creidhe home in time. Eanna might say what prayers they needed, enact the ritual suitable for the occasion. She might call on the ancestors to help. But, when it came to it, what would really be needed was strong, expert hands and a calm, confident voice to keep control of the situation. Creidhe's hands, Creidhe's voice. And whether she would come in time, or whether she would come at all, Eanna did not know. She only knew the young man she had seen, sitting at her sister's knee as if he, too, were an infant entranced by a bedtime story, had had a very odd look about him, a look that chimed with her own memory of childhood tales. The long, bony hands, the pallor, the strange, deep eyes that seemed to mirror the liquid mystery of the ocean: were not these the marks of the Seal Tribe?

NINE

Recognition. Sacrifice. Expiation.
MONK'S MARGIN NOTE

Stay close by me," Keeper warned her as they made their way down the steep hillside toward the cove. "You must not go out alone here, not until after the hunt. It is not safe."

"But you said—" Creidhe began, scrambling to keep up with his long stride.

"No danger from others. I will protect you. It is the traps, those that are set for the enemy. There is not time for you to learn them all. After the hunt they are dismantled; new traps next season, so the enemy cannot remember. I will show you."

And show her he did, while Small One, apparently aware of where these sudden dangers lay and how to stay away from them, wandered about in his doglike form, sniffing at bushes and stones, racing after birds, and generally behaving just like a small hound enjoying an outing on a summer's day. The moment of changing back, Creidhe had not seen; she supposed that eventually she would get used to it, this slipping from one form to another when the time seemed right. There was a wonder in it outside her experience, and she wished her sister Eanna could see it. Eanna, being a priestess, might have answers

It was hardly warm; the westerly wind whipped the sea to scudding whitecaps and set Creidhe's long hair streaming.

All the same, the sun showed himself, rising high to remind them how close it was to midsummer, and the hunt.

Traps. So many traps, ingenious, clever, cruel: she had not imagined this stark landscape could conceal such pitfalls for the unwary. Creidhe blessed the ancestors for depositing her here unconscious and unaware, so she had not attempted to find her way across the shore, up the hill, into the shelter of cave or hollow. For the truth was, there was nowhere safe, save those precise ways along which Keeper led her. There were hidden pits floored with spikes of sharpened bone; there were sudden drops from ledges that appeared quite safe, but were in fact kept slippery with coatings of some fishy-smelling substance; there were rocks suspended from long cords, which an unwary step on a particular point released to come hurtling toward the hapless victim, perfectly placed to crush his skull. How these worked she was not quite sure, and she did not ask. Keeper took her up by a place where puffins nested, to show a fine view of the big holm to the west. The waves washed in fiercely here: beyond that islet was a straight view to the farthest margin of the world. They climbed back down to the rocky hillside near the narrow bay. Tunnels pierced the ground on which they stood, a network of shadowy passages, some natural, some enhanced by the work of man. So far they had observed no sign of the other tribe on their wanderings.

"There are many underground ways," Keeper told her gravely, "some safe, some perilous. Last season, this where we stand"—motioning to an opening between the rocks before them, wide enough to admit a man—"led to a sheltered cave where three warriors might be concealed together. At low tide there is an escape at the other end, allowing a retreat and regrouping. They learned this last time and made use of it."

"And this time?" This time would be different; the grim set of his jaw made that clear.

"This time, when the last man enters, the rock shifts; that can be done by an adjustment, a lever, which is worked from above. It traps them within. They will find the lower entry narrower now, the right size for a rabbit or gull to pass through. Of course, it still admits the tide."

"I see," said Creidhe, shivering. Keeper's eyes were cool; evidently this sort of thing was quite routine for him. What kind of world had she strayed into?

"There are more," Keeper said. "Up the mountain, behind the waterfall, along the cliffs. Where we came down, many places where the ground will give way under a careless foot; on the shore, many spots where rocks and sea will trap a man; on the hillside, paths that lead to nowhere, ways where the lightest mist will shroud all safe exits. They are fools to come here. There is no defeating the Isle of Clouds."

"What about the others? What about—?"

"I have more to show," he said, taking her hand. He was looking up toward the crags that crowned the island. "When you see, you will believe that you are protected here, you and Small One. There is still doubt in your eyes, Creidhe. You should not doubt me. I am true to my promises."

They walked up the slope, Keeper slowing his pace to accommodate her. Her legs ached; she was not yet recovered from her illness and what had gone before.

"Keeper?"

"What is it? You wish to rest?"

"No, I can go on. I wondered, have you a boat of your own? For fishing perhaps? Do you ever leave the island?"

He smiled; there was no gladness in it. His eyes were bleak. "For fishing, I need no boat," he said. "But I have boats. I do not keep them here, in sight. They are little used. I cannot leave the island."

"Because of him?" Creidhe watched as Small One dug in the earth by a low-growing bush, pursuing some scuttling creature. "Is there nowhere safe for him? The northern islands? Or right away, some place such as my own homeland? This is so—it is so isolated; you seem so alone."

"You are here now."

"Yes, but—" She did not finish this. To say, *I won't be here forever,* would be tempting fate. She could not say, *I'll only*

be here until Thorvald comes for me. That quite probably
was false. If she knew Thorvald, by now he was embroiled in
some ambitious scheme of his own and had completely forgotten her. Sam might come; Sam wouldn't forget.

"I cannot take him." Keeper had stopped in his tracks, his
eyes on her, his voice almost angry. "Nowhere is safe for
him. Nowhere but here. All want him. Asgrim's folk, to
trade away, so they can win peace. The Unspoken, because
of what he is. The brothers, the Christians, they are the only
ones who remain outside, the only ones who ever tried to
stand against Asgrim. But in the end they are powerless.
This is the only refuge. We stay here, my brother and I."

"Forever?"

"Forever. That was my promise."

Around the hill on the northern side, where it seemed all
was stark cliff and rocky pinnacle and knife-beaked,
swooping birds, he led her to a network of caves and crannies, a hidden place no invader could possibly discover, its
entrance was so dangerous, so marginal. Climbing down to
the opening terrified her, but she would not say so, not with
Keeper's hand holding hers, leading her, his feet nimble and
sure on the slick surface of the rock ledge, showing the way.
It was dark inside, but not so dark that she could not see
what was stored on numerous shelves hewn from the walls
of this narrow, shadowy cavern. Here was an armory fit for
a seasoned battle troop, if somewhat outside the mode of
the weaponry her father and his men employed in the Light
Isles. There were many narrow throwing spears, apparently
carved from bone, with grips of woven twine cunningly
braided and knotted, decorated with tufts of feathers. There
were arrows of a similar make, and also some of pine,
which he must have salvaged. The bows, she thought, came
from the Long Knife people, for they were of a more familiar type, of fine seasoned hardwood, doubtless a gift from
the sea, since trees grew sparsely in these wind-harried islands. Knives were set in a rack of driftwood lashed with
rope; each was in a sheath of leather or padded wool or
some other material, and when Keeper drew one out to
show her, she saw how the iron gleamed, with not a trace of

rust. Her father would have been impressed; the proper care of weapons was something he valued. There were no hewing axes here. As a Wolfskin's daughter, Creidhe recognized that most of this armory consisted of weapons to be used at a certain range. She did not see a sword, or a shield, or a thrusting spear.

"Not so many left here now," Keeper said casually, testing the edge of a knife with his finger. A drop of blood appeared. "I have moved most of them out, since the hunt is near. It is necessary to have sufficient in place, here and there, since Asgrim's men may attack from different quarters. Spears, darts, stones. Too late to move them once his men land on the island."

"I see," Creidhe said after a moment. "What are those?" She had noticed another kind of missile, something akin to an arrow but longer, and barbed, with the bone tip discolored somewhat. She reached out to indicate what she meant, and Keeper grabbed her wrist, pulling her hand sharply back. Her heart thumped. She realized he had the strength to snap her arm.

"No!" he hissed. "A touch will kill. I'm sorry. I hurt you. Here, show me." He released his grip, taking her hand in both of his, touching the wrist. His palms were callused, the fingers roughened, but his touch was gentle. "Are you injured?"

"No," she whispered, her heart still racing.

"It is poison. You frightened me."

"I'm not hurt. It was stupid to think of touching them. Keeper, you have enough weapons here for a whole army." There was a question that followed this, if one were to be logical about things, but that was not the question she asked. "Where is Small One?"

"He will not enter here. He fears iron."

"Oh." She looked into his strange eyes, eyes in which the unfathomable depths of the ocean could be glimpsed. It was dim in the cavern, but his eyes were bright. They seemed to bear their own light within, changeable and perilous. "What about you? You are his brother; his kinsman, anyway. Does not cold iron make you, too, uneasy?"

He was still holding her hand, his fingers warm and strong. Common sense told Creidhe she should be frightened, and she was, but not of him.

"I would be lying if I said no. My blood shrinks from this metal. But I am Keeper, warrior and guardian. Five times I have survived the hunt; I have been true to my vow. I cannot afford to give in to my fear, for Asgrim would soon find and exploit such a weakness. So I make use of the weapons they leave behind. I have taught myself to hold them strongly, to cast them as if I were not afraid."

"I'm finding it harder all the time to believe that Asgrim is your father."

"I wish it were not so. But it is true. I am his son, as Sula was his daughter. It were better that such a man never take a wife, nor engender children. I will kill him. This summer, next summer, the one after. I will make an end of him for what he has done."

Creidhe felt suddenly cold. His voice had been flat and final, as if he were merely setting out the inevitable. "I'd like to go back now," she said quietly. "I'm getting tired."

"Come." Keeper turned, still holding her hand. "This way: we go out here, along the far ledge. Keep hold; look up, not down. A quick way back to the shelter, then you should rest. Too much for you."

"I'm all right." But she wasn't, not really; especially not when they edged along a narrow shelf in the rocks—that part was all right, she knew he would not let her fall—and Keeper pointed ahead and upward, and she saw the skulls. She stared, and blinked: they were still there. For all the myriad birds that thronged the ledges of the northern cliff face, jostling for room, this was one place where no gull roosted, where not a chick sat fattening on the nest, nor a parent dived with succulent fish in beak. Yet there were shelves here, many of them; safe, deep niches and cracks offering sheltered purchase. There was no room for birds. Each corner of space, each nook and cranny was already occupied by the clean-picked, hollow-eyed skull of a man. They sat in rows, in twos and threes, here one alone, here a pair leaning drunkenly together. Some were old, crumbling, toothless; some were newer, a tuft of hair, a patch of dried-up skin adhering to the naked bone. One wore a leather cap with ear flaps, though there was little left for it to shelter. Many bore signs of injury: a gaping split between the eye sockets, a smashed cheek, jaws that met less than cleanly. Creidhe stood stock-still on the ledge, transfixed. There were so many, too many to count. All had been set here, gazing out across the sea. Trophies. Markers. A testament to the years of survival.

"I think I'm going to be sick," she said, closing her eyes. Placed here one by one, season by season, hunt by hunt. Placed here by a man who walked between traps as sure-footed as a creature of instinct; who traversed cliff and cave as easily as some being from story, not quite human. Whose hunt was this, exactly?

"Come." Keeper's voice was firm, kind. "You will not be sick; just open your eyes and follow me. I've got you safe; you will not fall. The shelter is just up there."

And of course she wasn't sick, and she didn't fall, because he was Keeper, and if he said he would protect her, she knew it was true. She also knew, with a very odd feeling in the pit of her stomach, that she was indeed deeply afraid. Of what exactly, she was not sure; it seemed foolish to name it fate, destiny, doom, yet those were the words that kept coming into her head. When they reached the shelter, Small One was there before them, sitting by the fire, a child swathed in a threadbare blanket, rocking to and fro, humming so softly the tune could hardly be heard.

"Rest," Keeper said. "Lie down; I have asked too much of you. I wanted to show . . . I forgot how it is . . . we have been here a long time . . ."

"Don't be sorry. It is better that I have seen this." Creidhe sat down beside the child; she was cold now, and wrapped her own blanket around her shoulders. "Keeper?"

"Mmm?" He was making up the fire, setting water to heat. She wondered where he had got the pot from, the implements of cooking. Gifts from the sea? More trophies of the hunt?

"There's nobody else here on the island, is there? Just you and—Foxmask."

He flinched, his mouth tightening. "Don't use that name." His tone was cold.

"Very well. But it's true, isn't it? There is no other tribe; the whole thing, the whole hunt, every year, it's just you, one man against all of them."

"I am Keeper." The simple statement of truth, delivered without emphasis, was breathtaking in its courage.

"By all the ancestors," Creidhe breathed, "one man, holding out against so many. It is . . . terrible. It is like a thing of legend, an ancient story too strange to believe. Yet this is true. I saw them, I saw the men you have killed. I have to believe it."

"You disapprove? I act in accordance with a solemn promise. I must protect my brother."

"Yes, but . . ." It was hard to get her mind around it, though the truth had been creeping up on her for a long time now, since well before he had led her to his secret cave, shown her his implements of war, his wall of dead faces. The man who had done this was the same man who held the child with hands as gentle as a mother's, the same man who had fashioned garments for her while she lay sleeping, who had listened spellbound to her story. That man had killed and killed again, summer after summer. He had robbed the Long Knife people of their sons, brothers, fathers.

She felt a slight pressure against her side; the child was leaning on her, thumb creeping to mouth again, his lids drooping. Ingigerd had given up sucking her thumb at two and a half, having come to the realization that there were many more interesting ways to fill the day.

"I need to ask you something," Creidhe said, "and you probably won't like it."

"Go on." Keeper's eyes were wary.

"He is your kin, I understand that: Sula's child. I know how cruel they were to her, and I understand how angry that must have made you. You must have been very young when you stole him away: twelve, thirteen?"

He bowed his head. "Young, yes. Not yet a man."

"What you did was the act of a man, and I honor your courage; few would have attempted as much. But I look at

him now and I do not see a little boy like those of my home
islands, bonny, active, merry. To me he seems—deeply sad.
He's so thin, and so easily frightened. Here on this island he
leads a lonely life, for all he has you to keep him company.
Please don't be offended, I can see what you have sacrificed
for him. Indeed, I see your whole existence bent to his
preservation. But this child is no ordinary child. He is not
solely of your own lineage, Asgrim's lineage, but also of
theirs. Whatever we may think of their barbaric treatment
of your sister, this is the child of the Unspoken. This is Foxmask. Have you ever asked yourself, would it be better for
him if you had left him where he was?"

Keeper stared at her across the fire; his eyes seemed very
dark now, his pale features a mask of shock and hurt. Creidhe
shrank from that look: it was as if she had pierced him with
one of those barbs, the poisoned ones. She struggled on.

"To the Unspoken, Foxmask is a seer, a wise man, venerated, respected. With them he would have a special place;
he would be loved and guarded. Wouldn't he be safer there
than here? Besides, if he were returned, there would be
peace. There would be no more need for traps, for spears.
There would be no more need for killing. The women of the
Long Knife people could see their children grow and flourish. If you took him back, he would be happy. And you
would be free."

She waited, thinking Keeper would not reply at all, so
wounded was his expression. The child was nestling close
now, almost asleep; she gathered him onto her knee, rocking him. He was so slight, he felt like a cat, a little bird, a
bundle of frail bones and skin. His hair was like a nest, tangled and filthy. She wondered if she could comb the knots
out.

For a while Keeper stood there staring at her, quite silent.
Creidhe was not sorry she had spoken; this had needed saying. But she was sorry she had hurt him. The child was his
life's purpose. She was probably the first outsider to set foot
on his island save in war, and he had had no cause to trust
her. Yet he had taken her in. Now the weapon she had cast
had pierced his armor with deadly accuracy.

Keeper bent to the fire. He set on fuel, poured hot water into a bowl, added cold from a bucket set near, glanced across at her.

"You are cold," he said. "I have exhausted you. Perhaps you would like to wash, to warm yourself . . . I have forgotten such ways, it has been long . . . I think we offend you, myself and my brother . . . We are dirty, unkempt . . ."

Creidhe managed a smile. "You don't offend me at all. You merely startle and perplex me. I don't know what to make of you. I'm deeply sorry if I have upset you, I have the greatest respect for the way you have looked after the child. It's just that—this place, it's so remote, and—never mind. It's really none of my business. I have an unfortunate habit of interfering in other people's lives. Thorvald says I'm naturally bossy." She could hear herself prattling like a nervous child. "And yes, I would love to wash, I am used to doing so every day. And I'd like to do something with your brother's hair, comb it, maybe cut it, but only if you say yes."

"Do as you wish, as long as he is not frightened. I have made many errors. I knew nothing of the raising of children; all I could do was try to learn by myself. Now, I will go for fish while you wash. I have not quite forgotten what is correct." His tone changed, darkened. "Creidhe?"

"Yes?"

"Will you show us the web again tonight? Tell more?" The look in his eyes was different now; there was a hunger in it that sent a shiver through her whole body, a shiver that was not fear, but something else entirely, a heady, dangerous feeling that was new to her.

"Yes, if you want."

"Thank you. And I will tell too. I will tell you why my brother cannot go back, why that would be crueller for him than an exile here among the puffins and seals. Not now; please wash and rest. Tonight, when he sleeps again."

While the child slumbered by the fire, Creidhe stripped, washed as well as she could in the small quantity of warm water Keeper had provided, and scrambled back into her clothes. There was no sign of her original garments, and she deduced they had been too damaged to salvage. Laid away in yet another cave, she suspected, was a stock of tunics, breeches, cloaks and boots removed from the owners of those rows of sightless eyes out there on the cliff face. How else had he fashioned garments for herself and for the child, how else clothed himself as he grew from a boy to a man? So, she must ask him another favor. One could not wear a single set of clothing indefinitely, not even on an island at the end of the world with only three inhabitants.

She longed for soap; the supply she had brought from home was long gone, and she had carried none in her pack when she set out from Council Fjord. All the same, she felt a great deal better. Her hair was at least somewhat clean now, though sorely tangled. She was tempted to get out the shears and cut it short, but decided instead to give the long, damp locks a thorough combing, then plait them tightly. After a visit to the privy, which was a somewhat alarming hole in the rocks with a vast drop to the foaming ocean below, Creidhe settled with comb in hand and began the long, tiresome business of restoring her hair to some kind of order. She glanced across at the sleeping child. She hardly knew where she would start with him, but a face wash, surely, would not scare him unduly. When he woke she would try.

She had watched Keeper as he went to fish, a tall, thin figure in his fluttering, faded garments, walking in long strides down the bare, windy hillside to the western margin of the island. He seemed to pass like a shadow over the landscape, treading so lightly he would leave no tracks behind him. So young: not even as old as Thorvald, who had often seemed to her a great deal less than grown up. What a life for a boy to choose for himself. It shut off so many possibilities, for him and for that poor little scrap there, who seemed less powerful visionary than fragile outcast. What could their future possibly hold? And yet Keeper was strong. One could not pity him. There was a core in him that was surely unbreakable; perhaps he was strong enough for his small kinsman as well. Keeper wore death lightly; in the midst of blood and terror, he still found time for tenderness, he still watched over Small One as father and mother, brother and friend. It seemed to Creidhe, as she dragged the comb through her wind-knotted hair, that there was no way for this tale to end save in sorrow. For, whatever she might wish, whatever Keeper might wish, Asgrim's men would come. As surely as sun follows moon across the sky, as surely as summer comes on the heels of spring, the hunt would unfold, and a new season's blood would stain the lonely shore of the Isle of Clouds. To wish that they would not come was to wish death on the children of Asgrim's tribe, to wish more grim losses on young mothers like Jofrid.

It was necessary to use the shears after all, just a little: some knots simply refused to be undone. Creidhe snipped here and there, consigning the remnants to the fire. The rest of it was smooth enough. It was the best that could be managed; the days of washing her hair with soft soap and rinsing it in chamomile water had faded to a dream. She bound it into a neat plait, fastened with twisted strands of embroidery wool. On the blankets Small One still slept, curled neatly, cheek on palm. She tried to imagine him in Hrossey with her own family, sitting on Brona's knee playing a little game with a loop of string, or following after Ingigerd as her sister headed off across the yard to visit the goats in the walled infield. She pictured him riding on Eyvind's shoulders, or cuddled in Nessa's lap. But he did not fit there; the child that appeared in her thoughts was another, a sturdy, fair-haired lad whose bright eyes and sweet smile showed him to be of her own kin, not Kinart who was lost long ago, but another like him: her own brother, a brother she did not have. Small One, she thought, had no family but Keeper; perhaps needed no family but Keeper. All the same, he lay there vulnerable as a chick in the nest, and she feared for him. In his human form he seemed to her entirely without resources.

Keeper had said rest. She found she did not want to sleep; dark images floated in her mind, just below the surface, and she would not give them the open door that sleep provided.

So she unrolled the Journey, took up her needle and began steadily to sew.

Later, when the child woke, she spoke to him quietly, showed him water and cloth, mimed washing her own face. His big eyes were watchful, grave; she could not tell how much he understood. He was far dirtier than Keeper. Probably the young warrior swam in the sea. Creidhe damped her cloth in the water she had warmed, wrung it out, dabbed at the child's face.

"Good boy," she murmured. "You will feel much better; I know I do." It sounded foolish; what relevance had this small ritual of domesticity in such a wild and marginal place? "Good, that's it. Now your ears . . ." He was so little. Creidhe marveled again at the odd, triangular face; the neck like the stalk of some tender plant; the neat, long-fingered hands with their grimy, broken nails, hands that were a miniature version of Keeper's. The eyes, too, were the same, darkest green and fluid, like light through deep water. "There, that's better. Now I'm going to try combing your hair." She showed him the comb, pulling it through the un-bound tassel at the end of her long plait. "See, mine's tidy now, I did it while you were sleeping. Sit here in front of me, and I'll see what I can do. It may pull a bit. Tell me if it hurts and I'll stop."

It must have hurt considerably; this hair had possibly not seen a comb since Small One was an infant of one year old. Creidhe itched to cut it short, to slice off the knots and twists, the filthy debris woven through it, weed, feathers, twigs, to take a brush to the crusted scalp. But that could not be attempted; without the iron shears, the only way was slow, meticulous combing. She sighed and made a start, and to distract the child she sang as she worked. Her sister Ingigerd loved songs; she knew plenty now, and would join in enthusiastically when Creidhe and Brona reached the chorus. Creidhe sang one about a fisherman who caught a cod so big it nearly sank his boat on the way home. She sang one about the Hidden Tribe, back in the Light Isles, and the importance of leaving out milk and sweet cakes on certain nights of the year so they wouldn't play tricks on you. She sang one about the sun and moon and why they followed each other across the sky. By then she had combed out a small section of the child's hair to dark, fine floss. He had remained quite still on the ground before her, submitting silently to the ordeal. It had not been possible to do it without pulling; she wondered, really, why she was inflicting it on him. Who cared if he was unkempt and dirty, save herself?

"That's enough for today," she said gently, laying a hand on his shoulder. "You're a very good boy; my sister would have been squirming and complaining by now. She's about your age, but she's bigger than you and has long yellow hair like mine. Can you understand what I'm saying to you, Small One?"

He looked at her, round-eyed, aware, at least, that she was addressing him.

"I want to help you if I can. I could teach you songs, stories. Other things, too. Numbers. Games. Lots of things, if you want." Who knew how long she would be here? Surely anything that helped this waif become more like a normal child had to be good. It was clear she wasn't going to be much use to Keeper in his other activities, but this, at least, she could offer.

Small One's hand crept out to rest on her sleeve a moment, the fingers thin and pale as hazel twigs. Then he got up and went to the entry to stare down the hill, waiting for Keeper. Creidhe shivered as she moved to tidy away the bowl, the cloth; to put the little comb Sam had made for her back in her bag. Without one another, these two were incomplete. They needed one another for survival. Without Keeper, Small One would soon die: of cold, of starvation, of a broken heart. Without Small One, Keeper would have no purpose in life, no reason for going on. When Sula extracted his promise from him, she had surely not known how she limited her brother's future: how much he would deny himself, to keep faith.

* * *

They sat by firelight, Keeper, and Creidhe, and Small One. The Journey had changed again. It had silenced Keeper; he studied it with somber eyes. Creidhe observed that his hair was damp, and tied back from his long, strong-boned face with a cord. It had been thus when he returned from fishing, his gleaming catch slung over his shoulder. She had seen the glance he gave her, the shy admiration in it, the undercurrent of something a great deal stronger. She could feel the reflection of it in her own gaze. Perhaps Keeper knew little of the world beyond this island, little of how folk lived their lives. All the same, she realized that beside him, the young men she had known in Hrossey were children.

Supper was over now and Small One sat on her knee, perched where he could see the pictures. Creidhe wondered if the child had words at all; perhaps he had been born half-made and would not have grown up like other boys even had he been raised in a less unusual manner. She knew about children with deficiencies. Back home, she had delivered two infants of this kind herself. One young mother had been kicked by a cow while her daughter was still in the womb. That girl had survived, but was slow to walk, slow to talk, slow to understand. Then there was Moya, who lived near a haunt of the Hidden Tribe, an underground chamber where they were known to congregate after dark. Moya's infant had been born deaf. The story went that the mound dwellers had taken away his power of hearing because they were sick of the sound of Moya's voice, she and her man being known for their fierce disputes. Probably the Hidden Tribe thought they were doing the child a favor.

The Journey was fully unrolled. Keeper still stared at the part she had made today, where rows of faces gazed forth, each captured in the moment when breath ceased, each showing what gripped his mind in the instant before shadow took him: *my child, I will never see her again . . . my wife . . . my home shore . . . this hurts, let it end . . . I am afraid . . . the darkness comes . . .* Around this swathe of unquiet spirits Creidhe had embroidered a barrier that might have been rock, or smoke, or some manifestation that was not of this earth; whatever it was, it was clear these men were confined by it, condemned to be held there forever staring out, each reliving eternally the moment of his death. Above them Creidhe had made sun and moon, rainbow, clouds, birds flying. Whatever the strange perplexity of man's behavior, the long rhythms of earth and sky go on regardless. In the end, the little lives that play out below are not so very significant.

"Tell of this," Keeper said, his fingers reaching to touch a screaming mouth, a staring, ghastly eye. "Tell why you have made this." His voice was tight, almost accusatory; he would not meet her gaze.

"No," Creidhe said, "not for the child's bedtime story. I have not fashioned this to make some point, some comment. Sometimes I set down what is in my head; this is what I saw today, not merely the objects, but the essence of them. Sometimes these images seem to—make themselves. Often I am not quite sure what the stitches will show until I am finished. It is not for me to explain this to you or to anyone. You must look, and consider, and make of it what you will."

Keeper shot her a sidelong glance. "You think I do wrong," he muttered. "That is what this tells me. You think me savage and cruel."

"You weren't listening. The Journey does not show what I think. It shows what is to be seen. Do not assume that I judge you, Keeper. I try not to judge anyone. Instead, I take what action seems right to me, and in between I make my embroidery."

"There is too much power in this." Still his eyes were fixed on the tiny stitches, the small, wild faces, the agonized mouths. "It hurts me."

"Then look away. I have a tale for Small One, and it starts at the other end of the Journey. See, Small One, here is a boy of much your size and age. He was my brother, as you are Keeper's. Well, not quite the same; Kinart and I had the same mother and father."

She had intended to tell only a brief story, in which the young Eanna and Kinart and Creidhe met their friend Thorvald and went on an adventure, crossing a field with a large bull in it. But the tale flowed on, and did not stop until she reached the point when it must: when her brother, at not quite five years old, had wandered away from his family one day on the shore and had been found limp and white in the shallows, shawled in sea wrack. Creidhe had been less than four at the time. She remembered every detail, and although she was not a crying sort of girl, she came very close to it as she told of her father's terrible grief, and her mother's stoical acceptance that, at last, the Seal Tribe had come to claim a payment long due to them.

"It was because they had helped my mother with a magical task," she explained, her voice choking on the words, "the making of a special harp from the bones of a murdered man: a harp that sang the truth. The testimony of that instrument saved my father's life, and it saved the future of our islands. At the time, the women from the sea asked Nessa for no payment; indeed, they made her a gift. But she had always believed they would come back to claim what was due to them, and they did. She paid with the life of her only son. I'm sorry," Creidhe blinked and wiped her eyes. "I did not intend to tell such a sad story at bedtime. It was a long while ago."

She felt the child stir and raise his small hand to touch her wet cheek, as softly as the brush of a feather. She put her arms around him, gently so as not to frighten him, and closed her eyes a moment. Home was a very long way away. Within her, somewhere, that three-year-old remained, watching helpless as death transformed her sunny world.

"You have many tales of those you call the Seal Tribe?" Keeper's voice still sounded strained; there was no doubt she had upset him. Still, he could hardly expect her to be nonchalant about that panoply of weapons, that wall of skulls.

"Many. There are parts of the Light Isles where they are said to dwell; Holy Island, where the Christian hermits have their community, is one such place. Though the coming of the brothers drove the sea people away from there, I think."

"Have you ever seen them?"

"No; few people have. The women are said to be very beautiful, and seductive: many a fisherman has yearned to have one for a wife and come to grief because of it."

"Why would these folk steal a child only to let him drown?"

Creidhe bowed her head, cuddling Small One. "I don't know," she whispered. "The old women say the Seal Tribe don't feel love and loss as we do. A human child is nothing to them. I suppose they took him in payment and then found they had no use for him. We should not be speaking of this in front of—"

"That story is false," said Keeper flatly.

Creidhe was astounded. "No, it isn't," she protested. "My mother was there, she knows—"

"Not all of it. But it is wrong to say these sea people let your brother drown. That is a terrible deed, a murderous deed. That is not the way it was."

"How can you possibly know that? How can you be so sure?"

"I know, as you know your web shows truth, even when a force outside yourself guides your needle. I am sorry your brother drowned; I understand your father's grief." He was gazing at Small One now, his eyes shadow-dark. His expression stopped Creidhe's heart, so full of love and fear was it. "Your Kinart died by accident, no more. The folk of earth and ocean do not demand cruel fees from those who honor them. That is not the way of it. Men and women of good heart have no reason to fear such folk."

"You can't know that. These tales cannot take shape without some grain of truth—"

"The tales are wrong. They come from fear. But you should not fear. It is the tribes of men that are heartless, not the ancient ones."

"Men can be cruel, it's true," Creidhe said, thinking of Somerled. "But they can be good and noble too, brave and strong. My father is like that." She glanced at Eyvind's embroidered image, with which the Journey began: the stalwart, sunny-haired warrior with the wolf pelt on his shoulders. "And there are all sorts in between: men who strive to be valiant, or loyal, or virtuous, and who keep failing; men who start life with advantages and waste them. Women who are selfish, or lazy, or jealous; others who are wise and loving. All sorts."

She began to roll the Journey up once more; today's additions were dark, full of sorrow, but that was not of her choosing; she could only make truth as she saw it.

"You are sad," Keeper observed. He had not come to sit close by her this time, but remained a few paces off, standing, arms folded. The wind was stronger tonight, its eddies seeking them out through cracks in the stone walls, making the flames of their hearth fire flicker and tremble, and setting the feathers on Keeper's tunic shivering.

"Not sad exactly." Creidhe thought about this. "I think what I feel goes beyond sadness. I feel—powerless. There is a great pattern here of blood and death and loss; I would give much to be able to change that, and yet I cannot see any way it can be done. I fear for my friends, across there with Asgrim; I have no idea what has become of them. I fear for Small One, and for you—the risks you take are so great my mind can scarcely encompass them. I am a long way from home, Keeper; it seems everything that happens carries me away just a little farther."

"You wish the ocean had not brought you to my island?" His face was in shadow; she could not read his expression.

"Strangely, I cannot say yes to that. All along I believed I had some part to play in Thorvald's journey, and although I have been separated from him, I still believe that to be so. I just hope I find out what it is soon. What you showed me today alarmed me. These are unquiet spirits, Keeper. I do not think you are a cruel man. But it is a cruel vengeance not to let them rest, at the last."

"They brought this on themselves." Again, the flat statement of fact.

"Certainly they came here knowing they faced death. The hunt is a time of blood. But they came to try to win peace for their tribe, to salvage some hope of a future. Not to hurt Foxmask, only to return him to where he belongs. I do not like what Asgrim did; I did not like what he intended for me. But I can understand their reasons. Keeper, I delivered a child while I was in Brightwater, a boy who would have died without my skills in midwifery. I could not understand the terror that gripped the young mother even after her son was safely born. Then the Unspoken came, the voices, and sang him away. He died there in her arms, a boy who had been whole and sound a moment before. It was cruel, terrible. This was the third infant Jofrid had lost that way. Can't you understand why Asgrim's men would act to stop that happening again? If this continues, the Long Knife people are finished."

Keeper stared at her. "You argue for the folk who would have sold you to their enemy?"

"I do not support that," Creidhe said, shivering. "If I did, I would not have tried to escape. I have blood on my hands as you have: men drowned that day because of what I did. But I understand Asgrim's desperation. In such times, men take action that may be judged extreme in years of peace. What I do not understand is why, having defeated your adversary and killed him, you would not then allow him rest. If you sunder a man's head from his body, he cannot move on. You condemn his spirit to roam the wilderness, alone and crying."

He did not reply, and now Small One wriggled down from her knee and wandered off, out to the open hillside. Creidhe stood up, thinking to follow him, for it was late and in the half-dark the ground was treacherous.

"No need to go," Keeper said quietly. "The moon rises; he will watch, as he does when it is full. Later he will sleep. Sit down; there is a tale you must hear."

Creidhe sat, hands folded in her lap.

"When Asgrim's people first came to the islands, there was peace," Keeper said, squatting down beside her and using his long hands to illustrate his story. "The Unspoken had their seer, their Foxmask; they listened to his wisdom, and it helped them live well, reading the winds and tides, sowing seed by the moon and reaping at the right time, tending their creatures and their children. A hard life, but orderly. The islands were almost empty; there was plenty of room for the Long Knife people, and they settled and lived their lives. Each clan kept to its own islands; the fishing grounds were shared. Foxmask was a very old man. He was blind, and his legs were twisted and useless. He did not go abroad; the Unspoken tended to his every need, brought him food, kept his hut snug and dry. When they sought counsel they came to him. At the turning of the seasons he would sing for them, and in those songs he would set out what was important for the right living of their lives."

Creidhe nodded; this much she had heard already from Brother Niall.

"Then Foxmask died. There was no other to take his place, no child of a fair-haired mother whose skin rivaled the snow for pallor. Without the wisdom they needed, the Unspoken grew wild and dangerous. It was not long before war broke out with the Long Knife people, a conflict in which many died over the course of the years. Then they took my sister, and for a little, the war ceased." Keeper closed his eyes.

"You need not speak of this, if—"

"It seems simple to you, doesn't it?" His tone was bitter. "Sula cannot suffer anymore; she is gone. Give them the child, then, let them place him in the position of love and respect that Foxmask deserves, and all will be well. Best for him; best for all. That is what you think."

Creidhe did not reply.

"Part of what you see for my brother is true. If Asgrim's men took him and passed him to the Unspoken, Small One would indeed become a venerated seer, as his predecessor was. But first they would break his legs and put out his eyes."

"*What?*" Creidhe's voice was a strangled whisper.

"This ritual was to occur as soon as he was weaned from his mother's breast," Keeper said flatly. "I took him away just in time. They believe, you see, that to perform his role fully, Foxmask must be as the old man was. I know this. I walked among them. To do what I did, it was necessary to earn their trust. They believe thus, that to close the body's eye is to open further the eye of the spirit. To take away the ability to walk is to anchor the seer in the heart of his tribe. No matter whether this lore is true or not. If he goes back, they will do it. I do not believe he could survive such an ordeal."

"Oh, no . . ." Creidhe could hardly speak. That frail child, who had curled so trustingly on her knee: no wonder Keeper guarded him with such violent dedication. "Oh, no . . ."

"Asgrim knows this. Perhaps his men know it as well. Yet the Ruler does not understand why I took my brother. For Asgrim, to sacrifice a child for the good of the tribe is entirely justified. Even his own kin. He has shown that he cares nothing for the bonds of blood. It was not his legacy that bound me and Sula together, that binds me now to her son."

"I don't know what to say," Creidhe whispered, clutching her arms around herself, "save that I am sorry I doubted your wisdom; had I been in your position, I hope I would have had the courage to do the same. This is . . . it is sad beyond belief. There are no answers here." It was inevitable; the hunt would go on, and men would be killed, and Keeper would put his life at risk over and over. Her mind showed her Asgrim's men advancing, to be cut down one by one, their bodies strewn across the island. Thorvald and Sam were with Asgrim; would they, too, lie in their blood before this summer was over?

"It is not always sad," Keeper said. "The hunt is but once a year, and over quickly. We have long times of calm. Winters are hard; sometimes he is sick, coughing and choking, and that troubles me. But good times too. After the hunt we can walk our island freely, without fear of attack. The Isle of Clouds is a place of beauty and holds many wonders. A forest of stone; a perch as high as an eagle's nest. Creidhe?"

"Yes?"

"I have tried to teach him, to show him how to fend for himself. Tried to remember to talk to him, so he can learn words. Sometimes I forget; sometimes I think he cannot learn. I can protect him from Asgrim's men; I can keep him safe from attack. But what if I fell from a height, or drowned while fishing? What if I took an illness and died? Then he would be all alone. You say I have done wrong somehow, that he is not like other children. Then I have failed him, and I have failed my sister. This makes me sad; it makes me afraid."

Creidhe reached out, put her hands around his. "No," she said. "I was mistaken. In you he has the best example he possibly could." She forced tears back; this was not a time to be weak. "You love him, and you are strong. You understand the island and the patterns of survival in this place; that, you surely can teach him. And . . . if I am here long enough, I can help a little. Maybe I can teach him to talk, and some other things. I could try, anyway. If you were happy with that." Despite everything, despite Thorvald and Sam and all she had left behind, there was no choice in this.

His mouth curved in a smile. "Happy, yes," he said, eyes sliding away from hers in what seemed a sudden, inexplicable attack of the same shyness that had beset him earlier. She still held his hands between hers; now he moved his fingers to the outside, so his larger hands enveloped her smaller ones, and she felt the strength in them, a warrior's strength.

Light was filtering in through the entry; the moon was rising. They sat in silence, hands locked together, as the shadowy space turned silver-gray about them. Keeper's face, ever pale, now seemed suffused with an unearthly glow, his eyes strangely bright, his skin translucent with light. Creidhe could see from the wonder in his face that she, too, had been transmuted thus; it was as if he saw a goddess before him. Her breath faltered.

A song came lilting through the silence, a song of such magical purity Creidhe wondered for a moment if Keeper's eyes told the truth and some spirit of the night had indeed chosen to honor them with its presence. The notes rose in a great, perfect arch, aching in their intensity, and hung in the air, sounding from rock and bush and hillside, echoing from ocean and moon and star, then falling away in wondrous cascade to ringing silence. And again the song rose, stopping the heart, flooding the eyes with tears, bathing the spirit in a balm of deep wisdom. As the singing went on, the brightness in the shelter intensified, pulsing, glowing, radiant and strong. Creidhe was aware of Keeper rising to his feet, and of the two of them walking together out to the open. They stood there hand in hand, watching the full moon move up the pale summer sky in shining certainty; watching Small One as he sat cross-legged on the rocks, eyes fixed on that disc of light. Watching and listening as Small One offered his wondrous, wordless anthem to the beauty of this celestial spirit, made his music for her solemn dance. Keeper's arm crept around Creidhe's shoulders, hers around his waist. They stood in utter silence as the melody rose and fell again, noble, sweet, full of ancient power.

The wind had died down; the island was quite still, not a rustle, not a cry. The dark water of the western ocean shone in the strange light, glittering and perilous. It seemed to Creidhe such a song must reach to every corner of the world: to Asgrim among his warriors, dreaming of the hunt; to Thorvald and Sam, wherever they were; to the Unspoken, sick with longing for their seer's return. It seemed to her such an anthem of loveliness must reach even as far as the Light Isles, and beyond. If she had ever doubted Small One's abilities, she doubted them no longer. Perhaps he would never learn human speech; perhaps never play as other children did. After this, that seemed of no account at all.

The song drew to a close, falling away in a ripple of decoration, a filigree of little notes swirling around the great strong cadence of it. Small One gave a huge yawn and blinked. Creidhe and Keeper moved apart; neither, perhaps, had been aware of how they had been standing, bodies pressed close, arms wrapped, until now.

"Rest," Keeper said, picking up the child. Small One put his arms around the young man's neck and his head against his breast as if he were an ordinary lad tired out after a day's fun and games, and not a powerful vessel for the moon's ancient voice. "Time for bed."

The child was asleep the moment he put his head down.

Then Keeper looked at Creidhe in the firelight, eyes liquid, dangerous, and Creidhe looked back at him unblinking, though the music of her heart was wild and urgent. After a moment he turned away, retreating to the other side of the fire pit to unroll his blanket, and Creidhe settled to sleep by Small One. The song was finished, but in the soft moonlight that touched their slumber, the memory of its power and beauty still lingered. *This is eternal: ever changing, ever the same. The song calls me forth, and bids me farewell. I die and am reborn. I sing the pattern, whole, clean, pure; I sing the One Story.*

With a certain difficulty, for they were no longer young, the two hermits carried Colm home on a board and laid him to rest not far from the garden he had tended with such energy and love. Breccan found words for prayer; Niall stood with head bowed and palms together, and the fair, peaceable cadences warred in his mind with other, darker thoughts, thoughts that were less of sorrow and acceptance than of blood and revenge. Afterward Breccan gave him a cup of ale, made him drink it, poured him another.

"You wish to render me senseless in order to save me from myself?" Niall asked his fellow hermit, not meeting his eye.

"No, old friend. I merely hope to loosen your tongue a little. Primitive means perhaps, but I, too, am weary and sad. God has gathered our young companion home; Colm is in the best of hands now. Still, I feel his loss, and the girl's terrible fate among the Unspoken. Man's wickedness is strong in this place; at such times doubt assails me. It is not so difficult for me to understand your thoughts. We've known each other a long time. You should talk. This is best not kept within."

"It is a curse," Niall said, staring into his ale. His face was expressionless. "All that I touch turns to dust. It is a darkness I bring with me. I thought on these remote isles to escape it, but it seems I cannot do so. I thought, by inaction, I might hold to what I promised, that I might wreak no more havoc in the world. A contemplative life seemed safe. But it follows me wherever I go, this shadow from the past; there is no place where I can hide from it. What do you think? Is this some devil I carry within me? I've never had time for such fancies, you know that well enough. Had I your faith, this would be simple. To trust implicitly in a deity of love and forgiveness is to smooth one's path greatly; one abrogates responsibility that way. I would do that if I could. But a man cannot feign belief; he cannot pretend faith."

"Such times, such losses are by no means easy," Breccan said gravely, "even for a man who knows God's mercy. Believe me, one remains entirely accountable for one's actions: more so, in fact. You think I am untouched by grief or guilt for what has occurred? I saw Creidhe assaulted. I'm an able-bodied man, Niall. Do you imagine I do not ask myself, could I have done more? Could I have saved her? Do you think I do not wrestle with my conscience over the decision to take her away from here, risking attack in open country? Still, it is true, God's love sustains me through my times of doubt and darkness. As it does you, my friend, whether you know it or not. You do not recognize how much you have changed over these years of exile."

"That's just it," Niall said in a whisper. "I haven't changed at all. I've simply improved my self-control. I know the solutions, I ache to put them in place, every part of me screams, *Act, act now, take control here and put it right.* But I must not act. I've shown once before what I could do, what power I could wield, and what it led to. I swore I would take a different path. I will not break that oath."

They sat awhile by their small fire; the ale jug slowly emptied. Outside, the sky was dimming to the eerie half-dark of the summer twilight, and a full moon hung above the sea, pale and lustrous.

"You know," Breccan observed, "there's a flaw of logic in your argument."

"Yes," said Niall.

"What is it that triggers this curse of yours? Action or inaction? What is it you're supposed to have done wrong? We could hardly have refused to shelter the girl, knowing what we do of Asgrim. It was I who took her away, not yourself. It was Colm who volunteered to walk over to the encampment. I don't think you can claim to be the sole cause of this particular disaster, Niall."

"No," said Niall, "perhaps not. But I ask myself, why did Creidhe and her friends come to the Lost Isles in the first place?"

"Ah. The past follows us. True, certainly, and the past cannot be remade. You would do well to remember that, and to remember that you are not the same man who came to this shore long years ago, nor yet the same man who once confronted Asgrim with the truth of his wickedness and was shunned ever after. I do not forget how you welcomed myself and young Colm; how you provided for us despite your own evident desire to dwell entirely in solitude. God's grace worked in you then, Brother; it does so now. He has touched you despite yourself."

"You think?" The tone was bleak.

"I know it, my friend. Now, enough of this. We should not dwell on the past, save to learn the lessons it has for us. We can, however, influence the future. Somewhat against my better judgment, I believe this is a matter we cannot simply let slide."

Niall glanced sharply at him, dark eyes suddenly alert. "What are you proposing? That we convert Asgrim to a man of peace?" His tone was caustic.

"I would not go so far as to suggest that," Breccan said mildly. "Only God can perform such a feat. However, I am not prepared to let Colm's murder pass without at least expressing my outrage to the probable perpetrators. I also believe Creidhe's abduction should be reported formally to Asgrim in his role as Ruler of the Lost Isles; never mind that he doubtless knows already, there is a correct way for such things to be done, and it's time he was reminded of that. The boy did not deserve such a cruel end. Creidhe should have been offered the Ruler's protection, not scared into flight. We owe it to them to tell Asgrim as much, I think."

"You would go to Council Fjord, after what has happened?"

"He's not likely to make an end of all three of us," Breccan said dryly. "I thought we'd catch the lads tomorrow on the way over from Brightwater. Walk with them. That makes an attack less likely. What do you think?"

Niall was silent. It was the intense silence of a man who longs to say yes, and fights with the inner conviction that he must say no.

"Besides," Breccan added quietly, "we owe it to Creidhe's friends, the two young men, to let them know our version of what happened. We could speak to them of her time with us. Such small details can be of some comfort, you know. We should see them, I am sure of it."

Niall stared at the earthen floor. "Asgrim will never let us in," he said flatly. "He fears our influence over the men. We wouldn't get past the outer perimeter of the camp."

"Come now," Breccan said, "with your talent for deviousness, I'm sure you can think of a way."

Niall gave a bleak smile. "No doubt I can," he said grimly. "But I think it's you who are the devious one, Brother."

The two lads had no particular allegiance. They were ten or eleven years old, expert fishermen and bird catchers, and they wrote their own rules. As providers of food and bearers of messages they had earned themselves a degree of safety on the island, for the fact was, they were indispensable. When Niall and Breccan walked into Asgrim's camp around midday they had the boys close by them, so close that any act of violence toward the brothers was likely to injure a lad as well. Besides, Breccan had a fine joint of mutton over his shoulder and Niall bore a round of goat's cheese, and Asgrim's men were hungry. That did not stop two enormous guards from stepping onto the path in front of them, thrusting spears pointed at chest level.

"Where do you think you're going?" Skapti growled. "No admittance to the camp!"

"Especially not to your kind," rumbled Hogni. "You

boys, off with you, the Ruler's got a message for Gudrun, wants it taken straightaway."

The lads, paid in advance with a promise of more to come, did not move. Niall and Breccan stood silent. Other men were approaching now from farther down the path.

"What do you want anyway?" demanded Skapti.

"The Ruler won't see you," Hogni said. "Nothing's changed. No need for prayers here, we've got no time for them."

"We're here to see the two men from the Light Isles," Niall said crisply. "Thorvald and Sam. Are they close at hand?"

He expected an immediate refusal. They had never been admitted to Asgrim's camp before; even the settlement at Brightwater had been forbidden ground in recent years, though that had not stopped them from going there in the Ruler's absence. But to Niall's surprise, mention of the two young men seemed to change things. One guard looked at the other; they muttered under their breath.

"Will you ask Thorvald if he will see me?" Niall inquired politely. "I'm happy to wait here, and to accept his answer."

More muttering, in which the names Asgrim and Thorvald could both be heard. It was not possible to see ahead into the encampment, for the bulk of the two big men and others who had come up behind them blocked the way.

"We've brought a contribution for your supper," Breccan said, "and it's heavy. Please take it; you're welcome to it, whether our request is met or not. Preparation for war makes hearty appetites, I'm sure."

"Thanks," grunted Hogni. "Here." Meat and cheese were borne away by eager hands. "I'll go and find Thorvald for you, ask him what he thinks. You stay here, and no funny business."

"Funny business?" Niall's brows lifted extravagantly. "I wouldn't know where to start."

Skapti remained, spear point trained on Niall's heart. His expression, though, had altered "Thorvald a friend of yours?" he asked diffidently.

"Not exactly. A connection, one might say. A friend of a friend. Good warrior, is he?"

"The best," said Skapti simply. "The best we ever had. Fine leader: hard but fair, you know? Clever. And not afraid to put himself on the line. The sort of man you'd follow anywhere."

Niall could not reply.

"Interesting," said Breccan into the silence. "An incomer, too. That's a turn of the tide."

"You could say that," Skapti muttered. "Not so much of a turn that we've started letting priests into the camp, though. Don't think you're suddenly welcome here."

"Ah, well," said Breccan, smiling, "one always lives in hope. What about the other lad, Sam, isn't it?"

"He's all right. Good on the boats. Useful."

"I pray," Breccan was suddenly serious, "that he, and you, and all of them come through this summer safely, my friend. These are testing times. You will have heard that we, too, suffered a loss."

"That's nothing to do with me." Skapti's mouth closed like a trap, and his small eyes became distant.

They waited awhile. Now that the group of men near them had dispersed, it was possible to see ahead down the track to the bay where Asgrim had his shelter and outbuildings, his safe strand for boats, his flat ground for the rehearsal of war. There were men training there now, shooting arrows at straw targets. Niall watched them. There was quite a lot of noise: shouting, laughing. Nonetheless, the activity was disciplined. The red-haired man moved among them, encouraging, making suggestions, demonstrating. It was clear from the way men stopped to listen to him, attentive and serious, from the way they gravitated toward him, from the way they glanced over to check if he was watching before they loosed the bowstring, that he was a leader. It could be seen immediately in his stance: upright, relaxed, confident, yet always finding time to listen when they had something to tell him, always ready with a word of praise when they had earned it. Niall watched him, and presently saw the message delivered, and the young man turn his head to look back up the hill to the place where they waited by the path. The hair was Margaret's, deep auburn, glossy and well kept. The dark, wary eyes, scrutinizing, assessing, calculating, those were the mirror of his own.

"All right?" murmured Breccan, behind him.

Niall nodded. He would have to summon the capacity for speech now, for the young man was coming up the hill toward them, the second bodyguard at his side. Behind him the games of war went on. There was no sign of Asgrim.

"Good day to you," the red-haired man said, stopping on the path before them, his expression neutral. His features were pale and intense, the jaw firm, the mouth thin-lipped. He wore plain, serviceable clothes, woolen tunic and breeches, light leather boots, a good belt; as leader, he seemed to have few pretensions. "Hogni tells me you brought us meat; thank you for the gift, the men are becoming weary of fish. We don't allow visitors to the camp. I thought Asgrim had made that clear." He glanced at the two boys. "Off you go, lads," he said, the tone somewhat kinder. "Take a bite to eat, then see the Ruler. He has messages for you." This time the boys obeyed instantly, slipping away without a word. "Well, now," the young man went on, looking the two hermits over with a keen eye, "I see what you are, and wonder if perhaps I've been less than courteous. Still, rules are rules, and it's close to hunt time. My name is Thorvald. I can't welcome you to the camp. I will ask you why you're here. It's a long way just to deliver a bit of mutton the lads could have carried. Your names?"

"I am Brother Breccan and this is Brother Niall. We do have an errand here. We wish to report an unlawful killing. Our young companion, Colm, was set upon as he traveled this way a few days since, and done to death, his body left out on the hillside unattended."

Thorvald frowned. "I'm sorry to hear that. I respect your kind; we have folk such as yourselves in my homeland, men of wisdom and learning. This is regrettable. But it's Asgrim you should report it to, not me. I am war leader here. I am not Ruler."

No, thought Niall, heart beating fast, *but you should be.*

"We know that," he said, finding his voice with some effort. "But it's you we've come to speak to. We had cause to provide shelter to your friend, Creidhe, just before she was taken. We offer our sympathies to you. Her abduction was a terrible blow; if there's the slightest possibility she can be brought back, be assured we will do all we can to help you. Creidhe spent a few days with us, and we spoke at some length. There were certain matters . . ." It was not possible to go on. As Niall spoke, the young warrior's control had slipped badly, his pale face turning still whiter, his eyes betraying an anguish that awoke Niall's own memories, painfully.

"I see you do not yet know the full story," Thorvald said quietly. "I have to tell you that Creidhe is dead. The vessel of the Unspoken capsized into the Fool's Tide. I'm told she herself made that happen. All on board were drowned." His dignity was astonishing; he spoke with courteous restraint, making a valiant effort to mask his own evident distress. Niall's heart had turned cold at the news. If intellect had taken precedence over feelings, as was habitual for him, he might have believed death a better ending for that lovely girl, so full of vitality and warmth, than what awaited her among the Unspoken. The heart, however, had involved itself despite him. This was a grievous blow.

"I'm so sorry," Breccan said, his ruddy features creased with distress. "I can hardly believe this. Such a lively, courageous young woman. We should speak more of this—"

"I think not," Thorvald said. "This is past. The hunt comes soon, a matter of only days. That will take all our will, all our energy. What point can there be in going over what has already occurred? That would only awaken unrest and undermine our confidence. You think to offer prayers, maybe, for those who are lost. Prayers change nothing. We have a task before us here, and our minds must be on that alone." Niall could see how much this speech cost the lad; Thorvald's knuckles were white, even as his voice sounded with level assurance.

"We have made our own prayers," said Breccan. "What

we had in mind was more along the lines of advice. Advice, and information."

"Thorvald?" Skapti hissed. "Ruler's on his way up."

It was true; Asgrim could be seen approaching up the path, his dark features thunderous.

"Yes," Thorvald said absently. "Yes, thank you. Advice? What kind of advice does a priest give a soldier? To beg forgiveness from the gods at the moment the spear takes him in the heart?" His tone was bleak, too bleak for a young man, but Niall did not miss the spark of interest in his eye.

"Don't dismiss us lightly," Niall said in a whisper. "We can help you. You may be in danger here, more danger than you realize."

And at that moment Asgrim strode up to them grim-faced, his knife in his hand.

"Skapti! Hogni!" he snapped, and the two guards fell in on either side of the hermits, weapons at the ready. "I'll handle this, Thorvald," the Ruler went on smoothly. "I know these men; they are meddlers and troublemakers, for all the gifts they bring. They have nothing of value to us. I'll see them escorted on their way. Go on, son; the men need you back there."

Thorvald's eyes were still intent on Brother Niall's; there was a question in them. "These men have a murder to report," he said, "and perhaps something about Creidhe as well. I think we should hear them, troublemakers or not. We can hardly assess the information they bring if—"

Asgrim's brows crooked in a frown. "A murder, you say? How unfortunate. Very well, I will allow them a hearing, in private, in my quarters. If there's anything that concerns you, I will let you know. That seems fair. Off you go now, I can hear Einar calling you. They seem to believe they can't manage without you."

Thorvald stood his ground. "I'd like to speak with these men myself," he said.

Asgrim's little smile did not reach his eyes. "This is not relevant to your role here, Thorvald. I will deal with it.

Later, perhaps, you may get your chance. I hope you understand me."

For a moment Thorvald looked him straight in the eye, unmoving. Then he said, "Very well," and turned away, heading back to the men.

"Hogni, Skapti," the Ruler's voice was sharp, "take these two to my quarters. Then stand guard outside. They're not to speak to anyone, and no one's to speak to them. Understood?"

"Yes, my lord."

But when they reached Asgrim's hut, that was not quite the way of it. Breccan was taken to the anteroom, where he sat quietly on a bench while Skapti loomed in the entry, leaning on his spear. Hogni ushered Niall inside the inner chamber and the Ruler followed. Hogni went out; the door closed firmly. This, it seemed, was to be a private audience for one.

"Well now." Asgrim's voice was a mockery of an affable host's; his eyes were venomous. "Here you are in the middle of my encampment, in express defiance of my orders that you stay away from any settlement of the Long Knife people. I did not take you for a fool, *Brother*. Yet this seems an act of utter stupidity. You've seen the forces we keep here; they're extremely well armed, and their orders don't include being kind to priests. Oh, I expect you have a small weapon about you somewhere, hasn't that always been your way? I thought of asking my guards to search you, but I decided against it. Nasty injuries only complicate things. Besides, I don't believe you're here as an assassin; aren't you sworn to remain outside the affairs of men? A vow of inaction? No, I think you're here for information. Unfortunately I have none to offer. You'll leave, the two of you. You'll leave promptly, and you won't come near this place, or my men, again. Is that understood?"

There was a brief silence. Niall held himself straight and kept his eyes on Asgrim's. His fingers touched cold iron within the folds of his robe; he could indeed kill, should he have the inclination. He had been better taught than the Ruler could possibly imagine.

"The boy's dead," he said evenly. "Colm. That lad's been with Breccan since he was a child. He was outside all this, an innocent. You can't pin that killing on the Unspoken; what possible reason could they have for it? It's your work, Asgrim. Colm was silenced. You know what I'm talking about. What were you planning—a neat trade with your enemy, to let you off another summer of pointless losses? Was that in your mind the moment the girl stepped on shore with her head of hair the color of ripe barley? I'll wager your men came running to you then. They'd have seen the opportunity as you did. Another chance. You failed the first time; your son made sure of that. At twelve years old he was more man than you'll ever be. You lost that chance. Now here was another girl, one you knew you must make completely sure of."

"Where is this going, Niall?" Asgrim asked wearily. "What do you hope to achieve here? To persuade the Long Knife people that their best hope lies in hunt after hunt, season after season of bloody mayhem? This is pointless."

"And so," Niall went on as if the Ruler had not spoken, "you removed her companions as swiftly as you could, you confined her to the settlement with Gudrun as watchdog, and you set up a deal. Unfortunately, it seems the girl proved somewhat more courageous than anyone anticipated, and the result was death for her, and another failure for you. You've demonstrated your ineptitude twice over. That's not counting the hunt, an exercise in futility if ever I saw one."

"There's not a single one of my people would not support what I did," Asgrim said, "and you know it. You've been here long enough to understand how it is. Confronting me in some misguided attempt to goad me into an admission of guilt is a waste of time. I don't deny what you set out. We do what we must for survival here. Some actions seem cruel; they are for the greater good."

"Your record so far has hardly proven that."

"You think you could do better?" There was an edge to Asgrim's voice now; of the two men, it was the other who had stayed calm and controlled.

"I know so. I told you that last time, when it was your own daughter's life in the balance."

"Huh! A weakling priest whose whole existence is based on standing by to watch while others do the hard work, take the hard decisions? I know about you, Niall. I know more about you than anyone on the islands. I remember the day you came here."

"I, too. Perhaps we have not changed so very much since then. The welcome, I recall, was less than warm."

"You certainly weren't much of a priest then, and I doubt that's altered over the years. You don't need to tell me why you're here today, I know already. You want to see the boy. Thorvald, I mean. Tell him tales about me, my wickedness, my evil ways; persuade him not to help me. Is that it?"

"He and his friend deserve the truth. I imagine they bear quite a burden of guilt that the girl was lost."

"Guilt, guilt, we all carry that, it's part and parcel of man's very existence. In Thorvald's case, Sam's too, it's working itself out very conveniently in aggression. You can't see them. Thorvald's busy. He's proven more than useful to me. With him in charge, we've a chance this season, a good chance. I need him for the hunt. You can't talk to him."

"I see." Niall folded his arms. "This interests me, Asgrim. It's plain at a glance the young fellow's very able; your men follow him with a sort of dedication in their eyes, and I think I detect a new spring in their step and a definite improvement in their aim. There's something odd about this. Creidhe told me her friends were only here at the camp to earn the price of a length of wood. I understand, of course, that you retained them here until your unfortunate bargain with the Unspoken ran its course. Creidhe is dead now, but here's Thorvald in charge of your army, no less, and all set to risk his life in another man's war. Now why would a clever young fellow do such a thing?"

Asgrim gave a slow smile. "Because he thinks I'm his father," he said softly. "Ah, now I've achieved what I never managed before: I've reduced you to silence. Does it hurt? This skill, this dedication, this youthful energy all turned to my own cause; I've gained all that through the lad's fervent belief that he's at last tracked down the man who abandoned him before ever he was born. That's what he came here for; that was what he got in return for his friend's extremely poorly timed demise. He can think of nothing else now but proving himself worthy. He believes that if he does well enough, there will be some formal recognition at the end of it. An open-armed embrace, perhaps, along with a promise of future power."

"You have not told him the truth?" Niall could hear his own voice shaking. All of a sudden he felt deathly cold.

"Of course not. He's invaluable. I told you. A fine war leader, a genuine rallying point for the men. Of course I haven't told him."

"And after the hunt?"

Asgrim did not reply. He toyed with an empty ale cup on the table, his eyes avoiding the other man's.

"Answer me, Asgrim. After the hunt?"

"Well, well, my old adversary, I have touched a nerve, haven't I? And it doesn't take a lot of wit to deduce why. Indeed, all is explained: your harboring of the girl, the risky dispatch of the youth to bear a warning to Thorvald, your foolish trip here today . . . Who would have thought that a man of such studied detachment as yourself might actually have some sort of heart underneath? I can hardly believe it. After the hunt he'll go home, of course. Or not, as the case may be."

Niall clasped his hands together to keep them still. Once, long ago, he would have had no need of such primitive aids. He had been expert in this type of game. Surely he had not changed so much. "Or not?" he queried, brows raised. "You can hardly afford to let him stay, I imagine."

"Well, no," Asgrim said. "His value lasts precisely until the moment the hunt is over. After that he goes, one way or another."

Niall drew a deep breath and let it out slowly. "Let me talk to him," he said quietly. "Please."

Asgrim chuckled. "By all the gods! The aloof, the impenetrable Brother Niall begging? I never thought I'd see the day. Of course you can't talk to him. I think we've just enumerated at least three reasons why. A man shouldn't go about fathering children if he's going to turn his back on them, now should he?"

Niall regarded him levelly. "You'd know all about that, of course," he said.

"Hold your tongue! You're in no position to judge me. Besides, may I remind you that we are in my own quarters, with armed guards just beyond that door? I'll tell you what's going to happen here. You and your companion are going to make a rapid and unobtrusive exit while my forces are over on the cliffs in the south practicing their skills with ropes and weights. You're going to walk straight home, and you're going to stay away from here, and from Brightwater, until the hunt's well and truly over."

"I am not subject to your rule, Asgrim," Niall said quietly. "I made that clear from the first day I set foot on this island. I didn't think much of you then, and the years have done nothing to improve my opinion."

"Nonetheless, you will do as I say. If you do not, you will soon find yourself burying yet another companion. Then it will be as it was for you in the early years: a very lonely life indeed. If that is not sufficient warning for you, be in no doubt that your disobedience will do nothing to improve Thorvald's future prospects. Accidents occur quite frequently among fighting men. You'll go now, and you'll keep your mouth shut. Is that understood?" Asgrim's eyes were hard, his mouth tight. Niall had learned long ago how to read a man's face, his stance, his gestures. Beneath that well-kept mask of authority, he recognized fear.

"Your words are plain enough. I'll do as I'm bid, for now. It's just possible you may find others less obedient, Asgrim. I sense a change here; I think you feel the same. Is it hope your men have suddenly discovered? They will not relinquish that so easily, merely at your whim."

"You talk nonsense. You always did. I have no more patience with this. My guards will escort you up the hill. Go quickly, and count yourself fortunate that I let you go at all."

"Your hospitality, as always, is like none other," said Niall smoothly as Asgrim opened the door and they walked into the anteroom. Breccan still sat there, calm and quiet, his wooden cross between his hands. He had been murmuring prayers, perhaps, and the guards listening. The weapons had been set by; both men seized them as Asgrim came out.

"Take them to the top of the hill," the Ruler commanded, "and make sure they don't come back."

The men had moved away from the practice ground; now they were scaling the cliffs at the far end of the bay. They could be seen clearly from the hill path, organized in teams of four, one at either end of the line for safety, others creeping up or making their way down, a spider's dance of strength and grace. From the shore the red-haired man watched them, a straight, square-shouldered figure in his plain warrior's clothes, his back to the shelter and the track where Niall and Breccan climbed up and away. Nobody noticed the hermits' departure. The men were intent on their drill, focused on getting it right, and Thorvald had all his attention on his forces, no doubt praising their successes and correcting their weaknesses. It was plain to see he was a born leader.

They reached the brow of the hill.

"It's all right," Breccan told the guards. "You can leave us here; we'll head straight for home."

"No sneaking back," Hogni warned. "He means what he says."

"We know when we're not wanted." Breccan's voice was calm. "I'll pray for you."

"No need for that," mumbled Hogni.

"No harm in it either," said Breccan. "Well, we'd best be off. I hope you enjoy the mutton."

Niall had been silent all the way. To risk his own safety was nothing; he held his life of little value, and in fact only went on with it because of a promise. Others' well-being was quite a different matter. These hulking warriors might themselves be the instruments of whatever penalty Asgrim meant to inflict for disobedience. All the same, he had seen the way they spoke to their young leader, the look on their faces as they watched him.

"Tell Thorvald to be careful," he said softly. "He must be very careful. Tell him I regret greatly that we could not speak together."

"Not here to pass on messages," Skapti growled, and with that the two guards turned on their heels and headed back toward the encampment.

"Home," said Breccan firmly. "The cow needs milking, the chickens need feeding, and I need some quiet contemplation, a good supper and an early night. Come on. It's a long way for a couple of fellows past their prime."

Niall made no reply. He was gazing back down the hill.

"That's a fine young man," Breccan commented. "A son any father would be proud of. There seems a great strength in him, despite all that has befallen him."

"Yes," Niall said. "It is his father who lacks strength. It's as if my heart has been skewered and put to roast over a fire. How can a man stand back at such times and not attempt to intervene? And yet, to take action is to wreak yet more havoc. My mind can scarcely encompass it: Creidhe dead, that brave girl, and the boy at Asgrim's mercy . . . I should go back. I should confront him. But I cannot. What ails me, that I bind myself thus with my own promises?"

"Time," Breccan said, laying a hand on the other man's shoulder. "Give yourself some time. Do not speak of skewers and fires. You've only just discovered you have a heart. Let it beat a little."

They began to walk across the lower slopes of the fells, where rank grasses and pale, straggling flowers were cropped by rangy, long-locked sheep. For a considerable time they moved on in silence. Eventually Niall said, "There's an answer to this, I know it. An answer quite outside Asgrim's comprehension. And I have a feeling it doesn't lie in prayer."

TEN

In times of darkness, the faithful man prays for light
In times of confusion, he prays for clarity
I pray simply that someone may be listening

MONK'S MARGIN NOTE

We're as ready as we'll ever be," said Thorvald, watching the little wavelets as they washed onto the shingle close to his boots. "And just as well. They tell me it'll be only days now."

Sam nodded assent. "Knut reckons you can see it on the water. A calming. Not safe to go across yet, but soon. Not that it's ever plain sailing in the Fool's Tide. Still, there'll be a chance of getting back in one piece, if we time it right. Wouldn't want to linger."

"Tomorrow we'll take the boats along to Little Bay," Thorvald said. "There are still a couple of old huts there, I'm told. We can camp on shore until the sea's right for the crossing to the Isle of Clouds. We need to be ready for it; ready to sail at dawn, when the critical day comes."

Sam looked at him. "Excited, are you?" he inquired dourly.

"No, Sam. I'm not excited. I'm merely doing what a leader does: anticipating what may happen, and making sure we're all ready for it."

"A leader. Yes, you've become one of those, haven't you? Just like your father. Not so surprising, that. I worry about you, Thorvald. What happens when all this is over?"

Thorvald folded his arms, glancing sideways at his friend. Sam was looking like his old self, earnest, honest, perplexed. It was a relief after the mask of dedicated aggression he had worn since they heard the news of Creidhe.

"I thought you wanted this battle," Thorvald said. "A few days ago there was no stopping you. What happened to all that talk of blood and vengeance?"

Sam did not reply. He began to walk along the beach, scuffing his boots in the dark sand. Thorvald walked beside him. The light was dimming and birds cried overhead, winging to shelter under a violet sky.

"As for afterward," Thorvald kept his tone light, "why don't you tell me?"

"All right then." Sam's voice was gruff. "We come back victorious, so Asgrim's problems are all solved. He says thank you and offers to load the *Sea Dove* with provisions. We wave good-bye and sail off home. We break the bad news to Creidhe's family and make an enemy of Eyvind for the rest of our lives. Then we pick up where we left off, as best we can. How does that sound?"

"In keeping with your own common sense, Sam. That's how it sounds."

"The question is, would you be happy with that? Now, after all this?"

Thorvald could not suppress an outburst of bitter laughter. "Happy? When was I ever happy?"

They walked on in silence awhile, passing the shadowy forms of the small boats drawn up on shore and the larger bulk of the *Sea Dove*. The hull looked perfect; you could hardly see where the patching began and ended.

"How can you say that?" Sam asked suddenly. "As if losing Creidhe didn't change a thing for you, as if that's nothing in your long personal tale of unfairness and misery? That's rubbish, Thorvald. You should forget all that and just do what you have to. That's my opinion."

Thorvald was momentarily shocked into silence. Then he said, "I thought that was just what I was doing. You can't deny I've kept myself busy here."

"That wasn't fair of me," Sam muttered. "It's just, you're not the only one feeling bad. When she died it was like a light going out. I don't expect you to understand; your head's full of schemes and strategies, stuff that's beyond ordinary fellows like me."

There was a pause; they stood on the rocks at the far end of the bay, under the lowering cliffs where they had tested their skills in perilous ascent and descent.

"Are you saying," Thorvald asked, "that you think I care for nothing but this chance to prove myself, to lead and win for Asgrim? I would have gone home; I told him so. I told them all. You heard me."

Sam did not reply.

"I can't afford to be weak, Sam. They rely on me; the whole thing relies on me. I didn't seek that out, it just happened. Now there's no choice but to go through with it. But . . ."

"But what?" Sam growled, clearly unconvinced.

Thorvald's voice was no more than a thread. "You think it was nothing to me, to lose Creidhe. That's what you seem to be telling me. Sam, I did not imagine such a hurt could be possible. It was like—it was like the cutting off of a limb, the gouging out of an eye. After that, I can never be complete. Do you hear me? Is that enough for you? Now leave me alone, there's a battle to be won here, and I have no room in me for anything but that."

Sam made no move. He stood on the rocks, solid, steady. Thorvald stared out to sea; in the dim light, the waves could be seen breaking white over the offshore skerries.

"I'm sorry," Sam said quietly.

Thorvald drew a deep breath. "No," he said. "It is I who should be sorry, and I should thank you as well. You've given your time and your energy and your fine boat, and I've doubtless been so wrapped up in myself that I've hardly spared you a word. You're a true friend, Sam. I don't know why you put up with me. I do have to go on with this. I hope you understand that."

Sam nodded. "For your father, yes. And for Creidhe."

"And for myself. I don't see how I can do otherwise. As for afterward, we must go home, of course. What else could we do? I hope your deckhand is still waiting for you in Stensakir."

"As to that," said Sam, "I have a volunteer who's all too keen to find a new home away from all this, and honest work to go with it: young Knut. But all in good time. We've our battle to fight, two battles, really; one with this tribe on the Isle of Clouds, and another with the sea. Can't really say I'm looking forward to either."

"Are you afraid?" Thorvald asked.

"Not of the sailing part; that'll be hard, but I'm pretty sure the *Sea Dove* can handle it. The fighting part's a different matter. What about you?"

Thorvald considered this. "I'm not afraid of the hunt," he said slowly. "I don't think I'm afraid of dying either; my life is not such a wondrous thing, after all. But the thought of failure terrifies me, Sam. We cannot lose this time. I must ensure the men come through this. I must take Foxmask. That's what matters: to capture the seer and win peace for these people. That is what I must do. Until I have achieved it, I cannot think of home."

On the Isle of Clouds a fine mist hung low in the air, blotting out the landscape, drenching rock, bush and grass. The wet did not stop Keeper from fishing; he went out early, as soon as the sky was light enough, and came back dripping, with a string of fine haddock in his hand. Small One had been out, too, in his doglike form; now he shook himself vigorously, sending droplets spraying all around the small shelter.

Keeper put down the fish, took up a sack laid close at hand and rubbed his disheveled hair to some semblance of dryness. It stood up from his head in wild confusion. His clothing steamed before the fire that Creidhe had rekindled.

"Only a few days now," he remarked. "Three, four maybe. When the sky clears, I will show you where you must hide, you and Small One, when they come."

"Oh," said Creidhe. This was real; one could not pretend otherwise. "Not here then?"

Keeper looked at her, eyes somber. "Here is not safe," he said. "Too open, too easy to find. I will move you to another place and leave you there. Two days they will be on the island; the night between, they stand offshore in their boats. For that time, I cannot come back to you. You must stay hidden and quiet. It is hard for Small One. Better this season, because you are here."

"Oh." There seemed to be no more to say. She imagined the child, confined, mute and afraid, to some place of hiding all alone. Waiting for his brother to come back. Waiting to see if he would ever come back.

"What is it?" Keeper asked, squatting down beside her and starting to prepare the fish. "Are you afraid? If you stay hidden there is nothing to fear. Small One will be good. I have taught him what he must do. I would not leave you so long, but there is no other way. I cannot risk leading them back to him. Or to you, Creidhe."

She nodded, feeling the awful inevitability of it all, that crushing sense of doom she could not shake off, however hard she tried to apply common sense to the situation.

"Let me do that, since you caught them," she said, for there was no doubt practical activities such as cooking were a powerful help in such moments of doubt.

"As you wish." He passed the knife, watched as she continued the process with small, well-practiced hands. When she glanced up she saw that he was smiling, a smile of such disarming sweetness it made her heart turn over.

"What?" she asked him. "What is it? Didn't you believe I could perform such an everyday task? I do this all the time at home."

Keeper nodded; the smile had faded, but still he watched her. "I had thought others might wait on you," he said diffidently.

"They might, I suppose," said Creidhe, "if I asked them to. We have a lot of men and women who work in our household. But I love cooking, just as I love weaving and embroidery and teaching children. I do such work because I think it is important; because it is a joy."

Keeper nodded. "Such tasks lie at the heart of our existence," he said.

Creidhe felt a flush rise to her cheeks, echoing some

warmth deep within her. It was most disconcerting to hear this feral young man putting her own most private thoughts into words. "Yes," she said, cutting the fish into smaller pieces. "Such work binds folk together; gives them something to hold onto; makes many pieces into one fine whole. Like a good soup, where the sea and the garden and the fields offer up their best and you put it together with thanks and with loving hands, and make something new of it to share with the people you care about. Or a song." She glanced at Small One who now sat, blanket-wrapped, by the fire. "His song comes from earth and air and flame; from the depths of the ocean and the moon and stars. His is a greater gift than those we ordinary folk can offer. He opens our minds to the voices of the ancient things. I never thought to hear that. Not from a little child."

Silence fell between them. Creidhe put the fish in the pan with a splash of the seal oil he had in a jar, and set it on the coals at the edge of the fire. "You need breakfast today," she remarked, studying Keeper's gaunt features, his pallor, his shadowed eyes. Perhaps he had smiled, for a moment; nonetheless, the hunt was close. She still couldn't believe what he must do. "Small One too. I'd like to put a bit more flesh on him. If I were at home I'd feed him cheese, porridge, vegetables."

Keeper did not reply. The fire spat and sizzled as drops of rain fell down through the smoke-hole in the roof. Outside the hut, the mist was so close not a single landmark could be seen. On such a day the Isle of Clouds, with its precipitous terrain, its cliffs and fissures, was a place where only a fool would walk abroad.

"I intend no criticism, Keeper," Creidhe said. "I know you cannot provide such food for him here."

"He is thin. Weak. I know this."

"He's healthy enough. What choice do you have?"

"Sometimes their boats carry provisions," Keeper said. "Bread, meat, cheese. That can be stolen. If I can, I will do so this time."

"Oh, don't," Creidhe said hastily," don't take any extra risks, please—"

Now he was regarding her very closely indeed. "This is what I do," he told her, sounding puzzled.

"I would be very unhappy," Creidhe explained carefully, "if you put yourself in any greater peril just because I said the child needed more to eat. As it is, I'll be worrying about you every moment until all this is over. Please be as careful as you can."

"You should not be afraid. You will not be left to care for him on your own. Five times I have done this already; I have become expert at it."

"It's not being left to look after Small One that's worrying me. It's you. Don't you ever think you may get hurt, that you may be captured or killed? You spoke to me before of accidents, of illness; clearly you have considered those possibilities. This is far more dangerous. You put yourself at terrible risk."

"I think of it, yes. Beforehand only. Once it begins there is no room in my mind for such concerns. I will not be killed. This follows a pattern, every year the same. I know the pattern. I am ready for whatever they do."

She said nothing, merely put out her hand and curled her fingers around his. After a moment his other hand came over, rested on hers. The touch sent a thrill through her; her heart quickened.

"I am of no significance, save as his guardian," Keeper said. "Only he is important, his safety, his well-being. And now, yours." He spoke matter-of-factly. At the same time his thumb moved against her wrist, tentative, gentle, as if to give her a different message, one he would not put into words.

"The thing is," said Creidhe, finding it suddenly difficult to match his calm tone, "you may say you don't matter. But you can't stop other people worrying about you, not just because they depend on you, but because you mean something to them. Small One loves you. You are his family; you are his world, Keeper. He does not see you simply as guardian and provider. For him you are father and mother, brother and dearest friend."

"And you?" he said in a whisper.

"I don't know." Creidhe's voice was scarcely stronger. "After all, I've only been here a few days . . ." Nonetheless, somewhere inside her was a truth she feared greatly to recognize, a truth that had something to do with Thorvald, and something to do with the bond she had seen between her parents, still powerful and true after so many years, and a lot to do with accepting that the girl who had left the shores of the Light Isles in a quest to help a friend was gone now, replaced by a woman with entirely different needs and entirely different expectations. How could she have changed so much, so quickly?

"I should not have spoken thus," Keeper said tightly, withdrawing his hand. "I have been a long time away from others. Forgive me if I have forgotten what is right. Of course you do not wish to be here. Of course you wish to be at home with this father, the golden-haired warrior; with this mother, the far-seeing priestess. With your sisters, and your fine companions. There you have everything; here is nothing. Please forgive my hasty words."

Creidhe felt again that chill, the cold breath of what was to come. In all those years since he had taken the child away, she realized, Keeper had never once considered himself save as Small One's guardian. The promise he had made to Sula had been all his existence. And now, after so long, it had changed. She had changed it; had disturbed the balance of his life. What could she say to him? That she felt a bond here that was stronger, fiercer, more compelling than any she had known before? How could she put that into words? What words were adequate for such a turmoil in the heart, such dark tides in the flesh? It was ridiculous; a practical girl, the kind who never forgot to take a knife and a flint and a comb when she went traveling, did not allow such surges of feeling to sweep away all her common sense.

Keeper had risen to his feet and moved to the entry, where he stood looking out into the morning mist. It was as if the whole island were drenched in tears.

"I could say many things to you." Creidhe found her voice, though she faltered over the words. "So many things a whole day would not hold them all; a whole night would not allow them all to be spoken. I will not tell them this morning. After the hunt perhaps there will be time, and I can make a start. There's only one thing I will say now. It doesn't seem to make any difference that I've only just come here, that I don't really belong here, that I've known you and Small One so short a time. Common sense plays no part in this. I felt the call of this island long before I first set foot in Brightwater, a call that was ancient and powerful beyond my wildest imaginings. Something brought me here. And now I must tell you that while you are out there, I will hold you in my heart every moment. My fear for you is not as guardian and provider, but as a man I have come greatly to admire, a man of unbelievable courage, of wondrous strength and kindness. I've never met anyone like you before. So, your hurt will be my hurt. If you were killed, it would be . . . it would change the rest of my life, Keeper. It would change who I am. That's all I can say." Her voice was wobbling; she struggled to maintain control. "And this fish seems to be cooked. We should eat; it's best to follow the patterns of the day, even at such times."

Later in the morning the mist cleared and Keeper took her up the steep crag, guiding her on a path he seemed to know, though to Creidhe no track at all was visible. Small One scampered about; one might almost wish he would remain in this other form, for as creature, not child, he seemed a great deal more self-sufficient. Nonetheless, Creidhe was acutely aware that he was a child, a boy of six, born of a very young and undoubtedly human mother. The transformations were a kind of disguise that sometimes proved convenient, but that was all. Small One could not be asked to put on one semblance or another. In this, he was his own master.

"Don't look down," said Keeper, striding up the hill before her. His mood had altered completely since their earlier exchange; he had a spring in his step, a light in his eyes.

It occurred to Creidhe that this change might perhaps be attributed to something she had said. This both pleased and alarmed her. "Wait until we reach the top."

Creidhe's energy was all in matching his pace; looking was the least of her concerns. Her legs ached. Small One circled her, then bounded ahead.

"Not far now," said Keeper, not in the least out of breath. "Here, take my hand." And when it became clear to him that he had tired her, that she was struggling to keep up but would not tell him so, he said simply, "Come," and picked her up in his arms as if she were no more of a burden than Small One might be. Creidhe had no choice but to put both arms around his neck and her head against his shoulder. She was not at all sure how she felt about this; confused was probably the best way of describing the flood of sensations such closeness awoke in her. Once Keeper held her, his pace quickened; it became clear that he had, after all, been slowing his steps to accommodate her. Now they moved up the steep path with astonishing speed; the additional weight was apparently nothing to him, and he traversed the precipitous, rocky slope with never a foot set awry. Small One clambered, jumped, wriggled; barked, once, at some newly discovered creature under a stone. The sun peeped out between the clouds, brilliant gold-white, and they reached the top of the hill.

"Close your eyes a moment," said Keeper, setting Creidhe carefully on her feet again, facing him. His hands were around her arms; she had hers on his shoulders, and it was suddenly difficult to breathe, though he was the one who had just run up the crag, not she. "Now turn around; don't look until I say."

Creidhe obeyed, feeling his hands lightly around her waist now as he placed her before him, facing outward.

"Now," he said. "Open your eyes. Is not this the loveliest sight in the world? We stand here at the end of man's journeying; we look back from the edge of his farthest voyaging. I love this place, Creidhe. It is the meeting of earth and sky, the resting point of oceans. From where we stand, all stretches out. If I had a song such as Small One carries within him, I would sing it here for the winds to carry to the corners of the earth."

Creidhe nodded; she had no words. They looked east toward the Lost Isles; the tall, stark shapes of the islands seemed to drift in swathes of mist today, like places that existed only in legend or in ancient memory. The sea washed about them, silver, slate-gray, fierce deep green, changeable as a living creature, with more moods than there were pebbles on the shore. Above them the sun shone, bathing the bare rocks of the hilltop in pale light, touching Creidhe's hair to glittering gold. Westward, the other way, they could see the long slope down, the last, wave-struck holm where puffin and gannet crossed and crossed again on the wind, and beyond, the wild ocean path to the end of the world. That way lay realms of ice, pods of great whales, monsters and maelstroms. That would be an adventure such as only a madman or a visionary might essay.

It may have been a long time they stood and gazed, or not so long. Deep inside her Creidhe felt that strange sense of rightness, the deep certainty of time and place that comes but seldom in man's cluttered existence. But she was not unaware of the more immediate situation, which perhaps she should have taken steps to avoid: the fact that Keeper's arms had crept around her from behind and now crossed themselves firmly over her chest, holding her close; the fact that she was leaning back, so that the whole length of her body touched his. His mouth was against her hair; her hands rested over his as if they belonged nowhere but there. This closeness filled her with sensations both wondrous and heady; this was no dream, no vision or imagining, but real and strong, awakening every corner of her body to vibrant life. She did not move; he stood still as stone. Each sensed, perhaps, that for them there would not be many such moments of utter content.

Eventually Keeper said, "The boats—look over toward Council Fjord. They have gathered the boats near the western end, ready to sail at dawn on the day the water stills. Can you see?"

'She narrowed her eyes; the sea was bright in the high summer sunlight, and it was a long way.

"Seven, eight . . . I count nine of their small craft," Keeper said. "And another: a boat I have not seen before. It is larger and sturdier than theirs."

Creidhe could not see a single one; perhaps living wild sharpened the senses. Nonetheless, her heart sank. Some things, one did not need to see to understand. "Sam's boat," she said. "The *Sea Dove*. What else could it be?"

Keeper's arms disengaged themselves; he stepped away from her, shading his eyes with his hand, gazing across the Fool's Tide. "A fishing vessel, I would guess," he said. "This could carry many men. Asgrim has seized it, perhaps, to aid his venture."

Creidhe said nothing; the conflict of feelings within her made words impossible.

"You think not?" Keeper's tone was sharp. "You think your companions fight alongside the Ruler, willing participants in the hunt? Did you not say these men were not warriors?"

"I don't know what to think. Sam would not easily give up the *Sea Dove*. I hope no ill has befallen them. Why would they come here? That would be so wrong. Even Thorvald would not do such a foolish thing, surely."

Keeper looked at her, eyes shadowed, jaw tight. "They come for you," he said.

It had been in the back of her own mind, though she would not speak it; the very thought aroused such delight and pain, such elation and horror, she thought she could not encompass it without running mad. *Common sense,* she told herself. *Apply common sense.* "I don't think so," she managed. "How could Thorvald know I am here? Surely they believe I drowned; there was one of Asgrim's men watching from the shore when I overturned the boat. They should have gone home. I thought they would go home." Her voice was shaking. Thorvald still here, so close, just over the water and about to sail for this very shore: what could possibly compel him to make such a choice? And Keeper was here beside her, Keeper with his strong hands and his lean, fine body; Keeper with his shy words and his wonderful smile; Keeper with his traps and his tricks and his formidable array of weapons, about to face up to all of them, to all of the warriors that eight, nine, ten fine boats could carry ... Thorvald and Keeper ... Somewhere in her thoughts, the Journey unfolded, and she could see what must be next, and her very spirit shrank from it.

"There is no doubt in my mind," Keeper said flatly. "He comes to fetch you home. What else? He knows that you still live. He need not see the proof; he knows it in his heart." His tone was bleak, the voice of a man who is accustomed to loneliness.

"I shouldn't think so," Creidhe told him. The brightness and beauty of time and place had turned to shadows around her. "Thorvald tends to act according to the intellect; he disregards feelings usually." Still, he had come to the Lost Isles. What had that been if not a desperate quest to mend a broken heart?

Keeper had his back to her, studying the distant boats that she could not see.

"If your friend comes for Small One," he said, "I will kill him."

There was no answer to that. The doglike creature stood by Keeper's side now, small, untidy, its pointed ears scarcely level with his knees, it was such a little, scrawny thing. Beyond the two of them sky and sea and glittering brightness stretched away and away, a wondrous swathe of light and shadow, a picture of eternity. Surely the ancestors had laid a special hand on this place, marking it out, keeping it safe; surely that hand stretched, too, over the man she saw before her and the child he loved so fiercely. Surely, surely they must be safe. Creidhe would not believe the images she saw in her mind, the images that clamored to be put into wool and linen, to be woven into the Journey: the pictures she would not let herself create. As for Thorvald, he had always made his own decisions, and he must take his chances.

"Come," Keeper said abruptly. "We will go back. Can you walk down?"

"Of course."

He did not take her hand now, but went ahead without offering to help her. Something in the set of his shoulders and the look on his face kept her silent all the way down to the shelter. It was only when they were back inside that she asked him, "Weren't you going to show me the hiding place? I'd better know where it is, hadn't I? It can't be very long now."

Keeper was not even attempting his usual routine, raking out the coals, setting water to heat. He stood leaning against the rock wall, staring ahead of him, mouth set in a line. It was Creidhe who moved the pot onto the fire and tended to the child.

"I hope," she said carefully, "that you haven't suddenly decided you can't trust me. I won't deny that I am upset about what you saw, and about what you said. I fear very much for Thorvald. For Thorvald and Sam. They are old friends, and I don't want them hurt. I miss my family; I did not sail all the way to the Lost Isles thinking I might never go home again. Those things are true, and you need to understand that." She sat back on her heels by the fire, looking up at him. He had not moved; he would not meet her eyes. "But despite those things, I meant what I said before. All of it. And I give you my solemn promise that I will hide with Small One during the hunt, and make no noise, and guard him as best I can. If Thorvald comes here looking for me while the hunt is on, then I suppose he will sail away again without me. That's just the way it is. I would not give Small One up to Asgrim's men, Keeper, not now I know what the Unspoken intend for him. I am deeply hurt that you would believe that of me, even for a moment."

There was a long silence. Then he said, very quietly, "Your hurt is my hurt, Creidhe."

She nodded; a lump came to her throat.

"And yours mine, as I have told you," she said. "Your joy my joy, if ever we get the chance to find it. I will look after him for you."

"Creidhe?" The tone had changed again; now it was fierce, urgent. He moved to squat down by her, very close.

"Yes?" Her hands continued their practical work, putting fuel on the fire, pouring water.

"I have told you I will not be defeated. It is true. All the same, if—if such a thing should happen, I want you to take him. Take him away safe, right away, take him home to your own island, where they cannot reach him—"

She could hear the unsteadiness in his voice, and that alarmed her far more than his words. "Of course I will," she said. "I give you my promise. I swear by—what was the vow you made, it was a lovely and solemn one—by wind and wing . . ."

"By stone and star." He finished it for her. "Thank you, Creidhe."

"It will not be needed," she told him firmly. "You will be safe. The ancestors hold you in loving hands; the Isle of Clouds protects you. Keeper, you had better show me this hiding place today. We don't have a lot of time."

"Soon, yes. Do not be afraid. Soon over. Then there will be time for us. Now I must go again for fish, enough for your days alone. We do not make fire while they are here."

He moved to the entry, then turned back to look at her; the chill was gone from his eyes. "I ask too much of you," he said. "This man, Thorvald, I hear the softness in your voice when you speak his name. I see the change in your face. You made a long journey for him. Father and mother, sisters and homeland, all of this you left behind to follow him. Because of him you were taken and you nearly drowned. Now he comes for you at last, and you must hide from him. How can I ask this? When the sea brought you to my island, I did not understand these things. How can you be silent when your man comes here and calls to you?"

"I don't know." Now it was Creidhe's voice that was shaking. She looked across the fire at Small One; the child had her comb in his hand and was making an attempt to pull it through his wind-tangled hair. It was no simple task; he was cross-eyed with concentration. "I don't know how I will do it; I just know I will do it, because I must. Now you should go if you have to catch enough fish for several days. I suppose we'll have to make it into some sort of a soup."

By firelight, later, they sat quietly as the child fell asleep, tucked small and neat in his nest of warm cloaks and blankets. All that could be seen of him was a tuft of dark hair.

"You did not show the web tonight," Keeper said. "No story."

"Today I hadn't the heart for it. Neither the sewing nor the telling."

"What you see troubles you? Alarms you?" He had an uncanny knack of picking up what she had chosen to leave unspoken.

"Something like that. I did not want to frighten Small One, so close to the hunt. Sometimes images come that seem dark and foreboding. They are best not given form."

Keeper was finishing the binding on his knife, tucking the ends of the cord beneath, biting a loose thread off with sharp, white teeth. "My brother is in the web," he commented. "Does that mean all will be well with him, that he will survive?"

Creidhe shivered. "Fashioning the Journey does not make the future," she told him. "I am not a goddess or spirit, whose needle maps out the lives of men and women, whose tapestry has the power to change what is to come."

There was a little silence.

"Are you sure?" Keeper asked.

"I am an ordinary woman. I am not a seer like my mother, nor a priestess like my sister, nor even particularly good or brave. I assure you, I have no such powers. The Journey is just my way of setting down what I feel, and sometimes my feelings are very strong. My voyage to the Lost Isles shows how ordinary I am, how lacking in deep wisdom. I thought I could help Thorvald. I thought he needed me. It seemed terribly important to be with him, to stand by him; indeed, I had thought of little but him for some time past." She considered this, finding herself somewhat reluctant to look back at the Creidhe of last spring, a Creidhe in whose mind the prospect of marriage and settling down had loomed very large. "When I stowed away on Sam's boat, I behaved like a silly girl," she said.

"Silly?" Keeper's hands stilled; he regarded her solemnly, considering this. "I do not think you could be silly, Creidhe. If you are not yourself a goddess, then the hand of a goddess touches you; I have seen this since you first came into sight, floating to the shore of my island. You have so many deep things within you—wisdom, and kindness, and love."

"All the same," she struggled on, twisting her hands together, "it was foolish of me. I thought Thorvald would see—I thought it would become apparent to him, that he and I—I thought he would change. That I could change him. But that's not how it works. Either a man learns, and changes by himself, or he never changes at all. Thorvald is like his father, driven by some kind of darkness inside. If he ever grows beyond that, it will not be because of me."

Keeper did not comment. The knife was finished; he sat now with knees drawn up, arms around them, and stared into the fire.

"I'm sorry, I'm babbling on again," Creidhe said. "This can be of no interest to you."

"It is of interest. He is like his father? His father changed. He told me what he had been."

Creidhe was astonished. "Thorvald's father spoke to you of his past? Of why he was exiled? When?" Keeper could have been no more than a boy.

"I was unhappy. They befriended me: the two hermits, and the boy with them. I would have stayed there but for Sula. Asgrim forbade me their house. Niall challenged him; the Ruler did not like that. When I got home, there were beatings. I wished, then, that Niall was my father. He is a good man."

"He murdered his brother," Creidhe said. "He was king, once, in my homeland. He was responsible for some very evil deeds. But you're right. He's living proof of how a man can change. Though Niall himself would deny that. He would say that underneath, he is the same man he always was . . . I've just thought of something."

"What?"

"When we first heard of the Ruler, it was clear Thorvald thought Asgrim might be the father he was searching for. I thought that myself when I met him. He is of the right age and general appearance, and he's a man of authority as Somerled—Thorvald's father—was. If Thorvald has convinced himself the Ruler is indeed his father, that would explain why he stayed, why the *Sea Dove* is out there among Asgrim's fleet. Thorvald's trying to please him, and to prove himself." Images of blood and death assailed her once more; she put her hands over her eyes, but failed to shut them out. "If only I'd had the chance to talk to him, to tell him he was wrong."

"Why would he believe this?" Keeper's tone was puzzled. "As soon as he spoke of it, many men would tell him it could not be so. I am Asgrim's only son; Sula was his only daughter. Any man of the islands could attest to that. I do not understand this."

"No," Creidhe said. "Thorvald is not the easiest man to understand, nor the easiest man to love. I don't know why Sam and I put up with him really. He wanted it kept secret. Wanted to find out what kind of a man his father was, before he told him. You see, Somerled left the Light Isles without knowing of this son. Thorvald himself only found out who his father was last spring, when his mother thought he was ready to know the truth."

"His mother?"

"I call her Aunt Margaret, though she is not my blood kin. A fine, courageous woman, expert in all the crafts of needle and loom. She taught me all I know. A very lonely woman, who loves her son dearly, but finds it hard to tell him so."

"It is a sad story," Keeper said. "A man who might be a fine father now, but is deprived of the chance. A man who does not deserve to be a father, yet earns the loyalty of this son who is not his son. A twisted story much like my own. Yet I cannot pity this Thorvald. I dislike him greatly."

Creidhe said nothing. There was a question she dearly wanted to ask, but she did not know how to put it; it was a delicate matter.

"I—" she began.

"I—" said Keeper at the same moment. Both fell silent; neither attempted to frame their words again. Creidhe moved to her side of the fire, arranging her bedding next to the sleeping child. Keeper unrolled his blanket on the other side, as was his habit. Between them the embers glowed, cradled by the stones; tonight the fire's warmth did not seem to offer a great deal of comfort, for there was a deeper chill in Creidhe's heart, the touch of approaching shadows.

She lay there awhile, looking up through the narrow opening to the gray-blue of the summer twilight. There was no need to turn her head to know that Keeper, too, lay wide-eyed and wakeful, not three strides away beyond the fire.

"Keeper?"

"Yes?"

"I have a question for you, but I don't know if I should ask it."

A pause.

"And I have a question for you," he said. "You must ask first. If I can, I will answer."

"I was thinking—I was wondering if you would tell me about the time you went to bring Small One back from the Unspoken. I know it would be hard to talk about. I was thinking perhaps you might tell me."

"Are you sure you wish to know this?"

"Yes."

"After they took her"—his voice was very low, but the words came quickly, almost as if he had wished to tell this a long time—"I would have gone right away, you understand. I thought I could fight them, could save my sister, if I followed swiftly enough. I had my weapons, I had a little boat, I ran to the shore. He stopped me. My father stopped me. He locked me up; I could not go."

"Perhaps he feared to lose you as well. But didn't Asgrim go after them himself? He and his warriors?"

"Huh!" An explosion of scorn. "None followed the Unspoken. Asgrim held me prisoner a long time, in our own house. Would not let me out, though I raged against him, pleaded with him. By the time he set me free it was too late. They had put the seed of their child in her; they had destroyed her innocence."

Careful, very careful here. "What about your mother? Didn't she try to do something?"

A little silence.

"My mother was gone long since. When we were very small, almost too young to remember."

"Tell me the rest, Keeper."

"It was winter; I could not go. The waters were wild, the winds whipped hard and cold. I waited; I held my silence. I hated him that season. My bitterness was like a poison in my veins. When I could, I went up the hill to Brother Niall. Sweet words and silence were there, kindness and open hearts. Every time, Asgrim brought me back. Then spring came, and I took my boat and went to find her."

Creidhe heard what was in his voice, and longed with every corner of her body to get up, to take those few steps around the fire pit, to wrap him in her arms and offer what little she could in comfort. The power of her yearning astonished her; it silenced her completely. She lay still, heart pounding, pulse racing.

"I had learned a little wisdom over the time of waiting. I knew I could not rush in, a child with my small weapons, and hope to bring Sula home. So I sailed there, and walked up to their settlement, and spoke words of greeting, though the taste of them was sour in my mouth. I persuaded the Unspoken that I was a friend, a youth merely, and no threat to them. So they let me stay, and I saw my sister."

"You were there so early? Even before Small One was born?"

"Yes, Creidhe. I stayed with her, helpless to bring her away, for Sula was frightened and sick and full of despair. She was but one year my senior, and what they had done had hurt her, not just in the body but deep in the spirit. She would have taken a knife to her wrists or walked into the sea. I stayed close by her. She endured and bore her son. Once he was there, things changed. Sula was weak, she was sick, but she loved him from the first. No matter that he was the child of the Unspoken, the offspring of an unspeakable act of cruelty. He was hers; the moment she first looked into his eyes, he had his place in her heart. And in mine, Creidhe."

"I understand," she said softly. "It must have been very hard for you; so hard I can scarcely believe you endured it."

"I wanted to bring her away, to bring the two of them to safety. But Sula was thin, pale, like a little shadow, scarce able to walk more than three steps. She flinched at every sound; she feared to leave the small hut they had allotted her. She knew that when the child ceased drinking her milk, when she could no longer feed him, they would take him away. She knew that if they tried that I would fight them, and that I could not prevail against so many. They would perform the ritual wounding, and Small One would become Foxmask. If he survived it. We knew that before this day, we must take him away."

"But she died," Creidhe said in a whisper.

"She died. She had never been herself while I was there, not even before the child was born. She was like a dried-out husk of my sweet, merry sister. What girl of those tender years can endure such treatment and not go mad? She held on until her son was close to one year old; until, in secret, she had taught him to eat other foods, to nourish himself on what was provided for her, fish, eggs, vegetables. I helped her when I could, but it was no simple matter. For a young man to be in a woman's hut was unusual. Perhaps I seemed still a child; at any rate, they let me stay close by, close enough to recognize when she was deathly sick. Sula knew it was time; I spoke to her of escape, and she silenced me. She knew she would never escape. She made me plan it; she helped me work out what to do, she told me how to care for the infant, though she herself was little more than a child. I wept; I would not agree that she was dying. But I knew it, and the Unspoken knew it. They gathered, like carrion eaters around the still-warm corpse of a beast."

Creidhe was close to tears. She waited in silence.

"It happened earlier than they had expected, in the night, after a day of whale killing and a feast. All slept; all but Sula and me. She slipped away in the darkness; I saw the spirit creep out and the empty thing it left behind. I snipped a lock of my sister's hair and put it in my tunic. I set shells on her dead eyes. Then I took the child, and crept down to the shore, and sailed away in one of their boats before the early sun rose from the eastern sea. He lay quiet in the bows, watching the sky; even then, he knew what to do. We sailed to the Isle of Clouds. The Fool's Tide stilled to let us pass."

Creidhe had known what happened: the bare bones of it. It was a different matter to hear it spoken thus. The simplicity of it, the sorrow, the stark courage wrung her heart.

"She entrusted him to me," Keeper said. "I have kept my promise."

"Why did you go to the Isle of Clouds? Why not back home, where there were folk who could help you? I know your father had been unkind to you, but—"

"You do not understand," Keeper said. "He sold her; As- grim sold her. Traded her for a promise of peace. Exactly the same as the bargain he made for you. I know this. The Unspoken told me."

Creidhe was quite unable to speak.

"It is true." Keeper's voice was level. "The Ruler cares nothing for the ties of kinship. It was our mother's blood that bound Sula and me together, the same blood that binds me to her child. It was our mother's blood that called me here to my island. Asgrim despised us, my sister and I. We were not the children he wanted: a biddable daughter, an obedient son. In Sula, he saw only a white-skinned, fair- haired girl, a treasure he could use to win a reprieve from the battles, the raids, the fell charms the Unspoken used against his people. No matter that she was his own daughter. In me, he saw a boy who dreamed, a son who would rather talk to Christian priests than wield worldly power, a child whose mother's blood was all too apparent in his strange eyes and his refusal to obey. He saw the one who would prevent him from achieving his goal. I could not take Small One home. Asgrim would simply have handed him straight back to the Unspoken."

"He traded her, knowing what they would do to her? His own daughter? By all the ancestors, no wonder he thought nothing of using me the same way! Has the man no heart?"

"He chose unwisely," Keeper said quietly. "All went awry for him. Another man could have made this right. Asgrim cannot. He treads a path into darkness. If I do not kill him, another will. This season, next season. None can trust such a man."

"He chose unwisely? Chose what?"

"When he chose her. My mother. He could not hold her long. She went back to the sea."

Creidhe had known it, perhaps. It was there in Keeper's eyes, his hands, the strangeness that could not quite be defined.

"I did not wish to tell you this." His voice was hesitant.

"About your mother? Why not?"

"Because you will be afraid. What you said, about your family, about your brother who was drowned . . . now you will fear me. I did not intend to tell you."

"I think I knew," said Creidhe.

He was silent.

"Keeper?"

No reply.

"I am afraid of the hunt," Creidhe said, "and of what may happen. But I could never be afraid of you."

She heard his breath released in a rush, a great sigh. It became apparent to her that he had indeed dreaded this moment; that her trust was precious to him. And oh, how she wanted to be over there beside him, holding him, not here alone with her body on fire and her head spinning with feelings that thrilled and terrified her. To apply any sort of logic to the situation was an impossibility. They said the Seal Tribe could do that; they were supposed to be expert at seduction, at enthrallment. She would not believe it of

Keeper, with his shy sweetness. There was no magic here, she thought, but the natural enchantment of a man and a woman who fitted together so perfectly that they might be the two halves of one whole. Some might say such a mating was solely a thing of story, invented just to dazzle. But Creidhe knew it was not so, for she had grown up alongside its very embodiment: Eyvind and Nessa, each the perfect completion of the other.

It wasn't going to be easy to sleep. She shifted restlessly, turning from one side to the other.

"Keeper?"

"Yes?"

"Didn't you have a question to ask me?"

"Yes. But I cannot ask. It is—I cannot—I do not seem to have the words for it. I know I will offend you. I cannot speak it . . ."

She heard him move as she had, rolling from back to front, rustling his bedding; she saw without needing to look how he lay open-eyed and wakeful, staring up at the sky. It was not so hard to guess the nature of the question.

"Your tale was a sad one," she said softly, "too sad for a bedtime story, though it is a tale of great courage. You saved him; you kept your promise. But I think we need another story tonight, and I will tell it, if you agree."

"Please."

Creidhe could hardly hear him. He was too far away; further than he should be. Still, she would not move.

"I spoke of Aunt Margaret, Thorvald's mother," she began.

"I do not wish to hear a story of Thorvald. I am tired of him."

Creidhe found that she was smiling. "It is not so much a tale of him, though he is in it. You should not interrupt me. This is a story you will like in the end. Aunt Margaret taught me to spin, to sew and to weave. I love weaving; I'm supposed to be quite good at it. My blankets and wall hangings get given away as wedding gifts or as offerings to visiting officials such as the chieftains of the Caitt or the Jarls of Rogaland. It makes me proud that my work is valued, but sad, too, because giving it away is like saying good-bye to a part of myself."

"But," said Keeper, "then you share your gift for happiness with others; the beauty you make travels widely, and gladdens many hearts. That is good. I have interrupted the story again; I ask your forgiveness."

"Well," Creidhe went on, "just before I left home to come here, I finished making a blanket. It was a little different from the others; I chose the pattern and the colors for myself, and as I worked on it I . . ." she was blushing in the darkness, glad he could not see her, "I did not think of it on some nobleman's wall or decorating a fine lady's chamber. I always imagined it on my own bed: the bed I would share with my husband on our wedding night."

Silence.

"The blanket was a fine, deep blue; I made the dye myself. There were bands of red in it, a pattern of narrow stripes, and a border I fashioned on the strip loom, with trees and creatures. Every part of it was done with love; if you could tell the tale of what I dreamed as I made that blanket, it would be full of sunshine and warmth, of sweet embraces, of joyful homecomings, of laughing children and the smell of new-baked bread. Of kisses and gentle touching, of sighs that stop the breath, of . . . a whole world of happiness, I wished into that swathe of bright wool, Keeper. When it was finished, I rolled it up and stored it away at Aunt Margaret's house, and went home. Then I packed my bag and followed Thorvald to the Lost Isles."

Not a sound. His inclination to interrupt had deserted him now.

"I was a different girl then," Creidhe said carefully. The next part of this was going to be very hard to put into words. "I thought I loved him. I thought that was what love was, caring so much about someone that it didn't matter if he hurt me, if he ignored me, if he snapped at me. I thought it didn't matter if he placed no value on the things I cared about. My dreams told me of a time when that would change; when he would see me for what I really was, and

we would lie under that blue blanket together, man and
wife, as I had always imagined it would be. He has been my
friend and companion since we were tiny children. When I
stepped onto that boat, I still believed he would change: that
we were destined to be together. Thorvald can be—he can
be a fine man, loving and kind, when he remembers."

"I do not like this story, Creidhe."

"You want me to stop?"

There was a pause. "No," he said. "I will hear the rest."

"It was not Thorvald who changed, but me. Coming here
changed me. Our boat nearly sank on the way over. There
was a storm, and Sam was hurt. Thorvald was angry with
me. Then we reached the Lost Isles, and Asgrim took the
boys away. After that I learned about loneliness, and fear,
and how it feels to be unable to help, even when you've always believed that you could deal with anything. I've
learned how you can't count on your friends; I've learned
how strangers can become friends. When I came to the Isle
of Clouds I learned quite new things. Here I found courage,
loyalty and endurance, where I had expected only wildness.
I found imagination, kindness and generosity. I saw a
beauty I had never known existed in this world." Her hand
went out to rest on the sleeping form of Small One, rolled in
his threadbare blanket. "I saw that love can survive even in
the harshest of circumstances. That a child can keep faith
though his resources are tested beyond what most men
could endure, that he can remain true all the long years until he himself becomes a man. All this I have learned."

Keeper made no sound.

"And . . . and I discovered I had been deluding myself as
I sat at the loom dreaming my fair dreams of the future. You
do not make a man, or a woman, into someone you can
love; you do not adjust the other to fit your vision of the perfect mate, the one you would hold to you above all others.
He is himself; he will not change at your will. He makes his
own path. Over a long time I have come to recognize that
this is so. Such a pairing might lead in time to a life that was
satisfactory: a partnership of friends, in which familiarity
and trust played a role. There are many such. It is not so

with my mother and father, the wise woman and the golden-haired warrior. They looked and knew; what is between them is eternal, deep, a bond that cannot be denied. It can still be seen in their eyes, in their every touch." Her voice shrank to a whisper. "I have learned that I can accept no less than that."

There was a long silence.

"This is the end of your bedtime story?" Keeper's voice sounded quite odd, as if his thoughts were in some way making it difficult for him to speak.

"Not quite," Creidhe said. This tale would be told far better by touch: by the soft brushing of fingers, of lips, by the whisper of breath and the slow movement of the body. But she could not do that, not yet. "There is only one more part to it. Every night I have dreamed, here on the Isle of Clouds: so many dreams, some dark and ominous, some so sweet that when dawn came I yearned not to wake. Often I dream the same dream that was in my mind last winter as I wove that blue blanket. And I have to tell you, the man who shares its warmth with me now, while I sleep, is not Thorvald. Since you first touched me, I have known it could no longer be so."

She heard a sudden, abrupt movement, then utter silence.

"I do not imagine we can keep this up for long," she said, "your blanket on that side and mine on this, I mean. But, Keeper . . . dear one . . . I think that we must wait a little longer. The hunt is very close. I'm afraid for you, and for Small One, and for Thorvald and Sam as well. I will do as I promised; I will guard the child. What you have to do appals and terrifies me. I cannot understand how you can survive it, year after year. That is what gives me pause now, though I long to lie by you, to touch and . . ." She was not managing this very well at all; her feelings were threatening to get the better of her common sense. She took a deep breath. "What is between a man and a woman should be done in joy," she went on. "Until we have come through this dark time, we should wait, I think. Otherwise we would come together in desperation, we would seek one another in order to shut out fear, to banish shadows awhile. I don't

want it to be like that. I want it to be a thing of gladness, of
sunshine, of hope, the way I imagined it when I wove the
blue blanket." Gods, her heart was going like an axe cutting
wood, and her face felt hot as fire. She could never, ever
have spoken thus to Thorvald; she was not even sure she
had done the right thing now. Just possibly, this was not
what had been on Keeper's mind at all. He had a terrible
trial facing him; perhaps his thoughts were all of ambushes,
of sorties and sudden deaths. She could hardly bear to think
of it.

"I . . . I like this answer very well," Keeper said. It
sounded as if he was smiling. "It seems I did not need to ask
the question. I wonder if I have dreamed this, Creidhe."

"No," she said shakily. "You're awake. We both are, and
likely to stay that way awhile, I should think."

"It is such a short distance, from this side of the fire to
that," he said. "And yet, a world away. I had never thought it
could make such a difference where I set my blanket down."

"It won't be so long," Creidhe whispered. "A few days,
that's all. Goodnight, Keeper."

"Goodnight, dear one." His voice was soft in the half-dark.

Sleep did not claim her until it was close to dawn. By then
Keeper had gone, perhaps to set his blanket down elsewhere, perhaps to perform a patrol of his traps and bolt-
holes, his weaponry and lookouts. She did not wake until he
came back well after sunup, with Small One at his heels.

He smiled at her, a smile full of sweetness and sorrow,
and then he said, "We must go now. This morning. I will
take you to the place of hiding. They come tomorrow. I see
it on the water."

Creidhe's heart shrank as she scrambled out of her blankets, eyes still bleary with sleep. "Tomorrow? So soon? I
thought—"

"Yes," Keeper said gravely. "I, too, thought it would be
longer. We must gather all that is here: blankets, clothing,
the implements of cooking, all that can show signs of our
presence. Later I will erase all traces of the fire and cover

our tracks." He fell silent, watching her. "I am sorry," he said eventually. "Sorry that you must endure this because of me. You must not be frightened."

This time Creidhe could find no words of reassurance. Tomorrow was real; tomorrow looked her straight in the eye. Tomorrow was Thorvald facing Keeper with a sword in his hand and a mission in his heart. If Thorvald won, she could go home to her family. If Thorvald won, Small One would be handed to the Unspoken. And Keeper would die; she knew he would fight to the death before he let them take the child. In the back of her mind, she could hear his voice, stern, certain. *If your friend comes for Small One, I will kill him.*

As she folded blankets and cloaks, Creidhe struggled to apply a measure of calm to her thoughts. She considered what her parents would do if faced with such a situation. Nessa, still truly a priestess for all her life among family and folk, would seek aid in meditation, in divination, in trance and prayer. Nessa would act according to the wisdom of the ancestors. Creidhe was no wise woman. Sometimes what appeared in the Journey did seem to her to reflect an ancient wisdom that flowed into the woolen images quite independently of herself, but that was no help now. She knew what the Journey demanded next. It was starkly clear in her mind, and it turned her chill with foreboding. As for Eyvind, he would never have allowed matters to reach such an extreme. If he had to deal with this, he would gather all the parties together in a council, and ensure they brought their concerns into the open. He would insist they stayed there until a satisfactory solution was reached. That was his way, a path of justice and fairness. It was all very well in the Light Isles, a place of thriving, peaceful settlements, of well-tended boats and fields full of healthy stock. Who would have the strength to impose such ordered thinking on the autocratic Asgrim and his terrified people, or on the eldritch tribesmen of the Unspoken? How could the same council table ever hold the Ruler, and his son, and the folk who had stolen and defiled young Sula? If only Brother Niall were here, or Breccan. Creidhe longed for their calm, practical voices and their wise advice.

"Creidhe?" Keeper had finished gathering up his pots and pans, his fire irons and his ragged blanket. The fish they had cooked last night was ready in a covered crock.

"Is it time to go?"

"Take this," Keeper said. He held out the knife he had been working on, a sharp, useful-looking weapon whose bone hilt now bore an intricate binding of cord—twists and knots and turns that seemed to Creidhe a delicate, formal semblance of the tumbling waves of the western ocean and the long-limbed creatures that lived there.

"Thank you," she said, taking it in her hands. "I hope I will not need to use it." She glanced at Small One, who was making an attempt to fold his own blanket the way she had done hers, neat and square. Tongue between his teeth, he knelt and patted the threadbare wool flat with his small, long-fingered hands. "I intend that he and I will remain out of sight and quite silent until they are gone. I'm not used to hurting people. I'm not sure I—"

"Shh," Keeper said. "Just take it. It will ease my mind to know that you have the means to defend yourself, and him. All will be well; the hiding place is hard to find, and the Long Knife people become quickly frightened on the Isle of Clouds."

The hiding place was indeed hard to find: a shadowy cavern accessed from a ledge still narrower and more perilous than the one that led to Keeper's armory, and situated high on the southern flank of the island's steep hill. He had already put water there in skin bottles, and had laid a motley selection of old cloaks on the stone floor, sheepskin and felted wool and soft leather, the spoils of other hunts in other, earlier summers.

"It is small," said Keeper, "and you cannot make fire; you can burn no lamps. The two of you must sleep close to stay warm. I am sorry, truly. I regret this greatly."

Small One had carried his own blanket to the cave. Now he was laying it out by the wall, tugging it straight. It was clear he understood exactly what was happening and what was required of him.

Creidhe looked around the cramped space. The narrow entry left the cave in semidarkness even now, in full morning. She eyed the water skins, the pot of congealing fish, the hard ground where, she knew, the bedding they had brought would do little to alleviate aching backs and strained necks. She studied the child, who had seated himself cross-legged on his blanket and was staring at her with his ocean-deep eyes, pools of fluid darkness in the odd, triangular face. She thought of Sula.

"It's a very good place, Keeper," she said firmly. "It's snug and secure. I'm sure we will be safe here. Have you ever thought of just—of just hiding along with us, until they go away? Surely they would not find you here."

"When all are dead, there can be no more hunt. I will fight until they cease to come to my island. I have promised. And now I must go, Creidhe. There is much to be done today."

"Oh—you're going now, already? Can't I help you, just until the sun goes down? It is so soon—"

"Best that you stay here." His voice was firm but gentle; his eyes gave her another message, in which love and pain, desire and confusion were all present. "You can talk to him today, until nightfall. After that, you must be silent until it is over."

"You will not be with us tonight?" Despite her best efforts, Creidhe's voice came out small and wobbly.

"No, dear one. I must leave you now, and I will not return until they are gone from this shore. From now, from the moment I walk away from here, I must think only of the hunt; my mind must hold nothing but that. I regret—"

"Stop it!" Creidhe cut his words short. "Stop apologizing, as if this were your fault! Of course you regret. We all do, all three of us are sorry that we cannot be together, that we cannot walk about in the sunshine, and be close to other folk, and live our lives without fear. These islands are a crazy place, to generate such misery and terror. One day that will change. We'll make it change. Now you'd better say good-bye to Small One and go before I start to cry. I would rather not do that; I don't want to upset him."

Nonetheless, tears pricked her eyes as she watched Keeper kneel down, a long, lean figure in his feathered garments, and gather the scrawny child into his arms. His hands were careful, stroking the disheveled dark hair.

"I must go now, little brother," Keeper said softly. "You will be brave, I know, as you always are, and quiet and good. And this time you will not be alone. We have Creidhe now; we have light in our dark place. Creidhe will stay with you until I return. With her, you will be safe. Good-bye, Small One."

The child said not a word, made not a sound as Keeper set him back on the blanket and stood to face Creidhe.

"I must go now."

"Yes." And she should let him go, she should let him leave this place with nothing in his head but strategies for survival. Yet, as he stood pale and solemn before her with his eyes full of shadows, she found she could not simply stand aside and let him pass.

"You must say farewell to me too," she whispered.

"Yes," said Keeper, not moving. His own voice was hardly stronger. "But I have no words for it."

"No need for words." Creidhe took a step toward him and, twining her arms around his neck, she touched her mouth to his. Just a little kiss, she had told herself, just a brief good-bye kiss so she had something to hold onto while he was gone. But his lips parted against hers, his breathing quickened, his arms came around her in fierce possession and Creidhe realized that little kisses were no longer a possibility. She clung to him, her body pressing tightly against his, her mouth hungry, her hands clutching: so much for waiting until the time of desperation was past. Keeper's fingers had wound themselves into the long, bright strands of her hair. There was a kind of fire burning in her body now, the same she had felt last night when she had spoken words of love to him, but deeper, harsher, wilder in this moment of parting. Somewhere within her was the knowledge that, if her dark visions represented truth, she would never hold him thus again.

At length they both drew breath, though breath came hard and unsteadily, and they stepped apart, still clasping each other's hands, reluctant to sever that final bond. Creidhe looked into Keeper's eyes, seeing that alongside the daunting strength, the astonishing courage, the long-sustained loyalty, there was fear: the fear of his own mortality. He gazed back at her as if to commit her features to the deepest corner of his memory so that, even in the midst of battle, he would carry her with him.

"May the ancestors guard you, dear one," Creidhe whispered. "May they watch over you every moment, and bring you back safely to us."

Keeper bowed his head, lifting her hands to touch them briefly with his lips. "Good-bye, Creidhe," he said softly. "Know that, whatever happens, you have brought joy to my island, a joy I did not know was possible. Now I will go." And abruptly, so abruptly it stopped her heart, he released her hands, turned, and was gone.

She would not weep, not even with the warmth of his body still imprinted on her flesh, not even with the taste of his kiss still fresh and urgent in her mouth. She would not weep, because of Small One. Creidhe settled on the blanket and gathered the child onto her lap, where he nestled close, his head against her breast, one small hand grasping her hair. She felt the quick thud of his heartbeat, saw the emptiness in his eyes, a sorrow he would not give voice to, for he had promised to be good and quiet and, like his kinsman, Small One kept his promises. Creidhe thought of those other years, when he had been younger and had done this quite alone.

"Well, now," she said, "we don't have to be completely quiet until sunset. That's good. I thought I might tell you a story, one my sister Brona sometimes tells, about a warrior who went out to slay a big earth-troll and found a lot of new friends on the way, very strange friends. Would you like that? Good. It happened like this . . ."

* * *

At midsummer, the nights were short indeed in the Lost Isles. The men stood by the sea, waiting for the moment when the sun would emerge from his place of hiding below the eastern rim of the world, and it would be light enough to know if Einar had been right. Thorvald could feel his heart thumping in anticipation; it was necessary to remind himself that he must stay calm, whatever happened. A leader who could not control his own feelings had no hope of controlling his men. He breathed slowly, looking out over the gray expanse of water that lay between this western shore of the Isle of Storms and the distant, shadowy mass of the Isle of Clouds. Nearer at hand, across the sheltered waters of Council Fjord, he could see the two islets that lay by the fjord's opening; the steep, spiked ridge of Dragon Isle and the squat form of the Troll's Arch. Beyond them spread the Fool's Tide, where Creidhe had drowned.

The pale sky flushed suddenly with rose, and with a deep orange, and with bright gold.

"Here we go," muttered Einar, gaze intent on the water that lay below them, the sea path from this shore to that cloud-wreathed isle in the west.

Asgrim said nothing. He stood by Thorvald's side, arms folded, mouth tight. Thorvald could imagine what the Ruler was thinking: *Another dawn, another chance. Maybe this time, this year it will be different. Maybe we will win, and the time of suffering will be over. Let it be today.* And with that thought, another to rein it in: *Perhaps we will lose again. Has not that been the pattern of this five times over? I do not want to watch my men die. I cannot bear to fail again. Let it not be today.* It seemed to Thorvald that would be the manner of the Ruler's thinking. As for himself, his thoughts were orderly now. His mind held all his strategies, his plans, his knowledge of men and terrain and task. He had answers for whatever the Isle of Clouds could throw at them. He had confided in Einar and in Orm. He had told Hogni and Skapti as much as they needed to know. His final strategy was a desperate one, and to this only Sam was a party. It would be put into place if all else failed; with luck, there would be no need to take such a risk.

The sky brightened. One bird sang; another answered. Above them, light blossomed, and the chorus of chirps and whistles became a swelling, wordless anthem to the dawn. Another night was past; a new day was come. The waters of the Fool's Tide turned from slate to pearl to the pure, pale blue-green of a duck egg. For a little, the small knot of men stayed silent, frozen in place by the immensity of the moment. Then Asgrim drew a long breath and let it out in a great sigh, and Einar, with a fierce grin creasing his scarred features, said, "Looks like we're on, men."

After that, things followed a well-rehearsed pattern, every aspect in accordance with Thorvald's meticulous planning. The rest of the men were waiting by the boats, which were already packed in preparation, for Einar had predicted this would be the day on which the rare lull in the waters of that roiling strait made the Fool's Tide briefly navigable to skilled sailors. The men did not need to be told the signs were good; they saw it in the eyes of their leaders, and hastened to launch their collection of small craft in the predetermined order. Most of these vessels could hold two or three men at best, and for each boat Thorvald had designated a leader. These were the most level-headed of the group: Orm, Wieland, Einar, Skolli. The *Sea Dove* could carry a far larger complement, and on her Thorvald would travel with Sam, Knut, Hogni and Skapti and several other men.

Asgrim was not coming. The Ruler, in a decision that had shocked them all to silence, had announced that, this summer, he was entrusting the mission to Thorvald, as a father might to a son. His own presence would only confuse the chain of command. He knew Thorvald's battle plans and thought them sound. He would wait at Council Fjord for their return, and ensure preparations were made to tend to any wounded. It was best that way.

This had made jaws drop in amazement. In Thorvald's case it had also caused a wave of feeling, which he fought to suppress. Asgrim's recognition flooded him with warmth. It vindicated his actions and gave him back his identity. But beneath the surge of joy other, cooler impulses remained; for him, it would ever be rare for the intellect to be entirely overruled by the heart. Asgrim was cruel and unpopular. He did have good reasons for the way he ruled, but after the hunt those reasons would cease to exist. As a war leader, Asgrim was inept. He had proved it five times over. As chieftain of the Long Knife people he was scarcely better. Folk were unsettled, fearful, restless. They did not trust their Ruler. His recognition of his son did nothing to alter that. After the hunt, Thorvald thought, there would be changes. The Long Knife people must have just rule, genuine peace, a voice in the making of decisions and judgments. These men, Einar, Wieland, Knut, these decent, courageous men did not deserve a tyrant. No bond between father and son was more important than setting that to rights.

But first, this strange battle must be won. Two days, they would have, and the night between; two days until the waters of the Fool's Tide began to shift and stir once more, and its erratic currents to tear and suck at any craft a foolish sailor thought to steer across its turbulent surface. Two days, the seer captured, and a minimum of losses: that was what Thorvald had promised them. If he did not make good that promise, he told himself as they launched the *Sea Dove* into Council Fjord, he deserved nothing from Asgrim and nothing from the men. If he could not achieve victory, he did not deserve to be their leader.

At first they rowed; the waters of the fjord were sheltered from the prevailing winds, and progress under sail was erratic and sluggish. Once past the arms of land that jutted out westward, once level with the Troll's Arch and the monstrous, jagged shape of Dragon Isle, they felt their sails filled by a kindly wind, a wind such as Thorvald had not known before in the Lost Isles, steady and warm from the east. The prows of their vessels split the ocean smoothly, a creamy wake trailing behind. There was no longer a need for oars. The Fool's Tide stretched placid and gleaming around them, resting, sleeping, holding its breath to let the intruders by. Now that they were on the sea, there were few birds about; the gaggles of gulls that formed a daily escort to the fishing boats of the Long Knife people were nowhere to be seen. Without the harsh, small music of their cries the air seemed empty, the high clouds more distant; and when Thorvald looked back, the tall shape of the Isle of Storms, with its bare-topped crags and its sheer, rough-hewn cliffs, was receding as if into a dream. And before them in the west, closer and closer in its soft violet and shadow-gray and deep impenetrable green, loomed the mysterious form of the Isle of Clouds.

ELEVEN

I copy the psalms: my penmanship is satisfactory.
Year by year I set them down, in this quiet house. I write, I
eat, I sleep.
Today, within me something stirs and shivers. A dark change
beckons.
De profundis clamavi ad te Domine . . .

MONK'S MARGIN NOTE

It had been a night of no sleep. Now, standing immobile against the rock wall, shadow on shadow, Keeper watched them come. All was in readiness. After five hunts, he scarcely needed to think what must be done; his every sense was tuned to the dance of protection and survival, combat and death. Somewhere deep within himself, he had locked them away, his little one, whose frail form he could still feel in his arms, his goddess, whose sweet kiss he could still taste on his lips. They were not forgotten, but set apart until the days of the hunt were over once more and he could allow them back into his thoughts. Today, tomorrow, all was fleetness of foot, sharpness of eye, quickness of wit and a faultless aim. Today, tomorrow, one warrior must become an army.

The wind was favorable to Asgrim's men. The small boats were making good speed across the deceptive calm of the Fool's Tide and would reach his island when the sun was high. It was one of those rare, fine days that came from time to time in summer, white clouds scudding high across blue sky, and a real warmth in the air. There would be no rain today. That made Keeper's task more difficult; mist and rain gave him advantage, for he knew the island's treacherous slopes as a child knows his mother. Of the skulls he had kept, close to half had been those of men who died, not from his own spears and arrows, his own traps, but by falling from a cliff path or walking into a deep, sudden hole in the rocks. Where he could, he had retrieved their remains. Asgrim's men had warm cloaks, leather boots and sheepskin jackets. They had spears and knives. Nothing could be wasted on the Isle of Clouds.

When they were close, but not so close that they would see him, Keeper moved to a different vantage point, where he had a supply of arrows ready. He narrowed his eyes, looking out through a slit between the rocks that sheltered this cup-like retreat some way above the landing place. There was one boat in particular he watched, one that stood out by its sheer size alongside the low, simply constructed vessels of the Long Knife people. This boat was sturdy, well made, a craft any fisherman would be proud to call his own. There were several men on board. Keeper knew every one of his enemies by name, for he had lived among them until he was twelve years old. As the boat came closer, he identified Hogni and Skapti, who towered above the rest. Knut was on board, and others he recognized. They were lowering the sail now, taking up the oars to guide their vessel into the narrow bay. And, after all, he did not know them all by sight. The tall, fair fellow who was giving the orders was a stranger to him. The one who stood in the bows, spear in hand, scanning the rocks above the shore for signs of life, had hair as red as a winter sunset, and a look of fierce determination on his face. They were come, then; Creidhe's friends had made the choice to be his own enemies. He could not allow himself to dwell on this. They were here, and if they crossed his path they would die.

Last year, Keeper had attacked the moment Asgrim's forces came within range, taking five men with his arrows before the invaders had completed the ascent to the level ground above the shore. This year, his plan was to wait. He never took the same path twice; surprise was one of his principal weapons. He would track them until they split up, as they surely must if they intended to search for Small One. He would follow one group, then another, and let the island play its part. At nightfall they would retreat to the boats. The Long Knife people were afraid to stay on the Isle of Clouds after dark. Tomorrow they would try again, until the moment when they must sail for home before the lull on the waters was replaced by the surging turbulence that was the strait's usual pattern. He would pick off as many as he could today. He knew them; they were a dispirited crew, easily frightened, easily confused. By tomorrow he would have trophies to add to his collection, and the enemy would be much weakened. Then it would just be a matter of cleaning up.

He watched. His hands ached to pick up the bow, to sink an arrow in the broad back of Skapti or the strong chest of Einar, who was assembling a small group of men beyond the rocks there. Keeper's gaze sharpened. This was a departure from the usual way of things for Asgrim's forces. They seemed to be organizing themselves, forming up into three parties, and at the same time there were men posted at strategic points, armed with bow or thrusting-spear. The look on their faces was different too. Keeper sensed danger in those set jaws, those fierce eyes. Danger and challenge. Where had that come from? No time to ponder; he must move, quickly and invisibly, following one or other of their small squads, whichever looked most threatening. They were leaving men to guard the boats; the big, blond fellow was among those staying behind. Creidhe had said he was a fisherman; that was his boat. Before, they had never set a watch on the shore.

The groups moved off, fanning out across the hillside. They went cautiously, some prodding the ground for traps,

while others covered their comrades with shields and
weapons facing outward. The shields were new; in earlier
hunts, they had borne no more than two or three between
them. Someone had been busy. Keeper watched; in a moment, he would follow. His eyes were on the red-haired
man. Creidhe had said, *Thorvald is no warrior*. It was evident that Creidhe had got it wrong. Keeper could see that in
an instant. It was Thorvald whom they followed, Thorvald
to whom they glanced for direction. Keeper could guess
who had planned this careful advance, this ordered defense.
It was not Asgrim who had changed the expressions on their
faces. Creidhe's friend was not only a warrior today, he was
the battle leader. And the Ruler was not here.

Keeper moved. He went by cliff face and tunnel, by rock
cleft and shingly slope, ducking, sprinting, clinging, dodging. Year by year, season by season he had practiced his
shadow-swift navigation of the rocky, precipitous terrain.
He passed over it like a ghost, like a breath of wind.

Skapti's party went around the northern side of the island, skirting the cliffs, looking in holes and fissures and
caverns. Hogni's group set off to the southeast. Here the
hillside offered a broad view of the isles where the Unspoken had their strange dwellings. And Thorvald's warriors,
with Einar in the lead, went up the center, still under shields,
still bearing their weapons as if, at long last, they had
learned how to use them. They reached a ridge part way up
the steep, grass-covered fells skirting the Old Woman.
There they dropped behind the cover of a rocky outcrop,
perhaps to plan their next move. The advance had been well
executed, smooth and orderly. But Keeper had been quicker.
He was poised, now, far above where they lay believing
themselves concealed. Here, in this cleft of the rocks, he
had throwing spears and the darts he had coated with a poison gleaned from a certain rare shellfish. Those had been a
gift; the island had provided him with its own forms of assistance. He judged the enemy would come on upward, taking their time, perhaps spreading out farther to check for
possible hiding places. If they investigated the caves on the
northern side they would find a few surprises. They would

not reach the hidden chamber on the southern side, where his two precious ones were hidden. He had made quite sure of that.

They'd avoided the more obvious of his traps so far; that showed more intelligence than he'd expected. Clearly, this Thorvald thought he was clever. Keeper would let him go on deluding himself awhile. Then he would show the red-haired man what a fool he was to believe any man could outwit the Isle of Clouds.

"Stay down," Thorvald hissed. "If they've got any sense, they'll wait until we're spread out as far as possible and then strike. What's the likelihood of sending a couple of men up the gully there and having them cover us with their bows from the top?"

"I'll go," someone volunteered.

"I'll come with you," said a second man.

"Go on then," Thorvald whispered. "Slowly. When you get up there, crouch down behind the big rock and keep a sharp lookout. If anything moves, shoot it."

"What if it's him?" someone asked. "Foxmask?" This was a young voice, with an uneasy note in it.

"That's hardly likely," said Thorvald. "They'll have him under lock and key somewhere, chained up in a cave or bolted into a hut. Anything that moves is the enemy. Apart from us, of course. Now go."

The two men wriggled away, keeping low as they clambered up the cleft in the rocks. The others waited in silence. When the climbers were perhaps two thirds of the way up, there came a rattling, rolling sound from higher on the hill, and a shower of small pebbles cascaded down over Thorvald and Einar and the rest of their party. They put their shields up to cover their heads, or crouched with arms protecting skulls as the trickle of gravel became a shower of stones and then a thundering rain of rocks, from fist-sized pieces to great chunks heavy enough to crush a fellow's head. The noise was deafening; Thorvald thought he could hear a voice in it, a growling like a sleeping giant abruptly awoken: *Who dares set foot on my island?* And he heard a cry of pain as well, from one of the two men caught in the gully. At least one of the missiles had found its mark.

The flood of stones dribbled to a halt; one or two small pebbles still rolled crazily down the hillside.

"Keep down," Einar said in an undertone. "After that they'll expect us to back off. Egil, get up there fast and see who's hurt. Thorvald? What do you want to do?"

"Where do you think they are?" Thorvald ventured a quick look over the rocks that concealed them, turning his head to scan the hillside above. There were many vantage points up there, clumps of tortured bushes, grotesque rock piles, tricky undulations of the land. It was not possible to tell where the enemy was hiding, but one thing was certain: that had been no natural rockslide.

"Einar?"

It was one of the younger men, Ranulf. His face was pale as milk and his voice shook.

"What?" Einar snapped, scowling.

"Didn't you hear it?" Ranulf whispered. "The voice?"

"Shut up," said someone else testily. "Of course we heard it. If we let that stop us, we'd never get anywhere. You have to learn to shut your ears in this place, or you'd go crazy."

A gust of wind passed over them, full of the smell of the sea. Above, birds circled, screaming. Whatever had silenced the gulls that morning as the boats had set out on their venture, it had not stilled this island's inhabitants, for the sky was alive with wings.

Egil crept back, expression grim. "Thorkel took a hit on the head; out cold, can't see what the damage is. I'll go back up and help get him down. Skolli's all right, just shaken. Looks like they're up yonder to the south, behind that outcrop, the one that looks like a fist. You'd never attack them there; they've got too big an advantage. Shall I go now?"

"Bring Thorkel down," Einar said. "And be quick about it. You'll need to carry him back to the boats, we can't leave him here. Take him down, then get back up to us as fast as you can. Take young Ranulf with you, and watch out for traps on the way, they're everywhere. Skolli will stay with us; we're going on." He glanced at Thorvald. "That's unless you want to change the plan?"

Thorvald shook his head. "No. But not straight up, in full view. Egil's right; that would be inviting attack. If I were the enemy, I'd plan to follow up with arrows, pick us off the instant we come into view. If Asgrim were here, what would you do next?"

"Retreat and regroup," Einar said. "It makes sense. Moving up looks like suicide."

"Mmm," Thorvald said. "And retreating is just what the enemy expects us to do. Gather the men close. I have an idea . . ."

On the southern flank of the island, Hogni's men edged their way along a narrow path, trying hard not to look down. The coastline of the Isle of Clouds was, if anything, more hostile to intruders than their own Isle of Storms, which had its share of heart-stopping precipices and needle-sharp rock pinnacles. At one point Wieland went ahead to test a promising-looking path, broader and more level, which seemed to lead straight to the high vantage point that was their goal. He had taken one step, two steps onto the flat rocks of the ledge when his foot slipped oddly, his arms flailed for balance, and in an instant he had slid off the path and over the edge, plummeting toward the frothing waves far below. He shouted, and the sound echoed strangely around the crevices and crannies in the rocks, as if a whole chorus of unseen men screamed in alarm together. Hogni braced himself. The rope around his waist, joining him to Wieland, snapped violently taut. Behind Hogni, two other men sprang to support and steady him, to share the weight. They caught their breath shakily, then hauled as they had practiced on the cliffs by Asgrim's encampment. It was a quick, efficient job; soon enough, a white-faced Wieland emerged over the lip of the precipice to stand before them shaken and bruised but otherwise unhurt. The ledge had been slathered with some substance that rendered it slick as a weed-covered skerry yet could barely be detected by the eye.

"So, not that way," Hogni remarked. "I wonder what they've got hidden up there? All right, we take the long route. It'll be ropes again at the end; looks like the only path to the top is straight up."

They went on. In every man's mind, though nobody said it, was the knowledge that it had been Thorvald who had insisted on the ropes. But for that, Wieland would be dead, and Jofrid would have neither babes nor husband at her hearth. One of the men was whistling under his breath, a furtive sound that was part defiant victory song and part the expression of a body trembling with nervous tension.

"Shut up," hissed Hogni, and they moved forward in silence, each step cautious, every eye intent on the hillside above, the track before and behind, scouring the bare landscape for any sign of the enemy. It was clear their opponents had expected them to pass this way; it could be assumed, then, that warriors were waiting up ahead. Their own party was vulnerable here in single file, where well-aimed arrows could take them one by one. The ropes, then, would be something of a disadvantage.

"Quick as you can," Hogni said. "As far as that rock that looks like an old crone with a big nose. That's where we start to climb. Einar's team will be well up the hill by now; we want to reach that upper ridge when they do, and check who's seen what. Step lively."

Skapti's men took the northern route, avoiding the cliff paths, for on that side of the island they were scarcely navigable; it was considered less of a risk to make a way on open ground, sprinting from cover to cover and hoping all the time that the enemy was somewhere else. They made good progress, though the climb was taking its toll; their legs ached, and the farther they went with no sign of their adversary, the more jittery the men became. They had been ordered not to speak, and they followed their orders; only a fool would go out of his way to attract attention here. But a man could not silence

his thoughts, and all of their thoughts were the same: *It was
there, by that patch of scree, we lost Kolbein last year. Over
there where the bushes curl under the wind's blast, we saw
Havard die of a poison dart. That way lie the cliffs where four
men fell to their deaths in the second hunt.* Skapti saw what
was in their eyes and was powerless to change it, for the same
images tormented him: so many comrades lost, so many
good men slain, and all for nothing. Beneath that litany of
losses, for Skapti, another tune played: a song of blind obedience, of terrible guilt, of deeds done and lies told that
weighed heavy on him. He blinked and set his jaw. He was a
warrior, and today he was a leader. He had no time for this.

"Forward, men," he hissed, and they moved on up the
stark hillside. In this part of the island, the contours dipped
into pockets here and there, places well shielded by rocks,
where reasonable shelter might be found. There were remnants of stone walls and crumbling, derelict huts. They
stopped in one such small refuge to catch their breath, leaving a man on watch outside; this might be a snug hiding
place, but it was also an ideal spot to be cornered. The back
door, if you could call it that, opened onto a sheer drop
down a bird-thronged cliff to raging waters below. Skapti
looked around for signs of the enemy; such a good bolthole
would surely bear some clues, some evidence of tenancy.
He performed a cursory search, but could see nothing. They
sat a brief while, resting their legs, sharing the contents of a
water skin, checking their weapons, whispering what words
of reassurance they could find for one another. All agreed
that, given the choice between this unsettling advance
through a landscape which seemed, not deserted, but watching, breathing, waiting, and an open onslaught by armed
warriors, they'd take the attack any day.

Time to move on. Skapti opened his mouth to give the order, then paused. One of the younger men, Hjort, was twid-
dling something between his fingers, a tiny scrap of cord or
thread, which only caught Skapti's attention because of its
bright, unusual hue, a rich red-violet. Such an item seemed
greatly out of place in this landscape of dun and gray and
green.

"What's that?" Skapti asked curtly. "Hjort?"

"Bit of wool, that's all."

"Give me a look." Skapti took the little thread from the other man and held it up, feeling the softness and the regularity of the yarn. Sewing wool: a women's thing, and dyed fine as any lady's best. "Where'd you get this?"

Hjort was looking guilty now; he had no idea what had sparked this sudden interest. "It was just lying around. On the rocks over there."

Skapti strode across the small shelter, peering at the rock shelves, searching for more clues, but there was nothing to be found. After a little, he said, "All right, not a lot here. We'd best be off if we're to reach the top when the others do. Follow me." He slipped the little scrap of wool into his pouch and, spear at the ready, walked out of the refuge, calm-faced. But inside, Skapti was less than calm. Guilt clawed at him, regret and confusion worried at his heart. This was something he could never show to Thorvald. It was a message from the gods, for him alone, to remind him of the evil he had done. For he had seen what the other men had not noticed, or had not understood: a single, long thread of hair twisted around the flower-bright wool, hair that was as fair as ripe wheat in sunlight.

The three teams met at a certain point high on the flank of the Old Woman, where the ground levelled slightly. A grassy hollow behind low, tattered bushes allowed a gathering place; on either side they posted men with bows at the ready. Clouds were massing overhead now. The sun was here, then gone, here, then gone, as fickle as a bored young wife. Thorvald's group had reached this designated meeting place first. Hogni asked Einar how they had done it, and Einar said, rubbing his back, "Don't ask." It had been a case of going one by one, using decoys, and climbing rather faster than any of them was accustomed to. Even the smith, Skolli, was panting, and he had a chest on him like a stout ale barrel.

It was time for a quick exchange of what information they had gleaned. Thorvald spoke first.

"They were overlooking us, at a vantage point above a big overhang. They hurled stones; as you see, we're three men down, but Egil and Ranulf are unharmed, and should be on the way back by now. We don't know if Thorkel was just stunned, or more seriously injured. The fellows down at the boats will do what they can for him. I expected the enemy to follow the stones with arrows, but they didn't press their advantage. By the time we got up to the place where they'd been, there was nobody there. No sign but boot marks on the earth. Hogni?"

Hogni grimaced. "Nearly lost Wieland. Saved by the rope. Fellows did well. Came up the steep way, stiff climb. Nothing else to report. No sign of the enemy. Only thing is, I'd say they've got something down in those caves to the south that they don't want us laying hands on. The path Wieland was testing was greased slick as a lump of raw blubber. Why bother with that spot, well off the beaten track, unless it leads somewhere special?"

"These folk aren't stupid," Einar said. "Some of the traps must be randomly placed. I mean, what've they got to hide except the seer? I don't buy your argument, Hogni. It's too obvious."

"All the same," put in Thorvald, "the information could be useful. We must consider every possibility, however slight the evidence. Thank you, Hogni. Skapti, what about you?"

Skapti was looking ill at ease. "We're all here, no losses, no injuries. Nothing to report, except . . ." The big man hesitated.

"Except what?" snapped Thorvald.

"Well, we did find an old hut that looked like a good hide-out, sheltered and dry, with a spring near at hand and an outlook down to the anchorage. I'd have expected them to make use of it. There's precious little in the way of hospitable corners in this accursed place. But if they'd been there, they'd done a good job of covering their tracks. There was just one thing left behind."

"What?" Thorvald was growing impatient; the sun was well past its midpoint and they had made very little progress.

Hjort opened his mouth to speak, but Skapti was quicker.

"Small scrap of wool from a tunic or cape," he said. "There'd certainly been someone there."

There was a short pause, then Thorvald said, "Thank you. I can use this information. Now, men. We don't have much to go on. There hasn't been an attack as such; I don't count the defensive measure of the rock fall. We haven't even seen the enemy, far less encountered them. Any theories as to why they didn't attack us down at the bay, while we had our hands busy hauling up the boats? What are they waiting for?"

There was silence for a while. Thorvald could almost see his men thinking.

Einar spoke, his scarred features grave. His fingers twisted the shell necklace he wore, perhaps a charm of protection. "Looks to me as if they plan to wear us out first, then attack when we're at our weakest. I'd predict they move on us just before dusk."

Hogni nodded. "Got to attack sooner or later; just a matter of time."

"No mist today," observed Orm. "No rain. Other times, they've always attacked in the mist. When it comes down, it's as if they can still see and we can't. Took three of our men with those narrow bone spears last year. Drove four of our fellows off a ledge in the second hunt. Unusually fine today; that's why they're holding back. Should give us an advantage."

"Anyone else?" Thorvald was thinking fast, adapting his plans by the moment. Nobody spoke. "Very well," he said, "we've been through this before, but maybe we need to rethink it. Your estimate of the enemy's numbers is—thirty? Forty?"

"More of them than us," Einar said. "We've lost a good number of men every year since this began; the enemy just keeps on going. Plenty of them, that's plain."

"What's the biggest number of them you've ever seen to-gether?" Thorvald asked. "I know their manner of attack is informal, secretive; still, I need some idea."

"Thing is," said Skapti, "they're very quick. Like some-thing not quite human. You'll see one of them dart across between the rocks, or scuttle off over the cliff face, or dive under the water, but as soon as you see him, he's gone."

"Mostly, all we see is the spears and arrows coming out of the mist," added Orm. "The island protects these folk. It hides them."

"I understand that," Thorvald said, "and I know they don't engage you in hand-to-hand combat; from what you've told me, they've developed techniques that make that unnecessary, impossible even. The terrain most cer-tainly aids them, I see that for myself. Now answer me something. Is it fair to say you've never actually seen more than one or two of these tribesmen at a time? Cast your memory back. Think carefully, and be quick about it, we need to move." He looked around at the circle of men where they sat on the rocks or squatted on the grass. They were good fellows, loyal and courageous. A pity they were not just a little more clever. He could almost wish Asgrim were here.

"What about the voices?" someone asked. "The voices come from all around; more voices than we've got men, women and children on the Isle of Storms."

Thorvald was about to reply that nobody ever got killed by a voice, then recalled what he had been told about the Unspoken and the deaths of the newborn. "You are war-riors," he said. "Shut out the voices; they are no more than devices conjured to unman you and make you forget your own strength, your own courage. Shall I tell you what I be-lieve?" There were nods, encouraging grunts. "I think it very possible this enemy's numbers are far less than you imagine. I see it in their manner of attack. They are nimble and fit, they know the island, they are clever and well pre-pared. By means of these qualities, and with the aid of the weather, they can succeed in repelling your conventional attacks indefinitely, though I suspect you greatly outnumber them. I wonder why they do not simply go to ground and wait until the Fool's Tide forces us home. For some reason, this enemy continues to harry us as best he can. Now, men, I've made it plain to you already what we must do here. We will not allow this pattern to continue. We will turn this hunt on its head. We'll use these tribesmen's own tactics against them. Small groups, three or at most four, staying under cover, looking for anything these people may have left behind: weapons, clues, the wherewithal to make their traps. They must eat and sleep somewhere, they must leave traces of fire, unless they gobble their fish raw from the sea. Be vigilant; be watchful for any sign at all. Split up now and follow your leaders' directions. Any of the enemy you find, capture if you can. We want the seer, and only these people can tell us where he is. If you have to kill, kill. Press onward across the island and work as a team. Cover your comrades. You're looking for the enemy, and you're looking for Foxmask. Don't lose sight of who's doing the hunting here. Einar, Hogni, Skapti, you'll each appoint two other leaders from your groups as we planned, and split the men up."

"What about you?" inquired Hogni in simple curiosity.

"I'll be on my own," Thorvald said tightly. "And there's just one more thing."

They waited.

"We're not going back to the boats at dusk. We're staying up here."

"What!" someone burst out, and the others hushed him, but there were looks of shock and alarm all around.

"We always stand offshore overnight," Svein said in a horrified whisper. "Nobody sleeps on the Isle of Clouds."

"And so," Thorvald said, "what territory you gain on the first day must be traversed again on the second. No wonder you've never found the seer. And I didn't say anything about sleeping. We'll leave the fellows guarding the boats, and any wounded. The rest of us will gather up here. Those are my orders. Einar knows this, as do your other leaders. They've all agreed to it. If you want to win, you stay on shore. The enemy seems to like surprises. We're going to surprise him tonight. Now go. We meet back here at dusk."

There wasn't much to go on: two tiny clues, and his own growing conviction that, bizarre as it seemed, they were dealing here not with a whole tribe of savage warriors but, at most, a mere handful. It did not make much sense, considering the massive losses of earlier years. But superstition and fear can play a large part in such conflicts, and the more Thorvald considered the unfolding of the day, the more he convinced himself that he was right. This enemy was exceedingly clever. He had made excellent use of the advantages he had: speed, mobility, the terrain and, in other hunts, the natural propensity of the Isle of Clouds to attract mist, rain and high winds. Very probably, the only thing that had limited his assaults today was the clear weather. The Long Knife people had undertaken hunt after hunt despite their losses, their lack of cohesion as a fighting unit, their lamentable weapon handling and the misguided leadership of Asgrim. This dogged persistence had not served the Ruler's people well. The enemy knew how to use his wits. The only way to defeat him was to do the same. Numbers didn't matter here.

Thorvald reviewed the day. So far, they had lost no men: a considerable improvement on Asgrim's record to date. They had traversed a substantial part of the island: that, too, was pleasing, but insignificant unless they pressed the territorial advantage by remaining on shore overnight. They had not found Foxmask. Without that, in the final analysis, they had achieved nothing. So, a couple of clues and a hunch. Very well, he would work on that.

Some time later, when the sun was already low in the west and a faint, bright haze hung over the sea, not so much a mist as the ghost of one, Hogni's group of three men encountered Thorvald at a spot where the southern cliffs crumbled away alarmingly and a little spring sent a long, graceful plume of water down to the distant rocks below. On the banks of this streamlet, mosses and small creeping plants swathed the damp stones, and from time to time tiny birds darted down to scoop up a beakful of the clear water before launching themselves skyward once more. Thorvald was lying on his belly, close to the edge, peering down over the rock face. When he heard the others approaching, he wriggled back to safety.

"Anything?" he asked.

Hogni squatted down beside him, a solid figure in his worn leather garments, which had perhaps once been a uniform of some kind. "Saw one of them," he said. "Not so far from here. He led us a chase, kept us running. He didn't fire, though he had a bow and quiver on him. Young fellow, wild-looking. Thought we had him cornered once, but he disappeared among the rocks, and we couldn't find exactly where he'd gone in. Caves, tunnels, place is riddled with them. Think you may be right; these folk are trying to wear us out before they strike." Hogni glanced up at the sky. "Need to be soon, though. Day's passing."

"Maybe they'll attack at night," Svein offered. "They know the place, after all, and it's not as if it gets really dark this time of year."

"What about you?" Hogni asked, small eyes intent on Thorvald. "No prizes for guessing why you're over here; those were my own thoughts entirely. Seen anything? Heard anything?"

"Not a whisper," Thorvald said. "All the same, I think you were right. There are caves of some sort down there, and they warrant inspection. The question is, how? After what happened with Wieland, we'd be stupid to trust the ledges, and the cliff face looks like it's falling to bits."

"Ropes," Hogni said. "We've got a couple. I could hold you, if you're willing to try. Of course, if they're in there, it'll be a bit like dangling a chicken leg in front of a starving dog. I know which end of the rope I'd rather be on."

Thorvald considered the options. The light was dimming; still, there would be time. It was a high risk, but if his instincts had served him well, this could be the turning point.

"One try, I think," he said. "I've never acted as bait before; it'll be a first. All I want to do is look, this time. We need to be reasonably sure the seer's in there before we spend time worrying about how to get him out."

"Funny," remarked Hogni. "Just a boy, isn't he? Foxmask, I mean. Boys are noisy; I know it. Got a couple of my own, not that I've seen much of them in a long time. And this one's what, six, seven years old? How do they keep him quiet, that's what I want to know?"

"Not an ordinary sort of child," said the fourth man, Paul. "He's a seer, after all. They say he's half a boy and half a creature; that he changes himself by sorcery. That's what the name means: Foxmask. He hides himself by turning into an animal."

"A fox?" Thorvald queried, brows raised. "Not much of a disguise. In these parts he'd have more luck as a mackerel or a puffin."

"It's an old name," Svein said. "Another fellow had it before him. Goes back a long way."

"Still," Hogni said doggedly, checking the rope he had fastened around his waist, "it's a fact, children aren't naturally quiet. If he's there, you should hear something. Keep your ears open. Now come on, men. Svein, you anchor the end of the rope. Paul, keep your bow drawn and your eyes open, and tell me the instant you see anything. We're exposed to attack here, and that fellow went to ground not so far away. We'll give this one shot."

Over the edge, hands and feet searched, groping, clutching for purchase, the rope not taut yet, but held firmly from above. Thorvald knew Hogni could support his weight in case of a sudden fall, and that the three men had the strength to haul him back up. That did little to still his thumping heart or steady his breathing as he climbed cautiously down the vertiginous, damp cliff face. He went to the west side of the waterfall, avoiding the slickest patches. It was not possible to be covert here. Pebbles fell, small pieces of crumbling stone dislodged under finger or toe to hurtle down to the rock shelves far below. Perhaps this was a stupid idea. Very likely it was. On the other hand, if the enemy were as clever as Thorvald suspected, he might well choose to hide his treasure in this unlikely and inaccessible part of the island. So, keep moving, down and carefully down again, feeling the rope paid out from above, finding a crevice for the toe, the root of a tenacious plant for the stretching hand, and searching, searching across the expanse of uneven rock for any sign of a cave or hollow large enough to house anything more than a gull's nest. And listen: for behind the cries of birds, the plashing of the waterfall, the thunderous beating of his own heart, there must be clues. A child's whisper, a muted footstep, a chink of metal: if his intuition served him right, surely those who lay hidden somewhere within this desolate rock wall must reveal themselves in some small way, if only he had his ears open to it. Just a little longer . . . just a little . . . He clung to the rocks, still as a dead man, waiting.

The Journey lay spread out on the ground, jewel-bright colors glowing dimly in the faint light from the cavern's narrow opening. Creidhe had not intended to look at her work before the hunt was over, for to look was to picture the images she had not made, the terrible things that had lodged in her mind and refused to go away. But it was a long day, and the enforced silence made the time pass still more slowly. She could not tell stories, or sing songs, or even move about very much for fear of revealing her presence by a footstep, the rustling of clothing or some accidental piece of clumsiness. And they could hardly sleep the whole day away; that was to invite a wakeful night in which the fears that already beset Creidhe were likely to redouble themselves through the time of darkness.

Small One worried her. It was not that the child was likely to give them away by making noise; he was, if anything, unnaturally obedient to Keeper's request, uncannily understanding of what was required of him. It was the look of utter sadness on his strange, small face that wrung her heart, a grief that seemed to go beyond the fear of being hunted and

caught, the terror of knowing Keeper was out there in a battle
so unequal it seemed impossible that he would survive it yet
another year. Small One's eyes held all that and more; there
was something stronger there, a sorrow as deep as the message of joy and wonder she had heard in his song. His eyes
told a tale that had nothing at all to do with being six years
old and shut up in a cave in the semidark and not allowed to
talk. There were ancient things in this small seer's mind,
tides of the spirit that Creidhe knew were beyond her comprehension. All that she could do was try to comfort him, and
hope in that to find a little reassurance for herself.

So they studied the Journey, using hands and eyes to exchange a kind of commentary. Small One had traced with
his fingers the tales Creidhe had told before: Eyvind the
warrior and his clever friend Somerled; Eyvind earning his
wolfskin and later becoming a leader of men. Then there
was the tale of little Kinart, whom the Seal Tribe had taken
and drowned. Maybe. And Creidhe and her sisters; Creidhe
leaving home, sailing away; Creidhe upsetting a boat, and
reaching the Isle of Clouds. Small One's hands rested softly
on the dark wools that made the island's picture, the seal-
gray, the deep green, the dusky violet. Now he had reached
the place where his own image was shown, little more than
a pair of eyes in the shadows. He laid his fingers there, then
pointed to himself. Creidhe nodded. *Yes, you are here in the
Journey. I could not make the island without putting you
there.*

The child found Creidhe's image in the embroidery, a
limp figure sprawled over an upturned boat. In this depiction, pale hands stretched up from the water to guide the
battered craft to shore. Small One smoothed the golden hair
of the woolen figure with his fingers, then reached to stroke
Creidhe's long plait, which hung forward as she bent to
peer at the Journey. Creidhe nodded again, knowing what
would be next.

Small One's hand moved across the stitches Creidhe had
made since she reached the island: himself in doglike form;
the dead skulls with their silent, screaming mouths; the

mist, the rain, a little fire with a cooking pot beside it. He glanced up at her, eyes wide. His hand reached out again, touching the empty linen beside those last images as if he were searching for something. He gestured to the cave's opening, where a mellowing of the light suggested the sun was sinking toward the western ocean; looked at her, face as anxious as a chastised puppy's. There was no need at all for words. His message was clear. *Where is he? Where is my brother? Why haven't you put Keeper in your web?*

And when she could not answer, not so much because of the need for silence as because she had no answer she could give him, Small One became more agitated than she had ever seen him before. Still without a sound, he tugged at Creidhe's bag, tried to pull out the roll of cloth where her wool and needles were stored, and when he could not, he mimed for her what she must do. *Now, do it now, put my brother in your picture, now, today!* His eyes were terrified, his mouth quivering, his hands frantic as they tried to show her what he wanted. Creidhe reached to take his hands in hers, but Small One pulled away violently. Creidhe's own heart was thumping. She motioned to the cave opening, tried to show him, *I can't see to sew, there isn't enough light in here,* which was undoubtedly true. But it was not the real answer. She could not give him that. *I will not make the next part, for in it I see death. I know Keeper was wrong when he said I had the power to change the future with my needles and my colored wool. That cannot be so, how could it be? If I thought it was true, I would have made his image long ago. I would have shown him well and smiling, with one hand in mine, the other in yours, Small One. But I will not sew anymore, for what would creep onto the linen would not be that fair image but another, darker one. It would grow there despite me.* Indeed, it was right before her now, even with her eyes open. How could this hunt end without a loss that would tear her heart in two? Creidhe felt hot tears well from her eyes and roll down her cheeks; she tried to blink them back, but they would not obey. She covered her face with her hands; this was no good at all, she was the grown-up here, and should be strong. A moment later, she felt Small

One edge onto her lap and put his arms around her neck. She took her hands down to hug him in return, and when she did, she could feel that he, too, was weeping, his frail body shuddering in great, convulsive gasps, but still without a single sound. He wept as if his whole spirit were filled with grief. Creidhe cradled him, rocking in place, longing for words to comfort, for a little song, for the knowledge of what was wrong, so that she could help him. That other night, when he had sung the moon's stately dance across the sky, Small One had seemed powerful, old and wise. Now, huddled in her arms, he was a miserable, lonely child. Creidhe held him close, shut her eyes tight and prayed to the ancestors with all her will. *Please make this right. Please make this as it should be. Don't let Thorvald kill Keeper. And don't let Keeper kill Thorvald. And please let the child be happy, however things turn out. He doesn't deserve this; he's only little.*

In time, Small One fell asleep against her breast, his eyelids heavy with tears, and she wrapped him in blankets and settled him as comfortably as she could. Then Creidhe moved closer to the entry, watching the light change as the sun sank toward the west. She willed Keeper to hear her silent message. *Your brother loves you; you are everything to him. And I love you. I wish I had told you. Please be safe, wherever you are. Every moment I hold you in my heart. Know that; know it deep inside you.*

The light outside was orange, then red. Gulls exchanged echoing cries; there was a faint, watery music from the stream that tumbled down the cliff face not far from their hiding place. Creidhe sat very still. Her breathing slowed; her heart became steady. She would not help either Keeper or Small One by working herself up into a state of panic. She could not influence what happened now. She had promised to guard the child, and she could do no more than that.

There was a sound outside, above the cave entry, and a stone came bouncing down not two strides before her face. Creidhe sucked in her breath in alarm. Silence now. Perhaps it had been nothing but a natural crumbling of the cliff's already decaying surface. But no: now she heard a definite movement above, like a boot slipping, and a whole shower of pebbles cascaded past the opening. Creidhe froze. To move back, deeper inside, was to risk being detected by making some slight noise. To stay where she was meant being seen instantly if there was indeed a man on his way down here on some kind of search mission. It was most certainly not Keeper, who could traverse any kind of terrain with the sure-footed stealth of a wild creature.

Another small stone. The sounds from above had ceased. With painful slowness, Creidhe eased back on all fours, creeping toward the shadows of the inner cavern where the child lay sleeping. Where the child now rolled over restlessly, rubbing his eyes in his dreams, and gave a soft whimper before settling again into fitful slumber. So faint, so small a sound: so deadly a clue. Who was out there? Had they heard Small One's cry? In the half-darkness Creidhe's fingers stretched to grasp the twine-bound hilt of the knife Keeper had given her and, clenching her teeth in a strange mixture of anger and sheer terror, she crouched in place, waiting.

There was a shout from the clifftop, harsh and wordless, a cry of pain. The rope jerked violently, then steadied. Thorvald clung on, heart thumping. A moment later a voice came from above, Paul's voice, yelling,

"Get back up here quick!"

He obeyed. The note of horror in those shocked words allowed no other course. He climbed, slipping, fumbling, doing his best to minimize his reliance on the man who held the rope; who knew what was going on up there? For all his efforts, Thorvald lost his grip once, and dangled for the terrifying space of three heartbeats high above the wild seas at the cliff's base. The rope held firm; thank the gods for Hogni.

"Quick, hurry!" the voice yelled once more, and Thorvald lunged for the root of a clinging bush, caught, gripped tight, and began to haul himself up again. Heart hammering, body running with sweat, he clambered up the last few

feet and edged onto the level ground where his companions
stood. Only they didn't stand, not anymore. Svein was
sprawled facedown on the rocks, motionless save for a little
twitching of the hands. There was a long, pale arrow lodged
in his back. Paul was fitting a new arrow to his own bow,
hands shaking, as he stared away across the sloping grass-
land before them, where it seemed nothing stirred. And
Hogni, now fumbling to unfasten the rope that still bound
him to Thorvald, was gray-faced and shivering.

"What—?" Thorvald began, untying his own end of the
rope and dropping to his knees beside the wounded man.
He turned Svein over, and knew immediately that it was too
late: this warrior had death in his eyes, and nothing could
bring him back. Behind him, Paul was loosing arrows me-
thodically and cursing under his breath.

Hogni knelt down on Svein's other side, reaching to
close the eyes whose stare had become suddenly fixed and
opaque. "Thorvald?" the big warrior whispered.

Thorvald felt himself go suddenly cold, a chill that
seized him bone deep. He looked across the fallen man's
body; took in Hogni's small, terrified eyes, the tremor in his
strong hands. Just below the shoulder, the point of a slender
shaft emerged from Hogni's chest; this finely crafted missile had pierced his heavy leather tunic as easily as a sewing
needle through fine wadmal cloth. Thorvald rose slowly to
his feet. He forced himself to walk around, to see the other
end of the long dart protruding from Hogni's back; to observe the dark, oily coating that still smeared its graceful
form along with the big man's blood. Svein had died
quickly, in the space of that frantic struggle back up the
cliff. Hogni had been hit, yet Hogni had held the rope, he
had covered his comrade and followed his orders, even with
the knowledge that he held death in his body.

"Got Svein in the heart." Hogni's voice was a hoarse
thread of sound. "Paul winged the fellow, I think. Heard a
cry, then he bolted away again." His speech began to falter.
"Get . . . shelter. Need . . . talk . . . brother . . ."

"Maybe we can do something," Thorvald said, trying to

recall anything he had ever learned about poisons and their antidotes. "I can get the dart out; maybe if we cut the wound, then bind it tightly, and—"

"Not a hope," Hogni wheezed. "Not this stuff . . . seen it before . . . bit of time, not a lot . . . walk down now, while . . . can . . . Skapti . . ."

Thorvald's heart shrank. There was no point in disputing what must be truth.

"We should remove the dart, at least," he said. "That will make you more comfortable. Here—"

"No!" gasped the wounded man. "Don't touch it . . . wait . . . Skapti . . ."

"Very well," Thorvald said, his heart thumping. "We'll wait for your brother. Can you walk, Hogni?"

"Strong enough . . ." the big guard whispered.

"Paul!" Thorvald called. "Come on, we have to get him to shelter. Svein must be left for now. And we'll just have to hope those wretches are content with the damage they've done. By all the gods, they'll pay for this tomorrow. Come now," speaking to Hogni, who had risen to his feet and, swaying, placed one arm around Thorvald's shoulders and the other around Paul's, "let's find our comrades before the light goes. It grieves me to leave a fallen warrior behind, but we've no choice."

"I'll bring a couple of fellows up at dawn," Paul said. His voice sounded odd; when Thorvald ventured a glance, he saw that the archer's face was drenched with tears. "Bury Svein if we can. There's been enough of our men left lying in this accursed place without proper rites."

Then Hogni gave a shuddering moan, and a great tremor passed through him, and Thorvald and Paul walked onward in the failing light, the big man staggering between them. As for the enemy who had stalked them, and shot his venomous bolts with such cruel and deadly effect, he had vanished as if he were no more than a shadow.

Higher up, in the darkness of a shallow cave, Keeper sat alone. His arm ached where Paul's arrow had torn his flesh;

he had wrapped a strip of cloth around the wound, for he must leave no drop of blood behind him to reveal his passage across the hillside. He willed the throbbing pain into the back of his mind where such distractions belonged. It was essential to stay alert, to keep a step ahead.

They had surprised him. They had come dangerously close to the place where his dear ones lay hidden. That man Thorvald was clever. Keeper's hands had itched to take up his bow again, to loose a single shot and sever the rope on which Creidhe's friend dangled from the clifftop near the secret cave. There would have been satisfaction in seeing the red-haired man fall; rock would have smashed him, sea taken him. Those who trespassed on this island, those who sought to harm Small One deserved no better. But Keeper could not shoot; with this slicing wound to the upper arm, his aim could not be relied on, and to attempt and miss would have been to expose himself to swift counterattack. Thorvald must wait.

The men were gathered together now. He could hear them talking, and he could hear the sounds the wounded man was making. The poison could take a while if a warrior was strong. Keeper could attack tonight; the island would help him, sending voices in the darkness, using all its tricks and traps. But Asgrim's forces were substantial and gathered together with sentries posted, and Keeper had made an error. He had allowed himself to be wounded. That would limit his ability to strike true and to maintain the assault once begun.

So, not tonight, not against all of them at once. In other summers they had been easily frightened, quick to scatter, simple to pick off one by one as they fled. This year, Keeper could see it was different. This year they had a real leader: the incomer, the interloper, the arrogant Thorvald, meddling in a dispute that was none of his concern, and doing it with astonishing competency. Such a man cared nothing for Small One, save as a trophy of war, a prize to be won. And he cared nothing for Creidhe. He had treated her with contempt and was not deserving of her loyalty.

Keeper narrowed his eyes in the half-dark, listening to

the quiet voices of the men sheltering in the hollow below him. What would Thorvald do tomorrow? How would such a man proceed? He tried to focus on that, but his mind would not cooperate. He imagined, instead, Small One and Creidhe quiet in their little cave, hearing the sounds from outside, knowing someone was coming, holding one another close, frightened and alone. He remembered Small One's last, clinging embrace. He felt Creidhe's kiss, the wondrous, thrilling touch of her soft body against his, full of tenderness and promise. Keeper closed his eyes. He had sworn he would not think of them, not until it was over; the hunt required all his strength and all his will. Yet they were in his heart, filling it to bursting, driving out all else but the vision of a happiness he had never believed possible, and with it a fear redoubled.

And after all, his answer was before him, his plan and his strategy. He must not attack, but set a guard. To kill in numbers was good, since it reduced Asgrim's capacity for future hunts. But what was essential was to protect his treasure: to keep Small One safe, and to ensure Creidhe was not taken. Before first light he would station himself under cover near the southern clifftop, above the waterfall. If Thorvald returned there, Keeper would kill him. If others came with him, they too would die. There was only a day left, only one more day and the enemy would be gone. It would be the time of peace once more, and he could fetch his dear ones home.

"How long?" asked Thorvald in an undertone. It was some time later; they had reached the meeting place well after the others, and now Hogni sat propped against a great stone, shivering in febrile bursts, while an ashen-faced Skapti sponged his brother's forehead with a wet cloth. The others were gathered around, grim and quiet in the strange twilight of the summer night. Not all of the band was here, for Svein had not been the only loss. A man from Einar's party had been felled by a cunning rope snare that tripped him. His long fall had ended abruptly on rocks an impossible distance below the spot where his companions stood shocked and helpless. And one of Orm's group had stopped a spear: one of their own weapons returned to them by the enemy. Helgi had suffered a gurgling, choking death in his own blood. The men were silent; nobody was attempting to sleep. At either end of the hollow where they had come together, two patrolled with bows and throwing spears, though in the half-light finding a moving target would not be easy.

Skapti had dealt with the poison dart. Hands protected from the venomous coating by a strip of thick wool torn from his own tunic, he snapped the fine shaft a handspan from his brother's laboring chest and drew the other part out from Hogni's back with an unpleasant sucking sound. Hogni did not cry out; he was a warrior and well practiced in endurance. Simply, his breathing squealed a little, and his big fists clenched tighter. Thorvald bound the wound: such a small puncture, yet enough to rob this stalwart giant of his share in the future they all longed for.

Now they were waiting like ghosts gathered together in the twilight, without fire or shelter, without laughter or tales or a jug of ale to help them celebrate the lives and deaths of good men. Thorvald felt their eyes on him, and he imagined their thoughts: *You did this. You killed him, with your fine battle plans, your little sorties of men, sent out like lambs to the slaughter. This was to be our great victory. Now Svein is dead, and Alof and Helgi. Now we must watch Hogni die. What right have you to think yourself any better than Asgrim?*

"How long has he got?" Thorvald asked again, from where he sat cross-legged by the dying warrior's side. "Are you sure there's nothing we can do?"

"He's a big man, and the dart hasn't drawn much blood," Einar said under his breath. "That's bad for him; means it'll take longer. Some time in the night. Let's hope the enemy doesn't decide to attack."

"Isn't there—?"

Skapti shook his head. "A man doesn't survive this," he said, his voice harsh with grief. "Mostly, they go quick. My brother's fighting it. It's the only way he knows."

A convulsion passed through Hogni's large frame; his arms flailed up and out, his back arched, his feet drummed on the earth. Then he was still again, his wheezing breath the only sound save the faint, high cries of night-hunting birds. It was evident from the smell that he had lost control of his bowels; Einar moved quietly to perform what cleaning was possible here in this confined space.

"Thorvald?" Skapti's voice was as small as a child's, and held no trace of anger.

"What is it?"

"Could you ask the fellows to move away a bit? Not far; it's just, there's some things I need to tell him, before— some things I need to get out in the open, while he can still understand. Not you, Einar, you stay. Hogni? Can you hear me, lad?"

"No need . . ." Hogni's words came out on a hiss of labored air.

"Yes, there is," Skapti said soberly. "Got to tell you this or I can't go on, so shut up, will you, and let me do it. Thorvald?"

After moving the men away a little, Thorvald himself had stayed by Wieland and Orm, not quite out of earshot, but at least a respectful distance from the two brothers.

"Need you close by," Skapti said. "If you don't mind."

Wordlessly, Thorvald returned to Hogni's side. He held one of the big guard's hands, Skapti the other, while Einar damped the cloth from a water-skin and touched it to Hogni's pallid features.

"I'll be quick," Skapti said. "You know how it's always been," glancing at Einar, "me and my brother, special guards to the Ruler, watching over him, attending to his business. Long time: since we were youngsters. The only thing is, there was more to it than that. For me, that is. Special business: things you never knew about, Hogni. I don't like keeping secrets, especially not from my own brother. Doesn't sit well with me. But I did it. The stuff Asgrim made me do, I couldn't tell you about; you'd have despised me. The first time, he persuaded me it was the right thing to do, so the attacks would end. 'You're my right-hand man, Skapti,' he said. 'Let's do this for peace.' So I did it, without telling, and it seemed all right, but it went wrong. After that he had a hold on me. He knew how upset you'd be if you found out I'd lied to you. And he told me it was right, what we did; that we needed to do it for the Long Knife people, for all the children we'd lost. He said we could bring the bad years to an end. The first time, with Sula, I believed him; the other things I did because he scared me into it. But the last time, when Thorvald's little friend went, it was different. I felt sick; I felt like something dark and filthy had crept inside me. Knew then I'd been wrong. Wrong all along to do Asgrim's dirty work, wrong not to tell you the truth, Hogni. The Ruler's an evil man. I should have stood up to him."

Thorvald's skin was crawling with horror, although he had only partly understood. Hogni lay quiet for now, eyes fixed on his brother's strong-jawed face.

"Put it into plain words, Skapti," Thorvald said sharply. "What do you mean, the first time, the last time? First time for what, exactly?"

Skapti bowed his head. "Thing is," he said, "everyone thought Sula was abducted, stolen; they did wonder why Asgrim didn't rush off after her, but he wasn't a man you'd easily ask these things. I was the only one who knew he'd made a deal with the Unspoken; the only one save Asgrim himself and the girl's brother, young Erling. The Ruler's daughter wasn't captured, she was sold. Asgrim traded her to the enemy for a promise of peace."

There was utter silence. Thorvald could see from the look of revulsion on Einar's face and on Hogni's that neither had known this fact about the man they had followed as Ruler and battle leader. Farther back, where the other men sat huddled by the rocks, there was not a sound. Thorvald was certain they had heard every word. He summoned the strength to ask the question that must come next.

"And Creidhe?" He could not keep his voice quite steady.

"You see," Skapti said, openly weeping now, "I'd started believing it was the right thing, almost. Asgrim's good at bringing you around to his way of thinking. He locked his son up, wouldn't let the lad go off after Sula. The boy nearly went crazy. Good boy; bit of a dreamer, though, never liked fighting, couldn't handle a weapon to save himself. Everyone thought he'd end up a hermit, like those fellows up the hill. Finally he was let out, too late for the girl, but he took himself off to find her all the same, moment the weather allowed it. Thing was, while the Unspoken had her, we did have peace for a bit. And it was good. We'd almost forgotten how good it was. Then the boy took Foxmask, and it all started again."

"Tell me about Creidhe," Thorvald said, struggling for calm.

"We knew the moment she set foot on the island. The hair, you see. They made her cover the hair up; had to wait, so Asgrim could make a deal for us, be quite sure they'd leave us alone once they got what they wanted. Kept her a while, till he could arrange another meeting with the enemy."

Thorvald sat motionless as a chill ran slowly through him, a cold realization that made a mockery of all his own efforts at leadership here. He could not speak.

"Got you and Sam out of the way," Skapti went on. "Then he had his meeting, gave them his terms, got their agreement, set up a time and place. Told me what I had to do. In the end the girl made it easy for me, went out walking with just a priest for company. I was there. I made sure the Unspoken had her safe, watched them head off in the boat. She called out to me, asked me to help her. Already, I knew in my heart it was wrong. We all want peace, but not at that cost. Such a sweet girl, and so brave. Would've made a fine little wife for some lucky man. When I saw her tip up the boat and get away from them . . . when I saw her go under the water . . . I knew I'd done an evil thing. I'd been wrong the first time, wrong the second. Wrong when I killed a young fellow who was on his way to tell you the truth, Thorvald. Slaying a man in battle's one thing. Cold-hearted murder's different. The gods gave me a sign today, reminded me what sort of a wretch I am. Better I'd let Asgrim make an end of me than hand over an innocent girl to those savages, not once but twice. Better I was never born than do the things I've done." Skapti scrubbed a big hand across his wet cheeks. "Now I've told you, brother. I don't expect forgiveness. I don't deserve that. Just wanted you to have the truth before you go. Brothers shouldn't have secrets."

Thorvald was looking at Einar now; Einar met his gaze with an expression in which regret, apology and helplessness were all present.

"You knew," Thorvald whispered. "You all knew from the start what he intended for Creidhe, and none of you attempted to stop it. You accepted my help, you befriended me and Sam, and all the time you were party to Asgrim's plotting . . . By all the gods, I can scarcely believe this, and yet I must. I see the truth in your face, Einar; I hear the unmistakable ring of it in Skapti's voice. I suppose the injury that prevented Sam from walking back to Brightwater was no accident either. Perhaps you did not understand what Asgrim had done to his own daughter, but every one of you was complicit in Creidhe's capture." There was more, but he bit back the words, for he was still their leader, and a leader does not lose control. *You never wanted my help, and neither did my father. He kept me in the encampment merely so that I could not know what he intended for Creidhe until it was too late. He lets me lead you now only because Creidhe outwitted him and I became suddenly useful.*

"Skapti . . ." Briefly, they had forgotten a man lay dying before them.

"What is it, brother?"

"Getting . . . cold . . ." Hogni whispered. Tremors ran through his limbs, more frequent now, a twitching, shuddering sign of what was to come. His skin was gray and slick with sweat, the eyes already sunken. His teeth chattered.

"Here." Wieland stood behind Thorvald, a thick woolen

cloak in his hands. Thorvald took it, spread it over the dying man.

"Thorvald . . ." breathed Hogni. "Got to . . . forgive . . . got to . . . change . . ."

But Thorvald could not reply. A darkness had come into his mind, a churning chaos of fury and hurt and disappointment and grief that stopped his tongue and made him rise and turn away, walking to the rim of the hollow to stand alone, looking out into the night. His father had lied to him. They had all lied to him. He had believed these men trusted and respected him, he had believed they thought him worthy of the leadership that had so oddly fallen his way. He had been naïve, stupid, deluded. He had been a fool, blinded by his little successes with the ropes, the spears, the fine speeches of hope. He was misguided and selfish, just like his father. How could he have forgotten Somerled's tale, a tale of single-minded ruthlessness, of fierce ambition and bloody carnage? Somerled had murdered his own brother for leadership; he had come close to destroying Nessa's people so he could set a crown on his own head. Somerled might have a new name now, but he was the same man. Thorvald kicked savagely at the rocks. People didn't change. They couldn't. He'd been a fool to believe his father would ever recognize him publicly, an idiot to think Asgrim could ever love him. The man had never cared about kin. He didn't know what love was. He'd probably forgotten Margaret the moment their little encounter was over, their casual little encounter that had, so unfortunately, spawned a luckless son with no more value in the world than his father. For a son *was* his father: there was no escaping it. Hadn't he demonstrated that today, with three men out there broken on the slopes of the Old Woman, and a good soldier lying here in the throes of a slow death by poison? He was cursed by the gods; he had known it the moment his mother told him the truth, and he knew it now, bitterly, finally. He had failed Creidhe, he had failed the men, and he had failed himself. His mission here was nothing but a lie.

"Thorvald?"

"Leave me alone!" he growled, not turning to see who it was that spoke.

"Thorvald, you must come back. You must hear us."

"What's the point?" Thorvald snapped. "What can any of you have to say to me?"

"Every man deserves a hearing," Wieland said quietly, stepping into view. "Hogni's dying, and he wants his leader by his side."

"I am no leader," Thorvald said fiercely. "You all knew that. You all knew why Asgrim brought me to the encampment. It was a sham, a device to divert me from his real game. He is your leader, not I."

Wieland looked at him, somber-faced. "That's just where you're wrong," he said. "Come back, and we'll explain it to you. Don't let Hogni die with the memory that you turned your back on his brother, Thorvald. He needs to see your strength, and your recognition of his. Come on, man."

They'd gathered in close again; there was a space on the rocks among them where it was clear Thorvald was expected to sit, not far from where Hogni now lay with his head on his brother's lap and his eyes closed. From time to time his body twitched and jerked as the poison worked deeper, and Orm and Einar moved in to hold the thrashing limbs, lest the big man harm himself or others.

"Hurry up," Skapti whispered, looking up at Wieland. "He needs to hear it, and we don't have long."

"We want to tell you what's in our minds," Wieland said, eyes on Thorvald. "You haven't understood, you've got it wrong. We're not denying the truth, and we're not making excuses. Yes, we did know what Asgrim intended for the girl, and we didn't like it. But we didn't know your friend, she was a stranger to us, and it's a lot easier to sacrifice a stranger than one of your own, that's the honest truth."

"Sounds as if sacrificing his own wasn't a problem for the Ruler," Orm put in. "Can't credit it, myself; that he'd give them his own daughter."

"Thorvald," Wieland went on, "you have to understand how it's been for us. All I can tell you is my own small part of the story. I don't like to speak of it, but I see I must tonight. It's the only way I can explain to you. Been married six years; my wife's called Jofrid, Orm's sister she is, lovely girl. Been sweethearts since we were twelve years old. Wed the year before the first hunt. Jofrid loves children; the other women are always asking her to help with theirs, she's good with them. Quiets the fractious ones, charms the shy ones. The autumn after the first hunt, we were expecting a child of our own, our first. I'd made the cradle, Jofrid sewed a lot of little things, we could hardly wait. The night she gave birth, the voices came; they sang our son's spirit away, and he was born dead and cold. That was the punishment for our failure in the hunt.

"The next season it was Hjort's wife who lost a child, and Einar's daughter gave birth to a weak, deformed infant that died soon after. The year of the third hunt, Jofrid was pregnant again. I begged Asgrim to let me take her away, try to sail east to other shores so she could bear the infant in safety. The Ruler wouldn't let us go. Boat didn't belong to me, after all; besides, he needed every able-bodied man for the hunt. So we stayed, and it happened again. The first time we'd cried together, and hoped for another chance. The second time, Jofrid went quiet. Didn't want to talk about it, not to me, not to the other women. She might have talked to the Christians, but Asgrim wouldn't let them anywhere near the place. That fellow Niall had challenged him more than once, and he didn't like his authority questioned. Jofrid changed. It was like having a ghost in the house. She packed away the cradle, she folded the little garments and put them in the bottom of a chest. It was as if our child had never been.

"We failed again in the fourth hunt. Three babes died that year, all sung away before the sun rose on their second day. Jofrid attended those childbeds, but I did not get the story of them from her. She was closed in on herself, frightened to speak, frightened even to think. She wouldn't care for other women's children anymore; she didn't even want to look at them. Then there was the fifth hunt, a year ago. The pattern was the same. We came back fewer, and without the seer.

And by late autumn, Jofrid had another child in her belly."

Wieland paused; his voice had faltered here and there, as though he would weep if he could. A man was dying; other sorrows must be put aside for now. "They say your friend, Creidhe, was the one who delivered my son safely," he went on in a voice no louder than a whisper. "Saved him, when he would have been strangled by the cord. Saved him, so that the Unspoken could come and sing him to death in Jofrid's arms. My boy, my little son. And I could not be there by my wife's side to dry her tears and to grieve with her. I could not protect her, I was powerless to keep death away from my own children." Now Wieland could not hold back his tears; he fell silent, his features working. Orm reached out and put a hand on the younger man's shoulder.

"I do not tell this to excuse what we did." Wieland fought for control and found it, squaring his shoulders, dashing the tears from his cheeks, where five neat, parallel scars marked the years he had endured the hunt. "We all know it was inexcusable, a cruel violation of the laws of hospitality and those that should protect the innocent. I tell it only to explain that we are real men, with real hearts. We have our wives and families, our sweethearts, our old folk. We have our fishing boats, our sheep, our small fields. At least, we had those things: not much perhaps, but all we needed for content. That's all we ask for now: the life we once had, and our belief in ourselves. The chance to see our little ones grow up."

"I don't know why you're telling me this." Thorvald heard his own voice as if it were a stranger's, harsh and cold. "It's nothing to do with me. What small significance I may have had in this power game of Asgrim's died with Creidhe. I am no part of this."

"Wrong . . . Thorv . . . wrong . . ." It was Hogni who spoke, eyes still closed, hand clutching his brother's so hard the knuckles were white.

Thorvald moved to kneel by the dying man; here, at least, he must make pretense a little longer that he still had a part to play. "What is it, Hogni?"

"You . . . lead . . ." Hogni gasped. "You . . . win . . ."

"How can I lead?" Thorvald asked quietly, taking the big guard's hand again. "I'm nobody. My leadership is based on a lie. I'm nothing."

"You . . . lead . . . Promise me . . ." Hogni forced his eyes open; dying he might be, but their expression was fiercely challenging. "Promise!"

Thorvald's heart clenched tight; the blood thundered in his temples. "How can I promise?" he whispered.

Hogni's eyes closed. He said no more.

"One thing." Thorvald found his voice again. He looked at Skapti, who held his brother cradled in his strong arms. Skapti's eyes were red and swollen; moonlight showed the streaks on his broad face. "I forgive your brother for what he did, Hogni. Skapti has performed terrible acts, it is true. That it was at Asgrim's bidding does not excuse him. Creidhe was very dear to me; she was a part of me. Her loss weighs heavily on me, and on Sam. But Skapti has paid a high price, and will pay it until the day he dies. He need not bear the burden of my hatred as well. I forgive him. He has my friendship; indeed, he never lost it."

Skapti gave a big sigh, and a nod. Hogni did not respond; for a moment, Thorvald thought he had slipped away from them in silence. Then his eyes snapped open again, eerie in the pale light, harsh and commanding. "You . . . lead . . ." he said clearly. "Promise . . ."

Thorvald was mute. He would make no promises he could not keep.

"We need you, Thorvald," Einar said. "We can't do this without you."

"Me?" Thorvald snapped scornfully. "Asgrim's puppet, whom all of you led along with your lies? I don't think so." Curse it, he was sounding like a petulant child deprived of a treat. Why couldn't they just leave him alone? What more could they want from him?

"Thorvald," Orm said, rising to his feet, "you're the best leader we ever had. You're our only chance of winning this."

"Our only hope of getting rid of Asgrim," Einar added.

"Lead us tomorrow," put in Wieland, "and lead us afterward. We're sick of being too scared to say no. Help us find Foxmask, and then help us find what we once had and lost."

"Thing is," Skapti said, as his brother slumped, limp and pale, against his broad chest, "we never had hope until you came."

"But—"

"Oh, it started the way you said, you and Sam being kept there to stop you interfering. But we soon saw what you were. You made time for us. You cared about us. You were clever, and not slow to share what you knew. You had ideas, you saw far ahead. You stood up to him, to Asgrim. There's only one other man ever did that, the whole time he's been Ruler. You stood up to Hogni and me, even though you knew we could beat you to a pulp. You're our leader, Thorvald. You have to go on."

There was a muted chorus of agreement: whispers, murmurs, nods. Not too loud: they were on the island, in the night, and not one of them had forgotten the enemy.

Thorvald felt glad of the dim light, for he could tell his cheeks had flushed scarlet in a lamentable lapse of self-control, and tears pricked his eyes. "How can you say that?" he burst out. "I'm just like him! I'm no better than Asgrim! I promised you minimal losses, and we've already had three men killed. We sit this moment by the deathbed of our finest. And we still don't have the seer. So far, I've done a pretty poor job." Nonetheless, he felt a warmth creeping back with painful slowness to some inner part of him: his heart, perhaps.

"Thing is," said Skapti with a note of apology, "none of us really believed that part, minimal losses and so on. Proper battle, men do die. You'd never manage it without some casualties. Sounded fine, though; gave us courage. We trust you, Thorvald. It's the second part of the promise that matters. Find the seer. Lead us tomorrow, take Foxmask, and then come home and put things right. Say you'll do it. It's what he needs to hear."

At that moment Hogni began to convulse again, this time

more wildly, and Thorvald found himself leaning across the violently arching body while Einar held the poisoned man's legs and Skapti, sobbing, made his embrace of support into one of control, pinioning his brother's arms to his body. By the time the spasm was over, Thorvald realized he could no longer stem the flow of his tears. He lifted one of the big guard's hands and held it to his own wet cheek.

"Hogni," he said quietly, "I hope you can hear me. I don't know if I can do a good job. I think I might be just like Asgrim all over again. Chances are I will be. All I can say is, I promise to give it my best effort. I hope that's enough for you. And you're a lucky man. You've got the finest brother and the most loyal set of comrades a fellow could ever hope for. Rest well now, big warrior. Thor waits for you; his call rings strong in your ears. Rest now."

They took their turns then, one by one, in between the cruel convulsions that twisted Hogni's body ever more strongly, to say their good-byes with a word, a touch: all simple, all powerful, each one a blessing in its own way. When they were finished, they sat again, silent in their circle, and at last the spasms died down, and Hogni lay still and quiet as a sleeping child in his brother's arms. The moon was past full, but bright and cold; it shone on the dying warrior's strong, blunt features and softened the pain in his small eyes, the deep furrows of endurance around his tight mouth. It looked down in silence on the moment when the mouth relaxed at last, and the eyes grew fixed, and the hands opened, gently releasing their grip on his brother's.

Skapti had wept all his tears. He laid Hogni down, covered his face with a cloak, and sat beside him, legs stretched out, eyes closed in complete exhaustion. For a long time nobody spoke. Then Einar told them it was time to relieve the fellows on guard, and Ranulf and Hjort went off to do it, while the others shifted and stretched and handed around a water bottle.

Thorvald rose to his feet, regarding his men. It was necessary to say something now, quickly, before their expectations formed into more than a general desire to retain him as leader. They wouldn't be pleased, not in the short term;

too bad, they'd need to get used to accepting his decisions, even the ones that seemed wrong at first.

"Men?" he said quietly. Their heads turned; in an instant, he had their full attention. "I'll keep this short," Thorvald told them. "We're four men down, and we still don't have the seer. I've no intention of losing any more of you; I'm going to need all the support I can get back at Council Fjord. I have every intention of capturing Foxmask. I will not sail home without him. I will not let Hogni's sacrifice, and Svein's and Alof's and Helgi's, be for nothing. It's been a high price to pay; I will accept no less than victory in return. Now here's what we're going to do. As soon as it's light enough, Paul will arrange two teams to bring Svein's and Helgi's bodies back down. Alof must be relinquished to the sea; he lies beyond our reach. The rest of you are heading straight back to the boats at dawn. Once our fallen comrades are safe on board, you're going home. There will be no more losses here. We must look to the future, a future in which all of you have a role in rebuilding this broken community."

"Hang on," said Skolli. "That doesn't make sense. How can the seer be taken if we just up and go? The Fool's Tide will stay calm until dusk tomorrow if it follows the usual pattern. We needn't give up before afternoon."

"We're not giving up," Thorvald said, feeling his lips stretch in a mirthless smile. "We're merely offering the enemy a little of his own favorite tactic: surprise."

"You mean we hide the boats somewhere and come back in?" Paul asked.

"*You* don't," Thorvald said. "You, and Einar, and Skapti, and the rest of you do just what I say. You turn your backs on the Isle of Clouds and sail home to Council Fjord. You quit this shore for the last time. I give you my word that you will never have to endure the hunt again."

There was a silence while this sank in. Nobody seemed quite prepared to ask the obvious question. In the end it was Skapti who spoke, Skapti who still sat sprawled, eyes closed, beside his brother's body.

"And what'll you be doing?" he asked pointedly. "Plan-

ning a little solitary heroism? Think we'd let you get away
with that?"

Thorvald smiled. "Me, a hero? Hardly. I have a plan. Sam
and I will stay, with one boat. Paul's guess was half right.
We'll hide, and wait. I've a good idea where the seer may be;
I think I came close to finding him today, before the enemy
took Svein and Hogni. But I plan no heroics, no solo cliff
scaling, no spectacular feats of arms, I assure you. Merely
surprise. What the enemy will see is our departure, followed
by a long period during which all is quiet. I plan to wait until
they are quite certain we are gone and the seer is safe. I plan
to wait until they come out into the open. Then I will capture
the child and sail for home."

"Hmm," said Orm. "How long is a long period?"

"Until the day after tomorrow, if need be," Thorvald said.
"Until the enemy knows the Fool's Tide is no longer safe to
cross."

Einar whistled. "That's insane, Thorvald! Nobody gets
over the Fool's Tide after the days of calm are past! Why do
you think we only hunt once each summer?"

"Sam's a fine sailor," Thorvald said with a great deal
more confidence than he felt. "This is the only way. Now,
those are my plans. And my orders. Collect our dead, see
they reach the boats, look out for your comrades on the way
down, and be off as early as you can. Knut will sail the *Sea
Dove*. Einar will be in charge. There are to be no more
deaths. Any questions?"

"I've got one," Skolli said. "Don't you think the enemy
will be watching us when we sail off? Counting boats, if
not men? If you plan to get home, you'll need to keep one
boat in the anchorage here; how can that be secret? They'll
move down and slaughter the two of you the moment you
make an appearance."

"Sam's working on that," Thorvald told him with more
confidence than he felt. "While we've been up here, he and
Knut have been exploring the shoreline, looking for other
bays, trying to find the enemy's own craft. They've got to
have one or two; how else do they fish? If we can, we plan

to get away in one of theirs. As for staying unseen, there are only two of us, and we'll be careful."

"Odin's bones, Thorvald," Skapti growled, "first you say you'll lead us, and the next moment you're sending us all away and doing it on your own. Give us a chance, can't you? We want to help. We owe it to him," he glanced at Hogni's still form, "and to the other lads we've lost. How can you do it, just the two of you? Sam's no fighter, for all he may think so."

"You've got a job," Thorvald told him. "You need to get Hogni home and make sure he's sent to greet the Warfather in the way he'd want it done. Same for the others. Besides, you're one of my leaders. The fellows will need you on the boats, and on the other side. Those are my orders, Skapti."

"We'd all stand and fight beside you, if you'd let us," Einar said. "But staying after the water changes, that's madness. Won't you think again?"

"It's the only way," Thorvald said. "I never thought my heart would dictate my path for me, but this time it's giving me a sure message. I'll take Foxmask and I'll bring him back. Not by battle, not by hunting, not by cleverness. Just by waiting. You must trust me."

"We do," said Einar heavily. "What about Asgrim? What do we tell him?"

"Tell him whatever you like," Thorvald said. "The truth would be good. Tell him a Ruler of these isles will never again attempt to buy peace at the price of a girl's life. Tell him there are going to be changes."

"You'll stay on, then?" Skapti's voice was still hoarse with weeping. "Even after this?"

"First I have to deal with Foxmask. Afterward there will be time to speak of other things. Now rest, and think of home. Those of us who have led you will stand guard awhile and keep vigil for our fallen brothers. Tomorrow you leave this shore for the last time. That is my promise to you."

Then the men lay down, or settled with their backs against the rocks, and Thorvald and Skapti kept watch at the south end while Einar and Orm stood at the north. The moon passed across, remote and pale, and it seemed at times a faint music echoed from her cool, distant form, not so much a song as the memory of one, an eerie, half-caught vibration of the air, subtle, beguiling, frightening in its power. The song crept into the head of every man there, touching his dreams, sifting his thoughts, making him sigh or moan or stop his ears with his fingers. Some of the younger men wept, afraid; others comforted them with muttered words. Wieland had his hands over his face, though he sat still as a stone.

At the southern guard point, Skapti stared out into the night, silent. As for Thorvald, who stood close by, his mind was a turmoil of dark thoughts. He was a leader after all; it seemed he was wanted, respected, loved even. That set a warmth to the heart, a flush to the cheek; it put fine words on the lips, words that paid fitting tribute to the men's loyalty. And he could take Foxmask. He knew it, not with his intellect but deep in the belly, as an animal knows its chosen prey. He could and would succeed; all that he needed was patience, and Sam's ability to get them across the Fool's Tide. Of course, there was the possibility that Sam and Knut had not found a vessel for the taking. If that were so, he'd have to use one of their own, a small one, and hope the enemy wasn't counting. They would manage, one way or another.

It was not this part of it that clawed at his mind and would not let him savor the joy of knowing he was, after all, accepted and valued for what he was among this fellowship of men. It was *afterward* that troubled him. He knew how he wanted it to be: himself as leader, supported by the wisest of them, Einar, Orm, Wieland, a council that would govern fairly. Peace, prosperity, attention to the best practices for fishing and farming, a treaty with the Unspoken; later on, better ships, trade with the Light Isles and farther afield . . . Oh yes, he had no trouble seeing his future and theirs, a bright prospect stretching before them. He could do it; they could do it.

There was just one flaw in that enticing picture. He was

Asgrim's son: Somerled's son. While that gave him some kind of claim as Ruler, it also stamped him with his father's legacy. Somerled had acquired power of this kind in the Light Isles, and used it to kill, to destroy, to ride roughshod over what had existed there since ancient times, for no better reason than his own quest for absolute authority. Somerled had come here and sought power again under a different name. As Asgrim, he had led his people into a spiral of loss and defeat, heartbreak and waste. Thorvald was that man's son. He was made in Somerled's mold; he had felt it in his blood, this darkness, this fierce urge for recognition, for control. It had made him blind to Creidhe's peril. It had made him cruel to his mother. At heart, he was just like his father: give him enough power and he might well kill and wreck and burn just as Somerled had done. Who was to say he might not play cruel games with folks' lives just as Asgrim had done, the man who had sold his own daughter? Sula had been Thorvald's half-sister: strange, to think of that. And the boy, what had they said his name was, Erling? A kind of brother. He had never had a brother, nor a sister. He did not suppose the lad had lasted long, here in the harsh environment of the Isle of Clouds. Not if he was a dreamer as they'd said. The natives would have made quick work of him. But the child he had stolen away still lived. Thorvald sensed it. He thought he had heard it, a tiny sound from that cave this afternoon, like a sleepy sigh. He was sure it was not a bird; he was sure it was not his imagination. Death had intervened before he could investigate further; Thorvald's curiosity had killed Hogni, immobilized as the big man was by the need to hold the rope firm. Thorvald had made his comrade into a standing target.

So, he had to go on. He owed it to Hogni; he owed it to all of them. He had to go on, and if he turned into his father all over again, he'd just have to hope that someone had the gumption to finish him off before he did too much harm. Or that he would know when to end it himself. He had no loyal friend to send him off into exile when he grew into a danger. Sam would go home. Creidhe was dead. He was alone among his men, alone with the prospect of a power that thrilled and terrified him. How can a man not become his father? How can he find the strength to deny the blood that courses through his veins, dark and compelling, tugging at the mind, filling the heart, polluting the spirit? Without Creidhe to steady him, without Sam to anchor him, how could he ever travel this path and not lead them all into darkness?

TWELVE

Set your quill down, Brother; cover your ink pot.
This text is graven on the heart
With knife and blood.

MONK'S MARGIN NOTE

As the light began to fade on the second day, Creidhe forced her cramped limbs to obey her and moved to gather their meager supplies together. It had been quiet for a long time; only the piping songs of birds could be heard above the sound of the waterfall. Today no stones had fallen, no careless boot had disturbed the crumbling rocks above their cavern. She had heard no shouting, no whispers, no furtive exchanges. Nothing: it was as if the Isle of Clouds were deserted save for herself and the child. Her heart was faltering and a chill had possessed her, though she kept her expression calm for Small One's sake. If what her dreams told her was truth, she knew she would have to make her own way out of this precarious hiding place; she would have to ensure the child climbed safely back along the impossible ledge across which Keeper had brought them. The supplies must also be transported out. If he did not return, she must do it. If he did not return, her heart would break.

She'd had plenty of time to imagine a future on the island, just herself and Small One, braving the winter storms, the hunger, the loneliness. She had considered the alternative: giving the child up for the ritual maiming that would probably kill him. Increasingly, that had been on her mind. It could never be; she would not allow it. Creidhe drew a deep, shuddering breath, and closed her eyes. *I know now. I know why you fight so fiercely for him. And if I must, I will do what you did. He deserves no less.* A lonely life; a hard life. She had been so lucky, so rich in comforts. Last spring, before she stepped onto the *Sea Dove* and into a different world, she'd have been shocked to think of spending two days and a night quite silent in a tiny cave, using a bucket to relieve herself, eating nothing but a mess of cold fish that was definitely past its best. At home, she had taken her soft woolen blankets for granted. She had prided herself on the fine meals she had cooked to please her father, never really thinking just how fine it was to have flour and butter and vegetables at hand whenever you wanted them.

Small One was ready. He had folded his blanket neatly and put on his shoes. He watched her solemnly, a wary expression in his deep green eyes. The low light of late afternoon crept through the cavern's opening, touching his pale features with the semblance of a healthy color. Creidhe had spent some time working on the child's hair, having little else to keep her hands busy, and now it stood out from his fragile skull in a fine, dark nimbus. She noticed that Small One had replaced the scraps of weed and little feathers she had combed out.

The Journey was rolled up and ready to go; her bag was neatly fastened. Her own blankets were folded by the wall, the buckets covered. She would wait a little longer. Not too long; the summer days stretched out, but they must still reach the clifftop and make their way across the island to the shelter before it was too dark. Climbing up there, Creidhe thought dryly, was going to have a lot more to do with prayer and gritted teeth than with skill. Small One would be safer in his animal form: a pity she could not bid him change.

Just a little longer, and now that it was so late, surely past the time when the Fool's Tide must change back again, making safe passage to Council Fjord an impossibility until next summer, they might as well sit near the opening and let the sun touch their faces. She settled, leaning back against the rock wall and gazing out to the south where the islands of the Unspoken arose like huge, dark whales from the sea. Small One crouched beside her, clutching his blanket. They made no sound; they had promised to be quiet until Keeper returned, and perhaps, despite all her misgivings, despite Small One's earlier anxiety, the impossible might still happen. She would wait until she could wait no longer.

Creidhe found her mind turning in patterns like a child's, making bargains with the spirits that were no less heartfelt for their foolishness. Long ago, it had been: *If I stitch this seam perfectly, perhaps Father will let me ride to Stensakir with him tomorrow. If I lend Brona my best shawl, even though I know she'll probably lose it, maybe Thorvald won't be cross with me anymore.* Now, crazily, it was: *If I am patient, if I don't cry, if I believe, then perhaps Keeper will not be dead. Please let him not be dead.*

Small One's features showed neither apprehension nor hope. He simply sat waiting for what might come. So entangled was Creidhe in the dark web of her thoughts that in the event Keeper caught her quite by surprise, swinging around the entry silent as a shadow, dropping to crouch by Small One and touch a long, dirty hand to the child's fine hair, to bestow a kiss on his pale brow, and then turning toward her with a smile that was all dazzling white teeth and eyes alight with joy.

"It is over," he said simply. "They are gone."

Then Creidhe saw the rough binding around his left arm, where blood stained the rags, and the livid bruise on his temple, and she struggled to speak, but could find only a wordless sound of relief, love and confusion. No tears: she had promised herself that. She would be strong, as these two were.

"Come, dear ones," Keeper said. "We will go home now."

The impossible ledge, then, was traversed with feet light as a gull's, the cliff face scaled as if on wings. His hand in hers was like an anchor, like a song, like the touch of the sun after a long, cold winter. The day was suddenly beautiful. When they reached the top Keeper paused, still grasping her hand, to gaze out over the water, turning his back to the setting sun, narrowing his eyes toward Council Fjord.

"Can you see them?" Creidhe asked, a shadow touching her, for there was another question to be asked, and its answer could quench her elation instantly.

"No, Creidhe. They sailed very early, soon after dawn. I thought it was a trick, designed to flush me out, leave me open to attack. So I waited. There was work to be done here; I have cleansed the island of their presence."

She did not ask if he had added trophies to his wall. It did not take much imagination to picture how his day had been spent.

"Are you sure, then, that they are really gone?"

"They are gone. I have watched, and counted the boats as they sailed away. All have left these shores, your companions' vessel among them. And now the Fool's Tide is calm no more; there will be no safe passage across the strait before next summer. It is our time of peace."

Small One had made his way up the cliff unaided. He stood at a distance, himself staring out to sea, but he faced southward, toward the isles of the Unspoken. He appeared quite calm. After his first, clinging response to his kinsman's return, he had shown no sign of emotion. And now Creidhe had to ask the question.

"Thorvald," she forced the word out. "Was he here? Did you—?" It was not quite possible to put this into words. She shivered, seeing Keeper's eyes narrow, his mouth tighten.

"He was here. He led them; they followed his orders."

"*Thorvald?*" This could not be true; surely Keeper had got it wrong. "Thorvald is no warrior. Besides, we don't even belong here—"

"He was their leader, Creidhe. A capable leader: the Long Knife people fight better for him than they ever did for Asgrim. Still, I am here, and they are gone."

"Keeper, you must tell me. Did you—?"

He regarded her solemnly. "I did not kill your friend," he said, "although I could have done. There were four men in his party; I accounted for two and let the others take their chances with the island. He lives, and is gone from here."

There was nothing to say. Relief washed over her, closely followed by regret, confusion, even a kind of tender amusement as she saw the look on Keeper's face, where pride and jealousy were both evident in the bright eyes, the thin line of the mouth. And under it all, desire: a dark urging that would, very soon, be strong enough to overrun all of those other feelings. Here on the island there was nothing to get in its way, no customs, no family, no expectations. She felt its tide within her, and read its reflection on Keeper's face as they turned to walk back down to their old shelter. She knew it in the touch of his hand on her waist as he helped her down a steep incline; she heard it in his breathing and in her own. This had almost been denied them; the stark images of her dreams had made its fulfillment seem impossible. That it was granted despite those visions of death and loss would make their union sweeter still.

He had prepared for her return, and the child's; he had not come to fetch them until all was ready. The fire burned between the flat stones, and fresh fish were laid out ready for cooking. There was warm water. He had said to her, *We will go home*, and that was how it felt, in this last corner of the world, where the walls were the ancient stones that made the island's fabric, and the smoke-hole opened to a sky now dimming to the indefinable color of the long summer dusk. Keeper took out his knife and prepared the fish; Small One sat opposite, cross-legged, solemn, watching. And Creidhe, observing that Keeper had not set out his own blanket but left it crumpled in a corner, took his, and hers, and rolled them out side by side. He glanced at her, eyes bright, saying nothing.

"Will you let me clean that wound for you, while the fish is cooking?"

"It's nothing."

"Will you let me do it?"

"If you wish."

He was oddly diffident about it, and when Creidhe began

the process she understood why. It was not the wound itself, a deep gash probably inflicted by an arrow: that was easily washed and dressed with a strip torn from an ancient garment Keeper had produced. The problem was the closeness, the touching, especially once he removed his shirt to allow her access to the well-muscled arm the arrow had sliced. Her hands shook; his breathing faltered. His other arm came around her, his fingers stroked her hair; her lips touched his bare shoulder, her eyes closed as she tasted the salt sweetness of his skin. The fish sizzled on the coals; Small One sat silent, watching gravely.

"I wanted you last night," Keeper whispered. "In the darkness, I wanted you. I tried to put you from my thoughts, but could not."

"Nor I, you," Creidhe murmured, her hand creeping around his waist, feeling the warmth of his lean body.

"I wonder if you are able to tie a knot," Keeper said, "or whether I must fasten this bandage myself."

"You're laughing at me." Creidhe was a little taken aback. She forced herself to return to the task in hand, a blush rising to her cheeks.

"I have offended you?" Now he was looking wary again, shy as a wild creature. If there were rules for this, Creidhe thought, he had never had the opportunity to learn them; he had been twelve years old when he left his tribe for this life of exile.

"Terribly," Creidhe said with mock gravity, managing to tie the ends of the bandage and tuck them in reasonably neatly. "Perhaps you should find another shirt, if you have one. It's customary to dress up on such a night. And I would like a little time alone, if I may. I'll keep an eye on the fish."

Keeper nodded, solemn as an owl. He rose and, taking Small One's hand, made his way out of the hut without another word.

It was, Creidhe realized, her wedding night. She had imagined such a time over and over as she sat dreaming before her loom. She had pictured herself in skirt and tunic of fine wool, woven in a warm, soft blue, with a narrow border of heart's-eye. It would be spring, and she would wear a circlet of matching flowers on her head. She would wash her hair with chamomile and brush it until it shone. Brona would help her get ready; her family would watch with pride as the vows were spoken. There would be music and dancing and feasting; one of Zaira's cakes, for certain. Later, in the quiet of the bedchamber, the undressing, the sweet exchange of touches . . . before, she had not really thought so much of what came after that. There had been a kind of blur between that moment and the waking to the dawn, warmed by her husband's body and the blue blanket. Those dreams were a girl's fantasy, lovely but unreal. They were as far from tonight as the earth is from the stars. Even the man in them had been wrong.

Tonight there was no wedding finery; there were no herbs to cleanse the hair and body; no woolen coverlets, no soft bed. There was only the night and the island. Creidhe stripped off her clothes and, shivering, washed as quickly as she could in the remnants of the warm water. She could not even change her shift. She rubbed herself dry on one of the old cloaks and struggled back into the skirt and tunic Keeper had made for her. The fish was cooking well; she turned it on the coals. She loosed her hair and combed it out, then gathered it with a cord at the nape of the neck, letting it fall down her back unplaited. That was it: a bride's preparation. She lifted the fish in its wrapping of weed and set it on a platter, wondering vaguely if she would ever eat bread again.

When the others returned, Keeper was wearing a different shirt. It was much like the first, old and ill-fitting, but bore no bloodstains. He had washed his face and hands in the stream, and had made an effort to tidy his wild hair. He stood in the entry, hesitant, with Small One a step behind him.

"You look—very handsome," Creidhe said, studying him. "I'm proud of you. I wish I could take you home to meet my parents; that's the way it's done, usually. But all the family we have here is Small One. Shall we eat this fish?"

Keeper said nothing, but his eyes, fixed on her, spoke for

him well enough. *You are my goddess.* That look silenced
Creidhe; it robbed her of any appetite for the fish, though
she made herself eat it. He had taken some pains to ensure
this feast was ready and his hearth warm for her, even after
two grueling days of battle. She would not hurt him for the
world.

"Strange," he observed after a while. "I cannot eat."

"No," said Creidhe. "Yet the fish is very good."

"I cannot eat," Keeper said again, eyes bright. "And yet,
there is a hunger in me. A fierce hunger."

"Yes," Creidhe whispered. "I feel it too. We have a child
to put to bed first."

The moon was waning now. Nonetheless, tonight it
seemed Small One had a need to watch its progress across
the sky, and to greet it once more with song. Creidhe had
expected the child would be exhausted after the tension and
discomfort of that time of waiting, worn out with worrying
about Keeper's safety, glad to be back in the hut and curling
up in his own corner once more. She had expected him to
fall asleep the moment he finished his supper. Instead, he
left the shelter and went to sit on the rocks outside, straight-
backed and small, with the moon shining in his strange
eyes. Creidhe had made the mistake of forgetting, briefly,
that this was not an ordinary six-year-old. One could not
begin to imagine what visions the small seer had in his
head, what tides of feeling flowed in his spirit. His song began softly, with a sadness in the shape of it. It was no anthem of victory, no triumphant tale of another hunt won,
another dark trial survived. It was a lament. Perhaps the
wordless music told of what could not be; perhaps it remembered the men who had shed their blood on the island
this summer, and all the years before. Creidhe did not know.
She watched Keeper across the fire, and he gazed steadily
back at her. Neither made a move. Both recognized that
they could not touch again until Small One slept, for to do
so now was too dangerous. Once their hands clasped again,
once their lips met, once their bodies pressed close, there
could be no stopping the fire that had sprung up between

them until it burned to its natural conclusion. And that, thought Creidhe, might be quite a quick process once they allowed it to begin. Not that she had any experience of such matters, but it seemed to her that holding back was going to be an impossibility.

Small One's song sounded through the night air, piercing and sorrowful, telling of loss and loneliness, of hurt and misunderstanding and waste. Creidhe bowed her head; it did not seem right for her heart to be so full of joy, for her body to glow thus with anticipation, while the child gave voice to this music of deepest melancholy.

"Always he sings thus, after the hunt," Keeper whispered. "Always the same. It is not for you and me."

"Then who is it for? Himself?"

"Perhaps. There are no words in it; I think each listener takes a different message. He is sad, maybe, because the hunt must continue, year after year."

"Or for the men killed," Creidhe suggested.

Keeper spat on the ground at his side. "They are nothing," he said, his voice held quiet as the child's song rang on, out in the night. "Why would he grieve for them?"

Creidhe did not answer, for to do so honestly would be to cause bitter offense to Keeper, and she would not wound him, not ever. Especially not tonight. But she asked herself a question in silence, a question that had no good answer. *If he is so sad, does that not mean he wishes the hunt had ended differently? Perhaps all he wants is to go home. And perhaps, for him, home is not the Isle of Clouds.* This powerful creature, whose song traveled straight to the heart, was at the same time just a little boy. How could he understand what the Unspoken intended for him? How could he know that to travel back to his birthplace, the wellspring of his wisdom, was to give up sight and movement, perhaps to sacrifice his life before ever he grew to be a man? The yearning to return seemed to her a powerful part of the song. Promises were difficult and perilous things. Just possibly, what held the seer to the Isle of Clouds was no more than a child's undertaking to his brother, to be quiet, to be good.

* * *

"What in Odin's name is *that*?" hissed Sam, who was struggling to find a comfortable position for his long-limbed body in the depression under the rocks where the two men had sheltered for the night. "It sounds like those voices they're always talking about, the ones that come to steal souls. If we ever get back across that wretched strait and then home, I'll take great pleasure in personally throttling you, Thorvald, you stubborn wretch. Give me an honest storm on the open sea any day." He put his hands over his ears and squeezed his eyes shut. "It's as if it's right inside my head. No wonder Asgrim's people are so frightened. This is a cursed place, and I can't imagine how you bullied me into staying. When I agreed to that, I didn't know we were letting the others take the *Sea Dove*."

Thorvald sat cross-legged, straight-backed, maintaining his calm by careful breathing, though that distant, piercing song threatened the balance of his thoughts, speaking as it did of death, blood and errors. "You're the best sailor in the Light Isles, Sam," he said. "Of course you can get us back to Council Fjord. Of course you can do it. Even in *that*."

He jerked his head in the direction of the small boat hauled up on the shore not far from the place where they had concealed themselves. While Thorvald had led the men in their fruitless quest for the seer, Sam and Knut had followed their own set of orders. As Thorvald had suspected, the enemy had boats on the Isle of Clouds, hidden away in a narrow inlet whose only landward exit was a challenging climb up steep rock walls where sharp-beaked birds nested. Shallow hollows and indentations allowed the craft to be stored in semishelter. The boats had lain where they were a long time; it did not appear that the enemy ventured out to sea with any frequency. Nonetheless, all seemed efficiently maintained, some bearing signs of eccentric but effective repair work. Sam had chosen the strongest. There was one pair of oars and a sail of sorts. The vessel was small, light, a craft suited to shore fishing in calm seas. Beside the *Sea Dove* it was a gnat to a gull, a vole to a hunting dog. Thorvald sighed. Sam was right; in the *Sea Dove*, they might have had a fair chance of getting safely across the strait, even after the time of lull was over. In this shell of wattle, driftwood and skin, they'd need every scrap of seamanship they had, which in his case was next to nothing, and every bit of luck the gods deigned to bestow upon them. It had been the only way, however. The *Sea Dove* was large, strong, conspicuous among the flotilla of smaller boats. The enemy wasn't stupid. To count craft coming in and craft going out was only common sense, as Einar had pointed out. The number of boats would match. The number of men would not, but Thorvald thought that hardly mattered. They had lost four; if one or two more had disappeared before the vessels quit the shore for the last time, it was unlikely the enemy would notice it, or if they did, understand what it meant. To remain here once the Fool's Tide had ceased to be navigable was, on the face of it, utter stupidity. The rest of Thorvald's campaign, though unsuccessful in its primary objective, had not been foolishly planned or carelessly executed. They had gained ground; they had lost far fewer men than was usual for Asgrim; they had retreated in orderly fashion and sailed away with no further casualties. The enemy would judge him on that; this foe would have no idea of the surprise that awaited him. Them. How many were there? Ten, five, as few as three? Few, Thorvald thought, very few. Given the right moment, he knew he and Sam, between them, could take the seer.

"*Shut up, shut up,*" muttered Sam, hands clapped over his ears. He was the picture of misery, huddled in his cloak, eyes squeezed shut as if, by not seeing, he might cease to be tormented by that eldritch voice.

"Sam," said Thorvald, "don't forget, I owe you a favor. I did promise, remember, when I offered to pay, and you said no."

Sam growled something.

"What?"

"I said, forget it." Sam's tone was constrained, almost angry. "What I had in mind can't happen now. Forget favors. If I reach home in one piece, I'll be content enough."

"What did you have in mind?" Thorvald asked. Not only was he curious, but he, too, welcomed the distraction from the song that echoed in his mind as if to awaken all that lay hidden there.

"Nothing," growled Sam. After a moment's silence, he added, "Creidhe's gone. You can't bring her back, so you can't repay the favor. Now let's drop the subject, shall we?"

Thorvald was silenced. Life was full of small surprises. With the music drifting around him, he allowed himself to dwell, briefly, on another kind of future, one that might have been expected if there had been no voyage, no battle, no Long Knife people, no Asgrim. It was a life that followed a pattern such as fellows like Sam welcomed, a life in which one worked and wed and raised children, in which one farmed or fished or participated in councils. He tried to imagine that cottage in Stensakir with both Sam and Creidhe in the doorway. He pictured Creidhe waiting on the jetty as the *Sea Dove* sailed in at dusk, Creidhe with Sam's child in her arms. That was stupid. Wrong. It made him angry to think of it.

"What's biting you?" Sam asked, eyes open and fixed on Thorvald in the shadows.

"Nothing," Thorvald snapped. He was annoyed with himself for losing control so easily, and over something so unimportant. Creidhe was dead; he had to accept that. Let Sam have his little dreams, then; they were harmless enough.

"Made you angry, I see that," Sam said flatly. "No point getting upset. It would never have happened, her and me. Doubly impossible, it was."

"Why's that?" Thorvald could not stop himself from asking.

"Well, it's obvious. Eyvind and Nessa were on the lookout for a suitable match for her, and another for Brona in a year or two's time. They weren't looking at fishermen, nor even at clever fellows such as yourself, Thorvald. It was chieftains and lords, the princes of the Caitt, maybe some petty king of the Dalriada. Stands to reason. Nessa's daughters carry on the royal line of the Folk; their sons could be some sort of kings, and since Nessa's got no boys of her own, that's doubly important. Who's going to choose me as the father of royalty? Dreams, that's all it was."

Thorvald felt his lips stretch in something approximating a smile. "Of course, we know Creidhe had a mind of her own," he commented. "If she had her eye on a certain fellow, I dare say she could talk even Eyvind around, given time."

There was a silence.

"Sam?"

No reply.

"Sam, what is it?"

"You know," Sam said in a tone that was oddly muffled, "for a clever man, you've got some remarkable blind spots. Creidhe, want me? Impossible. She never thought of me that way for a moment."

"You can't be sure—" Thorvald began, though privately he agreed with this.

"I can be sure, sure as I am that the sun goes down at night. Creidhe never had room in her heart for anyone but you. It made me sick sometimes to see all that love wasted on a man too wrapped up in his own concerns even to notice her. I'd have been there when she needed me. I'd have given her anything she wanted."

"Oh yes," Thorvald spat before he could stop himself, "a two-roomed cottage, and a husband who talked of nothing but fishing, and a new babe in her belly every spring: a fine sort of gift that would have been."

Once these words were out, he could not take them back. It became impossible to sit by his friend anymore. Thorvald got up and stumbled down the shore in the half-dark, to stand gazing across the murmuring water with his fists clenched tight. Curse friends, curse the island, curse that unsettling song that now swooped down to a plangent ending, leaving only its echo behind. Curse this cruel darkness within him that made him hurt those who sought only to tell him the truth. Curse his father for making him the man he was.

"Thorvald?" Sam had come down quietly to stand on the rocks by his side.

"Leave me alone."

"Best come back up," Sam said softly. "We could be seen here. No point in wrecking what little chance we have."

"Shut up."

"You're a man, not a child." Sam's voice was remarkably even.

"I don't want to talk about this." *And I will not shed tears, for you are right: I am a man.*

Sam waited a little, and then he said, "They're honest things. A house, food on the table, a babe in the cradle. You shouldn't scoff at them. They're the things Creidhe wanted. Even so, I knew I had no chance. Different for you. If you'd put your mind to it, you could have made a case for yourself: educated, clever, the son of a nobleman. Suitable enough, if the lady happens to favor you."

"Huh!" Thorvald attempted a nonchalant shrug. "Me? I'd have been bottom of Eyvind's list, well after you, my fine fisherman. He had only to look at who my father was to rule me right out of contention. Bad blood. You know what Somerled did in the Light Isles. You've seen what he's done here. I told you about Sula, and about Creidhe. That man's son is not husband material for the royal line of the Light Isles. He's not a fit partner for any woman. I'm sorry I spoke to you as I did. I can't swallow those words now. They were cruel and heartless, because that's what I am. I'm a man just like my father."

There was a brief pause, and then Sam said mildly, "That's the stupidest thing I ever heard. I don't believe it for a moment."

"It's true. I feel it like a shadow I carry inside me, which I can never overcome. I'm not a good person to have as a friend, Sam. You've only got to look at where we are and what we're doing to know that."

"Shall I tell you what I think?"

"If you have to. It can't change the truth."

"I think you bear no resemblance at all to Asgrim. I look at him and I see a tired, dispirited leader who's resorted to fear as his only way of keeping control; a man who's so worn down by defeat after defeat that he's lost sight of what's right. Why else would he give up his own daughter like that? I look at you and I see a clever, capable fellow who thinks about himself just a bit too much. A man who sets his standards high, and punishes himself if he doesn't quite match up to them. A man who keeps himself to himself and sometimes doesn't recognize that he needs his friends. A fellow who's afraid to laugh, afraid to love, afraid of his own heart, because it's the hardest thing to set controls on. You know what? I see a man who's very like his mother, and not at all like Asgrim. Not that you're Lady Margaret all over again, either. A man's himself, when it comes down to it. It's our own path to make, Thorvald, it's not governed by some quirk of our ancestry. You've started to move ahead here. I saw the way the fellows looked at you yesterday. You've started to change things, change them for the better. I'm sorry Creidhe's not here to see that. I'm sorry you'll never get the chance to tell her what you told me: that losing her was like losing part of yourself. Oh yes, I remember that; how could I not? Now come on, we should get back under cover. That wretched singing's stopped, and we're a lot more likely to attract attention standing out here talking. And I do want to get home. There's a powerful wish in me to sit before my little hearth fire again."

"Even without Creidhe?"

Sam did not reply, and after a while the two of them went back up to the overhang and settled uncomfortably into the meager shelter it offered. They could hear the sea grumbling to itself, the perilous message of the Fool's Tide. There was no need to speak of tomorrow; they had planned it carefully, and each knew his part. In time, Sam fell into a half-sleep, but Thorvald sat wakeful, the sound of the waves a background to his recall of Sam's astonishing speech.

Sam was a simple man and saw things in simple terms. One did not expect a deep analysis of one's own situation from such a man. One did not expect him to expose, in clear and uncompromising terms, what was undoubtedly the truth. A kind of truth anyway. If one could believe it to be the whole story, one might find a great deal of reassurance in it. Hope, almost. Such feelings were somewhat strange to Thorvald; they did not visit him often. He was not entirely sure that he welcomed them. He sat quietly in the darkness, pondering this and waiting for morning.

Worn out by the power of his inner voice, the child fell asleep as soon as he lay down. Keeper and Creidhe stood watching him for a little. Now that the moment was here, Creidhe felt a strange uncertainty, for despite the clear messages her body had been giving her for some considerable time now, this was new territory, uncharted waters, and she was not entirely sure of the best way to move forward. She knew the basic elements, of course; she had grown up on a farm. She knew a few of the subtleties, too, for Eyvind and Nessa had been a fine pattern, a tender, comfortable example. She had seen their care for each other, their sweet touches, and the messages their eyes carried, still full of passion and promise even now, with five children born and years of service to the islands' community shared. All the same, to know something in theory does not necessarily mean one can do it with confidence. She felt, in a word, shy.

"What you said," Keeper's tone indicated he shared her confusion, "about it being customary to wash and change our clothes, I mean . . . I think perhaps there should be more to it. If I remember well."

"More?"

"Words," he said. "Words of a promise. Should there not be that? A ring, or other token?"

Creidhe smiled, seeing his pallor and the dark solemnity of his eyes. It was she who must take the initiative here and move things along, nerves or no nerves. "There are words," she told him. "You must take my hands, like this, and then we should say what we vow to each other, what we promise." All of a sudden, as Keeper folded her small hands within his long, thin ones, she became very still, aware that his seriousness was entirely appropriate. This moment was a turning point; it was the end of *I*, the beginning of *we*. To experience such a moment was to give a precious gift, and to receive one in return.

"You must speak first." Keeper's voice was constrained. "I do not know what to say."

The words came unsought; Creidhe spoke quietly, for Small One lay curled in his blankets not two paces from where they stood with hands clasped and eyes locked. "I promise that I will be yours, and love you, and stand by you as long as we live," she said, her voice shaking.

Keeper cleared his throat nervously. "I swear that I will guard you and love you always," he said. "That I will cherish and protect you. My walls will shelter you, my hearth fire warm you, my feet walk beside yours until our journey's ending. I give you my solemn vow."

"I thought you said you didn't know what to say," Creidhe whispered. "That was beautiful. Now you've made me cry."

"Oh, no—oh, no, please don't—"

Alarmed, Keeper put up a hand to wipe away the tear that rolled down her cheek, and was immediately encircled by her arms, for she could not hold back any longer. Her lips against the hollow of his neck, her whole body on fire, she murmured, "We should not end it thus, with our vows half spoken. I would say, I swear this by stone and star . . ." Her mouth brushed his skin, drunken with delight. She felt his hands stroking her back, then pressing her hard against him. And she heard his words, still tender and shy, for all the power in his lean, strong frame.

"I swear it by wind and wing. This promise binds me until death, and beyond. You are my dear one, my goddess, my wife."

"And you are my lover and my husband, the other part of me. And I think it is time, at last, to try this . . ."

When it came to it, inexpert as they were, they managed

to work it out with no difficulty at all. Eager hands dealt swiftly with the impediments of tunic or belt or skirt; ardent lips imprinted their subtle message on the soft skin of shoulder, of breast, of the secret crevices of the body; breath turned to sigh, to gasp, to half-formed murmurings of love and need. It was true, neither had attempted this particular task before, but they were young and healthy, and they were made for each other. Through the narrow opening above the hearth, the waning moon gazed down on the fine patterns of it; his thin, rough hand tracing pathways on her pearly skin; her wheat-fair hair falling like a golden torrent across his wiry body; their lips clinging, teasing, tasting until, all too soon, there was no longer a possibility of delay, and they came together in dark, sweet urgency. Keeper moved as the sea moves, steadily, strongly, the fierce tide of his need held, somehow, in check by his reverence for her, his goddess, his wife all pink and gold and white as he had first seen her revealed by firelight, yet now, astonishingly, here in his arms, her cheeks flushed with passion, her lips, her hands, the soft readiness of her body inflaming his desire. And Creidhe, who might have expected a little pain, and perhaps some disappointment as is quite usual for a young woman on her wedding night, discovered with a warm flood of delight that in this, she was her father's daughter, generous in the gifts she gave her partner and robust in her enjoyment of those he bestowed in return. So, at last, he thrust hard, and she rose to meet him, and the two of them trembled and cried out as Keeper released himself deep inside her, and Creidhe's own body responded in arching, aching fulfillment. After that, they were silent. Dazed, shocked, disbelieving, they lay in each other's arms as their hearts gradually slowed from the ferocious drumbeat of that moment, and the moon shone above them, remote and impartial, and the small snuffle of the child's breathing was the only sound in the stillness of the summer night.

Keeper moved after a little, rolling to his back, ensuring Creidhe could rest her head on his shoulder and curl against him in what comfort was possible on the earth's hard bed.

He pulled the blanket up over her. And very soon she was sleeping like a child herself, her arm stretched across his chest, her hair a soft whisper against his skin, her lips curved in a secret smile. But Keeper was wakeful, staring up at the sky, and his thoughts were on tomorrow, and on next summer, and on all the years to come.

Creidhe woke early. For a little she lay still, considering the sensations in her body, the satisfied aching that was an entirely new feeling, Keeper's warmth against her, his breath against her brow, stirring her hair. He was sound asleep, curled around her as if in protection. It was cold in the hut; the fire had died down to a mound of powdery ash. And Small One was nowhere to be seen, his blanket scrunched in a heap, his boots set neatly by the wall in his own corner. Shivering, Creidhe crept from under the covers, careful not to wake Keeper, and struggled into her skirt and tunic, slinging a warm cloak over the top. She thrust her feet into the small boots that had once been Sula's. There were embers still glowing beneath the blanket of ash; she blew them to life, setting sprigs of dry heather on top to catch the first small flames. There was a supply of driftwood at hand, and turf as well; Keeper was a good provider.

She shuddered, thinking how it would have been if her visions had proved true and he had fallen to Asgrim's forces in the hunt. How could she have managed, alone here with the frail child through the winter? The thought of that was terrifying. Keeper was a man, strong and capable, skilful and clever. Above all, he possessed a powerful will for his self-appointed mission. But he had been twelve years old when he came here, a child himself. How could one ever comprehend such fierce commitment, such single-minded dedication to this life of struggle and sacrifice? He had lived it alone, but for his small, silent kinsman: alone all these long years with the wind and storm, the stark cliffs and the pounding seas. Perhaps it was the blood he bore, his mother's blood, that made such endurance possible. She had been of the Seal Tribe, that race held in both awe and

fear by the folk of Creidhe's homeland. The folk of the Seal
Tribe were alien, with their ability to exist on land or in the
ocean, their deep fear of iron, their bodies that were similar
to those of men and women, yet subtly different. But for his
strange, long fingers, his pallor and his deep, changeable
eyes, Keeper seemed every bit a man; the joyful completion
Creidhe had experienced last night as she savored every
corner of his lean, muscular body, the way the two of them
had fitted so perfectly together, moving as one, seemed to
prove it without doubt. Perhaps he was more Asgrim's son
than his mother's child, though he would never recognize
that himself. It was not Keeper who was Other here, but
Small One, the seer whose mother had borne the blood of
both Seal Tribe and Long Knife people, and whose many
fathers were the men of the Unspoken, those who would
claim him as Foxmask and make him theirs forever by the
act of ritual maiming.

A chill passed through Creidhe as she knelt there. The
fire had caught the kindling and was burning with a reassuring brightness, setting a warm, rosy light on Keeper's pale
features as he slept on. The hunt was over. They were safe
for now, this small family so newly yet so unmistakably
hers. But there would be other summers and other hunts.
Right now, she would feel happier if Small One were back
indoors where she could keep an eye on him. It must be
freezing cold outside, and he hadn't put his boots on. What
was he doing?

She went out into the morning. The mist clung low across
the land; she could see for a certain distance, perhaps
twenty paces, before the white curtains of damp veiled the
hillside completely. Small One, in his doglike form, stood a
little way down the slope, ears pricked up as if in anticipation. Creidhe opened her mouth to call him, then bit back
her words as shock froze her in place. Emerging through
the shreds of mist was a man, a tall, fair-haired man whom
she recognized, though the broad cheeks and sunny smile
that had marked Sam's countenance in Stensakir were now
replaced by a leaner, harder look, the look of a warrior. He
had a spear in his hand, and it was plain from the way he

gripped the shaft that he had learned how to use it. Small One turned tail and came pattering back toward her. And now, behind Creidhe and to the left, there was a tiny sound: a single footstep on the small stones of the hillside. She turned and met Thorvald's gaze where he stood not four paces away, bow drawn, mouth set grim, dark eyes wide in chalk-white face, their shocked expression no doubt a perfect reflection of her own. For what was this feeling that surged through her, delight or anguish? Sweet reunion or sheer, mindless terror?

They spoke as one, unsteadily, uttering each a single word: the other's name. Behind her Creidhe could hear Sam striding toward them, less careful now to be quiet; she could hear Small One's little, quick feet. An instant later Keeper was in the doorway of the hut, a look on his face that silenced all of them, for he had the appearance of some ancient, terrible force of nature, dark and implacable. He was completely naked, without weapon or defense, and yet Creidhe saw Thorvald take a step backward. At that moment the image seized her once more, chill and inevitable: it was not yesterday, in the hunt, it was now, this morning, it was true after all, the terrible vision the ancestors had shown her. One night, she had been given, and now the dark thing would unfold, and Small One would be taken. . . . Thorvald's grip on the bow had not wavered for an instant, not even at that moment of heart-stopping recognition. Now she saw his fingers move slightly, preparing to release the arrow straight into Keeper's chest. Now she saw the subtle movement of Keeper's right hand, where he held a little loop of leather, a single round stone, all there had been time to grab as he had awoken suddenly to danger. Behind her, Sam's steps drew closer. Small One now scampered around Creidhe's feet, apparently heedless of peril.

Even the ancestors must be wrong sometimes, surely, surely they could not be so cruel? It must be possible to change things. Why else had she felt such compulsion to come on this voyage? Thorvald's fingers tightened on the bowstring; Keeper's hand came back, ready to release the missile. Creidhe's voice was suddenly released.

"No!" she screamed, and flung herself forward, oblivious to all but the need to stop them, to save them, to save all of them, whatever the cost. She felt herself moving as if on wings, as if on the breath of the west wind, her hands outstretched, her feet hardly touching the earth, such was her fierce urgency. Then there was a searing pain in her left arm, and a numbing blow to her head, and she sank into darkness.

Thorvald was a leader. Even in such a moment, he would not allow himself to forget that. Creidhe lay crumpled on the stony ground. Blood flowed from her arm, where his own arrow had ripped her flesh, but it was that cleverly hurled stone that had felled her; she had taken the missile meant for him. Sam's face was contorted with anguish, he was about to cry out. With a sharp, economical gesture, Thorvald silenced him. They had a moment to act, no more. For the enemy was off guard. As Creidhe fell, the fellow had uttered a terrible cry like a wild creature's howl of pain, and leaped to her side, heedless of Thorvald and Sam closing in on him. Now he crouched over her limp form, cradling her head, his long fingers touching the place where the stone he had flung with his cunning sling of leather had struck her hard on the temple, raising a swollen, angry lump on the pale skin. His eyes seemed blinded by shock. His hands were visibly trembling, as if what he had done was the worst act of evil imaginable: as if he had brought down a goddess. Beside him the little dog stood watching, round-eyed and still.

Thorvald glanced at Sam and gave a nod. Sam took two steps forward, and as the wild-looking fellow started, awareness returning suddenly to his strange eyes, and began to rise to his feet, the butt of Sam's spear struck him on the back of the head and he sprawled senseless on the ground. The wind stirred his matted hair, its chill touch merciless in the cold, sharp light before dawn. The doglike creature moved closer, whining, and licked the fallen man's white face.

"Creidhe!" gasped Sam, casting the spear down, rolling the warrior's body away with his foot and kneeling to lift her in his arms. "Odin's bones, she was alive all this time, and a prisoner here!" He put his fingers to her neck, and bent his ear to her mouth. "Sweet Freya be praised, she's still breathing! Quick, we must stop this bleeding. What on earth did she think she was doing?"

Thorvald blinked back sudden tears. She was alive. His heart was seized by such a confusion of feelings he could not begin to make sense of them. Easier, then, simply to do those things he knew must be done. Even now, even after this, there was still a mission, and he could not move on until it was completed. "The seer," he croaked. "We have to find the seer . . ."

"What?" Sam's voice was a snarl. He was tearing a strip from his shirt, big hands deft, binding the slicing wound on Creidhe's arm, taking off his cloak to wrap it around her shoulders. Her hair, unbound, flowed across his knees like a stream of gold.

"We have to find him. He must be close. I'm not leaving here without him." Turning his back, Thorvald stooped to enter the little hut, where a neat fire burned between stones. The interior was crude but bore signs of domesticity: there was fish ready for cooking, cloaks hanging from the walls, pots and pans. There was space for sleeping. He saw the way that was laid out, the tumbled blankets where it was clear two had lain but recently, and room for another on the far side, one that wore child-sized boots. He thought of Creidhe lying here at the mercy of that feral creature. All the evidence told him she had not only been captive in this hovel, but had been used: there was no doubt this primitive pallet had been the place where the fellow had had his satisfaction of her. Fury arose in him, nearly overwhelming the discipline he had learned to impose upon himself. He slung the bow on his back and drew the dagger from his belt. The enemy was only one. Deep inside him, he had sensed it all along. This man had condemned that honest soldier, Hogni, to a slow, cruel end by poison. This wretch had stolen Thorvald's dearest of friends, Creidhe, his loyal shadow, whom he had disregarded so many years, had snubbed and snarled at, not recognizing how he loved her until he believed her dead. And all this time she had been here, alive, and captive to this spawn of evil. This wicked creature had taken her, he had despoiled her, he had treated an innocent girl like any common whore. And now he would die. How could it be otherwise?

Thorvald stepped out of the hut. The fellow still lay motionless with the little dog standing anxiously by. Sam was wrapping Creidhe in his cloak. The expression on his face made Thorvald uneasy, for it was the look of a man who has made a decision and has no intention of having his mind changed for him.

Thorvald knelt by the fallen warrior, knife in hand. This would be instant: a simple drawing of blade across throat, and he would be avenged for Creidhe, for Hogni, for Svein and Alof and Helgi, for all of Asgrim's men who had died in the long years of the hunt. Easy: quick. The little dog whined again, staring at him with its odd, deep eyes in the neat, triangular face. By Thor's hammer, it was like no dog he had ever seen in his life, nor like a cat, nor yet quite like any creature he could recognize. It was like something from a tale of magic and mystery, something that did not belong in the world of men, old, wise, strange beyond belief . . . Thorvald felt the hair stand up on the back of his neck and a chill course through him as he gazed into the liquid depths of those eyes. By all the gods, he had it, the victory was his . . . He found he had been holding his breath, and let it out in a long, gusty sigh. His hand, clutching the dagger, was shaking like a leaf.

"Get on with it!" snapped Sam. "We're off back to Council Fjord and then straight home. Creidhe's hurt, and she's cold, and I'm getting her back to the Light Isles if I die in the attempt. A pox on your seer. I'm not giving him an instant more of my time. If you're going to finish that fellow off, just do it, will you, and let's be away down to the boat, for there's still a nightmare crossing ahead of us."

Sam was right, of course. By some miracle, Creidhe had
been restored to them, and he had another chance to get
things right, to tell her how he felt, to make up for his errors . . . They must get her to safety. He must act swiftly,
and go. Thorvald looked down at the fallen man's face, a
strong, thin face marked by a hard jaw, a tight mouth still
grim in unconsciousness, long dark lashes and unkempt
hair. He laid his knife against the naked throat, the fine
knife his men had made for him in token of his leadership,
a sign of their respect and trust. What was he waiting for?
He was a warrior, wasn't he? This should be as easy as
slaughtering a goat or sheep, easier in fact, since the victim
lay passive, offering his flesh for the sacrifice. But Thorvald's hand would not move. For in those grave, disciplined
features was the shadow of another man's face; this wild
fellow bore the mask of Asgrim in the jaw, the cheek, the
strength of the bones. This was the Ruler's son. This was
the youth who had stolen Foxmask long ago: the boy they
said had been a dreamer, with no talent for the games of
war. That boy had survived to become a man, and in the
process had taught himself to be a whole army. Such was
the strength he had possessed deep within: a fortitude to
marvel at. Furious hatred and a reluctant admiration warred
in Thorvald's heart. For what he had done, this man deserved death. There was no doubt what Skapti or Einar or
Skolli would have done here; would expect Thorvald to do.
But his hand was frozen; he could not make the weapon do
its work.

"Come on!" yelled Sam, an edge in his voice.

The doglike creature sidled closer. It was touching Thorvald's knee; he could feel a faint shivering coursing through
its body, almost like the movement of a body of water, a
trembling, constant vibration. Thorvald knelt motionless
with the knife in his hand. If this was Asgrim's son, it was at
the same time his own brother. He felt no bond of kinship;
indeed, he felt disgust, loathing, and a will to make an end
of the fellow and his acts of wanton violence. But he could
not kill his own brother. To do so was to prove himself in-

deed no better than the wretched Asgrim who had sired the
two of them, for was it not in penance for the act of fratricide that Somerled had been cast out of the Light Isles forever, to make his way by star and skerry to this distant
corner of the world? Here he had wrought his accursed life
anew as Asgrim, Ruler of the Isles.

Thorvald slid his dagger back in its sheath and rose
slowly to his feet. He was not his father. He was his own
man, and would make his own choices. As for this half-
brother who had caused such upheaval and loss, this savage
creature who had stolen Creidhe from him, he must take his
own chances.

"Thorvald!" yelled Sam. "I'm leaving right now, and if
you're not at the boat by the time I'm ready to sail, Creidhe
and I are going without you. I mean it."

He did, too; there was no denying the new note in his
voice, a note of determination and of hope reborn, despite
the voyage ahead. There was hope for himself as well, Thorvald thought, watching the strange, small creature as it
nudged the fallen man with its nose and looked up as if for
some reassurance. There were good grounds for hope. He
had Foxmask. Astonishingly, Creidhe was alive. And across
the Fool's Tide, in Council Fjord, his men were waiting. The
wind blew fiercely from the west, stirring the warrior's wild,
dark locks and touching his naked, white body with its chill
fingers. He'd hardly needed to consider the knife, Thorvald
thought; the weather would finish the fellow off soon enough
if he was left out here.

The little creature whined. Down the hillside Sam had
disappeared into the mist, carrying Creidhe in his arms.

"Oh, all right," muttered Thorvald, not sure whom he was
addressing. Over the time of preparation for the hunt he had
become stronger. Last spring, he would not have been able
to drag a grown man into the hut as he did now, without becoming breathless from the effort. He laid the fellow down
in the spread blankets, trying not to think of Creidhe, for if
he did that, his anger might get the better of him again. He
covered the man up with what was at hand, cloaks, blan-

kets, skins, other items of clothing. He laid some turf on the fire. That was enough; he owed the fellow nothing, brother or no brother. The lad had chosen to come here, after all; let him take his chances on the Isle of Clouds, if he liked the place so much. As for the fierce tribe, the savage army Asgrim had believed he faced, one man, his own son, that was all it had taken, one man and the island. Thorvald would not tell the others the truth about that; why lessen what must be their joy at achieving the longed-for victory?

Now he must go; Sam's threats had not been idle ones. He stooped to gather up the small creature, but it had edged away now and was tugging at something that lay by the wall, a strap or belt. No, it was a bag, neatly packed and fastened shut: a familiar bag, the very one Creidhe had carried with her from the Light Isles, holding the unlikely and foolish items she had chosen to bring, notably her embroidery linen and colored wools. Who but a girl would think it appropriate to carry such trifles on a journey to the end of the world?

The creature was growling now; it had gripped the bag's strap in its little, sharp teeth and would not let go. By all the gods, thought Thorvald, he'd better be right about this and not end up walking into Asgrim's encampment with nothing more than some puny runt of a dog. He thought he was right. He had listened with care when the men discussed the nature of what they hunted.

"All right then," he said cautiously, reaching for the bag and praying the creature would not decide to sink its teeth into his hand. "We take this as well. I dare say Creidhe would be quite cross if we left it behind; she sets a high value on her handiwork. Here, I'll carry it on my back, and you under my arm—"

But that was not to be. The creature watched him take up Creidhe's belongings, then scampered out of the hut. Thorvald's heart sank. The thing was tiny and agile; it could lead him a merry dance in the hills and crevices of the island while Sam sailed back to Council Fjord, taking away his only means of escape.

But when he came out of the hut, leaving the fallen warrior lying motionless by the fire, the doglike creature was
heading off down the path to the anchorage. It stopped from
time to time to glance back, as if to check whether Thorvald
was following. There was no need to capture it, to confine
it, to force it to leave the Isle of Clouds. It was quite apparent that Foxmask had decided to go home.

It was a long time since the white-haired man had learned
how to keep a small boat afloat in open sea. He had been
young and hale then, his locks as dark and glossy as polished oak wood. He had learned quickly, the choice being
to die, and break a promise, or to sail, and live, and remain
true. He had learned the hardest way possible. Such a lesson is never forgotten. Now his hands moved efficiently,
rigging mast and sail, loading what he had brought with
him: less, even, than the basic tools for survival they had allowed him when they cast him out into lifelong exile all
those years ago. He had water today, and a spare cloak, and
some rope. No food: he didn't expect he'd be needing that.
No fishing gear. This voyage had one purpose only.

He launched the small craft from the shore of Blood
Bay, pushing it through the dark sand of the tidal flats and
into thigh-deep water before clambering aboard. The process was less than graceful; he was no longer a young man,
though, he thought grimly as he took up the oars, neither
was he yet so old that he could not act when it at last came
time for it. He had waited long enough for fear that such a
decision might cause him to break a vow he must never for-
swear. Long ago he had promised the dearest friend he ever
had, his only true brother, that when he made landfall on
his perilous journey he would strive to be all he could be:
wise, balanced, a true leader of men. But how could a
flawed creature such as himself keep this solemn promise,
other than by sealing himself off from the world of affairs?
There was a craving in him for control, for respect, for the
admiration of men. He sensed that, however powerful he

became, it would never be enough to satisfy him. Better then, surely, to close off any possibility of power, lest he break his oath and bring darkness on them all. Yet the desire for control had never truly died over the years as he labored in the guise of holy brother, fashioning his days around the hours, from matins to compline, wielding his pen in scholarship, not in the secret messages of strategy and intrigue. He had mixed pigments, he had embellished his pages with delicacy and wit. He had copied the scriptures for Breccan. He had even made maps for the Ruler, just to keep his hand in, so to speak. He had learned that to milk a cow and to dig a vegetable patch in the right spirit were, to the faithful, true acts of prayer. And he had watched Asgrim's pathetic efforts to establish a community here, had observed the inequities and follies of the governance the Ruler imposed on the frightened islanders. He had stood by as the Long Knife people battered themselves into hollow ruins of men in their futile struggle against the enemy they had not begun to study, the foe they had no hope of understanding.

He could not intervene. To step in and take Asgrim's place, as he had longed to do, was surely to become once more the leader he had shown himself to be in the Light Isles: one who knew no way to govern but by cruelty and terror, a Ruler less fit for the title than Asgrim himself. He had come close at times. Once, when he was new here, and the knowledge of kingship lost was raw and painful in his mind, he had confronted Asgrim and read the fear in the other's eyes, a fear that awakened bitter memories. Niall had withdrawn, opting for solitude, for a scholarly detachment. And later, when the Ulstermen had come, and he had discovered to his astonishment that friendship of a kind was still possible for him after all, there had been the boy, Erling. A keen mind, a strong will, for all the lad's dreamy ways: Niall had discovered in himself a desire to protect the youth from his father, to allow him a chance, at least, to grow and learn, free from the harsh controls Asgrim saw fit to impose on this son who was not the son he had wanted.

There had been a spark of something rare in Erling. Breccan had seen it, too, as the boy questioned scripture endlessly, searching to find meanings in the tales of Christ and his disciples that were not present in the pattern of his own life among the Long Knife people. Well, Erling had certainly broken the pattern, but not in the way Breccan had hoped, which was that the boy might join them in the hermitage and commit himself in time to their own vows of poverty, chastity and obedience. Erling had surprised everyone. He had endured his father's beatings, the abuse, the imprisonment, biding his time until he might escape. Then he had stolen the child away from the Unspoken. He had astounded them all by removing the seer neatly and effectively beyond the reach of anyone. Such an act of furious courage, of dedicated self-sacrifice, was surely the stuff of legend.

The problem was, Niall told himself as he set the little boat on a southward course toward the Isle of Shadows, the real problem was that Erling's heroism had achieved nothing beyond a momentary denting of Asgrim's iron-strong authority. The voices still came in the night; children still perished. The hunt went on, with its harvest of death and despair. The seer had probably died that first winter, out on the Isle of Clouds in the mist and rain. The lad might not have fared better, for an ability to argue points of logic and a fondness for stories were not the best gifts to carry into a life of struggle with cold, hunger and loneliness. There probably was no seer anymore. But others still clung to their belief in him. The Unspoken had faith, the Long Knife people hunted, the crazy feud continued. In time, it would destroy them all.

Before, Niall would have stayed in his hermitage, observing, considering. He would have watched the boats sail out at midsummer and return the next day with somewhat fewer men on board. Breccan would have prayed for Asgrim's warriors, and he himself would have knelt quietly by his brother's side, respecting his faith. If God chose to reward the courage of the Long Knife people with failure and loss, who was he to criticize?

But it was different now. He had let them take the girl,
Eyvind's own daughter, whom he should have protected,
that bonny young woman with his dear friend's butter-
yellow hair, his guileless blue eyes, sweet as a cloudless
summer sky, his heartbreaking goodness and simplicity.
She was the very pattern of her father, yet more, for she also
had Nessa's quick mind, her depth of understanding. Now
Creidhe was dead: his fault, Somerled's fault, Somerled's
touch again, turning all to ashes. He could have acted earlier, and he had chosen not to. He must act now. It was too
late for Creidhe, but not too late for the boy. No, not a boy:
a man. His son. His son, Thorvald, the image of Margaret in
his regal stance, his air of contained authority, his proud
features and fine auburn hair . . . Yet it had been Niall's own
dark, troubled eyes that had gazed back at him from that
guarded young face, his own eyes full of a conviction and
purpose he had never been able to harness as Eyvind had
wished him to. Asgrim might be ashamed of his own son.
For Niall, that was not at all the way of it. He had recognized from that first shattering moment that his heart was
not, after all, frozen forever; that this young man was himself as he should have been, a fine leader untrammeled by
the dark fetters of the past that Somerled had never been
able to shake off. If he could have shouted so the whole
world could hear, he would have cried out, *He is my son.*

So now it was time to act. Asgrim might choose to pursue
the hunt year after year, tossing away the lives of his men
like so many broken tools. He would not be allowed to
waste Thorvald thus. Thorvald would live; he would be a
leader such as these folk had never known before.

Niall had considered his plan a long while. He thought it
would work, with no real damage to anyone that mattered.
What was a seer, after all, but someone who could give the
people reasonable advice as to how they might best live
their lives? The details of it were unimportant. Nine out of
ten men of Rogaland had fair-haired mothers. The rest, that
was nothing: probably no more nor less than a wretch such
as himself deserved. Certainly less than the punishment he

had inflicted on his own brother in a time when he had known only the lust for power, the bitter struggle to make himself into what he believed he must be: a king of men. The ritual could be endured. In its way, it might even be rather interesting, if he were able to remain conscious while they performed the surgery.

The little boat scudded across the ocean, bobbing like a toy in the deep waters between the Isle of Storms and the southern islands, mysterious home of the Unspoken. Niall gazed about him, committing all to memory: the myriad hues of the water; the wide, pale sky dotted with gulls; the steep, dark forms of the islands, fringed with bird-thronged cliffs. The day was a sweet one; the sun had a real warmth in it, the air was fresh, and seals swam to left and right of his boat as if in escort.

He would have liked to see Thorvald again, just once, before they took away his sight. He would have liked to look at his son and tell him how proud he was to have sired such a fine young man; how sorry he was that he had not watched him grow up. Foolish, that was. No boy wanted Somerled as a father. Thorvald was the leader he was precisely because his father had not been there during those growing years. He had been free of his heritage. Margaret had done a good job. Niall wished he could have told her so.

Breccan would not be happy. Breccan would find him gone, and sorrow for him, and pray for him. If the Ulsterman could see him now, Niall thought, finding there was a smile on his face with nothing at all of bitterness in it, Breccan would be surprised. For there were four things the white-haired man had brought with him on this last voyage from the Isle of Storms. The first was the cloak, since he must stay warm enough to use his hands effectively. The boat could not sail itself. The second was the rope; it was foolish to travel without rope. Third came water to keep him alive in case of emergency. Fourth was the wooden cross that hung around his neck. He had found he could lay down quill and parchment easily, knowing he would never write again. The last psalm was finished, copied in perfect completion, the capitals done with leaves and flowers, and here and there in the text, the places where his thoughts had challenged the confines of the manuscript, yearning and reaching and breaking free of the borders. That work was done now. There would be no more letters, no more maps. A man does not write in darkness. There would be no more sailing, no toiling in the gardens, no walking to settlement or lakeshore or hilltop. That was accepted; the choice to end that life was all his own. And yet the cross still hung about his neck, a simple thing of ash wood that had seemed, until the day he met his son, no more than the meaningless symbol of a faith that would belong always to others like Breccan and Colm, never to himself. Somerled, adherent to a god of peace and forgiveness? Somerled, converted by a red-haired Ulsterman to a path of goodness and light? The idea was so ludicrous that surely even Eyvind, the truest and most tolerant of friends, would laugh in disbelief if he could hear it. And yet, the cross: he reached to close his hand around it, to shut his eyes in prayer. *De profundis clamavi ad te, Domine* . . . Always, before, no more than the words, polite echo of Breccan's and Colm's, the motions only, to make a template for his days, so he could bear to go on living this shell of a life, this travesty of an existence . . . Yet now, no echo but the true word, whole, fierce, majestic, striking a terror to the heart, for this awful voice told him of sacrifice and redemption, of the laying down of a life infinitely more valuable than his own, of the salvation, not just of a couple of hapless tribes on a far-flung group of islands, but of all mankind, forever. This voice whispered in his ear like the rolling of distant thunder, speaking of fathers and sons. This voice made him weep and tremble. It made him grow still with the longing for grace.

And so Niall sailed steadily on, and the southern isles loomed closer and closer as the sun passed overhead. Gulls screamed; the water parted under the vessel's bow. His left hand touched the warm wood of the cross, his right held the steering oar as the wind carried him toward his destiny. The moment of darkness, the moment when all hung in the balance, would be the moment of awakening; the shadowing of human vision would be the bright dawn of the soul, bought with love and sacrifice. The voice sang in his spirit, at once terrifying and comforting. For this, he had waited all his life.

Creidhe began to fight a way out of the mists of unconsciousness. Sounds came first: the creak of a sail, footsteps on wood, Sam's voice, curt, tense. Then an awareness of movement: a surging up and down, familiar from that unspeakable time of confinement on the *Sea Dove*. It felt as if a knife was jabbing into her temple. She was lying on something soft, a cloak, laid over a ridged, uncomfortable surface: the boards of a boat's planking, probably. Her arm was hurting. There was something tied around it, tight and awkward. As vision returned through the fog that wreathed her eyes, memory came with it, sharp as a kick in the belly. *Keeper* . . . *Small One* . . . Creidhe sat up abruptly, and nearly vomited from the pain. She tried for words, but found none. The little boat, not the *Sea Dove* but a tiny, frail craft of driftwood and animal skins, was being tossed about with a violence that far surpassed the storm they had endured on their voyage from the Light Isles. Water sprayed everywhere, fine and drenching; while she gathered her breath, a wave washed over them, and she was lying in a cold puddle, her clothing instantly wet through. It was then she saw Thorvald, his hands grasping a scoop or bucket, his features tight and fierce as he stooped to bail the flood from this toy of a craft. The wind whipped at his auburn hair and tore at his clothing with greedy fingers. There were voices in it, howling, angry voices: *You think to cross the Fool's Tide, you, a mere man, and an incomer? Fool indeed!* Beyond him Sam could be seen struggling with the sail, keeping his balance as a true seaman does, reading the surge as if it were an extension of his own body. Creidhe forced herself to her knees; made her head turn this way and that, despite the pain, made her eyes search from bow to stern and into every corner of the boat, refusing to believe what she sensed must be true: surely even Thorvald would not do this, surely the ancestors would not allow it . . .

She saw only the two men, and the churning sea all around them, and behind them the Isle of Clouds, already vanishing into the mists of memory, as if it were all no more than a dream, a silly girl's fancy that she could change the pattern of something so ancient, so grand and terrible; could somehow, if she were brave enough, if she loved enough, make it all come out right. A cry of pure anguish came from her lips. The primitive, wrenching wail froze Thorvald where he crouched with bailer in hand, and made Sam pause, white-faced, even as he struggled to keep the small craft from spilling them all out into the sea.

The eldritch scream became a torrent of words. Creidhe could hear her own wild babbling, could feel herself clutching at Thorvald's clothing and shouting her furious grief into his face as he stared at her, his blank expression showing he barely comprehended the sense of what she was trying to tell him. But now she had started, she didn't seem to be able to slow down. "Where is he? Where are they? What did you do to them? You've killed him, you've killed him, haven't you, you've destroyed him for your own gain, your own pride—how could you, Thorvald? You've left Small One all by himself, I promised to look after him, I promised, he's only little, he can't—"

Thorvald slapped her across the face. It was a calculated blow, not painful, just hard enough to bring her tirade to an abrupt halt. She stared at him, shocked into silence. In that moment, he seemed like a stranger.

"Where is he, Thorvald?" she whispered, her fingers still clutching tightly at the breast of his tunic. "What have you done? Answer me!"

He had heard her all right, she could see it; he had understood those words above the wind's howling and the angry music of the Fool's Tide.

"Now, Creidhe," he said carefully, "you've been through some terrible times, I can see that, and we'll talk about it when Sam's got us safely back to Council Fjord. It's dangerous on these waters; you need to sit down and be quiet, and let us sail the boat—"

"Tell me! Tell me what you've done! Where is he? Where is—?"

"Creidhe, stop it. You're safe now, it's all right. We're here, we'll look after you. It's a shock, I know. For us, too. We thought you were dead—"

"Thorvald!" Creidhe said through gritted teeth. *"Where is the child?"* And at that moment she saw the ears, small, pointed ears like a dog's, the only part of the seer that was visible in the bows of the boat, behind her little bag and two other packs. Small One was here; they had taken him. They had taken him and now they would hand him over to Asgrim. If they had taken him, that meant Keeper was dead.

"Creidhe?" Thorvald's voice had softened just a little. "It'll be all right now, I promise you. It's all over. We have you safe." It was the tone of a man who tries to reassure a frightened woman that all is well, believing that should be enough for her; believing she cannot possibly comprehend the true meaning of affairs, and that therefore there is no point in trying to explain them. She thought, too, that he was fighting a battle with his own anger, with his own tumult of feelings. But there was no room for sympathy in her. Not now.

"Creidhe?" Thorvald asked quietly. "Did you understand me?"

The next question must be spoken, though she knew its answer already; it was there in the strange, numb chill that had seized her body, and in the hard, cold thing that had lodged itself in her heart.

"Tell me," she whispered. "Tell me, Thorvald. What did you do? What happened to the man who was with me on the island?"

Sometimes lies are necessary, even when you are a leader. For Thorvald, this was one of those moments. He could hardly bear to look at Creidhe, to gaze into those eyes, which surely should have been relieved or grateful or apologetic: they had saved her, hadn't they, her and the seer? But the eyes were furious, accusatory and tragic. Before their awful power his courage seemed to shrink, and he struggled for words. He hadn't wanted to hit her; it had been the only way to stop her flood of crazy talk and calm her down. She was hysterical; if he did not control her she might end up tipping this small craft over as she had the vessel of the Unspoken, and drowning them all in these voracious waters. His anger was not for her, but all for the man who had abused her, had held her prisoner, had turned her into this babbling mockery of her old self. He had struck her, when deep within him all he had wanted to do was put his arms around her, to offer affection and comfort. But there was no time for that; they were scarcely halfway to safety, and it was plain Sam fought every instant to keep them on course through these erratic currents, these insanely gusting winds. He must answer her. And there was only one possible answer, for she had been hurt, abused and terrified out of her wits, and now she needed to know she would be safe. She needed the certainty of that.

"The man who held you captive? The wretch who took the seer and started all this? I killed him. It was that or die myself, and Sam along with me. This is over, Creidhe. It's over, and we're taking you home."

He hoped, for a moment, that the deathlike grasp she had on his clothing might turn to a reaching for comfort; that he might, however briefly, embrace her, perhaps merely as a brother would, anything, any way he could show her what his confounded tongue, his too-carefully schooled eyes were unable to do for him. But Creidhe let him go, put both hands over her face, and subsided into a terrible, still silence, a withdrawal that spoke of a state of profound shock. She seemed beyond weeping, beyond comfort, beyond any help at all. Then Sam shouted an order, and Thorvald grabbed the steering oar as it swung wildly across, and it was no longer possible to do anything but follow Sam's commands as the vessel plowed its crazy, tenuous course through the surging waters. This was a battle, two men and a makeshift curragh against the Fool's Tide—the tales had been true; there was no predicting what would come next out here, a gust of freakish wind, a sudden whirlpool, sucking like a ravenous creature of the deep, an impossible, eddying current tugging them toward rocks. Sam looked furious; his brows were drawn together in a stormy scowl, his amiable mouth set in a thin line of anger. When Thorvald glanced back toward Creidhe, somewhat later, he saw that the odd little creature had crept out unobserved from its hiding place and now sheltered in her arms, reaching up from time to time to lick her blanched face, where the bruise Thorvald's blow had made was flowering rose and purple on her delicate skin. Her eyes were fixed to the west, empty and strange, gazing back to the steep, wild shores of the Isle of Clouds. In that moment, she seemed to Thorvald like a being from some dark tale of ancient memory: as remote as a goddess.

The sea punished them all the way to Dragon Isle and the Troll's Arch; almost to the very mouth of Council Fjord. Sam's face was gray with exhaustion, and Thorvald obeyed his commands without any conscious thought. Creidhe sat slumped on the decking with the little doglike creature in her arms. Her clothing was wet through and her hair lay in saturated strands across her bowed shoulders. It was as if she were suddenly blind and deaf, as if she had no understanding of the peril they were in or the horror of the situation she had faced on the island. She did not seem to realize that they had saved her. It came to Thorvald that perhaps her experiences had unhinged her mind; she had certainly had nothing to say that made any sense. But he could not think of that. Once they passed the Troll's Arch the water would be calmer; surely these conflicting currents could not follow them into the shelter of the fjord, where high, layered cliffs offered protection from all but the most cruel of westerly winds. They were nearly there, and they had Foxmask. He allowed himself, cautiously, to think ahead: to see Einar and Skapti and the others at the moment they knew victory was theirs, and a future of peace no longer an impossible dream. That would be sweet indeed. That would be enough, to shake their hands and see the warmth come back to their grim faces, and to hear the joy in their weary voices. He would be content with that; let the future take care of itself.

"Worst of it's over," Sam observed in something like his normal voice as he moved to take the steering oar. "Once we draw level with Dragon Isle there's only one rough patch, and we can sail to the north of it, all being well. Might not be sleeping with the fishes tonight after all. Hope Knut's looked after my boat."

As Thorvald relinquished his place, edging forward, he blinked in amazement and heard, over the ceaseless voice of the sea, Sam's gasp behind him. The little boat was working her way steadily toward the shelter of the fjord. To starboard loomed the steep, jagged shape of Dragon Isle, and ahead the squat form of the Troll's Arch came closer, with the rock-layered slopes of the Isle of Storms rising solid and dark behind it. But he was not watching those things, for on the boat was unfolding a wonder: in Creidhe's arms where she sat silent was no dog nor cat nor woodland creature, but a little ragged child with stick-like limbs and a head of wild, dark hair. Thorvald's heart pounded. Such a transformation could surely not be real, and yet undoubtedly it had occurred right here before his eyes. A fierce satisfaction filled him. His instincts had been sound: they had indeed rescued the seer, and the mission was all but accomplished.

"Thor's hammer!" exclaimed Sam in tones of hushed incredulity.

"We've got him," croaked Thorvald. "We've got Fox-mask."

It takes but an instant for sun to turn to shadow, light to dark: only an eye blink, if the ancestors will it so. They were passing the narrow gap between the islets, troll and dragon. Thorvald saw the child reach up its skinny arms to wrap them around Creidhe's neck, hugging her tightly. He saw Creidhe's fingers stroke the disheveled locks, moving with great gentleness. He watched as the seer pressed his pale, triangular face against Creidhe's cheek, not a kiss exactly, but a gesture of affection, of respect . . . of farewell . . . and then, quick as a flash, the small boy scrambled to the side of the boat, clambered to the rail, and leaped out into the swirling currents that edged the Fool's Tide. Frozen in utter disbelief, the three of them stared as the child's thin arms moved, pale as willow wands, in the turbulent water; as the current swept him toward that narrow southward channel. Then, abruptly, the ocean swallowed him, and Foxmask was gone.

Thorvald seized a desperate lungful of air, as if he himself were drowning. "Put about!" he yelled. "Stop, turn back!"

Sam stared at him unmoving. "I can't," he said heavily. "No leeway, and it's a following wind. Unless you want to smash the boat and drown the three of us."

It was true; that channel was scarcely navigable save on the calmest of days and under oars. Besides, the wind had already borne them level with the Troll's Arch. And even if they could follow, what was the point? There was no sign of the child. Even supposing, by some miracle, the boy survived a brief span in the chill waters, how could they hope to find him? Sam was right. To attempt any kind of pursuit would be a pointless sacrifice of their own lives.

A tumult of feelings welled in Thorvald's heart: bitter, blinding rage, anguished disappointment and a chill recognition of failure. He could feel himself shaking, and he could not hold back his words. "How could you do that?" he shouted at Creidhe. "How could you let him go? You've ruined everything!"

Creidhe stared back at him, ashen-faced, her eyes wide and strange. She said not a word.

"Don't you understand what this means?" Thorvald's own voice came out harsh and uncontrolled, and he fought to temper it. "There are good men on the Isle of Storms, men who've battled and suffered for years over this! That child was their last chance of peace! I gave them my word that I'd bring him back!"

"That's enough," Sam growled. "Shut your mouth and make yourself useful, we're not out of danger yet."

But Thorvald didn't seem to be able to stop. Creidhe's silence, her blank, wide-eyed expression, filled him with terror, for it seemed to him confirmation of a truth he had almost been able to forget: somehow, his own ill touch had made everything go wrong, and now the quest was lost, the Long Knife people condemned to struggle on through misery and heartbreak, and his own dear friend was turned into an empty shell before his eyes. This was his doing. He had failed them all. He crouched by Creidhe, gripping her by the shoulders. "What's got into you, don't you understand anything?" he hissed. "When I came here to find my father, I didn't expect to be the bearer of the worst news he'll ever get: that we found the seer at last, then let him slip through our fingers! How am I supposed to tell the men that?"

"Thorvald!" roared Sam. "Leave her alone!"

Tears welled suddenly in Creidhe's eyes, spilling down her cheeks. She made no attempt to wipe them away, but stared at Thorvald, mute as before. Perhaps she really had gone crazy. Thorvald shivered. That would be fine news to bear home to her father.

"Odin's bones, Creidhe," he snapped, "say something, can't you?"

"What should I say?" Her voice was small and remote.

Thorvald drew a deep breath and released it slowly. This was not her fault; he was wrong to accuse her, wrong to be angry. He had been leader. The responsibility, in the end, was all his own. "I'm sorry," he said. "I forgot myself. The truth is, I have lost this battle, and we must bear my father's people tidings of defeat, not of peace."

There was a moment's silence, and then Creidhe started to laugh, a dreadful, mad laugh that set his teeth on edge. Her sweet, guileless eyes had darkened with a terrible bitterness.

"Your father's people," her words tumbled out in a breathless, halting voice, "that's very funny. In the name of your father's people you set yourself up as a war leader; you invade the island, thirty warriors against one; you kill a man who only ever acted for love of his kin; you seize an innocent child and try to bind him to a future of unutterable suffering! Was it your father who bid you do this, Thorvald? Was it truly?"

He stared at her, trying to make sense of her words. "What do you mean, unutterable suffering?" he asked. "The

seer came with us willingly, you saw that. You saw how thin
and weak he was; it's a miracle he survived that wild existence on the Isle of Clouds. The Unspoken would have
cherished him. Foxmask is their most venerated seer; he
would have been treated as a king, as a god."

Creidhe's eyes had turned cold with fury. "That's so like
you, Thorvald. You always did rush into things without
waiting to find out the details first. No wonder you were so
eager to lead these men. No wonder you seized on the idea
Asgrim was your father. Clearly, he never bothered to tell
you what would happen to Foxmask when you passed him
over to the Unspoken. He didn't tell you about the ritual,
did he?"

There was a moment's charged silence. Grim-jawed, Sam
eased the little boat to the north of a patch of water whose
ruffled surface showed danger below: a submerged skerry or
a last remnant of the treacherous currents of the Fool's Tide.

"What ritual?" Thorvald kept his voice calm and careful,
though there had been an icy premonition in Creidhe's words.

"The maiming. The Unspoken would have blinded and
crippled Small One, to make him the same as the old seer
was, the one whose death started all this in the first place."
Creidhe sniffed and scrubbed a hand across her cheek.
"They believe he cannot sing his prophecies unless he un-
dergoes that torture first. But he can; I've heard him. He can
do it. He . . . he could do it."

Thorvald swallowed. He almost wished Creidhe had maintained that strange, cold demeanor, for it was becoming difficult to watch her now that she was openly weeping. Abruptly,
she had become her old self, the girl who had shadowed his
steps when they were children, the young woman for whose
death he had not allowed himself to grieve aloud. "That is terrible," he said more gently. "No, they did not tell me. I expect
the men did not know. Did you let him go because of this?
You must realize he could not survive long in these waters."

"Let?" Creidhe queried. "There's no *letting* with Small
One. He makes his own choices. I did not expect him to do
what he did. Not even after he saw Keeper die. There's a
grief in this that you can never understand."

"Creidhe—" Thorvald hesitated; she was only a girl, after all. "Surely it would have been better if the child had gone back to the Unspoken, cruel as it seems to say it. We could have won peace for the Long Knife people, man, woman and child alike. There have been many deaths of infants among them over the years of the hunt, babes sung away by the Unspoken before they saw a second day. Can you say it is justified for that to go on, for the sake of one small boy? Asgrim's people have suffered season after season of loss. I do not know how I can give them this news. How can I face it? How can I face my father?"

"Thorvald," Creidhe said, holding him with her gaze, "Asgrim is not your father."

That chill again. He had not missed it when she had implied this before. "What do you mean? Of course he is. He as good as said it himself—"

"He is not your father. What about the scar?"

"Scar?" echoed Thorvald as the sail crackled in the wind, and they ducked out of the way. "What scar?"

Creidhe stared at him, blue eyes wide. "You mean you didn't know? Aunt Margaret didn't tell you?"

"Tell me what? What are you talking about?"

"She didn't; I see that. I never thought to mention it. I just assumed you would know. It's a sign of blood brotherhood, the same my own father bears on his left forearm. Somerled's arm is marked with its twin. I've seen it."

Thorvald stared at her. "Then—" he began.

"I've seen it here in the islands, and the man who bore it was not Asgrim."

"But—" Thorvald's head reeled. The encampment, the training, the work he had done with the men . . . Asgrim's grudging expressions of trust, the Ruler's implied recognition of kinship . . . all lies, all pretense, all yet another demonstration of his own ineptitude, the shadow inside him that turned all he touched to dust. It could not be true. It must not be true.

"Freyr's bollocks," observed Sam. "What a turnaround. Bit of a relief, I should think, to find out the Ruler isn't your father after all. Not a father I'd much care for myself. Question is, if it's not him, who is it?"

"What about the map?" Thorvald asked suddenly, clutching at straws. "I saw the map, Asgrim had it in his sleeping quarters, with pens and pigments. It was done in the same hand as the letter he left my mother, I'm sure of it—"

Creidhe's lips curved in a joyless smile. "Another man made the map, Thorvald. A man with a scar on his arm. He is your father. He is Somerled, though he goes by a different name now. A long time has passed since he sailed away from the shores of Hrossey. That was a desperate voyage: a voyage to turn a man's hair white with terror."

There was the unmistakable ring of truth in her words. A strange calm settled over Thorvald, as if a violent storm had passed, sweeping everything before it, leaving a landscape scoured clean of markings.

"A white-haired man," he said. "The hermit. You expect me to believe Somerled—*Somerled*—became a Christian? A man who tortured his own brother to death and imposed a rule of terror and blood on the Light Isles?"

"I don't care what you believe," Creidhe said tightly. "Brother Niall is your father. Much can change in eighteen years, Thorvald. A boy can grow to a man. He can learn courage and devotion and sacrifice, or he can learn only how to be selfish and blind. A girl can learn how wrong she was about what things are important, about what things are so precious that to lose them is like death. Perhaps a man can learn that forgiveness is possible, even for the darkest acts of wrongdoing. You should ask him."

Thorvald did not reply. An image was in his mind, a memory of dark eyes staring into his with penetrating intelligence, of a voice both soft and incisive, of features austere with self-discipline below that tonsured head with its snowy hair. He had thought the priest an old man. The fellow had wanted to speak with him alone . . . he had not taken that opportunity, he had let Asgrim overrule him, not understanding . . . Creidhe was right, he had been blinded by what he had convinced himself was the truth. It was he who was the fool.

"Creidhe?" Thorvald spoke softly.

She looked at him, eyes red and swollen.

"I'm sorry," he said, forcing the words out, feeling the bitterness of it deep in his heart. "I'm truly sorry."

"For what you have done"—Creidhe's words were like drops of ice, clear, cold—"I can never forgive you, Thorvald. Never."

After that, there was nothing more to be said, though it was somewhat unjust of her, Thorvald thought, to blame him for the child's demise. Perhaps it was the whole ill-considered venture she meant, a journey that had proved nothing to him save the truth about his own inadequacies. In silence, they sailed the little boat between the sheltering arms of land and into the safety of Council Fjord.

THIRTEEN

Thor's hammer!" exclaimed Sam. "A welcoming party! Now that I wasn't expecting." For sailing toward them in the center of the long bay, making steady progress against the wind, was the neat, compact form of the *Sea Dove*. As their own small craft drew closer, they could see familiar figures on board: Orm at the tiller, towering, broad-shouldered Skapti in the bows, and, sitting on a bundle in the central hold, a man in the coarse brown habit of a Christian hermit, with an expression of desperate anxiety on his amiable countenance.

Now I must say it, Thorvald thought. *Now, already, I must find the words. I must tell them I have broken my promise: that I have failed them.*

But as they drew alongside the *Sea Dove*, and Skapti reached down with a hook to hold the curragh against the larger vessel's side, Breccan called to them, his voice tight with distress.

"Thorvald! You must help me!"

A tale emerged, a garbled, extraordinary story. All the same, the white-faced cleric told it with the undeniable voice of truth. Breccan spoke of a man gone, sailed away alone to the southern isles in a crazy quest to offer himself to the Unspoken as seer . . . a man who was no seer, but who nonetheless had such a persuasive tongue, such a gift with words, that he might, just possibly, succeed in his bizarre mission . . . a hermit who was prepared to sacrifice his own sight, his own mobility quite willingly if it would end the years of futile waste and heartbreaking loss on the islands . . . who was prepared to be a blind cripple, if it would save his son.

"You see," Breccan said simply, "he knew that even if you survived the hunt, Thorvald, your days were numbered. The Ruler fears you: this season, he has found you useful to his purposes, but in the longer term your skills, your power, the leadership you offer his men are deeply threatening to his authority. How could Asgrim let you live beyond this summer?"

"Like to see him try anything now," muttered Skapti. "Things have changed."

"By doing this," Breccan went on, "Niall intends to end the war and allow you to take control more easily. That is what I believe. He himself has stood outside the world of affairs these many years, for fear of what he might begin if he acted against Asgrim." The Ulsterman was struggling to explain calmly, to control his shaking voice. "But he could not stand by and watch his son perish. He hinted at this before, but I could not credit it; it is a crazy, wild scheme, and Niall is a man of cold logic, of meticulous planning and tight controls. I did not believe he would go through with it. He timed it well; kept me up late, so that I slept past matins. He was long gone by the time I woke, and in this wind he may already be nearing the shores of the Isle of Shadows, where they have their place of ritual. We need the *Sea Dove*, Sam, with you to sail her. And we need you, Thorvald. Niall won't listen to me, nor to a single one of the Long Knife people. But he will surely hear the voice of his son. You must turn him from this dark course. To act as he intends is to condone the violence, the primitive ritual, the heathen practices of these lost souls."

And as Thorvald stared back at him, stunned into silence, Breccan looked beyond him, and saw who it was they carried with them in the little boat of latticework and skins.

"Creidhe! By all the saints!"

Thorvald noticed, in the ensuing flurry of activity, that Skapti could not stop staring at Creidhe, and that the big guard seemed to have tears in his eyes. He observed that Breccan moved with perfect balance on the boat, unsurprising, he realized, in view of that long voyage from the shores of Ulster. Thorvald and Sam clambered up onto the *Sea Dove*. There was a brief dispute.

"Creidhe can't come with us," Sam said flatly. "She's been hurt, she's exhausted, and besides, the moment those savages set eyes on her you know what they'll decide. They're taking a chance, trusting the word of an enemy, if they choose the priest. With Creidhe they've got their fair-haired girl all over again, the means to recreate their cursed Foxmask. And there's not many of us. She must stay here."

"I can take her ashore on the small boat if you want," Orm offered, glancing at Thorvald. "But—"

"I'm coming on the *Sea Dove*." Creidhe's tone was chill and final. "I must be there. I must be there at the end." She stood in the rocking curragh, her hands grasping the rope that Skapti had lowered to help them climb up. "You owe me, Thorvald," she said.

Thorvald opened his mouth to argue, then shut it again.

"You can't leave Creidhe here with Asgrim," Breccan observed mildly. "That would be the same as handing her over to the enemy."

"I'm coming with you." Creidhe began to climb, but Skapti reached down, gripped her by the arms and, with one expert heave, lifted her bodily onto the *Sea Dove*. Orm climbed down into the curragh.

Thorvald found his voice. "You'd better tell them," he croaked as Orm took up the oars, heading for the tidal flats where a number of men seemed to be waiting. "Tell them I failed in the mission. We found Foxmask all right; for a little, we had him. But . . ." He glanced at Creidhe. "But he escaped us, at the end. Tell them I'm sorry. Tell them I'm more sorry than I've ever been in my life."

Orm gave a nod, and pulled on the oars, and the little boat slipped away shoreward. On the *Sea Dove*, Creidhe sat silent and blank-eyed once more. She looked as if part of her were missing; as if something had plucked out the vibrant core of her being, leaving an empty hollow inside her. Skapti had taken off his own thick felt cloak and put it around her shoulders, and she huddled in it, shivering. Sam was doing something expert-looking with the sail, and gesturing for the big guard to take the steering oar. The *Sea Dove* trembled, steadied, and moved off westward again. The sun had not yet reached its midpoint. Perhaps there was still enough time.

"Thank you, Thorvald," said Brother Breccan quietly. "It was such joy for him to find he had a son. He has great pride in you."

Thorvald bit his lip, afraid to speak lest he lose his last vestige of self-control. For all his efforts to discipline it, his heart seemed to be busily tearing itself to shreds.

"I see how difficult it is," Breccan went on, seating himself by Thorvald, well out of the way of the brisk, efficient activities of Sam and Skapti. "If we took no action here, if we let Niall follow his own course, there might be peace in the Lost Isles. The killings, the stealing away of souls, the terror and bloodshed might be at an end. We could achieve that simply by doing nothing. And you would be a hero to these folk."

Thorvald stared at him. "He must not do it," he whispered. "He must not sacrifice himself. A victory bought at such a cost is not worth winning."

Creidhe's eyes were on him. Their blue depths seemed full of truth, as if she could see right into his heart, and a sadness came over him that was deep and abiding, for it seemed there were no answers here, no real ones. Who was he to meddle in such grand and perilous matters, such ancient patterns of power and faith? What had he done in this place but add sorrow to sorrow? Thorvald closed his eyes, for he could not bear to look at Creidhe, or at Breccan, or at a single one of them, lest he see only a reflection of his own wretchedness in their gaze.

So far, so good. Niall's quick ear, his gift for language had served him well. The tongue was the same, though different in inflection and emphasis, with a certain spitting crispness to some sounds; the Unspoken had quickly understood his purpose. Whether they were prepared to accept the offer remained to be seen. He was weary; the long sail had sapped his strength. He thought, as they marched him up from the stony shore to a flat expanse of sward before the low buildings of their settlement, that there were certain small goals he could set himself, which might make this a little easier to endure. He wished to retain some dignity. He would give himself a pattern for the management of fear, and of pain. Patterns were always useful. Not to scream, that was his first goal. Not to lose control of his bladder and bowels: that might become difficult at a certain point. Not to change his mind and beg for mercy. He knew he could manage that one, the most important one. He need simply picture his son, a man infinitely more deserving of a future than himself, a man who would not have existed but for him. His one fine achievement: his one good legacy. To preserve Thorvald, he could endure much. He could endure whatever they did to him.

They put him in a low, dark hut, with men standing guard outside. He waited. After a long time, a tall old man came in and squatted by his side, dark eyes fixed on his, craggy face ash-white in the shadows. There were questions then, not so very many of them, but all difficult to answer. If Niall got this wrong they would send him away, and it would all have been for nothing. He must not get it wrong. He must not falter. Had he not always been a master at games, a subtle wearer of masks, a skilful manipulator of others' beliefs and emotions? So he made guesses, gave answers and thought he saw the old man's strong features relax a little, his strange, deep eyes grow warmer. The inquisition over, the elder withdrew. There was another endless time of waiting.

He could hear the men of the Unspoken conferring in hushed voices, but he could not catch the words. From time to time they strode past the entry to the hovel where he sat, and once or twice looked in: thin, scarred faces; dark, deep-set eyes; necklaces of bone; clothing of skins, rank-smelling as if incompletely cured. Niall waited, and while he waited he muttered to himself the words of the psalm he had copied as his last act of scholarship in the world of see-ing men: *speravit anima mea in Domino* . . . And after a while the tiny, powerful voice seemed to speak again, a breath of reassurance, a murmur of hope, and his thunder-ing heart slowed a little, his head cleared somewhat, his breathing steadied. Faith . . . a man must have the faith to pass this over to a higher power, to trust in one whose wis-dom must surpass that of mortal man, to let it go . . . finally, to relinquish control and accept as God's will whatever must come . . . How could he do that, he who had ever exer-cised his own controls, carved his own path, been master, not just of his own fate, but the fate of all those who stepped into his shadow? *Faith,* murmured the voice, terrifying in its simple truth. *Hope . . . Love . . .*

And though Niall thought he could keep the pattern he had set himself, and mask the signs of weakness as they performed the dark acts of the ritual, before this terrible whisper he trembled like a birch in a spring storm. To lay his heart open thus and let the light touch him at his core was the hardest thing he had ever done. In the shadows of the little hut, Brother Niall knelt on the earthen floor, the cross between his hands. His lips moved in prayer. "See, the door is open at last," he breathed, and felt hot tears flow from his eyes like the water of a blessing. "Be welcome here . . ."

He was not sure how much time had passed. He judged, by the sun's position, that he had knelt there long. His joints were stiff; the men of the Unspoken had to haul him to his feet. His mind felt empty, clean as if new washed; the things they were doing seemed to have little connection with him. Indeed, he hardly understood their purpose. They stripped off every item of his clothing: his coarse-spun robe, his sandals, the shirt and small-clothes he wore underneath for warmth. His fingers moved to clutch the cross as one man severed the cord that held it. Then he let it go. There was a purpose to this, though it had escaped him for a moment. It came to him again with brutal clarity, and he could not suppress a shudder. It seemed they intended to perform it now, straightaway. So soon; he had not thought it would be so soon. He had passed the test. Whether he could maintain this role remained to be seen. He hoped that he could, so the peace would endure. Let the cross be taken, for he held its power inside him now, and he thought that would shield him against much. They slipped a robe over his head, fine dark wool sewn with many small shells. They offered him a bowl of strong-smelling liquid to drink. He was thirsty; he took a mouthful, then pushed it away.

"Take, take," the tallest man was urging him, a frown creasing his brow. "Hard, the pain—take, sleep—"

But Niall would not drink, for it seemed to him this must be endured in its full terror and grandeur, or he would learn nothing. Besides, he did not wish his senses dulled in a drug-induced torpor, his lids closed by false repose, not even for an instant. Until the last, he would have his eyes open to the sky, to the light, to a world he had never understood was beautiful until the day he saw his son.

They led him out, not as a captive now, but with a respect verging on awe. Many folk were assembled around the edges of the sward, and he could see that there was a great stone in the center, a monumental flat slab of granite, the lush grass around its base studded here and there with summer flowers, small and bright. Yellow, pink, blue, red, each was a sweet reflection of the season's kindness. Sheep watched him from the stone-walled field beyond, rangy, long-coated sheep with mild eyes and busy, chewing mouths.

They led him closer, and the people began to chant. There were women here, gaunt, wild-eyed women as feral as the men, and clad in the same rough animal hides, with tunic or leggings of crudely woven wool beneath. He saw no children. By the stone slab the old man waited. His hair was as long and twisted as the wool of those tough island sheep, and in his deep, dark eyes could be read iron-strong purpose, and alongside it, both respect and compassion. There was a short, squat fellow beside him, with ropes in his hands.

"No need to bind.me," Niall said. His own voice had a faraway sound, as if it belonged to another man, in another life. "I've come here of my own free will."

"Hard for you," the tall man muttered, lifting his brows. "None can keep still against the blinding."

"Then hold me with your hands." Niall glanced at the second man, trying for a reassuring smile. He was not sure he could recall how such an expression was formed; all of a sudden he was feeling quite odd. His heart refused his request to slow down; his breath faltered.

The short man nodded. "I hold you," he grunted. "And others. Will be quick."

Niall lay down on the stone, on his back. The sky was dazzling bright, but he would not shut his eyes on this last glimpse of day. It was a blue arch above him, as blue as Eyvind's gaze that had so astonished him with its guileless beauty, long ago in Rogaland. Another pattern established itself in his mind as the short man placed his strong hands on either side of Niall's head, holding it still, and he felt the grip of four others on his arms, his legs, as if the pain of this might cause his whole body to jerk convulsively and set the knife off course. Perhaps they would not use a knife but some other implement, a spoon-like device, or even sharp-nailed fingers. He had not looked to see what tools they had at hand. A new pattern, he told himself, forcing his breathing slower. He would endure this as Eyvind would, his one true friend, his brother of the heart, the man he would wish to have been were there any choice at all in such matters. Eyvind, emphatically no Christian, was yet the very pattern of faith, hope and love: their true exemplar, as child and man. Eyvind would lie still and silent; Eyvind was strong. Let this priest, or whatever he was, use his knife as quickly and cleanly as Eyvind himself had done, the first time Somerled had ever seen him, slaughtering a goat in a moment of pure, perfect sacrifice to Thor. That swiftly slashing blade, merciful in its certainty, those warm blue eyes had changed Somerled's life forever. Let today's enactment mark another change: in the shadow of blindness, in the shattering of his bones, let his spirit walk forward into light.

"You are ready, brother?" the tall man murmured.

Niall could not nod in response, for his head was held in those two strong hands as in an iron vise. He swallowed and, with a certain difficulty, found his voice.

"Do it," he whispered.

A desperate journey: four men sailing, pushing the boat to her utmost, straining to make what speed they could to the shore where, Breccan had told them, the Unspoken had their place of deep ritual. The Ulsterman knew it; in the early days, his kind had taken their message even to the heart of this pagan realm. Indeed, they had persisted for some time, until it became quite clear to them that these particular ears would be deaf forever to the word of God. They had retreated; their purpose in this isolated place was not a mission to convert the heathen but primarily prayer, solitude and self-denial in the mode of those who had sought God's voice in the deserts of the Holy Land. Still, Breccan remembered the place, and directed them to it with quiet efficiency.

The wind was westerly, the sailing tricky even now they had passed beyond the oddities of the Fool's Tide. Even so, with Sam's knack for coaxing the best from his boat despite contrary conditions, they made good progress. Seals crossed

in the white wake the *Sea Dove* left behind her. The small
curragh Niall had taken would be far slower, so they had at
least some chance of reaching their destination in time. On
the other hand, Niall's path was shorter, a direct way southward from Blood Bay. The day had brightened; the sun
shone pale gold in a wide expanse of summer blue.

Creidhe could not stop shaking. The men moved about
her briskly, and she saw their sideways looks, their frowns
as they assessed her, but this did not seem to have any
meaning. Nothing seemed to make sense anymore. Her
mind was turning in tangled circles: *If I had not come to the
islands, if I had not been there, they would not have caught
Keeper unawares. If I had not tried to stop them, Keeper
would have lived. If Keeper had lived, they would not have
taken Small One, and Small One would not have done what
he did . . . It was my fault . . . and now both of them are
gone.* The grief of that was in her somewhere, a tight, cold
knot deep inside. The screams, the fury, the tears had done
nothing to diminish it. She knew she would hold it forever;
it had become a part of her, as Keeper and Small One were.
Forever . . . Keeper's vow whispered in her heart: *My walls
will shelter you, my hearth fire warm you, my feet walk beside yours until our journey's ending.* For him, the ending
had come cruelly soon.

She had known. She had seen it, in the visions, in the
stitches she refused to make, the images she would not fashion. And yet, Small One had urged her to complete her
work. *Put him in your web, now, now!* Perhaps if she
had . . . perhaps if she had dared . . . no, that was foolish. If
the ancestors willed she should lose the two of them, her little family, her dear ones, then that was how it unfolded. No
girl with needle and colored wools had the power to gainsay
such ancient wisdom. Still, she had not thought, when she
felt the compulsion to follow Thorvald, when she felt the
sharp pull of the Isle of Clouds there on the path above
Brightwater, that it would end in such sorrow. She had
found her heart's joy here in this lonely place. And Thorvald had killed him; it was Thorvald, the center of her world

for as long as she could remember, who had shattered her happiness. That was what the hunger for power did to a man: made him a mindless killer.

Creidhe shifted uneasily, feeling the wind's bite through the thickness of Skapti's cloak. She was being unfair, of course. The terrible, cold grief that had possessed her had not quite driven out her powers of reasoning. If Thorvald had not killed, Keeper would have made an end of him, and of Sam too. Keeper had taken countless lives in his mission to protect his small kinsman. It would have been Thorvald's sightless eyes, and Sam's, staring down at her from those shelves on the northern cliffside, if Thorvald had not acted to defend himself.

She glanced at Thorvald now where he took his turn on the steering oar; he was pale as chalk, his dark eyes narrow and fierce, his tight mouth bracketed by lines of tension. She understood what he felt; hadn't she always? To find his father at last, and perhaps to lose him so cruelly before they could meet, and embrace, and speak freely together, that was terrible indeed. But it was no more terrible than the death of Keeper, and the drowning of Small One. Once, she had not been able to look at Thorvald without feeling her whole self suffused by love and longing. Once, she had been little more than a child. She knew what love was now; she knew what loss was. Her eyes passed over her old friend and away, and she could not find a shred of sympathy in her heart. If she still stayed by him, if she obeyed the compulsion to be at his side on this last voyage into the unknown, she did not do it for Thorvald, but for the white-haired priest who was his father. In this realm of grim strangers, Niall had been a voice of wisdom, of kindness, of sanity. She had seen something in him that seemed to chime with her father's words as Eyvind spoke of that fierce, lonely child who had been his friend and his enemy so long ago. What was it he had said? Something about a spark of greatness, of goodness, hidden so deep few could see it. It seemed to Creidhe the perilous voyage, the seasons of loneliness, the long testing of the spirit these isles had imposed on Somerled had forged a new man, one who still held that spark, now grown to a blaze of warmth and compassion, whatever he himself might say. It was for this man's sake, and for her father's, that she was here now, watching as the shore of another island drew closer, and the men worked to lower the *Sea Dove*'s sail and ease her into the bay under oars. Creidhe was not frightened, or apprehensive, or regretful. She was no longer angry or aggrieved. There was simply the cold, hard stone of loss in her chest, and the voice of the ancestors breathing in her ear, bidding her go on. Her feet must tread this path; in time, she would understand why.

The men sprang over the boat's side, weapons in hand. Even Breccan bore his heavy staff. Here, there was no resistance; the Unspoken had not so much as a single sentry posted at their landing place. There was a path leading up across the rocks; higher on the hillside there seemed to be turf-roofed buildings, and from somewhere above, a low, rhythmic chanting could be heard, a powerful sound that resonated deep.

"A ceremony," Breccan said, white-faced. "Perhaps they enact the ritual even now. Come, we must hurry."

"Be watchful," warned Thorvald. "If we rush in blindly we do nobody any good. Keep your weapons ready, and look about you. Leave the talking to me. Skapti, we're going to need you."

"You can't leave Creidhe on the boat alone," hissed Sam.

"She must hide," Thorvald said curtly. "Skapti's the best fighter among us, we can't do this without him. I'll need all of you."

"I don't like this," Skapti muttered, glancing at Creidhe with little, anxious eyes before he, too, jumped out of the boat into knee-deep water and followed the other men to shore. "Stay down out of sight, lass. We won't be long."

Creidhe waited a certain time before she followed them: not so long that they were gone from view, but long enough so they would not simply turn and march her back to the *Sea Dove*. She hitched up her skirt, but it still got wet through as she waded to the narrow strip of dark sand marking this island's safe landing place. There were long, low boats here, the twins of the vessel she had capsized out in the Fool's Tide, killing its men. Creidhe shivered, stooping to wring out the folds of her skirt. Perhaps she was being foolish. Perhaps she should obey Thorvald, who seemed to believe himself in charge here. Was it true that she was no more than a meddling nuisance, best hidden away where she would do no more harm?

A white-plumed sea bird glided above her, calling plaintively into the empty sky. The chanting rose and fell, a stark, echoing sound that seemed as old as the bare hilltops of the islands, a thing beyond human memory. Creidhe smoothed her damp clothing. The sweet notes of color on the hem—Keeper's careful, small stitches—sent a pain like a barbed arrow through her heart. *Walk on*, the bird seemed to cry. *Walk on*, sang the voices from the hillside above her. Creidhe made her back straight, held her head high. As Thorvald and Sam, Skapti and Breccan moved with stealthy purpose up toward the place of ritual, Creidhe came silently behind them, as calm and pale as a spirit woman. The bird that flew above her was joined by a second and a third, their voices making a music that flowed with the chanting, and below those sounds of the island came another: the hushed, wild, endless song of the sea. Creidhe's steps were silent; all the same, at a certain point, Sam turned his head to look behind him, and nearly dropped his knife.

"Creidhe!" he hissed in horror, and at that moment the men reached the top of the track.

Creidhe saw Thorvald freeze in place, looking away from her; she saw Skapti raise his arm, spear poised to throw. Breccan's hand tightened on his staff, but he would use it only to defend himself, she knew that. A moment later the chanting faltered and ceased and shouts erupted, the voices of the Unspoken in outrage, in ferocious challenge, and she could see Thorvald gesturing to the others, *no, don't attack,* and sheathing his sword, and putting his hands up, empty, as if to say to the enemy that he had come in peace. She could hear an angry swell of noise, growing to a roar; that was to be expected. One did not lightly interrupt a solemn ritual. Now two of the Unspoken appeared and seized Thorvald by the arms. Skapti was shouting at his leader, demanding to be allowed to use his weapons or at least his fists, and the roaring grew louder, the dangerous sound of a crowd frustrated of a long-desired goal. Creidhe began to run, scrambling up over loose stones. She reached the top of the path and halted, staring.

There was a wide expanse of open ground before the low stone buildings of the settlement here. Grass grew lush and green, dotted with small, bright flowers. The sward was trampled now, for there was indeed a large circle of folk here, men and women, gaunt, wind-weathered and wild, clad in crudely woven garments covered with skins. Some bore ornaments of bone around the neck, strung on strips of leather; most wore their hair long and twisted into knotted strands, with here and there a small bead or decoration, again of pale bone, white or cream or yellow. Their eyes held a single expression: furious outrage. It was clear the unexpected visitors had disrupted a gathering of deepest solemnity.

A group of men stood in the center of the circle, five or six of them, and among them there was one who was tall, old and commanding in his presence. This elder was staring directly at Thorvald, eyes blazing with anger. In his hands was a neat, small implement of bone, something between a knife and a scoop. It was glistening red. And now, as Creidhe's heart thumped with horror, although she had thought she could feel nothing again, the other men shifted, revealing what lay between them.

On a vast slab of rock a man lay sprawled on his back, a thin robe of fine wool covering his body. He seemed relaxed, as if in sleep; he was not chained, or tied, or bound in any way, though red marks on his arms and legs suggested he had but recently been held hard in place by those lean, dangerous-looking fellows who still waited close by his side. His head was shaven in front, the same as Brother Breccan's; from where she stood transfixed, Creidhe could see the white sweep of his hair, pale as a swan's feathers, and the bright stain of blood that ran down his blanched face to stain the snowy locks scarlet. She felt herself gasp with shock and release her breath in a shuddering, sickening rush. Then Thorvald, Thorvald who was a master of self-control, Thorvald who might have cared nothing for the world at all, so little was he accustomed to revealing of his heart, let out a great cry, threw off the grip of the fellows who held him as if they were straw men, and launched himself across the space to the ritual stone. He moved like a thunderbolt, like a fury, like a bird winging for home. In that moment, nothing in the world could have stopped him. The men who stood by the stone stepped back at the look in his eyes.

Skapti moved. Spear in hand, he surged across the space to Thorvald's side, a massive, furious presence. Thorvald was bending over the slab, speaking softly. Creidhe saw him lift the wounded man's head and slip a careful arm beneath his shoulders. The elder's expression had tightened alarmingly, and now the other men around him drew their knives on some unspoken command. Beside Creidhe, Sam shifted his own blade in his hand. Immediately, all around the circle, weapons appeared, implements of sharpened bone, of leather, of hard stone. In a moment this would erupt into a chaos of blood and death. That could not be. It was not meant to be.

"Stop!" Creidhe cried out, and, taking a step into the circle where all could see her, she slid back the hood of the thick felt cape she wore, Skapti's cape, to reveal her long, shining hair, bright gold in the sun of the summer afternoon. "Stop, all of you! You must not hurt this man further! He is a Christian priest and cannot be your true seer!"

The silence that followed was profound, a silence of shock, disbelief and wonder: a silence of something close to terror, as the men and women of the Unspoken stared, lean faces growing pale, mad eyes fixed on Creidhe's slender form in her wet clothes and her rough cape, and the fall of golden hair across her shoulders. Even the elder grew still. Behind him, Thorvald sat on the edge of the granite slab, cradling the injured priest in his arms. Breccan had moved closer and was using Thorvald's knife to rip cloth from his robe, trying to staunch the bleeding.

"Dead," the elder whispered, staring at Creidhe. "Lost in the Fool's Tide. Dead, but walking still."

"No," Creidhe said, finding it not so hard to hold his gaze, for she seemed beyond fear now. "I am alive, as you see, a flesh and blood woman, saved by the ancestors' intervention, and by an act of great kindness. Saved for this. Let the hermit go; you cannot use him now, the ritual has been interrupted. It is imperfect, and the spirits displeased. Take me instead. I offer myself willingly, if these hostilities cease as a result. I have nothing left to lose."

"Creidhe!" She heard Sam's horrified shout, saw from the corner of her eye how two men of the tribe seized the fisherman before he could move toward her. Breccan looked across at her from where he tended to his fellow hermit, his eyes wide with shock.

"You can't do this, Creidhe," he protested. "Perhaps you do not understand what will happen to you—"

"I understand," she said flatly.

. The elder had put down the foul implement he held; it lay on a smaller stone with others whose uses she did not want to guess—a long, serrated knife of pale metal; a heavy, short club; skewers of bone. He took two steps toward her and stared deep into her eyes. His long fingers came up to touch her bright hair, lingering over the silken strands; with his other hand he stroked her neck, where the pearly skin was exposed by the opening of the tunic Keeper had made for her. Somewhere behind her Sam snarled in helpless fury. Skapti took a step forward, his face like a thundercloud, and was halted by Thorvald's raised hand.

Another voice spoke, a voice rasping with pain, yet held in the tightest control.

"Creidhe . . ." Niall gasped, "not this way . . . I . . . I alone . . ."

"Hush." It was Thorvald speaking, Thorvald's voice as she had ever longed to hear it, tender and open. That tone was not for her, but for his father. "Hush, now. All will be well.

Brother—?" Thorvald turned to Breccan, and the Ulsterman took his place, supporting the wounded man. Creidhe held the elder's gaze; she could not yet look across to see what damage had already been done, but at least Niall still lived and was conscious. Perhaps, between them, the men might convey him to safety and healing. Perhaps there could be peace, and Thorvald would make something of his life.

"Do you accept this offer?" she asked the tall man calmly. "I am young and healthy. My mother bore five children safely. I and my sisters grew strong and well. Please let these men go unharmed. The war is over."

There was silence: a silence like the moment when the tide changes and all hangs in the balance. She looked at Thorvald. Staring at her, he seemed stripped bare of any defenses. If the tribe accepted her offer, she could win him this peace; he had his father, and the future lay before him bright and new, vibrant with possibilities. His pathway had opened at last, clear and straight.

"Creidhe—" he began, and halted, as if his words choked him. Pride, and confusion, and deep sorrow could all be read in his eyes. "Creidhe . . ."

"It's all right, Thorvald." She heard her own voice as a stranger's, small, cool and remote. "This is not your choice, it's mine."

"No!" His voice was a harsh whisper, his hands clenched tight. "No . . ."

"Come," said the elder, gesturing to the assembled folk, and two of the women walked forward to take Creidhe by the arms, apparently to march her away. Perhaps they would put her in a dark little hut, as they had Sula. Then, at night, the men would come. She registered the rank smell of the women's bodies, the rough, hard touch of their hands, the light in their eyes. For the tribe of the Unspoken, Creidhe was hope reborn.

"No!" Thorvald's tone had changed; this was a command. "No! You cannot take her."

The women paused, holding Creidhe between them. She could see the path to the shore where the *Sea Dove* lay beached; sanctuary, escape. She would not think of that.

"Cannot?" the elder echoed. "You are four; we are many. We are not afraid to die, not for this. For this, we have waited many seasons."

"You must not take her." Thorvald stepped forward, facing the elder; his hand moved to his sword hilt. "There must be another way. Creidhe is . . ." He faltered, and a fierce flush came to his cheeks, sitting oddly with the authority of his manner. "She's mine," he said simply. Creidhe stared at him. He was clever, there was no doubt of it; who else would have thought of using this argument, falsehood as it was? He was too clever for his own good.

The tall man glanced at the ritual stone where the Ulsterman sat by his fallen brother, wiping the blood from his sheet-white face. "One or the other," he said. "You cannot take both. The gods are angry; you came where you do not belong, and made the ritual imperfect. But we will keep the man, if the woman is yours. The mother of Foxmask must come to us pure, untouched, unsullied. How else can we know her child is a true son of the tribe? If the sun and moon woman is your wife, then she cannot serve us. We will take this man she calls priest. He is brave: worthy. We must complete the ritual."

"Then we will fight," said Thorvald, drawing his sword, "and you will discover the power of four against many. I'll die before I let you touch either one of them again. Skapti?"

Beside him, Skapti's mouth stretched in a grin that sent folk scurrying backward; his grip on the spear shifted, and he changed all at once from a lumbering, lumpish giant to a thing of beauty, alive with the tense, quivering readiness of a stalking predator. Across the circle Sam wrestled with his captors, shouting; Breccan held Brother Niall in his arms and could not help, though his lips moved in prayer, and perhaps, when it came to it, that was his strongest weapon to aid them. Creidhe saw what was to come in a clear flash of color, as if set down in neat, small stitches so the story would live on into a time when they themselves had faded from memory: a terrible, heroic stand, not four against many but, in truth, only two, Thorvald and Skapti back to back, fighting like wolves, like dragons, like battle heroes; Skapti and Thorvald falling in their blood while the others looked on helplessly; Thorvald hacked to death before their very eyes, Niall mutilated, the peace won at a cost beyond bearing. Wrong, all wrong: the ancestors were lying to her.

"No!" she screamed, wrenching away from the bony hands that restrained her. "No! This is not right, it can't be right, there has to be another way!" She stared wildly up into the sky, and a great cry came from deep in her belly, a shuddering wail of frustration and grief. Such a plea must surely be heard even by the gods themselves. It was a sound of primal pain. "Help us!" she screamed into the bright expanse above. Then she closed her eyes. The vibrant echo of her call hung in the air; around it, all was silent. No scrape of metal on metal, no footfall, no word now, no breath. Only the soughing of the wind, and the murmur of the sea.

And then, at last, the song. It crept to their ears like a sweet whisper of hope; it lodged in their heads like the voice of what was to come, bright with promise; it touched their hearts as a healing balm. The song fluted and chanted and tangled through the air, and birds fell silent before its loveliness. It was a little, simple thing; wordless, artless, yet its power was such that the folk of the Unspoken, every man and woman, sank to the ground, prostrate as if in the presence of a god. Sam, Thorvald, Skapti stood frozen. And Creidhe opened her eyes, gazing to the shoreward path.

A small, bedraggled figure stood there, legs and arms stick-thin; hair a tangled mess of dark strands dripping across his skinny shoulders. As she stared, transfixed, he shook himself as a dog does, and droplets flew all around him in a silvery spray. He came on, walking alone and steadily in his squelching wet shoes and his sodden, feathery garments, his delicate, triangular face pale and calm, his eyes like beacons, shining, confident and true. And still he sang, a chant sweet and wondrous and terrible in its power. As he came nearer, making a straight path between the assembled folk to the place where the elder lay by the stone in a posture of complete abasement, Small One's song

changed, warming to a joy that filled the heart and brought
tears to the eyes, and a smile transformed his features, a
smile of such happiness it clutched at Creidhe's vitals. The
child took two, three steps toward the ritual stone, and bent
to raise the tall man gently to his knees, as if it were Small
One who was the elder. Then the man, weeping, reached
out, and Small One set his thin arms around the elder's neck
and was enfolded in an embrace of such tenderness one
might have thought this was his own father. The long years
of exile were over. Foxmask had come home.

Creidhe's heart was beating like a drum, her skin was
clammy with sweat. The women had released her, prostrat-
ing themselves full length like the others. Now the folk of
the Unspoken rose from the ground and moved in to cluster
around the child and the man who held him in his arms. For
a little, the intruders were quite forgotten. Creidhe elbowed
her way to Breccan's side where he still sat supporting the
white-haired man. There was a little space by them; Thorvald stood in a pose of readiness, sword in hand, and Skapti
paced, brandishing the thrusting spear to ward off any who
might venture too close. But none watched them now; every
eye was on Foxmask, every ear tuned to the voice that still
sang on, filling the air with the music of lives made fresh
and paths once more true.

Creidhe bent close; it was the first clear sight she had had
of the injured man. He was so ghost-white one might have
thought him dead, save for the one dark, penetrating eye
blazing stark with endurance. His tight mouth was framed
by grooves of pain. He held himself quite silent. And where
his left eye had been, there was a hideous, open wound, a
gaping socket that welled with fresh blood and oozing gob-
bets of matter. Breccan's hands were shaking as he sought
to stem the flow. To bind the wound would be futile without
fresh linen or water or healing herbs.

Her father had spoken to her of Somerled's severe discipline, his astonishing self-control. This, however, went beyond anything she could have imagined. Niall could not
quite regulate his breathing; still, he had not cried out, not
once. Creidhe met that single eye, bright with pain, and

said, "He'd be very proud of you. Will be, when I tell him. Not just for today, but for everything. You've kept your promise."

She saw Niall's lips twitch in an attempt to acknowledge her words; he could not nod, would not speak, lest the effort cause him to scream aloud, or shed tears, or faint, and thus break what she suspected were terrible, self-imposed rules. Then his gaze went back to Thorvald, standing with weapon in hand, ready to defend to the death his father, his comrades, the oft-ignored companion of his childhood. There was such love in that look, Creidhe felt it even in her own numb and aching heart.

"We must get him to the boat and away to safety," Breccan said. "I need bandages and salves, and herbs for the pain. Do you think they will let us go now?"

But Creidhe did not answer him, for at that moment the mob of folk surrounding the elder and the child parted, and the song died away in a scatter of bright notes, and there was once again a deep, profound silence. She saw the elder set the child on the ground near the place where the implements of ritual were laid out in readiness. The stocky man with arms like tree limbs had taken up his ropes once more. Small One stood very still, eyes tranquil, hands relaxed by his sides. He was a child. How could he understand?

The elder turned toward Thorvald, facing the point of his sword unflinching.

"You must leave this shore," the tall man said gravely, gesturing with a hand to encompass Thorvald, and Creidhe, and the two priests, as well as the looming figure of Skapti behind them. "Take this man with you and tend to his wound. He is very strong: worthy of the honor we accorded him. A priest indeed, full of power in body and spirit. We would have welcomed him, revered him. You must do no less, for this is a man forged by a life of darkness into a true weapon of light. You must be guided by him, for he is wise. As for ourselves, this is our day of healing and of joy, for our true son is returned, our dear one of the spirit, our own Foxmask. We receive him into our hearts and are made whole again. It lacks but the deep ritual, and for that, outsiders may not be present." His eyes moved briefly to the skewers, the scoop, the club laid ready.

"Thank you." Thorvald's voice was that of a leader. He sheathed his sword and gestured to Skapti, who lowered the spear perhaps a finger's breadth; the big warrior's expression was still ferocious with challenge. "We will leave straightaway. My father's injury is terrible; he needs care urgently." There was a note of censure in the words.

The elder gazed at him unperturbed. "He is strong," he said. "Now go."

A glance across the circle, and Sam was released. They were free to leave. Skapti passed the spear to Sam and bent to take up Brother Niall in his arms. Thorvald began to lead the way toward the track.

"Creidhe?" Sam said gently. "It's over now. Time to go home." And he put a hand on her shoulder, as if to guide her.

"No!" Creidhe exclaimed, shaking him off with some violence. "No! It can't be finished like this, I promised Keeper—" She darted across the sward in Sula's little boots and snatched the child up in her arms. There was a gasp of shock from the assembled folk; Thorvald was suddenly still, and Skapti halted, bearing the wounded priest. The elder's eyes were fixed on the child; it was clear that from now on, the choices the tribe made would be Foxmask's. The little face was clear and calm. The deep green eyes, changeable as the sea, looked into Creidhe's, and Small One put up a hand to touch her cheek.

"I know the manner of your ritual." Creidhe spoke shakily, but pitched her voice so all could hear. "I understand the reasons for it. In order to tell his truths, to sing his songs, Foxmask must relinquish the sight of the world. Thus are opened the eyes of the spirit. To guide you on the right paths, the seer must cease to tread the flawed ways of man, and travel by visions and stars, by whispers and memories. But you must not damage this child. I could argue that he is small, frail and innocent. I could warn you that in seeking to prepare your seer for this role among you, you may simply end up killing him. But I know you will not heed such worldly truths, not from me. So I will let the seer himself speak for me. You heard his song today, as he stepped from the strong hands of the sea and came among you once more, full of love and wisdom, ready to give himself to your tribe as guide and wise one for the rest of his life. He loves you: that is clearly read in his eyes. He is already full of understanding, rich in knowledge of the patterns of the ancestors. Foxmask is only six years old, and yet his songs fill our hearts with healing hope. I heard him on thc Isle of Clouds, where I dwelt by his side before I came here. His voice sang the moon across the sky; it opened pathways I had never dreamed were possible. You have heard him today. Who among you could doubt the joyous note of homecoming in his song? Who could question the wisdom in it, an understanding as far beyond our own as the stars are beyond the little lamps we light to keep away the darkness? I say to you, this child is already wise; at six years old, he is the true elder among you. His spirit shines bright; he is filled with the light of the ancestors."

She felt the slight weight of the child in her arms, the tickle of his tangle of dark hair against her cheek; his thin arms were about her neck. Let them listen to her, she prayed; let them understand this truth, or her promise to Keeper would be entirely broken. "There is no need to blind the child," she went on, forcing her voice steady. "Already in him the eye of the spirit is fully open. There is no need to cripple him. Did he not come back to you, through the sea, all the way from the Isle of Clouds? Foxmask is home; he has come home by his own choice. He will not leave you again, but will serve you long and faithfully. I beg you, think on this, and do not harm the one who loves you best of all."

There was silence for a little, and then whispering and muttering among the folk. The man with the ropes had not moved. Perhaps he was aware of Sam's eyes fixed on him with a dangerous glint in them. The fisherman stood close at hand; there was less than a spear's thrust in it. The elder was frowning and rubbing his chin.

"Creidhe!" hissed Thorvald. "We must go, my father is hurt, I must get him to help."

She turned a little, regarding him without expression, her arms wrapped firmly around the small form of the child. "Then go," she said flatly.

"Don't be stupid—" Thorvald began, and fell silent as the tall man spoke. He was not looking at Creidhe, or at Small One, or at Thorvald, so clearly the leader of this band of interlopers. Instead, he met the one-eyed gaze of the man who lay bleeding in Skapti's strong arms.

"What do you say?" he asked, and there was a deep respect in his voice. "This is a girl, we cannot take her words as guidance. But the seer trusts her, he clings to her as to a friend of the heart. Our lore demands that Foxmask undergo the ritual. Yet there seems a truth in what she tells. What must we do?"

And Niall, summoning speech from the depths of his shocked and wounded body, answered him in a thready whisper. "Whose voice will you trust but the child's? Whose path will you follow but his? He speaks the word of God. Creidhe's telling the truth; she knows no other way. If her voice is not enough for you, ask the seer."

The elder inclined his head gravely. All eyes turned to the child in Creidhe's arms. Creidhe felt his little hand against her cheek again, his fingers cold, his touch gentle. He was saying good-bye.

"I hope this is right, Small One," she whispered. "As long as you are safe and happy . . . he would be content with that, I think . . ." For a moment she felt the child's fierce hug, and she held him in return; he was only six, for all his wisdom, and the way ahead of him was all of giving and sacrifice. The burden he would bear was not a light one. Then he pulled back, and she saw his odd little smile and the tranquil, soft gaze of his sea-green eyes. She set him on the ground; her hands touched his thin arms one last time, then let go.

He sang a new song. Its gentle sweeps of melody wove about them as they stood quiet. Its delicate grace notes wreathed the ancient stone as, at a gesture from the elder, the men of the Unspoken gathered up the instruments of the ritual, placed them in a skin bag, and bore them away. Its lilting phrases followed the small party of intruders as they made their way toward the shoreward track, and the men and women of the Unspoken fell back to let them pass. The song rose to fill the air with its brightness, with its sweet, strong message of love, loyalty, and acceptance, vibrating in the timbers of the *Sea Dove* as the men pushed her off the shore and out into the bay, sounding in her sails like a wind of truth as they set a course for Council Fjord.

Skapti and Thorvald sailed the boat; Sam was busy rummaging in his well-kept supplies, finding cloth for bandages, fresh water, and the means to make a splint, for it was apparent the loss of an eye was not the only injury Niall had sustained. His right leg was useless, the bones of the calf shattered by one well-aimed blow of that short, thick club. Sam found a strong cordial set away in a small flask of metal, stoppered with a bone plug wound with leather, and this time Niall drank without protest, swallowing the draft the fisherman offered him in two labored gulps. His breath came harder now; Creidhe wished he would allow himself to cry out, for his silence was costing him dearly. When the drink had done its work, and the lid grew heavy over the priest's single eye, they splinted the leg, Sam and Breccan between them, with Creidhe's deft fingers to knot the linen strips around the lengths of pine they used, wood set aside from the mending of the *Sea Dove*. A broken man was not so easily mended. Perhaps the limb would knit straight; with luck, he would walk again, though never as he had done. Niall remained conscious. Creidhe heard the whistle of his breathing and felt the trembling that coursed through his body. Such pain . . . Even her father, surely, would scream under such agony. And yet, looking up, she saw a peace on the priest's white features, an acceptance in the shadowed depths of his one dark eye that spoke of a joy transcending earthly pain. Whatever he had found today, it seemed a shield good and abiding, and of more than worldly strength.

When it was done, Sam turned his attention again to the boat, and Breccan settled by the injured man's side, with Creidhe opposite.

"Rest now," the Ulsterman said quietly. "This journey is nearly over."

Niall made a little sound, signifying thanks, or agreement.

Breccan's eyes were thoughtful, his amiable face serious. "The word of God," he mused. "You said, he speaks the word of God. How can that be? These folk are pagan, unbelievers. Their rites are savage and cruel. The maiming of children, the gouging of eyes . . . it is surely the devil's word we heard here, and not the truth our heavenly Father gives us. And yet . . . and yet, the child himself . . . The message, so powerful, so good . . . Did he twist my perceptions, to make me see dark as light? I do not understand it . . ."

"Brother . . ." Niall's whispering voice had lost its clarity; the strong draft made him slur his words, but still they heard him. "Much to learn . . . you and I . . . lifetime . . ."

Breccan glanced at Thorvald, now manning the steering oar, his features focused, intent, as the *Sea Dove* plowed her way back to the world of men. "You'll have other things to do with your life now, my friend," he said softly. "A time of change for you, I think. Your son has a great task ahead of him in this place. He'll need you." But there was a question in his tone.

"You think?" said Somerled, smiling.

It was night, but summer saw the sun hide just below the rim of the world, leaving a strange, cold light on rounded hill, on quiet lake, on the stone walls of hut and barn and sturdy longhouse. Near the western shore of Hrossey, the light filtered through the cracks in door and shutters, adding its coolness to the flickering glow of Margaret's small oil lamp.

She stood in the weaving room, the bowl of seal oil with its floating wick set by her on a stone shelf, and stared in the dim light at the piece stretched half finished on the loom. It was plain enough, no dyes, just the natural hues of the wool, white and cream and the rich, dark shade from her special flock of black-coated ewes. The design had simple stripes at the ends and an even, strong weave; Margaret was skillful, and such a piece as this would be highly valued. But she would never weave as Creidhe had done, with true magic in her fingers, with dedication in her heart as she devised the fine, bright dyes, the intricate border strips, the bold, lovely designs. It took more than skill to create as Creidhe did; it took love.

Margaret picked up the little lamp and walked barefoot into the long room, where all was neat and orderly, the table cleared, the fire banked up, the pots and crocks scoured and stored. In the tiny room that opened off this chamber her serving women slept, weary from the hard day's work in house and fields. The little maid she had brought with her on that long-ago voyage from Rogaland was a matron now, wed to a man of the islands and a mother of fine sons, with a farm of her own for them to work on.

Margaret shivered. The memories of that time hung close on nights like this, chilling her deep inside, banishing sleep. So many chances there had been, so many opportunities, and most of them wasted. All that she had carried out of that dark season was her son, and now it seemed he, too, was lost. It was high summer; the barley grew lush, the sheep were fat, even the wind had lost its sharp bite. But Thorvald had not come home; Creidhe's place before the loom remained empty. There was no joy in the house. In the brightest season of the year, her home was a place of shadows. Her bare feet whispered on the stone floor, moving to the spot where heavy shutters covered the single, narrow window of the long room. Her fingers slid the bolt aside; she pushed the shutters open with a creak and looked out.

No stars were visible; the brightness of the long summer twilight masked them from view. The landscape lay like a world of dreams, ordinary things made strange by that quirk of half-darkness, half-light. The compact forms of sheep were silvery hummocks merging with the grass; the roof weights moved in the slight wind as with their own life. A cloak, slung over a line to dry, spread wings like a creature poised to take flight to the invisible moon. The air came to her nostrils pure, cool and clear.

Margaret sighed. This was not good enough. How could

she go on like this? She was like a stream dammed in its course which fills and fills, building and building, and yet what held her seemed so strong it would never give, not if the weight of all the cares in the world pressed in on it. It was not right. On such a night, with the world laid out before her in its grand, mysterious wonder, how could she stand here like a shriveled husk of a woman, shut so tight around herself that all she could feel was regret? Oh, to be seventeen again and given the chance to try once more, to make her life anew. Margaret drew the shutters closed. How foolish, to wish such a thing. There were no second chances. If there were, who was to say she would not make all her errors twice over? There was only this life, now, and what years the gods might see fit to grant her. She pictured it: ten years, twenty if she were lucky. Middle age, old age, served out in obedience to her own tenets of restraint, control, order, discipline . . . served out alone, if Thorvald were lost, alone with neither father nor mother, sister nor brother, husband nor children around her . . . What did she have? Her skills, certainly, though they were not so much, when she had seen her pupil's work flowering bright and wondrous on the loom and knew she did not have it in her to match that. Still, she had taught Creidhe the elements, had tutored other girls who now plied their craft ably all over the islands. There was a certain satisfaction in that. Her household, her farm . . . both were well run, prosperous, orderly; the credit for that was principally another's, she felt. Her mind darted away, somehow reluctant, tonight, to dwell on Ash, for suddenly those thoughts had a danger in them. She had friends, old and true ones. But Nessa was heavy with child now, and her small family had seemed to close in on itself at this time of risk and worry. Without Creidhe, Margaret felt herself outside that tight circle of love and protection, and limited herself to offers of help with their stock, or gifts of wool or cheeses. She participated in the councils, sometimes, as widow of a former chieftain of the island and as a landholder in her own right, but such pursuits meant less each time. Perhaps, at six-and-thirty, she was starting to grow old.

Control, she told herself, and moved to take the lamp again and walk to her bedchamber. She made her breathing slower; forced back the tears that pricked her eyelids. Self-pity was not productive; it solved nothing. If logic, reasoning and force of will could not show her a pathway forward, then she must simply accept that her doom was to become a lonely dried-up spinster beset by shades of the past. It was a punishment: the gods' burden, set on her for what she had done. And yet, tonight, something stirred within her, like a tiny voice, a whispering song, terrifying yet wondrous, telling her it was not so . . . she was still alive, deep inside . . . she must simply breathe, and open her eyes, and change . . . it would be easy . . .

And so, as her feet passed by a certain doorway that was covered only by a coarse woolen hanging, Margaret paused without a sound. And within the chamber, the man who had lain awake, sharing her every step, her every moment of self-doubt, saw the light of her small lamp through the woven fabric and spoke softly from his narrow bed.

"Are you all right?" Ash asked.

Margaret swallowed, her heart suddenly racing. She did not know what words would come to her lips; perhaps a simple positive, then a flight to the sanctuary of her own quiet chamber. Yet his voice seemed to open something inside her, to touch a corner where sensation had long been absent.

"I can't get warm," she whispered, her teeth chattering as if the words themselves had made this true. The lamp shook in her hand; oil spilled onto the flagstones. A moment later he was in the doorway beside her, one hand reaching to take the lamp, the other clutching a garment, a rumpled shirt perhaps, in front of him to hide his nakedness. He had been careful, always, to observe the rules of conduct between steward and mistress; she had never seen him thus unclothed, not in all the years the two of them had shared this house. Those same rules should have constrained her to turn her gaze away rather than look on him. But Margaret found she could not. His body was pleasing to her: lean, compact, wiry, the frame of a man who has worked hard and seen little of indulgence. His chest was thatched with iron-gray hair; his shoulders were strong, his arms corded with muscle, for all his neatness of build. In the small light of the lamp his eyes met hers, steady and true, though she did not miss the wariness there. Words fled again; she did not know what she could say to him, for if she asked, and he said no, as well he might, she did not think they could ever be friends again. And he was her one true friend, her best companion; through all these lonely years he had proved it over and over, though she had given him scant recompense for his loyalty.

"I have said it before," Ash's tone was gentle, "but I must summon my courage, I think, and tell you again. I would serve you until my last breath leaves me: with my labors, with my hands, with every scrap of life I have in me." His voice shrank to a whisper, matching hers. "And with my body, if you wish. To warm you only, if you prefer. If there is one thing I have learned in this household, it is to exercise restraint."

He was a brave man, Margaret thought, feeling the tears she had held back beginning to spill, despite her.

"I would prefer—I—" Her voice was shaking; by all the gods, was this to be the way of it, that as soon as she lowered one part of her guard, all her defenses tumbled down? It was indeed as if she were seventeen again, and trembling before her first sweetheart.

Ash set down the lamp and reached to cup her face with his hand; her tears flowed unchecked between his fingers. "Tell me," he said.

Margaret drew a deep breath. She reached for the garment Ash still held before him and drew it away so it fell, discarded, on the cold stone floor. Her hands moved again, and he in turn drew breath, this time sharply.

"I might show you, perhaps," she said softly, moving closer so her body touched his own, feeling his warmth, his strength. Suddenly she was no longer afraid, no longer unsure. "Still, a lady does not act thus; so I was taught as a girl. Unless the man is her husband."

Ash said nothing; his lips were against her hair, his hands moved down her back, pressing her closer.

"I thought . . ." Margaret said, closing her eyes. Sensation, already, grew strong enough to crowd out discipline, control, cold logic. There was only his heart, thumping like a hammer against her, and the wondrous touch of his hands, and the hard vigor of his body, awakening her own as if she were indeed no more than a young girl, and he her first and only love. "I thought . . . you might agree to that . . . then this would be . . . it would be . . ."

"Later," Ash whispered. "We will talk later."

"Come, then," said Margaret, stepping back, taking his hand in hers, leading him along the dark hallway to her own chamber. "Come, and be welcome, dear friend."

"I am, I confess, somewhat out of practice." She heard his voice in the dimness of the quiet room; recognized from the tone of it that he was not altogether joking. She reached to unfasten the ribbon at the neck of her nightrobe, but Ash was there before her, fingers deft and sure. His body was close again: hot, hard, certain in a way that needed no words.

"I, too," she told him, slipping the gown over her head. "It's been a long time. Why have we waited so long?" Suddenly she knew how foolish that had been: so many years wasted, years that could have been full of love, of laughter, of joyful sharing. There could have been children.

"Hush," said Ash, drawing her down to lie by him, flesh on naked flesh, a sweet congruence of skin. Age, shyness, lack of practice became of no consequence whatever; the language of the body is immediate and powerful, and makes its own rules. "We waited for tonight, that's all. And for what's to come."

Much later, as the cold half-light began to change to the pale gold that presages the sun's creeping up from his shallow summer hiding place, Margaret heard Ash say against her temple, "I love you."

And she would have told him the same, but her self-imposed rules would not allow her to lie.

"I don't know if I can love anymore," she said, her fingers moving softly against the hollow of his back, where strong spine curved to well-muscled buttocks: his body was a delight, a whole world for discovery. "You know already that I have lain with my husband, and with another man. My dear, I never felt such delight as you have given me tonight. I had not dreamed such pleasure was possible."

"You honor me," Ash said, holding his voice quiet, for there were others in the house, and morning was coming. "You said . . . before . . . you spoke of marriage, I think. Did I hear you correctly? Would the lady Margaret, daughter of Thorvald Strong-Arm, stoop to ally herself to a housecarl? How can that be?"

"You heard correctly," Margaret said, catching the note of constraint in his words; somehow, she had upset him. "Though you are no housecarl, my dear, and you know it."

There was a silence. Ash had moved away from her in the bed; she was cold again. At last he said, very quietly, "Would you wed a man you do not love?"

She felt her heart turn over. He was her dear friend, so wise, so good and generous, and she had hurt him.

"I only said I do not know if I can," she told him. "All I can tell you is that I will never learn if I do not have you beside me. Indeed, I do not think I can go on at all without that. Something has changed tonight; the shadows have receded, as if a door were opened and sunlight let in. As if a barrier were broken and prisoners set free. I do not know what it is. I only know I do not want to spend another night in this bed alone, without your body to warm me, your arms to enfold me, your heart against mine. I only know I do not want to go forth in these islands again without you by my side, not as steward but as husband. It should have been so long since, when we were young. Perhaps this is love. Whatever it is, it feels like the first touch of spring sun, the smell of rain after long drought. In time, I will learn the truth of it. If you will help me." So sweet, so new, that sensation of letting go, of sharing, of knowing she need not do it all by herself, ever again.

"I love you," he said once more, so softly she could

barely hear, and folded her close. In a matter of moments the two of them slipped into sleep. They lay safe in each other's arms as the women of the household began to rise, and stir up the fire, and prepare for a new day.

FOURTEEN

His voice
A sigh in the west wind
A song in the waters
A whisper in the heart
His voice and a new day.

MONK'S MARGIN NOTE

By the time the *Sea Dove* came back to Council Fjord, the bodies of Helgi and Svein had been consigned to earth with due ritual. Prayers had been spoken for Alof, who drifted somewhere in the waves beyond the Isle of Clouds, forever parted from his home shore. For Hogni it would be different. Hogni was a warrior by trade and must have a warrior's rites.

"It can't be tonight," Einar told Thorvald as men hastened to the place where the *Sea Dove* was beached, and many willing hands helped to convey wounded priest and exhausted girl to the shelter above the bay. "They have to fetch Hogni's wife here; she lives right across the other side of the island, at Starkfell settlement, where the boats go over to the Isle of Streams. It'll be a slow walk back with the children. They're little lads; the younger was the last child born on the island before the hunt began. Besides, we've called a council for tonight. Asgrim didn't want it, but we all insisted. You have to speak up for us, Thorvald, and do it quickly before he takes a grip on things the way he did before."

"Tonight?" Thorvald's head was reeling with all that had

happened, so much, too much for one mind, one heart to hold at once. The seer restored, his father, Creidhe, and now the men, and this . . . He drew a slow, deliberate breath and squared his shoulders. "Yes, of course it must be tonight, I understand. You've done well to persuade him. I must make sure my father is attended to first; he's been terribly injured."

Einar's eyes widened. "Your father?" he echoed, turning his head to look as the men who were carrying the wounded hermit reached the shelter and disappeared inside. "The Christian is your father?"

"It's a long story. Now tell me quickly, are they all here, Wieland, Orm, Skolli? Will all speak out if I lead the way?"

"We'll speak all right." Einar's mouth stretched in a grim smile of satisfaction. "And we'll back you up with cold iron, if that's what it comes to."

"I hope force will not be necessary," Thorvald said. "He is but one man, after all." On the other hand, Asgrim had held the Long Knife people in his power throughout those years of hardship and grief. He was strong, and a clever talker.

"Don't worry about the hermit," Einar said. "Skolli has good hands for bone-setting, and there's a woman up there with a knowledge of herbs and such. Don't look so astonished, Thorvald. Every hunt brings losses. The women come to help tend the wounded, and to claim the bodies of the slain. At such times, Asgrim admits them to the camp. Besides, news travels fast. Once the word was out that you'd gone off south to confront the enemy, folk started walking in from Brightwater, from Blood Bay, from all over. People can feel change coming. They want to be here to see it happen."

It was still light when they gathered in the shelter, though the sun had set, for the sky held the pale, cool glow of the summer night. At the far end of the long chamber, Brother Niall lay on a pallet; Skolli had removed the makeshift splint, straightened the bones of the shattered leg as best he could, and bound the limb again while the white-haired man shivered and trembled and put his teeth through his lip, but cried out not at all. Now, a strong draft of soporific herbs had granted the hermit a merciful half-sleep, and he rested with hands relaxed and features peaceful. A wadding covered the gaping wound where his eye had been, with a strip of linen wound around the tonsured head to keep the dressing in place. By the pallet sat Breccan, pale but calm, and a silent, blank-faced Creidhe. Sam stood in the shadows nearby.

Asgrim was taking a long time to come down from his hut. After an initial greeting, a few congratulatory words, an expression of shock and wonderment at the sight of Niall wounded and Creidhe alive, he had retreated quickly to his private quarters, raising no protest as the communal sleeping place became shelter to women and Christians both. Perhaps, Orm observed tightly, the Ruler realized he'd backed himself into a corner, and was spending what time he had working out how he might extricate himself. Skapti was keeping vigil by his brother's body, which lay in a little anteroom off the main chamber. There were no personal guards, not anymore. And all of them knew the truth now, about what Asgrim had done to his own daughter. The question was, what was Thorvald going to do about it all?

It felt odd to be going through the normal routine, cooking fish, handing out platters, sitting on the earthen shelves to eat, men and women together. It was not a joyful feast; too many had been lost, too much endured. Still, voices buzzed with anticipation, not untinged with fear. This would be the first council held since the days before the war began; the first since long before the years of the hunt. Much depended on its outcome. The men knew Thorvald; the women did not, and their doubt showed in their eyes.

Time passed. Skapti came to join them. He sat by Thorvald's side, picking at a platter of food. After a while, Einar went outside and came back in again. They waited some time longer, until Thorvald, making a decision, rose to his feet.

"Einar, Skapti, go and fetch him," he said crisply. "Folk are weary; the sooner we begin, the sooner this can be concluded and we can all get some well-earned sleep."

"No need." The voice from the doorway was level, considered. "Let us begin, by all means. I see no real necessity for this, as I told Einar. There's nothing to discuss. However, since the men insisted, I suppose we must humor them." The dark eyes met Thorvald's, cryptic, unreadable. "Who's going to sit at the top, you or I?"

"I'm happy here, among my men," Thorvald said, matching the other's measured tone, though his heart was thumping and his palms were clammy. "By all means take your usual place."

Asgrim moved to the head of the long hearth. He wore a plain dark robe and a belt with a silver buckle; his hair was neatly tied back from his face, his hands relaxed by his sides. If he felt any misgivings, he gave no sign of it.

"Very well," he said. "I must admit I was somewhat surprised when Einar and others requested a formal council on the very heels of the hunt, and with one of our own still lacking the funeral rites due to him." A low rumbling sound emanated from Skapti, like a big dog's growl of warning. "I'd have thought strong ale and good fellowship were more in order on such a night," Asgrim went on, unperturbed. "Be that as it may, this gathering allows me the opportunity to congratulate the young man who, it seems, has saved us all. To see the *Sea Dove* sail in with her mission accomplished was a bright vision indeed." He turned once more to Thorvald, nodding with a certain graciousness. "The seer is returned to his people, and the years of the hunt are over. We thank you from the bottom of our hearts, Thorvald. This was never your battle. It was never your quest. We feel delight at the unexpected restoration of your little friend Creidhe. We are grateful to Sam for the part he and his fine boat have played in this. For your own valor and persistence, we lack adequate means of repayment. Of course, we'll make sure you are generously supplied for your return home, and the boat as well fitted as possible."

It was not necessary for Thorvald to respond. Several voices spoke, all of them angry.

"What do you mean, it was never his battle?"

"Return home? His home's here with us!"

"Let Thorvald speak!"

Einar's voice silenced them all, quiet as it was. "Not yet," he said. "Thorvald will speak after me. I called the council; under the rules of precedence, it's for me to set out the matter for discussion. Maybe some of you have forgotten that. It's been a long time."

"Very well." Asgrim's tone was icy.

"We all know what Thorvald did," Einar said. "Others, too; I've heard the full story, and it's clear that every single man, and woman, that sailed off on the *Sea Dove* today played a part in securing peace for us. There's no need for formal thanks or rewards. Thorvald understands how we feel. It's something too big to put into words."

There were nods, grunts of assent, glances and grins in Thorvald's direction. For all his measured words, Einar was nervous; his hands were clasped together behind his back, and the five-line scar showed stark against the pallor of his cheek. After this it would be six, but then no more. Wieland was sitting beside his wife, a thin young woman with a tired, sad face; his fingers were laced in hers, and she leaned against his shoulder.

"Anyway," Einar went on, "what I'm telling you is that this council is not to mark the end of the hunt, as such, nor to thank those who achieved it, since they know already the depth of gratitude we bear them. It's to decide what comes next."

The words hung in the smoky air of the shelter for a long moment.

"Next?" Asgrim echoed. "What do you mean?"

"The election of a Ruler." Orm had risen to his feet. "That's allowable when the people decide it. I can even remember how it's done, I think, if all these years without proper councils haven't driven it out of my head—"

"I see." Asgrim's tone was level still, his expression bland. "A challenge. And, of course, you are right. There

were rules, once. Such niceties can hardly be observed in
times of conflict such as we have endured. A conflict, I must
point out, that you have survived only because of the quality
of my own leadership, my unrelenting will to hold back the
enemy. Who among you would have done what I have done
for you? If not for me, many more would have perished.
The Long Knife people would have been finished years ago.
You can't do without me. Try it, and the Unspoken will be
on your doorstep again tomorrow with some new demand,
and when you can't meet it, they'll be back to take your
children, to sing them on their swift journey to oblivion—"

"Enough!" This time, astonishingly, it was Wieland who
cried out, Wieland who leaped to his feet, an accusatory finger pointed straight at Asgrim. "How dare you speak thus
before my wife, and before the other women of our people
who have seen their babes sacrificed thus? How dare you
darken their minds with your fearful lies? The war is over!
The seer is restored! We want no more of your falsehoods
and your cruelty!" The young man subsided back to the
earthen shelf, and his wife slipped her arm around his
shoulders. There was a chorus of voices, both male and female, all of them approving.

"Strongly spoken, lad," Asgrim said, folding his arms. "I
understand that emotions run high at times like these. It's
been hard for all of us. That's why it seems to me that now
is not the best time for formal debate of such weighty matters. You're not yourselves. We should give it a few days at
least, time to talk it through, time for Hogni to be sent to his
rest and the others accorded a mourning period of some
dignity. Besides"—he glanced to the back of the shelter,
where Breccan sat by his friend's side—"there are outsiders
here, folk who should not be admitted to such an assembly.
You speak of rules, Einar. That is one of the rules."

"Brother Niall is my father." Thorvald was astonished by
the pride it gave him to be able to say this, the courage he
felt flooding back as he spoke. Perhaps this would not be so
difficult after all. "I think you may find the rules allow him
to be here by virtue of kinship. Sam and I, incomers as we
are, are most certainly of your company of warriors, and

have earned our places among you. Brother Breccan's here to tend an injured man; Creidhe also. Let us proceed with this. I understand that, if there are candidates for leadership, they must be allocated time to speak, to set forth their claims each in turn. They may then request that two or three others speak in support of them. Then the people make a choice. Do I have it right?"

Asgrim looked at him. "It is a long time since my own election as Ruler," he said grimly. "I took the place of a man who died, and I was unopposed. What you suggest could be lengthy. If there were several contenders, we could be here all night."

"There's only two contenders." Skolli's deep voice cut across the chamber. "Yourself and Thorvald. And we need no setting out of claims to help us choose between you. It'll be over in a flash."

Asgrim's dark eyes rested again on Thorvald. "True?" he queried. "You seek to oppose me?" It was the tone that had ever made men shake in their boots.

"No," said Thorvald, provoking a chorus of shocked exclamations, which he silenced with a raised hand. "I seek to be leader of these men and women. I seek to guide and help them to a better future, a future in which all of us work together for peace and prosperity. I do not seek to oppose you. But if I am elected Ruler here, I want you gone from this place, never to return."

Asgrim's eyes had narrowed alarmingly.

"Since I have already begun," Thorvald went on, stepping up to stand by the Ruler, facing the assembled folk, "let this be my formal speech to you. We've won a great battle here; we've won ourselves a chance of a future. I don't need to tell you how precious that is. All of us understand we mustn't squander it; that we must work together to rebuild what was lost, and to seek new opportunities as well. I've fought alongside you. I've seen your courage and your comradeship, your vision and your commitment. Some of you here don't know me. I am an incomer; that is something I must ask you to accept. It makes no difference to my promise to you: that if you choose me to lead you, I will strive to ensure the best future for the islands, and for every man, woman and child here. You are fine people, and you deserve no less.

"I will not enumerate Asgrim's faults; if you don't know yet that he has undervalued you, insulted you by his lack of trust, and sought to frighten even the strongest of you into obedience, then nothing I can say is likely to sway your opinion. I simply offer myself as a replacement. I will not call myself Ruler. I cannot govern alone; if you choose me, I'll institute a council of elected people to advise me. We'll hold a Thing regularly to sort out our own disputes under due process of law, and we'll also discuss making a formal truce with the Unspoken, to guard against future trouble. That's for later. First, we need to make sure all are provided for, that crops are sown and harvested, stock tended to, boats and houses repaired. I'm told we owe a great debt to the womenfolk of the island for keeping all that going under great difficulty. You are hard workers, all of you: good workers. You are strong in spirit; I've seen that on the Isle of Clouds, and I see it in all of your faces here tonight. You've come through terrible times, and you've survived. If you elect me, I will help you to move on now, to make the best of this time of peace. I will give you a rule of justice and fairness. I will give all that is in me to give. I swear it."

A chorus of cheers greeted this speech, a clapping of hands and a thumping of boots on the earthen floor.

"Stirring stuff," observed Asgrim dryly. "I have no desire to make any emotive statements myself. I merely point out that Thorvald is a very young man and, despite his undoubted success in the hunt, entirely untried as a leader in times of peace. Don't let the euphoria of the moment warp your judgment or rob you of any common sense. What you decide tonight, you must live with for at least three years under the rules Einar is so fond of. Thorvald's not one of us. He's an incomer who reached this shore entirely by accident. He hasn't witnessed at firsthand the evil deeds our enemy can perform. He hasn't shared our heartbreak and sorrow. The women among you don't know him, and I see from the doubt in their eyes that they don't trust him. Who's to say what he'll become if you elect him to lead you? A tyrant? An ineffectual weakling? Put him in charge and anything could happen."

There was a general muttering around the hall, and then one of the women stood up, a tall, solidly built personage of indeterminate age, with scraped-back hair and a grim jaw.

"That's all very well, Asgrim," she said flatly, "but what can you offer us that's better? It sticks in the craw to hear you speak as if you represent the women here, after what you've put us through. We've obeyed your orders and lived by your rule a long time now, and our existence has been all fear and mistrust. You've made us act in ways we'd have shrunk from if we hadn't been too scared of your thugs to disobey." She shot a meaningful glance at Skapti. "Which of us would have let her husband go, her sons, her brothers, year after year, knowing they might come back crippled or never at all? Knowing it was hopeless all the time? Which of us would have allowed that if we hadn't been too frightened to speak up? You made us perform your own dark deeds, Asgrim, in the name of a peace that was not to be, not while you were in charge. You made us trick the girl so you could hand her over; made us conspire against a creature who had shown us nothing but kindness. Now they're saying it was the same with young Sula: your own daughter. That sickens me. It would sicken any right-thinking man or woman. But it's not your own evil deeds we spurn now, it's the way you turned us into something no better than yourself. I want the taint of that off my hands. I want the taste of it out of my mouth. As far as I'm concerned, any leader will be better than you, whether it's Orm or Einar or one of the others. If the men think young Thorvald's the one, I'll support them, and so will every woman here." She sat down abruptly, her face red.

"Well spoken, Gudrun," Einar said quietly. "Thorvald, I think we can consider that a speech in support of yourself. Is there anyone else who would like to add a few words?"

Many voices sounded; a forest of hands shot up.

"Who do you choose, Thorvald?" Einar was smiling.

"I would give all a chance to speak, if I could," Thorvald said, feeling the flush in his own cheeks. "But it's late, and we need sleep." His gaze moved over them: Einar himself, veteran of many battles; Skolli with his broad smith's shoulders; stalwart Orm and sad-eyed Wieland. Sam stood in the background, tall and fair. And there was one among them who sat quietly, not asking for consideration, merely fixing his small, reddened eyes on Thorvald in an expression as mournfully loyal as that of a devoted dog.

"Skapti," Thorvald said. "I wish Skapti to speak for me." And heard, in Asgrim's indrawn breath, that this was the last thing the Ruler had expected. The big warrior, undoubtedly, was the only one of them Asgrim had counted on as an unwavering ally.

Skapti rose to his full, considerable height. The assembly fell silent. "Man of few words," Skapti said. "Not a good talker. I've done some ill deeds, you all know about that, or if you don't, you'll find out soon enough. He made me do them," glancing at the Ruler, whose features had gone rigid as a mask, "but that's no excuse. Thought I was finished, done for. Nearly made an end of it myself. He pulled me back. Thorvald. Best friend you'd ever have. Best leader you could ever find. Thanks to him, I can go forward now, even without my brother." A tear trickled down his broad cheek; he dashed it away with a large hand. "Even without Hogni, I've something to live for. Thorvald gave me faith in myself, faith that I can do the right thing. He gave me hope."

"He gave us all hope," Orm said quietly.

"You can't go past him," Skapti said. "He's the best."

After that, it was quickly over. Asgrim, stony-faced, declined to appoint any man or woman to speak on his behalf. They took a vote; the outcome was entirely unsurprising. After the tumult of shouting, the acclamations, the pounding of fists and the drumming of feet had died down, Thorvald turned to the man who had been called Ruler. He chose his words carefully; best that this be concluded in a dignified manner, though his fingers itched to wring Asgrim's neck for what he had done to Creidhe.

"You're to be out of your hut and out of the area as soon as possible after daybreak," he said crisply. "You will not remain on the Isle of Storms, nor on the Isle of Streams. I will not have you near at hand to disrupt our endeavors. Your ill deeds have lost you the chance of any place in our community. We'll undertake not to harm you on your journey to wherever you intend to go." Thorvald's glance swept around the room, taking in the angry eyes of many of the men. "If you wish, you may take one of the smaller boats and sail from Council Fjord to your chosen destination. Please take your belongings with you. We intend a clean start."

Asgrim said not a word. His mouth was set in a line, his face ghastly pale. He must have expected a struggle; perhaps, defeat. Evidently he had not anticipated a repudiation as thorough as this. His dark eyes raked across the chamber, dangerous as a snake's, and then he turned his back on them and strode out the door. Einar made to follow, but Thorvald said, "No, leave him be. He'll do as we bid. He has no real choice."

By the time they awoke next morning, still weary after the brief rest but already talking among themselves of the new challenges, the work that lay before them, Asgrim was gone. His hut was empty, everything taken, bedding, small storage chest, weapons, quills, inks and parchments. One of the boats was gone as well; it seemed the Ruler intended to take his chances with the Fool's Tide, unless he planned to skirt the islets and head south. Wagers were made, jokingly, as to who would come off best in an encounter, Asgrim or the Unspoken. Then they turned their attention to more important matters. At midday a strong-faced woman walked into the encampment with two young boys at her side: Hogni's wife Gerd and her sons. At dusk all gathered by the water's edge to send her man to his long sleep.

They had built a fine raft of driftwood, and on this the big warrior lay covered by a warm cloak of blue-dyed felt, with his weapons by him: thrusting-spear, axe, knives, staff. He wore his leather helm and breastplate, his best winter boots, his sheepskin coat and thick wool trousers and tunic. Hogni's features were distorted by the manner of his death; there was no disguising that. But his brother had washed him clean with big, gentle hands, and combed his matted hair, and settled him as peacefully as he could. All knew the spirit no longer felt the pain of that last, cruel night when the poison worked its way through this strong body. That was an attack no human fortress could withstand.

They packed the raft with oil-soaked cloth, with dried bracken, with anything that would burn fast and hot. They waited on the shore in a place where the current would carry this small craft away, waited until the sun dipped below the edge of the world and the sky turned to the blue-white glow of the summer night. They were all there, all who had survived the last hunt: Orm, Einar and Wieland; Skolli the smith and Knut the fisherman with the incomer Sam by his side; the younger fellows, Ranulf, Thorkel, Paul, and more. Breccan was not present, nor the wounded Niall, who could not yet be moved. Creidhe, too, had remained in the shelter, but the other women stood by their men, grave and quiet. Hogni's wife, flanked by her sons, stood with Skapti and Thorvald, close by the place where her husband lay ready.

Now it was time. Skapti should have spoken the words of farewell, but when it came to it, he seemed unable to summon the power of speech. His mouth worked, his eyes filled with tears, his broad, strong features crumpled with sorrow. So it was Thorvald who spoke.

"Go forth, warrior, on your last journey." He did not cry out. His tone was not grand and ringing, but quiet, respectful, intimate: it was as if he spoke to Hogni alone, directly, honestly, as to a dear friend. Around him on the shore men swallowed, scrubbed their cheeks, blew their noses. "You were ever brave and strong, honest and forthright. You taught us well; we all had bruises to prove it at one point or another. You gave all that you had for us; all that you were. Rest now, secure in your brother's love, in the love of your woman and your sons. Go now on your journey, borne on the wind from the islands. Go straight to the god's right hand, for you died as you lived, a true son of Thor. Know that in this place your children will grow in peace and security, for we will make a new world for them, all of us together: a world in which such seasons of blood and sorrow cannot come again. Now it is time to say farewell. Come!" Thorvald glanced at Skapti, and at Einar, and at the two young lads of seven or eight who stood wide-eyed by their mother's skirts. They all moved forward and set hands to the raft, easing it down into deeper water; the sea washed to their knees, to their thighs, and the little boat was free to go.

"Careful," Thorvald said to the smaller boy, who stumbled in the half-light, in danger of falling in the chill water. "Here, take my hand."

Skapti gave one final heave, and as the raft began to drift out to sea, the others waded back to the dark sand of the tidal flats where Orm now stood with a lighted torch, and the archer, Paul, by his side. But Skapti stood with the sea around his knees, watching as the little raft bore his brother away, farther and farther from the shore, westward on his last, long journey.

Then Paul fitted a certain arrow to the string, and drew the bow strongly, and Orm touched the brand to the tip of the arrow, setting it aflame. The bowstring twanged; the arrow arched through the air, out over the sea, winging swift and true. A flicker, a flaring, and at once the raft was engulfed in fire, robing the fallen warrior in a garment of light. Hogni burned long; they watched him pass down Council Fjord, a glowing vessel of flame, toward the hidden shapes of the Troll's Arch, and Dragon Isle, and out into the grip of the Fool's Tide. They watched until the raft shrank to a pinprick of light in the summer twilight, then winked out altogether.

The children were shivering, yawning, worn out by the strangeness of it all. Their mother shepherded them close; when Thorvald spoke to her she looked him straight in the eye, as if assessing the worth of this man for whom her husband had given his life.

"He was a brave man and a good one," Thorvald said quietly. He looked at the two boys. "We'll make sure you are provided for, all of you," he added, not sure how this would be done, but knowing that from now on such things would be his responsibility, and that he must learn quickly. "Now you should rest and get warm. There's a fire in the sleeping quarters, up yonder." That building had once been the meeting hall of the Long Knife people, in a time before the hunt. It would be satisfying to restore it to its original purpose.

"We will go home," Gerd said. Her weary features were full of courage; it was the same look Hogni himself might have given at such a moment. "Tonight, to Brightwater. Tomorrow, to Starkfell. We have been long enough away; there are stock to tend to."

Thorvald was about to protest that it was night, and a long walk, and a dangerous path. But he bit back his words; all around him the men were settling small packs on their backs, fastening cloaks tighter, and picking up staves to aid the climb. And Skapti now came out of the water, wiped his nose on his sleeve, and took the hands of the small boys in his own.

"Time to go," said the big guard. "If that's all right with you."

"Of course," Thorvald said. "Of course you must go. Take what time you require. But don't forget that I need you here, Skapti. I rely on you to help me and advise me. I'll be calling a council before next full moon, and I want all the men to come."

"I'll be there." Skapti's eyes were bright.

"And in the meantime, all of us must think of the future, of what there is to do, and how best to accomplish it. We'll all play a part in that. I'm sorry Hogni isn't here to see it, bitterly sorry."

"He sees it," Skapti said. "Make no doubt of that. Now we'd best be off. Come on, lads, step lively."

Asgrim's tale was not quite finished. Thorvald and his party remained at Council Fjord for a few days, waiting until Niall was well enough to be moved. Some of the men, those with no families, stayed on to help. Most set off for their homes, to tend to farm or boat or other livelihood, and to spend time with their kin before the long work of rebuilding the broken community began in earnest. On the second day, Thorvald was sitting outside the shelter with Sam and Knut, working on some improvements to the *Sea Dove's* sail, when Paul came running into the encampment, stumbling over his words in his haste to impart some news. He did not seem distressed, merely overexcited. They sat him down, gave him ale, waited as he got his breath back. The other men, alerted, gathered around to hear what he had to tell.

Paul's family lived in an out-of-the-way place, a tiny settlement on the northwestern margin of the Isle of Storms, set on a clifftop high above the sea. He'd headed off that morning, planning to reach the farm before dusk and give his mother a surprise. He'd taken a cliff path for much of the journey; it wasn't the safest way, but it was definitely the quickest, and Paul knew the terrain well. That was how he'd seen it: Asgrim's boat.

"He was sailing north," the archer said, "and making good progress. From his position, I reckon he must have been holed up at Little Bay, and headed out this morning. Probably aiming for the outer islands; only a scattering of folk there, and perhaps he thought they'd take him in, since they know little of what happens in these parts. The wind was favorable. He'd got around the northern edge of the Fool's Tide, and the weather was set fair. Me, I'd have liked to make use of my bow to pick him off cleanly, but Thorvald had given him an undertaking, and besides, he was probably out of range. Out of harm's way. Or so I thought." He took a swig of his ale and wiped his mouth with his hand.

"What happened?" Knut asked eagerly, for all sensed some wonder here, some dark conclusion. It could be seen in the teller's eyes.

"Strangest thing I've ever seen," Paul said in a tone suddenly hushed with awe. "Calm sea, steady breeze, boat under perfect control. Then there were . . . there were hands, or arms, or . . . I don't know what to call them, but they were there, all around his boat, dragging, pulling. I heard him cry out. It was a little enough sound in all that ocean. And then . . . and then they broke the boat apart under him, tore it up, shredded it to fragments. Last thing I saw was a . . ." Paul gulped, "a woman, something like a woman, reaching up and putting her arms around his neck, only it wasn't like a wife does to her husband, you take my meaning, but more like an executioner with a victim . . . she was choking him even as she bore him under . . . A moment later, all there was to see was little bits of wood floating on the surface. Perfect calm."

For a little, all were silent. The image in their minds robbed them of words.

"The Seal Tribe," Knut said eventually, his voice shaking. "They came for him."

"Of course, his wife was one of them," said Paul, nodding. "Retribution, that's what it was. Look what he did to his own daughter. Her daughter. Had to catch up with him some time. All the same, I regret that arrow. There'd have been satisfaction in that."

Thorvald shivered. It was just, perhaps; on the other hand, he would not wish such an end on any man. The islands, it seemed, delivered their own punishments, in their own time.

A cottage was provided in Brightwater, roomy and dry. There was a tiny, private chamber for Creidhe, not much more than a storage corner, with a shelf for sleeping. Gudrun had offered her a bed, and so had Jofrid, a Jofrid not yet restored to joy, for her losses would shadow her always, but at least a young woman who now had hope in her eyes. Wieland stayed close, watching over his wife like a hen with a lone chick. But Creidhe would not go with the women of the village. So she was lodged with Breccan and Niall, and with Thorvald and Sam, until it was time to move on. Niall ran a fever, and between them Breccan and Creidhe were kept busy sponging his burning body, administering drafts, and making sure visitors made as little noise as possible. Thorvald had a lot of visitors, for all the respite he had decreed before his council. Men sought his advice on their sheep, their boats, their sons living in the far islands. They told him of their wives' anxieties, their children's fears. They asked him to speak at an old man's burial rite. They talked of building a temple, of refurbishing the council house, of seeking to emulate the *Sea Dove*'s neat construction in the making of boats, if only they could procure the timber. Some of them began to talk of trade and of treaties. Thorvald listened, commented and praised them for their initiative. He offered grave advice. Sam watched him with wonder. Was this the same man who had raged against the dark heritage of his blood, back home in Hrossey? Was this the lad who had barely known what he was doing when he borrowed the *Sea Dove* and its hapless master and set off on that foolhardy journey into the unknown?

Sometimes Brother Niall was lucid, though he lay weak as a new lamb, his face dewed with sweat. When those times came, Breccan and Creidhe rested, and it was Thorvald who sat by his father's side, dabbing his brow with a damp cloth, holding his hand and speaking in a low voice. At such times an expression could be seen on Niall's face that was quite new to him. He had ever worn a mask, knowing it could not protect him from the world's barbs, but recognizing it could at least conceal the way they wounded him. If he had felt love before, and perhaps he had done, long and faithfully, that mask had hidden it well. Now he set such artifice aside. It was wondrous indeed to see the gaze his single eye turned on his newfound son, and the reflection of that gaze in Thorvald's own eyes.

Niall wanted to go home. He wanted his quills, his inks, his parchments; he wanted the quiet of the hermitage, the empty sweep of hillside under the pale sky. He talked about the cow, the chickens, the little garden Colm had made.

"Soon," said Breccan. "When you are well again."

Sam had nearly finished provisioning the *Sea Dove* for her journey home to the Light Isles. The Long Knife people were generous; the boat would make this trip far better supplied than she had been on her wild voyage from Stensakir.

They would take a different course this time, Sam said: more east than south at first, to skirt the shores of the Northern Isles before the run home. Knut was coming, not simply because, without Thorvald, Sam would not be able to manage the craft in open seas, but for change, adventure, opportunity. The young fisherman's eyes were bright with anticipation. In a day or two they would be ready.

There had been some discussion among the Long Knife people about Creidhe. At least four of the unwed men had made careful inquiries as to whether the fair-haired woman was planning to remain in the islands and, if so, whether it was really true that she was not betrothed to either Sam or Thorvald, but no more than their friend. The answer seemed to depend on who was asked. They gave up approaching Sam, who nearly bit their heads off with his curt response that Creidhe was going home with him, of course, and they should know better than to ask him such a stupid question. And Skapti, quizzed on the subject when he returned to Brightwater, seemed to believe there was an understanding between the girl and Thorvald, which their new leader had stated in no uncertain terms when he bargained for her release among the Unspoken. Word of this spread quickly and the men stopped asking. However, Skapti himself was heard to comment that if Creidhe was indeed Thorvald's sweetheart, the two of them had evidently had a falling out, for the girl was a shadow of herself, picking at her food, wan and exhausted, and she never exchanged so much as a word or two with Thorvald, though there were many times when his eyes followed her with a certain expression in them that the big warrior thought he knew well enough. He'd been that way inclined himself for a little. He knew how foolish that was now, a bit like a stray dog looking at a princess. Besides, he'd Hogni's family to worry about, Gerd and the lads. There was no time for dreams. He was sorry the girl looked so sad. There was a tale there that nobody knew, nobody but Creidhe herself, and she had it locked up tight.

* * *

"Father?" Thorvald asked as he sat by the pallet while all the others slept.

Niall moved his head a little so he could read his son's features. "What is it?"

"Breccan said you can be moved in a day or so, now the fever's broken. He must go back to the hermitage, at any rate; he has to resume tending the stock, the boys can't be spared any longer. But—"

"But what, Thorvald? Does it embarrass you to have a cleric for a father? You see some other path for me, perhaps one where I limp forward with a sword in my hand and a patch over my eye?"

Thorvald flushed. "I waited a long time to find you," he said, glancing around the room as if to check nobody was awake to hear him. "All my life. I had hopes you might choose to stay here, by me. To help me. I have a great deal to learn. I can pretend to be the leader they want, strong, wise, just. But in truth, I know nothing at all. I've been making it up as I go along. It was Creidhe who won their battle for them in the end, not I."

"Ah," Niall said with a crooked smile, "a little humility. That's good to see. It's a quality I could have done with at your age, and lacked entirely. Thorvald, you *are* the leader they want. They have chosen you. They respect and love you. If the truth astonishes you and makes you humble, that's just as it should be. You will spend your life becoming worthy of their trust."

There was a silence.

"Father?"

"Mmm?"

"I'm not sure I can do it on my own."

"You're not on your own. You're surrounded by good, strong men and women, willing and loyal, whose hearts are bent only on a future of peace and prosperity. Besides, I won't be far away. I expect I'll manage to hobble down the hillside occasionally; and my door will always be open to you."

"It's not the same. You have a wisdom beyond mine; an authority far greater, if you choose to use it. It's you who should be leader of the Long Knife people. Should have been so years ago, I think, when first you came to the Lost Isles."

"Oh, no. Oh, no." Niall's face grew somber. "Never that. I challenged Asgrim, it is true. But I drew back from wresting power from his hands, misguided as he was. Do not forget what you know of me, Thorvald. I am as I am now. But I have performed deeds to make men shrink with horror. I was indeed blind in those days, and walking a path as twisted and awry as any the Devil himself could devise. If you wonder why I do not seek power in the world of men, that is half the answer. A man whose hands have taken his own brother's life is not fit to lead. A man who cannot act without bringing darkness to all he touches should set himself aside; should place himself where he cannot be tempted to interfere. I became a hermit. I ceased to seek out Asgrim; I let him follow his own path. Until the day I sailed for the Isle of Shadows."

"What changed your mind?" Thorvald whispered.

And Niall said simply, "Love."

After a little, Thorvald took his father's hand in his, swallowing, and asked him, "You said that was half the reason. What was the other half?"

"I discovered that God has a sense of humor. All those years I played the part of priest: I stood by my brethren and mouthed the words they spoke in true faith; I copied the scriptures not because I believed a single word of them, but simply so I would not lose the skills I had at reading, scribing and translation. I argued philosophy with Breccan: there was genuine pleasure in that. I tried not to let my cynicism confuse the boy. I found a certain calm in the pattern of their days; the order and discipline of their life suited me. But I was no Christian. My mind was full of doubt and disbelief. I have seen enough of the dark acts men can perform. I have felt such shadows in the core of my own being that I could hardly be swayed to believe in a god of goodness and light, however eloquently Breccan pleaded his case. Until now."

"What do you mean?"

"God's joke: he saved it until the last, testing my resistance to him all those years. It was simple, Thorvald, simple and shattering. You came, and Creidhe told me I had a son, and I saw you, the one fine thing I had made. I had known nothing of your existence before then. Something changed within me; something opened, a tiny crack, a little chink. It is all God needs. I ceased to resist him, and I heard his voice. He laughs now, I imagine. He has won this battle, and I am truly his." Niall's eye was bright. It seemed to Thorvald the light that shone in the priest's pale features owed little to the flickering glow from the oil lamp. This was an illumination soul deep.

"I cannot think what to say," Thorvald told his father, "save that if this news makes its way home to Brother Tadhg in the Light Isles, he will be even more astounded than I."

Niall grinned. "Ah, Tadhg. Creidhe told me he still lives, roaming the islands with his little satchel and his book of tales. How I feared that man! He had extraordinary power; God's love was ever strong in him. Yes, he will be amused. And delighted. He once offered to teach me the ways of his faith and I would not listen. Thorvald?"

Thorvald caught the change in his father's tone and did not respond. He knew what was coming.

"What happened with Creidhe? She won't talk to me or to Breccan. It seems she won't talk to anyone. I heard her on the Isle of Shadows, proud and strong, facing the Unspoken, protecting the child with all she had to give. But after that, such a terrible change . . . the bonny, smiling girl she once was has become a wraith, dispirited and hopeless. She has suffered some hurt we know little of, I'm aware of that. But Creidhe is resilient and courageous, like her father. I cannot understand this. Couldn't you reach her?"

Thorvald's brief laugh was bitter with self-mockery and full of pain. "I? I am the last person she will confide in, Father. I was her friend once. She came here solely for me, to protect and guide me. I thought her foolish for that, but it was I who was the fool. It was Creidhe's intervention that won us the peace. But something has changed. She's been hurt and frightened. She was captive on the Isle of Clouds, and there's no doubt in my mind the fellow used her. It seems to me that she does not recognize, yet, that she is safe."

"Fellow?"

"There was a warrior there; he held her and the child prisoner. He'd been a long time without a woman, I imagine." Thorvald could hear the anger in his voice. "I think it was Asgrim's son."

"Erling? That dreamy, quiet lad, still alive after so long on the island? But yes, it does make sense; who else would have the love, the drive to preserve the child all those long years?"

"Love," echoed Thorvald with some bitterness. "He did not show much love to Creidhe; he abused her, defiled her. You've seen what she has become."

Niall was silent for a little. Then he said, "This sits at odds with what I knew of the boy, Thorvald. Still, it is a long time, and men change when their circumstances are extreme. He perished in your last battle, I take it? A sad ending for such a peaceable young man."

"I begin to believe it is not the same," Thorvald said, "for this was no peace maker. He was a killer, professional, expert and ruthless. He deserved the punishment we meted out. In truth, he deserved more."

Niall waited.

"I came close to killing him," Thorvald said with a certain reluctance. "In the end something stayed my hand. Very probably he did not survive. He was wounded, and I left him where he lay." The full truth he would not tell, lest he appear weak.

"I see. So it is over for him, and over for Creidhe, the dark and dangerous times behind her. And yet, she still seems sunk in despair. I ask myself why? From what I saw of her earlier, when we witnessed the cruel death of an infant she had struggled to save, Creidhe does not seem a person easily thrown into despair."

"I thought"—there was misery in Thorvald's voice—

"that once the seer was safe, once she knew he was content and would not be harmed, she might forgive me for my meddling. That it might be as it once was between us."

"And how was that?"

"It was . . ." Under his father's searching gaze, Thorvald struggled for words to tell the truth. "All those years, since we were little children, she followed me, like a constant shadow, always there, listening, waiting, walking in my footsteps. When I was sad she comforted me. When I was hurt she helped me. She was younger; often I grew impatient or angry, and drove her to tears or to silence. But I . . . I got used to it, to having her near. I took her entirely for granted, Father. Until I believed her dead. And then I . . ."

Niall waited.

"I could not believe how it hurt. I could not understand how a man could suffer such a blow and still go on."

"But you did. Go on, I mean."

"The men needed me," Thorvald said simply. "My feelings were unimportant. My grief, my guilt . . . they were of no matter, not when the future of the Long Knife people was in the balance. I shut them within me and got on with things."

"And now Creidhe has returned and you still take her for granted?" Niall's brows arched in query.

"No!" said Thorvald fiercely. "Never! When I knew those fellows were talking about her—was she going home, was she likely to wed one of them—I was so angry I had to go off by myself to save from setting my hands around their necks and throttling them."

"Why, Thorvald? Such talk seems not unreasonable in the circumstances. She's a comely girl, and there is a certain shortage of marriageable women here."

"I never gave it much thought before," Thorvald whispered. "Marriage, I mean. My mind was on other things. Besides, I knew Eyvind would never allow . . . but when they started to talk . . . How could Creidhe wed someone else? It just wouldn't be . . . it wouldn't . . ." He faltered to a stop.

"But you will not tell her how you feel?"

"You've seen her, Father. She cares nothing for me anymore. She cares nothing for anyone. It's as if part of her is lost, some vital core removed. I don't know how I can help her."

"You must let her go home," Niall said quietly. "Back to her family, back to her own people."

Thorvald bowed his head.

"Thorvald, she's not for you. Such fair souls as this, they touch us deeply, they enchant us with their transparent goodness and beauty. We are drawn to them like moths to the lamplight. Perhaps we want to own them, as much as we can, hoping some of that magic may pass to us and make us a little better, a little brighter. But they are not for you and me, son. Ours will always be a pathway of doubt and struggle. That is our nature. You've a task here among the men, a fine and worthy one, and you'll do it well. Perhaps in time you will wed and raise children of your own, perhaps not. But you must smile, and thank your two friends for their bravery and their support, and bid them farewell when the *Sea Dove* sails. We have our own road to tread."

And though Thorvald hardly understood his father's speech, for it was as if he spoke not of his son or of Creidhe, but of others entirely, it did seem Niall's words bore the wisdom of his long experience, his years of contemplation and study.

"You're tired, Father," Thorvald said. "It's late. You should try to sleep now." He settled Niall on the pallet, easing a goose-feather pillow under his head.

"Thorvald?"

"Father, you must stop talking and rest if you want to get well—"

"I need a pen and ink and a parchment. Tomorrow. You must—"

"You're not well enough to write. Not yet."

"There's nothing wrong with my hands. Tomorrow. Please."

Thorvald sighed. "I suppose someone can fetch what you

need. Is it so urgent to begin your transcriptions once more? There are years ahead for scholarship."

"I must write a letter. Before the *Sea Dove* sails."

"Oh."

"Your mother deserves that at least. I treated her as thoughtlessly as you did Creidhe. It will be hard for her when the *Sea Dove* returns without her son."

"She won't care." Thorvald knew even as he said it that this was not true.

"Nonsense," said Niall, reaching to clasp his son's hand as Thorvald tucked the blankets in. "Though they may not put it into words, mothers always love their sons. Margaret was ever a self-contained girl. That was one of the things I liked about her. Make sure you get the pen and ink in the morning."

"Yes, Father."

Keeper awoke to a deathly quiet. He knew instantly that they were gone, for he felt the island's rhythms and balances in every fiber of his being; he was attuned to them. The place was deserted, save for the seals and the birds. And himself.

All the same, he searched. He searched as he had prepared for the hunt, with meticulous care, with cold purpose, with nimble feet and a predator's acuity of sight. He scoured the island from rocky shore to dizzy crag, from hidden bay to deepest cavern, until his legs trembled with weariness and his vision blurred with exhaustion. Then he went back to the shelter and made a halfhearted attempt to clean the crusted blood from his head wound. He sat by the cold hearth with his hand on the necklace he wore, a pale, faded thing woven from strands of his sister's long hair. Small One's boots stood by the wall; his short cloak lay crumpled on the ground. Keeper reached for the blanket on which Creidhe had lain in his arms only this morning; he lifted the worn fabric to his face and thought he could smell her faint, sweet scent still lingering there. He did not weep.

He sat empty, silent. Small One was taken. Keeper had broken his promise. Creidhe was gone. It was his own blow that had struck her; he had wounded her. And now they had torn her away from him. He sat there long, wondering if he would ever move again, wondering if grief and guilt would steal away the man he had been, a fighter, a guardian worthy of the name he had chosen for himself, and leave behind only a shell to be broken and dispersed by the wind. Almost, he gave in to sleep, for if he lay here on the earthen floor with the blanket clutched close, perhaps he would dream fair dreams of his goddess. Perhaps he could shut out the vision of Small One cold, hurt, bleeding, frightened, the image of Creidhe running, falling, lying pale and still on the stony hillside. Perhaps he could forget the triumph in the eyes of the red-haired man. But he did not sleep, for it seemed to him a vigil must be kept. So he sat open-eyed, and in time came the song. It came from far away, so far away it was almost beyond the margins of hearing, and yet he heard it as if Small One had meant it for him alone. It was a fragment borne on the wind, a scattering of notes already fading as they reached him, and yet he understood them deep in his heart.

Tears did come then. The sweet, wordless melody told him Small One was alive, safe, content. But the tears were of grief, too, a terrible, chill regret that tore at his vitals, enough to make him cry out in pain. Small One was home, returned to the Shadow Isle. And the child was happy. Whatever they had done to him with their knives and clubs while Keeper lay here senseless, useless, still the seer's song rang out its message of peace and forgiveness, love and hope. And that was most bitter of all, for it told Keeper he had been wrong. It seemed that what he had thought protection had been imprisonment. He had believed the life he had made for Small One was better, freer, safer. All that he had done was keep the child away from his true place. All that time, all those years as he watched his small kinsman grow, and shielded him from harm, and guarded him as fiercely as a wolf her young, he had seen the look of sadness in the child's eyes and had not known that its cause was himself. He had bid Small One hide and be silent as the hunt raged around him, and the boy had obeyed him. Does not a good child obey his elders? Yet all the time, in the seer's strange, deep mind, there must have been a terrible, secret sorrow. As the seasons passed, as they survived each summer's hunt, Small One's sadness must have deepened, knowing this most loyal of brothers would never let him go home.

The bitterness of it ate at Keeper. The song ended, and he sat motionless, staring unseeing at the cold hearth, the threadbare blanket clutched against him. There was no denying the truth. The task that had been his life's purpose had been misguided, hollow and cruel. There had been no need for men to be wounded and to die. There had been no need to fashion himself into a warrior. There had been no need of him at all.

In the morning he walked down to the hidden cove where he kept his boats. The best one, the only one he had ever used, was gone. The others were damaged, their skins slit, their timbers broken; even supposing he might call on his mother's people, and they might be prevailed upon to gentle the Fool's Tide and let him pass over, he could not do so until he had made a craft strong enough to cross the treacherous strait. And what then? He had seen the look in that man's dark eyes, a fierce, implacable glare of ownership. There was a bond between them, his goddess and her childhood friend; did they not appear together in her web, where he himself had never earned a place? It was not Keeper she had leaped to protect in that last, desperate bid to cheat the gods. It was the red-haired man. By the time he had made a boat, she would be gone, whisked back home to her own island, safely out of his reach. He knew this as he knew the tides: in his blood.

There was nowhere for him to go. With sinking heart, he recognized this. Asgrim's people loathed him: for every life he had taken in the long years of the hunt, there would be a man waiting on that shore for vengeance. He could not follow the child. He would never see his little one again, for the Unspoken have long memories, and though they had wronged Sula terribly, he himself had dealt them a heart wound when he robbed them of the seer. He could not live among men. He did not know how. He knew only the island, and the hunt.

Such discipline as he had kept does not die easily. On the second day after he lost his dear ones, Keeper knew he was cold and hungry, and that the oozing wound on his head needed attention. He made a choice: the only kind he knew. Be strong or give up. Live or die. He made fire, built up a mass of glowing turf, left it burning safely between stones. He fetched fresh water. He went for fish, catching them in the manner of his mother's people, with soothing words and his hands. He killed them with respect and gratitude, for their kind had sustained him and the child long. He bore his catch back to the hut and set it to bake in the coals.

Then he made himself put the place to rights. Blankets and cloaks were folded and stacked. The hardest thing was storing away Small One's little boots, his warm cape, the sheepskin hat he had been reluctant to wear. Nonetheless, Keeper did it. These garments would not be needed anymore. Perhaps he would look at them sometimes; perhaps not. As reminders they were unnecessary. The pain of this loss would never leave him; it was lodged deep in the bone. It came to him that there would no longer be a ready supply of leather boots, of warm clothing, of iron implements and useful lengths of timber on the island. The hunt was over. He'd need to be frugal.

He ate the fish. When he was done, he sat gazing into the fire awhile, thinking that if he let his mind drift he might see her again, grave and quiet on the other side, watching him across the flames with her sweet blue eyes full of mystery and enchantment. But he could not see her. Perhaps, for the rest of his life, she would walk only in his dreams.

After a while Keeper took up the knife he had used to gut the fish, and weighed it in his hand, considering. Then, quickly before he could change his mind, he reached to sever the small thing he wore around his neck, and it fell into his hand, a whisper-soft trifle of woven hair. He held it a moment, and in his mind he said, *I'm sorry. But we were wrong, the two of us.* And he cast the necklace into the fire.

The next day he visited a cavern farther away, where many items from the hunt were laid by. Among them, hidden deep, were the remnants of the clothing Creidhe had worn on the day the Fool's Tide carried her to the island. They were too tattered and damaged to be worn, but he had washed and dried them and set them here; how could he discard anything that had touched her skin? Now he brought them out and found a little knife, a bone needle, and his carefully hoarded twine, and he cut and stitched and fashioned a garment for himself, one that could be worn secretly beneath his shirt, close to the heart. He put it on, and thought he could feel her against him, warm, gentle, giving, strong. He set his materials away and returned to the hut, where all was neat and orderly. He ate and slept. Next morning he fetched implements for digging and for shifting stones, and walked to the place he had chosen, and began to build. No matter that they had taken her. No matter that they would carry her across the sea, too far for him to follow. Creidhe had made him a promise. He, too, must keep faith.

The message came when Eyvind was in council at his own house. He and Ash had five other men with them, representing the different settlements of Hrossey and the islands to the south. The threat from the Caitt people was real enough, for all those chieftains' assurances of peace; today this small council debated, quietly and urgently, the topic of just who could be trusted. It was understood by Eyvind's household that such discussions were not to be interrupted. So, when Nessa herself drew aside the woolen hanging across the doorway and stepped into the room, her husband got up at once, his composure failing to disguise the sudden pallor of his face. On the other side of the table, Ash rose slowly to his feet.

"She's home," Nessa said simply. "The boat came in to Stensakir last night. Sam sent a boy to tell us. They'll borrow horses from Grim and be here by midday."

Eyvind did not smile, but his eyes were bright as he reached to take his wife's arm, to walk with her out of the chamber into the privacy of the hallway.

"I'll ride out straightaway to meet them," he said, seeing the longing in Nessa's eyes, the way she clutched her hands tightly together over the swell of the child she carried. If not for that, she would herself have played a part in today's council. "Ash will come with me . . ."

"Eyvind?"

He waited.

"We must send a message to Margaret. I have a man ready to go. Creidhe is home safely, and Sam, and another man. But Thorvald did not come with them. I don't know how to give her such news."

"Where is Thorvald? Is he safe?"

Nessa shook her head. "There was nothing said of that. We must wait until Creidhe arrives home."

Behind them Ash had emerged, silent, from the council chamber. Eyvind turned toward him.

"I'd have asked you to ride with me toward Stensakir," he said gravely, "for it seems the *Sea Dove* has come back at last, and my daughter with it. But it is not all good news, I'm afraid."

"What has happened?" Ash was already taking his cloak from the peg in the hallway, preparing himself to leave.

"We don't know," Nessa said softly. "Only that Thorvald is not with Creidhe and Sam. We must wait for them to reach us. But we cannot let Margaret hear this news by chance. I have a man ready . . ."

"I will tell her." Ash's quiet voice allowed for no argument. "And I will fetch her back here. That's what she will want: to hear what has happened from Creidhe herself. I should go now, right away. This is welcome news, in part at least; I am happy for you." His spare, lined features were as well controlled as always; like Margaret, he never gave much away.

"I'm sorry," said Nessa, putting a hand on his. "Truly. Perhaps this is not as bad as it sounds. Ride safely."

The kitchen was a bustle of activity, most of it Brona's.

As Nessa returned to the council room to offer an explanation on her husband's behalf and bid the men a courteous farewell, her daughter assumed quick control of the
serving women, ordering the preparation of mutton with
garlic, and setting her own hands to the making of a special pie with eggs, goat's cheese and dried mushrooms.
Eyvind rode off to the northeast somewhat faster than his
wife liked to see him travel, though Nessa understood his
urgency. For herself, the feeling in her breast was as much
anxious pain as joyous relief; all this long time she had
yearned for Creidhe's return, had worried and prayed and
waited for this day, but now there was a strong sense in
her of something awry. It was not simply the fact of
Creidhe coming back without Thorvald, though Nessa
knew this in itself was cause for disquiet. She had long
understood the inclination of her daughter's heart. This
was deeper, darker, a whispering of the ancestors. Something was wrong.

Brona sang, finishing the pie with a neat latticework of
pastry on the top. She looked flushed and pretty, her hands
neat and deft as she worked. Beside her Ingigerd stood
watching, solemn as a little owl.

"It's very possible Creidhe won't be hungry," Nessa commented wryly from the doorway. "If they've had a long
voyage, she may simply want to sleep. You have flour on
your cheek and on your skirt, daughter. Perhaps you'd like
to brush your hair and change your clothes. Ingi and I will
set that to bake for you."

Brona glanced up, a deep flush spreading across her fine
features, so like her mother's. She said nothing.

"Of course," Nessa went on solemnly, "Sam may very
well decide to head back to Stensakir and leave Eyvind to
bring Creidhe home."

"I'm not—" Brona began, then bit back her words.
Sometimes her mother's ability to see beyond the obvious
was disconcerting. "It's just—"

"I'm teasing you, Daughter." Nessa was smiling. "I expect he will come, being a responsible sort of man. Go and

put on your good things. I'm glad to see you smiling. I can scarcely believe they are here at last."

But after Brona had darted to kiss her mother on the cheek and flown away to her chamber with Ingigerd at her heels, Nessa's smile faded. She set the little pie to cook and stood by the fire to warm her hands and stare into the flames. Despite the heat of the room, there was a chill inside her that would not go away.

Sam's features were set tight with anxiety as he rode, and there was a hard knot in the pit of his stomach. Eyvind's presence only made it worse, for after the first embrace of greeting, golden-haired father and daughter locked in each other's arms on the side of the track while he stood by holding the horses' reins, there had been little said, and he could see Eyvind looking at Creidhe not with delight and relief, but with disbelief and shock. Apart from that greeting to her father, Creidhe had not spoken at all. It was Sam who had told Eyvind, briefly, that Thorvald was well and had decided to stay in the Lost Isles. It was Sam who had introduced Knut, who rode with them, and explained his presence. Now it seemed to Sam that it might be he who would have to recount the whole tale not just to the formidable Eyvind but to Nessa and to Thorvald's mother as well. For Creidhe's silence was not only of today. During the long voyage home, while he and Knut coaxed and wrestled and guided the *Sea Dove* across the northern ocean and back to the Light Isles, Creidhe had been shut deep within herself, mute, frozen. She could understand him; she had moved when told to, she had helped with the boat on the rare occasions he'd needed to ask. She had prepared food for the two men but had eaten little herself. No wonder Eyvind stared. His bonny daughter was ash-pale, her rounded face gaunt and drawn, almost as if she were an old woman. The sweet blue eyes had lost all their brightness. It had been thus, Sam reckoned, ever since the day they had rescued her from the Isle of Clouds. Apart, that was, from

the brief, strange scene when she had challenged the Unspoken over the fate of the seer. But she'd not been herself
then either. That day she had seemed to him fierce, proud
and distant. She had seemed like a queen. And as soon as
she knew the child was safe, she had become as she was
now, as if all the life had been drained from her. How was
he going to explain that?

As it happened, when the four of them rode up to the
longhouse where Eyvind and Nessa lived, and Sam saw the
family gathered outside the door to meet them, his eyes fell
first on Brona, fifteen years old and dressed in her good tunic and skirt of green-dyed wool, with a matching ribbon
tying her long, dark hair. She smiled, a generous, shining
smile of uncomplicated delight. Her skin was brown from
the sun, her cheeks flushed pink; her gray eyes danced with
life. She ran to hug her sister as Creidhe got down with
Eyvind's help. Then Brona turned to Sam, looking up at
him shyly through her long lashes. Sam couldn't take his
eyes off her. It was a long time since he had seen such a picture of simple, healthy goodness; the sight sent a surge of
pleasure through him. Perhaps, after all, his old world did
still exist.

"Welcome home, Sam," Brona said. The smile, now,
seemed to be for him.

"You're looking well, Brona."

"You look tired. And you'll be hungry. I made a pie."

Like a ray of sunshine, Sam thought. Like a breath of sea
air. He followed her into the house, summoning his
courage. If he must tell the tale alone, tell it he would, and
truthfully. He had played a part, after all: a bigger and
bloodier one than he would have dreamed possible when he
sailed away from Stensakir on Thorvald's dark mission. He
would tell them, and then it would be over, and he could get
on with things.

But it was Creidhe who told the tale, her voice clear and
precise, with a cool detachment that held her family silent
through the whole strange account. They sat over a meal;
nobody ate much. Creidhe's story was hard to believe, but
they knew she did not lie, and besides, neither Sam nor

Knut contradicted her. There was a point at which Sam attempted to interrupt, as if a part of the tale had been left untold; nobody missed the look Creidhe gave him, a look that silenced the fisherman instantly.

They had to believe it. The three had reached distant islands, where the young men had been bound to train as warriors, since the *Sea Dove* was damaged and wood must be earned to mend her. In time, Thorvald had somehow become a war leader, and had led his forces to victory against another tribe. And he had found his father. That gave him two reasons for staying when the others sailed for home. Somerled was a priest, a Christian. He had been in danger and they had rescued him. He had a different name now. After it was over, Sam and Creidhe had bid Thorvald farewell and sailed for home.

"Brother Niall—Somerled—is a good man; he has a place in the islands, and his faith, and now he has his son as well." Creidhe's tone had altered a little; momentarily, her listeners caught an echo of her old warmth. "And Thorvald has changed. In some ways. He has more of a part to play there than he ever did in Hrossey." She was speaking directly to Margaret now, a Margaret who, despite her outward calm, could be seen to be clenching her hands tightly and hanging on every word.

"The men seem to respect him greatly," Creidhe went on. "He will do well, I should think."

"Creidhe," Eyvind put in carefully, "where were you while Sam and Thorvald carried out the preparations for war? What were you doing?"

Creidhe looked at her father, eyes wide and blank. "Nothing much," she said.

Sam opened his mouth; Creidhe glanced at him; he shut it again.

"You're tired, daughter," said Nessa, who wore a little frown on her brow. "We ask too much of you too soon, I think. Why not go and rest now? There will be time for more talk later. She looked at Sam and Knut. "Please accept our hospitality for the night. It's a long ride back after such a journey."

"Thank you," Sam said, "but we'd best be off home, I

reckon. I've been too long away; I want to sort out the boat, and find Knut lodgings, and get about the business of fishing again as quick as I can. But I'll be back this way soon. If that's all right." He could not help glancing in Brona's direction as he said it; she was sitting with her small sister on her lap, and flashed a smile at him, her eyes alight.

"You'd be welcome," Nessa said, though Eyvind made no comment. "We have you to thank for our daughter's safe arrival home, though the voyage itself was a wild and foolish endeavor."

"Which, undoubtedly, my son persuaded you to undertake." Margaret's dry tone did not conceal the fact that she was on the verge of tears. "I, too, thank you, Sam; and you, Knut, for coming with them. We're happy to see you home. I must hope Thorvald will pay us a visit some day. Distance makes that less than likely, I suppose."

Creidhe spoke into the sudden silence. "I have a letter for you, Aunt Margaret. I was given it to deliver."

Margaret looked at her, dark eyes watchful, as if to defend herself from further hurts.

"It's not from Thorvald," Creidhe added, and took a little scroll from the pouch at her belt. It was neatly tied with a scrap of scarlet cord.

Margaret's hand was shaking as she took it. "Excuse me," she said, and rose to her feet, making for the outer door. The men got up respectfully. By the doorway, Margaret paused, turning back toward them. Her face was pale; her eyes glittered with tears. "Ash?" she said, and reached out a hand, and he crossed the room in three strides, setting his arm around her shoulders in full view of everyone. Their news was learned thus, without any need for words. They went out, and the door closed behind them.

"I'm all right, Mother," Creidhe protested as Nessa tucked the covers over her in the dimness of the little sleeping chamber she shared with Brona. "Really. I think you're the one who should be resting, with that child growing apace.

Are you sure it isn't twins? You should have told me before."

"I hardly knew it myself at that stage." Nessa's expression was very serious as she sat by the bed, scrutinizing her daughter's sunken features, her dull, lifeless eyes. "I'm so glad you are home, Creidhe." She had longed to speak to Creidhe of the child, of her fears about the delivery, and about the price the Seal Tribe might seek to extract from her. Creidhe would understand these things in a way Eyvind could not. Creidhe would offer kindness, reassurance and brisk, practical advice. But she could not burden Creidhe with her own concerns. It seemed to her that this daughter, formerly so strong and capable, had become in little more than a single season as delicate and fragile as a new-laid egg. They must tread carefully; they must take time. "Sleep now," Nessa said, smoothing Creidhe's hair back from her temple. "You're home."

"Mother?" It was a whisper.

"Yes?"

"Don't let Father ply Sam with questions. I've told you what happened. There will be more in Brother Niall's letter. But that's all. Sam needs to get back to the way things were. He'd never have gone at all but for Thorvald."

"And you?"

Creidhe gazed up at her. "Me?" she asked blankly.

"What will you do?"

"I don't know," Creidhe said, and closed her eyes.

For a while it seemed to Nessa that Creidhe was grieving over the defection of Thorvald, to whom she had been deeply loyal since their infancy; Thorvald, whom she had followed to the ends of the earth. Eyvind had done his best to get the truth out of Sam, with limited success. He discovered Creidhe had been held captive, briefly; that there was a possibility she had been hurt, misused, during that time. On hearing this, Eyvind had come close to venting his fury on Sam himself, for not protecting her, for not preventing such an outrage, but Sam's natural dignity and obvious contrition

cooled the older man's anger. It was clear the fisherman had
done his best; plain, also, that whatever had happened in
that remote place had not just damaged Creidhe but had
changed all of them profoundly. Thorvald a leader of men:
that was a little hard to swallow, for although the lad was
clever and able, he was also moody, volatile, subject to
bouts of black self-loathing. Would one choose to follow
such a man? Sam was different too: harder, older. And
Somerled. That was most startling of all. Somerled a hermit. Somerled a Christian who, Margaret revealed after
reading her letter, had made a choice to follow ways of solitude and scholarship rather than run the risk of being se-
duced by power again. Somerled had indeed kept his
promise; he had become the man Eyvind had once entreated him to be. It was strange and wondrous. It was
deeply soothing to the heart, as if at last the threads of a
great tapestry were tied and finished and the work revealed
to be a thing of beauty, once gone darkly awry, now set
straight and fair. He would be truly happy, Eyvind thought,
despite his anxiety for Nessa, if it were not for Creidhe. The
change in her was shocking, frightening; it caused him deep
unquiet.

They all agreed she must be given time, and so, as harvest month came and went and the days grew shorter and
the winds colder, they moved around her with care, avoiding awkward questions, not asking too much of her, sparing
her the need to attend such public gatherings as weddings
and festival days. And they saw, to their dismay, that time
alone was doing little to heal whatever hurt it was Creidhe
bore. She walked through a semblance of her old routine,
helping in the house, going to Margaret's to spin and
weave. She made no new designs, working only on those
Margaret set her. She kept herself tidy, and treated them all
with a distant courtesy. This seemed a mockery of the old
Creidhe, as if a changeling pretended to be the girl they had
known and loved, without understanding what it was that
had made her the vibrant, glowing center of any room she
entered. That quality was not beauty or charm, not kindness
or goodness or generosity, but all of these with something

extra thrown in for good measure, something elusive whose name nobody knew, but whose loss everybody grieved.

In time, they began to come to terms with it. While Creidhe was away, Brona had assumed many of her sister's household responsibilities, and she kept them now, planning in advance so they would be ready for visitors, supervising Ingigerd, preparing special meals. It was to Brona that small Ingi turned now, next after her mother; this youngest sister was shy of the new Creidhe, who had no will for the telling of tales, the ready hugs of comfort, the laborious brushing and braiding of tangled hair. As for Nessa, she was looking inward more and more as her time came closer. She hid her distress so as not to worry Eyvind more than she need do. And Eyvind ceased to cast around for likely suitors when he traveled about the islands consulting the landholders and attending councils, for it was plain that was no longer appropriate and perhaps never would be. There was Brona, of course. It was plain what Brona wanted; Sam had become a frequent visitor, and although he spoke with Creidhe alone sometimes, and seemed to be able to coax a little animation to her features, he spent most of his time gazing at Brona, and she at him, with an expression that was quite unmistakable. And Eyvind, who had never considered that Nessa's daughters, born of the ancient royal line of the Folk, might marry farmers or fishermen, looked at Creidhe, wan and dispirited, and looked at Brona, sparkling with health and happiness, and knew he would have to say yes when Sam finally plucked up the courage to approach him on the matter. Not yet, though; let them wait a little and prove this was strong and real. Next summer would be quite soon enough.

When it lacked but a single turning of the moon until Nessa's babe was due, her eldest daughter, Eanna the priestess, arrived at the longhouse with her little cat in a basket and settled to stay awhile. Her presence brought calm; the young wise woman was deeply respected in the islands as guardian of the ancient ways of the Folk. This faith had endured alongside the other, newer beliefs, the rituals of Odin, Thor and Freyr that Eyvind's people had brought from their homeland, and the Christian teachings spread by Brother

Tadhg and his fellows. Eyvind's family followed the old ways, despite his childhood in Rogaland and his young life as a warrior servant of Thor. The islands had changed him; Nessa had changed him.

Eanna had consulted the ancestors on the subject of Creidhe. She held certain images in her mind as she watched her sister; considered certain wisdoms she had kept to herself thus far. Because of her position, Eanna was lodged in a small, separate dwelling house, but she took her meals with the family. The cat had deserted her for now and attached himself to Ingi, who carried him around tirelessly, showing him every corner of house and yard, stable and walled field. Eanna observed. Her family was unhappy, deeply so, for all their surface calm. There were secrets. True, some things are destined to be secret, and should remain so. But not this, whatever it was. This was tearing her strong family apart. Nessa was pale and anxious, Eyvind too quiet, the child tiptoed around Creidhe as if she were a ghost. Brona was the only one who seemed happy at all, and even she was looking worn out.

Eanna took her chance in the afternoon, when Nessa had gone to rest, on her husband's orders, and the women were busy out of doors. Brona had taken Ingi off to gather the eggs; a meaningful look from her eldest sister had told her this expedition should not be rushed. Eanna sat with Creidhe on a bench before the cheerful glow of the turf fire.

"I must—" Creidhe began, getting up.

"No." Eanna's voice was quiet but firm; it was a tone that could not be disobeyed. "Stay here. I want to talk to you."

Creidhe sat down again, mute. Her fair hair was pulled back severely from her face and plaited painfully tight. There was no color in her cheeks at all. Her hands twisted together in her lap.

"Brona tells me you've stopped making the Journey," Eanna said.

Creidhe blinked; the question had startled her.

"Why, Creidhe?" Eanna asked.

Creidhe began to speak, faltered, tried again. "I can't," she said dully.

"Can't? Why not?"

"Because . . . because I can't see what's next." There was a hopeless sound to Creidhe's voice, a terrible resignation. "There's only a blank, as if it went wrong and just stopped. I don't know what to do."

This, Eanna suspected, was the most anyone had got out of her sister since her return home. The family's kindness did not seem to have helped much. Perhaps the time for kindness was over.

"This is extremely selfish, Creidhe."

Creidhe did not respond.

"What about Mother? The last thing she needs right now is you mooning about the place wrapped up in your own sorrows, when she has this child to worry about. She's so concerned for you she's losing sleep, sleep she badly needs. You were never selfish before."

"She doesn't need to worry. She doesn't need to concern herself with me." Creidhe's tone had not changed.

"No? Then try to act a bit more like a real live woman and less like a cloth doll, can't you? If you'd stirred yourself to think about Mother a single moment, you'd know she's terrified about the birth, terrified the child will die, full of fear that the Seal Tribe will rob her of another infant in payment for the favor they once did her. And Father's afraid he'll lose her or the baby or both. Ingi seems to be pretending you're not really here: have you seen the way she avoids you? Is that good for a child? Whatever it was that happened, you must talk about it, get it out. You're hurting everyone. It has to stop."

Creidhe stared at her hands, offering nothing.

"Answer me, Creidhe." That tone again: not the voice of a sister but that of a priestess, ancient and commanding.

"They should be content," Creidhe said, not looking up. "Sam and I are back safely, Thorvald is happy, Somerled has become a good man . . . What more do they want?"

"They want the old Creidhe back. They want to put things right for you."

"The old Creidhe doesn't exist anymore. She's dead. She died when . . . when . . ."

Something, Eanna thought. Something at last, though her sister had sunk her teeth in her lip to stop it from coming out. "When Thorvald decided to stay, and sent you home?" she ventured. "That's what Mother seems to think."

Creidhe stared at her, blue eyes round with surprise. "Thorvald?" she echoed.

"You seem astonished," said Eanna dryly. "Yet you spent your whole childhood following him about like a devoted slave. You chose to go with him on his mad voyage. Surely you expected something out of it." It was cruel, maybe. But if cruelty would force Creidhe awake, would light some spark in her eye, if only one of anger, then she would use it.

"I wouldn't wed Thorvald if he were the last man in the world," Creidhe said in that small, cold voice. "I'm glad that he found his father, and his future, for Aunt Margaret's sake. But that's all. I hope I never see him again as long as I live."

"Creidhe," Eanna said quietly, "did Thorvald hurt you? Was it he who—?"

"Who what?" It was plain that Creidhe was not going to make this easier for her sister.

"Something Sam said—implied—to Father, that you had been harmed in some way when you were captive—that perhaps some man had forced you—"

"Sam doesn't know anything. He doesn't understand anything. And nor does Thorvald. All he could think about was winning his war and impressing his father. Even at the end he didn't understand what he had done when he . . . when he . . ."

Eanna moved closer, taking her sister's hands in hers. They were as cold as a corpse's. "Tell me, Creidhe. What did he do? What is too terrible to be set down in the Journey?"

Creidhe shook her head, closing her eyes. "I can't. I can't bring myself to tell you. Somehow, if I don't say, if I don't share it, I can keep him—them—as they were, alive inside me, deep down. I can see and hear them . . . If I talk about it I'll lose that last little scrap of life, and if I do that I don't think I can go on at all, not even pretending . . ."

It had been there, the truth at last. *I can keep him alive . . .*

Not Thorvald, not Sam, but another. And Eanna thought, just possibly, that she knew who it was.

"I have looked in the fire for you," she said slowly. "Made the patterns of augury, sought the council of Bone Mother. I have truths to tell you, sister, if you will hear them."

"There was no need," Creidhe said flatly. "It's too late to change it now."

"It's never too late," Eanna said. "All is change. And I did not do it for you, believe me, but for Mother and for Margaret, both so anxious for the children they love. The ancestors have much to say concerning yourself and your journey. It seems to me the truth is a great deal more complex than the tale you told the family."

"I told no lies."

"Perhaps not; and Sam is loyal to a fault. They tell me he refuses to fill in the blanks. I've seen a child in the story, a powerful child, and there is a young warrior. I did not speak to others of these two, because of what they are. Mother has reason to be anxious about the Seal Tribe. As I said, she fears for her child."

"That's nonsense!" Creidhe pulled her hands away from Eanna's. "They would never take him, and they didn't take Kinart either! The folk of the Seal Tribe love the islands, and protect all those who honor the ancient powers. They value life; they do not steal children. Those are simply the fireside tales of old people, told to keep infants away from dangerous shores. They will not harm Mother or her baby."

"You sound very certain." Eanna watched her sister closely.

"I am certain. He told me."

"Who?"

Silence. Creidhe closed her mouth into a tight line.

"Let me tell you something, Creidhe. I was shown a vision at last full moon, when I made a circle and kept vigil through the night. I saw a man, wild and fierce, chipping rocks with a heavy hammer, working as if to put his whole being into what he made. He wore distinctive clothing, dec-

orated with many small feathers. This was a lean, weathered
sort of man, with dark hair held back by a strip of leather.
Young; not so much older than yourself. The hillside where
he stood was steep and grass-covered; many birds flew
above. I could not see what he was making, perhaps a wall
to shield sheep, perhaps a hut for his stock. There was rain
falling, and he worked on as if he could not feel it. He
talked to himself as he labored, and your name was in it.
Often. He repeated it as if it were a kind of talisman. I have
seen this man before, in visions. The last time I saw him, I
saw you as well, sewing the Journey, with a little, ragged
child by your knee."

Eanna watched her sister. It was like the moment when a
dam begins to break its banks; first one tear trembled in
the blue eyes and fell down the pale cheek, and then another, and another, and in total silence Creidhe put her face
in her hands and wept. Eanna said nothing. She did not offer the comfort of touch or words of reassurance. Both of
them knew well that the visions of the ancestors show *was*
and *is* and *will be* mixed together, along with the cruel *may
be* and *might have been*. One interpreted their meaning as
if solving a puzzle, a puzzle that might have many possible
answers.

Creidhe's shoulders were heaving, her hands still
clutched tightly over her face, as if to try to contain the
flood of grief. She had held these tears back a long time.

"The Seal Tribe," Eanna said at last. "You weep for one
of the Seal Tribe."

"You don't need to worry," choked Creidhe. "He's dead.
Thorvald killed him."

Eanna absorbed this. Creidhe had said, *I can keep them
alive.* "And the child?" she asked.

"Well, and content . . . a great seer . . . he saved the people and made the peace. But it was too late for Keeper."

"Keeper. That is his name? And you love him." No judgment in the tone.

"With everything that I am." Creidhe spoke these words
in a tone that made her sister's spine tingle; it was not the
voice of a lovesick girl, but a deep, solemn swearing of

truth. "I never thought such a bond was possible . . . He did not deserve to die, he was so brave, so loyal and strong . . ."

"You saw him die? You witnessed it?" Cruel again, but she must press the advantage she had; Creidhe must tell it all.

"No. I was knocked unconscious. They told me later. He told me. Thorvald. They were enemies, one sworn to protect Small One—the seer—the other to hunt him down. It was my fault Keeper died." The voice very small now, like a child's. "I tried to stop them. If I had not done that, Keeper would have won. He was by far the better fighter. He never lost a battle, until that day."

"Then Thorvald would have died."

No response.

"You know, Creidhe," Eanna said carefully, "how hard the ancestors' messages are to decipher; one could spend a lifetime working them out. Indeed, some of us do just that. Tell me, is it possible you were wrong? Could this man still be alive, do you think?" She did not tell Creidhe her own interpretation of the vision, nor her certain belief that it had shown not *then* but *now*.

Creidhe shook her head. "Why would Thorvald lie? Why would he spare Keeper's life? Thorvald hated him for what he had done, for all the men he had killed over the years, for making the war continue. He never understood why Keeper did it, not even when he knew what the Unspoken intended for Small One. Of course he killed him."

"All the same."

"Don't seek to comfort me with false hopes, Eanna. That's cruel. I long to see your visions, to hear of them, to find solace in them. But I cannot believe them. I cannot think of any reason Thorvald would tell me such a thing if it were not the truth."

"Because he was jealous?" Eanna asked softly.

Creidhe stared at her a moment, and then burst into terrible laughter, a sound that chilled her sister, so full was it with bitterness. "Thorvald? Jealous? He never even saw me. Thorvald cares for nothing but himself."

"Didn't someone say he was a leader of men now? Well respected? A selfish man does not become such a leader."

"Maybe he has changed," Creidhe conceded reluctantly. "Just a little."

"And he may also have changed in his feelings for you. Would that make a difference to you, Creidhe?"

"Nothing can make a difference."

Eanna drew a deep breath and let it out in a sigh. Was that all this had been, an argument that simply came full circle?

"Now, Creidhe," the priestess spoke again, "I'm about to make a request and to give you some advice. I'm not going to tell you to stop the self-pity and find another good man; I hear in your voice that this was the only one, and I grieve for you, though unlike you I think nothing is certain. I ask you, as your sister, to speak to Mother today, to reassure her, and to promise her you will deliver her child expertly and safely as you always do. That may seem obvious to us, but she needs to hear it from your own lips. And you must explain to her about the Seal Tribe."

"But—"

"It doesn't matter how much you tell or how you do it. Just make sure she's not frightened anymore. She needs you, Creidhe. We all do."

"Not you, surely." The tone was dry.

"You'd be surprised," Eanna said. "Now the request. I want you to start working on the Journey again."

"I can't—"

"You said you don't know how it goes from now on. But I think there is a part of your work you did know how to make, but would not fashion, out of fear. If he is dead and the child safe, what is there to be afraid of anymore?" That, too, was somewhat less than kind; Creidhe's pale cheeks grew still whiter. "So, get your work out, sort your colors, make that small part at least. And listen for what the ancestors whisper in your ear, sister. No matter how dark the day, how crooked the path, they are always close. Make room for them in your heart, shattered and sorrowful as it is. They may surprise you."

FIFTEEN

. . . this contemplative life is far safer, believe me, both for myself and for others who may cross my path. I do not forget the past; I remember what I was. Looking at him, I feel no regret for the loss of what other men have: the warmth of family, the security of household and community, and a path to tread among men of affairs. That is our son's life, not mine. He need not fear me. I would never challenge him for power. Already he is a finer man than I could ever be, and for that I thank you from the bottom of my heart. I treated you badly; I knew no better. In return you have given me a priceless gift. I promise you I will guide him, advise him and love him as a good father should. That is all the recompense I can make you.

Know that my dark path is turned to light, not only by the return of this son I never knew I had, but by the love and guidance of a God whose existence, until last summer, was as much of a mystery to me as Thorvald's. I am unworthy of such joy: I greet each day with wonder. With all sincerity I wish you a life of equal contentment. For the making of this fine son, for nurturing him to become the man he is, you deserve no less.

EXTRACT FROM LETTER

It was spring once more: a whole year since Margaret had given her son the letter and sent him racing off across the ocean to find the man who was his father. Now the green hills of Hrossey were dotted with new lambs, and on the cliffs south of the Whaleback the small, bright blooms of heart's-eye flowered in profusion under a mild sun.

Creidhe was tired of weaving. She had made a number of heavy, plain blankets, and a wall hanging to be presented to a nobleman in Rogaland. Eyvind was sailing there in sum-

mer as part of a delegation seeking a trade arrangement
with the Jarls in that region. The hanging was not her own
design; the bold ideas that had once been her great strength
had deserted her. She no longer sought to create new dyes,
fresh shades of color, or to fashion intricate borders on the
strip loom. She had made what was required to Margaret's
specifications, and it was both expertly crafted and pleasing
to the eye, but it was not her own. Whatever she had lost
from within her when Keeper died, it was the same thing
that had created those works of magic and beauty. There
was no point even trying anymore. She just couldn't do it.

Today her back ached and her eyes had had enough of the
monotonous task: the work on the loom was very plain,
done in the natural cream of the fine wool Margaret's main
flock produced, and the only skill required was in keeping
the weave even. Creidhe got up, stretching, and walked into
the long room of Margaret's house. Margaret's and Ash's
house. She must get used to the fact that they were married
now; she must get accustomed to the astonishing sight of
Margaret happy. The two of them, who had shared the
house so long as mistress and steward, had been quite transformed by what had happened. They were like a pair of
young lovers, clasping hands as they passed, exchanging
shy smiles and whispered words. Creidhe had seen a warm
blush of awareness creep across Margaret's ladylike features; she had seen a look in Ash's steady gray eyes that signified, quite simply, ardent desire. They welcomed Creidhe
to their house, as had always been the case; they worried
about her as her own parents did. On the other hand, it was
always evident, when Creidhe made her excuses and
headed back home, that the two of them were glad to be left
alone together, save for the discreet, well-trained men and
women of the household. The bond between Ash and Margaret could be read in the way they moved, the way they
looked, in every note of their voices.

Creidhe was glad for them. But under this, there was something hard to bear, a wrenching reminder of the joy that could
be had in the finding of a perfect partner, and the deathblow

suffered when such a one was stolen away. She had tried, very
hard, to shut herself off from feeling. She had tried to be a little as Margaret herself once was, calm, distant, moving
through her days immune to pain or joy. This had not served
Creidhe well. It took only a small thing, perhaps observing
Sam and Brona as they shared a joke by the fire, or seeing the
way her father held his newborn son in his arms, as if the babe
were a treasure more valuable than all the gold in a dragon's
hoard, or noticing Ash's work-scarred hand move to touch his
wife's sleek auburn hair in a gesture of tenderness. These
things brought Creidhe's pain alive so vividly she thought she
would break apart, would shatter into brittle pieces, no longer
able to bear the intensity of it.

A whole year. It was plain her family had expected her to
be better by now, to have begun forgetting. But everything
had seemed to make it worse, to make her remember. The
birth of her small brother, Eirik: it had been a joyful occasion, for once Creidhe had reassured her mother about the
Seal Tribe, in a general sort of way, the delivery had been
accomplished calmly and easily. Eirik was a fair-haired infant of robust health and strapping build; plainly he took after his Wolfskin father. And Creidhe had thought of Keeper,
who had taken such care of his small, frail kinsman;
Keeper, robbed by Thorvald's quick blade of ever having a
son or daughter of his own to love as he had loved Small
One. She had clung, for a little, to the hope that she might
be carrying his child when she came home, but it had not
been so. A dark day, that had been, when her monthly
bleeding came on time; so dark she had come close to
spilling out the whole truth to Brona, just so she could
speak Keeper's name aloud. But she had not; Brona was
happy, and that had made Sam happy, and why would
Creidhe spoil their well-deserved joy in any way? What had
happened to her was not their fault. Besides, keeping the
truth inside, secret, seemed necessary; the worst thing, now,
would be to let her memories wither and fade. They were all
she had left.

She sat on the steps, her bag beside her, and let the afternoon sun warm her. Soon she'd head for home; it was a good day for walking, and the solitary journeys from her family's longhouse to Margaret's and back again were somehow soothing. Under the wide sky, with the sea's hushed music in her ears and the sweep of the gentle hillside before her, she was able to remember how small she was in the great memories of the ancestors, how tiny and insignificant her pain in the long tale of her people's history. It did not provide solace, but it brought acceptance just a little closer. She had not reached it yet, for acceptance seemed to her the death of hope. And without hope, what was there to live for? She had thought, at first, that she had no hope at all, but it could not be so: if it did not exist, somewhere within her, why had she bothered to come home? Why not walk off a cliff, or take a knife to her wrists, and put an end to the hurt once and for all?

There had been reasons to go on, of course: to deliver her mother's child, to see Sam and Brona married, to avoid causing her family any more sorrow. But she knew that even without these things she would never have made an end of herself. Life was too precious to be treated with such contempt. It was for the ancestors to decide how long or short a mortal span would be, not for each man and woman. If she still lived, even with such grief, there was a purpose to it. And purpose was hope, in a way.

All the same, she had not followed her sister Eanna's suggestion, not fully. She had taken the Journey out, looked at it, and put it away again. She had replenished her stock of colored wools, replaced needles she had lost, sharpened her little shears. But she had made not a single stitch. For this task, her hands seemed to have no will, her mind no pattern.

The sun was kind today; its warmth was easing her aching back, bringing life to her cramped hands. Little puffy clouds passed over; she could see their shadows skipping across hillside and drystone dike and rocky outcrop, then dancing away again. Light . . . shade . . . light . . . shade . . . A gull glided overhead, its voice high and harsh. A silent voice, fierce in its entreaty, spoke behind that call, chilling her blood. *Put him in your web, now, now!* Small

One had believed it, and Keeper had believed it. It seemed possible even Eanna, a wise woman who surely should have known better, believed that Creidhe with her needle and wools had some power beyond the ordinary. Could she have saved him? Had she indeed needed only to set his image on the linen to determine whether he walked onward in his own journey or fell lifeless under Thorvald's sword? Creidhe shivered. She was no goddess, for all Keeper's sweet words. She was flesh and blood, ordinary, weak, helpless . . . and it was too late . . .

Cold logic spoke inside her: the voice of her sister, the priestess, or perhaps her own voice. *If it is too late, then surely to do it now can cause no harm. Why not try? Why not finish what you have begun? Then, at least, the effort of spinning and dyeing and setting aside these materials will not have been wasted. Take your work out again. Thread your needle. See if your hands will fashion one stitch, or two, or three. Not to go on with this is exactly the same as death. It means you're given up on life. Move your Journey onward. Keeper deserves no less.*

It was strange to find, after so long away from this most cherished of tasks, that her fingers obeyed her instantly, that the choice of color and starting point and pattern happened as it always had with the Journey, seemingly without any decision on her part; how her hands worked ever more quickly and her eyes scanned the blank expanse of linen ever more intently as the images that would fill it formed themselves whole and complete in her mind, ready for needle and wool to give them physical form. She sewed as the sun sank into the west, as the breeze got up and the ewes headed for shelter with their lambs at heel. She sewed as the sky cooled and darkened; she went on until she could barely tell sea-blue from weed-green, scarlet from rich purple. At some point Ash came out with a warm cloak and laid it around her shoulders; he had lit a lantern and put it on the steps nearby. A little later Margaret brought soup and bread and set them beside her. A man rode away to the north, probably with a message to let Nessa and Eyvind know she'd be staying the night here. Apart from that they left her undisturbed. She was hardly aware of time, of place, of the cold or the darkness, only of the need to make this, a need now as fierce and pressing in her as Small One's silent entreaty that long-ago day when the two of them had waited in hiding as the hunt raged above them on the slopes of the Isle of Clouds.

She was lying curled up on the steps when Ash and Margaret went out to check again, some time after supper. Her cheek was pillowed on her hand; the other hand clutched the length of embroidered linen to her breast. Needles and threads were safely stowed; Creidhe was ever an orderly worker. Her breathing was calm; her long lashes were closed peacefully over the blue eyes. She was sleeping as soundly as a child.

While Ash carried Creidhe to the bed his wife had prepared, Margaret gathered up the Journey and the little bag and bore them indoors, out of the dew. This embroidery had long been Creidhe's most prized work, and her most secret. All the same, it was more than Margaret could manage not to look at it now. When Ash came back to the long room, she was standing by the table with the bright expanse of delicate color, of intricate, mysterious detail laid out before her in the warm glow of a lamp. Margaret was stock still, entranced.

"Look," she said simply. "Just look."

All was there: all of a life, and all of the unseen life of the heart, the sweet, the terrible, the strange visions of the spirit. Here was family, with its strength and its warmth, its joys and its losses. Beyond family, the images showed a more distant past in which two boys marked their flesh with a hunting knife and swore an oath in blood. The images moved on through time. They did not make a story. Sometimes they did not even show what could be judged real or possible, but always they made a picture of truth. Nobody, looking at this wondrous piece of work, could doubt that. Here was Creidhe herself, flying through the sky, her hands reaching out to touch the moon. Here Thorvald, alone. His small figure was made with great care, the red hair blown into wild streamers by the wind, the eyes shadow-dark, the expression forbidding. Their boat, the voyage, the images of steep, stark islands, lonely in a cold sea. One isle was shrouded in perpetual mist, encircled by birds. Then stranger things: eyes hidden in the bushes, a wall of screaming faces, hands in the water, guiding a little craft through wild seas.

Creidhe had left a blank space before she began again, as if there were a certain part of this tale unknown or undecided. On the right of this empty expanse of linen she had fashioned today's work. Here was a picture of such joy and loveliness it put a lump in Margaret's throat to see it. A man and a woman flying, or floating, hand in hand; he dark, lean, fierce in appearance; she of rounded form, blue-eyed, with long hair dancing in a golden cloud around her dazzled features. They seemed to hang in air, the two of them, and about them was a cloud of small things, fine, beautiful things, as if Creidhe would show here all the wonders the world held, if only one would open one's eyes to them: birds of many kinds, and shining fish, and beetles with glowing carapaces. There was a creature like a dog, or a cat, or maybe a fox: Margaret remembered foxes from Rogaland, and this had that same look, bright-eyed and wary. Flowers and grains and grasses, creeping mosses and fronded ferns. Heart's-eye vibrant in its purple-pink, and celandine, and buttercups. Here, too, were works of man: a scrap of writing in neat black ink, though Creidhe herself could not write; a garment edged in that same heart's-eye shade; a pair of little boots, like a child's. Amidst the circling frieze of wonder, the two gazed at one another as if they were the only man and woman in all the world. It was only later, when the first shock of this stunning tapestry of life had passed, that the viewer noticed another figure there: at the bottom, cross-legged on a flat stone, a little ragged child, singing.

"We've all been terribly wrong," Margaret whispered, her fingers moving to touch the bright hair of the joyous, soaring girl. "She did not find cruelty and abuse on that island, she found love."

"Found it and lost it," said Ash. "But what goes here?" He was looking at the blank part, the part Creidhe had chosen not to make.

"I have no idea," Margaret said. "Either she does not know what happened, or is reluctant to set it down. He died, perhaps. Or sent her away, though that seems unlikely if she has made his image truly here. I suspect Eanna may know a little more, but the wise woman keeps her own counsel, she always has. Most certainly, Creidhe's sorrow is not for Thorvald; what love she felt for my son has been quite eclipsed by this. There is such power in these images. It is as if the gods spoke through her. I can understand why she held back from doing more; and why, once begun, she could not stop until she finished it."

"I wonder," mused Ash. "I wonder if it really is finished?"

After a year in the Lost Isles, Thorvald was learning caution. All the same, the boat was ready, a fair copy of the *Sea Dove*, and the fellows eager to put her to the test in open seas. There was no doubt they badly needed to establish some contact with realms farther afield, particularly with the Light Isles, now more often known by their Norse name of Orkneyjar, Isles of the Seal. They needed wood for boat-building—he knew Eyvind had an agreement with the Jarl in Freyrsfjord for a supply—and good quality iron. They needed breeding stock to replenish what had been lost in the years of the hunt. They had not much to offer in return, but that would change in the future; Thorvald would make sure of it. Meanwhile, a voyage to those shores, just to open preliminary discussions, was desirable. Once there, it was best if Thorvald started the process by approaching those influential men he knew personally, such as Grim and Thord. And Eyvind. He was not looking forward to seeing Eyvind again, but that challenge must be faced some time, and the sooner the better, Niall told him. Eyvind would be angry, no doubt. But Creidhe had been home a long while, provided the *Sea Dove* had weathered the voyage, and her father would be reconciled, in part, to Thorvald's actions. Eyvind might be strong enough to take your head off with a single blow, but that didn't mean he was actually going to do it. The Wolfskin was a leader; furious he might be that his daughter had run away, but he would still be keen to listen. Creidhe was probably married with a child on the way, joked Ranulf, and would have forgotten Thorvald entirely. Thorvald did not respond to this. He had business with Creidhe as well as with her father, business that took up a great deal more of his thoughts than he wished.

They left in spring. After the crossing to the Northern Isles they sailed southward, and when the Light Isles came in sight they hugged the western coastline all the way to the sheltered bay of Hafnarvagr. There they left the *Swiftwing* at anchor and procured horses for the ride north to Thorvald's home. He made it plain to his companions that this journey was to be undertaken in a precise order: first his mother, so she would not hear of his arrival from others; then a message sent to Eyvind and Nessa, a formal message from himself as emissary from the Lost Isles, requesting talks on matters of trade and treaties. Then Creidhe, if her parents had not already wed her to some likely nobleman and sent her off to Caithness or all the way to Rogaland. Creidhe alone and in private. He'd have to beg that from Nessa.

It nagged at him, irritating as a burr next to the skin: the need for her, the memory of her, the knowledge that he had somehow failed her. The fact that she had not forgiven him: he had never asked her what it was that he had done that was so terrible it shattered their old friendship. He hoped time, and home, and the support of her family had changed her mind; that it would be the old Creidhe who stepped through the doorway of her parents' house, her arms open in welcome, her blue eyes alight for him. There was a girl in the Lost Isles, daughter of one of the leaders from the northern region, who had come to the last two councils with her father, lodging in Brightwater. Thorvald had not exchanged more than a few words with her, but he had seen the way she watched him, coolly, gravely, as if assessing what he was made of. She had smooth dark hair and serene gray eyes, and nothing at all of the giggling, mock-shy demeanor other girls showed in his presence. He liked that. He liked her. But she was not Creidhe, and never could be.

Up to a certain point, all went to plan. Skapti, Ranulf and Orm exclaimed in wonder at the smooth and gentle contours of the land, the sleek, fat sheep, the walled fields of bere and oats shooting lush and green. There was a sharp westerly wind, carrying rain; Ranulf, shivering, commented that the weather, at least, was just like home. Still, it was a fair place; it seemed more than likely, Orm reckoned, that Knut would have settled and found a wife, and have no inclination at all to make the journey back.

So far, so good. They reached Margaret's longhouse and dismounted in the yard. Thorvald felt unaccountably nervous, as if he were still that impulsive youth who had spat words of black resentment at his mother, then sailed away with no explanation whatever. When Ash appeared in the doorway, his plain features alive with astonishment, Thorvald's manner was more curt than he had intended.

"Ash, I see you haven't moved on. Please tell my mother I am here, with three companions. I hope they can all be accommodated."

He was not sure how Ash was going to respond; it almost seemed the poker-faced housecarl was suppressing a smile of amusement. As it was, Ash did not get the chance to speak, for Margaret appeared beside him in the doorway and, an instant later, was running toward Thorvald in a most un-Margaret like way, and he dismounted and felt her arms come around his neck in an embrace such as she had not offered him since he was a tiny child. He might almost have let tears fall, had he been that kind of man. It was good. It was remarkably good. Beside them, he was aware of Ash welcoming his companions as if he were master of the house, and extending an invitation to stay as long as they wished, since the buildings were spacious and could easily accommodate visitors.

Thorvald had done no more than blink with surprise when his mother drew back, releasing him, and moved to

Ash's side, and the two of them reached out to each other, clasping hands like a pair of courting youngsters.

"We're married now," Margaret said, her smile something new and, Thorvald was forced to admit, pleasing to see. "I need to tell you straightaway, so there's no misunderstanding."

"Oh." Thorvald could not think what to say. Once, he would have found the very idea repugnant. His own mother, Lady Margaret, daughter of Thorvald Strong-Arm, wed to a—a serving man? But he had had time for reflection since last spring. As child and youth, he had scorned Ash's contributions to his education even as he endured the endless practice sessions in armed and unarmed combat, horsemanship and strategy. He had come to realize, over the season of the hunt, that without Ash's expert teaching, his patient tutoring in the arts of war, it would have been impossible to win the trust of Hogni and Skapti and the other men. He could never have led them into battle. Ash had not always been a housecarl. If he had stayed with Margaret all those years, it was by choice. Thorvald saw in the calm gray eyes, now turned toward his mother in reassurance, that Ash had stayed because of love. How could her son grudge Margaret a moment's happiness? He himself had hardly made things easy for her, or for Ash himself.

"Well, this is good news," he made himself say. "What a surprise. I offer my congratulations to you both."

"Are you home for long?" Margaret asked, and Thorvald felt overwhelming relief that he did not need to explain that this was a brief visit, that he would never return to pick up the pieces of his old life.

"Perhaps one turning of the moon. I need to speak of trade matters; I will tell you more once we're settled. Mother, how is . . . ?"

"How is Creidhe? Not very well, Thorvald. Changed terribly. Still struggling to make sense of it all, I think. She told us very little. Sam's fine. He's courting Brona, and happy as a pig in clover."

"Creidhe is not yet wed then?" They were going up the

steps now, and he spoke quietly, for his mother's ears alone. He tried to keep his voice cool and dispassionate.

"No, Thorvald," said Margaret, and it sounded to him, oddly, as if she felt sorry for him. "She's very sad; too sad to consider such a prospect. We've all been extremely worried." It was a statement of fact, without censure. Then they were inside, and he had to introduce the others properly and could not ask her more.

They sent a messenger, and while they waited for an answer the household moved with brisk efficiency around them, preparing a fine meal of roasted beef accompanied by a particularly good ale. Skapti, grinning, flirted with the serving women; Orm engaged Ash in a long discussion about sheep, and Ranulf subsided into a comfortable seat by the fire, ale cup in his hand, feet stretched to the flames' warmth. Thorvald passed on certain messages to his mother and heard her own news. A son born to Eyvind and Nessa; a decision coming soon, as to which ties must be put first, those with Rogaland or with Caithness; a great council at Freyrsfjord in the summer, which Eyvind would attend, though he was reluctant to part with small Eirik for long: what if the child learned to walk, he had protested, and he was not there to see it?

A messenger from Eyvind's household came promptly; he must have been despatched straight after the other arrived. They were to ride on in the morning. Eyvind could not summon all the landholders in less than three days, but he wished to see Thorvald alone, tomorrow. Nessa and Eyvind were glad Thorvald was home safely and sent their regards to Margaret and Ash.

Only Skapti went with him. Ranulf had a monstrous headache and could not leave his bed, and Ash wanted to show Orm his two best rams, and talk to him about wool. Thorvald was somewhat relieved; today's meeting would not be easy. Perhaps only Skapti had an idea what it meant to him.

It was not such a long ride. The rain was gone; in time they came up over a rise and there before them, across a patchwork of neat, walled fields, were a fine heather-thatched longhouse and outbuildings set around a courtyard where folk moved about purposefully, some leading horses, some with dogs at heel. Thorvald did not see anyone he knew among them. The two men rode down the hillside. Thorvald rehearsed in his mind what he would say to Eyvind. His belly churned with trepidation, as if he were no leader of men but a foolish youth caught out in some piece of mischief.

"Thorvald?" Skapti said quietly. He was pointing down toward the stone dyke that circled the outermost field, where two small figures could now be seen, baskets in hand, stooping to gather herbs that grew in the damp by a little stream. Two figures; no, three, for one girl carried an infant on her back in a sling, an infant with the same wheaten-fair hair as her own. Thorvald's heart seemed to halt in its tracks a moment, then beat again. Without a word he turned his horse, and Skapti followed. A little later, both girls stood upright, watching them come.

The men rode up to the wall and dismounted. There was a charged silence; Thorvald and Skapti were both staring at Creidhe, a Creidhe they scarcely recognized, for she was so thin and pale she looked like a ghost. Whatever had ailed her, those last days in the Lost Isles, had clearly not been cured now she was home. Her eyes were shadowed, her lips set tight. The sight of the rosy, cheerful Brona standing by her sister's side only made Creidhe's woeful state the more shocking.

Brona found her voice. "Welcome home, Thorvald. It's good to see you. And you—?"

"Skapti," the big man mumbled, ducking his head in a kind of bow. "You'll be Creidhe's sister."

"Yes, I'm Brona. Betrothed to Sam. I've heard lots about you. Didn't you once flatten Thorvald in a fight? Or maybe that was your brother. Sam tells me he was a great warrior too." Brona glanced at her sister, then at Thorvald.

"Creidhe, I'm going to take my basket back to the house, I'm sure we've picked enough. I'll show Skapti where the stables are and introduce him to Mother."

Creidhe was silent, staring out toward the sea, away from Thorvald.

"Shall I take Eirik?" Brona offered.

"It's all right," Creidhe said, not turning. "He's asleep. I'll bring him up soon." And indeed, the infant slept deeply and peacefully on his sister's back, his small, blond head drooping against her neck, one thumb plugged firmly into his mouth. His eyelids were soft with dreams.

Brona headed off briskly toward the longhouse. Skapti followed, leading the two horses. Whether it was what Eyvind would have wanted or no, Creidhe and Thorvald were left alone.

Thorvald sat on the wall. She stood by him, looking away.

"A fine boy," he commented, glancing at the infant. "Your parents must be pleased."

She said nothing. The silence drew out.

"You look terrible," Thorvald said eventually. "Sick. Sad. I don't know what to say to you." It was the truth; there was no point in disguising it.

"You need not say anything, Thorvald." Creidhe's voice was flat.

He tried a new tack. "My father is well. So is Brother Breccan. He has a small following now among the people of Brightwater. He has great hopes of baptising three or four by next Yule. Both wished to be remembered to you."

Creidhe acknowledged this with a nod. It was better than nothing.

"So Sam and Brona are to be married," he said. "Your father agreed to that? I'm surprised. Sam and I always believed Eyvind would accept no less than Jarls for you and your sisters. I'm happy for Sam; he's a good man, a good friend. I always thought it was you he preferred."

She looked at him then, eyes wide, expression wary. "Strange, isn't it, how we think we know what we want," she said. "And how wrong we can be about it. For a long time I thought you were the only man in the world. If I'd seen another girl so much as look at you, I would have wanted to kill her. Then, for a little, I despised you. Now I just wish you would go away, and stay away."

For a while Thorvald could not speak. Her words had hurt him more than he could have imagined possible. Creidhe gazed out westward, features devoid of expression.

"You've made it quite clear what you think of me," he managed eventually, "and I suppose I must accept that, though I had hoped—I had entertained a slight hope that things might be different between us, that they might be as they were before—"

"How was that, Thorvald? You getting on with your life and me following you, invisible until you decided you needed me for a little comfort? Was that what you expected?" She had turned back toward him now; the anger in her eyes was at least better than that terrifying, blank indifference. "I pity any girl who marries you. She'll always come second, or perhaps third. After yourself and whatever quest currently absorbs you."

Thorvald swallowed. "This is not like you, Creidhe." He knew the words were feeble.

"It is like me. I am simply not as I was. If you don't care for the way I am now, look to your own actions for the reason. It doesn't matter anyway. After today we need never see each other again."

"Creidhe!" The word burst out, vibrant with feeling; he could not hold it back. "Don't say that!"

"I have said it."

"At least tell me—at least give me the chance—"

"Tell you what?" Her voice was cold and tight.

"What I'm supposed to have done that's so terrible, what it is I can never be forgiven for. I had hoped for more than friendship from you. I was deluding myself to think that possible, obviously. But to lose even your friendship, that would be like—like—" He faltered to a stop, alarmed to hear such words spilling from his lips, and he a seasoned leader of men.

"Like losing a part of yourself," Creidhe said quietly. "I cannot believe you still haven't worked it out, Thorvald.

You were always so clever, so good at puzzles. You would have given up Foxmask to the Unspoken, even though their intention was to blind and cripple him. All for your own glory. That was bad enough. But in seeking to take the seer, you dealt me a heart wound. You killed the man who was the other part of me. You snatched away his happiness and mine with a single stroke of your sword. Because of you, I'll lead only half a life. Because of you, Keeper never knew an existence beyond the terror of those lonely years on the island and the dark days of the hunt. That was what you did. You can't change it now. You can't bring him back." Her voice was itself like that of a seer, hollow and ringing. Her words made his heart quail. She was wrong about him, deeply wrong, and he longed to explain. He longed to tell her everything, how perhaps his quest had begun in a desire to impress Asgrim, to prove his own worth, but had changed to something far bigger: the will to bring peace, to give the men back their pride in themselves, to build a new community. He ached to tell her all that he had learned. But that was of no matter now. You can't bring him back, she had said. If he read her aright, he could indeed do just that. He could restore to her the very thing whose loss had leached the life from her spirit and emptied her eyes of joy; in doing so, he must lose her forever.

"Creidhe," he said carefully, knowing there was no choice in this at all, "for the sake of the bond we once had, the friendship we shared all those years, I beg you to listen to me now. This is important; you can't know how important. Please don't turn away; please don't go silent again. Who is this man Keeper? Do you mean the fellow who held you prisoner on the Isle of Clouds? Asgrim's son, Erling?"

"He didn't like that name," Creidhe said quietly. Thorvald did not miss the change in her tone; it had softened, warmed. "He called himself Keeper, because that was his life's purpose, keeping his sister's son safe. He called the child Small One. Never Foxmask: he lived in horror of what the Unspoken would do to the boy if they got their hands on him."

"Wrong, in the end."

"Wrong, yes; but he did not live to know that. And they would still have done it."

"But for you. You were very brave that day. You spoke to them like a goddess."

Something unaccountable happened then: tears began to stream down Creidhe's wan cheeks in total silence. She put up her hands to scrub them away, as a child might. On her back her small brother slept on, oblivious. Thorvald was transfixed; the sudden change from the cold expression of judgment to this flood of grieving filled him with anguish. She was his dear friend and he could not touch her, could not offer a simple embrace of comfort. She loathed him. She had said so.

"Creidhe." His voice was urgent. "Stop it. Stop crying, please, I can't bear it. And listen to me. You must listen." His mind was racing ahead to the remoteness of the island, the vagaries of the Fool's Tide, the fellow's feral nature, the tally of men slain: clearly, the thing was impossible, ridiculous. Still, he must tell her. "Sit down, here." He fumbled for a handkerchief, passed it to her, his hands shaking. "That's better. Let me see your face, Creidhe. You must look at me while I say this."

She raised brimming eyes to him; her cheeks were wet, her lips trembling.

"I lied to you, Creidhe. I've only ever done that once, and I did it because I thought it was for the best. I thought you'd been held prisoner and abused. I thought the way you were behaving was because of that: shock and terror. So I lied."

"Wh-what are you saying?"

"I would have killed him. He accounted for four men that hunt; he had slain many more over the years, good men, honest men like Skapti's brother, who died slowly and cruelly from poison. I thought the fellow had taken you by force. I stood ready, sword in hand, as he lay senseless before me. But don't forget, I still believed Asgrim was my father then. That made this man Erling a kind of brother. When it came to the point, I couldn't do it. I couldn't kill my brother. So I dragged him to the shelter and left him."

Creidhe was mute, her eyes wide with shock, staring into his. He knew, in that moment, that her happiness was infinitely more important to him than his own.

"He's still alive, Creidhe. He was the only one on the island, wasn't he? Some of the fellows have been saying they've seen smoke from a little fire. They talk about the Seal Tribe, as fishermen do. There's certainly someone there on the Isle of Clouds; it can only be your Keeper."

Her eyes blazed. Her cheeks flushed scarlet. Her mouth curved in a smile of such joy it brought tears to his own eyes. An instant later she had sprung to her feet and thrown her arms around him, and, cruelly, Thorvald felt her body pressed to his own, frail and thin, but nonetheless providing a piercing reminder of how things might have been if he had not been so blind.

"Oh!" Creidhe breathed. "Oh, Thorvald, oh, Thorvald, thank you! How soon can we go back? We must be there by midsummer, because of the tide—oh, Thorvald, my dear, my friend, you can't know how happy I am! But to think, all this time he's been there alone, he must have thought—oh, how terrible, with Small One taken, and me gone as well, he would have believed—but he didn't give up, he waited for me—when can we leave?"

To anyone watching from a distance, and several members of Creidhe's family were doing just that, the scene would have had a single, obvious interpretation. A discussion, an argument, tears, then a fierce embrace, moderated somewhat by the presence of small Eirik: what else but a lovers' falling-out, ended in the best way possible? Then Creidhe practically skipping back to the house despite the child on her back, Creidhe leading Thorvald by the hand, Creidhe with her thin features radiant and blissful: how else might one read so dramatic a change?

Nessa waited by the steps. She was a wise woman, a priestess, for all she had set aside the formal observances for a life as wife and mother, councillor and arbiter. She, at least, knew that things are seldom as they seem on the surface.

"Mother!" Creidhe called, beaming. "Mother, I'm going back! He's alive, he's still there waiting for me!" And she threw her arms around Nessa, hugging her with a strength that seemed suddenly, miraculously restored to her. Eirik awoke and began to utter infant sounds that suggested hunger; he was a strapping child. Nessa looked over her daughter's shoulder and into Thorvald's dark eyes. She saw the hurt on his face, the wounded, lost look, turn at some silent self-command to the composed, guarded expression of a man of affairs, a leader. He was, beyond doubt, his father's son.

"Welcome, Thorvald," Nessa said, reaching to help Creidhe unfasten the bindings that held the child. "It's good to see you."

"Thank you. I'm glad to be back, though somewhat nervous, I have to say. Creidhe has more news for you; it's unlikely to please you, I fear, nor her father."

Nessa took Eirik in her arms; he was damp and beginning to squall. "Creidhe can tell me first, and then we'll speak to Eyvind together," she said, heading indoors. "After this small tyrant is fed, I think. My husband's out in the fields; you have a little time to gather your thoughts. Brona will fetch you some ale." She paused, taking in the white-knuckled tightness of his clenched fists. "Thorvald," she said, "this has been a very worrying time, a difficult time for us all. I have to say to you, anything that can bring such a smile to Creidhe's face and put such a spring in her step must be acceptable to Eyvind. Whatever it may be. Even if it means we must lose her again."

"It's ridiculous," Eyvind said, pacing up and down the short length of their bedchamber. "It's too far away. We'd never see her again."

"Ask yourself," said Nessa, "if you would travel such a distance if it were I who lived on that far isle. Ask yourself if you would allow anyone to stop you."

"What has the fellow to offer?" Eyvind demanded, glowering. "From what Creidhe tells us, he knows nothing but fighting. What sort of a life can such a man make for our daughter?"

Nessa did not offer a reply, but simply looked at him. Her lips curved in a little smile.

"It was different with us," he said after a pause. "I did my best to change. You helped me change."

"And Creidhe will help Keeper, if there's a need," Nessa said tranquilly.

"Maybe. But this is not an ordinary man; this is some strange combination of man and sea creature. What would their children be? How could they ever live a life among men and women? It's unthinkable."

"From what Creidhe tells me," Nessa said, "Keeper is man enough."

"You're not married," Eyvind told his daughter sternly. "The alliance you're proposing is not sanctioned in any way. Your reputation—"

"We have exchanged vows, Father," Creidhe said. "Solemn vows under moon and stars, promises witnessed by the ancestors themselves. We are husband and wife, forever. No oath could be more binding."

"What if you have a child?" Nessa asked her daughter in the privacy of her sleeping quarters. "How can you manage that, alone on this island, so far from anyone? Capable as he sounds, Keeper's unlikely to be much help with that. How can you look after an infant properly without a warm house, and good food, and folk to support you? Aren't you afraid of what might happen?"

"We'll manage," Creidhe said with complete confidence. "Don't forget, Keeper had the care of his sister's child since Small One was not much older than Eirik is now. He's a good provider, Mother."

"We'll never see you again," Eyvind said to Creidhe, baldly. His tone was desolate. "You'll never come home. It's plain this fellow is wild and alien; he can never live among men."

"You surprise me, Father," said Creidhe, taking his hand. "You've always been generous in your assessment of men. How can you say such a thing when you have not even seen Keeper?"

"I've heard more than enough," Eyvind growled.

"He can learn," Creidhe said. "It won't be quick; he's lived alone on the island, save for the child, since he was twelve years old. It will take time. But we will come back some day. Do not say never."

"I would sail with you if I could," Eyvind said to Thorvald. "At least that way I could meet the fellow and assess him before I gave my consent. I don't like the sound of him, for all Creidhe's ecstatic descriptions. He sounds entirely unsuitable."

Thorvald held his tongue, though privately he agreed wholeheartedly.

"Curse this council! Curse this trip to Freyrsfjord! The timing could hardly be worse."

"We cannot delay our return," Thorvald said. "As we've told you, Creidhe must cross to the island by midsummer or the tides make it too dangerous." They had been careful to keep from Nessa and Eyvind the precise truth about the Fool's Tide: that there were in fact only two days of the year when it might be easily passed. "And the council's crucial. Rogaland can offer you excellent trade prospects; protection, too, in times of war. You must be there to reinforce that."

Eyvind regarded him quizzically. "You realize, of course, that the Norwegian king may take it into his head to give us an overlord, one of his preferred chieftains, set in place as Jarl of the Light Isles? That would be quite a price to pay for their fine timber and their protection against invaders from the south."

"All the same."

"All the same, you're right; my mind is made up, and I must go there and put my case."

"There's nothing to stop you from sailing to the Lost

Isles another summer, and seeing for yourself that Creidhe is well and flourishing with her new husband." There was a question in Thorvald's tone.

"Would he want that, do you think?" Both men knew Eyvind was not referring to Keeper.

"Oh, yes," Thorvald said softly. "I'm in no doubt at all of that. He's thirsty for news of you."

"I don't know," Eyvind said. "Even after all these years, even after so many changes, I don't know if I could bear to see him."

"A good father would have said no," Eyvind told Nessa. His tone was heavy. "A good father wouldn't have given such a proposition a moment's consideration."

"How could you say no? You've seen how she looks. I imagine I once looked at you that way: as if you held the sum of my happiness."

"*Once* looked at me?"

"And still do, my dear, believe me. And Creidhe will look thus at her Keeper even when they are middle-aged and set in their ways, as you and I are."

"Middle-aged?" Eyvind raised his brows. "You still look about Creidhe's age to me, and as mysterious and lovely as the first time I saw you." He glanced at the child sleeping on her lap. "We've been so lucky. So lucky."

"Yes," agreed Nessa softly. "We cannot deny our daughter the same happiness."

"Strange," Nessa observed, watching the little boat sail away from Hafnarvagr. "The Seal Tribe did take one of my children after all."

"I thought you wanted her to go. It was you who persuaded me."

"I do want her to go. I want her to be happy. That doesn't make it hurt any less. I'll never see her children; I'll never meet her daughters, who carry on the royal line I vowed to protect."

"Don't say never." Eyvind's tone was gentle. "I heard Eanna say once, all is change. Creidhe will come home one day, and her man with her. I'm sure of it."

Beside them on the shore Ingigerd, seven years old and relishing her new role as big sister, was struggling to prevent the wriggling Eirik from crawling over the edge of the track and down into the sea. Brona and Sam stood arm in arm, waving as the vessel grew smaller and smaller on the silvery waters.

"Well then," said Margaret shakily, wiping her eyes, "this calls for some good ale, and a fire, and some talk among friends. Our door is open to you all; let's ride there and celebrate, and enjoy one another's company."

"Celebrate?" echoed Eyvind. "I'm not sure there's much cause for jubilation."

"Of course there is, Father," said Brona, chuckling. "Two daughters off your hands in the same season? What more could you ask for? Come on, let's go. I'm getting hungry. Aunt Margaret tells me there's spice cake." Eyes dancing, she led the way back to the horses, and the others followed her.

It was a rare quality his daughters had, Eyvind thought: a gift for happiness. He could not think where it had come from. If he had to let them go to see that bright flame flourish and grow, then so be it. Who was he to hold them back?

"You're not to drop anchor," Creidhe told the men sharply. "You're not to beach her either. Just hold her still and let me down over the side with my bags. Then go. No waiting around."

"Creidhe," protested Thorvald as they edged the *Swiftwing* into the narrow inlet that was the one safe landing place on the Isle of Clouds, "that's ridiculous. We must at least be certain he's here, and prepared to receive you. Besides, you can't carry everything. We must come ashore with your supplies. You're going to be here a whole year." While they had waited at Council Fjord for the lull in the Fool's Tide, he had ensured the boat was loaded with full provisioning for Creidhe's stay on the island. As her friend, and as leader here, he was bound to do no less.

"I'll be here longer than that," Creidhe said. "And I'm not taking the supplies. All I need is my little bag and that roll of bedding."

"Odin's bones, Creidhe," Thorvald ran his fingers through his hair in frustration, "there's no grain on this island, no vegetables, no proper shelter, no cattle . . . You must take the sack of flour at least, and the crock of onions. You must take the tools. And we can't just drop you in the water, we have to get you ashore—"

"Keeper will provide for me."

"Creidhe—"

"He will provide for me. This is important, Thorvald. You can't understand how important. It's to do with what he is; with what he has done here. To take those things he cannot offer me is to insult him, to challenge his very reason for being. I will go with no more than I carried last time: the clothes I stand up in and my little bag. That's all."

"What about that?" Thorvald challenged, pointing to the roll of bedding, covered in oiled cloth, which she had insisted on bringing. "You didn't have that before."

Creidhe blushed. "That's different. It is of my own choosing. A gift. You must not come ashore. Don't forget, he's known only the hunt. He has cause to feel much bitterness toward you. We cannot be sure he will not strike the moment your foot touches his land; that has long been his way."

In the end they compromised. While Thorvald and Orm held the boat in waist-deep water, using the oars to keep her from beaching, Skapti went over the side into the sea. Creidhe clambered over the rail, the bag on her back, the bundle under her arm. Skapti carried her to the shore, set her on the wet sand, and waded noisily back to the boat.

"Good-bye," called Thorvald, but it seemed she did not hear him. She stood there a moment looking up the steep, rocky path toward the level ground far above. The bay was little more than a deep fissure in the cliff, the track a challenge to the fittest legs. There was no sign of life on the island save the birds that wheeled in the sky, filling the air with their echoing cries. Creidhe took a deep breath and began to climb.

She did turn, once, but it was not to wave him farewell. She set the bundle down and gestured sharply. The meaning was plain: turn the boat, sail away, get out of sight as you promised. They edged the *Swiftwing* back under oars; not out of sight, not yet, but far enough so that Creidhe turned again and resumed her climb. Thorvald had no intention of leaving until he had some idea, at least, that she would be safe.

As Creidhe neared the top of the path, a figure appeared above her. He was there in an instant, standing dark and still as a man made of stone. He bore a spear in his right hand, a bow over his shoulder, a quiver on his back. The breeze stirred the small feathers that decorated his clothing; it sent strands of hair across his fierce, gaunt features. A chill gripped Thorvald, a memory of death. He could scarcely breathe.

Creidhe halted, looking upward. She dropped the bedding on the track and opened her arms. As for Keeper, his utter stillness did not last beyond that moment. Casting the spear aside, flinging the bow to the ground, he covered the distance as fast as a running deer. He reached her and paused. Then he took one step forward, and they put their arms around each other, not passionately, not wildly, but in an enfolding of utmost gentleness, and it seemed to Thorvald that what he saw was indeed two parts of one self, come wondrously back together. There was a rightness about their still posture, the sense of a perfect fit: Keeper's head bowed over Creidhe's, her brow against his neck. Thorvald felt such a confusion within him that it made him sick and faint. *I'll never feel this again*, he thought, astonished. *This tumult of emotions, this rending of the heart: I'll never feel it again.* And he thought that, as he was to be a leader of men, perhaps this was just as well. But as a man, he felt the loss of it, for it was like the passing of springtime in all its turbulence and promise. Then he turned away, and barked an order, and they set sail for home.

* * *

". . . they took him . . ." Keeper was whispering against her hair. "They took him . . . they took Small One away . . ."

"I know," Creidhe said, feeling the drumming of his heart against her, savoring the sweet warmth of him. "He's safe, Keeper, he's well and happy. He went of his own choosing. They did not harm him. There was no maiming, no blinding."

"You were there?" he asked her, astonished.

"I was there, and I stopped them. I thought you were dead, dear one. There was nobody else to help him."

"I did wrong, Creidhe. Wrong. All this time . . ." He was growing agitated; she felt the trembling in every part of him.

"Hush," Creidhe said. "We have many stories to tell before we make sense of it all. You acted from love, that's the only thing that matters. And so did he; why else did he stay here, save for love of you, his only family? Dear one, I've come a long way. Can we go home now?"

They climbed to the top of the track together, and he gathered his weapons and took the roll of bedding under his arm. Creidhe noticed a change in him; he was thinner, as she was, and his features harder somehow, as if he had aged far more than a year since last she saw him. His hair was different. It was combed neatly, and tied at the nape with a strip of leather. Only a few strands escaped to fall across his brow. She reached up to touch the dark locks at the temple, to brush the wisps from his eyes.

"You look—beautiful," she told him. "I'm so glad you waited. I'm so glad, I can't find words for it."

"How could I not wait?" Keeper whispered. "Such a vow as we made is forever. I would have waited until the end of time. Longer, if I could."

They walked on. It became apparent to Creidhe that the path they took was not the one that led to the old shelter, the place where she had fallen to a skillfully hurled stone.

"Where are we going?" she asked him.

A sudden shyness crept into Keeper's voice. "I made you a house, as I promised," he said. "A good house, warm and safe. Big enough for the three of us, though Small One is gone."

Creidhe smiled. "I suppose we'll have a little son or daughter of our own, some time," she said. "By next summer, if the ancestors look kindly on us. Our house will be full."

That silenced him completely, but Creidhe did not miss the change in his eyes, the hesitant, sweet smile that curved his solemn mouth. This, she thought, would be a powerful step toward putting things right at last.

The house was set in a sheltered fold of land by a little stream. He'd been right; it was roomy and well made, with a roof of grass thatch held down by hanging rocks, and walls of shaped stones. Creidhe could see timbers here and there; these, perhaps, had once been part of a boat. There were two rooms; the larger held a central hearth where a small fire smoldered. There was a dry place for storing turf, and pegs for hanging clothes, and neat stone shelves. There was a broad sleeping platform big enough for two.

Creidhe exclaimed with delight. "It's wonderful! I love it! And I have just the thing . . ." She motioned to him to set the bundle down on the platform. "Could you unfasten this, please? You may need to slit the binding with a knife; I think the knots have tightened . . ."

Nothing was wasted on the Isle of Clouds. Keeper did not cut the twine, but undid it with long, deft fingers. The contents of the bundle unrolled partly, a bright expanse of blue and red wool.

"It's exactly the right size," Creidhe said, a lump in her throat as she watched the play of expressions on his face, as she saw memory alive in his liquid green eyes. "I must have made it for just this bed, all that time ago."

Keeper unfolded the blanket fully. It covered the sleeping platform from side to side, from head to foot. His fingers moved over the fine weave, the vivid deep blue, the heart's-blood red, the intricate border of tiny trees and creatures.

"For me?" he breathed.

"For you. For my husband."

* * *

It is not always the case that dreams come true. Indeed, more often they give us warped and twisted versions of the truth, showing us what we wish were so, or what we fear may be to come. It was not thus for Creidhe. When she awoke next morning on the Isle of Clouds, it was exactly as she had dreamed it over the loom, fashioning this lovely thing of colored wool, weaving her fair visions into her work. Almost exactly. The early sun crept through the doorway of Keeper's fine house, touching the blue blanket to vibrant, glowing life. She lay warm beneath it, her body languid and pliant, full of an aching sweetness. Her husband's arms were firm and strong around her, shielding her from all harm. And if he was not the man who had lain there in her dreams, no matter. He was her only love, her heart's desire. Without him, she would have spent her whole life incomplete. Who should lie with her under the blue blanket, but he?

She stirred against him, smiling, and felt his hand tighten in her hair, drawing her closer. His need for her was great; of the two, he had been hurt far more. She must tread softly, go slowly, and help him all she could. In time, perhaps he might be ready to venture forth, to try new pathways, to meet a wider circle. He had skills that unscrupulous men might seek to exploit; there were dangers to be faced that, as yet, barely had form. They needed time. Surely, if they lived their lives well, if they understood how blessed they were, the ancestors would grant them that.

AUTHOR'S NOTE

In location, geography and terrain, the Lost Isles bear a close resemblance to the Faroes, a group of eighteen islands situated approximately halfway between Norway and Iceland. But *Foxmask* is not a novel about the Faroes. The setting and characters exist somewhere between history and mythology, and the Lost Isles themselves are part real, part imagined. The place names used in this book include loose translations of the actual names for various parts of the Faroes and pure inventions. For example, the Isle of Streams (Streymoy) and the Witch's Finger (Trøllkonufingur) are close to the existing Faroese names. I renamed many places in keeping with the nature of the story.

You can find the locations of the events in *Foxmask* on a map of the Faroes, though I have taken some creative liberties with the terrain and distances. The westernmost island of Mykines, which wears a semipermanent shawl of cloud, is the Isle of Clouds, and the inland lake of Sørvágsvatn with its precipice and waterfall, is Brightwater. Council Fjord is really Sørvágsfjørdur, and the town of Sørvágur marks the approximate location of Asgrim's encampment. Windswept Vágar has become the Isle of Storms, and Midvágur is Blood Bay. This village is still the scene of some of the bloodiest occurrences of the *grindadráp*, in which pods of pilot whales are herded to the beach for slaughter.

As for the Fool's Tide, these days a small ferry makes the trip from Vágar to Mykines regularly, excepting in the worst weather. The permanent population of Mykines, where Keeper built his wife a house, is fifteen hardy souls, along with large numbers of puffins, gannets and other birds. The island does indeed have just one rather tricky landing place. The sea crossing is rough, and I did the trip by helicopter, a common form of transport in the Faroes.

We passed over layered, rock-crowned peaks that still bore caps of snow in May. The strait between Vágar and Mykines is dangerous for small boats. It features in the old accounts of St. Brendan's voyage, and in Tim Severin's tale of its reenactment, *The Brendan Voyage*, as particularly difficult to navigate. Legends grow up easily around such perilous places; the stories of the Fool's Tide and the Seal Tribe are just such coded warnings, designed to keep fishermen out of harm's way.

The first book in this series, *Wolfskin*, dealt with a Viking voyage to Orkney and was in many respects based on real or possible history. *Foxmask* is a little different. We do know that the Faroes were settled by people from southern Norway and Orkney at around the time this book is set. It is also known that Irish monks made their way to these distant islands, very probably well before the Norse arrivals. It's an inhospitable realm, and was settled by the hardiest and most tenacious of people. The weather is extreme, the narrow channels between the islands dangerous, and the land marginal for farming. The fishing is unsurpassed. Written records of this early settlement are few and far between, with most accounts being set down hundreds of years after the fact.

So, how much of the story of *Foxmask* is true, or could be true, and how much is pure fantasy? The following are at least possible, or even probable: the existence of isolated hermitages on the islands and the voyages there of intrepid Christians such as Breccan; the presence of settlers like Asgrim and his Long Knife people, scratching a living from the sea and from their tenacious island sheep whose dreadlocked, multicolored descendants wander those hills today. The voyage of Thorvald, Sam and Creidhe in their fishing boat from Orkney is also possible, though it would have been a testing trip with such a small crew. Still, if St. Brendan could do it in a curragh of ox skins from the west coast of Ireland, they could do it in their sturdier craft, provided the weather was on their side.

The people of the Seal Tribe are based on a number of

folkloric sources. The existence of such ocean creatures, neither benign nor inimical to man, just profoundly Other, is alluded to in the old tales of many island-dwelling races.

As for the Unspoken and their small seer, Foxmask, those spring purely from imagination. History does not tell us whether there were any folk dwelling in the Faroes prior to the coming of the Christians, but there could have been. I created a race in keeping with the highly challenging nature of that environment. Had they existed, I have no doubt their culture and beliefs would have been enmeshed with the forces of nature on which their survival depended.